Great Australian Writers

ALAN MARSHALL

KENNETH COOK

NENE GARE

KIT DENTON

Dad,
Happy Christmas 1990
love from Lesley a Lance
xx

Great Australian Writers

ALAN MARSHALL
I CAN JUMP PUDDLES

KENNETH COOK
WAKE IN FRIGHT

NENE GARE
THE FRINGE DWELLERS

KIT DENTON
THE BREAKER

HEINEMANN

I Can Jump Puddles first published in 1955 by Longman Cheshire Pty Limited
Wake in Fright first published in 1961 by Michael Joseph Limited
The Fringe Dwellers first published in 1961 by William Heinemann Limited
The Breaker first published in 1973 by Angus & Robertson Publishers, Sydney & London

This edition first published in 1987 for
William Heinemann Australia by

Octopus Books Limited
59 Grosvenor Street
London W1

ISBN 0 7064 3251 7

Printed and bound in the United Kingdom by William Clowes Limited, Beccles

Contents

ALAN MARSHALL
I CAN JUMP PUDDLES

PREFACE

This book is the story of my childhood. In these pages I have described those influences and those incidents that helped to make me what I am.

But I wanted to do much more than record the experiences of a little boy faced with the problem of his crutches; I wanted to give a picture of a period that has passed. The men and women here described are a product of that period and they too are passing. The influences that made them self-reliant, forthright and compassionate, have given way to influences that can develop characters just as fine, but the mould has changed and the product is different .

To give a picture of life at that time, I have gone beyond the facts to get at the truth. I have sometimes altered scenes, made composite characters when this was necessary, changed time sequences to help the continuity and introduced dialogue that those who shared my experiences of the horse-days may find confusing.

I ask their pardon. A book of this nature demands a treatment that facts do not always supply; the truth it seeks to establish can only be revealed with the help of imagination.

ALAN MARSHALL

To
My Daughters
HEPHZIBAH AND JENNIFER
who can jump puddles too

CHAPTER 1

When my mother lay in the small front room of the weather-board house in which we lived, awaiting the arrival of the midwife to deliver me, she could see tall gums tossing in the wind, and a green hill, and cloud shadows racing across the paddocks, and she said to my father, 'It will be a son; it is a man's day.'

My father bent and looked through the window to where the dark, green barrier of the bush stood facing the cleared paddocks.

'I'll make him a bushman and a runner,' he said with determination. 'By God, I will!'

When the midwife arrived he smiled at her and said, 'I thought the little chap would be running around before you got here, Mrs Torrens.'

'Yes, I should have been here half an hour ago,' said Mrs Torrens brusquely. She was a heavy woman with soft, brown cheeks and an assertive manner. 'There was Ted greasing the gig when he should have had the horse in.' She looked at mother. 'How are you, dear? Have you had any pains yet?'

'While she was speaking,' my mother told me, 'I could smell the myall-wood handle of your father's stockwhip hanging on the end of the bed, and I could see you wheeling it round your head at a gallop like your father.'

Father sat in the kitchen with my sisters while I was being born. Mary and Jane wanted a brother to take to school with them, and father had promised them one called Alan.

When Mrs Torrens brought me out for them to see, I was wrapped in red flannelette, and she placed me in father's arms.

'It was funny looking down on you there,' he said. 'My son ... There was a lot of things I wanted you to be able to do – ride an' that. I wanted you to have good hands on a horse. Well, that's what I was thinking. Running, of course ... They reckoned you had good limbs on you. It seemed funny, me holding you there. I kept wondering if you would be like me.'

*   *   *

I had not long started school when I contracted Infantile Paralysis. The epidemic that began in Victoria in the early 1900s moved into the country districts from the more populated areas, striking down children on isolated farms and in bush homes. I was the only victim in Turalla, and the people for miles around heard of my illness with a feeling of dread. They associated the word 'Paralysis' with idiocy, and the query 'Have you heard if his mind is affected?' was asked from many a halted buggy, the driver leaning over the wheel for a yarn with a friend met on the road.

For a few weeks the neighbours drove quickly past our house, looking hurriedly, with a new interest, at the old picket fence, the unbroken colts in the stockyard and my tricycle lying on its side by the chaff house. They called their children in earlier, wrapped them more warmly and gazed at them anxiously when they coughed or sneezed.

'It hits you like a blow from God,' said Mr Carter, the baker, who believed that this was so. He was the Superintendent of the Bible Class and proclaimed in his weekly announcements, as he faced his pupils with a sombre look:

'Next Sunday morning at Divine Service the Rev. Walter Robertson, BA, will offer up prayers for the speedy recovery of this brave boy sorely stricken with a fell disease. A full attendance is requested.'

Father, after hearing of these words, stood in the street one day tugging at his sandy moustache with a nervous, troubled hand, while he explained to Mr Carter just how I happened to catch the disease.

'They say you breathe the germ in,' he said. 'It's just floating about in the air – everywhere. You never know where it is. It must have been just floating past his nose when he beathed in and that was the end of him. He went down like a pole-axed steer. If he'd been breathing out when that germ passed he'd'd've been right.'

He paused, then added sadly, 'Now you're praying for him.'

'The back is made for the burden,' murmured the baker piously. He was an elder of the Church and saw the hand of God behind misfortune. On the other hand he suspected the devil of being behind most of the things people enjoyed.

'It's God's will,' he added with some satisfaction, confident the remark would please the Almighty. He was always quick to seize any opportunity to ingratiate himself with God.

Father snorted his contempt of such a philosophy and said, with some savagery, 'That boy's back was never made for the burden, and, let me tell you, this won't be a burden either. If you want to look for burdens, there's the place to look for them.' And he tapped his head with a brown finger.

Later, standing beside my bed, he asked anxiously, 'Have you got any pains in your legs, Alan?'

'No,' I told him. 'They feel dead.'

'Oh, hell!' he exclaimed, his face stricken.

He was a lean man with bowed legs and narrow hips, the result of years in the saddle, for he was a horsebreaker who had come down to Victoria from outback Queensland.

'It was the kids,' he used to say. 'There's no schools outback. Only for them, by cripes, I'd never have left.'

He had a bushman's face, brown and lined, with sharp blue eyes embedded in the wrinkles that came from the glare of saltbush plains.

A drover mate of his, who called in to see him one day, exclaimed, as father crossed the yard to greet him, 'By cripes, Bill, you still walk like a bloody emu!'

His walk was light and mincing, and he always looked at the ground ahead of him as he walked, a habit he attributed to the fact that he came from 'snake country'.

Sometimes, when he had a few drinks in, he would ride into the yard on some half-broken colt and go rearing and plunging amongst the feed boxes, gig shafts, and the remains of old wheels, scattering the squawking fowls and giving high, larrikin yells:

'Wild cattle and no brands! Let them ring! Ho, there!'

Then he would rein the horse back on its haunches and, snatching off his broad-brimmed hat, would swing it round in some mock acknowledgment of applause while he bowed towards the kitchen door where mother generally stood with a little smile upon her face, a smile that was a mixture of amusement, love and concern.

Father was fond of horses, not because they were the means by which he earned his living, but because of some beauty he saw in them. He liked studying a well-built horse. He would walk round it slowly, his head on one side, looking carefully at every feature, running his hands down its front legs, feeling for swellings or scars that would show it had been down.

'You want a horse with good, strong bone, and plenty of daylight under him,' he used to say, 'one that stands over a lot of ground.'

He thought horses were like human beings.

'Yes, it's a fact,' he had said. 'I've seen them. Some horses sulk if you as much as touch'em with a whip. So do some kids ... Box their ears and they won't talk to you for days. They hold it against you. They can't forget, see! By hell, it's true of horses too! Use the whip on some of them and you make a jib. Look at the chestnut mare of Old Stumpy Dick's. She's tough in the mouth. And I mouthed her, mind you. It just shows you ... It's in her like in Stumpy. Whoever mouthed him made a proper mess of it. He still owes me a quid on that job. Well, let it go ... He's got nothing.'

His father had been a red-headed Yorkshireman, a shepherd, who had migrated to Australia at the beginning of the '40's. He married an Irish girl who arrived at the new colony in the same year. They say he strode onto the wharf when a ship laden with Irish girls seeking work as domestics arrived in the colony.

'Which one of you will marry me, now?' he called out to the girls lining the rail. 'Who'll take a chance with me?'

One strong, blue-eyed colleen with black hair and broad hands eyed him speculatively for a moment, then called back, 'I'm willing. I'll marry you.'

She lowered herself over the ship's side, and he caught her on the wharf. He took the bundle she carried and they walked away together, his hand on her shoulder as if he were guiding her.

Father was the youngest of four children and inherited the temperament of his Irish mother.

'When I was a kid,' he told me once, 'I caught a teamster fair behind the ear with a paddy melon – if the juice gets into your eyes it can blind you, you know. Well, this fellow went sort of half cranky and came at me with a waddy. I made for our hut yelling, "Mum!" This bloke meant business, mind you – by hell, he did! I had nothing left when I reached the hut. I was done. But mum had seen me coming and there she was waiting with a kettle of boiling water swinging easy in her hand. "Keep back," she said. "This is boiling. Come any closer and I'll let you have it in the face." By hell! it stopped him. She just stood there with me clinging to her skirts and watched him till he went away.'

Father was earning his own living at twelve. His education had been limited to a few months' schooling under a drunken teacher to whom each child attending the slab hut that served as a school, paid half a crown a week.

After he started work he drifted round from station to station, horsebreaking or droving. His youth and early manhood were spent in the outback areas of New South Wales and Queensland, and it was these areas that furnished the material for all his yarns. Because of his tales, the saltbush plains and red sandhills of the outback were closer to me than the green country where I was born and grew to manhood.

'There's something in the back country,' he once told me.

'You're satisfied out there. You get on a pine ridge and light a
fire ...'

He stopped and sat thinking, looking at me in a troubled way.
After a while he said, 'We'll have to think up some way to stop your
crutches sinking into the sand outback. Yes, we'll get you up there
some day.'

CHAPTER 2

Not long after I became paralysed the muscles in my legs began to
shrink, and my back, once straight and strong, now curved to one
side. The sinews behind my knees tightened into cords that tugged
at my legs till they gradually bent and became locked in a kneeling
position.

The painful tension of the twin sinews behind each knee and the
conviction that if my legs were not soon straightened they would
always remain in their locked position, worried my mother who
kept calling on Dr Crawford to prescribe some treatment that
would enable me to move them normally again.

Dr Crawford, uncertain of how Infantile Paralysis developed,
had watched my mother's attempts to bring life back into my
legs by massaging them with brandy and olive oil – a cure recom-
mended by the school teacher's wife, who claimed that it cured her
rheumatism – with a slight frown of disapproval, but, after remark-
ing 'It can't do any harm', left the question of my immovable legs
till he had made further enquiries about the complications being
experienced by victims in Melbourne.

Dr Crawford lived at Balunga, the township four miles from our
home, and would only visit patients in outlying districts when the
case was an urgent one. He drove a jogging grey horse in an Abbot
buggy with the hood half raised, so that the lining of scalloped
blue felt, acting as a background, presented him to the best advantage as he bowed and flourished his buggy whip to those who
passed. The Abbot buggy established him as the equal of a
squatter, but not the equal of a squatter who had an Abbot buggy
with rubber tyres.

He was a man with a readily available knowledge of the simpler diseases.

'I can say confidently, Mrs Marshall, that your son has not got the measles.'

But Poliomyelitis was a disease of which he knew very little. He had called in two other doctors for consultation when I first became ill, and it was one of these who announced that I had Infantile Paralysis.

Mother was impressed by this doctor, who seemed to know so much, and turned to him for further information, but all he would say was, 'If he were a son of mine I would be very, very worried.'

'I'm sure you would,' said my mother dryly, and never had any faith in him from then on. She believed in Dr Crawford who, when the other two doctors had gone, said, 'Mrs Marshall, no one can tell whether your son will be crippled or not, or whether he will live or die. I believe he will live, but it is in God's hands.'

This pronouncement comforted my mother but my father reacted in quite a different way. It brought from him the observation that Dr Crawford had now admitted he knew nothing about Infantile Paralysis.

'Once they tell you you're in God's hands you know you're done,' he said.

The problem of my contracting legs was one that Dr Crawford eventually had to face. Troubled and uncertain, he beat his pudgy fingers in a soft tatto upon the marble top of the washstand beside my bed while he looked down on me in silence. Mother stood beside him, tense and still, like a prisoner awaiting sentence.

'Well, now, Mrs Marshall, about these legs ... M-m-m-m, yes ... I'm afraid there is only one thing we can do. He's a brave boy. that's fortunate. We just have to straighten those legs. the only way is to force them down. They must be forced straight. The question is: how? The best way, I think, would be to lay him on the table each morning then press your weight upon his knees till they straighten. The legs must be pressed flat on the table. Say, three times. Yes, three would be enough, I think. Say, two on the first day.'

'Will it be very painful?' my mother asked.

'I'm afraid so.' Dr Crawford paused, then added, 'You will need all your courage.'

Each morning when my mother laid me on my back on the kitchen table, I looked at the picture of the frightened horses that hung upon the chimney above the mantelpiece. It was an engraving of a black horse and a white horse crowding together in terror while a jagged streak of lightning projected out of the dark background of storm and rain and hung poised a few feet in front of their distended nostrils. A companion picture on the opposite wall showed them galloping madly away, their legs extended in rocking-horse fashion and their manes flying.

Father, who took all pictures seriously, sometimes stood looking at these horses with one eye half closed to aid his concentration while he assessed their value as hacks.

Once he told me: 'They're Arabs all right, but they're not pure. The mare's got windgalls, too. Look at her fetlocks.'

I resented any criticism of these horses. They were important to me. Each morning I fled with them from jagged pain. Our fears merged and became a single fear that bound us together in a common need.

My mother would place her two hands upon my raised knees then, with her eyes tightly closed so that her tears were held back by her clenched lids, she would lean her weight upon my legs forcing them down till they lay flat upon the table. As they straightened to her weight my toes would spread apart then curve down and round like the talons of a bird. When the sinews beneath my knees began to drag and stretch I would scream loudly, my eyes wide open, my gaze on the terrified horses over the mantelpiece. As my toes curved in their agonised clutching, I would cry out to the horses, 'Oh! horses, horses, horses . . . Oh! horses, horses . . .'

CHAPTER 3

The hospital was in a township over twenty miles from our home. Father drove me there in the brake, the long-shafted, strongly-built gig in which he broke in horses. He was very proud of this brake. It had hickory shafts and wheels, and he had painted a picture of a bucking horse on the back rail of the seat. It wasn't a very good picture and father was in the habit of excusing it with the explanation, 'He hasn't quite got into it, see. It's his first buck and he's off balance.'

Father put in one of the young horses he was handling and tied another to the shaft. He held the shafter's head while mother placed me on the floor and climbed in. When she had seated herself she lifted me up beside her. Father kept talking to the horse and rubbing his hand along its sweating neck.

'Steady, boy! Whoa, there! Steady now!'

The antics of unbroken horses never scared mother. She sat with an unconcerned expression upon her face while stubborn horses reared, came down on their knees or bounded off the road, grunting with the violence of their exertions to rid themselves of the harness. She sat on the high seat, bracing herself to every plunge or sway, one hand clutching the nickel rail at the end. She would lean forward a little when the horses backed violently or be jerked back against the seat when they plunged forward, but she always retained a firm grip on me.

'We're right,' said mother, her arm firmly around me.

Father released his hold on the bit and moved back to the step, slipping the reins through his hand, his eyes on the shafter's head. He placed one foot on the round, iron step and grasped the edge of the seat, paused a moment calling, 'Steady there!' to the restless, nervous horses, then suddenly swung himself into the seat as they reared. He loosened the reins and they plunged forward, the colt tied to the shaft by a halter pulling sideways, its neck stretched, as it bounded awkwardly along beside the harnessed horse. We shot through the gateway with a scattering of stones and the grating, sideways skid of the iron-shod wheels.

Father boasted that he had never once hit the gate posts in his bounding departures, though splintered grooves hub-high in the wood suggested otherwise. Mother, leaning over the mudguard so that she could see the gap between hub and post, always made the same remark: 'You'll hit one of those posts one of these days.'

Father steadied the horses as we bounced on to the metal roadway from the dirt track that led to our gate.

'Steady now!' he called, then added for mother's benefit, 'This trip'll take the gas out of them. The grey is by The Abbot. All his get are the same – they're always on the bit.'

The warm sun and the noise of the wheels on the roadway sent me to sleep, and the bush and paddocks and creeks moved past us, veiled for a moment in the dust stirred by the feet of our horses, but I did not see them. I lay with my head against mother's arm till she woke me three hours later.

The gig wheels were crunching the gravel in the hospital yard and I sat up, looking at the white building with its narrow windows and strange smell.

Through the open doorway I could see a dark, polished floor and a pedestal bearing a bowl of flowers. But there was a hush about the building, a strange quietness that frightened me.

The room into which my father carried me had a padded seat running round the wall and a desk in one corner. A nurse sat at the desk and she asked father a lot of questions. She wrote his answers in a book while he watched her in the way he would have watched an untrustworthy horse that had its ears back.

After she had left the room taking the book with her, father said to mother, 'I never come into one of these places without feeling like telling them all to go to hell. They strip the feelings from a man like you skin a cow; ask too many qustions. They make you feel you shouldn't be here – as if a bloke's trying to put something over them, or something. I don't know ... '

After a little while the nurse returned with a wardsman who carried me away after mother had reassured me that she would come in to see me when I was in bed.

The wardsman was dressed in brown. He had a red, lined face, and looked at me as if I wasn't a boy but a problem. Carrying me into a bathroom he lowered me into a bath of warm water. He then sat on a stool and began to roll a cigarette. After he lit it, he said to me, 'When did you last have a bath?'

'This morning,' I told him.

'Aw, well, just lie down in it. That'll do.'

Later, I sat up in the cool, clean bed in which he had placed me and pleaded with mother not to go. The mattress on the bed was hard and unyielding and I could not gather the blankets into folds about me. There would be no warm caves beneath these blankets nor channel pathways for marbles, winding about on the quilt. There were no protecting walls close to me and I could not hear the barking of a dog nor the noise of a horse munching chaff. These belonged to my home and at that moment I wanted them desperately.

Father had already bade me goodbye but mother lingered. She suddenly kissed me quickly and walked away, and that she could do this was to me incredible. I did not see her leaving me of her own will but leaving me because of some sudden, monstrous circumstance over which she had no control. I did not sing out to her or beg her to return, though this was what I longed to do. I watched her go, unable to make any effort to prevent her.

The man in the next bed watched me in silence for a little while after mother had gone, then asked, 'Why are you crying?'

'I want to go home.'

'We all want that,' he said, then he turned his gaze to the ceiling and sighed and said, 'Yes, we all want that.'

The ward in which we lay had a polished floor, light brown between the beds and down the centre, but dark and shining beneath the beds where the feet of nurses never disturbed the covering of wax.

The white, iron bedsteads, facing each other in two rows along the walls, stood on thin legs resting on castors. For a few inches around each castor the floor was bruised and dented with these little wheels that spun round distractedly when nurses moved the bed.

The blankets and sheets were drawn tightly round each patient then tucked in beneath the mattress so that they formed a binding across him.

There were fourteen men in the ward. I was the only child. After mother left me some of these men called out to me and told me not to worry.

'You'll be all right,' a man said. 'We'll look after you.'

They asked me what was wrong with me and when I told them, they all discussed Infantile Paralysis, and one man said it was murder. 'It's bloody murder,' he said. 'That's what it is. It's bloody murder.'

This remark made me feel important and I liked the man who said it. I did not regard my illness as being serious, but as a temporary inconvenience, and in the days that followed I met the painful periods with resentment and anger that quickly turned to despair when the pain was prolonged, but once the pain stopped it was quickly forgotten. I could not sustain a depressed state of mind for very long. There was too much to interest me in my surroundings.

I was always pleasantly surprised to see the effect my illness had on those people who stood beside my bed looking down at me with sad faces and who saw my sickness as some terrible calamity. It established me as a person of importance and kept me contented.

'You're a brave boy,' they said, bending down and kissing me then turning away with mournful expression.

I used to puzzle over this bravery which was attributed to me by those I met. To be described as brave, I believed, was to be decorated. I always felt impelled to change my expression when visitors called me brave, the pleased expression that was natural to me being inadequate to carry the description.

But I was always afraid of being found out and it began to embarrass me to accept these tributes to my courage, tributes which I knew I had not earned. The sound of a mouse gnawing behind the skirting boards of my room always frightened me and I was frightened to go out to the tank to get a drink at nights because of the dark. Sometimes I wondered what people would think if they knew this.

But people insisted I was brave, and I accepted this attitude with some secret, though guilty, pride.

In a few days I identified myself with the ward and the patients and began to feel superior to new patients who entered the ward awkwardly, confused with the rows of watching faces, homesick and longing for a familiar bed upon which to sink.

The patients talked to me, using me as a butt for their jokes, patronising me, as adults do children, and calling out to me when subjects for conversation evaded them. I believed everything they told me and this amused them. From the security of their long experience they looked down on me, imagining that because I was guileless I was incapable of understanding references to myself. They spoke about me as if I were deaf and could not hear their words.

'He believes everything you tell him,' a youth across the ward explained to a newcomer. 'You listen. Hey Smiler,' he called to me, 'there's a witch down the well near your place, isn't there?'

'Yes,' I said.

'There you are,' said the youth. 'He's a funny little beggar. He'll never walk, they tell me.'

I thought the youth was a fool. It amazed me that they imagined I would never walk again. I knew what I was going to do. I was going to break in wild horses and yell 'Ho! Ho!' and wave my hat in the air, and I was going to write a book like *The Coral Island*.

I liked the man in the next bed. 'We'll be mates,' he said to me not long after I arrived. 'How'd you like to be mates with me?' 'Good,' I said. Because of the coloured picture in one of my first books I had an idea that mates should stand together holding hands. I explained this to him, but he said it wasn't necessary.

Each morning he would raise himself on his elbow and say to me, emphasising each word with a beat of his hand: 'Always remember, McDonald Brothers' windmills are the best.'

I was pleased that now I knew what make of windmill was the best. Indeed, this statement became so fixed in my mind that, thereafter, it always affected my reaction to windmills.

'Does Mr McDonald and his brother make them?' I asked.

'Yes,' he said. 'I'm the original McDonald. I'm Angus.'

He suddenly sank back on his pillow and said petulantly, 'God only knows how they'll manage with me away – orders and that. You've got to keep your eye on things.' He suddenly called out to a man across the ward, 'What's the paper say about the weather today? Do they reckon there's going to be a drought or not?'

'The paper hasn't come yet,' the man said.

Angus was the tallest and biggest man of the twelve patients in the ward. He was suffering from some complaint that caused him pain and sometimes he would sigh loudly or swear or give a deep groan that frightened me.

In the morning, after a resltess night, he would say to no one in particular, 'Aw, I had a hell of a night last night!'

He had a large, clean-shaven face with deep creases joining his nostrils to the corners of his mouth. His skin was smooth like tanned leather. He had a flexible, sensitive mouth that easily broke into a smile when he was not suffering pain.

He used to turn his head on the pillow and look at me for long periods in silence.

'Why do you take so long to say your prayers?' he asked me once; then in answer to my look of astonishment he added, 'I've watched your lips moving.'

'I have to ask a lot of things,' I explained to him.

'What things?' he asked.

I became confused, and he said, 'Go on. Tell me. We're mates.'

I repeated my prayers to him while he listened, gazing at the ceiling, his hands clasped on his chest. When I had finished he turned his head and looked at me. 'You haven't left anything out. You've given Him the lot. God'll think a hell of a lot of you by the time He's listened to all that.'

His comment made me feel happy and I decided I would ask God to make him better too.

The long, involved prayer I repeated each night before I went to sleep was the result of an increasing number of requests I was making to God. My needs grew greater each day and, as I only dropped requests when they were answered, the new pleas were so far in excess of those that were answered that I began to dread the necissty of going through it again and again. Mother had never allowed me to miss Sunday School and from her I had learnt my first prayer which was a little composition beginning, 'Gentle Jesus meek and mild', and which ended with the request to bless various people, dad included, though in my heart I always felt he didn't need blessing. But later, when looking at a perfectly good cat that someone had thrown away, I became frightened at its rigid stillness and was told that it was dead. In bed at nights I thought of mother and father lying still with lifted lip like the cat, and I prayed with anguish that they mightn't die before me. This was my most earnest prayer that could never be missed.

After further consideration I decided to include Meg, my dog, in a requst to preserve her till I became a man and was old enough to stand her death. Feeling troubled that I might be demanding too much from God I added that, as in the case of Meg, I would be satisfied if both my parents lived till I was a man of, say, thirty. I felt that at this great age I would be past tears. Men never cry.

I prayed to be made better, always adding that, if He didn't mind, I would like to be cured before Christmas, two months away.

The pets I kept in cages and in enclosures in our backyard had to be prayed for, since, now that I couldn't feed them or change their water, there was always the danger of this being forgotten. I prayed that this might never be forgotten.

My corella, Pat, an irascible old cockatoo, had to be let out of his cage each night for a fly round the trees. Sometimes neighbours complained about him. On washing days he would land on their clothesline and pull out the pegs. Angry women, seeing white sheets lying in the dust, threw sticks and stones at Pat, and I had to pray that they would never hit and kill him.

I also had to pray to be made a good boy.

After Angus had commented on my prayers he asked, 'What sort of chap do you think God is? What does He look like?'

I always pictured God as a mighty man dressed in a white sheet like an Arab. He sat on a chair with His elbows on His knees looking down at the world, His eyes darting rapidly from person to person. I never associated Him with kindliness, only with severity. Jesus, I thought, would be kind like dad, but would never swear like him. The fact that Jesus only rode donkeys and never horses was disappointing to me.

Once dad, after removing a pair of new boots he had been 'breaking in', slipped on his Gillespie's Elastic Sides and exclaimed with feeling, 'These boots were made in heaven.' Thereafter, I believed that Jesus wore Gillespie's Elastic Side boots.

When I had finished explaining these things to Angus he commented that maybe my picture was closer to it than his was.

'My mother always spoke in Gaelic,' he said. 'I always saw God as a stooped old man with a white beard, surrounded by a lot of old women knitting and talking in Gaelic. God always seemed to have a patch over one eye, and mother would say, "It's them there larrikins throwing stones." I couldn't imagine God doing anything without first consulting mother.'

'Did your mother smack you?' I asked him.

'No,' he replied reflectively. 'She never smacked us kids but she was very severe with God.'

To a patient who said something to him from a bed on his left hand side, he answered, 'You needn't worry. I won't destroy his faith. He'll think it out for himself when he's a man.'

Though I believed in God and devoted part of my evening to addressing Him I regarded myself as being independent of Him. He could quite easily have offended me so that I would never have spoken to Him again. I was frightened of Him because He could send me to be burnt in hell-fire. The Superintendent of our Sunday School had described this. But more than hell-fire I feared becoming abject.

When Meg got staked in the shoulder while chasing a rabbit I felt that God had let me down badly and resolved that in the future I would look after Meg's welfare myself and blow God. I didn't pray to Him that night.

Whenever father mentioned God he criticised Him, but I like father's attitude since it established him as someone upon whom I could rely if God failed me – he had bound up Meg's shoulder. But his manner, when God was mentioned, sometimes troubled me.

Once when he took a mare to Old Waddy Dean's stallion, Waddy asked him what colour he would like the foal to be.

'I know a way of making it any colour I like,' Waddy boasted.

'Can you make it a colt or a filly?' father asked him.

'Ah, no!' said Waddy piously. 'Only God can control the sex.'

To me, who was listening, father's reaction to this statement seemed to question God's power over horses, though it left me with a great faith in father. Men like father, I thought, were stronger than any God.

But men in hospitals were different from men out of hospitals. Pain robbed them of something, something I valued but could not define. Some called out to God in the night and I did not like it. I felt that they should not have to do this. I did not like to admit to myself that men could experience fear. When you became a man, I thought, fear and pain and indecision just didn't exist.

In the bed to my right was a heavy, awkward-moving man whose hand had been crushed in a chaffcutter. During the day he walked round the ward talking to the patients, going messages for them, or bringing them things they needed. He advanced upon you with a large, wet smile, leaning over the bed in a fawning way. 'You all right, eh? You want anything, eh?' His manner disturbed me; maybe because his kindness, his offers to help, sprang not so much from a natural compassion as from fear. There was a danger of him losing his hand, but God was good and would surely look after those who helped the sick.

Mick, the Irishman in the bed across the ward, always waved him away from his bed in a friendly way.

'He's just like a water dog,' he said once when the patient was out of the ward. 'Every time he comes near me I feel like throwing him a stick to bring back.'

In bed he was restless, tossing, sitting up and lying down again. He patted his pillow, turning it this way and that and frowning at it. When night came on he took from his locker a little prayer book. The expression upon his face changed and his body suddenly became still. He brought from some inner reserve a suitable serious ness in which he clothed himself like a garment.

Around the wrist of his crushed and bandaged hand he had wound a chain bearing a small crucifix. He raised this metal cross to his lips and pressed it there with a still intensity. He must have felt he was not sufficiently devout in his reading because two deep lines appeared between his brows and his lips moved slowly forming the words he read.

One night, Mick, after watching him for a moment, evidently felt that this man's piety emphasised his own lack of it.

'Who does he think he is?' he said, looking towards me.

'I don't know,' I said.

'No one can say I neglected the faith,' he muttered, looking hard at one of his fingernails. He bit it, then added, 'Not often, I haven't.'

He suddenly smiled. 'There was my old mother now – God bless her. A finer woman never lived, though I say it myself. Yes, it's a fact. Others'll tell you that. Ask anybody round Borlic. They all knew her. I used to say to her on the fine mornings, "God is good, mum," I'd say. "Ah, yes! but the devil ain't bad, Mick," she'd say. Yes, they don't breed them that way now.'

Mick was a short, alert, nuggety man who loved talking. He had hurt his arm in some way and was allowed to get out of bed and go to the bathroom each morning. When he returned he would stand beside his bed looking down on it while he rolled up the sleeves of his pyjamas as if he were going to sink a posthole, then he would clamber in, prop pillows at his back, rest his hands on the turned-down sheet in front of him and look round the ward with a pleased expression of anticipation upon his face.

'He just sits there waiting for someone to start him off,' was how Angus described it.

Sometimes Mick would look at his arm with a puzzled frown and say, 'I'm damned if I can understand it! There it was right as rain, then I heaves a bag of wheat on the dray and it goes on me. You can never tell what's wrong with you till it comes on you sudden like.'

'You're lucky,' commented Angus. 'Two or three more days and you'll be down in the pub. Did you hear about Frank?'

'No.'

'Well, he died.'

'Get out! Fancy that now!' exclaimed Mick. 'It just shows you. One minute you're running round happy as Larry: the next minute you're cold. He was all right when he left on Tuesday. What happened to him?'

'He collapsed.'

'This collapsing's bad the way it gets you,' said Mick, and became silent and gloomy till the breakfast tray arrived; then he brightened up and said to the nurse handing it to him, 'Tell me now, is there a chance of you ever falling in love with me?'

The nurses with their white, starched aprons and pink frocks, their scrubbed hands smelling of antiseptics, went swiftly by my bed on their flat-heeled shoes, sometimes smiling at me as they passed or stopping to tuck in my blankets. Since I was the only child in their charge they mothered me.

Father's influence led me into sometimes seeing people as horses, and as I watched the nurses going up and down the ward they seemed like ponies to me.

On the day father brought me to the hospital, he had given a quick glance over the nurses – he liked women – and commented to mother that there were some good shafters among them but they were all shod wrong.

When I heard trotting horses going past the hospital I thought of father and I could see him sitting on a horse that reared and plunged and he was always smiling. He wrote me a letter and in it he said:

'It's keeping dry up here and I've had to start feeding Kate. There's whips of feed on the creek flats yet, but I want to keep her in good nick for you when you come back.'

When I read the letter I said to Angus McDonald, 'I've got a pony called Kate,' then, repeating father, 'She's a bit ewe-necked but she's honest.'

'Your old man breaks in horses, doesn't he?' he asked me.

'Yes,' I said. 'He's easy the best rider in Turalla.'

'He dresses flash enough,' muttered McDonald. 'I thought he was out of a buckjump show when I saw him.'

I lay thinking over what he said, wondering whether it was against father or for him. The way father dressed pleased me. His clothes suggested he was a man who moved quickly. When I helped him put the harness away, the neatsfoot oil left marks on my clothes and hands, but it left no mark on father. He took a pride in his clothes. He liked his moleskin trousers to be white and unmarked and his boots were always shining.

He liked good boots and regarded himself as a judge of leather. He was always proud of the boots he was wearing – generally elastic sides. When he took them off as he sat in front of the kitchen stove each night, he would examine each one carefully, flexing the sole with his hands and pressing the upper this way and that, searching for signs that his boots were beginning to wear.

'The upper on this left boot is better than the one on the right,' he told me once. 'Funny, that. It'll go before the left one.'

He often talked about Professor Fenton who ran a buckjump show in Queensland and had a waxed moustache. The professor wore a white silk shirt and a red sash and could do a double 'Sydney Flash' with a stockwhip. Father could crack a whip but not like Professer Fenton.

While I was thinking about these things he came walking down the ward to see me. His steps were short and quick and he was smiling. He held one arm across his chest where, beneath his white shirt, something bulky was concealed. Standing beside my bed he looked down at me.

'How are you, son?'

I had been feeling contented but he brought with him the atmosphere of home and I suddenly felt like crying. Before he came, the old post and rail fence upon which I used to stand to watch him handling horses, the fowls, the dogs, the cats – all these had moved away beyond my immediate interest but now they seemed close and real to me and I needed them. I needed mother, too.

I didn't cry but father, looking down at me, suddenly tightened his lips. He thrust his hand within his open shirt where he had been holding something to him and suddenly pulled out a struggling thing of soft brown. He lifted the blankets and pushed it beneath them against my chest.

'Here, hold this against you,' he said fiercely. 'Clutch that to you. It's one of Meg's pups. It's the pick of the bunch and we're calling it Alan.'

I wrapped my arms around its warm, snuggling softness and held it to me, and my need passed from me in a breath. I felt a surge of pure happiness and, looking into my father's eyes, I passed it on to him, for he smiled at me.

The pup moved against me and I looked down beneath the arch of blankets I had formed with my lifted arm and there it lay with its bight eyes watching me, and, seeing me, it wriggled with a quick friendliness. The eager life of it moved into me, refreshing and strengthening me so that I felt no weakness at all. Its weight upon me was good and it smelt of home. I wanted to hold it forever.

McDonald, who had been watching us, called to Mick walking down the ward with a towel across his arm, 'Keep the nurses talking out there, Mick,' and to father he said, 'You know what they are – dogs in here ... No understanding ... That's the trouble.'

'That's so,' said father, 'five minutes'll do him. It's like a pot to a thirsty man.'

CHAPTER 4

I respected men. I regarded them as capable of overcoming any difficulty, of possessing great courage. They could mend anything; they knew everything; they were strong and reliable. I looked forward to the time when I would grow up and be like them.

It seemed to me that father was typical of all men. In those periods when he acted in a way I considered unusual for a man, I felt he did so consciously and that his object was to amuse people. I was sure that, on such occasions, he was always in control of his actions.

This explained why I was not afraid of a drunken man.

When father was drunk, which was rarely, he still retained, I imagined, a perfectly sober and grown-up side of the character he was presenting to onlookers even though he did not reveal it.

When, on arriving home from a prolonged visit to a pub, he flung his arm round mother's waist and, with a 'Ho, there!' swung her round the kitchen in a wild dance lit with whoops, I watched him with delight. A drunken man was a romping, talking, laughing man who staggered for the fun of it.

One night two nurses came into the ward guiding between them a drunken man that the police had brought to the hospital. I looked at him in astonishment, afraid of what had happened to him, for he was being directed by something within him he could not control. Tremors shook him and his tongue was loose in his open mouth.

As he was led through the open door he looked up at the ceiling and shouted, 'Hallo. What are you doing up there? Come down and I'll have a go at you.'

'There's nothing up there,' said one of the nurses. 'Come on.'

He was a prisoner walking between them. He went blundering towards the wall like a blind horse, but they guided him into the bathroom.

When they had bathed him and put him into his bed next to Mick's the sister gave him some paraldehyde. He made strange noises when he swallowed it and cried out, 'Hell!' then added plaintively. 'That's crook. That's terrible crook stuff.'

'Lie down now,' the sister ordered. 'Nothing will touch you here. You'll soon be asleep.'

'The coppers tried to tack it on to me,' he muttered. 'Me mate came at me first ... Well, yes, that's right ... Where the hell am I? You're a nurse, aren't you? Yes, that's right ... How are ya? We been on the booze for weeks ... I'll lie down ... I'll go quiet ... '

The sister, with her hand on his shoulder, pushed him gently back on to the pillow, then went away.

When she had closed the door he lay quietly for a moment in the half dark then sat up stealthily and looked at the ceiling. Then he looked at the walls and the floor beside him. He felt the iron framework of his bed as if he were testing the strength of a trap.

He suddenly noticed Mick resting on his pillows watching him.

'Goodday,' he said.

'Goodday,' replied Mick. 'You've been in the rats, have you?'

'Rats is right,' said the man shortly. 'What do they slug you in this joint for the night?'

'It's on the house,' said Mick, 'You're jake.'

The man grunted. He had full, sagging cheeks covered with a greyish bristle. The flesh around his eyes was swollen and inflamed as if he had been crying. His nose was large and fleshy, pitted with sunken pores, dark-centred, as if each of them clasped the root of a hair.

'I might know you,' he said to Mick. 'Ever been to Mildura? Ever been on the Overflow, Piangle, Bourke ... ?'

'No,' said Mick, reaching into his locker for a cigarette. 'I've never been up that way.'

'Well, I don't know you then.'

He sat staring ahead of him, his hands moving purposelessly upon the bedclothes. Suddenly he whispered urgently, 'What's that over there? Look! Near the wall! It's moving!'

'It's a chair,' said Mick glancing at it.

The man lay down quickly and pulled the blankets over his head. His bedclothes were shaking.

When I saw him do this I too lay down and put my head beneath the blankets.

'Hey!' I could hear McDonald speak to me but I did not move. 'Hey, Alan!'

I pulled the blankets away from my face and looked at him.

'It's all right,' he assured me. 'He's been on a bender and he's got the DT's.'

'What's that?' I asked him, my voice shaking a little.

'Too much booze. He's seeing things. He'll be right tomorrow.'

But I could not go to sleep and when the night nurse came on I sat up to watch her as she walked down the ward.

'Come here, sister,' the man called to her. 'I want to show you something. Bring a candle here.'

She walked over to his bed, holding her lantern high so that she could see him. He had pulled back his blankets and was holding his finger tight against his naked thigh.

'Look! I've got it here. Look!'

He lifted his finger and the nurse, bending forward with the light of the lantern full on her face, gestured impatiently. 'It's a freckle. Go to sleep.'

'It's no freckle. Look, it's moving.'

'Go to sleep,' she said, giving him a friendly pat on the shoulder.

She pulled the blankets over him. She was so calm and unconcerned that it comforted me. In a little while I was asleep.

When I woke up in the morning I lay for a moment thinking sleepily of the eggs in my locker. I had counted them the day befoe but, with my mind still bemused with sleep, I couldn't remember how many were there.

Breakfast in the hospital was a meal patients ate without enjoyment.

'You eat it to keep alive,' Angus explained to a new arrival one day. 'You couldn't eat it for any other reason.'

It consisted of a plate of porridge and two thin slices of bread bearing a scraping of butter. Those patients who could afford to buy eggs or had friends or relatives with fowls kept a supply of eggs in their locker. They treasured these eggs and became concerned when there were only one or two left.

'I'm getting low in eggs,' they would say, peering frowningly into their lockers.

Each morning a nurse walked down the ward carrying a basin.

'Come on. Hand out your eggs. Who's having eggs for breakfast?'

Patients would sit up hurriedly at the sound of her voice and lean towards their lockers, some stiffly and painfully, others weakly with drawn faces, and they would open the cupboard doors and reach in for the brown paper bags or cardboard boxes that contained their eggs. They would write their names upon the eggs they intended giving her then sit hunched forward in their beds looking around them as they nursed their eggs in the grey dawn light like sad birds in their nests.

It was necessary to write your name on the eggs you gave the nurse, for disputes often occurred and a man with a supply of large, brown eggs might claim he was given a pullet's egg when, after cooking, they were returned to their owners. There were some patients who took pride in the freshness of their eggs, and they would sniff suspiciously at the ones returned to them and argue they had received the staler ones of another patient.

Those patients who did not have any eggs always watched this morning ceremony with wistfulness that was sometimes resentful. Then they lay back and sighed or complained about the bad night they had had. Many patients shared their eggs with these unlucky ones.

'Now, here's three,' Angus might say to the nurse. 'One is for Tom over there, and one for Mick. The other's mine. I've marked them all. And tell the cook not to hard-boil them.'

The eggs were always returned hard-boiled. No egg cups were provided and you held the warm egg in your hand while you gouged into it with a spoon.

Mother sent me a dozen eggs a week and it delighted me to be able to call to a man across the ward, 'I'm putting in an egg for you this morning, Tom.' I liked to see the smile on his face when I told him this. My dozen eggs went very quickly; then Angus would give me one of his eggs each morning.

'You hand out eggs like a Buff Orpington,' he used to say. 'Hang on to some of them. I'm getting short.'

I was trying to work out what patients didn't have eggs when I suddenly thought of the new arrival who now, when it was light, did not seem so frightening. I sat up quickly and looked across to his bed but he was hidden beneath the blankets.

'What's he doing now?' I asked Angus.

'He's still seeing things,' answered McDonald, who was un-wrapping a small piece of butter he had taken from his locker. 'He was crook last night. He got out of bed once. Mick said he's as weak as a cat this morning.'

Mick was sitting up and yawning, accompanying his yawn with a doleful cry. He scratched his ribs and said, answering Angus, 'He's weak all right. No wonder ... The cow kept me awake half the night. How did you sleep, Mac?'

'No good. I've got that pain again. It's got me licked. It can't be my heart because it's on the right side. I told the doctor but he didn't say what it was. They tell you nothing.'

'It's a fact,' said Mick. 'I've always said there's no one feels the pain like yourself. I rolled on my arm last night and had the devil's own job to stop from yelling out. This bird here,' he nodded towards the new patient beneath his blankets, 'thinks he's crook. Well, he had a hell of a good time getting crook. I'll swop my arm for his guts any day.'

I liked listening to this talk in the morning but often had difficulty in understanding what was said. I always wanted to know much more.

'What did you roll over on your arm for?' I asked Mick.

'What for!' exclaimed Mick in surprise. 'What do you mean "What for"? How the hell do I know? I rolled on it because I thought it was my good arm. You're a funny little beggar, you are.'

The man in the bed beside him groaned and Mick turned and addressed the mound of bedclothes.

'Yes, you're done, brother. You're going to push up daises tomorrow. All good things come to an end, more's the pity.'

'Don't say that to him,' protested Angus. 'You'll frighten hell out of him. Do you want an egg this morning or not?'

'Make it two and I'll pay you back next week when me old woman visits me.'

'She mightn't bring you any.'

'And she mightn't at that,' said Mick nodding his head resignedly. 'It's a funny thing but a man never marries a woman as good as his mother. I've seen it scores of times. Women today are all the same. They're going back; anyone will tell you that. You go into my old mother's pantry back home now. Hell! A mouse couldn't push his way through the jars of pickles and jams and bottles of sauce and hop beer – all made with her own two hands. You ask any woman today to make you a pot of jam ... ' He gestured contemptuously, then added in a change of tone. 'She'll bring in the eggs. Give me two. I'm hellish hungry this morning.'

The drunk suddenly sat upright and flung back the blankets as if he were going to leap out of bed.

'Hey! Pull 'em over you again,' ordered Mick. 'You played up enough last night. Stop there. They'll strap you down if you bolt now.'

The man pulled the blankets back and sat clutching at his hair. He stopped and said to Mick, 'I can taste that medicine yet. Everything's jumping.'

'Do you want an egg?' I called out to him in a quavering, uncertain voice.

'The kid over there wants to know if you want an egg for breakfast,' Mick informed him.

'Yes,' he said still holding his hair. 'I'll have it. I'll have it. I've got to get me strength back.'

'He'll have it,' Mick called to me. 'Shove it in.'

I suddenly liked the man and decided to ask mother to bring me enough eggs for him too.

After breakfast the nurses hurried from bed to bed replacing the quilts they had removed the previous evening. They leant over each bed, the patients looking up at them from their pillows. The eyes of the nurses, as they concentrated on the movements of their hands, were not aware of the patients. They tucked in the bedclothes, smoothed them, patted them into creaseless bindings in preparation for the matron's tour of inspection.

Some of the nurses, if they were not in a hurry, would joke with us. Some of them were friendly, comfortable persons who gossiped with the patients and called the matron an 'old hen', and whispered 'Look out!' when the sisters came through.

One of these, Nurse Conrad, a dumpy little girl who often chuckled when she was talking to the patients, was a favourite of Angus's. He always kept an orange for her when anybody gave him some.

'There's a kind little girl, now,' he said to me one day when she smiled at him as she passed. 'I'll shout her to see "The Blanche Family", blowed if I don't!'

This travelling troupe of 'Instrumentalists and Master Entertainers' were on their annual visit to the town and the exciting posters announcing them had already been discussed by the patients.

'There's one thing I'll say about "The Blanche Family",' announced Mick, 'they give you a run for your money. There's a bloke there ... he was there last year and I'm tellin' ya, he's good ... This bloke played "She Wore a Wreath of Roses" on beer bottles, and hell! he brought the tears to your eyes. And only a little bloke ... Nothing to him ... You'd meet him in a pub and never notice him. By cripes, I'm sorry I'm missing it!'

The morning after they appeared Nurse Conrad, hurrying into the ward in the dawn light, was greeted by Angus, eager for news of her outing.

'Well, how did you get on?' he called to her.

'Oo! It was beaut,' she said, her plump cheeks shining from her morning bath. 'We had a second front seat.'

She paused for a moment to glance at the report book which rested on a desk near the doorway then hurried over to Angus where she began straightening his bedclothes while she told him about it.

'It was wonderful,' she said enthusiastically, 'and it was packed to the doors. The man who took the tickets at the door had a black cape on lined with red.'

'That'd be old man Blanche,' called Mick from across the ward. 'You can bet he'd be hanging round the dough.'

'He wasn't old.' Nurse Conrad was indignant.

'Well, his son, then,' said Mick. 'It's all the same.'

'Go on,' said McDonald.

'Did a little bloke there play "She Wore a Wreath of Roses" on beer bottles?' Mick wanted to know.

'Yes,' Nurse Conrad told him impatiently. 'But he played "Home Sweet Home" this time.'

'Were there any good singers there?' asked Angus. 'Did they sing any Scotch songs?'

'No, none of those. There was a man there – you'd scream at him – he sang "The Hob-nail Boots That My Father Wore". He had us in fits. And there was a Swiss man, all dressed like a Swiss and everything, he yodelled but ... '

'What's yodelled?' I asked.

I had been leaning over the side of my bed trying to get as close as I could to Nurse Conrad so that I could hear all she said. To me this concert was as exciting as a circus. Just to have seen the man wth the red-lined cape would have been a wonderful experience. Nurse Conrad now seemed a glamorous and interesting person as if seeing the concert had endowed her with qualities she had not possessed before.

'A man who can sing up high like,' she turned and told me quickly before continuing her story to Angus. 'I knew a boy in Bendigo. He was tall and everything ...' She chuckled and pushed a loose strand of hair beneath her cap. 'This boy – I don't care what anyone says – could yodel as good as this Swiss man. You know, Mr McDonald, I went with him and I could listen to him all night. I'll tell you what, I can't sing at all but I sing a lot to amuse myself, and, though I say it myself, I know a lot about music. I studied for seven years and I should know something. I loved last night, knowing about music and that. But this yodeller wasn't near as good as Bert, I don't care what anyone says.'

'No,' said McDonald flatly, 'that's right.' He seemed as if he didn't know what to say next. I wanted him to keep asking her questions but she turned and began tidying my bed. She bent over me and her face came close to mine as she tucked the edge of the blankets beneath the mattress.

'You're my boy, aren't you?' she said looking into my eyes and smiling.

'Yes,' I said tensely, unable to turn my gaze away and suddenly feeling I loved her. I was overcome with nervousness and couldn't say any more.

Acting on some impulse she bent and kissed my forehead then gave a little laugh and moved across to Mick, who said to her, 'An' I could do with a little bit of that myself now. I'm a child at heart, they tell me.'

'You, a married man, talking like that! What would your wife say? I think you must be a bad man.'

'Well, yes, an' I'm that too. I've no time for good men at all. The girls don't like'em either.'

'They do so.' Nurse Conrad was indignant.

'No,' said Mick. 'They're like kids. When my sister's kids do anything wrong their mother says, "You're growing like your uncle Mick." And they think I'm the best bloody uncle of the lot.'

'You mustn't swear like that.'

'No,' said Mick agreeably. 'I mustn't. That's right.'

'Now, don't crease your quilt. The matron is making her rounds early today.'

The matron was a stout woman with three black hairs sprouting from a mole on her chin.

'You'd think she'd pull'em out,' Mick observed one day after she had left the ward. 'But women are cranky that way. Once they pull'em out they reckon they're owning up to having them. So they hang on to them and pretend they're not there. Aw well, let her have 'em! She'd still win a Weight for Age even if she does carry a penalty.'

The matron walked swiftly from bed to bed closely followed by a respectful nurse who volunteered information about the patients she thought the matron should know.

'His wound is healing nicely, Matron. We have put this patient on to senega.'

The matron believed in cheering the sick.

'A few bright words work wonders,' she used to say, speaking the last three words with separate emphasis as if she were repeating a tongue twister.

Her uniform was always stiffly starched and dictated her way of moving so that sometimes she gave the impression of being animated by strings pulled by the nurse behind her.

When she finally appeared in the doorway the patients had finished their morning talk and were sitting or lying in some mood of expectation though subdued by the severity of their unrumpled beds, and brooding on their illnesses.

When Mick mentioned the matron, it was with irreverence, but now, as she approached his bed, his attitude was nervously respectful.

'How are you this morning, Bourke?' she asked with designed cheerfulness.

'Fine, Matron,' Mick responded cheerfully, but was unable to sustain it. 'That shoulder's crook but it's coming good, I think. I can't lift my arm properly yet. Is that anything serious like?'

'No, Bourke. The doctor is quite satisfied.'

She smiled at him and moved away.

'A hell of a lot of satisfaction you get from her,' muttered Mick sourly when she was out of hearing.

When the matron reached my bed she assumed the attitude of one about to say amusing and comforting things to a child for the purpose of impressing the adults listening. It always made me uncomfortable – as if I were being pushed on to a stage and told to perform.

'Well, how is the brave little man this morning? Nurse tells me you often sing in the morning. Will you sing for me one day?'

I was too confused to answer.

'He sings "Sh! Sh! Go out black cat",' said the nurse who had moved forward. 'He sings so nicely, too.'

'I think you will be a singer one day,' said the matron. 'Would you like to be a singer?'

She did not wait for me to answer but turned to the nurse and continued, 'Most children want to be an engine driver when they grow up. My nephew is like that. I bought him a toy train and he is so fond of it, the pet.'

She turned to me again, 'Tomorrow you'll go to sleep and when you wake up your leg will be in a lovely white cocoon. Won't that be nice?' then to the nurse, 'His operation is at 10.30. Sister will attend to his prep.'

'What's an operation?' I asked Angus when they had gone.

'Oh, they mess around with your leg ... fix it up ... Nothing much ... They do it while you're asleep.'

I could see he did not want to explain it to me and a feeling of fear touched me for a moment.

Once when father had left a young horse standing in the brake, the reins tied to the rim of the strapped wheel, while he went in to get a cup of tea, it had plunged and snapped the tightened reins and bolted through the gate leaving the smashed brake piled against the post as it galloped away free.

Father, who had dashed out at the sound, stood surveying the wreckage for a moment, then turned to me – I had followed him – and said, 'Well, blast it, anyway! Let's go and finish our cup of tea.'

I thought of this for some reason when Angus paused and made no further explanation. It came to me like a deep breath.

'Well, blast it, anyway!' I said.

'That's the spirit,' said Angus.

CHAPTER 5

Dr Robertson, who attended me, was a tall man who always wore his Sunday suit.

I divided clothes into two groups – Sunday clothes and those you wore the rest of the week. You could sometimes wear your Sunday suit during the week but only on special occasions.

My Sunday suit was a coarse, blue serge that came in a brown, cardboard box. It was wrapped in tissue paper and had a wonderful new smell.

But I didn't like wearing it because I had to keep it clean. Father didn't like his Sunday suit either.

'Let's get this darn thing off,' he'd say after returning from church, a place he rarely went to, and only then because mother insisted.

I was amazed that Dr Robertson wore his Sunday suit every day. Not only that, I counted them and found he had four Sunday suits so I concluded he must be very rich and live in a house with a lawn. People who had a lawn in front of their house or drove a rubber-tyred jinker or an Abbot buggy were always rich.

One day I said to the doctor, 'Have you an Abbot buggy?'

'Yes,' he said, 'I have.'

'Has it got rubber tyres?'

'Yes, it has.'

After that I always found it difficult to talk to him. All the people I knew were poor. I knew the names of rich people and had seen them driving past our place but they never looked at poor people or spoke to them.

'Here comes Mrs Carruthers,' my sister would yell, and we would rush to the gate to see her go past, a groom driving her pair of grey horses.

It was like seeing the Queen go by.

I could understand Dr Robertson talking to Mrs Carruthers but I could never get used to him speaking to me.

He had pale, sunless skin, darkening on the cheeks where the razor had slid over the sunken roots of his beard. I liked his eyes which were light blue with wrinkles around them that folded when he laughed. His long, narrow hands smelt of soap and were cool when he touched you.

He pressed my back and legs and asked me if it hurt, then he stood erect and looked down at me and said to the sister, 'Severe curvature there already. The muscles on one side of his back are badly affected.'

After he had examined my leg he patted my head and said, 'We'll soon straighten that.' And to the sister, 'A realignment of his thigh bone is necessary.' His hand moved to my ankle and he continued, 'The sinews here will have to be shortened and the foot lifted. We'll cut them in front of the ankle.'

He moved his finger in a slow stroke just above my knee.

'We'll do the alignment here.'

I always remember the movement of his finger since it marked the line of the scar I was to bear.

The morning before he operated on my leg he paused as he was passing my bed and said to the matron, who was accompanying him, 'He seems to have adjusted himself quite well; doesn't brood at all.'

'No, he's quite a bright little fellow,' said the matron, then added in a cheering-the-sick voice, 'He sings "Sh! Sh! Go out black cat"', don't you, Alan?'

'Yes,' I said, experiencing the confusion that always came to me when she addressed me in this fashion.

The doctor looked at me reflectively for a moment then suddenly stepped foward and pulled back my blankets.

'Turn over so that I can look at your back,' he ordered.

I turned over and for a moment felt his cool hands move down my curved spine in a questing way.

'Good!' he said raising himself and holding the blankets aloft so that I could turn over again.

When I faced him once more he rumpled my hair and said, 'Tomorrow we will straighten that leg of yours,' then he added, smiling at me in a way I thought was strange, 'You are a brave boy.'

I accepted his tribute without any feeling of pride, wondering what made him say it and wishing he knew what a good runner I was. I considered telling him but he had turned to 'Daddy' who was grinning up at him with his toothless gums as he sat in his wheelchair.

Daddy belonged to the hospital like a cat belongs to a home. He was an old-age pensioner with paralysed legs and he propelled himself round the ward, or out on the verandah, in a wheelchair that had a circular rail atached to the spokes. Daddy's thin, wiry hands would clutch these rails and turn the wheels with quick thrusts. He leant forward in the chair as he propelled himself rapidly down the ward and I envied him and saw myself dashing round the hospital in such a chair and, later, winning chair races at sports meetings and calling out, 'Take your lap,' like bike riders.

Daddy always took up his position beside my bed during the doctor's visit. He watched the doctor eagerly as he moved round the ward, keyed and ready to say something he had prepared to impress the doctor when he stopped in front of him. It was no use speaking to him at such times; he wouldn't hear you. Yet, at other times, he talked continually.

He was an old pessimist and complainer and didn't like having to bath each day.

'The Eskimos don't wash, and you couldn't kill them with an axe,' he'd say in defence of his attitude to water.

The sister put him in the bath each day and he regarded this as bad for the chest.

'Sister, don't put me under that squirty thing again or I'll get pneumonia.'

He had a face that shut into folds when he closed his mouth. His domed head was sparsely covered with fine, grey hairs, too thinly covered to hide his scalp which was shiny and blotched with brown.

He repelled me a little, not because of his appearance, which I found interesting, but because I thought he was rude, and because the way he spoke sometimes made me feel uncomfortable. Once when he said to the sister, 'Sister, I have had no overflow of the guts this morning. Does it matter?' I looked quickly at the sister to see her reaction but her face didn't change.

His complaints irritated me and I thought that sometimes he should say he felt good instead of always saying he felt bad.

'How are you, Daddy?' Mick sometimes asked him.

'Never been worse.'

'You're not dead yet, you know,' Mick would reply cheerfully.

'No, but the way I am it will be any tick o' the clock now, any tick o' the clock.' Daddy would shake his head mournfully and propel himself over to the bed of some newcomer who had not yet grown tired of his moaning.

He respected the matron and was always careful not to offend her mainly because she had the power to send him away to some old men's home.

'You don't last no time at all in them there places,' he told Angus, 'that's if you're sick. Once you're old and crook the quicker the govmint gets rid of you the better they like it.'

So he always spoke to the matron as agreeably as he could, anxious to placate her and to say things that suggested he was suffering from serious complaints that warranted his stopping at the hospital.

'Me heart feels as dead as mutton in me guts,' he told her once when she asked him how he was.

I got a picture of a butcher's block with a severed heart lying damp and cold upon it and I felt depressed and said to Angus, 'I am well today. I feel very well today.'

'That's the stuff,' he said, 'keep up the good work.'

I liked Angus.

That morning when the matron was making her rounds, she said to Daddy, who had wheeled his chair to the front of the fire that warmed the ward. 'Who crushed these curtains?'

The open window they covered was near the fireplace and the breeze had been wafting them towards the fire.

'I did, Matron,' admitted Daddy. 'I thought they might blow in the fire.'

'Well, your hands must have been filthy,' she said angrily, 'you've left black marks all over them. Always ask the nurse to tuck them back in the future.'

Daddy noticed me listening and later he said to me, 'You know, the matron is a beautiful woman. She saved my life yesterday but I think she's upset about the curtains, but, you know, if I had been in my own hut I'd have done the same with my curtains. You can't be too careful with fires.'

'My father has seen a house burnt down,' I told him.

'Yes, yes,' he said impatiently, 'he would ... The way he walks down the ward you'd reckon he's seen the lot. The flames catch hold of the curtains and away she goes – that's how it hapens.'

Sometimes a Presbyterian Minister visited Daddy. This dark-clothed man knew Daddy when the old fellow lived in a hut by the river. After Daddy had been taken to hospital the Minister continued visiting him and brought him tobacco and copies of the *Messenger*. He was a young man with an earnest voice who backed away like a nervous horse when any nurse revealed an intention to talk to him. Daddy was anxious to get him married and ofered him to several of the nurses. I had always listened without much interest to Daddy's praise of the man and to the reaction of the nurses when Daddy suggested they marry him, but when he put the proposition to Nurse Conrad I sat up with a sudden feeling of apprehension, anticipating she would accept the old man's offer.

'There's a nice single man for you,' Daddy told her. 'He's got a nice place – mightn't be too clean, but, still, you could clean it up. You've only got to say the word. He's a clean-living bloke, of course ... '

'I'll think about it,' Nurse Conrad promised him. 'Perhaps I'll go and look the place over. Has he got a horse and gig?'

'No,' said Daddy. 'There's nowhere to keep a horse at his place.'

'I want a horse and gig,' said Nurse Conrad lightly.

'I'm going to have a horse and gig some day,' I called out to her.

'All right, I'll marry you.' She smiled at me and waved her hand.

I lay back suddenly feeling excitingly old and full of responsibility. I had no doubts that now Nurse Conrad and I were engaged to be married. I adjusted my expression until I thought it resembled that of a brave explorer looking across the sea. I repeated in my mind several times, 'Yes, we'll charge it to your account'. I always associated this remark with being grown up. I often repeated it to myself when I wanted to feel a man instead of a little boy. I must have heard it one day when I was out with father.

The rest of that day I thought out plans for getting a horse and gig.

After Dr Robertson had left me, he said to Daddy, 'How are you this morning, Daddy?'

'Well, Doctor, I'm bound up as if I'm sanded. I reckon I should be drenched. Do you think a dose of salts'd shift me?'

'I think it would,' said the doctor gravely. 'I'll order you some.'

The doctor crossed the ward and stopped beside the bed of the drunk who was sitting waiting for him, his face with its twitching mouth stamped with anxiety.

'And how are you?' asked the doctor dryly.

'I've still got the shakes a bit,' said the man, 'but I'm good. I think I could go out this afternoon, Doctor.'

'I don't think you are quite clear in the head yet, Smith. Weren't you stark naked in the ward this morning?'

The patient looked at him in a stupefied way and then said in quick explanation, 'Yes, that's right. I did that. I got up to wash my feet. I was terrible hot round the feet. They were burning.'

'Maybe tomorrow,' said the doctor shortly. 'You may be able to leave tomorrow. I'll see.'

The doctor walked briskly away and the patient sat leaning forward plucking at the bedclothes with his fingers. He suddenly lay down.

'Oh dear!' he moaned. 'Oh dear me!'

After Dr Robertson had left the ward, mother, who had been waiting, was allowed to come in and see me. I felt shy and embarrassed as she walked towards me. I knew she would kiss me and I regarded this as a bit sissy. Father never kissed me.

'Men never kiss,' he told me.

I regarded displays of affection as a weakness. But I would have been disappointed if mother had not kissed me.

I had not seen her for a few weeks and she looked a new mother to me. Her smile, her comfortable figure, the fair hair that was coiled into a bun at her neck – all these were so familiar to me that I had never noticed them before; now I looked at her, noting these things with pleasure.

Her mother had been an Irish woman from Tipperary and her father a German. Her father had been a gentle and kindly man who had come to Australia with a German band in which he played the bassoon.

She must have resembled her father. She had his colouring. She had a pleasant expression and wore her character upon her face for all to see.

The wind and rain of many a winter's drive in the open brake had left fine lines upon her weathered face, a face that cosmetics had never touched, not because she did not believe in them but because she never had the money to buy them.

When she reached my bed she must have noticed my embarrassment because she whispered, 'I'd like to kiss you but there are too many looking so we'll pretend I have.'

When father visited me the conversation was dominated by him even though he was a good listener, but with mother I always took charge.

'Did you bring plenty of eggs?' I asked her. 'There's a poor man here with no eggs. When he looks at a chair it moves.'

Mother looked across at the man – I had glanced at him as I spoke – and said, 'Yes, I've brought you a lot.'

Then she felt in her bag and said, 'I've brought you something else too,' and she brought out a brown paper parcel tied with string.

'What is it?' I whispered excitedly. 'Let me see. I'll open it. Give it to me.'

'Please,' she prompted me, withholding the parcel.

'Please,' I repeated, holding out my hand.

'Mrs Carruthers sent it to you,' she said. 'We haven't opened it, but we're all waiting to see what is in it.'

'How did she bring it?' I asked, taking the parcel and placing it on my knee. 'Did she come to the house?'

'She drove up to the front gate and handed it to Mary and she told Mary it was for her little sick brother.'

I tugged at the string, trying to break it. Like father, I grimaced when putting effort into my fingers. He always did it when opening a pocket knife. ('I got it from my mother.')

'Dear me! what a face you're pulling!' mother said. 'Here, give it to me. I'll cut it. Is there a knife in your locker?'

'There's one in mine,' said Angus who had been watching us. 'You'll find it near the front, I think. Just open that drawer there.'

Mother found his knife and after she had cut the string I slipped off the paper wrapping impressively addressed to 'Master Alan Marshall' and looked excitedly at the lid of a flat box featuring pictures of windmills and barrows and waggons made from perforated strips of metal. I lifted the lid and there lay the strips and beside them, in smaller compartments, were screws and screwdrivers and spanners and wheels. I could hardly believe it was mine.

The toy was impressive but the fact that it came from Mrs Carruthers was unbelievable.

It could almost be said that Mrs Carruthers was Turalla. She had built the Presbyterian Church there, the Sunday School, the new wing of the Manse. The annual school prizes were donated by her. All the farmers were deeply in debt to her. She was President of 'The Band of Hope', 'The Bible Class', and 'The League of Australian Women'. She owned Mount Turalla, Lake Turalla, and all the best land along Turalla Creek. She had a specially padded pew in the church with a special hymn book bound in leather.

Mrs Carruthers knew all the hymns and sang looking up a little. But she sang 'Nearer my God to Thee' and 'Lead Kindly Light' in alto and for these she kept her chin down and looked stern because she had to go down very low.

When the Minister announced these hymns father would mutter
into the hymn book, 'Here she goes.' Mother didn't like him saying
this.

'She has quite a good voice,' she told him once when we were
having our Sunday dinner.

'It's good,' said father. 'I'll give her that. But she'll tag along
behind the field and still pip the lot of us on the post. She'll break
down if she keeps that up.'

Mr Carruthers was dead but, according to father, when he was
alive he was always protesting against something. When he protested he raised a pudgy hand and cleared his throat. He protested
against cows on the road and the decline in manners. He also
protested against father.

Mr Carruthers' father, representing an English company, had
landed in Melbourne in 1837 and made west from that town in
bullock drays laden with stores. It was said there was rich volcanic
land awaiting settlement in the open forest country a hundred miles
or more away, though the Blacks were considered unfriendly and
would have to be dealt with. The party had rifles for this purpose.

Mr Carruthers eventually took up hundreds of square miles of
rich land that, now divided into scores of farms all mortgaged to the
estate, brought in a large income in interest alone.

The large bluestone mansion he had built on a picked site was
eventually inherited by his son and on the son's death it became the
property of Mrs Carruthers.

The enormous house stood in the centre of thirty acres of parkland, a large area of which was laid out in gardens designed in
English style with ordered pathways and formal flowerbeds bloom-
ing under strict direction.

In the shade of elms and oaks, and sheltered by shrubs brought
out from England, pheasants, peacocks, and strange coloured
ducks from China pecked and scratched in the leaf mould left from
autumn fallings. A man in gaiters moved amongst them, his raised
gun occasionally bursting into sharp reports as he shot at the
rosellas and red lories that came in to eat the fruit on the orchard
trees.

In the spring, snowdrops and daffodils flowered amidst the dark
green of Australian bracken and gardeners wheeled laden barrows
between the hollyhocks and phlox. Their sharp shovels, striking at
the tufted grass and the heaped twigs and leaves rising to the base
of the few remaining gums, severed the roots of surviving green-
hoods and Early Nancies and they toppled and fell and were
carried away in the barrows to be burnt.

And the thirty acres were clean and smooth and orderly.

'The Blacks would never know it now,' my father said to me when we were driving past the gate one day.

From the gateway to the homestead a gravelled drive wound between rows of elm trees. Just inside this gateway a small cottage, 'The Lodge', housed the gatekeeper and his family. At the sound of trotting horses or the grating of carriage wheels on the gravel he would hurry from his house and swing open the gates and raise his hat to those who entered. Visiting squatters driving Abbot buggies and pairs, city visitors in leather-sprung carriages, ladies with thin waists sitting stiffly in phaetons, looking over the heads of prim little girls and boys poised on the edges of seats facing them – they all went past the gatehouse and nodded or smiled patronisingly or ignored the gatekeeper and his raised hat.

Half-way up the drive was a small fenced enclosure. Once tall bluegums had lifted their naked limbs high above the kangaroo grass and emu bush that grew there but now dark pines shaded it and the ground beneath them was padded with brown needles.

A red deer walked ceaselessly round the enclosure, following a worn track that skirted the fence. Sometimes it raised its head and bellowed hoarsely, and carolling magpies ceased their song and flew hurriedly away.

Across from the enclosure were the stables, large, two-storey, bluestone buildings with lofts and stalls and feed bins hollowed from the trunks of trees. On the stone cobbles that surrounded the buildings grooms hissed in English fashion as they currycombed the horses that stamped restlessly, flicking their docked tails in a useless attempt to rid themselves of flies.

A wide roadway led from the stables to the portico of the homestead. When a visiting Governor or an English gentleman and his lady came up from Melbourne to experience station life and see the 'real Australia' their carriages would stop beneath the portico while they alighted; then their grooms would drive the carriages down the wide approach to the stables.

On these nights the Carruthers would hold a ball in the big house and, from a backen-covered hill behind the mansion where a clump of wattles had escaped destruction, the more daring or wistful of Turalla's residents would stand looking down at the vast, lighted windows behind which women in low-cut gowns and carrying fans bowed to their partners in the opening of the Waltz Quadrilles. The music would come up to this little group of people and they would not feel the cold. They were listening to a fairy story.

Once when father stood with them holding a half-empty bottle, he began to give a happy whoop at the end of every swing in the set they were dancing behind the lighted windows and he wheeled round the wattles with the bottle as a partner, whooping to the music.

After a while a stout man wearing a gold watch chain from which hung a gold-mounted lion's claw, a mounted miniature of the man's mother and several medals, came out to investigate the whoops.

He ordered father away and when father continued whooping he swung a punch at father. In explaining what happened afterwards, father would say, 'I sidestepped him then came in quick and played up and down his ribs with the good old one-two-three like a xylophone. The wind that came out his mouth nearly blew my hat off.'

When father was helping the man to his feet and brushing his clothes, he said to him, 'I thought you had too many gee-gaws about you to be any good.'

'Yes,' said the man vaguely. 'Too many ... Yes, yes ... I feel slightly dazed ...'

'Have a drink,' said father handing him the bottle. After the man drank he and father shook hands.

'He was all right,' explained father afterwards. 'He'd just got in with the wrong mob.'

Father broke in most of Carruthers' horses and was friends with Peter Finlay, the head groom. Peter often visited our place and he and father discussed articles in the *Bulletin* and the books they had read.

Peter Finlay was a remittance man and could talk on anything. All the Carruthers were poor talkers. Their reputation for brains was based on their ability to say, 'Hm, yes,' or 'Hm, no,' at the right times.

Peter could talk quickly, with enthusiasm, and people listened to him. Mr Carruthers often said that Peter's gift for talking intelligently was the result of good breeding and that it was unfortunate he had come down in the world.

Peter didn't think he had come down.

'My old man lived according to ritual,' he told father. 'A hell of a ritual it was too. I had a hard job breaking away from it.'

Mr Carruthers found it difficult to entertain the important people he invited to his home. His evenings with these visitors were full of long, uncomfortable silences. A visiting Governor or a titled Englishman was not impressed by 'Hm, yes,' or 'Hm, no,' so Mr

Carruthers always sent down to the stables for Peter, when his guests were men of importance who expected their brandy to be drunk in an atmosphere of discussion.

When Peter received Mr Carruthers' message he immediately made for the big house where he entered by a back door. In a small room reserved for the purpose was a bed with a damask quilt and upon the bed, neatly folded, was one of Mr Carruthers' best suits. Peter would put the suit on, then present himself at the Drawing Room where he would be introduced as a visiting Englishman.

At the dinner table his conversation delighted the guests and gave openings for Mr Carruthers to say 'Hm, yes,' or 'Hm, no,' in an intelligent manner.

After the guests had retired Peter would take off Mr Carruthers' suit and go back to his room behind the stables.

Once he came to father and told him that Mr Carruthers would like father to put on an exhibition of riding for the benefit of some important visitors who were staying at the station and were anxious to see something of real Australia.

At first father was resentful at the suggestion and said, 'To hell with them,' but after a while he reckoned he'd do it for ten bob.

'Ten bob's ten bob,' he reasoned. 'You can't just turn your back on it.'

Peter thought this would be satisfactory to Mr Carruthers even if it was a bit high.

Father was undecided as to what 'real Australia' was, though he told Peter that if people wanted to see it they would find it by looking in his pantry. Sometimes father thought that poverty was the real Australia but he only thought this when he was sad.

On the day he was to present himself at Carruthers' he tied a red handkerchief round his neck and put a cabbage-tree hat on his head and rode a bay mare called Gay Girl who would buck if you touched her flanks with your heels.

She was sixteen hands and could jump like a kangaroo, so when the visitors were all nicely seated on the wide verandah, sipping drinks, father appeared galloping through the trees like a bush-ranger and whooping in a wild, frightening fashion.

'I came round the bend to the five-bar gate flat out,' he said, when telling the story. 'The take-off isn't bad – a bit of gravel but enough dirt for a grip. I steady her till her stride is balanced then put her at it. I've always said a grass-fed horse'll give you all you want in a burst. I'd only brought Gay Girl in and she is fresh as paint. Well, she takes off too soon, of course – being fresh, see – but, anyway, she's going to clout, I can see that; the gate's swung high –

you could walk under it. They reckon, you know, that Carruthers'd
sack a bloke for putting up a scraping gate. I wouldn't put it past
him.'

He gestured contemptuously, then went on:

'When I feel Gay Girl lift I go up with her to save her as much
weight as I can – you could've shoved your head between me and
the saddle as she rises. It's her front legs I'm worried about though;
once they're over I'm with her all the way.

'Hell, that horse could jump! S'elp me Bob! she gives a twist and
gets another two inches from the air. It don't stop her clouting with
her back legs but she's in her stride two bounds from where she
lands, and I'm sitting on her as snug as a brand.

'I reef her back on her haunches beside the verandah just in front
of this Carruthers mob and they're on their feet shoving back chairs
before they've swallowed their last mouthful of grog.

'Well, I jam my heels into Gay Girl's flanks then, and she's into
it, squealing like a pig. She tries to brush me off against a tree –
she's like that, a dirty bucker. I drag her round, flapping me hat
against her ribs and she bounds sideways on to the verandah. She's
a twisting bucker and every time she spins she knocks over a chair
or a table. There's glasses of grog flying everywhere, and blokes
jumping up, and women screaming, and some of the blokes jump
between me and the women with faces on them like they was
heroes, and women hang on to 'em, and the boat's going down, and
throw out the lifebelts, and kiss me goodbye, and God Save the
King, and all that sort of thing. Hell! you never saw the like.'

When father reached this stage of the story he began laughing
and didn't stop till he had wiped his eyes with his handkerchief.

'Aw, hell!' he said, taking a breath, then concluded, 'Well, before
I quieten her, I knock Sir Frederick Salisbury, or whatever his
name is, head over turkey into a clump of peacocks.'

'Did all this happen, dad?' I asked him once. 'Is it true?'

'Hell, yes ... Well, wait a minute ...' He screwed up his face and
rubbed his chin with his hand. 'Well, no, son, I suppose it isn't,' he
decided. 'Something like that happened but after you tell it a few
times you keep on making it better and funnier, see. I'm not telling
lies. I'm telling a funny story. It's good to make people laugh.
There's a hell of a lot of other things making them sad.'

'Is it like that about the deer?' I asked him.

'Yes,' he said. 'It is, a bit. I rode him but that's all.'

Why Mr Carruthers protested against father was because father
rode his deer.

'There he was going round and round and round,' he told me.

'Poor beggar . . . I was up there with some of the boys and I stood on the fence and as he passed beneath me I jumped on to his back. They reckon I wasn't game, of course.' He paused, looking ahead of him and stroking his chin, a faint smile on his face, then added, 'Hell!' in a tone that suggested a terrific reaction from the deer.

He would never tell me much about this escapade, which he seemed to regard as childish. All he would say when I asked 'Did he go?' was 'Did he what!'

But I asked Peter Finlay about it, thinking that father's reluctance to talk about it must have meant he was thrown.

'Did the deer toss father?' I asked Peter.

'No,' he said, 'your father tossed the deer.'

Later, someone told me the deer broke a horn on father and this was what annoyed Mr Carruthers who saved the deer's horns and put them over his mantelpiece.

After Mr Carruthers died, Mrs Carruthers sent the deer away, but, when I was old enough to go sneaking through the estate, you could still see the deep track it had made walking round and round.

It was because of these things and because of the awe in which everyone in Turalla, except father, held Mrs Carruthers that I looked at this box on the bed before me almost reverently, valuing it far more than any other gift I had received. It was valuable not because it could entertain me – a candlebox on wheels would have pleased me better – but because it was evidence that Mrs Carruthers was aware of my existence and that she thought me important enough for her to buy me a present.

No other person in all Turalla had ever had a gift from Mrs Carruthers – only me. And she had a rubber-tyred Abbot buggy and a pair of grey horses and peacocks and millions of pounds.

'Mum,' I said looking up at her, my hands still clasped round the box, 'when Mrs Carruthers handed Mary the present, did Mary touch her?'

CHAPTER 6

Next morning I was not given any breakfast but I did not feel very hungry. I was restless and excited and had moments of fear during which I wanted mother.

At half past ten Nurse Conrad wheeled a trolley, resembling a narrow table on wheels, beside my bed and said, 'Come on. Sit up now. I'm going to take you for a ride.'

She pulled back my blankets.

'I'll get on,' I said. 'I'll get on it.'

'No, I'll lift you,' she said. 'Don't you like me putting my arms around you?'

I looked quickly at Angus and then at Mick to see if they had heard.

'Go on,' Mick called out. 'She's the prettiest bell wether you're ever likely to meet. Give her a go.'

She lifted me in her arms and held me a moment, smiling down at me, 'I'm not a bell wether, am I?'

'No,' I replied, not understanding that a bell wether was the Judas sheep of the slaughter yards trained to lead those about to be slaughtered into the killing pen.

She laid me on the cold, flat top of the trolley and covered me with a blanket.

'Away we go!' she said gaily.

'Keep your pecker up,' encouraged Angus. 'You'll be back with us soon.'

'Yes, he's going to wake up in his own warm bed,' said Nurse Conrad.

'Good luck to you!' called Mick.

The drunk raised himself on an elbow and said hoarsely to me as we passed his bed, 'Thanks for the eggs, mate.' Then he added more strongly, 'Good on ya!'

Nurse Conrad wheeled me down a long corridor and through glass doors into the theatre in the centre of which stood a high table with thin, white legs.

Sister Cooper and a nurse were standing near a bench upon which steel instruments lay on a white cloth.

'Well, here you are!' exclaimed the sister walking over to me and stroking my head.

I looked into her eyes, seeking assurance there.

'Feeling frightened?' she asked.

'Yes.'

'You silly boy. There's nothing to be frightened of. In a minute you'll go to sleep and after a little while you'll wake up in your bed again.'

I could not understand how this was possible. I was certain I would wake up from any sleep if the nurses tried to move me. I wondered whether they were just saying this to fool me and that, instead of waking up in my bed, something painful was going to happen to me. But I believed Nurse Conrad.

'I'm not frightened,' I said to the sister.

'I know you're not,' she said confidentially as she lifted me on to the table and placed a low pillow beneath my head. 'Now don't move or you'll roll off.'

Dr Robertson entered briskly and stood smiling down at me as he massaged his fingers.

'"Sh! Sh! Go out black cat", so that's the song you sing, is it?'

He patted me and turned away.

'Abbot buggies and black cats, eh!' he murmured as a nurse came forward and helped him into a white gown. 'Abbot buggies and black cats! Well! Well!'

Dr Clarke, a grey-haired man with a tight-lipped mouth, walked in.

'The Council hasn't filled in that hole near the gate yet,' he said, turning to face a nurse holding his white gown up in front of her ready for him to slip it on. 'I don't know ... Can you rely on any man's word these days? This gown seems too big ... No, it's mine all right.'

I looked at the white ceiling and thought of the puddle near our gate that always came after rain; I could jump it easily but Mary couldn't. I could jump any puddle.

Dr Clarke had moved round to my head where he stood holding a hollowed, white pad like a shell, above my nose.

At a sign from Dr Robertson he saturated the pad with liquid he poured from a little blue bottle and I gasped as I drew a laden breath. I jerked my head from side to side but he followed my nose with the pad and I saw coloured lights, then clouds came and I floated away upon them.

*　　*　　*

I did not wake up in my bed as Sister Cooper and Nurse Conrad had promised. I fought through haze and a swinging world without comprehending where I was until suddenly, in a moment of clarity, I saw the ceiling of the theatre again. Then, after a little while, I could see the sister's face. She was saying something to me but I could not hear her. But, in a moment I could, and she was saying, 'Wake up.'

After I had lain quietly for a while I remembered everything and I suddenly felt cheated.

'I'm not in bed like you said,' I muttered.

'No, you woke up before we got you there,' she explained, then added, 'You mustn't move even the tiniest bit. The plaster on your leg is still wet.'

I became conscious of my heavy leg and the stone-like clasp of the plaster encircling my hips and waist.

'Lie still now,' she said. 'I'm going out for a minute. Watch him, nurse,' she said to Nurse Conrad who was putting instruments away into glass cases.

Nurse Conrad came over to me. 'How's my boy now?' she asked.

Her face was beautiful to me. I loved her plump cheeks, flushed like apples, and her twinkling little eyes tucked away beneath thick, dark brow and long lashes. I wanted her to stop with me and not go away and I wanted to give her a horse and gig. But I felt sick and I was shy and couldn't tell her these things.

'Don't move, will you?' she cautioned me.

'I think I might have moved my toes a bit,' I said.

The repeated warnings not to move made me want to move just to see what would happen. I felt that once I knew I could move I would be satisfied and stop.

'You mustn't even move your toes,' she said.

'I won't again,' I told her.

I was kept on the operating table until lunch time, then wheeled carefully to my bed where a steel framework held the blankets high above my legs and prevented me from seeing Mick across the ward.

It was visiting day and relatives and friends of the patients began to arrive. They strode down the ward laden with parcels, looking neither to the right nor the left, acutely conscious of the sick people each side of them as they kept their gaze on the patient they were visiting. The patients were self-conscious as they awaited the visitors approaching them. They looked away from them, pretending not to notice them until they stood beside their bed.

Those patients who had no friends or relatives to visit them did not lack for visitors. A Salvation Army lass or a Minister or a Priest would stop and talk to them – and then, there was always Miss Forbes.

Miss Forbes came each visiting day laden with flowers and tracts and bedsocks. She must have been seventy years old. She walked stiffly, helped by a stick, and she would tap this stick against the end of the bed of those who ignored her and say, 'Well, young man, I hope you're doing what the doctor tells you. That is the way to get well, you know. Now, here are some currant cakes for you. If you chew them well they won't give you indigestion. Always chew your food well.'

She always gave me a humbug lolly.

'They clear the chest,' she said.

She stopped at the foot of my bed as usual and said gently, 'So you have been under an operation today, have you? Well, the doctors know what they're doing and I'm sure it's all for the best. So never mind, there's a good boy. Never mind, there's a good boy.'

My leg was aching and I was lonely. I began to cry.

She was concerned and came quickly round to the side of my bed and stood there awkwardly, anxious to comfort me but uncertain what she should do.

'God will help you to bear your suffering,' she said earnestly. 'Here! I have some messages here.'

She took some tracts from her handbag and handed me one.

'You read that; there's a good boy.'

She touched my hand and walked self-consciously away, but she looked back at me several times, her face troubled.

I looked at the tract in my hand, feeling it might contain some magic, some sign from God, some inspired message that would enable me to get up and walk like Lazarus.

The tract was headed, 'Why Are Ye Troubled?' and it began, 'If living a stranger to God, you may well be troubled. The thought of death and judgment to come may well give you trouble. If this is your condition, God grant that your trouble may be greater and greater, until you find rest in Jesus.'

I didn't understand it. I put it on my locker and continued crying softly.

'How're you feeling now, Alan?' asked Angus.

'I feel heavy,' I said. After a while I told him, 'My leg is aching.'

'It will soon stop,' he said to comfort me.

But it didn't stop.

When lying on the operating table, the plaster around my right leg and around my waist still moist and soft, I must have lifted my big toe in some brief spasm but lacked the strength in my paralysed muscles to force it down again to its natural position. Some movement of my hip, too, had lifted the inside plaster bandage, setting it in a ridge that pressed like a blunt knife against my hip bone. Gradually over the next two weeks this ridge ground its way into my flesh till it touched the bone itself.

The pain from my lifted toe was unceasing but I got some relief from my torn hip when I lay still with my body twisted a little. Even in the short intervals of sleep that came to me between the waiting periods of pain, I had dreams in which I moved through other worlds of suffering.

Dr Robertson looked frowningly down at me as he pondered on my descriptions of my pains.

'Are you sure it is your toe that is paining you?'

'Yes. All the while,' I told him. 'It never stops.'

'It must be his knee,' he said to the matron. 'He probably imagines it is his toe. And this pain in your hip ...' He turned to me, 'Does your hip ache all the time too?'

'It hurts when I move. It doesn't hurt when I lie still.'

He pushed against the plaster above my hip.

'Does that hurt?'

'Oo!' I exclaimed, trying to move away from him. 'Oo, yes!'

'Hm!' he muttered.

A week after the operation, an angry defiance that had enabled me to bear the pain gave way to despair, and the fear I had of being thought a baby did not help me any more. I began to cry more often. I cried silently, gazing open-eyed through my tears at the high, white ceiling above me. I wished I was dead, seeing in death not a frightening absence of life, but a sleeping without pain.

I began repeating over and over again in my mind in a jerky rhythm, 'I wish I were dead, I wish I were dead, I wish I were dead.'

I found, after a few days, that by jerking my head from side to side to the rhythm of the repeated words, I achieved a mental distraction that brought relief from the pain. By keeping my eyes open as I flung my head from side to side on the pillow, the white ceiling quickly became blurred and the bed upon which I lay rose on wings from the floor.

Beyond this first dizzy state was a nebulous, clouded place wherein I swung in mighty curves through darkness and light free from pain but gripped by nausea.

Here I remained until the will to continue tossing my head was lost to me and I slowly returned, moving towards formless shadows that shimmered and swayed and then materialised into the beds and windows and walls of the ward.

I usually sought this relief at night but sometimes, if the pain was bad, I did it in the daytime when the nurses were out of the ward.

Angus must have noticed me jerking my head from side to side for one day he asked quickly, just as I had begun moving my head, 'What d'you do that for, Alan?'

'Nothing,' I said.

'Come on, now,' he said. 'We're mates. What makes you jerk your head? Are you in pain?'

'It stops the pain.'

'Oh!' he said. 'Is that it! How does it stop the pain?'

'I don't feel it. I get giddy an' that,' I explained.

He did not say anything but later I heard him telling Nurse Conrad that something had better be done about it.

'He's game,' he said. 'He wouldn't do that unless he was crook.'

That night the sister gave me the needle and I slept without waking but next day the pain continued and I was given doses of A.P.C. and told to lie quietly and go to sleep.

I waited till the nurse had left the ward and then began rocking my head again. But she had expected it and was watching me through the glass door.

Her name was Nurse Freeborn and no one liked her. She was strict and efficient and only did what she had to do.

'I'm not a servant,' she said to a patient who asked her to hand me a magazine. Sometimes she would say, 'Can't you see I'm on my rounds?' when asked to do something that would hinder her for a moment.

She came back swiftly.

'You naughty boy,' she said sharply. 'Stop doing that at once. If ever you shake your head like that again I'll tell the doctor and he'll give it to you. You mustn't do that. Now you lie quietly. I'll be watching you.'

She strode away, her lips compressed, but looked back at me once more before she passed through the doorway.

'Remember, now, if I catch you shaking your head again, look out.'

Angus scowled at the doorway.

'Did you hear that?' he said to Mick. 'Fancy her being a nurse. Hell ...'

'Her!' Mick gestured contemptuously. 'She told me I was suffering from Imaginitis. I'll give her Imaginitis. Next time she chips me I'll tell her off, you see if I don't. Take no notice of her, Alan,' he called to me.

A local infection began to develop in my hip where the plaster had cut into the flesh, and in the next few days it reached the stage where I suddenly felt a boil had broken high up somewhere on my leg. The dull ache of my toe had been hard to stand that day and now this burning sensation in my hip ... I began sobbing in a hopeless, tired manner then I noticed Angus watching me with a troubled expression. I raised myself on my elbow and looked at him in a way that must have revealed my desperation for his face suddenly showed concern.

'Mr McDonald,' I said, my voice trembling. 'I'm sick of pain. I want it stopped. I think I'm busted.'

He slowly closed the book he was reading and sat up looking towards the ward door.

'Where's the bloody nurses?' he called out to Mick in a savage voice. 'You can walk. Go out and get them. Send Daddy for them. He'll do. This kid's had enough. I'd like to know what his old man'd say if he was here. Hop out and tell one of the nurses I want her, Daddy. Hurry up.'

In a little while a nurse came in and looked enquiringly at Angus.

'What's the matter?'

He nodded towards me. 'Have a look at him. He's crook.'

She raised my blankets and, seeing the sheet, she lowered them again without speaking and hurried away.

I remember being surrounded by the doctor, the matron, and the nurses and I remember the doctor sawing and hacking the plaster from my leg, but I was burning hot and giddy and I didn't remember father or mother coming. I remember father bringing me some parrot feathers but that was a week later.

CHAPTER 7

When I again became conscious of the ward and its inmates there was a stranger in Angus' bed. Both Angus and Mick had been discharged the week I had been ill. Angus had left me three eggs and a half jar of pickles and Mick had given Nurse Conrad a jam tin full of bush honey to give to me 'when I came good again.'

I missed them. The ward seemed to have changed. The men who now lay in the white beds were too ill or too subdued by their unfamiliar surroundings to sing out to each other and they had not yet learned to share their eggs.

Daddy was gloomier than ever.

'This place is not what it used to be,' he told me. 'I can remember arguments going on in this ward – you never heard the like. Clever blokes, too, some of 'em. Just take a look at this mob. You wouldn't give two bob for the lot. They come in here with guts ache then roll their eyes like they got consumption. They won't listen to a bloke's troubles; all they think of is their pains and aches. If I wasn't gonner die any tick o' the clock I'd ask the matron to let me go. An' she's a beautiful woman, mind you!'

The man in Angus' bed was very tall and when Nurse Conrad tucked in his blankets just after he had arrived, she exclaimed, 'My! You are a big man!'

He was pleased. He smiled self-consciously and looked round the ward to see if we had all heard, then he settled deeper into the bed, stretching his long legs so that his toes thrust the blankets through the bars at the foot and clasping his hands behind his head.

'Can you ride?' I asked him, impressed by his size.

He looked at me quickly, then, seeing I was a child, he ignored the question and continued his survey of the ward. I wondered whether he thought I was cheeky, then, feeling indignant, I convinced myself I didn't care what he thought.

But he always spoke to Nurse Conrad.

'You're all right,' he'd say to her.

He didn't seem able to say much else when she waited for him to continue. Sometimes he would try to grab her hand when she was taking his pulse and when she jerked it away he'd say, 'You're all right.'

She always had to be careful when standing near his bed or he'd slap her on the back and say, 'You're all right.'

'Don't do that again,' she said sharply to him once.

'You're all right,' he said.

'And following up with that remark doesn't smooth it over either,' she said looking at him with some cold knowledge in her eyes.

I couldn't make him out. He never said 'You're all right' to anyone else.

One day he spent the afternoon frowning and writing on a sheet of paper and that night, when she was removing his quilt, he said, 'I've written a piece of poetry about you.'

She looked surprised, then suspicious.

'Do you write poetry?' she asked pausing in her work and looking at him.

'Yes,' he said. 'It comes natural to me. I can write poetry about anything.'

He gave her the sheet of paper and she read the poem, a pleased expression growing on her face.

'That's real good,' she said. 'It is. It's real good. Where did you learn to write poetry?'

She turned the paper over and looked at the back then read the poem a second time.

'Can I keep this? It's real good.'

'That's nothing.' He waved a deprecating hand. 'I'll write you another tomorrow. Keep that. I can turn 'em out any time. I don't have to think. It's natural to me.'

Nurse Conrad turned to fix my bed, placing the sheet of paper on my locker while she folded the quilt.

'You can read it,' she said, noticing me glancing towards it. She handed it to me and I read it slowly and laboriously.

NURSE CONRAD
Nurse Conrad comes and makes our beds,
And wonders why we get it into our heads
That she is the nicest nurse in the hospital,
And I'm telling you this is gospel,
Because no other nurse is as pretty as her,
Or half as nice to the patients who suffer.
She always comes at your call,
And is loved by everyone, one and all.

When I finished reading it I didn't know what to say. I liked what it said about Nurse Conrad but I didn't like him saying it. I thought it must be good because it was poetry and they made you read poetry at school and our teacher was always saying how good poetry was.

'It's good,' I said wistfully.

I wished I had written it. A horse and gig seemed nothing beside a man who could write poetry.

I felt tired and wished I was home where no one wrote poetry and where I could jump on Kate and go trotting round the yard while father called out, 'Sit up straight now ... Keep you hands down ... Head up ... Get the feel of her mouth ... Push your legs forward. Right. That's good. Straighter still ... Good on you.'

If Nurse Conrad could only see me on Kate.

CHAPTER 8

My leg from the knee to the ankle was now in a splint and my foot and waist were not confined in plaster. The pain had gone and I didn't wish I were dead any more.

'The bone is slow in knitting,' I heard Dr Robertson tell the matron. 'The circulation is poor in that leg.'

One day he said to the matron, 'He's pale ... No sunshine ... Put him in a wheelchair each day and let him sit in the sun. How would you like to ride round in a wheelchair?' he asked me.

I could not answer him.

That afternoon the sister pushed a wheelchair beside my bed. She laughed as she saw the expression upon my face.

'You'll be able to race Daddy now,' she said. 'Come on; sit up till I get my arm round you.'

She lifted me into the chair, lowering my legs gently till they rested against the woven cane back of the lower framework. My feet could not reach the wooden support that projected like a shelf at the bottom of the leg-rest. My legs dangled uselessly, the feet pointing downwards.

I looked down at the support, feeling disappointed that my legs were too short to reach it. I could see myself chair-racing under a great handicap but I had no doubt father would rig up a rest that I could reach, and my arms were strong.

I was proud of my arms. I grasped the wooden rails that circled the spokes but I felt giddy and let the sister push me through the ward door, down the corridor and out into the bright world.

As we passed through the door leading to the garden, the fresh, open air and the sunshine poured itself over me in one immense torrent. I rose to meet it, sitting upright in my chair, facing the blue and the sparkle and the gentle push of the air against my face, like a diver rising from the sea.

For three months I had not seen a cloud or felt the sun upon me. Now they were returned to me, newly created, perfected, radiant with qualities they never possessed before.

The sister left me in the sunshine near some sheoak trees and though there was no wind I could hear them whispering together as father said they always do.

I wondered what had happened to things while I had been away, what had changed them so. I watched a dog trotting along the street on the other side of the high picket fence. I had never seen such a wonderful dog, so pattable, so full of possibilities. A grey thrush called and its note was a gift to me. I looked down at the gravel upon which my chair rested. Each grain had colour and they lay there in their millions, tossed into strange little hills and hollows. Some had escaped into the grass which skirted the pathway and the grass stems leant over them in lovely curves of tenderness.

I could hear the shouts of children at play and the clip-clop of a trotting horse. A dog barked and away out over the resting houses there came the whistle of a train.

The foliage of the sheoaks drooped like coarse hair and through it I could see the sky. The leaves of the gum trees glittered, throwing off diamonds of sunshine that hurt my eyes, unprepared for such brightness.

I hung my head and closed my eyes and the sun wrapped itself round me like arms.

After a while I raised my head and began to experiment with the chair, grasping the rails like Daddy and trying to turn the wheels, but the gravel was too deep and the pathway was flanked with stones.

I became interested in seeing how far I could spit. I knew a boy who could spit across a road but he had a front tooth out. I felt my teeth but none of them were loose.

I studied the sheoaks and decided I could climb them all except one and it wasn't worth climbing.

After a while a boy came walking up the street. He clattered a stick along the pickets as he walked and he was followed by a brown dog. I knew the boy. His name was George and his mother brought him each visiting day to the hospital. He often gave me things – comics, cigarette cards, and sometimes lollies.

I like him because he was a good rabbiter and had a ferret. He was kind, too.

'There's lots of things I'd give you,' he told me once, 'but I'm not let.'

His dog's name was Snipe and this dog was so small he could go down burrows but he could fight anything so long as he had a fair go, George told me.

'If you want to be a good rabbiter you've got to have a good dog,' was one of George's convictions.

I agreed with this but thought a greyhound was good to have if your mother would let you keep it.

This fitted in with George's ideas on greyhounds. He told me darkly that 'Women don't like greyhounds.'

This was exactly what I thought.

I regarded George as being very clever and I told mother about him.

'He's a good boy,' mother said.

I was a bit doubtful about this and hoped he wasn't too good.

'I don't like a siss, do you?' I asked him later. It was a searching question.

'Hell, no!' he said.

It was a satisfactory answer and I concluded that he wasn't as good as mother thought.

The sight of him coming along the street filled me with joy.

'How's it goin', George?' I yelled.

'Not bad,' he said, 'but mum said I gotta come straight home.'

'Aw!' I exclaimed, disappointed.

'I gotta bag of lollies here,' he informed me in the tone of one mentioning a commonplace.

'What sort?'

'London Mixture.'

'They're the best, I reckon. Are there any of those round ones – you know – with hundreds and thousands stuck on 'em?'

'No,' said George, 'I ate 'em.'

'Aw! did you!' I murmured, suddenly depressed.

'Come over to the fence and I'll give you what's left,' George urged me. 'I don't want 'em. We got hundreds at home.'

It was a request I would not have thought of refusing but after an automatic but futile struggle I told him, 'I can't walk yet. They're still curing me. I'd do it if I didn't have a splint on but I've got a splint on.'

'Well, I'll pitch 'em over,' announced George.

'Good on ya, George!'

George stepped back on to the roadway to take a run at it. I watched him approvingly. If ever there was a boy who demonstrated by text-book preliminaries that he was a perfect thrower, that boy was George.

He eyed the distance, loosened his shoulders ...

'Well, here she comes!' he cried.

He began his run with a graceful skip – the touch of a perfectionist – took three long strides and threw.

Any girl could have thrown better.

'I slipped,' George explained in a tone of exasperation. 'Me darn foot slipped.'

I didn't see George slip but there was no doubt he must have slipped and slipped badly.

I looked at the bag of lollies lying some eight yards away from me on the grass and said, 'Listen! How about you going round to the gate and coming in and getting them?'

'I can't,' explained George. 'Mum's waiting for the suet to cook. She said I gotta come straight home. Leave them there and I'll get them for you tomorrow. No one will touch 'em. By hell I must go!'

'All right,' I said resignedly, 'that'll have to do.'

'Well, I'm off,' called George. 'See you tomorrow. Hurroo.'

'Hurroo, George,' I called abstractedly. I was looking at the lollies and trying to work out some way of getting them.

Eating a lolly was, to me, a delightful experience. When father paid his monthly bill at the store he always took me with him and after the storekeeper had handed father the receipt, he would say to me, 'Well, my little man, what would you like? I know – lollies. Well, let's see what we can do.

He would twist a piece of white paper into a cone and fill it with boiled lollies and give it to me and I would say, 'Thank you, Mr Simmons.'

I always kept the lollies for a while before I looked at them or ate them. The hard feel of them beneath the paper, each little bump representing a lolly, the weight of them in my hand, these were so full of suggestion I wanted to enjoy them first. Besides I always divided them with Mary when I got home.

Boiled lollies were good but I was allowed, as with those given to me by the storekeeper, to keep on eating them till the bag was finished. This lowered their value a little, suggesting, as it did, that they were not valued by adults.

There were lollies so expensive I was only allowed a taste. Once father brought a thrupenny cake of milk chocolate and mother gave Mary and me a square each. The taste of that milk chocolate dissolving on my tongue was delightful and I often recalled it as one would a significant event. 'I'd sooner milk chocolate than chops any day.' I told mother as she bent over the wire griller.

'Some day I'll buy you a cake of it,' she told me.

There were times when a man gave me a penny for holding his horse and when this happened I would run to the baker's shop, where lollies were sold, and stand gazing into the window at the display of Rum-rum-go-goes, Milk Poles, Silver Sticks, Cough Sticks, Sherbet Suckers, Licorice Straps, Aniseed Balls and Snowballs. I did not notice the few dying blowflies lying on their backs between the packets and straps and sticks, feebly moving their legs and sometimes buzzing. I only saw the lollies. I would stand there a long time quite unable to make up my mind what to buy.

On these rare occasions when some squatter gave me thrupence for the same job, I was immediately surrounded by my school mates who passed on the news from boy to boy with shrill cries, 'Alan's got thrupence.'

Then came the important question, 'Are you going to spend it all at once or keep some for tomorrow?'

On the answer to this depended the extent to which each boy would share in my purchases and they awaited the decision with restraint.

My answer, in the form of an announcement, was always the same, 'I'm going to spend the lot.'

It was a decision that invariably brought forth yells of approval then scuffles to decide who would walk each side of me and behind me and in front of me.

'I'm your mate, Alan ... You know me, Alan ... I gave ya the core of me apple yesterdee ... I got here first ... Let go a me ... I always been mates with Alan, haven't I Alan?'

It was recognised in our school that, so long as a boy was clutching you, he had some claim on you or, at least, was entitled to a consideration of any demands he made. I walked in the centre of a little, compact group, each boy attached to me by a resolute hand. I clutched the thrupence.

We came to a halt in front of the window and now I was deluged with advice.

'Remember, ya get eight aniseed balls for a penny, Alan ... How many of us are here, Sam? There's eight here, Alan ... Licorice straps go the furthest of any lolly ... Sherbert suckers are beaut ... You can make drinks out of sherbert suckers ... Let go a me ... I was beside him first ... Fancy, thrupence! You can have a lend of me shanghai any time you want it, Alan.'

I looked at the bag of lollies on the grass. The thought that it would be impossible for me to get them of my own accord was an alternative I did not consider for a moment. Those lollies were mine. They were given to me. Blow my legs! I would get them.

The chair was standing on the edge of the pathway that skirted the grassy plot on which the lollies were lying. I seized its arm-rests and began to rock it from side to side till it hung poised on a slanting wheel at the end of each sway; then I gave an extra lift and it crashed to its side, flinging me face downwards on the grass. My splinted leg struck the stone border of the pathway and the sudden pain made me mutter angrily and pull some grass out by the roots. The pale roots, holding in their clasp a lump of granulated soil, seemed, in some strange way, a comforting thing. In a moment I began to drag myself towards the lollies, leaving behind me as I progressed, some pillows, a rug, a comic. . . .

I reached the paper bag, grasped it in my hand and smiled.

Once, when I had climbed a tree to put a pulley rope over a limb for father, he called out delightedly from below, 'You did it, By hell, you did it!'

I did it, I thought, and I opened the bag, and after a moment's pleased inspection, extracted a conversation lolly upon which I read the words, 'I love you'.

I sucked it appreciatively, taking it out of my mouth every few moments to see if I could still read the words. They faded, became a line of meaningless depressions, then vanished. I held a little pink disc in my hand. I lay on my back looking through the branches of a sheoak and crushed the lolly between my teeth.

I felt very happy.

CHAPTER 9

The consternation that seized the nurses who found me lying on the grass surprised me. I could not understand the summoning of the matron, the gathering round my bed and the mixture of concern and anger that marked their interrogation.

I kept repeating, 'I tipped myself over to get the lollies,' and when the matron insisted on me answering, 'But why? Why didn't you call a nurse?' I answered, 'I wanted to get them by myself.'

'I can't understand you,' she complained.

I wondered why she couldn't. I knew father would. When I told him, he said, 'Couldn't you have sort of climbed out of the chair without tipping it over?'

'No,' I said, 'I couldn't use my legs, see.'

'I see,' he said, then added, 'Well, you got them anyway. I

wouldn't have called a nurse either. She would have got them all right but then it would have been different.'

'It would have been different,' I said, liking him more than ever.

'But don't hurt yourself next time,' he warned me. 'Be careful. Don't tip yourself out for lollies again. They're not worth it. Tip yourself out for big things – like a fire or something. I'd have bought you some lollies but I'm not holding too good this week.'

'I don't want any this week,' I said to comfort him.

For the next few weeks I was watched very carefully when I sat in the wheelchair on the verandah; then one day the doctor arrived carrying a pair of crutches.

'Here are your front legs,' he told me. 'Do you think you could walk on these? Come on and we'll try.'

'Are they really and truly mine?' I asked him.

'Yes,' he said, really and truly ...'

I was sitting in the wheelchair out in the garden and he pushed it on to the grass under the sheoak trees.

'This is a good place. We'll try here.'

The matron and some of the nurses had come out to see me attempt my first walk on crutches and they gathered round while the doctor placed his hands beneath my arms and lifted me up from the chair, holding me erect in front of him.

The matron, to whom he had handed the crutches, placed them beneath my armpits and then he lowered me till I was resting my weight on the armpit rests.

'Are you right?' he asked.

'No,' I said, suddenly unsure of myself. 'I'm not right yet. I'll be right in a minute.'

'Take it easy,' he instructed me. 'Don't try and walk yet. Just stand. I'm holding you. You can't fall.'

My right leg, the one I called my 'bad' leg, was completely paralysed and swung uselessly from the hip, a thing of skin and bone, scarred and deformed. I called my left leg my 'good' leg. It was only partially paralysed and could bear my weight. For weeks I had been testing it while sitting on the edge of my bed.

The curvature of my spine gave me a decided lean to the left but resting on the crutches pulled it temporarily straight, and my body lengthened so that, standing, I appeared taller than when sitting down.

My stomach muscles were partially paralysed but my chest and arms were unaffected. In the years that were to follow I came to regard my legs as not worth much consideration. They angered me, though sometimes they seemed to live a sad life of their own apart from me and I felt sorry for them. My arms and chest were my pride and they were to develop out of all proportion to the rest of my body.

I stood there uncertainly for a moment looking ahead towards where, a few yards away, a bare patch of ground was worn in the grass.

I will get there, I thought, and waited, not knowing exactly what muscles to call upon, conscious that the crutches beneath my armpits were hurting me and that I must move them forward and take my weight for a moment on my good leg if I wanted to walk.

The doctor had taken his hands away but he held them apart one each side of me, ready to grab me should I fall.

I lifted the crutches and swung them heavily forward, my shoulders jerking upwards to the sudden jar as my weight came down on the armpit rests once more. I swung my legs forward, my right leg dragging in the dirt like a broken wing. I paused, breathing deeply and looking at the bare patch of earth ahead of me.

'Good!' exclaimed the doctor as I made this first step. 'Now again.'

I went through the same movements again, then three times more till at last I stood achingly upon the patch of earth. I had walked.

'That will do for today,' said the doctor. 'Back into your chair. You can have another try tomorrow.'

In a few weeks I could walk round the garden and though I had fallen a few times I had acquired confidence and was beginning to practise leaping from the verandah, seeing how far I could jump from a line scraped on the path.

When I was told I was going home and that mother was calling for me next day I was not as excited as I had thought I would be. The hospital had gradually taken the form of a permanent background to my thoughts and activities. My life had become ordered and I felt, in an unexpressed way, that in leaving the hospital I would lose the security I had acquired there. I was a little afraid of going and yet I was eager to see where the street that passed the hospital led to, what was going on down there beyond the rise where shunting trains puffed and trucks banged together and cabs carrying people with bags came and went. And I wanted to see dad breaking in horses again.

When mother arrived I was dressed and sitting on the edge of my bed looking at the empty wheelchair I would not be able to ride in again. Father didn't have enough money to buy a wheelchair but he had made a long, three-wheeled vehicle out of an old peram-

bulator and mother was wheeling this. She was to take me down
the street where father had left a waggonette in the pub yard while
he got a pair of horses shod.

When Nurse Conrad kissed me goodbye, I wanted to cry but I
didn't and I gave her all the eggs I had left and some *War Cries* and
the parrot feathers father had brought me. I had nothing else to
give her but she said that was enough.

The matron patted my head and told mother I was a brave little
fellow and that, in one way, it was fortunate I was crippled so
young in that I would now have no difficulty in adjusting myself to
a lifetime on crutches.

'Children are so adaptable,' she assured mother.

Mother, looking at me, seemed possessed by some deep sadness
when the matron said this, and she did not reply to her which I
thought was rude of mother.

The nurses waved to me and Daddy shook my hand and said I'd
never see him again. He'd be gone any tick o' the clock now.

Mother had wrapped me in a rug and I lay in the pram clutching
a little lion made of clay that Nurse Conrad had given me.

She wheeled me on to the street and pushed me along the
pathway and over the rise. There weren't the wonderful things I
thought there would be over this rise. The houses were no different
from other houses and the railway station was just a shed.

She pushed me over a kerb and through a gutter then up again,
but somehow one of the wheels went over the edge of the paving
and the pram tipped over and I fell into the gutter.

Mother's efforts to raise the pram from where it lay half on top of
me, and her anxious demands to know whether I was hurt were lost
to me. I was too busy searching for my clay lion and there he was,
sure enough, underneath the rug with his head broken off as I had
expected.

A man had dashed forward in answer to mother's call.

'Could you help me lift my little boy back?' she asked him.

'What's wrong?' exclaimed the man seizing the pram and lifting
it with a quick heave. 'What's wrong with the kid?'

'I tipped him over. Be careful! Don't hurt him; he's lame!'

This last exclamation of mother's shocked me into a sudden
awareness of my part in this unnecessary excitement. The word
'lame' was associated in my mind with limping horses and suggested complete uselessness.

I raised myself on my elbow in the gutter, looking at mother with
an expression of astonishment.

'Lame, mum?' I exclaimed with some force. 'What did you say I
was lame for?'

CHAPTER 10

The word 'crippled', to me, suggested a condition that could be applied to some people, but not to myself. But, since I so often heard people refer to me as crippled, I was forced to concede that I must fit this description, yet retained a conviction that though being crippled was obviously a distressing state for some people, with me it didn't matter.

The crippled child is not conscious of the handicap implied by his useless legs. They are often inconvenient or annoying but he is confident that they will never prevent him doing what he wants to do or being whatever he wishes to be. If he considers them a handicap it is because he has been told they are.

Children make no distinction between the one who is lame and the one who has the full use of his limbs. They will ask a boy on crutches to run here or there for them and complain when he is slow.

In childhood a useless leg does not bring with it a sense of shame; it is only when one learns to interpret the glance of people unable to hide their feelings that one experiences a desire to avoid them. And, strangely enough, this unshielded glance of distaste only comes from those who have weak bodies, who carry with them a consciousness of some physical inferiority; it never comes from those who are strong and healthy. Strong and healthy people do not shrink from the cripple; his state is so remote from them. It is those under the threat of helplessness who quail when confronted with it in another.

A useless leg, a twisted limb, is freely discussed by children.

'Come an' see Alan's funny leg. He can put it over his head.'

'How did you get your sore leg?'

The pained mother, hearing her son announce bluntly, 'Here's Alan, mum. His leg is all crooked,' hastens to stop him saying more, forgetting she is facing two happy little boys, her son proud of his exhibit, Alan happy to be able to provide it.

A crippled limb often adds to the importance of its owner and he is sometimes privileged because of it.

In circus games I accepted the role of donkey – 'because you have four legs' – with a great display of kicking and bucking, enjoying being able to do this and seeing my four legs as being most desirable.

Children's sense of humour is not restricted by adult ideas of good taste and tact. They often laughed at the spectacle of me on crutches and shouted with merriment when I fell over. I joined in their laughter, gripped by some sense of absurdity that made a stumble on crutches a hilarious thing.

When high paling fences had to be negotiated I was often pushed over and a collapse of those taking my weight was regarded as extremely funny, not only by those helping me but by myself too.

I was happy. I had no pain and could walk. But the grown-up people who visited our home when I returned did not expect me to be happy. They called my happiness 'courage'. Most grown-up people talk frankly about children in front of them, as if children are incapable of understanding references to themselves.

'He's a happy kid despite his affliction, Mrs Marshall,' they would say as if surprised that this were so.

'Why shouldn't I be happy?' I thought. The suggestion that I should be other than happy troubled me in that it implied the presence in my life of same disaster I did not recognise but which would catch up on me some day. I wondered what it was and at last concluded they imagined my leg pained me.

'My leg doesn't hurt,' I'd say brightly to those who expressed surprise approval of my smiling face. 'Look!' and I would lift my bad leg with my hands and place it over my head.

This made some people shudder and my puzzlement increased. My legs were so familiar to me that I viewed them as one would normal limbs and not as objects that raised a minor revulsion.

Those parents who told their children to be gentle with me or who felt they should correct what they considered an unfeeling attitude in their children, only succeeded in confusing them. Some children, subject to the counselling of parents anxious to 'make things easier' for me, would sometimes protest against the treatment I was getting from their mates.

'Don't bump him; you'll hurt his leg.'

But I wanted to be bumped and though I was not naturally aggressive I developed an aggressiveness to counter what I regarded as unnecessary and humiliating concessions.

Having a normal mind my attitude to life was that of a normal child and my crippled limbs could not alter this attitude. It was when I was treated as someone different from the children with whom I played that my development had to include provisions to meet these influences that would have harnessed my mind to my crippled body.

There is not a state of mind peculiar to crippled children and differing in its attitude to life around them from that of children with sound bodies. Those who stumble on crutches or fall or automatically use their hand to move a paralysed limb are not thinking in terms of frustration and suffering nor are they occupied with the difficulty of getting from one place to another; they are occupied with their object in going there as are all children who run across a paddock or walk up a street.

Suffering because of being crippled is not for you in your childhood; it is reserved for those men and women who look at you.

My first few months at home left me with some awareness of these things but my knowledge was instinctive rather than the result of reasoning.

After the spaciousness of the ward I had to adjust myself to life in a house that suddenly seemed as tiny as a box.

When father lifted the pram from the waggonette and wheeled me into the kitchen I was astonished how it had shrunk. The table with its plush, rose-patterned cover, now seemed to fill the room so completely that there was hardly space for my pram. A strange cat sat licking itself on the brick hearth before the stove.

'Whose cat?' I asked, surprised that this familiar room should contain a cat I had not sponsored.

'It's Blackie's kitten,' explained Mary. 'You know – she had them before you went to the hospital.'

Mary was anxious to tell me everything of importance that had happened since I left.

'And Meg has had five pups and we're calling the little brown one Alan. He's the one dad brought into the hospital to show you.'

Mary was excited at my return and had already asked mum if she could take me for walks in my pram. She was older than me and was a devoted, thoughtful person who sat hunched over a book when she wasn't helping mother but who became full of indignant energy when called upon to defend some ill-treated animal, a crusade that took up a lot of her time. Once when a horseman, leaning from his saddle, flogged a lagging and exhausted calf that was unable to keep up with its mother, Mary stood on the top rail of our gate and screamed at him with tears in her voice. When the calf went down, its sides streaked with brown saliva, Mary sped across the track and stood above it with clenched hands. He did not hit it again.

She had dark hair and brown eyes and was always jumping to her feet to get you things. She claimed she was going to be a missionary some day and help the poor Blackfellows. Sometimes she decided she would help the heathen Chinese but she was a little frightened of being massacred.

The *Bulletin* sometimes had pictures of missionaries sitting in pots being cooked by Blackfellows and I had told her it would be better to be massacred than cooked, mainly because I didn't know what massacred meant.

Jane was the eldest in our family and she fed the fowls and kept three lambs a drover had given her when they were too tired to travel. She was tall and walked with her head up. She helped Mrs Mulvaney, the baker's wife, to look after her babies and she was paid five shillings a week and could buy anything she wanted after she gave mum some.

She had gone into long skirts and put her hair up and she had a pair of tan lace-up boots that went right up almost to her knees. Mrs Mulvaney thought they were very smart and I thought they were smart, too.

When I walked with her she used to say, 'Now, be a little gentleman and raise your cap to Mrs Mulvaney if we meet her.'

When I kept thinking about raising my cap I always raised it but I didn't keep thinking about it much.

Jane was at Mrs Mulvaney's when I arrived home so Mary told me all about the canaries and Pat, the corella, and my pet possum and the king parrot that still hadn't grown a tail. She had fed them every day and hadn't missed once and she had put in two new salmon tins for the canaries' water. The bottom of Pat's cage needed scraping but that was all. The possum still scratched you when you held it but not so much.

I sat there in my pram – mother had hidden my crutches as I was only allowed to use them for an hour each day – and watched mother spread the cloth and set the table for dinner. Mary brought in wood for the stove from the woodbox on the back verandah where the rotting boards hushed the sound of her skipping feet.

Now that I was home the hospital seemed far away, and all that had happened to me there was slipping from reality and remaining in my mind as a story I had experienced. The little things that were now happening around me were re-entering my life with a new vividness, a new magic. The hooks on the brown dresser from which mother was now taking the cups were strangely impressive as if I had never seen the bright curve of them before.

A lamp with a fluted column, a cast-iron base and a pink

Edwardian globe stood on the safe beside which my pram was standing. At night it would be taken down and lit and placed in the centre of the table and there would be a circle of bright light beneath it on the cloth.

The safe had sides of perforated zinc and the smell of food came through the holes. Upon the safe there was a sheet of tanglefoot, an oblong of heavy, brown paper covered with a brown sticky substance for catching flies. The sheet was thickly covered with flies, many of them struggling, some buzzing as they beat their wings in a blur of movement. In the summer the flies were thick in the house and you kept waving your hand above your food to keep them away. Father always placed his saucer on top of his cup of tea.

'I don't know,' he used to say, 'most people can drink their tea after a fly has been in it; I can't.'

A big, black kettle with its spout gaping like a striking snake steamed on the stove and above the stove was the mantelpiece girded with a mantel drape of brown baize now dulled by smoke and steam. A tea caddy and a coffee tin with a picture of a bearded Turk upon it stood on the mantelpiece and above the mantelpiece was the picture of the frightened horses. It was good to see this picture again.

Above me on the side wall was the large, framed picture of a boy blowing bubbles that came as a supplement in the Christmas *Pears' Annual*. I raised my head and looked at him with a new interest, my period away from him having quite removed the dislike I had had for his sissy curls and old-fashioned clothes.

A pincushion of blue velvet spiked with pins hung from a nail beneath this picture. It was stuffed with sawdust and you could feel the sawdust when you squeezed it.

Behind the back-verandah door was another nail from which hung old almanacs and on top of them the latest Christmas gift from the storekeeper, a cardboard pocket for letters that was flat and in two pieces when we got it. Father had bent one of these pieces, upon which red poppies were twined round Mr Simmons' name, and thrust its corners into slits on the larger piece, and there was the pocket. Now it was full of letters.

Two other doors opened into the kitchen. One led into my bedroom, a small box-like room with a marble-topped washstand and a single bed covered with a patchwork quilt. Through the open door I could see its newspaper-covered hessian walls that always swelled and subsided when wind buffeted the house, as if the room were breathing. Blackie, the cat, used to sleep at the foot of my bed, and Meg slept on the bag mat beside it. Sometimes, when I was asleep, mother would sneak in and hunt them out, but they always came back.

The other doorway led into Mary's and Jane's bedroom, a room the same size as mine but containing two beds and a chest-of-drawers with a swinging mirror suspended between two little top drawers in which Mary and Jane kept their brooches.

Opposite the back-verandah door was the entrance to a short passage. Worn, plush curtains closed this passageway from the kitchen, dividing the house into two sections. Here in the kitchen half you could jump on chairs and make a row and play bears under the table if you wanted to, but the front section beyond the curtains was never used for playing nor entered with dirty clothes or muddy boots.

The Front Room opened off the passage and here the linoleum shone from scrubbing and the freshly-raddled fireplace was neatly packed with wood ready for lighting on winter nights when we had visitors.

The walls of the Front Room were covered with framed photographs. There were frames made of shells, of velvet-covered wood, of pressed metal, and there was one made of cork. There were long frames containing a row of photographs and large, carved frames in one of which a fierce man with a beard stood with one hand resting on a small table standing in front of a waterfall. This was Grandfather Marshall. In the other big frame an old lady in a black lace shawl sat stiffly on a rustic seat in an arbour of roses, while behind her a thin man in narrow trousers gazed sternly at the photographer as he rested his hand on her shoulder.

These two unsmiling people were mother's parents. Father, after looking at the picture, always said grandfather had big knees like a foal, but mother said it was the narrow trousers.

Father always read when sitting in the Front Room. He read *Not Guilty – A Defence of the Bottom Dog*, by Robert Blatchford, and *My Brilliant Career*, by Miles Franklin. He valued these two books that Peter Finlay had given him and often talked about them.

'I like books that tell the truth,' he sometimes said. 'I'd sooner be sad with the truth than happy with a lie, blowed if I wouldn't.'

He came in from the loosebox, where he had been feeding the horses, and sat down on the horsehair chair that always pricked me through my trousers when I slid on it, and he said, 'That last bag of chaff I got from Simmons is full of oats. It's the best bag I've had from him this year. Old Paddy O'Loughlan grew it, he reckons.' He smiled at me. 'How do you like being home, old chap?'

'Oo, it's good!' I told him.

'Yes, it's good all right,' he said, grimacing as he tugged at his elastic-side boots. 'I'll wheel you round the yard after and show you Meg's pups,' he added.

'Why don't you buy some more of that chaff before it all goes?' mother suggested.

'Yes, I think I will. I'll book it up. Paddy's crop was short and all head.'

'When can I have another go on my crutches?' I asked him.

'The doctor said you must lie down for an hour every day, Alan,' mother reminded me.

'That's going to be a job,' father muttered as he examined the soles of his boots.

'We'll have to make him.'

'Yes, that's right. Don't forget now, Alan; you must lie down every day. You can have a go on your crutches every day though. I think I'll have to pad the tops with horsehair. Do they make you sore under the arms?'

'They hurt,' I said.

With his boot held in front of him he looked at me for a moment with concern in his eyes.

'Pull your chair over to the table,' mother said to him. She came and pushed my wheelchair to a place beside him, then stood erect and smiled down at me. 'Well,' she said, 'we have two men back in the house again, eh! I won't have to work nearly as hard now.'

CHAPTER 11

After lunch father wheeled me round the yard. He pushed the pram close to Pat's cage and for a moment the need to clean the floor rested disturbingly on me, then I looked at Pat. The old corella was sitting hunched on his perch rubbing his bills together with the familiar grinding sound. I put my finger through the netting and scratched the back of his lowered head and the white powder from his feathers came on to my finger again and I could smell the parrot smell that always evoked the crimson flash of wings in the bush. He took my finger gently in his powerful bill and I felt the quick little tapping pushes of his dry, rubbery tongue.

'Hallo Pat,' he said and his voice was mine.

And the king parrot in a cage near him still bobbed up and down, up and down on his perch, but Tom, the possum, was asleep. Father lifted him out of the dark, little box in which he slept and he opened his large, tranquil eyes and looked at me before curling up again in father's hand.

We moved over to the stable where I could hear horses snorting chaff from their nostrils and the sharp sound of their iron shoes striking the rough stone floor as they moved.

The stable was sixty years old and seemed as if it would collapse with the weight of its straw thatch. It leaned to one side even though the uprights that supported it were trunks of sturdy gums topped by a fork in which the undressed beams of the roof were resting. It was walled with upright slabs split from the trunks of trees felled beside it and you could peer between them into the dark stalls that smelt sharply of horse manure and urine-damp straw.

Ropes tied to iron rings in the wall held the horses as they fed from feed troughs made from heavy logs hollowed with an adze and squared with a broad axe.

Beside the stable, under the same heavy, thatched roof, now noisy with nesting sparrows, was the chaff house, its rough board floor inches deep with spilt chaff. Next to it was the harness room where, on wooden brackets projecting from the slab wall, hung sets of harness – horse collars, hames, reins, breechings and saddles. Father's buckjump saddle, a Kinnear, hung on a special peg, its projecting knee pads waxed and shining.

At the foot of the wall, resting on the grooved and squared log supporting the slab uprights were tins of neatsfoot oil, harness black, bottles of turpentine, Solomon's Solution and drenches. Currycombs and brushes lay on a shelf built on to the wall and two curled stockwhips hung on nails beside it.

The Thatched roof continued over the buggy shed where a three-seated buggy and the brake were kept. The brake was tipped back and the two long, hickory shafts passed under the eaves and pointed towards the sky.

The back door of the stable led into the horse yard, a circular enclosure fenced with rough-hewn seven-foot posts and split rails. This high fence sloped outwards so that a bucking horse could not scrape father's legs against the rails or crush him against the post. In front of this yard grew an old, red gum tree. In blossoming time flocks of lorikeets searched its flowers for honey, sometimes hanging upside down on the outer branches or circling the tree in screeching groups when startled into flight. Against its twisted trunk leant the broken wheel of a dray, rusty waggon axles, buggy springs with broken shackles and the weather-worn seat of a gig from the torn cushions of which projected tufts of grey horsehair. A pile of worn and rusted horseshoes rested against one of its uncovered roots.

A clump of wattles grew in one corner of the yard and beneath them horse manure lay thick on the ground, for the horses father was breaking camped here in the shade when the days were hot. Each stood with a lowered head and a lax hind leg and they switched their tails at the flies brought there by the smell of the manure.

Close to the wattles was the road gate and across the dirt road-way was an area of bushland, a refuge for the few kangaroos that still refused to retreat back to less settled areas. The messmate and stringybark trees sheltered patches of swamp where black ducks gathered and from where the booming of bitterns could be heard on still nights.

'The bunyip is out tonight,' father would say when he heard them, but they made me afraid.

The store, post office and school were almost a mile away along the road and here the cleared land was squared with rich dairy farms owned by Mrs Carruthers.

A large hill, Mt Turalla, rose behind the township. It was covered in bracken and scrub and at the top was a crater down which the children rolled boulders that went bounding and crashing through ferns till they came to rest on the bottom far below.

Father had ridden to the top of Mt Turalla many times. He said that horses reared on its slopes were always sure-footed and worth a couple of quid more than those reared on the flats.

After he had told me this it became one of my convictions, solid within me like a rock. Everything father told me about horses was retained firmly in my mind and became part of it like my name.

'I have a half-draught colt here,' he said as he pushed my pram into the stable. 'It shows the whites of its eyes and I've never known a horse that showed the whites of its eyes that wouldn't kick the eye out of a mosquito if it got half a chance. It belongs to Brady. It'll kill him one day, you mark my words.'

'Whoa there!' he called to the horse that had flinched forward with a flattened rump. 'See! He's ready to lash out now. I've mouthed him, he's not going to be hard in the mouth, but I'll bet he'll go to market when I get him in the brake.'

He left me and, moving over to the horse, ran his hand down its quivering rump.

'Steady, now. Whoa there. Whoa, old boy. Steady ...' He talked gently to the horse and in a moment it stood quietly and turned its head to look at him.

'I'll put a kicking strap on him when I harness him up,' he said. 'That look means nothing.'

'Can I go with you when you put him in, dad?' I asked him.

'Well, yes, you could,' he said slowly as he began to fill his pipe. 'You could help me break him in by holding him an' that. You would be a great help to me, but,' he tamped the tobacco down with his finger, 'I reckon I better take him for one or two runs first. Not far ... An' they won't be proper breaking-in runs, of course. But I'd like you to watch him from the ground first and tell me what you think of his gait when I bring him past you. I want you to do a lot of that for me – telling me how they go an' that. You've got a feel for a horse. I don't know anybody that's got as good a feel for a horse as you have.'

'I'll tell you what he's like!' I exclaimed suddenly eager to help him. 'I'll watch his legs like anything. I'll tell you what he does and everything. I'd like doing that, dad.'

'I knew you would,' he said lighting his pipe. 'I was lucky to get you.'

'How did you get me, dad?' I asked him, wanting to be friendly and companionable with him.

'Mother carried you round inside her for a while then you were born,' he told me. 'You grew like a flower beneath her heart, she says.'

'Like the kittens Blackie had?' I asked.

'Yes, like that.'

'It makes me feel sick, a bit.'

'Yes.' He paused, looking out through the stable door towards the bush, then said, 'It did me, too, when I first heard of it, but after a while it seems good like. You can't beat seeing a foal running beside its mother, pressing against her – you know ... They push against her while they run.' He pushed against the post to show me. 'Well, she carried it before it was born. And it bucks round her like it wanted to get back. It's a good thing, I reckon. It's better than just being brought to your mother. It's well thought out when you come to think of it.'

'Yes, I reckon it is, too.' I quickly changed my view. 'I like foals.'

I felt that I loved horses carrying foals.

'I wouldn't like to be just brought,' I said.

'No,' father answered. 'Neither would I.'

CHAPTER 12

Father wheeled me into the yard and told me to watch him greasing the buggy.

'Did you know it was the picnic on Saturday?' he asked me as he jacked up one of the wheels.

'The picnic!' I exclaimed, excited at the thought of this annual Sunday School gathering. 'Are we going?'

'Yes.'

A sudden stab of disappointment changed my expression. 'I won't be able to run,' I said.

'No,' said father abruptly. He spun the raised wheel with a violent jerk of his hand then watched it revolving for a moment. 'It doesn't matter.'

I knew it did matter. He had always told me I was to be a runner and win races like he used to do. Now I wouldn't be able to win any till I got better and that wouldn't be till after the picnic.

But I didn't want to make him sad so I said, 'Anyway, I suppose I would have looked back again.'

I had always been the smallest and youngest competitor in the children's races at the Sunday School picnic and the handicappers all co-operated to ensure I passed the tape ahead of the older and bigger boys running against me. They always gave me half-way start, an advantage I really didn't require as I could run swiftly when it was not demanded of me, but since I was never known to win a race they were always anxious to help me.

Father always entered me in these races with great confidence. On the morning of the last picnic, when I could run like other boys, he had explained exactly what I had to do when the pistol went off and I had so impressed him by my enthusiastic reaction to his advice that he had announced at the breakfast table, 'Alan will win the boys' race today.'

I heard this prophetic statement as one would a pronouncement of fact from a god. Dad had said I was going to win a race today so I was going to win a race today. Any other alternative was impossible. I spent the next hour before we left in announcing this fact to any horsemen who passed our gate.

The picnic ground was on the banks of Turalla Creek, three miles away, and, on this particular day a year ago, father drove us there in the three-seated buggy. I sat with mother and father in the front seat and Mary and Jane sat facing each other in the back.

The farmers and bush people driving to the picnic always regarded the journey there as providing them with an opportunity to display the quality of their horses and along the three miles to the creek buggy wheels spun and gravel flew from swinging hooves as one challenged the other to race for the glory of his horse.

The actual roadway was a metal one but following the wide stretch of grass along the three-chain road was a track made by those drivers who studied their horses. It consisted of three deep, continuous depressions in the soft earth, the two outside ones for the wheels of the vehicles and the wider, centre one for the feet of the horses. It wound round stumps, skirted ponds and squeezed between trees until at last, where some deep drain barred the way, it joined the metal again.

But never for long. It would move out again on to the grass when the obstruction was passed and continue its twisting course till it disappeared over an horizon hill.

Father always drove on this track with its dips and hollows and the buggy swayed and rocked delightfully as he 'touched up' Prince with the whip.

Prince was a raking chestnut with a Roman nose but father said he could go like a bat out of hell. He was a square-gaited trotter with broad hooves and he often 'struck' when trotting – the shoes of his hind feet would strike those of his front with a sharp clicking sound.

I liked to hear it. I liked my boots to squeak when I walked, for a similar reason. Squeaking boots established me as a man and Prince's clicking shoes established him as a horse that could go. Father didn't like this habit of Prince's and he had his front shoes weighted to cure him.

When Prince got on to the dirt track and felt father rein him back – 'pull him together', father called it – his ears came back, his rump lowered and he threw his powerful legs in long swinging strides that made the buggy wheels sing behind him.

And I wanted to sing too for I loved the bite of the wind on my face and the sting of the thrown dirt and gravel on my cheeks. I liked to see the grip of father's hands on the reins as he strove to pass gigs and buggies in which men he knew leant forward shaking loosened reins or using their whips as they called urgently to horses straining to reach their top.

'Hup! Hup!' called father, this breaking-in cry of his carrying with it some urgent, powerful appeal that horses responded to and fled from with increasing speed.

Now, sitting in the sunshine, a rug over my knees, watching him grease the buggy, I thought of this day, a year ago, when he had beaten McPherson in a race down the Two-Mile Flat.

For some reason father never looked back at drivers who challenged him. He looked ahead down the track he was travelling, a smile on his face.

'A bad bump can throw you back a yard,' he told me once.

I always looked back. It was exciting to see the head of a powerful horse at your buggy's wheel, the flare of his nostrils, the blown foam that streaked his neck.

I remembered looking back at McPherson.

'McPherson's gaining, dad,' I warned him as a yellow-wheeled jinker in which a sandy-bearded man was bringing his whip down on the flanks of a pacing grey, came pounding along the metal a length to the rear of us where we sped along the dirt track now beginning to converge on the made road.

'To hell with him!' muttered father. He stood up in front of the seat, leant forward and shortened his reins then gave a quick glance ahead to where, a hundred yards away, the dirt track met the metal road in the crossing of a drain. Beyond the culvert the dirt track moved away from the road again but on the culvert only one could pass.

'Into it, you beauty!' yelled father and he flicked Prince with the whip. The big horse flattened into a more extended stride as the track drew parallel with the road.

'Get to hell out of it!' yelled McPherson. 'Draw out or be damned to you, Marshall.' Mr McPherson was an elder of the Church and knew all about hell and the damned, but he didn't know very much about Prince.

'I've got you bloody well licked!' shouted father. 'Hup! Hup!' And Prince gave that little bit more that father knew he had. The flying buggy cut in under the nose of McPherson's grey, skidded on to the metal, crossed the culvert in a whirl of dust and was back in the silence of the dirt track while McPherson cursed behind us, his whip still flailing.

'Blast him!' exclaimed father. 'He thinks he should have beaten me. If I'd been in the brake I'd have left him standing.'

Father always swore a lot on his way to the Sunday School picnic.

'Remember where we're going,' mother reminded him.

'All right,' said father agreeably. 'Hell!' he exclaimed. 'Here comes Rogers with his new roan. Hup! Hup!'

But we had topped the final rise and the picnic ground was below us. And beside it was the creek. The angled shadow of a huge railway bridge that spanned it trembled on the water and lay motionless on the wide stretch of grass that moved back from the water's edge.

Children were already playing on this flat area. Adults were bending over baskets, unpacking cups and plates, lifting cakes from nests of paper and arranging sandwiches on trays.

Horses tied to a fence that curved over a nearby rise rested with drooping heads and hanging, unbuckled harness. Some tossed nosebags as they snorted the dust from their nostrils. Below, in the shadow of the bridge, buggies and gigs with empty shafts stood in the gaps between the piles.

Father drove our buggy between two groups of these towering columns and we tumbled out almost before his 'Whoa there!' and a pull on the reins had stopped the horse.

I made for the creek at a run. Just to look at it gave me pleasure. The moving water made curved ridges against the upright stems of rushes. The flat leaves of reeds moved their pointed tips to and fro on the surface and from the bottom of deep pools silver bubbles sometimes came wriggling upwards and broke on the surface amid expanding ripples.

Old redgums grew on the banks and their limbs curved over the water, some of them so low that the current tugged at their leaves, dragging them with it then releasing them again. The dry trunks of fallen trees lay with their rooted butts on the edge of the grassed hollows where once they had stood erect. You could use these weathered root spikes as steps and climb to the top; then you could look along the trunk and see where it disappeared beneath the water. They were cracked and bleached by sun and rain and I liked to touch them, to look intently at the texture and grain of the weathered wood seeking for possum scratches or just so that I could imagine what the tree was like when it was growing.

On the far bank of the creek bullocks stood with lifted heads among the tussocks and looked at me. A blue crane rose heavily from a clump of reeds; then Mary came and told me I had to go back to the buggy and get ready for the race. This was the race I was going to win and I told her about it as I clung to her hand while we walked across the grass to where mother was sitting on the ground beside the buggy preparing lunch. She had spread a cloth on the grass and father was kneeling beside it carving slices of meat from a cold leg of lamb. He always suspected meat bought from butchers and claimed that mutton was never any good unless it came from a sheep slaughtered while it had a full stomach and was fresh from the grass.

'They get knocked about by dogs and are jammed in yards,' he used to say. 'They bruise the hell out of them. You can't leave a sheep go without a feed for a couple of days without it losing condition.'

Now he muttered over the leg of lamb as he turned it this way and that on the plate.

'When this lamb was alive,' he said to me, 'it was as long in the tooth as I am. Sit down and have a bit.'

After lunch I followed him round till the bell rang for the boys' race.

'Come on now and I'll lead you in,' he said, suddenly turning from the man to whom he was talking. 'See you later, Tom.' He waved to the man and, taking my hand, he walked with me to where Peter Finlay was busily shepherding a group of boys into an orderly line.

'Back you go,' Peter kept repeating, his outstretched arms moving up and down with a jerky movement as he walked up and down in front of them. 'Don't jostle. Spread out. That's better. There's no hurry. Take your time. We'll let you know when to get set. Back further ...'

'Five to four the field,' father said to him as he pushed me forward.

Peter turned round. 'Ah!' he exclaimed, looking down at me with an amused smile. 'Is he going to jib today?' he asked father.

'No, he's rearing to go,' father told him.

Peter glanced along the track upon which we were to run then said, 'Shove him up near that far tussock, Bill. He'll have a chance from there.' He patted me on the head. 'Now you show your old man how you can go.'

I was interested in all the preparation and bustle for a race I was to win. Boys jumped up and down on their mark or leant forward with their fingers on the ground. Father told me I wouldn't have to do that. I followed him down between two long lines of people. All the people I knew were standing there watching us and smiling. Mrs Carter was there: she had given me a lolly once. Now she waved to me.

'Run hard, Alan,' she called out.

'Here's the place,' said father. He stopped and, bending down, took off my shoes. The grass felt you'd like to jump up and down on it when you stood on it with your shoes off. I jumped around on it.

'Steady now,' father said, 'A prancing horse never wins anything. Stand still here and face that tape down there.' He pointed to where at the far end of the two rows of people two men were holding a tape across the track. It seemed a long way away, but I wanted to reassure him. 'I'll get there as quick as anything.'

'Now, listen to me, Alan.' Father squatted on his heels so that his face was close to mine. 'Don't forget all I've told you. When the pistol goes bang you run straight for that tape. And don't look back. As soon as you hear the bang, you run. Run hard like you do at home. I'm going to stand over there near these people. Now I'm going. Keep looking at the tape and don't look back.'

'I'll get a prize when I win, won't I?' I asked him.

'Yes,' he said, 'now get ready. The pistol will go off in a minute.'

He walked backwards away from me. I didn't like him going away. There were too many things to remember when he wasn't there.

'Ready!' he suddenly called out to me from where he stood in front of a line of people.

I looked back to see why the pistol didn't go off. All the boys were standing in a line. I was out of all the fun up there on my own and I wished I was back with them. Then the pistol went off and they were all running. It shocked me to see how quickly they began to run. They were racing with their heads back but they hadn't started to race me yet. You can't race anybody when they're not with you.

Father was yelling 'Run! Run! Run!'

Now they were all round me and it was time to race them but they wouldn't wait for me and I ran desperately after them feeling angry and a little bewildered. The tape was down when I reached it and I stopped and cried. Father ran to me and lifted me in his arms.

'Dash me rags!' he exclaimed in exasperation. 'Why didn't you run when the gun went off? You looked back and waited for the boys again.'

'I had to wait for them to race them,' I sobbed. 'I don't like winning races on my own.'

'Well, don't cry over it,' he said, 'we'll make a runner of you yet.'

But that was a year ago.

Maybe he thought of this as he spun the wheel of the buggy and I sat there in my pram watching him with a rung over my crippled legs.

'You won't be able to run this time,' he said at last, 'but I want you to watch them running. You stand near the tape. Run with them while you watch them. When the first kid breasts the tape you breast it with him.'

'How, dad?' I did not quite understand what he meant.

'Think it,' he said.

I thought over what he said while he went into the harness room for a tin of axle grease. When he came out he placed it on the ground beside the buggy then wiped his hands on a piece of rag and said, 'I had a black bitch once – a half-bred kangaroo dog. She could run like the son of a gun. She could stay with any flying doe and'd bail up an old man 'roo in a hundred yards. She'd scatter a mob then race up on one and toss it by grabbing the butt of its tail while it was in the air. She never went for their shoulder like other dogs. But she never missed. She was the best dog I've ever had. A bloke offered me a fiver for her once.

'Why didn't you sell her, dad?' I asked.

'Well, you see, I reared her from when she was a pup. I called her Bessie.'

'I wish we had her now, dad,' I said.

'Yes, I do, too, but she got staked in the shoulder and put it out or something. She had a hell of a lump on it afterwards. She was never any good after that. But I took her out just the same and she did all the barking and the other dogs did all the running. I've never seen a dog get so excited over a course. And she never chased them herself, mind you.

'I remember how we bailed up an old man 'roo once and he had his back to a tree and when Brindle – he was another kangaroo dog I had – when Brindle went in the 'roo ripped him from his shoulder to his flank and Bessie yelped as soon as the 'roo got him. By hell, she did! I've never seen a dog throw herself into scraps and courses like her. Yet she only did it by barking an' that.'

'I like you telling me about her, dad,' I said, eager to hear more.

'Well, you've got to be like her. Fight and run and race and ride and yell your bloody head off while you're looking on. Forget your legs. I'm going to forget them from now on.'

CHAPTER 13

The children who lived further down our road called for me each morning and pushed me to school in the pram. They liked doing it because each one had turns in riding with me.

Those pulling the pram would prance like horses and I would yell out, 'Hup! Hup!' and wave an imaginary whip.

There was Joe Carmichael, who lived almost opposite us – he was my mate – and Freddie Hawk, who could do everything better than anyone else and was the hero of the school, and 'Skeeter' Bronson, who always said that he'd 'tell on you' when you hit him.

Two girls lived up our road; Alice Barker was one. All the boys at the school wished she was their girl but she liked Freddie Hawk. Maggie Mulligan was the other girl. She was a big girl and knew three terrible swears and would say the three of them together if you got her wild. She would clip you on the ear as quick as look at you and I liked her wheeling me in the pram better than anyone else because I loved her.

Sometimes, when we played 'bucking horses' the pram tipped over and Maggie Mulligan would say the three swears and pick me up and call to the others, 'Here! Help me chuck him back before someone comes.'

She had two long red plaits down her back, and sometimes boys at school would yell out, 'Ginger for pluck' at her and she would sing back at them, 'Long nose eats the fruit. You're lousy as a bandicoot.'

She wasn't frightened of any boy and she wasn't frightened of bulls either.

When McDonald's bull got out and started fighting with one of the road bulls we all stopped to watch them. McDonald's bull was the biggest and he kept pushing the road bull backwards till he got him against a tree then he drove at his flanks. The road bull bellowed and turned to get away. Blood was running down his back legs and he made up the road towards us with McDonald's bull on his heels, goring him as he ran.

Joe and Freddie and Skeeter lit out for the fence but Maggie Mulligan stopped with me and wouldn't let go the pram handle. She tried to pull me off the track but she didn't have time and McDonald's bull gave a side toss with its horns as it passed and sent the pram flying, but I fell on ferns and wasn't hurt and Maggie Mulligan wasn't hurt either.

But the wheel of the pram was buckled and Maggie Mulligan put the Fireman's lift on me and carried me home and she only had four spells because Joe and Freddie counted them.

At school they always left my pram near the door and I walked into the schoolroom on my crutches.

The school was a long, stone building with high, narrow windows and you couldn't see out of them when you were sitting down. They had wide sills covered with chalk dust. In one of these alcoves stood an old vase with some dead flowers in it.

There were two long blackboards, one at each end of the room.

Beneath each blackboard were ledges on which rested pieces of chalk, dusters to clean the board, large setsquares and rulers.

A fireplace full of dirty record books was let into the wall between the two blackboards, and above the fireplace was a picture of a group of blood-stained soldiers in red coats, all looking outwards and leaning forward with their rifles projecting over the dead bodies of other soldiers lying limply at their feet. In the centre of the group, higher than the others, stood a man holding a banner on a long pole. He was yelling out something and shaking his fist. It was called 'The Last Stand' but Miss Pringle didn't know where they were standing. Mr Tucker said it represented British heroism in full flower and he tapped the picture with a long stick when he said it so that you would know what he was talking about.

Miss Pringle taught the Little Ones and Mr Tucker taught the Big Ones. Miss Pringle had grey hair and looked at you over her glasses. She wore a high whale-bone collar that made it hard for her to nod her permission for you to go out and I was always wanting to go out because then you could stand in the sun and look at Mt Turalla and hear magpies. Sometimes there were three of us outside together and we would row over who was to go back first.

Mr Tucker was the head teacher. He did not wear glasses. His eyes frightened you even when you hung your head and refused to face them. They were sharp and hard and cold and he used them like a whip. He always washed his hands in an enamel basin in the corner of the room and after he had washed them he would walk over to his desk and stand behind it looking at the pupils while he dried them on a small, white towel. He dried each finger separately, beginning with the first finger. His fingers were long and white and threaded on sinews you could see beneath the skin. He rubbed them briskly without losing the effect of deliberation and as he rubbed them he looked at us with his eyes.

No one moved while he dried his hands, no one spoke. When he finished he would fold the towel and put it in the desk drawer and than he would smile at us with his teeth and lips.

He terrified me as a tiger would.

He had a cane and before he used it on a boy he would swish it twice through the air and then draw it through his closed hands as if to clean it.

'Now,' he would say, and his teeth would be smiling.

To be able to stand the cuts was evidence of superiority. Boys who cried from the cuts were thereafter unable to boss any other boy in the playground. Even smaller boys stood up to them, confident they could lick them. My pride demanded I establish myself in some field children valued and since most of these fields were closed to me I developed a disdainful attitude towards being caned even though I had a greater fear of Mr Tucker than most of the pupils. I refused to jerk my outstretched hand back as the cane came down, as some boys did, nor did I grimace and fold my arms after each cut, having no faith that it eased the pain or made Mr Tucker give you fewer cuts then he intended. After the cane I could not clasp the hand-grips of my crutches, my numbed fingers refusing to bend, so I placed the backs of my hands beneath the grips and could get back to my seat in that way.

Miss Pringle did not use a cane. She used a broad strap, split at the end into three narrow tails. These tails were supposed to sting more than a single strap but she soon discovered that this was not so and thereafter she held the strap by its divided end and belted us with the broad section.

She kept her lips tightly closed and didn't breathe when she wielded the strap but she couldn't hit very hard. She often carried it round the class with her, striking her skirt with it now and then in the way a stockman cracked a whip to frighten cattle.

She was calm when she strapped you but Mr Tucker was seized with a savage urgency when he felt called upon to flog a boy. He would bound to his desk and fling back the broad lid with a bang, yelling, as he searched for the cane among the roll books and papers in the desk, 'Come out here, Thompson. I saw you pull a face when you thought my back was turned.'

No one worked when he caned a boy. We all watched in a stricken silence, numbed by fear of an anger we could not understand or explain. His reddened face and changed voice seemed to us evidence of terrible intentions and we quaked in our seats.

We knew how he saw Tompson pull a face behind his back. The glass on the picture above the fireplace reflected those behind him and when he looked at it he did not see the dead soldiers or the man screaming as he clutched the flag; he saw the faces of the children.

The children often discussed the cane and the strap. One or two of the older boys spoke with authority on the subject and we listened to them with respect.

They would remind us that a horse hair placed in a tiny split at the end of the cane would split the entire cane in two after the first blow on a boy's hand. Hearing this, I would have dreams of climbing through the window of the deserted school, inserting the horse hair and escaping unnoticed. I could see, next day, the thwarted, furious expression on Mr Tucker's face as he gazed at the split and useless cane in his hand while I stood smiling, with outstretched hand in front of him waiting for the blow I knew he could not deliver. It was a most satisfying picture.

But to insert that horse hair meant breaking open the locked desk and this we could not do. So we rubbed resin on the palms of our hands, believing that this rendered the hand so tough no cut could hurt it.

I gradually became the authority on resin, describing the amount to use, the method of application, the varying qualities of resin, in a tone that showed I was a veteran and could not be contradicted.

But, later, I turned to wattlebark, soaking my hands in the brown liquid made from pouring hot water over the bark. I claimed this tanned the hands, and displayed my palms, calloused from constant rubbing on the crutch grips, to prove it. I made many converts and a bottle of wattlebark liquid was worth four marbles or six cigarette cards provided it was almost black.

At first I sat in the gallery at Miss Pringle's end of the room. The gallery consisted of rows of desks standing on rising tiers till, at the rear, they had risen half-way to the roof. The desks each held six children and had backless seats attached to them. They were disfigured by initials, circles, squares and gashes carved into the wood with pocket knives. Some had round holes cut through the top and you could drop a rubber or pencil through into the open compartment below. Six inkwells rested in holes bored to secure them and there were grooves beside these inkwells for holding pens and pencils.

The Little Ones used slates to write upon. The slates had a hole bored through the top of the frame, and a string, to which a piece of rag was tied, was passed through this hole and tied to the slate.

When you wanted to clean the slate you spat on it and rubbed the writing away with the rag. After a while the rag began to smell and you got a new piece from your mother.

It was the custom to work up a good spit by sucking the inside of your cheeks and working your jaws. A big spit was reason for pride and you showed it to the boy next to you before you tilted the slate and guided the moving spittle this way and that till the wet trail it left behind it reduced it to a size where further experiment was boring. You then wiped your slate with the rag and paid attention to Miss Pringle.

Miss Pringle believed that constant repetition of a fact embedded it in your mind for ever, complete with full understanding of all it implied.

You first learned the alphabet by repeating it each day, then in a sing-song voice the whole class chanted, 'C-A-T, cat; C-A-T, cat; C-A-T, cat.'

That night you told your mother you could spell 'cat' and she thought it was wonderful.

But my father didn't. He said, 'To hell with "cat"! Spell "horse",' when I confronted him with my new knowledge.

I learned quickly when I set my mind to it but I was a giggler and a talker and was constantly being caned. I left each class with something still unlearned and I began to hate school. My writing was bad, according to Miss Pringle, and she always clucked her tongue when she looked at my spelling. Freehand Drawing appealed to me because then I could draw gum leaves and my drawings would be different from everyone else's. For Ruled Drawings we drew cubes and mine were never square.

Once a week we were given a lesson called 'Science'. I liked this lesson because then we were allowed to stand round the table and you could push and shove and have fun.

Mr Tucker opened the cupboard containing some glass tubes, a spirit lamp, a bottle of mercury and a leather disc with a piece of string attached to the centre. He placed these things on the table and said, 'Today we are concerned with the weight of air which is fourteen pounds to the square inch.'

This didn't make sense to me but the fact that I was standing beside Maggie Mulligan made me wish to shine so I proffered the information that my father had told me the fuller you are with air the lighter you are and you couldn't sink in the river. I thought this had some bearing on the subject but Mr Tucker slowly put the piece of leather back on the table then looked at me with his eyes so that I could not face him and said through his teeth, 'Marshall, I would have you know that we are not interested in your father or in any observation made by your father even if such observations proclaim the stupidity of his son. Would you please attend to the lesson.'

He then wet the leather disc and pressed it on the desk and none of us could pull it off except Maggie Mulligan who ripped the guts out of it with one yank and proved air didn't weigh anything.

She told me when she was wheeling me home that what I said was right and that air weighed nothing.

'I wish I could give you a present,' I told her, 'but I haven't got anything.'

'Have you got any comics?' she asked.

'There's two under my bed,' I said eagerly. 'I'll give you both of them.'

CHAPTER 14

My crutches were gradually becoming a part of me. I had developed arms out of proportion to the rest of my body and my armpits were now tough and hard. The crutches did not chafe me any more and I could walk without discomfort.

I practised different walking styles, calling them by the names applied to the gaits of horses. I could trot, pace, canter and gallop. I fell frequently and heavily but learned to throw myself into positions that saved my bad leg from injury. I typed the falls I had and when beginning to fall always knew whether it would be a 'bad' or 'good' fall. If both crutches slipped when I was well advanced on my forward swing I fell backwards and this was the worst fall of all since it often resulted in my being winded or twisting my bad leg beneath me. It was a painful fall and I used to thump the earth with my hands to keep from crying out when I fell in this manner. When only one crutch slipped or struck a stone or root, I fell forward on to my hands and was never hurt.

I was never free of bruises or lumps or gravel rashes and

each evening found me attending to some injury I had received that day.

But they did not distress me. I accepted these annoying inconveniences as being part of normal living and I never for a moment regarded them as a result of being crippled, a state which, at this period, I never applied to myself.

I began walking to school and became acquainted with exhaustion – the state so familiar to cripples and their constant concern.

I always cut corners, always made in as straight a line as I could to where I wanted to go. I would walk through clumps of thistles rather than go round them, climb through fences rather than deviate a few yards to go through a gate.

A normal child expends its surplus energy by cavorting, skipping, spinning in circles or kicking stones along the ground as it walks up the street. I, too, felt the need to do this and I indulged in clumsy caperings and leaps as I walked up the road just because of a need to express how well I felt. People seeing me expressing my joy in living so clumsily regarded it as pathetic and stared at me with pity so that I immediately stopped till they were out of sight then threw myself into my happy world again, free from their sadness and their pain.

Though I was not aware of it, my values were changing and from having a natural respect for those boys who spent most of their time reading, I became absorbed in physical achievement. I admired a football player, a boxer, a bike-rider far more than those with impressive mental achievements. The tough boys became my playmates and my conversation often suggested aggressiveness.

'I'll punch you fair in the eye after school, Ted; you see if I don't.'

I talked in terms of violence yet shrank from demonstrating it. I could not punch a boy in the eye unless he first punched me.

Violence of any kind was abhorrent to me. Sometimes, after seeing a man flog a horse or kick a dog, I would creep home and put my arm around Meg's neck and hold her tightly for a moment. It made me feel better as if her security embraced myself.

Animals and birds were never long out of my mind. Birds in flight affected me like music. I watched dogs running, with an almost painful awareness of the beauty of their motion, and a galloping horse made me tremble with some emotion I could not define.

I was not aware that in this worship of all action that suggested power and strength I was building up a compensation for an inability to indulge in such action myself. I only knew I felt an uplift of spirit when I witnessed it.

Joe Carmichael and I hunted rabbits and hares together and with a pack of dogs we went tramping through the bush and across open paddocks, and when we roused the hare and the dogs gave chase I watched with a keen pleasure the kangaroo dog's undulating run, his lowered head close to the ground, the magnificent curve of his neck and shoulders and the swinging, leaning turn of him as he came round after the dodging hare.

I began walking into the bush in the evenings so that I could smell the earth and the trees. I knelt among the moss and fern and pressed my face against the earth, breathing it into me. I dug among the roots of grass with my fingers, feeling an intense interest in the texture of the earth I was holding, the feel of it, the fine, hairlike roots it contained. It seemed magical to me and I began to feel that my head was too far above it to appreciate to the fullest the grass and wildflowers and ferns and stones along the tracks I walked. I wanted to be like a dog, running with my nose to the earth so that there would be no fragrance missed, no miracle of stone or plant unobserved.

I would crawl through ferns by the swamp's edge, making tunnels of discovery through the undergrowth, or lie prone with my face close to the curled fronds of bracken newly emerged from the creative darkness of the earth, gently clasped like babies' hands. Oh! the tenderness of them; the kindness and compassion of them. I would lower my head and touch them with my cheek.

But I felt confined, restricted in my quest for some revelation that would explain and appease the hunger I possessed. So I created dreams, for in these I could roam as I willed, unhampered by an unresponsive body.

After tea, before it was time to go to bed, in that first expectant darkness when the frogs from the swamp began their chirping and early possums peered out from hollow limbs, I would stand at our gate looking through the rails at the bush across the road where it stood motionless against the sky, waiting for the night. Beyond it Mt Turalla hid the rising moon on those nights I loved the best and its huge shoulder was sharp against the glow.

Listening to the frogs or a mopoke or the chirr of a possum, I would launch myself out into a powerful run through the night, galloping on four legs, my nose to the earth as I followed a rabbit's trail or the tracks of a kangaroo. Maybe I was a dingo or just a dog living a life of its own in the bush – I was never quite sure – but I was never separate from the bush through which I loped in tireless strides. I was part of it and all that it offered was mine.

In this escape from the reality of laborious walking I experienced speed that was tireless, leaps and bounds that were effortless and the grace of movement I recognised in men in action and in the running of dogs and horses.

As a dog running through the night I experienced no effort, no fatigue, no painful falls. I raced through the bush with my nose to the leaf-strewn earth, bounded a length behind speeding kangaroos, turning as they did, leaping to bring them down, hurtling over logs and creeks, passing from moonlight to shadow, twisting and turning, my body firm with tireless muscle and animated by an intense and joyful energy.

In my hunting dreams my imagination stopped at the seizing of a rabbit or kangaroo; it was the chase in which I gloried, the merging of my identity with the bush.

I could not imagine exhaustion in uncrippled bodies. Exhaustion, to me, was a condition arising from walking on crutches and had no part in the lives of normal people. It was my crutches that prevented me running all the way to school without stopping, that increased the beat of my heart when I climbed a hill, and made me cling panting to a tree while other boys continued on. But I didn't resent my crutches. I could not feel that way. I left them behind in my dreams but I returned to them without resentment.

In this period of adjustment the two worlds in which I lived were equally enjoyable. I gained from each the stimulus to pass into the other. The world of reality forged me; in the world of dreams I swung the blade.

CHAPTER 15

Freddie Hawk could run and fight and climb and use a shanghai better than anyone else in the school. He was a champion at marbles and could pitch a cigarette card further than the other boys. He was a quiet boy who never boasted and I was devoted to him. He was saving cigarette cards and only had one to get to complete the set of 'Arms and Armour of the British Empire'.

He kept this set in a tobacco tin and once or twice a day he would take out the little pack, wet his thumb, and count them while I watched him. There were always forty-nine.

I wanted to get him that missing card and would accost every man I met: 'Got any cigarete cards, mister?' but without result.

After I had concluded that it must be the rarest cigarette card in the world, a horseman I stopped as he was passing our gate drew if from a packet and gave it to me.

I could hardly believe I had it. I read the number several times – thirty-seven; that was right. Freddie didn't have number thirty-seven.

Next day I waited impatiently on the road for him to appear and began yelling the news to him when he was a quarter of a mile away. When he was close enough to hear me he began to run and when he came up I handed him the card.

'I got it from a bloke on a horse,' I told him excitedly. 'He says to me, "What are you saving?" and I says to him, "Arms and Armour of the British Empire," and he says, "By hell I might have one of them!" and by hell, he did too. Now you've got the set.'

Freddie looked at the card then turned it over and looked at the number. He then read through the description of the Armour it pictured and remarked, 'It's it all right, b'cripes!'

He took his tobacco tin from his pocket and opened it. He placed the new card in its correct position in the pack, tapped the pack on a post to straighten it, liked his thumb, and counted the cards slowly, saying each number aloud. I repeated the number with him.

'Fifty!' I exclaimed triumphantly at the end of the count.

'It looks like it,' he said.

He again tapped the pack against the post and counted them again, beginning with the last one.

'Now you've got the set, Freddie,' I said happily when he had finished. 'And they're all goodies.'

'Yes,' he said. He placed the pack back into the tobacco tin. 'Fancy – the bloody set.' He held the tin at arm's length and looked at it, smiling.

'Here, take it,' he said, suddenly thrusting the tin into my hands. 'They're yours. I saved 'em for you.'

He rarely played with me at school, being too intent winning marbles or cigarette cards or spinning tops.

I was a poor marbles player and always lost. Freddie had a

Milky Really worth a bod and he gave it to me so that I could play 'Reallies Up'. Each boy competing placed a Really in the ring but only the best players would risk such valuable marbles. Each time I played I lost the Milky Really and I would go to Freddie and say, 'I lost it again, Freddie.'

'Who to?' he would ask.

'Billy Robertson.'

'All right,' Freddie would say and he would go and win it back for me and say, 'Here it is,' then he would return to his own game again.

He always moved over when I was having a row with a boy and he would stand there listening while he kicked the gravel with his foot. Once when Steve McIntyre told me he'd kick me on the backside, I said to him, 'It's the last backside you'll ever kick,' and Steve got back to take a run at me. Freddie had been listening and he said to Steve, 'The bloke that boots him boots me.'

Steve didn't want to kick me after that but when we were marching into school he whispered to me, 'I'll get you after school, see if I don't.' I lashed out with my crutch and got him on the shin before he drew back and after that all the kids began taking sides and some said I wanted a punch on the nose and some said Steve wanted one.

My row with Steve had started when we were all struggling to get a drink at the square iron tank that held the school's water supply. A large tin pannikin with a rusted bottom hung on the tap and beneath the tap the spilt water had collected in a depression worn by the boots of the children. Those clamouring for a drink stamped in this muddy pool like cattle at a trough.

At playtime in the summer there was a rush for the tank, girls and boys pushing and shoving, grabbing the half-full pannikin from the lips of those already drinking and pouring the contents down their own throats while a score of hands were reaching towards them. As the drinking ones discarded the pannikin it was seized and drained by others.

There was a constant yelling for recognition. The one drinking was appealed to, threatened, denounced or reminded of obligations he had forgotten.

'Here on the outside, Bill . . . I'm here . . . Hand it over. I lent you my Really. After you, Jim . . . Hey, Jim, after you . . . There's enough in it for the two of us. Get out of the bloody road, look who you're pushing . . . I got here first. I'm next. You go to hell!'

Water was spilt down dresses, shirts . . . Boys emerged hopping on one leg and holding shins with their clasped hands: 'Oo-oo-oo.'

Girls yelled, 'I'll tell on you.' Those who had drunk forced their way out from the crush wiping their wet mouths with the backs of their hands and grinning triumphantly.

I fought with the others. In matters such as this no concessions were made to my crippled limbs and I was knocked over or pushed aside with complete disregard of my crutches.

I encouraged this attitude by talking in terms inappropriate to my powers. 'I'll fix you in a minute,' I would threaten the school bully to his astonishment.

It was recognised that I was prepared to follow up my threats by action but until my row with Steve McIntyre I never had to make good my threats.

Steve hit the pannikin upwards when I was drinking and soaked me with water and grabbed the pannikin out of my hand. I punched him in the stomach then fell over since it jerked the crutch from beneath my arm. While on the ground I grabbed his legs and tipped him into the mud. But he got up before I did and was going to have a go at me then but the bell rang.

For a week after that we exchanged threats, each surrounded by a group of mates whispering advice. It was recognised that I had powerful arms and Steve's advisers openly proclaimed that if you kicked the crutches from beneath me I was done. This was denied by the boys on my side who were of the opinion that I was at my best when on the ground. I didn't know when I was at my best but I was completely incapable of thinking in terms of defeat.

'Say he knocks me out,' I explained to Freddie Hawk. 'Well, when I come round I'll have another go at him.'

My reasoning was based on a simple premise, 'If you don't give in, you're never beaten.' Since nothing on earth would make me give in I must win.

Freddie, counting marbles into a cloth bag with a tape on it remarked, 'I'll fight him for you and I'll give you another Really.'

I couldn't agree to this. I wanted Steve McIntyre for myself. I had to fight him or else I would be a siss. If I didn't fight him the kids would never again take any notice of what I said.

I explained this to Freddie who then suggested I fight him with my back against a stone wall, because then, whenever he missed me, he would bash his hands against the stones.

I thought this was a good idea.

When I got home from school that night I told mother I was going to fight Steve McIntyre behind the old stump in Jackson's paddock next day.

She turned from the stove where she was cooking and exclaimed, 'Fight? Are you going to fight?'

'Yes,' I said.

She shifted the big black kettle on the stove and said, 'I don't like you fighting, Alan. Can't you get out of it?'

'No,' I said, 'I want to fight him.'

'Don't,' she pleaded with me, then sudenly stopped and looked at me with a troubled expression arrested on her face while she stood thinking.

'I . . . What does your father say?'

'I haven't told him yet.'

'Go down and tell him now.'

I walked down to the stockyard where father was walking round and round behind a young, nervous horse that was dragging a post behind it. The horse's neck was arched and there was froth around its mouth where it champed the mouthing bit. It moved in starts and father kept talking to it.

I climbed on to the rail and said, 'I'm going to fight Steve McIntyre tomorrow.'

Father reined the horse in and moved up to it where he began patting its neck.

'How do you mean – fight?' he asked. 'Are you having a go at him with your fists?'

'Yes.'

'What's the row over?'

'He chucked water over me.'

'That's not so bad, is it?' he asked. 'I like water fights, myself.'

'He keeps chipping me.'

'Well, that's not too good,' he said slowly, looking at the ground. 'Who's back-stopping you?'

'Freddie Hawk.'

'Yes,' he murmured to himself. 'He's all right,' then added, 'I suppose you've got to lock horns with someone.' He looked up at me. 'You don't go round looking for fights, do you, son? I wouldn't like to think that.'

'No,' I said. 'He picks me.'

'I see,' he said. He looked at the horse. 'Wait till I let this colt go.'

I watched him unfasten the breast plate and drop the trace chains; then I climbed from the fence and waited for him at the stable door.

'Now, let's get this straight,' he said when he came out. 'How big's this McIntyre kid? I don't remember him.'

'He's bigger than me but Freddie reckons he's got a tail.'

'Yes,' argued father, 'but what happens when he hits you? He'll play hell with you while he keeps out of reach. You might get one chop at him but a lift under the chin'd flatten you like a tack. And not because you can't fight, mind you,' he hastened to add. 'You're the sort of bloke who could go like a threshin' machine. But how are you going to keep standing? How do you hang on to your crutches and paste him at the same time?'

'Once I'm down I'm set,' I told him eagerly. 'I'll pull him down then. He'll never get away.'

'How about your back?'

'It's all right. It doesn't hurt. If he kicked me on it, it'd hurt, but I'll lie on it.'

Father took out his pipe and looked thoughtfully at his fingers pressing tobacco into the bowl.

'Pity you couldn't fight him some other way. How'd you go with shanghais or something like that?'

'Oo! He's good with a shanghai,' I hastened to inform him. 'He can kill a tomtit across the road.'

'How about sticks?' father suggested doubtfully.

'Sticks!' I exclaimed.

'Well, if you had a go at him with sticks, you've got something your way. You're stronger in the arms than he is. You could sit down facing him on the grass and have a lash at him that way. When they say "Go!" or whatever they say, king him. If he's yellow like you say he'll toss it in after he collects that first hit.'

'What if he won't fight with sticks?'

'Just work him along to have a lick at you with sticks,' father explained. 'If he still jibs at it, call him yellow in front of the other boys. He'll rise to that hook. Take him gently. Don't lose your temper. Swipe him on the knuckles if you can. If he's like his old man he's a soda. I see his old man down at the pub the other day poking in as if he'd like to have a go at someone. When old Riley invited him out on the grass he closed up. This kid'll be like him. You see the look on him when you tell him it's sticks not fists.'

That night, through the open door of my bedroom, I saw father talking to mother as she sat darning my stockings, and I heard him say to her, 'We've just got to toughen him, Mary. You know that. He's got to learn to take it on the chin no matter how it's dished out. Save him from this and he's going to get it fair in the neck later on. It's a cow, but there you are. We got to cut out working for the kid; we got to work for the man. I want him to try the lot no matter what the risk. Half the time it's a matter of risking his neck or breaking his heart; I choose to risk his neck. That's how I see it anyway. I may be wrong, but I'm staking all I've got, I'm right.'

Mother said something in reply and he answered, 'Yes, I know, I know. We've got to take that risk. It frightens hell out of me too but I reckon the worst he'll get is a lump on the head and a cut or two.' He paused, then added, 'I wouldn't like to be the kid McIntyre,' and he threw back his head and laughed gently with the lamp light on his face while mother watched him.

CHAPTER 16

Fights were always held after school. On those days when a fight was to take place an air of excitement and tension seized each child and the girls kept threatening to 'tell' and the school's known tell-tale-tits were subjected to a tirade of abuse that resulted in offended girls switching their pigtails and marching off with their noses in the air while those pupils who despised the tell-tale watched them balefully.

But it took courage to tell when almost the entire school were in favour of the fight and those girls with reputations as betrayers made a few bluffing marches to the school door where they stopped in indecision and exchanged slanderous remarks about the pigs of boys watching them.

The girls did not attend the fights, it being considered too brutal an exhibition for their genteel minds but they watched from a distance and swore excitedly among themselves, so Maggie Mulligan told me.

She always came to the fights. She walked with the group that surrounded me on our march to Jackson's paddock and took the opportunity to convey her allegiance to me in a hurried whisper, 'If he licks you, I'll lick his sister.' No remark could have established her loyalty more.

'I'll belt hell out of him,' I told her confidently.

I had no doubts as to the outcome. I was an interested observer rather than the central figure of the preparations made by the boys on my side. The division in loyalties was quite plain. Each boy had been asked whose side he was on and the school was about equally divided.

Steve McIntyre had, at first, scorned to fight with sticks but the
suggestion had been so enthusiastically received by all the boys
who heard me make it that he couldn't very well refuse especially
after I had denounced him as yellow and given him the 'Coward's
Blows' by tapping him three times on the shoulder while I chanted,
'One-two-three you can't fight me.'

So sticks it was, and Freddie Hawk cut me a beauty. The wattle
from which it had been cut had no grubs in it, so Freddie told me in
the manner of an authority. It was three feet long and thick at one
end.

'Hold it by the thin end,' Freddie ordered. 'Swing it like you're
going to hit a cow. Get him behind the ear, then swipe him another
on the nose.'

I listened with respect to Freddie. I was sure there was nothing
he did not know.

'Behind the ear is a good place,' I agreed.

Spies brought information from one camp to another and it was
said Steve was going to hit straight down 'like he was chopping
wood!'

'There's only going to be two hits,' he boasted. 'I'll hit him and
he'll hit the ground.'

'Like hell!' Freddie greeted this information from a reliable
informer with contempt. 'What's Alan doing while he's chopping
him!'

Freddie and Joe Carmichael who were back-stopping for me had
measured the sticks, one against the other, so that neither of us
would have an advantage.

Steve's supporters surrounded him in a compact group when we
were all gathered behind the big stump in Jackson's paddock.
Maggie Mulligan reckoned Steve was showing signs he'd like to
quit. But Freddie didn't.

'He fights best when he's howlin',' he told me, 'and he ain't
howlin' yet.'

Before Steve and I sat down opposite each other, Steve took off
his coat, rolled up his shirt sleeves and spat on his hands. This
impressed everybody except Maggie Mulligan who reckoned he
was showing off.

I didn't take off my coat because my shirt had a lot of holes in it
and I didn't want Maggie Mulligan to see them. But I spat on my
hands just to show I knew it was the right thing to do, then I folded
my legs beneath me like a Blackfellow and swung the stick through
the air as if I was Mr Tucker swishing his cane.

After Steve finished spitting on his hands he sat opposite me, out of reach of my stick, so they made him come closer. I reached out my stick to see if I could reach his head and I could easily, so I said I was set. Steve reckoned he was set, too, then Freddie gave his final instructions.

'Remember,' he said, 'nobody is to tell old Tucker about this.'

Everybody promised not to tell old Tucker then Freddie said, 'Into it,' and Steve hit me on the head with his stick. It landed on my hair and skidded down my cheek taking skin with it. It was so completely unexpected that he hit me again on the shoulder before I finally realised we had started.

The blows I then delivered were inspired by a terrific rage and would have stopped a bull, so Maggie Mulligan said.

Steve fell over backwards to escape them and I threw myself forward and belaboured him furiously as he tried to roll away. His nose was bleeding and he let out such a bawl of pain that I stopped in indecision but Freddie Hawk cried, 'Finish him off,' and I began again, crying out between each blow, 'Have you had enough? Have you had enough?' until, between his howls I heard him cry, 'Yes.'

Joe Carmichael was standing beside me with my crutches and Freddie helped me up on to them and I was trembling like a young horse. My face was stinging and painful to touch and a lump was growing on my head.

'I beat him,' I said. 'Didn't I?'

'You knocked fog out of him,' said Maggie Mulligan, then added, leaning anxiously towards me, 'How's your bad leg?'

Father and mother were waiting at the gate when I got home. Father pretended to be mending it and he waited until the other kids went on up the road; then he came over to me quickly and asked, holding his eagerness back, 'How'd you go?'

'I beat him,' I said and somehow I felt like crying.

'Good on ya!' said father, then looked anxiously at my face. 'He's crow-picked you bad. You look as if you've been through a threshin' machine. How're you feeling?'

'Good.'

He held out his hand to me. 'Shake,' he said. 'You've got the heart of a bullock.'

When he shook my hand he said, 'Now mother would like to shake it too.' But mother picked me up in her arms.

Next day Mr Tucker looked at my face then called me out and flogged me for fighting and he flogged Steve McIntyre, too, but I kept remembering that father said I had the heart of a bullock and I didn't cry out.

CHAPTER 17

Joe Carmichael lived quite close to our place. After school hours we were rarely apart. On Saturday afternoons we always went hunting together and on week nights we set traps which we visited early each morning. We knew the names of all the birds in the bush around our homes; we knew their habits, their nesting places, and each of us had a collection of eggs that we kept in cardboard boxes half full of pollard.

Joe had a fresh, ruddy face and a slow smile that made grownups like him. He raised his cap to women and would go messages for anyone. He never quarrelled but always clung stubbornly to an opinion even though he did not defend it.

Joe's father worked for Mrs Carruthers, doing odd jobs round the station, and each morning in the dawn he rode past our gate on a pony called Tony. Each evening as darkness was falling he came riding home again. He had a sandy moustache and father said he was the most honest man in the district. Mrs Carruthers paid him twenty-five shillings a week but she took five shillings back for the rent of his house. His house was built on an acre of land and he kept a cow.

Mrs Carmichael was a thin, little woman with her hair drawn back in two tight wings above her ears. It was done up in a bun at the back. She washed clothes in round wooden troughs made from the halves of barrels and she always hummed a tune as she washed. The tune was always the same. It didn't go high or low but remained on an even key like an expression of contentment. It moved out from the washhouse on the summer evenings and greeted me as I came through the trees to their place and I always stood still to listen to it.

She made ketchup from the mushrooms we gathered. She would place them evenly on a tray and sprinkle salt upon them and little pink beads of juice would gather on their gills and this was the beginning of the ketchup.

She kept fowls and ducks and geese and a pig. When the pig was big Mr Carmichael killed it and put it in a tub of hot water and scraped the hair off it, then he salted it and hung it in a little hut made of bags. He lit fires of green leaves on the floor of this hut and smoke came out everywhere. After he did this the pig was bacon and he gave father some and father said it was the best bacon he had ever tasted.

Mrs Carmichael always smiled at me when I came there and said, 'Sure, it's you again.' Then she would say, 'I will give you and Joe a piece of bread and jam in a minute an' I will.'

She never seemed to notice my crutches. She never mentioned them in all the years I knew her. She never looked at them or at my legs or back. She always looked at my face.

She spoke to me as if unaware that I couldn't run like other boys.

'Run down and get Joe now,' she'd say, or, 'You and Joe will be runnin' the fat off your bones with your rabbits and things. Sit down now and have a bite to eat.'

I was always wanting her house to catch fire so that I could dash in and save her life.

Joe had a brother, Andy, who was too young to go to school. It was Joe's job to look after Andy and Joe and I regarded him as a burden.

Andy was fair and could run like a kangaroo rat. It took Joe all his time to catch him when he wanted to boot him. Andy could dodge like a hare. He was very proud of being able to dodge and sometimes threw cow dung at Joe so that Joe would chase him. Joe couldn't run much but he hung like a dog to the trail once he started. He'd wear Andy down and just as he was going to grab him, Andy would let out a wail that brought his mother dashing from the washhouse.

'What are ye up to now?' she would call. 'Leave the boy alone. He's done ye no harm.'

Joe propped like a stock horse when he heard his mother's voice, and Andy would scuttle off with a grin on his face and cheek Joe from behind a tree.

Joe always contrived to get Andy a long way from home when he wanted to clip his ear. But Andy's howls could be heard half a mile and Joe had to shepherd him away from the house till they died down. Joe often remarked, 'Andy's not worth the worry of him,' but let anyone criticise Andy and Joe would shape up and dance around like Tommy Burns.

Joe had two dogs – Dummy and Rover. Dummy was a pure-bred greyhound, a yellow dog that always yelped when you pressed his back. Joe attributed this to the fact the Dummy was once run over by a buggy and had never got over it.

'If it wasn't for him being run over,' Joe often explained, 'he'd win the Waterloo Cup any day.'

Dummy's accident didn't affect his speed in the bush and Joe and I were given to boasting about him when discussing dogs at school.

Rover was a mongrel that displayed a toothy grin when he wagged his tail. He grovelled at your feet, turned over on his back and wriggled his devotion when you spoke to him. We thought a lot of Rover.

I never took Meg hunting but I had a kangaroo dog called Spot. Spot wasn't as fast as Dummy but he was better through scrub and had tougher feet. He had been ripped by an old man kangaroo when he was a pup and had lost his heart for kangaroos after that. But he was a good rabbiter.

With the three dogs nosing through the grass and trees ahead of us, Joe and I set off every Saturday afternoon searching for rabbits and hares. We sold the skins to a bearded skin buyer who used to drive his horse and waggon up to Joe's each week. The money we received for the skins we placed in a tin. We were saving up to buy *Leach's Bird Book* which we regarded as the most wonderful book you could possibly get.

'I suppose the Bible's better,' Joe once conceded. Joe was faintly religious at times.

Beyond the belt of messmate skirting the swamp, was open bush country and beyond that, the grass paddocks of farms where we were always certain of putting up a hare.

On these hunting excursions Joe adapted his pace to suit mine. When plovers rose with warning cries from clumps of tussock, he would not rush ahead to search for their nest; he would walk side by side with me. He never robbed me of the pleasure of discovery. When he detected, before me, the crouched form of a hare in its seat, he would beckon me with violent gestures and make soundless contortions with his mouth that suggested urgent cries for me to hurry. I would swing towards him on my crutches, raising and lowering them with exaggerated care so that they came to rest in silence between each leap. Then we would watch it together as it crouched with its bulging, frightened eyes staring at us, its ears flattened along its back. The sound of the approaching dogs would make it tighten its ears, pressing them still lower to its hunched back till our simultaneous yell sent it in one bound on its race towards the distant rise where the long grass was.

'We'll rouse one here,' I said to Joe one sunny morning when we had set off with our lunches and were threading our way through tussocky grass with Andy close behind us. 'There's hundreds in here; you can tell by the look of it. Call Dummy. You keep back, Andy!'

'I want to stop with you,' said Andy, a note of rebellion in his voice.

'Don't start him off before we get properly going,' Joe warned me. 'If he starts howling now he'll rouse every hare for miles.'

Andy listened to this with satisfaction. 'There won't be a hare anywhere,' he agreed, nodding his head.

After a speculative glance at Andy I concluded not to press the point.

'All right,' I said, 'you come with me, Andy. I'm going up the rise to stop them going through the pop-hole in Baker's fence. Joe'll put 'em up. Don't let the dogs in till I yell "right", Joe,' I addressed him.

'Come behind here,' Joe yelled at Rover. Rover crawled to Joe's feet and turned over on his back in a plea for mercy. 'Get up,' ordered Joe sharply.

'Come on, Andy,' I ordered.

'Yes, you go with Alan, Andy,' said Joe. Joe was pleased to get rid of Andy.

When I reached the wire netting fence that followed the rise, I made Andy sit down against the small round hole in the netting on the edges of which brown hairs were caught in the spikes.

'You sit there, Andy,' I said, 'and they won't be able to get through.'

'They might charge me.' Andy was a bit uncertain of the wisdom of this manoeuvre.

'Charge, be blowed!' Andy exasperated me.

I walked back a little way and yelled to Joe, 'I've blocked the hole with Andy. Put one up now.'

'Fetch 'em out,' Joe called to the dogs.

Rover, who was always the first to discover a hare or a rabbit, suddenly threw off his humble demeanour and became full of aggressive energy. He dashed into the tussocks closely followed by Dummy and Spot who kept leaping high above the grass, their necks stretched, their heads turning as they searched the runways for that flash of fur that heralded an escaping hare.

Rover suddenly yelped and threw himself at a tussock from where a hare lifted itself in one graceful leap. The abject, cowering creature seeking to conceal itself in the grass was gone. Now its ears were erect and its run was confident. It gave three skips as if to balance itself before stretching out in a gliding run on the pad that led to the pop-hole.

Dummy, with Spot's head close to his flanks, came in silently, his body flexing like a bow. It curved and straightened with each bound; the head, independent of these movements, stretched forward with terrible purpose. For the first few yards his bounds were convulsive and made by violent effort; then he reached his running speed and moved with a curving and effortless rhythm.

Close behind him, Spot moved in similar fashion and further back the barking, yelping Rover, his long hair flopping, strove to keep them in sight, plunging through obstructing grass as if its resistance was directed and hostile.

The hare, not yet frightened into top speed by the first drive of a dog to seize it, sped along the track with its long ears fully erect, its head high. It still gave an occasional skip as it ran but near the pophole the yells of Andy and me scared it and it turned quickly away, dropping its ears in concealment as it sped off through the grass. Dummy, following fast, skidded round in a propping turn, the gravel flung by his tearing paws bouncing off Andy's sailor jacket and the arm with which he shielded his face.

Spot, a little to the rear, cut in behind Dummy and drove in for the kill, but the hare dodged swiftly, turning in its own length, and shot back between the two dogs. Dummy, now recovered from his turn, drew up on the hare and attempted to scoop it up in his open jaws as he over-ran it. But again the hare dodged and now, thoroughly frightened, it made off across the paddock with both dogs racing behind it.

'Sool'im! Catch 'im!' I yelled, following in bounds across the grass.

Joe, running in on an angle, kept yelling, 'Skitch 'im, boy! Skitch 'im!'

In the centre of the paddock Dummy took another turn out of the hare, then Spot, cutting a corner, brought it round once more with a drive that sent him skidding away from the hare that now made for the scrub with Dummy gaining on it with every bound.

Spot cut across towards the scrub and, as Dummy worked it round, he charged at the hare and followed it into the teatree and bracken with no slowing up of his speed.

'He'll lose him in there,' Joe panted as he came up to me.

We stood and watched the line of scrub then suddenly, from deep within it, there came a loud yelp, a howl, then silence.

'He's staked,' I exclaimed in fear, looking at Joe, hoping desperately that he would offer another explanation.

'Looks like it,' he said.

'He'll be killed dead,' said Andy in a frightened voice.

'You shut up!' snapped Joe.

We searched the scrub till we found him. He was lying on ferns with blood on his chest and the stake that pierced him had blood on it too. It was a broken-off limb of a tree, hidden by ferns and pointed like a dagger.

We covered him with scrub till you couldn't see him; then we went home and I didn't cry till I found dad in the harness room and told him.

'It's bad,' he said, 'I know that. But he wouldn't know what hit him.'

'Would it hurt?' I asked tearfully.

'No,' he answered in an assuring tone, 'He wouldn't feel it. Wherever he is now he'll still think he's running.' He looked at me thoughtfully for a moment then added, 'He'd be a sad dog if he knew you were cut up over him sleeping on the ferns out there in the bush.'

I stopped crying when he said this.

'It's only that I'll miss him', I explained.

'I know,' said father gently.

CHAPTER 18

Each day after school Joe drove his mother's ducks and geese to a pond a quarter of a mile away and each evening he drove them back again. They moved ahead of him in a rocking, white line, alive with eagerness and anticipation. When he drove them through the last clump of trees they increased their speed and began quacking, and Joe sat down.

I nearly always accompanied him and we sat together. We both enjoyed watching the ducks with lowered breasts enter the water then glide out with the tiny waves of the pond slapping and rocking them. In the centre of the pond they stretched erect and flapped their wings then sat back in the water with a comfortable wriggle of their tails and bodies before searching for the water creatures that inhabited the pond.

Joe reckoned there could be anything in the pond but I didn't think so.

'You never know what's in there,' Joe reflected at times.

On windy days we placed crews of ants in empty fish tins and sailed them across the pond, and sometimes we paddled round the edge looking for apus, that strange, shrimp-like creature with its moving gills.

Joe knew a lot about apus.

'They're very delicate,' he told me. 'They die if you put them in bottles.'

I wondered where they went when the pond was dry.

'God only knows!' Joe said.

While the ducks were enjoying themselves we wandered in the bush looking for birds, and, in the spring, climbing to their nests.

I was fond of climbing trees. Anything in the nature of a challenge always roused me, driving me to attempt things that Joe, under no compulsion to prove his physical fitness, would not wish to do.

I used my arms in climbing, my legs being of little use. My bad leg swung uselessly as I drew myself up from limb to limb and my good leg could only be used as a prop while my hands reached to higher branches.

I was afraid of heights but managed to overcome this by avoiding looking down unless it was necessary.

I could not monkey-climb up a trunk like other boys, but I could climb a rope hand over hand and when the lower limbs were out of my reach Joe would throw a plow-line over one of them and I would pull myself up on this double strand till I could grasp a limb.

When the magpies nested, Joe would stand below yelling a warning just before the birds attacked. I would climb to the limb, swaying in the wind, my face pressed close to the wood, drawing myself slowly along past forks and peeling bark towards the dark, round patch nestling in leaves against the sky and I would hear his yell, 'Here she comes!' and I would pause in my climbing, clinging with one arm and waving the other desperately above my head, waiting for the rush of wings, the sharp clack of a snapping bill, and the gust of wind on my face as the magpie lifted and shot skywards again.

If you could watch them making their gliding dive it wasn't so bad because you could strike at them as they came in and they would swerve away with a quick flick of their wings and a furious jab at your hand, but when your back was to them and you needed both hands to hold on with, they often struck you with their bills or wings.

When this happened to me I would hear Joe's voice below, full of quick concern.

'Did he get ya?'

'Yes.'

'Where?'

'On the side of the head.'

'Is it bleeding?'

'I don't know yet. Wait till I get a grip here.'

In a moment when I could free a hand from its grip on the limb I would feel my stinging head then glance at my finger-tips. 'She's bleeding,' I'd yell to Joe, both pleased and concerned with the evidence.

'Hell! Anyway you haven't got far to go now. About a yard ... Stretch out now ... A bit further ... No ... To the right a bit ... Now ... '

And I would slip a warm egg into my mouth and come down and we would look at it together as it lay on my palm.

Sometimes I fell, but lower limbs generally broke my fall and I was never badly hurt. Once when climbing with Joe, I slipped as I swung for a limb and grabbed Joe's leg instead. Joe tried to kick me loose but I clung to him like a goanna and we both went crashing down through the brances to land clasped together on the bark-strewn ground below, bruised and breathless but intact.

This fall made a big impression on Joe. In moments of reminiscing he would often remark, 'I'll never forget the bloody day you grabbed my leg and wouldn't let go. Now what did you do that for? I yelled "leggo".'

I could never give him a satisfactory answer though I always felt I was justified in clinging to him.

'I dunno,' he would say reflectively. 'A fellow can't trust you climbing; I'm blowed if he can!'

Joe developed a philosophical attitude towards the falls I had when walking with him. Immediately I plunged forward on my face, or tottered sideways before collapsing, or crashed on my back, Joe would sit down and continue his conversation knowing that, for a little while, I would lie as I fell.

Since I was nearly always tired, a fall offered me an excuse to rest as I lay stretched on the ground, and I would take a twig and search among the grass stems for insects or watch ants hurrying through the tunnels beneath the leaves.

We never mentioned the fall. It didn't seem important. It was part of my walking.

As Joe once remarked, in discussing my falls, 'You're not dead; that's the main thing.'

If I had a 'bad' fall Joe sat down just the same. He never made the mistake of coming to my aid unless I called him. He would sit on the grass, give one glance at me rolling in pain, then look resolutely away and say, 'It's a cow!'

In a minute I would lie quietly and Joe would look at me again and say, 'What d'ya think? Will we keep going?'

The term he used whenever he mentioned my falls was the term used by bushmen in drought time when their horses and cattle lay dying on the dry earth.

'Another cow went down today,' they would say, and Joe would sometimes say to father when father asked him how I was going. 'He went down near the creek and then he didn't go down again till we reached the stones.'

The big drought that struck Australia at this time introduced Joe and me to fear and pain and suffering we had never known before. In our experience, the world was a pleasant place. The sun was never cruel and God looked after the cows and the horses. When an animal suffered it was because of man; of this we were sure. We often reflected on what we would do if we were a cow or a horse and we always decided we would leap fence after fence until there was only bush around us and no people whatever, and here we would live in perfect happiness till we died peacefully in the shelter of trees with long, green grass to rest upon.

The drought started with the failure of the autumn rains. When the winter rains came the earth was too cold for growth and seeds did not sprout and the perennial grass was eaten down to the roots by hungry cattle. The spring was dry and when summer came in, dust was blowing across paddocks that in other years were covered in grass.

The road stock, horses and cattle, kept by their owners on the three-chain roads that laced the district, wandered for miles looking for feed. They forced themselves through fences into paddocks even barer than the roads they left to pluck a dying shrub or bush.

Farmers, unable to feed those aged horses they had retired to their back paddocks, and lacking the courage to shoot animals they had come to regard as part of their farms, turned them out on the roads to fend for themselves. They bought badges for them and the weight on their conscience was lifted.

The local Council only permitted stock on the roads when they had, hanging from their necks, a brass badge for which the Council charged five shillings. This badge entitled the purchaser to graze his beast on the road for a year.

On summer nights the jingle of the chains to which these badges were attached, could be heard through the bush as the horses and cattle wearing them came into the road trough to drink.

For miles along the roads branching out from the trough, bands of horses and cattle could be seen muzzling the dusty earth for roots or standing on the metal eating the dry manure left by chaff-fed horses that had been driven by.

Each mob seemed to keep to itself, always going along the same road, always searching the same lanes. As the drought progressed and the burning heat continued, the mobs grew smaller and smaller. Each day the weakest stumbled and fell and the others moved away from the rising dust of its struggling, walking slowly with dragging feet and drooping heads on and on and on till thirst turned them once more and they began the long trek back to the trough.

Along the roads they walked, magpies with gaping bills stood tottering on gum-tree branches, crows flocked across the paddocks cawing and circling as they sighted a dying beast, and over it all from horizon to horizon the haze of bushfire smoke and the smell of burning gum leaves hung disquietingly above the grassless earth.

Each morning the farmers went round their paddocks raising the cattle that were down.

'I lost three more last night,' a passing farmer would say to father. 'I expect another couple to go down tonight.'

Entire herds of dairy cattle died in the rented paddocks of their owners. They lay on their sides, the earth around their hooves kicked into new-moon holes as they struggled to rise. Day after day under the unclouded sun they kicked and kicked ... and dust rose above them and floated away. And their heavy breathing could be heard across the paddocks ... and deep sighs ... and sometimes a low moaning.

The farmers, hoping for rain, hoping for the miracle that would save them, left the struggling cattle for days. When death had almost come to a cow they killed her with blows then went to the stronger ones who lay lifting their heavy heads and dropping them again; opening wide, staring eyes, struggling to rise.

They placed ropes around them, lifted them with horses, levered them to their feet with planks, held them in an upright position with strong shoulders till the beasts could be left to stand unaided and live another day.

Men leant on gates looking at the blazing sunsets while behind them the empty bails of their cowsheds opened out on to paddocks of bare earth. They gathered round the post office at mail time, talking of their losses and debating how they could raise money to buy hay, how they could hang on till rain came.

Father was having a bad time. He had several of Mrs Car-

ruthers' horses to break in and she sent down chaff to feed them.
Each week Peter Finlay left four bags at our gate and father would
take a handful of the chaff and pour it from hand to hand blowing
the straw away with his mouth till a little pile of oats lay on his
palm. It pleased him when there were a lot of oats. 'Good stuff,' he
would say.

He seemed to spill a lot on the chaff-house floor when he was
filling the kerosene-tin buckets from the bags. Each evening Joe's
father came across with a hearth brush and a bran bag and he
swept up all the chaff that was spilt and took it home. He was
trying to keep his cow and his horse alive. Chaff was a pound a bag
when you could get it and this was his wages for a week so he could
not buy it. Joe went into the bush and cut swamp grass but the
swamps were dry and soon it was gone.

Joe and I were always talking about the horses we had seen that
were down. We tortured ourselves with harrowing descriptions of
the slow deaths taking place in the paddocks and bush around us.

For some reason I could not explain, the death of animals in
paddocks did not affect either of us as badly as did the death of
the road stock. The road stock, it seemed to us, were friendless,
deserted, turned out to die, while the cattle and horses in paddocks
had owners who felt for them.

On the hot summer evenings when the sky remained red long
after the sun had set Joe and I walked down to the road trough to
watch the stock come in. The horses came in every second night,
being able to survive two days without water. The cattle came in
every night but they gradually died round the trough, not being
able to range as far as the horses.

One night we sat looking at the sunset and waiting for the horses.
The road stretched straight through timber then into open country,
disappearing finally over a rise. On the rise were dead gums and
these were silhouetted against the red sky in sharp detail. The
strongest of winds could not move their dead limbs nor any spring
bring leaves upon them. They pointed their skeleton fingers at the
red sky, standing as still as death, and in a little while the horses
rose from behind the earth on which they stood and moved beneath
them, coming towards us with a clinking of neck chains and the
clatter of hooves on stones.

They walked down the rise, twenty or more, old and young, their
heads drooping, all stumbling a little. As they smelt the water from
the distant trough, they raised their heads, gathered themselves
and broke into a shambling canter. They did not crowd together as
they cantered – one stumbling horse could have brought down

several of them and once they were down they never rose again –
they cantered apart.

Not one of these horses had lain down for months. Some cantered
evenly, some rocked in their stride but they all kept well away from
each other.

As the trough came in sight some neighed, others quickened their
pace. One bay mare, with hipbones so sharply defined, so prominent, I felt they would surely pierce her dry skin, with each rib
showing distinctly on her sides, suddenly faltered in her stride. Her
legs crumpled, buckled beneath her ... she did not stumble and
fall; she collapsed, pitching forward a little so that her nose hit the
ground before she rolled to her side.

She lay still a moment then made a desperate effort to rise. She
rose on to her front legs, struggling to get her hind legs to complete
the lift, but they gave way and she fell back on her side once more.
As we hurried towards her she raised her head and looked towards
the trough. Even when we stood beside her she still looked towards
the trough.

'Come on,' I cried to Joe. 'We've got to raise her. All she wants is
a drink and it'll put strength into her. Look at her flanks. She's dry
as a bone. Let's get hold of her head.'

Joe stood beside me. We placed our hands beneath her neck and
tried to lift but she did not move. She was breathing deeply.

'Let her have a blow for a bit,' Joe advised. 'She might be able to
get up then.'

We stood beside her in the gathering dark quite unable to accept
the fact that she must die. We were restless and nervously irritable
with frustration. We wanted to go home but we were afraid to part,
for then we would be alone with the tormenting picture of her lying
there dying in the night.

I suddenly grabbed her head. Joe slapped her rump. We yelled
at her. For a moment she fought to rise then fell back and a
shuddering groan came from her as her head sank down to the
earth.

We couldn't stand it.

'What the hell is everybody doing?' Joe suddenly shouted
angrily, looking round at the empty roads as if expecting strong
men with ropes to dash forward to help us.

'We'll have to get her a drink,' I said in desperation. 'Let's go
and get a bucket.'

'I'll go,' said Joe. 'You wait here. Where is it?'

'In the chaff house.'

Joe set off running towards our house and I sat down on the

ground beside the mare. I could hear mosquitoes and the drone of heavy beetles in flight. Bats ticked above the trees. The rest of the horses had drunk and were slowly filing past me, making back to some far-away spot where some grass butts still lingered. They were like skeletons of horses clothed in skin and I could smell their musty breath as they passed.

When Joe came back with the bucket we filled it at the trough, but it was too heavy for Joe to carry back alone so I helped him. We lifted it a yard at a time. We held the handle together and swung it forward a yard then we would walk ahead of the bucket again and reach back and swing it forward once more until, after repeating this movement a score of times, we reached the mare.

We had heard her neighing her thirst as we got closer to her. When we placed the bucket in front of her she thrust her nose deep into the water and sucked so strongly the level fell swiftly around her nose as we watched it. In a minute she had emptied the bucket. We brought her another one and she emptied that, then another one ... But by now I was exhausted. I fell and was too tired to rise. I lay beside the mare, all my strength gone.

'Hell! I'll have to be carting you water next,' said Joe.

He sat down beside me looking at the stars and he sat there for a long time not moving or talking. All I could hear was the deep, sad breathing of the horse.

CHAPTER 19

One Saturday afternoon I stood near the gate and watched Joe running through the timber on his way to our place. He ran in a crouched position with his head tucked between his shoulders and, as he ran, he dodged behind trees and kept looking back as if pursued by bushrangers.

Flinging himself behind an old redgum tree, he lay flat on his stomach, peering from behind the bole towards the trees through which he had just been running. He suddenly flattened himself against the ground like a goanna and I looked and saw Andy running along the track.

Andy didn't dodge behind trees. He ran with an intense purpose that didn't demand concealment.

Joe wriggled in a circle round the tree to keep the trunk between him and Andy, but Andy was familiar with Joe's tactics and went straight to the tree.

Joe rose from behind the trunk and greeted Andy in tones of surprise.

'You, Andy? Cripes, I was just waiting for ya!'

He didn't fool Andy who had exclaimed with great satisfaction, 'Got ya!' when Joe appeared.

Joe and I had arranged to meet Skeeter Bronson and Steve McIntyre at the foot of Mt Turalla. We were taking the dogs, as foxes were often seen amongst the bracken that covered its sides, but our main object was to roll stones down the crater.

The huge rocks we levered from the crater's lip would hurtle down the steep sides of the crater, bounding high in the air, crashing into trees and leaving behind them streaks of torn scrub and fern. When they reached the floor of the crater they were travelling in springing leaps that carried them a little way up the opposite side before they came to rest.

The climb up the mount was an exhausting walk for me. I needed frequent spells that I always had when Joe was my only companion, but when other boys were with us they complained of these stops.

'Cripes! Ya not stoppin' again are ya?'

Sometimes they wouldn't wait and when I finally joined them at the top, the quick triumph of that first bound over the crest had gone and exclamations of excitement were finished.

I stole time for resting by claiming the attention of those with me. I would point to runs through the ferns and exclaim, 'I can smell a fox! He musta just passed! Follow him up, Joe!'

The discussion as to whether it was worth following the trail took time, and I would gain the rest I needed.

Skeeter and Steve were kneeling beside beside a rabbit burrow when we arrived at the clump of wattle where we were to meet them. They were looking at the tail and hindquarters of Tiny, an Australian terrier owned by Skeeter. Tiny's head, shoulders and front legs were submerged in the burrow and he was scratching vigorously.

'Did ya see any go in?' demanded Joe who had dropped to his knees in front of them with the authoritative air of the expert. 'Here! Give me a go!' He grabbed Tiny's hind legs.

'Pull him out and we'll feel down the burra,' I said, equally efficient as Joe.

'Any bloke who puts his hand down a burra is a fool,' said Steve rising to his feet and brushing his knees as if his interest in the burrow was now at an end. He had never forgiven me for my victory in our fight with sticks.

'Who's frightened of snakes!' I exclaimed contemptuously, lying on my side and thrusting my arm up the burrow while Joe held the struggling Tiny.

'Ya can feel the end of it,' I announced scornfully after wriggling my shoulder deeper into the burrow's mouth.

'It's a breedin' burra,' said Joe. He released Tiny who again dived into the burrow as I removed my arm. With the stump of his tail rigidly still he gave three long, investigating sniffs then backed out and looked up at us questioningly.

'Come on,' said Steve. 'Let's get goin'.'

'Where's Andy?' asked Joe. Andy was sitting on the ground between Dummy and Rover. He had been parting Rover's hair looking for fleas, an operation that Rover bore with a still, entranced expression on his lifted face.

'What did ya bring Andy for?' asked Skeeter with an expression of suffering on his face.

Andy looked quickly at Joe for a satisfactory explanation of his presence.

'Because I brought him, that's why,' replied Joe truculently. Joe never wasted any time on Skeeter. 'I'd punch him as soon as look at him,' was a frequent remark of his which expressed his opinion of Skeeter.

We followed a narrow horse-pad that girdled the side of the hill. It was a difficult path for me. The ferns that skirted it were high and offered stiff, tangling resistance to each swing of my crutches. Wide tracks presented no such problems and I always looked for them when I walked through the bush, but on Mt Turalla the tracks were all narrow pads, hip-high in fern. I kept one crutch swinging along the open pathway, my legs and the other crutch forcing their way through the growth.

I never considered my legs; a passageway for them was unnecessary. My weight only rested on my good leg for an instant before both legs swung forward again, but the state of the ground upon which my crutches rested, the obstructions opposing them, were important. A fall always came from a slipping crutch, or the striking of its tip on a stone, or its entanglement in grass or fern, never from the failure of my legs to complete their swing.

When Joe first began walking with me it worried him to see my legs bashing their way through ferns while an unobstructed track ran beside me. The movement of one crutch along this pathway seemed unimportant to him; it was the course my legs followed that was the measure of my comfort in his eyes and he often complained, 'Why don't you walk on the track where it's easy?'

After I explained it to him he remarked, 'It's a beggar, isn't it!' then never mentioned it again.

The strategy I used to distract Skeeter and Steve from their intention to reach the top without delay succeeded, and we all walked over the crest together. The unimpeded wind blew strongly against us and we breasted it with delight, sending loud yells echoing round the crater lying like a deep bowl in front of us.

We sent a rock bounding down its steep slopes, watching the falling flight of the stone with excitement. I longed to follow it, to see for myself what lay hidden down there amongst the ferns and trees that grew on the bottom.

'They reckon there might be a big hole down there with just a bit of earth covering it,' I said, 'and if you stood on it – hell! you'd go through into boiling mud and everything.'

'It's extinct,' said Steve with a typical lack of co-operation.

'It might be,' Joe argued aggressively, 'but just as like as not the whole bottom's sorta soft and ready to fall in. There's no knowin' what's down there,' he ended solemnly. 'By cripes, there's not!'

'I'll bet Blacks lived down there once,' said Skeeter. 'You'd see where they'd been if you went down. Mr Tucker found a Blackfellow's axe up here.'

'That's nothin',' said Joe. 'I know a bloke's got half a dozen.'

'I'm going half-way down,' said Steve.

'Come on!' said Skeeter eagerly. 'It'll be good fun. I'll go. Come on, Joe.'

Joe looked at me. 'I'll wait for you,' I said.

The slopes of the crater were littered with scoria and stones that long ago must have bubbled in some fierce heat before solidifying. They were lumps of froth turned into stone and they were so light they floated on water. There were outcrops of rocks with the smooth surface of an arrested liquid and round stones with cores of green gravel. Odd gum trees grew on the steep sides and there were large patches of bracken.

My crutches would not grip on this steep, crumbling earth and even where the tips rested firm it was impossible to leap down so steep a slope. I sat down with my crutches lying beside me, prepared to wait till they returned.

Andy was determined to go with Joe on this adventure.

'I can't go far with Andy.' Joe was making it easy for me. 'He'd knock up if we went to the bottom. I'll go half-way down.'

'I can walk like anything,' protested Andy, anxious to reassure Joe.

'We won't be long,' Joe assured me.

I watched them moving downward, Joe holding Andy by the hand. Their voices got further away till I could not hear them.

It did not distress me that I could not go with them. I believed I was staying because of my decision to stay and not because of my helplessness. I *never* felt helpless. I was exasperated, but my exasperation did not arise from my inability to walk and climb like Joe or Steve; it was directed against the Other Boy.

The Other Boy was always with me. He was my shadow-self, weak and full of complaints, afraid and apprehensive, always pleading with me to consider him, always seeking to restrain me for his own selfish interests. I despised him, yet he was my responsibility. In all moments of decision I had to free myself of his influence. I argued with him then, when he would not be convinced; I spurned him in fury and went my way. He wore my body and walked on crutches. I strode apart from him on legs as strong as trees.

When Joe had announced he was going to walk down the crater, the Other Boy spoke quickly to me in urgent tones: 'Give me a go, Alan. Go easy. I've had enough. Don't make me tired. Stop with me a little while till I get my wind. I won't try and stop you next time.'

'All right,' I assured him, 'but don't come at that too often or I'll leave you. There are a lot of things I want to do and you're not going to stop me from doing them.'

So the two of us sat there on the hillside, the one confident of his ability to do all that was asked of him, the other dependent on the first one's patronage and care.

It was a quarter of a mile to the bottom of the crater. I could see the boys scrambling down the slope, moving now to the right or the left seeking easier places or holding on to the trunk of a tree while they stood a moment looking around them.

I expected them to turn at any moment and come climbing back again. When I saw they had made up their minds to continue to the bottom I felt a sense of betrayal and muttered to myself in annoyance.

I looked at my crutches for a moment, wondering whether they would be safe there and if I could remember where I left them; then I turned on to my hands and knees and set off for the bottom where the boys were now calling to each other and exploring the flat area they had reached.

At first I crawled, crashing my way through ferns with little effort as I went plunging downwards. Sometimes my hands slipped and I fell on my face, skidding on loose earth till I was stopped by some obstruction. On areas of scoria I sat upright as in a sled and went sliding down for yards amid a cascade of gravel and bouncing pebbles.

Near the bottom the huge stones that once had rested on the top of the mount lay in piled confusion among the fern. Ever since the early pioneers had entered this country those who climbed the mount had been levering these heavy rocks from where they had been lying half-buried on the summit, and had watched them hurtling downwards till they rolled to a stop far below.

I found it difficult to cross this barrier of tumbled stone. I moved from rock to rock, taking all my weight on my hands to save my knees, but when I at length reached a less crowded area where I could crawl between them, my knees were scratched and bleeding.

The boys had watched me coming down and when I came tumbling through a belt of fern on to level ground, Joe and Andy were waiting for me.

'How in the hell are ya goin' to get up?' Joe asked as he dropped down on the grass beside me. 'It must be after three o'clock now and I've got to bring the ducks home.'

'I'll get up easy,' I told him shortly, then continued in a change of tone, 'Is the ground soft down here like what you thought? Let's roll over stones and see what's underneath 'em.'

'It's just like on top,' said Joe. 'Skeeter caught a lizard but he won't let you hold it. Steve and 'im keep talking about us when I'm not there. Look at 'em now.'

Skeeter and Steve were standing near a tree talking and glancing towards us with the unmistakable furtiveness of conspirators.

'We can hear you,' I yelled out. This lie was the traditional opening to acknowledgments of enmity and Steve replied with undisguised hostility. 'Who're *you* talking to?' he demanded, taking a step towards us.

'Not to you, anyway,' called Joe who regarded this answer as a devastating retort. He turned to me grinning happily, 'Didja hear me give it to him?'

'Look, they're off,' I said. Skeeter and Steve had turned and were beginning the climb up the side of the crater. 'Let 'em go. Who cares for them?'

Skeeter looked back over his shoulder and shouted a final insult. 'Both of youse are cranky.'

Joe and I were disappointed at the poor quality of this thrust. It was too uninspiring to rouse a spirited reply and we watched the two boys in silence as they picked their way through the stones.

'Skeeter couldn't fight his way out of a paper bag,' Joe asserted.

'I could, couldn't I, Joe?' piped Andy. Andy's estimate of his ability was always based on Joe's opinion.

'Yes,' said Joe. He chewed a grass stem then said to me, 'We'd better get goin'. I gotta get the ducks yet.'

'All right,' I said, then added, 'You needn't wait for me 'less you like. I'll be jake.'

'Come on,' said Joe rising.

'Wait till I just feel I'm down here,' I said.

'It seems funny, don't it,' said Joe looking round. 'Listen to how it echoes.'

'Hullo!' he yelled and round the side of the crater came faint 'Hullos' in answer to him.

For a little while we sent echoes tumbling from the slopes then Joe said, 'Let's go. I don't like down here.'

'Why don't you, Joe?' asked Andy.

'It's like as if it'll fall in on you,' he said.

'It won't fall in, will it, Joe?' asked Andy anxiously.

'No,' said Joe. 'I'm only talkin'.'

Yet it did seem as if the enclosing sides would topple over and down, shutting us off from the sky. From here the sky was no longer a dome that covered the earth but a frail roof resting on walls of stone and gravel. It was pale and thin, drained of its familiar blue and rendered insignificant by the mighty slopes that rose to meet it.

And the earth was brown, brown ... All brown ... The dark green of the ferns was swamped with brown. The still, silent boulders were brown. Even the silence was brown. We sat cut off from the bright sounds of the living world that lay over the encircling rim and all the while we felt we were being watched by something huge and unfriendly.

'We'll go,' I said, after a silence. 'It feels crook down here.'

I lowered myself on to the earth from the stone on which I had been sitting.

'No one will ever believe I've been down here,' I said.

'It just shows what fools they are,' said Joe.

I turned and began crawling back. In crawling up a steep slope the weight is thrown on to the knees and mine were already inflamed and tender. Coming down, my arms had taken my weight and no power had been demanded of my knees that merely supported me. Now I had to struggle with each yard I traversed and I quickly tired. I had to rest every few yards, sinking down with my face pressed to the ground and my arms lying limp beside me. In this position I could hear the beating of my heart coming from the earth.

When I rested Joe and Andy sat each side of me and talked but after a while we climbed and rested in silence, each occupied with his own problems. Joe had to help Andy, at the same time keeping pace with me.

I crawled on and on exhorting myself with silent commands to greater endeavour. 'Now!' 'Again!' 'This time!'

High up on the crater's side we stopped for one of our rests. I lay full length on the earth breathing deeply and from the ground against which my ear was pressed I heard two quick thuds. I looked up towards the top of the crater and there outlined against the sky were Skeeter and Steve and they were yelling in fear and waving their arms.

'Look out! Look out!'

The stone that under a sudden impulse they had sent rolling down on us had not yet gathered speed. Joe saw it at the same time as I did.

'The tree,' he yelled. He grabbed Andy and the three of us floundered towards an old dead gum that towered from the crater's side. We reached it just before the stone passed us with a shrill whistle and thuds that shook the ground. We watched it leaping wildly over ferns and logs away below us and then heard the sharp crack as it struck the boulders hidden in bracken. It broke in half and the two pieces separated and shot away from each other at an angle.

Steve and Skeeter, frightened by what they had done, had turned and were running over the crest.

'They're gone!' I said.

'Cripes! Didja ever see the like!' said Joe. 'They mighta killed us.'

But we both felt pleased that this had happened to us.

'Wait till we tell the kids at school,' I said.

We began our climb again feeling a little better and talking about the speed of the stone but soon we were silent again and when I rested Joe and Andy just sat there looking back at the crater below us.

It seemed to me we were all struggling together and their silence, like mine, was that of exhaustion.

I began spelling more frequently and when the sun was beginning to set and the sky was flaming red behind the opposite crest I had to sink to the ground after each painful, forward heave.

When finally we reached the top I lay on the ground while all my flesh twitched like that of a kangaroo from which the hide had just been taken.

Joe sat beside me holding my crutches and in a little while he said, 'I'm getting worried over those ducks.'

I rose to my feet, placed the crutches beneath my arms, and we set off down the mountain.

CHAPTER 20

It troubled father to see me returning exhausted from long walks in the bush. One day he said, 'Don't walk so far, Alan. Hunt in the bush round the house,'

'There are no hares there,' I said.

'No.' He stood looking at the ground and thinking. 'You've got to hunt, have you?' he asked me.

'No,' I said, 'but I like going out hunting. All the boys go hunting. I like going out with Joe. He stops when I'm tired.'

'Yes, Joe's a good bloke,' father reflected.

'Getting tired's nothing,' I said to him when he remained silent.

'No, that's true enough. I suppose you'll have to have a crack at the lot. Anyway, toss it in and lie down when you're done. You might have a champion horse but you've still got to spell him going up a long hill.'

He saved some money and began looking at the second-hand advertisements in the *Age*. One day he wrote a letter and a few weeks later he drove to Balunga and brought home an invalid chair that came up in the train.

It was standing in the yard when I came home from school and I stood looking at it in amazement. Father yelled out from the stock-yard, 'It's yours. Hop into the saddle and give it a fly.'

The chair was a heavy, cumbersome affair built with no regard to saving weight. It had two over-size bicycle wheels at the back and a small wheel in the front attached to the frame by a cast goose-neck. Two long handles, one each side of the seat, were attached to rods that were fitted to cranks on the axle. The handles were worked to and from, one going forward as the other came back. The right handle had a swivel attachment that enabled the rider to turn the front wheel to the right or left.

It took a heavy pull to start it moving but once it was in motion it could be kept moving by a rhythmic working of the arms.

I climbed into it and rode it round the yard in a series of jerky, forward movements, but after a while I learned to relax momentarily at the end of each sweep so that it ran smoothly along like a bicycle.

After a few days I could race it up the road, my arms working like pistons. I rode it to school and became the envy of my mates who climbed aboard with me, either sitting on my knee or facing one another sitting on the goose-neck. The one in front could grasp the handles lower down than my grip and help work them to and fro. We called it 'working your passage' and I would give anybody a lift who worked his passage.

However, those who sat in front, not having arms trained to thrusting on crutches, soon tired and I was left to work the handles witout help.

The invalid chair extended my range of movement and brought the creek within reach. Turalla Creek was three miles away from our home and I only saw it on Sunday School picnic days or when father drove that way in the brake.

Joe often walked to the creek to fish for eels and now I could accompany him. We tied our two bamboo rods beside the seat, placed a sugar bag on the footboard for carrying the eels, and set off with Joe sitting in front working his arms with short, swift strokes while high up on the handles my arms worked with longer sweeps.

Saturday night was our fishing night and we always left home in the late afternoon, arriving at McCallum's Hole before the sun set. McCallum's Hole was a long, dark stretch of water, deep and still. Redgums lined its banks and threw powerful limbs across the water. Their trunks were gnarled and twisted, charred by bush fires or bearing the long, leaflike scar left by a Blackfellow after he had removed the bark for a canoe.

Joe and I fashioned stories around these canoe trees which we examined eagerly, looking for the marks of the stone axe that had been used to cut the bark from the trunk. Some of the scars were small, no longer than a child, and we knew the bark from these had been used to fashion coolamons, the shallow dish in which the lubras placed their piccaninnies to sleep or in which they carried the vegetable food they gathered.

One such tree grew with its huge, coiling roots touched by the water of McCallum's Hole. On still nights when our floaters sat

motionlessly in a moonlight path on the water, the dark surface at
our feet would glitter with ripples then break and for a moment a
platypus would be floating there, watching us with sharp eyes
before it curved its body and returned to its burrow amongst the
submerged roots of the old tree.

They used to swim upriver against the current then float back,
their heads still facing the stream as they searched for worms and
grubs the current was carrying. Sometimes we thought they were
fish as they floated by with only their curved backs above the
surface and we would cast our lines towards them. If one took the
bait we pulled it out on to the bank where we touched its fur and
talked about how we would like to keep it, before we let it go.

Water rats also lived in holes beneath the tree. They brought up
mussels from the mud below and broke the shells on the flat surface
of one huge root from where we gathered the pieces and put them in
a bag to bring home to the fowls.

'It's the best shell grit you can get,' Joe told me, but Joe always
dealt in superlatives. He described my invalid chair as 'the best
made thing he had ever seen' and wondered why they never had
races for them.

'You'd be a champion, easy,' Joe assured me. 'Now, say you
were on scratch ... Well, that wouldn't matter a beggar. No other
bloke's got arms like you. You'd romp it in.'

He talked like this while we sat facing each other on the chair,
our arms moving rhythmically to and fro as we made for the creek.
We both felt very happy on this night for we had made a 'bob.'

Catching eels with a hook can be exciting but with a bob the
excitement is continuous and the catch much bigger.

A bob is made by threading worms on to a strand of wool till you
have one tremendous worm several yards long.

This heavy worm-string is then looped into a dropping bunch to
which the line is tied. It is not used with a float. It is cast into
the water as it is, where it sinks to the bottom and is almost
immediately seized by an eel whose file-like teeth get caught in the
wool.

When the one holding the line feels the tug he jerks the eel from
the water and it falls with the bob on to the bank beside him. He
then has to seize it before it escapes back into the water, cut
through the back of its neck with a knife and thrust it into his bag.

Eels are slimy and are hard to hold and sometimes two would be
jerked to the bank at once and Joe and I would dive after them,
grabbing them and losing then, then flinging ourselves upon them
again. While we were waiting for a bite we rubbed the palms of our

hands on the dry earth so that the dust adhering there would prevent our grip from slipping. The slime from the eels caked this dirt and after a while we had to wash it off then rub them in the dust again.

We lit a campfire when we reached the old tree and boiled the billy into which mother had already placed the tea and sugar. We watched flocks of ducks come swiftly up the creek, following each bend and rising steeply when they saw us.

'There's a power of ducks on this creek,' Joe said munching a thick corned beef sandwich. 'I'd like a penny for every duck, say, from here to Turalla.'

'How much do you reckon you'd have?' I asked him.

'A hundred pound, easy,' said Joe who always argued in round figures.

Joe regarded a hundred pounds as a fortune. 'You never know what you could do with a hundred quid,' he told me. 'You could do anything.'

This was an absorbing subject.

'You could buy any pony you wanted,' I said. 'Buckjump saddles! – Cripes! Say you wanted to buy a book, now. . . . Well, you could get it and if you lent it to anybody and they wouldn't give it back, it wouldn't matter.'

'Aw, you'd easy get it back,' Joe said. 'You'd know who had it.'

'You mightn't,' I insisted. 'No one remembers who they lend books to.'

I threw my crusts into the river and Joe said, 'Don't frighten hell outa the eels. Eels is terrible nervous and, what's more, there's an east wind tonight and they won't bite with an east wind.'

He stood up and wet his finger by thrusting it into his mouth. He held it upright in the still air and waited a moment.

'Yes, it's east all right. It feels cold on the east side.'

But the eels bit better than Joe anticipated. I had no sooner lifted the bob from the grass-lined tin in which we kept it and cast it into the water than I felt a bite on the line. I jerked the rod upwards and flung the bob with an eel attached on to the bank. The eel floundered on the grass then wriggled towards the water like a snake.

'Grab it!' I yelled. Joe grabbed it and held it squirming in his hands while I opened the pocket knife. I severed its backbone behind its neck and we placed it in the sugar bag which we put down beside the fire.

'That's one,' said Joe with satisfaction. 'The east wind musta died down – a good job, too. We'll get a lot tonight.'

By eleven o'clock we had eight eels, but Joe wanted ten.

'When ya got ten it makes out ya good,' he reasoned. 'It's better to say, "we got ten last night" than to say "we got eight".'

We decided to stay till twelve o'clock. The moon had risen and there was plenty of light to see our way home. Joe gathered more wood for the fire. It was cold and we were thinly clad.

'You can't beat a good fire,' I said, throwing dry gum branches into the flames till they billowed up higher than our heads.

Joe dropped an armful of wood and ran to grab the rod which had moved to the tug of an eel. He flung the eel out on to the bank where it fell near the fire, glittering with black and silver as it writhed away from the heat.

It was the biggest eel we had caught and I flung myself at it eagerly. It slipped from my grasp and slithered towards the water. I rubbed my hands desperately on the ground and crawled after it but Joe had dropped the rod and had seized it near the edge of the water. It wriggled in his hands, threshing its head and tail. Joe gripped it tenaciously but it squeezed through his hands and fell to the ground. He dived at it again as it was entering the water but he slipped on the mud and went into the creek up to his waist.

Joe never swore much but he swore now. It was funny to see him in the water but I didn't laugh. He crawled out on to the bank and stood up, his arms curved away from his sides as he looked down at the pool of water gathering at his feet.

'I'll get into a row over this,' he said in a tone of concern. 'By hell, I will! I'll have to dry my pants if it's the last thing I do.'

'Take 'em off and dry 'em at the fire,' I suggested. 'They won't take long. How did he get away from you?'

Joe looked back at the creek. 'That eel was the biggest eel I've ever seen in me life,' he said. 'I couldn't get me hands round it. And heavy! – Cripes, it was heavy! Did ya feel the weight of it?'

Here was a wonderful opportunity for creating an experience that could never be checked and Joe and I revelled in it.

'It felt like a ton,' I said.

'Easy,' Joe reckoned.

'What about the way it lashed round,' I exclaimed. 'You could feel it fighting like a snake.'

'It got round me arm,' said Joe, 'and I thought it was broke.' He paused then began taking off his trousers with great speed as if a bull ant had gone up his leg. 'I gotta get these dry.'

I thrust the end of a forked stick into the ground so that it leant almost over the fire where his trousers would dry quickly in the rising heat.

Joe took a piece of sodden string, a brass door knob and some marbles from his pocket and placed them on the ground, then he hung his trousers on the stick and began dancing up and down before the fire to keep warm.

I flung the bob back into the creek, hoping to catch the eel we had lost and when I finally felt a bite I jerked the rod with the power of one about to lift a heavy weight.

A wriggling eel, clinging to the bob, flashed high in the air above my head, came down in a curve behind me, and crashed into the stick holding Joe's trousers. The trousers fell into the fire.

Joe dived towards the fire then backed precipitately as a flare of heat burst against his face. He raised one hand to shield his face and tried to reach his trousers with the other. He suddenly raced round the fire swearing in an anguished fashion then grabbed the rod from my hands and poked at his flaming trousers in an effort to hook them and jerk them out. When at length he got the end of the rod beneath them, he was desperate for time and he gave such a tremendous heave on the rod that the trousers leaped upwards from the flames and described a rainbow of fire against the night before sailing on free of the rod and dropping with a sizzle and a puff of steam into the waters of the creek.

As the flames were extinguished a great darkness came upon Joe. The black patch of his sinking trousers could be seen against the gleam of the moving water before they disappeared, and he watched this patch, bending out over the water with his hands on his knees and the glow of the fire painting his bare behind a rosy pink.

'My God!' he said.

When he had recovered sufficiently to discuss his predicament he announced that we must get home quickly. He had lost interest in catching ten eels and was concerned over being seen without trousers.

'It's agin the law to leave your pants off,' he told me earnestly. 'If any bloke seen me without pants I'd be done. You can do a stretch quick and lively if you're caught without pants. Old Dobson,' Joe was referring to a local racing cyclist who had recently gone off his head, 'went to Melbourne and ran clean through it without pants an' they jailed him for hell only knows how long. We gotta get going. I wish it wasn't a full moon.'

We hurriedly tied our rods to the side of the chair, placed the bag of eels on the footboard and set off, Joe sitting on my knee in gloomy silence.

I had a heavy load and when we came to a hill Joe had to get out and push. But there were not many hills and I got slower and slower.

Joe complained of the cold. My exertions on the handles kept me warm and I was protected from the breeze of our passage by Joe who kept slapping his bare thighs to warm them.

Far ahead of us, on a long, straight stretch of road, we saw the lights of a buggy approaching us. We could hear the clock-clock of a jogging horse and I said, 'That sounds like old O'Connors's grey.'

'That'll be him,' said Joe. 'Pull up! You never know who'll be with him. Let me off. I'll hide behind the trees over there. He'll think you're on your own.'

I stopped the chair on the side of the road and Joe ran across the grass and disappeared into a dark clump of trees.

I sat there watching the approaching buggy, glad of the rest, and thinking of each section of the road ahead of me – the easy parts, the long rises, our lane and the last pull home.

When the candle lamps of the buggy were still a little way off the driver pulled his horse to a walk and when he came level with my chair he called out, 'Whoa,' and the horse stopped. He leant forward in the seat and peered at me.

'Good day, Alan.'

'Good night, Mr O'Connor.'

He looped the reins over his arm and felt for his pipe.

'Where you off to?'

'I've been fishing,' I told him.

'Fishing!' he exclaimed. 'Strewth!' He ground tobacco between his palms and murmured, 'It beats me what a kid like you wants to go round ridin' in that bloody contraption in the middle of the night for. You'll go and get yourself kilt. Look, I'm tellin' ya!' He raised his voice, 'You'll get bloody well run over be someone who's boozed – that's what'll happen to you.'

He leant over the mudguard and spat on the ground.

'I'm damned if I can make your old man out and there's a lot more can't make him out either. A kid crippled up like you should be home restin' in bed.' He shrugged resignedly. 'Well, it's nothin' to do with me I suppose, praise God! Have you got a match on you, now?'

I climbed from the chair, untied my crutches from beside the seat and handed him a box. He struck a match and held it to his pipe. He sucked vigorously with a gurgling noise as the flame rose and fell above the bowl. He handed me the box then raised his head with the pipe projecting upwards at an angle and continued drawing on it until a sudden glow came from the bowl.

'Yes,' he said, 'we all have our troubles. Here's me with the rheumatiz in me shoulder somethin' terrible. I know what it is . . .'

He gathered in the reins then paused and asked 'How's your old man goin' these days?'

'Pretty good,' I answered, 'he's breaking five of Mrs Carruthers'.'

'Her!' snorted Mr O'Connor. 'Hell!' then added, 'Ask him if he'll handle a three-year-old filly I've got. She's broken to lead. Quiet as a lamb too . . . How much does he charge?'

'Thirty bob,' I said.

'Too much,' he said firmly. 'I'll give him a quid – an' a good price too. She hasn't got a buck in her. You ask him.'

'All right,' I promised.

He pulled on the reins. 'I'm damned if I know what a kid like you goes round in the middle of the bloody night for,' he muttered. 'Giddup.'

His horse roused itself and moved off.

'Hurroo,' he said.

'Good night, Mr O'Connor.'

When he had gone Joe emerged from the clump of trees and came running over to the chair.

'I'm frozen stiff,' he muttered impatiently. 'If I bent me legs I'd crack 'em. What did he stop so long for? Quick, let's get goin'.'

He clambered on to my knee and we set off again, Joe shivering convulsively between exclamations of concern and anger at the loss of his trousers.

'Mum'll go stone mad. I've only got one other pair and the backside's out of 'em.'

I pulled and pushed at the handles with all my strength, my forehead pressed hard against Joe's back. The chair bounced along over the rough road with the long rods clacking together and the eels slipping from side to side in the bag at our feet.

'One thing,' said Joe seeking to comfort himself, 'I took everything out of the pockets of me pants before they were burnt.'

CHAPTER 21

A swagman sitting near our gate had told me he knew a man who had both legs off and yet he could swim like a fish.

I often thought of this man swimming like a fish in the water. I had never seen anyone swimming and I had no idea how you moved your arms to keep afloat.

I had a large, bound volume of a boys' paper called *Chums* in which there was an article on swimming. It was illustrated with three pictures of a man in a striped bathing suit and a moustache who, in the first picture, stood facing you with his arms stretched above his head; the next picture showed his arms stretched out at right angles to his body, and in the last picture they were by his side. Arrows curving from his hands to his knees suggested he moved his arms downwards in what the writer called the 'Breast Stroke', a name that was faintly distasteful to me since I always associated the word 'breast' with a mother feeding her baby.

The article mentioned that a frog used the breast stroke when swimming and I caught some frogs and put them in a bucket of water. The swam to the bottom, circled it, then came up again and floated with their noses on the surface and their legs widespread and still on each side of them. I did not learn very much from watching them but I was determined to learn to swim and on summer evenings began sneaking off in my chair to a lake three miles away to practise.

The lake lay hidden in a hollow with the steep, high bank rising in terraces for two or three hundred yards from the water. These terraces must have continued beneath the surface, for a few yards out from the edge the bottom dropped abruptly into depths where trailing waterweeds grew and the water was cold and still.

None of the boys at the school could swim nor could any of the men I knew in Turalla. There were no suitable bathing places in the district and only on very hot evenings, and under a strong incentive, were men tempted to go to the lake which was always regarded as dangerous. Children were warned to keep away from it.

However, groups of boys sometimes ignored their parents' instructions and splashed in the water round the edge trying to teach themselves to swim. If any men were present at these times they kept their eyes on me and wouldn't let me go close to the 'holes', as we called the place where the bed dropped away to deep water. They carried me from the bank to the shallow section, being concerned if they saw me crawling across the stones and through the belt of mud that skirted the edge.

'Here, I'll give you a lift!' they would say.

They concentrated the attention of all who were there upon me. When no men were present the boys never seemed aware that I crawled when they walked. They splashed water on me, plastered me with mud in our mud fights, or fell upon me and pummelled me with wet fists.

In our fights with mud I was a perfect target since I could not dodge or pursue the one who attacked me. I could easily have withdrawn from such battles; I could have called out 'Barley' and given them the victory. But if I had done these things I would never have been able to preserve an equality with them. I would always have been an onlooker, the victim of an attitude they reserved for girls.

I was never conscious of any reasoning behind my actions nor was I aware that I was directed by motives designed to give me equality. I acted under compulsions I did not recognise and could not explain. Thus, when faced with a determined boy throwing mud at me, I crawled straight towards him, disregarding every handful he hurled, till finally, when I was about to grapple with him, he would turn and flee.

It was so in fights with sticks. I moved straight into the fray and took the blows, for only in this way could I earn the respect given by children to those who excelled at games.

Swimming was an achievement upon which the children placed great value and it was the custom to proclaim you could swim when you could lie face downwards upon the water and draw yourself forward with your hands on the bottom. But I wanted to be able to swim in deep water and since other children so rarely went to the lake I began going out there alone.

I left my chair in a wattle clump on the top of the bank then scrambled down the grass-covered terraces till I reached the shore where I undressed and crawled across the stones and mud till I reached the sand. Here I could sit down with the water no higher than my chest.

The article in *Chums* said nothing about bending your arms and

thrusting them forward in a way that offered no resistance to the
water. My interpretation of the drawings was that you merely
moved your straightened arms up and down.

I reached the stage where I could keep myself afloat with a
mighty threshing but could not go forward and it was not till the
second year, when I discussed swimming with another swagman at
our gate, that I learned how to move my arms.

I learned very quickly after that until there came a day when I
felt I could swim anywhere. I decided to test myself out over the
'holes'.

It was a hot summer evening and the lake was as blue as the sky.
I sat naked on the bank watching the black swans far out on the
water, rising and falling as they rode the tiny waves, while I argued
with the Other Boy who wanted me to go home.

'You swam easily a hundred yards along the edge,' he reasoned.
'No other boy at school could do that.'

But I would not listen to him until he said, 'See how lonely it is.'

It was the loneliness that frightened me. No trees grew around
this lake. It lay open to the sky and there was always a still silence
above it. Sometimes a swan called out but it was a mournful cry
and only accentuated the lake's isolation.

After a while I crawled into the water and continued on, keeping
erect by moving my arms in a swimming stroke on the surface, till I
reached the edge of the drop into the dark blue and the cold. I stood
there moving my arms and looking down into the clear water where
I could see the long, pale stems of weeds swaying like snakes as they
stretched out from the steep side of the submerged terrace.

I looked up at the sky and it was immense above me, an empty
dome of sky with a floor of blue water. I was alone in the world and
I was afraid.

I stood there a little while then drew a breath and struck out over
the drop. As I moved forward a cold tendril of leaves clung for a
moment to my trailing legs then slipped away and I was swimming
in water that I felt went down beneath me for ever.

I wanted to turn back but I kept on, moving my arms with a slow
rhythm while I kept repeating over and over in my mind. 'Don't
be frightened now; don't be frightened now; don't be frightened
now.'

I turned gradually and when I was facing the shore again and
saw how far away it seemed to be I panicked for a moment and
churned up the water with my arms, but the voice within me kept
on and I recovered myself and swam slowly again.

I crawled out on to the shore as if I were an explorer returning home from a long journey of danger and privation. The lakeside was now no longer a lonely place of fear but a very lovely place of sunshine and grass and I whistled as I dressed.

I could swim!

CHAPTER 22

Our gateway was shaded by huge redgums. The scattered charcoal of campfires lay amongst the leaves, twigs and branches that littered the ground beneath them. Swagmen passing along the road often slipped their swags off their shoulders and rested here or stood looking speculatively at the house and the wood heap before coming in to beg some tucker.

Mother was well known to those swaggies whose beat passed our home. She always gave them bread, meat and tea without asking them to chop wood in return.

Father had humped his bluey in Queensland and was familiar with the ways of swagmen. He always called them 'travellers'. The bearded men who kept to the bush he called 'Scrub Turkeys' and those who came down from the plains he called 'Plain Turkeys'. He could tell the difference between them and whether they were broke or not.

When a swaggie camped at our gate for the night father always said he was broke.

'If he were holding well, he'd keep on to the pub,' he told me.

From the stockyard he often watched them carrying billies to our door and if they clung to the lid of the billy and didn't hand it to mother he would smile and say 'old-timer'.

I asked him what it meant when they held on to the lid while mother took the billy and he said, 'When you're on the track there's some people as wouldn't give you the smell of an oilrag. You've gotta work 'em along like you was a sheep dog. Say, now, you want tea and sugar – that's what you always want. You put a few leaves of tea in the bottom of the billy – not many, enough so she knows you're light on the tea. When she comes to the door you don't ask for tea. What you ask for is a drop of hot water to make some tea and you say "The tea's in the billy, lady." She takes the billy and you hang on to the lid, then you say, as if you'd just thought of it see, "You could stick in a bit of sugar if you don't mind, lady!"'

'Now when she goes to put the hot water in the billy she sees there's not enough tea in it to colour a spit so she chucks in some more. She mightn't want to but she don't like handing it back to a bloke weak as dishwater so she shoves in more tea. Then she chucks in the sugar and he's got the lot.'

'But why does he hold on to the lid?' I persisted.

'Well, you never get as much if they can cover it up. When there's no lid to hide what they give you they don't like facing you unless the billy is full.'

'Mum's not like that, is she, dad?'

'Hell, no!' he said. 'She'd give you the boots off her feet if you let her.'

'Has she ever?' I asked, interested in the picture of mother taking off her boots and giving them to a swagman.

'Aw, well ... No, if it comes to that. She could give them old clothes or boots but anybody'd give them clothes. It's tucker they want, especially meat. Giving tucker costs money. A lot of people'd sooner give 'em a pair of old pants their old man won't wear no more. You give them meat when you grow up.'

Sometimes a swagman slept in our chaff house. Mary was feeding the ducks one frosty morning and she saw a swaggie covered in a blanket as stiff as a board. He had frost on his beard and eyebrows and when he got up he walked round in a stooped position till the sun warmed him.

After that, when Mary saw a swagman camped at the gate, she sent me down to tell him he could sleep in the chaff house. I always followed him into the chaff house and when mother sent Mary out with his dinner she would send me out my dinner too. She knew I liked swagmen. I liked to hear them talking and hear about the wonderful places they had seen. Father said they pulled my leg but I didn't think so.

When I showed one old man my rabbit skins, he told me that where he came from the rabbits were so thick you had to sweep them aside to set the traps.

It was a dusty night and I told him if he put the *Age* over his face it would keep the dust off him. I slept out on the back verandah and I always did it.

'How much dust would it keep off?' he asked me as he raised a black billy to his mouth. 'Would it keep off a pound of dust now?'

'I think so,' I said doubtfully.

'Do you think it would keep off a ton of dust?' he asked, wiping drops of tea from his moustache and beard with the back of his hand.

'No,' I said, 'it wouldn't.'

'I been crossing outback stations where you got to sleep with a pick and shovel beside you when a dust storm's coming on.'

'What for?' I asked.

'So's you can dig yourself out in the morning,' he said, looking at me with his strange little black eyes that had lights in them.

I always believed everything I was told and it troubled me when father laughed at the stories I repeated to him. I felt it showed he was criticising the man who had told me.

'It's not that at all; I like the blokes that tell 'em,' he explained, 'but they're fairy stories, see; funny fairy stories that make you laugh.'

Sometimes a swaggie would sit over his campfire and shout at the trees or mumble to himself as he looked at the flames; then I knew he was drunk. Sometimes he would be drinking wine and sometimes methylated spirits.

There was a man called 'The Fiddler' who always held his head a little to one side as if he were playing a fiddle. He was tall and thin and was a three-strap man.

Father had told me that one strap round the swag meant a newchum who had never been on the track before; two straps meant you were looking for work; three straps showed you didn't want to find it; and four straps was a travelling delegate.

I always looked at the straps on their swags and when I saw the three straps on The Fiddler's swag I wondered why he didn't want to work.

He was a metho drinker and when drunk would call out to teams of horses he could see beyond his fire.

'Whoa there! Hold up! Gee, Prince. Gee, Darkie. Come over....'

Sometimes he ran round to the other side of the fire, swinging an imaginary whip with which he would flog some horse that angered him.

When he was sober he talked to me in a high-pitched voice.

'Don't stand there movin' from leg to leg like a hen in the rain,' he said once. 'Come over here.'

When I went over to him he said. 'Sit down,' then added, 'What's wrong with your leg?'

'I got Infantile Paralysis,' I told him.

'Fancy that now!' he said, nodding his head sympathetically and clucking his tongue as he put more wood on his campfire. 'Well, you've got a roof over your head, anyway.' He looked up at me. 'And a bloody good head it is; like a Romney Marsh lamb.'

I liked these men because they never pitied me. They gave me confidence. In the world they travelled, being on crutches was not as bad as sleeping out in the rain or walking with your toes on the ground, or longing for a drink you had no money to buy. They saw nothing but the track ahead of them; they saw brighter things ahead of me.

Once, when I said to The Fiddler, 'This is a good place to camp, isn't it?' he glanced round and said, 'Yes, I suppose it is – to a bloke who hasn't got to camp here.' He gave a scornful laugh. 'A cocky said to me once, "You blokes are never satisfied. If a bloke gives you cheese you'll want to fry it."'

'Yes,' I told him. 'That's me.'

'I've seen the time when I've been on the track and I've thought if I only had tea and sugar I'd be right; then when I've got tea and sugar I want a smoke, and when I've got a smoke I want a good camp, and when I've got a good camp I want something to read. "You don't happen to have any reading matter on you, do ya?" I asked this cocky. "I can see I won't get any tucker out of you."'

The Fiddler was the only swagman I met who carried a frying pan. He took it from his tucker bag and looked at it with satisfaction. Then he turned it over and looked at the bottom which he tapped with his finger.

'A solid pan, this . . .' he said. 'I picked it up near Mildura.'

He took some liver wrapped in newspaper from his tucker bag and frowned at it for a moment.

'Liver is the worst meat in the world to spoil your pan,' he said, pursing his lips so that his black moustache jutted forward contemplatively. 'It sticks like a plaster.'

Like all swagmen, he was preoccupied with the weather. He was always studying the sky and speculating as to whether it was going to rain. He did not carry a tent in his swag, just the usual two blue blankets rolled round a few tattered garments and two or three tobacco tins containing his possessions.

'A hundred and sixty points of rain fell on me one night near Elmore,' he told me. 'It was too bloody dark to move and I sat there with me back to a post just thinkin'. Next morning there was mud everywhere and I had to plough through it. There won't be any rain tonight; it's too cold. She's comin' up, though. Might strike here tomorrow afternoon.'

I told him he could sleep in the chaff house.

'What about your old man?' he asked

'He's all right,' I assured him. 'He'll make you a mattress out of straw.'

'That was him I was talking to this afternoon, was it?'

'Yes.'

'He struck me as a good bloke. He rigs himself out flash but he talked to me just like I'm talking to you.'

'Well, that's right, isn't it?'

'Course it's right. I think I will sleep in your chaff house,' he added. 'I been on a bender and I'm crook in the guts.' He frowned at the pan in which the liver was sizzling. 'I had terrible nightmares all night last night; dreamt I was on the track and the rain was comin' down hell for leather. Me billy had a hole in it and I couldn't make tea. Hell! I woke up sweatin'.'

Another swagman came walking down the road while we were talking. He was a short, thick-set man with a beard and his swag was long and thin. His tucker bag hung loosely in front of him and he walked with a heavy, deliberate tread.

The Fiddler looked up sharply and watched him approach. I could see by his expression that he did not want this man to stop and I wondered why.

The newcomer walked over to the fire and dropped his swag at his feet.

'Good day,' he said.

'Good day,' said The Fiddler. 'Where you makin'?'

'Adelaide.'

'There's a long lead ahead of you.'

'Yes. Got a smoke on you?'

'I'm on the butts. You can have a butt if you want it.'

'That'll do.' The man took the butt The Fiddler handed him, placed it delicately between his pursed lips and lit it with a glowing stick he took from the fire.

'Did you come through Turalla?' he asked The Fiddler.

'Yes. I lobbed here this afternoon.'

'What's the butcher and baker like there?'

'The baker is all right, plenty of stale buns, but the butcher's no good. He wouldn't give you a burnt match. He'll shove you on the Douglas for a flap of mutton.'

'Did you go to the back of the pub?'

'Yes. Got the butt of a roast there. The cook's all right – a big woman. You could line off bricks with her nose. Ask her. Dodge her offsider. He's a little bloke; wants a drink for anything he gets you.'

'Any Johns there?'

'No, but look out for the John at Balunga – that's further on –
he's crook. He'll dwell on you if you go on the grog.'

'I'm only holding a deener, so to hell with him!'

'You'll be all right further north,' said The Fiddler. 'I see they've
had rain up there so every cocky'll be in at the pubs. You'll get a
guts full there.'

He cut a thick slice of bread from a loaf mother had given him,
divided the liver and placed one of the pieces on the bread which he
handed to the man.

'Here, get that into you.'

'Thanks,' said the man. He munched at it for a while then asked,
'You don't happen to have a needle and thread on you, do ya?'

'No,' said The Fiddler.

The man looked at a split in the knee of his trousers. 'A pin?'

'No.'

'My boots are crook, too. What do they pay for harvesting round
here?'

'Seven bob a day.'

'That's right,' said the man sourly. 'Seven bob a day and they
pay you off on Saturday so they won't have to feed you on Sunday.
Have you got another butt on you?' he added.

'No, I'm hanging on to these,' said The Fiddler. 'There's a dance
on at Turalla tonight. You'll get plenty of butts round the door in
the morning. I reckon you'd better get movin' or she'll be dark
before you strike Turalla.'

'Yes,' said the man slowly, 'I suppose I'd better.' He rose to his
feet. 'Straight on?' he asked swinging his swag on to his shoulder in
one movement.

'Don't take the first turn, take the second. It's about two miles.'

When he had gone I said to The Fiddler, 'Wasn't that fellow any
good?'

'He was humping a cigarette swag,' explained The Fiddler. 'We
all dodge blokes with a swag like that. They never have anything.
They bot on you for the lot. If that fellow joined up with you, you'd
take all the skin off him draggin' him. Now show me where this
chaff house is.'

I took him up to the chaff house where father, having seen me
talking to him, had already thrown in some armfuls of clean straw.

The Fiddler looked at it for a few moments in silence then he
said, 'You don't know how lucky you are.'

'It's good to be lucky, isn't it?' I said, liking him a lot.

'Yes,' he said.

I stood watching him unroll his swag.

'S'elp me!' he exclaimed looking around at me. 'You hang round like a drover's dog. Hadn't you better go in and have tea?'

'Yes,' I said. 'I'd better. Good night, Mr Fiddler.'

'Good night,' he said gruffly.

A fortnight later he was burnt to death in his campfire eight miles from our place.

The man who told father about it said, 'He'd been on the metho for a couple of days, they say. He rolled into the fire in the night – you know how it'd be. I was sayin' to Alec Simpson on my way down here, I said to him, "It was his breath that caught fire, that's what it was." He musta been fair full of metho. Once his breath caught fire the flame would go curling down through his guts like a fuse. By the living Harry, he'd burn! I was just sayin' it to Alec Simpson – Alec bought my chestnut mare, you know. I was just sayin' before I came down here that that's how he went all right and Alec said, "By hell, I think you're right!"'

Father was silent a moment then said, 'Well, that's the end of The Fiddler, poor beggar; he's dead and gone now.'

CHAPTER 23

Most men patronised me when they spoke to me, their usual attitude towards children. When other adults were listening it pleased them to be able to raise a laugh at my expense, not because they wished to hurt me but because my ingenuousness tempted them to play on it.

'Been riding any buckjumpers lately, Alan?' they would ask, a question I considered a serious one since I did not see myself as they did.

'No,' I would say. 'I will be soon, though.'

This was considered by the one questioning me as worthy of a laugh and he would look towards his companions to include them in his mirth.

'Didya get that? He's going to ride buckjumpers next week.'

Some men were abrupt and curt with me, regarding all children

as uninteresting and incapable of being able to contribute anything
of value to a conversation. Confronted with such men I could find
no common level to communicate with them and I was silent and
awkward in their company.

On the other hand I discovered that swagmen and bushmen,
being lonely men, were often awkward and unsure of themselves
when a child spoke to them but when they were met with an
uncritical friendliness they were eager to continue the conversation.

One old bushman I knew was like that. His name was Peter
McLeod and he was a teamster who carted posts from deep in the
bush forty miles below our place. Each week he came out with his
laden waggon, spent Sunday with his wife, then returned again,
striding beside his team or standing upright in the empty waggon
whistling some Scotch air.

When I called out, 'Good day, Mr McLeod,' he would stop and
talk to me as if I were a man.

'Looks like rain,' he'd say, and I'd say it did too.

'What's the bush like where you go, Mr McLeod?' I asked him
one day.

'As thick as the hairs on a dog,' he answered, then added, as if
the remark were a communication with himself, 'Yes, she's thick all
right. By hell, she's thick!'

He was a tall man with a shining black beard and legs that
seemed longer than they should have been. His head bobbed when
he walked and his big arms hung down a little in front of him.
Father said he unfolded like a three-foot rule but father liked him
and told me he was an honest man and could fight like a tiger cat.

'There's none round here could beat him at his best,' he said.
'He'd lock horns with anyone after a few beers. He's a tough, hard
man with a soft heart but when he hits a man, the man stays hit.'

Peter hadn't gone to church for twenty years. Father said, 'then
he went to vote against the Presbyterians joining up with the
Methodists.'

Once a Mission came to Turalla and Peter, after a week of heavy
drinking, decided to become converted but he backed out like a
frightened horse when he found they expected him to knock off
drinking and smoking.

'I've been drinking and smoking to the Glory of God for forty
years,' he told father, 'and I'll keep on for the Glory of God.'

'That about sums up how he stands with God,' father said. 'I
don't think he bothers much about Him when he's carting posts.'

The bush Peter described to me seemed a magical place where
kangaroos hopped quietly through the trees and possums chirred at

night. It was the thought of an untouched bush that appealed to me. Peter called it 'maiden bush' – bush that had never known an axe.

But it was so far away. It took Peter two and a half days to reach the post-splitters' camp and he slept beside his waggon for a week.

'I wish I were you,' I told him.

It was September and I was on holidays, the school being closed for a week. I had followed Peter's team in my chair, wanting to see his five horses drink from the trough. He carried a bucket to the two shafters and I sat in my chair and watched him.

'Why's that?' he asked.

'Then I could see the maiden bush,' I told him.

'Hold up!' he sang out to the horse who was nosing the bucket he was lifting to her. She began drinking with a sucking noise.

'I'll take you there,' he said, 'I want a good bloke to help me. Yes, I'll take you any time you like.'

'Will you?' I asked, unable to hide my excitement.

''Course I will,' he said. 'You ask your old man if you can come.'

'When are you going?'

'I leave at five tomorrow morning from the house. You get down there at five and I'll take you.'

'All right, Mr McLeod,' I said. 'Thank you, Mr McLeod. I'll be there at five.'

I didn't want to discuss it further. I set off for home as fast as my arms would take me.

When I told father and mother that Mr McLeod said he would take me to the bush, father looked surprised and mother asked, 'Are you sure he meant it, Alan?'

'Yes, yes,' I said quickly. 'He wants me to help him. We're good mates. He said we were once. He told me to ask dad if I could go.'

'What did he say to you?' asked father.

'He told me to be down at his place at five in the morning if you let me go.'

Mother looked questioningly at father and he answered her glance.

'Yes, I know, but it'll all pay off in the end.'

'It's not the trip so much,' she said. 'It's the drink and the bad language. You know what it's like when men are shut up in the bush.'

'There'll be grog and bad language all right,' father agreed. 'Make no mistake about that. But that won't hurt him. It's the kid who never sees men grogging up who takes to it when he grows up. Swearing's the same – the kid who never hears bad language swears like a trooper when he's a man.'

Mother looked at me and smiled. 'So you're going to leave us, are you?' she said.

'Only a week,' I said, feeling guilty. 'I'll tell you all about it when I come home.'

'Did Mr McLeod mention anything about tucker?' she asked.

'No,' I said.

'What have you got in the house?' Father looked at mother.

I've got that round of corned beef for tonight's tea.'

'Toss it into a bag with a couple of loaves of bead. That'll do him. Peter'll have tea.'

'I've got to leave here at four,' I said. 'I mustn't be late.'

'I'll wake you,' mother promised.

'Help Peter as much as you can, son,' said father. 'Show him the breed holds good. Light his campfire for him while he feeds the horses. There's lots of jobs you can do.'

'I'll work,' I said. 'My word, I will!'

Mother didn't have to wake me. I heard the creak of a board in the passage floor as she came out of her bedroom. I jumped out of bed and lit the candle. It was dark and cold and for some reason I felt depressed.

When I joined her she had lit the fire in the stove and was preparing my breakfast.

I hurried into Mary's room and woke her up. 'Don't forget to feed the birds, will you, Mary?' I said. 'Let Pat out for a fly about five. The possum's got plenty of green leaves but you'll have to give him bread. You'll have to change all the water today because I forgot, and the parrot loves thistles. There's one growing behind the stable.'

'All right,' she promised sleepily. 'What time is it?'

'A quarter to four.'

'Oo, dear!' she exclaimed.

Mother had scrambled me an egg and I began eating it with unnecessary haste.

'Don't gulp you food down like that, Alan,' she said. 'There is plenty of time. Did you wash yourself properly?'

'Yes.'

'Behind the ears?'

'Yes, all round my neck.'

'I've put some things in this little bag for you. Don't forget to clean your teeth with salt every morning. The brush is in the bag. And I've put in those old trousers of yours. Are your boots clean?'

'I think so.'

She looked down at them. 'No, they're not. Take them off and I'll black them.'

She broke a piece off a stick of blacking and mixed it with water in a saucer. I stood fidgeting while she rubbed the black liquid over my boots, impatient to be gone. She brushed them till they shone and helped me put them on.

'I've taught you how to tie a bow,' she said. 'Why will you knot your laces?'

She carried the two sugar bags out to the buggy shed where I kept my chair and struck a match while I stacked them on the footboard and tied my crutches to the side.

The darkness had a bite of frost in it and I could hear a willy wagtail whistling from the old redgum. I had never been up so early before and I was excited with this new day that was still unspoilt by people, still silent with sleep.

'No one in the world is up yet, are they?' I said.

'No, you're the first up in the world,' mother said. 'Be a good boy, won't you?'

'Yes,' I promised her.

She opened the gate and I passed through almost at top speed.

'Not so fast,' she called after me in the dark.

Beneath the trees the darkness was like a wall and I slowed down. I could see the tops of the trees against the sky and I knew the shape of each of them. I knew where the holes in the road were and where it was better to cross the road and travel on the wrong side to avoid bad patches.

It was good to be alone and free to do as I wished. No grown-up was guiding me now. Everything I did was a direction from myself. I wanted it to be a long way to Peter McLeod's, but I wanted to get there quickly.

Once I had left the lane and passed on to the main road I could go faster and my arms were beginning to ache by the time I reached Peter's gate.

As I came down the track towards his house I could hear the iron shoes of the horses striking the cobblestoned floor of the stable. Though Peter and the horses were hidden in darkness I could see them with eyes created by sound. Tug chains clinked to impatient stamping, grains of chaff were snorted from nostrils and the stable door clattered as a horse bumped it passing out. Peter's voice yelled commands, a dog yelped and roosters began crowing from the fowlyard.

Peter was yoking up the horses when I pulled up in front of the stable. It was still dark and for a moment he did not recognise me.

He dropped the trace chain he was holding and stepped over to the chair, peering down at me.

'It's you, Alan. Strike me! what are you do – Cripes, you're not coming with me, are you?'

'You asked me,' I replied uncertainly, suddenly afraid I had misunderstood him and he had not meant me to come.

''Course I asked you. I've been waiting here for you for hours.'

'It's not five yet,' I said.

'No, that's right,' he muttered, suddenly thoughtful. 'Your old man said you could come, did he?'

'Yes,' I assured him. 'So did mum. I've got my tucker. Here it is.' I lifted the bag to show him.

He suddenly grinned at me through his beard, 'I'll hop into that tonight,' then changed his tone. 'Come on. Shove your cart in the shed. We've got to be on the road at five.' His face became serious again. 'Are you sure your old man said you could come?'

'Yes,' I insisted. 'He wants me to go.'

'All right.' He turned to the horses. 'Move over!' he cried as he placed one hand on a horse's rump and bent to pick up the trace chain with the other.

I put my chair in the shed and stood watching him, holding my two bags like a newchum-traveller about to board a boat.

The waggon was a heavy wood-waggon with broad iron tyres and brake blocks of redgum worked by a screw handle projecting from the rear. Its woodwork was bleached and cracked with sun and rain. There were no sides but at each of the four corners a heavy iron standard with a looped top was thrust into a socket in the bolster. It had a floor of heavy, loose planks that clattered loudly on bumpy roads. Some stays thrown on to the floor added to the noise. There were two pairs of shafts, one for each shafter.

Peter raised a pair of these with a heave, hooked the back chain that crossed the shafter's saddle on to the 'traveller' hook on the shaft then walked round to the other horse standing patiently beside its mate.

He yoked them noisily, yelling, 'Hold up!' 'Get over!' or 'Whoa there!' each time a horse moved or refused to respond to his hand.

The three leaders stood side by side waiting for him to hitch their connecting reins and hook up their traces. They were not so heavy as the two shafters. They were Clydesdales while the two shafters had Shire blood in them.

After Peter had yoked the horses he threw the nosebags and some bags of chaff on to the waggon, glanced into his tucker box to see if he had forgotten anything, then turned to me and said, 'That's the lot. Hop up! Here, I'll take your bags.'

I swung over to the front of the waggon, and, holding on to the shafts with one hand, I threw my crutches up into the waggon with the other.

'Do you want a hand?' asked Peter, moving forward uncertainly.

'No thank you, Mr McLeod. I'm right.'

He walked to the leaders' heads and stood there waiting. I lifted myself with my hands till I got the knee of my good leg on the shaft then reached up and grasped the crupper of the shafter beside me. I pulled myself up till I was resting on his rump. It was warm and firm and divided by the shallow valley of his back into two powerful mounds of muscle.

'Rest your hand on a good horse and the strength of him goes through you,' father had told me.

From the shafter's rump I swung over into the waggon and sat down on the tucker box.

'I'm right,' I called to Peter.

He gathered the reins from where they were looped on the off shafter's hames and clambered up beside me.

'There's a hell of a lot of men can't get into a waggon as good as you,' he said as he sat down.

He paused with the reins taut in his hands: 'Would you like to sit on a butt of chaff?' he asked.

'No, I like here,' I said.

'Gee, Prince!' he called. 'Gee, Nugget!'

The team moved forward with a jingle of trace chains and a creak of harness. Behind them the waggon lurched and rumbled. There was a faint light in the eastern sky.

'I like to get away at piccanninny dawn,' said Peter. 'It gives you a good working day then.' He yawned noisily then suddenly turned to me. 'Now, you're not running out on your old man, are you? He said you could come?'

'Yes,'

He looked gloomily at the road. 'I can't make your old man out.

CHAPTER 24

The leaders walked with slackened trace chains, only tightening them when we came to a rise or a hill. I thought this was unfair to the shafters.

'The shafters are doing all the work,' I complained to Peter.

'Once the waggon's moving, there's no weight in it,' he explained. 'This team could pull hell out by the roots if I ask 'em. Wait till we get the load of posts on, then you'll see them all pull.'

Dawn had broken and there was a pink glow in the east. From every clump of trees the magpies were carolling. I felt there could be nothing in the world more lovely than this – sitting behind a team of horses in the early morning and listening to magpies.

From a distant paddock came the voice of a man shouting at a dog, 'Go behind there!'

'That's Old Man O'Connor bringing in the cows,' said Peter. 'He's early this morning. Must be going out somewhere.' He thought a moment. 'He'll be going to Salisbury's clearing sale. Yes, that's it, and it'll be the Abbot buggy he's after.' His voice expressed annoyance. 'What does he want to be buying Abbot buggies for when he owes me ten quid for posts?'

He slapped the reins angrily against the shafter's rump. 'Get on there!' After a while he said resignedly, 'That's what you get for trusting a man; they go round driving Abbot buggies and I go round in a waggon.'

We passed through the deserted streets of Balunga as the sun was rising and soon we were following a track winding between timber that gradually grew thicker till only the bush was around us and the fences had gone.

The dust from the horses' hooves rose into the air and settled softly on our hair and clothes. The wheels brushed against the leaning scrub as we passed and the waggon lurched as the wheels dropped into holes worn in the track.

I wanted Peter to tell me stories of his adventures. I looked upon him as a famous man. He was the hero of so many tales told where groups of men gathered to yarn. In hotel bars, so father said, some men would say, 'You talk about fights! I saw Peter McLeod fight Long John Anderson behind the hall at Turalla.' And everyone would listen to his tale of the fight that lasted two hours.

'Yes,' the man would say, 'they carried Long John away on a hurdle.'

Peter had only been beaten once in his long career as a fist-fighter, and that was when he was so drunk he could hardly stand, and a farmer with a reputation for back-pedalling in a row had hopped into him to pay off an old grudge. His sudden, furious attack left Peter stretched out cold on the ground. When he came round the farmer had gone, but Peter was down at his cowyard before sunrise next morning, to the farmer's astonishment, and clutching the top rail with his two powerful hands he roared, with reddened face, 'Are you as good a man now as you were last night? If you are, come out here.'

The farmer stood transfixed, a bucket half full of milk hanging from his hand.

'I – er – I couldn't fight you now, Peter,' he complained plain-tively, gesturing with his hand to express complete surrender. 'You're sober. You'd kill me when you're sober.'

'You hopped into me last night,' asserted Peter, a little non-plussed by this attitude. 'Come and have a go at me now.'

'But you were drunk last night,' argued the farmer. 'You could hardly stand up. I'd never fight you sober, Peter. I'd be mad.'

'Well, I'll be damned!' exclaimed Peter, incapable of directing the situation. 'Come out here, you cow.'

'No, I won't fight you, Peter; not while you're sober. Call me anything you like.'

'What the hell's the good of that if you won't fight?' Peter was exasperated.

'I see your point,' said the farmer agreeably. 'Calling names gets you nowhere. How're you feeling?'

'Sore as a boil,' muttered Peter, looking round him as if for direction. He suddenly leaned wearily on the rail of the fence. 'I'm crook as a mangy dog this morning.'

'Wait till I get you a taste,' said the farmer. 'I've got some whisky in the house.'

Father reckoned Peter went home leading a crook horse the farmer sold him, but mother said the horse was a good one.

I wanted Peter to tell me some of these stories so I said, 'Father told me you could fight like a thrashin' machine, Mr McLeod.'

'Did he now!' he exclaimed, with a pleased expression on his face.

He sat thinking, then said, 'Your old man thinks a lot of me. We've got a lot of time for each other. They tell me he was a great runner once. I was looking at him the other day. He stands like a Blackfellow.' He changed his tone. 'An' he said I could fight, did he?'

'Yes,' I said, then added, 'I wish I could fight.'

'Aw, you'll be a good fighter some day. Your old man could scrap and you're like him. You can take punishment. If you want to be any good you've got to be able to take punishment. Look at the time I got into a push of the Stanleys. There's four of them and they can all go. I didn't know them but I heard of them. One of them – I think it was George – followed me round the back of the pub abusing me and when I talked fight he said, "Remember, I'm one of the Stanleys," and I said, 'I don't give a damn if you're the four of them. Put 'em up.'

'Well, we're no sooner into it than his three brothers come round, and I've got the four of them on my hands.'

'Were they all fighting you?' I asked.

'Yes, the lot. I closed in and threw one, and as he was going down I slipped my knee up into his belly and took his wind. The other three kept me pretty honest for a while, but I kept getting in low down – that's the only way to fight with your fists. Get him underneath. Don't worry over the face. If you want to paint him, do it after the wind is out of him.

'I got me back to a wall and gave them a different hand each time. I didn't have much up my sleeve, but I got 'em all down then chucked it. The game wasn't paying. I was taking too much punishment. But I got the verdict. Cripes, yes!' he said, pleased with the memory. 'It was a fight and a half.'

We were passing through a large clearing in the bush. A decayed dog-leg fence, erected from trees felled along its line, encircled the paddock, in which saplings and scrub marked the return of the bush. A disused, grass-grown track led from some sliprails to a deserted bark hut where thin saplings swept their leaves against the walls.

Peter suddenly roused himself from his thoughts and said, with a new eagerness, 'This is Jackson's place. In a minute I'll show you the stump where young Bob Jackson broke his neck. His horse bolted and threw him, then two months later Old Jackson wrapped a bullock chain round himself and walked into the dam. I'll show you the dam after. The stump's not far now. Just along here. . . . It's about twenty yards in from the fence. There was a lump came up on his chest as big as my head. He must have landed fair on the stump. Now, where is it?' He stood up on the waggon, looking intently into the paddock. 'There it is. Whoa there! Whoa, blast ya.'

The horses stopped.

'Over there on its side ... see it? Near that dead wattle.... Hold up!' he yelled to one of the horses which had lowered its head to pluck the grass. 'I must have another look at that stump. Come over and I'll show you.

We climbed over the fence and walked to a fire-blackened stump that lay with its blunted root-butts beside a grassed depression in the ground.

'They say this knob here caught him in the chest and he hit his head here.' Peter pointed to two prominent root-spikes on the stump. 'His horse ... Now, where did it gallop from? ... It came around here,' he waved his hand in a half-circle that embraced a stretch of the paddock. 'Over there a bit.... Then it turned at that messmate – he reefed it round there, I reckon – and made past that clump of fern, then came along this stretch of grass flat out. It must have shied from the stump here.'

He stepped four paces away from the stump and measured the distance with his eye for a moment. 'That'd be about where he left its back. It'd shy out here,' he waved an arm towards the fence, 'and he'd tumble to the right.' He paused a moment gazing steadily at the stump. 'He never knew what hit him.'

When we returned to the waggon, he told me that Old Jackson went queer after his son's death.

'It wasn't exactly cranky. He was just like he'd gone broke – sad all the time.'

When we came to the dam Peter reined in the horses again and said, 'Well, there it is. It's deep near the far bank. Of course it's silted up since then. He walked straight in and never came up. His old woman and the other boy cleared out after that. She felt it terrible. Now you wouldn't find a straw to clean your pipe with on the place. I brought in the cart and shifted her bits of furniture to Balunga. By hell, when she saw me she looked like the Relief of Mafeking. She filled up when I was leaving her. I told her Old Jackson was a white man if ever there was one. But my old woman reckons that makes it worse. I dunno....'

He started the horses then said, 'They say a bloke's brain system goes when he drowns himself. Maybe so ... I dunno.... But Old Jackson wasn't like that. He was a good bloke. All he wanted was a mate to say, "Give it another go", and he was right. The trouble was I was getting the horses shod that day.'

CHAPTER 25

That night we camped in a deserted shingle-splitter's hut. Peter unharnessed the team then took a pair of hobbles and a horsebell from a bran bag he had been carrying on the waggon.

I lifted the bell from the ground. It was a heavy, five-pound bell with a deep musical note. I rang it, listening to the sound that I always associated with clear mornings in the bush, when every leaf was wet with dew and the magpies were singing. I dropped it a few inches to the ground and Peter, who had been rubbing some neatsfoot oil on the hobbles, exclaimed sharply, 'Hell! Don't do that! You mustn't drop a bell. It ruins 'em. Here, show me.' He held out his hand for the bell.

I picked it up and handed it to him.

'This is a Mongan bell, the best bell in Australia,' he muttered, examining it carefully. 'I gave a quid for it and I wouldn't take a fiver for it. You can hear it eight miles on a clear morning.'

'Dad said the Condamine bell is the best.'

'Yes, I know. He comes from Queensland. The Condamine sends a horse deaf. It's too high a note. You bell a horse regular with a Condamine, he goes deaf. There's only two bells – the Mennicke and the Mongan, and the Mongan's the best. That bell's made out of a pit saw. And not just any pit saw, either. They pick one with a good ring in it.'

'What horse are you going to put it on?' I asked.

'Kate,' he said. 'She's the only bell horse I've got. The others can't ring it properly. She's got a long gait and shakes her head. She swings it when she walks. I bell her and I hobble Nugget. He's the boss and they all stop with him.'

He stood erect. 'I'm going to put the nosebags on them for an hour first. They only get roughage in the bush here.'

'I'll light the fire in the hut, will I?' I asked.

'Yes. Start her up and put on the billy. I'll be with you in a minute.'

When he came into the hut later I had the fire going and the billy boiling. He threw a handful of tea into the bubbling water and placed the billy on the stone hearth in front of the fireplace.

'Now, where's your corned beef?'' he asked.

I had bought my sugar bags into the hut and I took the round of beef in its newspaper wrapping from one of them and handed it to him.

He unwrapped, pressed it with one thick, dirt-blackened finger and commented, 'It's prime beef, this – a piece of silverside.'

He cut me a thick slice and placed it between two huge pieces of bead. 'This'll stick to your ribs.' He filled two tin pannikins with strong, black tea and handed me one. 'I've never seen the woman yet who can make tea. You can always see the bottom of the cup when a woman makes it.'

We sat before the fire eating our bread and meat. Between each mouthful Peter lifted his pannikin and took two noisy gulps of tea. 'Ah!' he would say contentedly as he put the pannikin down again.

After he had finished the last pannikin of tea he tossed the dregs into the fire and said, 'Now, how's this leg of yours at night? Do you have to tie it up or anything?'

'No,' I said, surprised, 'it's all right. It just lies there.'

'Go on!' he exclaimed. 'That's good. Does it hurt at all?'

'No,' I said. 'I don't know it's there.'

'If you were my kid I'd take you up to Wang at Ballarat. He's a fair marvel, that fellow. He'd cure you.'

I had heard of this Chinese herbalist. Most people round Turalla regarded him as the man to go to when all other doctors failed. Father always snorted when he heard his name mentioned. He called him a 'weed merchant'.

'Yes,' Peter went on, 'this Wang never asks you what's wrong with you. He just looks at you and tells you. I wouldn't've believed it, mind you, but Steve Ramsay told me all about him – remember Ramsay, the bloke that couldn't hold nothing on his stomach but his two hands?'

'Yes,' I said.

'Well, Wang cured him. Steve says to me, when I had the crook back, "You go to Wang and don't tell him what's wrong with you. Just sit there and he'll hold your hand. He'll tell you things that'll stagger you," and by cripes he did too. I took a week off and drove up and he looked at me like Steve said – I never told him nothin' – I was paying him – let him do the finding. I sits there and he sits there looking hard at me and holding me hand and he says, "What are you wearing that bandage for?" Yes, that's what he says all right. "I'm not wearing a bandage," I says to him. "You're wearing something round you," he says, "Well, I'm wearing a red flannel belt, if that's what you mean," I says. "You'll have to get rid of that," he says. "Have you ever had an accident?" "No," I tells him. "Think again," he says. "Aw, well, about a year ago I was thrown out of a gig and the wheel ran over me," I says, "but I wasn't hurt." "Oh yes you were!" he reckons. "That's your trouble. Your side is out of position." "Hell!" I says, "is that what's bloody-well wrong with me," then he gives me a packet of herbs for two quid and mum boils 'em up for me – terrible taste it was. I never got a pain after.'

'But that's your stomach,' I said. 'I want my legs and back made better.'

'It all comes from the stomach.' Peter spoke with conviction. 'You've got blown up or something – like a cow on lucerne – and there's something left there you gotta get rid of.

'Like that girl up country Wang cured. Everybody knows about that. She was so thin she couldn't throw a shadow but she ate like a horse. She had all the doctors licked then she went to Wang and he says, "Don't eat nothing for two days then hold a plate of steak and onions under your nose and breathe it in."

'Well, she does this and a tapeworm crawls out her mouth and keeps crawling out. They tell me it was a hell of a length. It keeps coming out till it falls all tangled-up on her plate. She got as fat a mud after. It must have been in there for years eating everything she swallowed. Only for Wang she'd of been well dead.

'Aw no, doctors know nothing when it comes to these Chinese herbalist blokes.'

I did not think there was any truth in what he said though his story frightened me.

'Father said anybody can be a Chinese herbalist,' I argued. 'He said all you want, to be a Chinese herbalist, is to look like a Chinaman.'

'What!' exclaimed Peter indignantly. 'He said that! He's mad! The man's mad!' Then he added in a less aggressive tone, 'Mind you, you're the only bloke I'd say that to. But I tell you this: a bloke I know – educated, mind you; he can read anything – he told me that over in China where these blokes come from, they're learn-ing for years. After they've finished learning they're examined by blokes well up in doctorin' an' that. These blokes examine them to find out whether they know enough to be Chinese herbalists. What they do – they take twelve of these blokes at a time – the blokes that are learning, see – they take these twelve blokes into a room with twelve round holes in the wall going through into another room.

Then they go out – anywhere . . . on the street, say . . . and they look
for people with twelve terrible diseases. Like, they'd say, "What's
wrong with you?" "Guts ache." "Right, in you come." Then someone else – "Me liver's gone." Good – in him, too. Then blokes –
say, with backache like I had . . . "Right, you'll do."

'And they get twelve like that and they take 'em all into the other
room and make 'em shove their hands through these holes in the
wall. See how it's comin' out? The blokes wanting to be herbalists,
they look at the twelve hands and they write down what each
bloke's got on the other side and if they get one wrong, they're out.'

He gave a scornful laugh. 'An' your old man says anyone can be
a Chinese herbalist! Still, we gotta lot of time for each other. He's
got some funny ideas, but I don't hold it against him.'

He rose to his feet and looked out the hut door. 'I'll hobble Kate
and let 'em out, then we'll turn in. She's going to be a pitch-black,
dark night tonight.'

He looked up at the stars. 'The Milky Way's running north and
south, anyway. It's gonna be fine. It's when she's east and west you
get the rain. Well, I won't be long.'

He went out to the horses and I could hear him yelling out to
them in the dark. Then he was silent and the soft notes of the
horsebell came to me as the horses moved out into the bush.

When he returned he said, 'I haven't had Biddy down here
before. She comes from Barclay Station. Horses reared in open
country are always frightened, their first night in the bush. They
hear the bark flapping. She was snorting a bit when I let her go.
Aw, well, she'll be all right. Now, what about a bed for you?'

He looked carefully round the earth floor of the hut then walked
over to a small hole beneath the wall. He studied it a moment than
took the paper in which the corned beef had been wrapped and
stuffed it into the hole with his fingers.

'Might be a snake hole,' he muttered. 'We'll hear that paper
rattle if he comes out.'

He laid two half-filled chaff bags on the floor and flattened them
till they formed a mattress.

'There you are,' he said, 'that should do you. Lie down there and
I'll chuck this rug over you.'

I took off my boots and lay upon the bags with my head resting
on my arm. I was tired and I thought it was a beautiful bed.

'How's it feel?' he asked.

'Good.'

'The oats might come through and stick into you. It's good chaff
that; came from Robinson's. He cuts it nice and fine. Well, I'll turn in.'

He lay upon some bags he had prepared for himself, yawned noisily, and pulled a horserug over himself.

I lay awake listening to the sounds of the bush. It was so good to be there I didn't want to sleep. I lay beneath my rug gripped by an exciting awareness. Through the open door of the hut the smell of gum and wattle released by the night came moving across my bed. The wild cries of plovers going over, the call of a mopoke, the rustles and squeaks and the possum chirrs of warning – these created a presence in the darkness and I lay there tense with listening, awaiting a revelation.

Then, softly through the other sounds, came the notes of the horsebell and I sank back relaxed into the chaff mattress, seeing, as I fell asleep, the long, striding gait and swinging head of Kate ringing her Mongan bell.

CHAPTER 26

The bush through which we travelled became more stately, more aloof. As the trees increased in height so did our isolation from them become greater. They thrust their pure, limbless trunks two hundred feet above the earth before crowning themselves with leaves. No struggling scrub cluttered their feet; they stood on a brown carpet of their own shed bark. Beneath them was a strange expectant silence, unbroken by bird cries or the chatter of creeks.

Our tiny waggon with its tiny horses moved slowly beneath them, sometimes scraping some huge root-spur as we followed a turn in the track. The jingle of trace chains and the soft thud of hooves on the springy earth were small sounds that did not venture beyond the nearest tree. Even the creak of the waggon took on a plaintive note and Peter sat in silence.

In patches of friendlier bush where beech trees grew the track dipped into creeks where the clear, shallow water ran sparkling over stones as smooth as eggs.

In open spaces where the thin, wild grasses scarcely hid the earth, mobs of kangaroos stood watching us, raising twitching nostrils to get our scent before bounding slowly away.

'I've shot 'em,' Peter declared, 'But it's like shooting a horse; it gives you a crook feeling.' He lit his pipe and added mildly, 'I don't say as it's wrong, but a lotta things that ain't wrong ain't right either.'

That night we camped on the bank of a creek. I slept beneath a bluegum and as I lay on my chaff bags I could see the stars beyond its branches. The air was moist, cool from the breath of tree ferns and moss and the horsebell sounded a clearer note. Sometimes it rang with sudden vigor when Kate clambered up a bank or slipped when descending to the creek to drink, but it was never silent.

'We'll reach the camp today,' Peter told me in the morning. 'I'm due there just before lunch. I want to load up this afternoon.'

The post-splitters' camp lay on the side of a hill. It came into view as we rounded a spur – an open patch shorn from a fleece of trees.

Above the camp, from which a scarf of thin, blue smoke was rising, the hill lifted to a skyline of bunched tree-tops glittering in the sun.

The track skirted this hill and emerged on to the clearing around which the heads of slain trees were piled in confusion.

In the centre of the clearing were two tents with a campfire burning in front of them. Blackened billies hung from a tripod over the fire and four men were approaching it from where they had been working on a fallen tree lower down. A team of bullocks stood at rest beside a stack of split posts, while the bullock driver sat on his tucker box beside the waggon eating his lunch.

Peter had told me about the men who were camped here. He liked Ted Wilson, a man with stooped shoulders, a wispy, tobacco-stained moustache, and merry blue eyes embedded in wrinkles. Ted had put up a slab house about half a mile from the camp and he lived there with Mrs Wilson and his three children.

Peter's opinion of Mrs Wilson was divided. He considered her a good cook but complained she liked 'howling about people who died'.

'She doesn't like blood, either,' he added.

It appeared that Mrs Wilson, after being bitten by a mosquito one night had left a patch of blood 'the size of a two-bob bit' on the pillow.

'The way she went on about it,' reflected Peter, 'you'd think a sheep had been killed in the room.'

Ted Wilson worked with three other men who camped on the site. One of them, Stewart Prescott, a young man of twenty-two, had wavy hair and wore snub-nosed ox-blood boots when he went out. He had a huckaback waistcoat with round, red buttons like marbles, and he sang 'Save My Mother's Picture from the Sale' in a nasally voice. He accompanied himself on the concertina and Peter regarded him as a great singer, but 'a proper darn mug with horses'.

People called Stewart Prescott 'The Prince' because of his flash clothes, and he gradually became known as Prince Prescott.

He had once worked in the bush below our home and had often ridden past our gate on his way to a dance at Turalla. Father rode into Balunga with him one day and when father returned he told me, 'I knew that fellow couldn't ride; every time he got off the horse he did his hair.'

Prince was always talking about going to Queensland. 'There's money to be made up there,' he used to say. 'They're opening up the land.'

'That's right,' father agreed with him. 'Kidman's opening up as much as he can get. He'll open up six foot of it for you after you've worked for him for forty years. Write and ask him for a job.'

Arthur Robins, the bullocky, came from Queensland. When Peter asked him why he left that State, he explained, 'Me wife lives up there,' an explanation that satisfied Peter. Peter asked him what Queensland was like and he replied, 'It's a hell of a place but you can't help thinkin' you'd like to go back there.'

He was a litle man with stiff, wiry whiskers in the midst of which a large nose stood naked to the weather. It was an undefended nose, red and pitted, and father, who knew Arthur, once told me that it must have tossed in the towel before Arthur was ready.

Peter thought Arthur looked like a wombat. 'Every time I see him I feel like hiding the spuds,' he told me.

Arthur did not mind comments on his appearance but he resented any reflection on his bullocks. He once told the barman at the Turalla pub, in explaining why he had just been fighting a mate, 'I stood him abusing me, but I wasn't going to stand him running down me bullocks.'

He was an alert, quick man given to seeking relief with the remark, 'It's a hard life.' He said it when he rose to begin work after a lunch or as he left to go home when an evening's entertainment was over. It was not a complaint. It expressed some long weariness that made itself felt when he was faced with his work again.

When Peter reined in the team near the tents the men were already filling their pannikins with black tea they poured from the billies on the fire.

'How are ya, Ted?' Peter called as he climbed from the waggon.

Without waiting for an answer, he continued, 'Did ya hear I sold the chestnut mare?'

Ted Wilson walked to a log, carrying his pannikin of tea in one hand and a newspaper-wrapped lunch in the other.

'No, I hadn't heard.'

'Barry bought her. I gave him a trial. That leg'll never come against her.'

'I don't think so,' commented Ted. 'She was a good mare.'

'I've never bred better. She'll take a drunk man home and keep to the right side of the road every time.'

Arthur Robins, who had joined the group when we arrived, shrugged his shoulders and commented, 'There he goes. As soon as he gets talkin' he breeds that mare over again.'

Peter glanced at him agreeably. 'How are ya, Arthur? Loaded up yet?'

'I'm a bloke who works, of course. I'm thinkin' of takin' on a horse team and givin' up work.'

'You'll die in the yoke,' retorted Peter mildly.

I had not got out of the waggon with Peter. I was looking for my pannikin and when I climbed down and walked towards the group each man looked at me with surprise.

Suddenly, for the first time, I felt my difference. That I should suddenly feel this way astonished me. I hesitated, momentarily confused. Then anger stirred in me and I swung towards them with quick, determined thrusts of my arms.

'Who's this you've got with ya?' asked Ted in surprise, rising to his feet and watching me with interest.

'That's Alan Marshall,' Peter informed him. 'He's a mate of mine. Come here, Alan. We'll bot some tucker off these blokes.'

'Goodday, Alan,' said Prince Prescott, feeling a sudden satisfaction at knowing me.

He turned to the others, eager to explain my crutches.

'He's the kid that got Infantile Paralysis. He was terrible crook. They say he'll never walk again.'

Peter turned on him angrily. 'What the hell are you talkin' about?' he demanded. 'What's wrong with you?'

This outburst astonished Prince. The other men looked at Peter in surprise.

'What's wrong with what I said?' asked Prince, appealing to his mates.

Peter grunted. He took my pannikin and filled it with tea. 'Nothing wrong,' he said, 'but don't say it again.'

'So your leg's crook, is it?' asked Ted Wilson, breaking the tension. 'You've gone in the fetlocks, is that it?' He was smiling at me and at his words all the men smiled.

'I tell you,' declared Peter impressively, standing erect with my pannikin held in his hand, 'if you could sole your boots with this kid's guts they'd last for ever.'

I had felt lost and alone amongst these men, a feeling that even Ted Wilson's words had failed to dispel. I had regarded Prince's remark as silly. I was determined to walk again, but Peter's anger gave it an importance it did not deserve, while at the same time rousing in me the suspicion that all these men felt I would never walk again. I wished I were home; then Peter's final remark burst upon me, and I experienced so great a feeling of elation that the effect of what had been said before was swept away in an instant. He had lifted me to the level of these men, but more than that, he had ensured their respect for me. This was what I needed.

I felt so grateful to Peter I wanted to express it in some way. I stood as close to him as I could and when I cut slices from the mutton he had cooked the night before I gave him the best piece.

After lunch the men began loading posts on to Peter's waggon and I went over to talk to Arthur, the bullocky, who was preparing to pull out.

His team of bullocks, sixteen of them, stood quietly chewing their cuds, their eyes half-closed as if they were concentrating on the working of their jaws.

The heavy yokes of river oak rested upon their necks with the keyed ends of the bows projecting above them. From the start-rings hanging from the centre of each yoke the lead chain passed from pair to pair till it reached the ring at the end of the waggon pole.

The two shafters were shorthorn stags with thick, powerful necks and heads like bulls. Their horns were short but the horns on the bullocks were long and pointed. The leaders were two Herefords, tall, rangy animals with mild, tranquil eyes.

Arthur Robins was busy preparing to pull out of the clearing. His huge waggon was laden with logs.

'Over ten ton there,' he boasted.

He wore faded dungarees and heavy, hobnail-boots with iron tips. His greasy felt hat had slits cut round the crown and through these he had threaded a strip of greenhide.

He shouted to his dog to come from beneath the waggon.

'Any bullocky who lets his dog walk under the waggon doesn't know his job. The bullocks don't like it. Go behind there,' he ordered as the dog slunk out. 'It makes 'em kick,' he explained to me as he pulled his trousers higher on to his hips and tightened his belt. 'Well, that's about the lot.'

He looked round to see if he had forgotten anything then picked
up his six-foot handled whip from the ground. He glanced at me to
see if I were in the way. Some of the pleasure I felt in watching him
must have been reflected in my face, for he lowered the butt of the
whip to the ground and said, 'You like bullocks, do you?'

I told him I did and, seeing he was pleased with me, I asked him
their names. He pointed to each bullock with his whip and gave its
name with some comment on its value in the team.

'Buck and Scarlet are the polers, see? You want thick necks on
the polers. Those two can move a load on their own.'

There was a bull in the team called Smokey and Arthur said he
was getting rid of him.

'If you yoke a bullock beside a bull, the bullock falls away fast,'
he said in confidential tones. 'Some say the bull's breath is too
strong, some say it is the smell of the bull, but the bullock always
dies in the end.'

He stepped closer to me, rested one of his legs by bending the
knee, and tapped my chest with his fingers. 'There's some cruel
bullock drivers in the world,' he said, his tone admitting me to
some familiar world of his own. 'That's why I'd sooner be a horse
than a bullock.' He raised himself and stretched his arm. 'But I
dunno; there's cruel teamsters too.' He paused, thinking a moment,
then added with some violence as if forcing the words from him,
'An' you don't want to take no notice of what Prince said either.
You gotta neck and shoulders on you like a working bullock. I've
never seen a kid walk better.'

He wheeled round with a shout and swung his huge whip.

'Buck! Scarlet!'

The polers moved into their yokes with slow, deliberate steps.

'Brindle! Poley!' His voice came back from the hills.

Down the long throat of each bullock in the team a moving lump
of chewed grass passed smoothly as they swallowed their cuds in
response to his voice. No bullock hurried. Each step they took to
move into the yokes was a calculated one and not a reaction to fear.

When the lead chain was tight and each bullock lay leaning on
its yoke with lowered head and taut hindquarters Arthur glanced
quickly along the double line then shouted for the pull.

'Gee, Buck! Gee, Scarlet! Gee, Red!'

The sixteen bullocks moved as one. They pressed forward into
the yokes with a slow power. For a moment of breathless strain the
reluctant waggon with its load of posts remained motionless, then
with a painful creaking it lurched forward and was under way
rocking and complaining like a ship at sea.

Arthur strode beside his team with his dog at his heels, his whip over his shoulder. Where the track began to drop before a sharp descent he hurried behind the waggon, turning the handle of the screw-brake with urgent speed. As the steel tyres bit into the huge redgum brake blocks a painful shrieking came from the lumbering waggon. The sound sped round the hills, echoing from side to side, filling the valley with its anguish and startling a flock of black cockatoos into flight. They passed over my head with a powerful beat of wings and their mournful cries merged with the shrieking of the brakes in some sad protest that continued till the birds passed over the timbered crest and the waggon had reached the floor of the valley.

CHAPTER 27

Ted Wilson's house was half a mile off the main track. Peter always brought a case of beer down with him each trip, and it was the custom for the men to gather at Ted's house the night he loaded up, to drink and yarn and sing songs.

Arthur, the bullocky, always camped within walking distance on this night and two sleeper cutters, the 'Ferguson Brothers', came over from their camp to have a drink and a yarn. Prince Prescott and the two other splitters were frequent visitors to the home, but on this night Prince brought his concertina and wore his huckaback waistcoat.

Ted rode on the waggon with Peter and me when we left the camp. When Peter called to me to climb aboard he turned to Ted and the three other splitters who were standing with him, and with his hand cupped to his mouth, said in a hoarse whisper, 'Watch this now! You watch him. This kid's a marvel; won't let you help him. This is what I was telling you about,' then dropping his hand, he addressed me in a voice intended to be casual, 'Righto, Alan. Up you go.'

Before he said this I had looked at the height of the load with some misgiving, but now that I had a reputation to live up to I approached the waggon with confidence. I clambered on to Kate's rump as I had before, but now the place I had to reach was high above me, and I knew I would have to stand upon her to reach a grip that would enable me to pull myself up. I grasped the end of one of the posts and dragged myself to a standing position with my good leg firm on her rump. From this height I swung myself to the top with little trouble.

'What did I tell you, eh?' Peter exclaimed, bending and thrusting a pleased face close to Ted's. 'See it!' He straightened and flicked a scornful finger. 'What's crutches to him – nothing!'

Peter and Ted sat with their legs hanging over the front of the load. The track to Ted's house was narrow and the branches of trees bent like bows as the bodies of the two men thrust them forward. As they passed, these branches sprang back and struck me sharply where I sat further back on the load. I lay on my back and watched them swish over me, delighting in the heavy rocking of the waggon and its laboured creaking. After a while the horses stopped and I knew we had arrived at Ted's home.

The house was built of upright slabs, the gaps between the slabs being packed with clay. A bark chimney filled one end and beside the chimney an iron tank was fed from a curled piece of bark that caught some of the rain water shed by the bark roof.

There was neither fence nor garden to shield it from the encroaching bush. A thin, stringybark sapling bowed over it in the wind, and ferns grew thickly before the unused front door.

Near the back door an upright log formed a stand for a chipped enamel basin. The stains of soapy water streaked its sides and the ground around it was grey and muddy.

Four possum skins, stretched and nailed to the back wall with the flesh side out, glistened in the evening sun and from the lower branch of a wattle nearby a hessian meat safe swung gently to and fro.

The trunk of a tree fern formed a step for the back door and beside this a piece of hoop iron had been hammered into the tops of two pegs to form a scraper for removing mud from the boots of those about to enter.

Back from the house four sapling posts, supporting a bark roof, formed a shelter for a gig, the harness for which was hanging on the dashboard.

Peter pulled his team up in front of the shelter and I climbed down. Two children stood watching me as I turned and placed my crutches beneath my armpits.

One little boy, about three years old, was completely naked. Peter, looping the reins before tossing them on Kate's back, looked down at him with a pleased and interested smile on his face.

'Well!' he exclaimed. He reached out his rough, horny hand and stroked the little boy's back with his fingers. 'What a smooth little fella, eh! What a smooth little fella!'

The child looked solemnly at the ground, sucking his finger and submitting to Peter's caress with a suggestion of wariness in his stillness.

'He *is* a smooth little fella.' Peter's fingers stroked his shoulders almost with wonder.

The other boy was about five. He was wearing long cotton stockings, but his garters had broken and the stockings hung round the tops of his boots like shackles. Braces made of rope supported his patched trousers, and his buttonless shirt only had one arm. His hair looked as if it had never been brushed. It stood straight out from his head like the hair on the back of a frightened dog.

Ted, who was unharnessing the horses, walked round from behind the leaders and, seeing his son, he stopped and looked at him critically, then shouted, 'Pull up yer socks! Pull up yer socks! Peter'll think you're some new breed of fowl I've got.'

The boy bent and pulled up his stockings while Ted watched him.

'Now take Alan here inside while we take out the horses. Tell mum we'll be in in a minute.'

The woman who turned from the open fireplace to look at me as I entered wore an expression that suggested she was wagging a tail. Her face was fat and placating and she wiped her soft, damp hands hurriedly on a black apron patched with flour as she came over to me.

'Oh, you pore boy!' she exclaimed. 'You're the cripple from Turalla, are you? Would you like to sit down now?'

She looked round the room, pressing her fingers against her full lips in a frowning moment of indecision. 'This chair here. . . . Sit here. I'll get a cushion for your pore back.'

She placed her hand on my arm to help me to the chair, lifting with such power that I had difficulty in keeping my armpit on the crutch. I staggered and, with a quick exclamation of concern, she seized my arm with both hands, looking towards the chair as if measuring the distance between me and salvation. I floundered to the chair, throwing my weight on the crutch she was not impeding while she held the other arm high in the air. I sank into the chair feeling confused and unhappy, wishing I were outside among men where my crutches seemed of little importance.

Mrs Wilson stood back from the chair and viewed me with the satisfaction of a woman looking at a fowl she has just plucked.

'There, now!' she said happily, 'Feel better now?'

I mumbled a 'yes' of relief at being free of her grip and looked at the door through which I knew Peter and Ted would soon be entering.

Mrs Wilson began questioning me on the 'terrible disease' I had. She wanted to know did my leg hurt, my back ache, and did my mother rub me down with goanna oil.

'It's so penetrating it will go through a bottle,' she informed me impressively.

She thought I might have a lot of acid in me and it might be as well for me to carry a potato in my pocket wherever I went.

'As it withers it sucks the acid out of ya,' she explained.

She considered the possibility of my collapse while there and told me not to worry because Ted had the gig. Then she took a saucepan of boiled mutton that had been resting on two iron bars across the fire, sniffed it and complained about how hard it was to keep meat fresh in the bush.

I began to like her after she forgot I walked on crutches and talked of her own diseases. She busied herself round the kitchen as she talked, placing the steaming mutton on a large plate on the table and mashing the potatoes she had tipped from another saucepan. Straightening her back as if it hurt she told me in the confidential way of one imparting a secret that she would never make old bones.

I became interested and asked her why, and she replied darkly that her organs were all out of place. 'I can't never have no more children,' she informed me, then added, after a moment's thought, 'Thank God!'

She sighed and looked abstractedly at the boy with the socks, who had been listening to us.

'Run and get Georgie's pants and shirt,' she said suddenly. 'They'll be dry now. I don't want him to catch his death of cold.'

In a moment the boy, whose name was Frank, brought them in from where they had been hanging on a bush outside and she dressed Georgie, who had been looking solemnly at me while this was going on.

His mother gave a final pat to his shirt then stood back and warned him. 'You come and tell me when you want to go anywhere next time. I'll smack you if you don't.'

Georgie kept looking at me.

When Ted came in with Peter he slapped Mrs Wilson so

boisterously on the rump that I felt a sudden concern for her organs.

'How's the old woman?' he cried happily. He looked at the table to see what was for tea, then said to Peter, 'This is a prime bit of mutton I got. I bought four ewes off Carter at half a crown a head. They were in good condition. Wait till you taste it.'

CHAPTER 28

When the table was cleared after tea and the Miller lamp hanging by a chain from the ceiling was lit, Peter brought in the case of beer and he and Ted worked out on a piece of paper what each visitor was to pay for 'the grog'.

'We'll crack a bottle before the others come,' Ted suggested after they had arrived at a figure, and Peter was agreeable.

Mrs Wilson put the two boys to bed in the other room where I could hear a baby crying. After a while it stopped and she came out fastening her blouse. The two sleeper cutters had arrived and were sitting on a form beside the table. Their greeting showed they liked her.

'We certainly been punishin' those wedges today, Missus,' one of them said to her, his big arms stretched out on the table as if they were too heavy for him to support.

'How're they splitting?' Ted asked him.

'Not bad. We're working on four-billeters. It's the quickest tree in the bush.'

I wondered why a four-billeter was the quickest tree in the bush and had made up my mind to ask him, but Arthur Robins and the three post-splitters arrived and Ted began filling the pannikins lined up on the table.

Each man had brought his own pannikin and though the pannikins varied in size Ted poured the same quantity of beer into each of them.

After a few rounds Prince Prescott began playing his concertina. He swayed his shoulders in an exaggerated fashion, sometimes throwing his head back and flinging his arms above him where, for a moment, the concertina jigged in and out before being swept down again. Sometimes he hummed a few bars of a song as if testing his voice against the panting notes of the instrument.

'He's not warmed up yet,' Arthur Robins told me in an undertone.

Arthur had sat beside me on a box near the fire. A gentle smile of anticipation never left his face. He was fond of songs with a kick in them, as he described it, and kept asking Prince to sing 'The Wild Colonial Boy'.

'What's wrong with the fella!' he exclaimed testily when Prince, absorbed in the 'Valetta', failed to hear him.

'Give us "The Wild Colonial Boy",' he demanded again in a louder voice. 'To hell with that thing you're playing!'

The concertina stopped with a wheeze. 'Righto,' said Prince. 'Here we go.'

As he began to sing Arthur leant forward on his box, his lips moving to the words and his eyes bright with pleasure.

> *'There was a wild Colonial boy, Jack Doolan was his name,*
> *Of poor but honest parents, he was born in Castlemaine;*
> *He was his father's only hope, his mother's only joy,*
> *The pride of both his parents was the wild Colonial boy.'*

This was father's favourite song and when there were men at our place and he had a few drinks in he would stand on the form and sing it, and when he came to the chorus he would shout, 'Stand up when you sing this. Get on your feet, men,' and when Prince broke into the chorus I took my crutches from against the wall and stood up, and I said with quick urgency to Arthur, 'Stand up!'

'By God, I will, boy!' he said, and he rose to his feet and crashed his tin pannikin on the table and he lifted his whiskery face and bellowed the chorus in a voice that should have come from a giant of a man. And I sang with him in high, unbroken tones and Peter and Ted and the sleeper cutters rose to their feet and sang too. We all stood up and the men crashed their pannikins on the table as Arthur had done and Mrs Wilson clutched her hands on her beast and whispered 'God love me!' in a tone of wonderment.

> *'Come, all my hearties, we'll roam the mountains high,*
> *Together we will plunder, together we will die;*
> *We'll wander over valleys, and gallop over plains,*
> *And we'll scorn to live in slavery, bound down with iron chains.'*

'Ah, there's a song now!' said Arthur huskily as he sat down and held out his pannikin for more beer. 'It puts great heart into a man when he can see no end to his labourin'.'

The song had infected Peter with a desire to contribute some-thing stirring to the gathering. He was too busy drinking to waste time singing a Scottish song, but he knew two lines of an Adam Lindsay Gordon poem that, throughout the evening, he repeated with an almost reverent respect.

They came to him now as he was standing filling a pannikin from a bottle and he sudenly stopped pouring and, holding the bottle and pannikin motionless in his hands, he gazed fixedly at the opposite wall and recited the lines in a deep, emotional voice.

> *'Between sky and water, the Clown came and caught her,*
> *Our stirrups clashed loud as we lit.'*

For a moment after he finished he continued staring at the wall.

Arthur screwed up his face and looked at him speculatively. 'He's still riding the Clown,' he concluded, then turned his atten-tion to his pannikin.

Whenever Peter recovered from the effect of his brief excursion into poetry he felt impelled to explain the quotation.

'You know what it means, don't ya? Some blokes miss it. This Clown is a fast jumper. He takes off well back, see, and he fairly flies over the waterjump. Now the other horse takes off first but the Clown, coming up fast, takes off behind him and catches him fair over the jump. That's what it means when it says "between sky and water".

'They land together. The other horse bores in as they land – you can bet that – and their stirrups clash. The Clown must have been a well-sprung horse, good bone with plenty of daylight under him. I'd like to meet the bloke that wrote it.'

He swallowed a pannikin of beer and smacked his lips as he looked at the empty pannikin in his hand.

After a time it was hard to stop Prince singing. He sang 'The Face on the Bar-room Floor', 'The Luggage Van Ahead', and 'What Will You Take for Me, Papa?'

Each song made tears run down the face of Mrs Wilson. 'Aren't they beautiful?' she sobbed. 'Do you know any more?'

'Aw, yes, Mrs Wilson, I know plenty more.' Prince dropped his head modestly as he spoke. 'I pick 'em up everywhere.'

'Do you know "The Fatal Wedding"?' she asked, leaning towards him hopefully.

'No, I don't know that one, Mrs Wilson. I will, though. I'll get hold of it all right. I know "Will the Angels Let Me Play?" Would you like to hear that?'

'Oo, yes!' said Mrs Wilson. 'It sounds lovely.' She turned to Peter and Arthur who were arguing whether a team of bullocks could pull more than a team of horses.

'You two be quiet now,' she demanded. 'Prince is going to sing us a lovely song. You can argue after. Go on, Prince.'

Peter dropped a hand with which he was emphasising a point and accepted the position. 'All right. Into it, Prince.' He leant back in his chair, his head nodding a little. 'Let down the sliprails,' he muttered.

Prince stood up and announced the title of the song; 'Will the Angels Let Me Play?'

He bent over his concertina that began wailing beneath the curve of his body, then he straightened, flinging back his hair with a toss of his head, and began singing in a nasal voice:

> *'In a yard where children were playing games one day,*
> *A little child on crutches was watching wistfully,*
> *Tho' she tried so hard she couldn't play as other children do.*
> *They said she was a bother and in their way too.*
> *One night when all was silent, the Angels came that way*
> *And took the little darling, whose sweet lips seemed to say:'*

Prince swept into the refrain with a throb in his voice.

> *'Mother, when I go to heaven,*
> *Will the Angels let me play?*
> *Just because I am a cripple, will they say I'm in the way?*
> *Here, the children never want me, I'm a bother, they all say.*
> *When I go to heaven, mother, will the Angels let me play?'*

As Prince sat down confident of praise to follow, Peter rose to his feet, staggered a little, then drew himself up and thumped the table, his glossy beard jutting out from his aggressive chin.

'That's the saddest darn song I've ever heard, but it should never have been sung in front of that kid here.' He pointed a dramatic finger at me, shaking it in emphasis. 'It's not the right song to sing in front of him.' He turned and leant towards me. 'Don't you take any notice of it, Alan.' He sat down heavily and poured himself another beer. 'Between sky and water the Clown came and caught her,' he muttered.

I was astonished at his outburst. I had not connected the song with myself. I was touched by the plight of the little girl and kept wishing I were there to play with her. As Prince's voice kept on I saw myself thrashing every child who said she was a bother. I wondered why she didn't tell them off herself and concluded she must be a very little girl. But that I should consider myself like her was ridiculous.

Prince was annoyed with Peter. Just when he was preparing himself for praise Peter criticised him.

'What's wrong with it?' he protested to Arthur. 'That song's all right. Alan knows he's crippled, don't he? So do we.'

Arthur stood up and leant across the table so that he could speak confidentially to Prince.

'That's where you're wrong, Prince; he don't know he's crippled.' He raised an emphatic finger to support each word with a gesture. 'He'll never know it if he lives to be a hundred.'

He drew himself up with lifted chin and firmly closed lips and looked at Prince sternly, anticipating disagreement from Prince, but Prince was suddenly humble, an attitude that changed the tone of Arthur's voice.

'I'm not saying it was a bad song,' Arthur continued, 'but why try and wake him up to what fools think?'

Prince admitted it would be better if I never woke up to fools.

'Oh, dear me!' exclaimed Mrs Wilson, who was listening. 'I've always said it's better not to know what's wrong with you. People with cancer an' that. . . . Oh, it's terrible, terrible. . . .'

Arthur looked thoughtfully at her for a moment then shrugged and said to Prince, 'Give us another song. What about something stirring like? Do you know that song about Ben Hall? There's a man now! Sing us that.'

'I don't know the words of it, Arthur. How's it go?'

Arthur drew a deep breath and tucked his chin well down on his chest. 'Only the robber rich men feared the coming of Ben Hall,' he sang in a quavering, uncertain voice. He stopped and wiped the back of his hand across his mouth. 'That's all I know, but, hell! it's a good song. You oughter learn it.'

'I wish you'd sing "There's Another Picture in my Mamma's Frame",' pleaded Mrs Wilson.

'Strewth!' exclaimed Arthur contemptuously, and hurriedly swallowed a pannikin of beer.

'I heard a fellow sing that at a concert at Balunga one night,' said one of the sleeper cutters. 'It brought down the house. This bloke that sang it came up from Melbourne specially. I forget his name

but they reckon he was a champion at singing. He used to get paid
for it.'

'I know two verses of it,' Prince said. 'Let's see if I can get the
tune. I've sung it once but ... Now, how's it go ... ?'

With his head on one side and his eyes closed he listened to the
notes he squeezed from the concertina, then suddenly smiled and
nodded. 'She's right. I've got it.'

'Quiet over there.' And Mrs Wilson looked at Peter and Ted who
were talking together but not listening to each other.

'This saddle was a bit knocked about – the girth was no good –
but I put it in the back of the cart ...' Ted's voice suggested his
remarks were confidential.

'I bought the grey for a fiver,' Peter broke in, holding a pannikin
of beer a few inches from his mouth while he gazed steadily across it
at the wall. 'I rode him twenty miles that night. ...'

'It was a Queensland saddle,' Ted interrupted, filling his
pannikin.

'He never turned a hair ...' said Peter.

'I bought a new girth ...' Ted went on.

'Never raised a sweat ...' Peter addressed the wall.

'Well, after that ...' Ted was approaching the climax.

'Shut up, you two,' said Arthur. 'The missus here wants a
song.'

Peter and Ted looked at Arthur as if he were an intruding
stranger.

'What ...' began Ted.

'Prince is going to sing another song.'

'Hop into it,' Peter consented agreeably. He settled back in his
chair and gazed at the ceiling. 'We're listening.'

Prince began singing:

> 'Come, my baby, tell me why you're crying,
> Don't you see it pains your papa so?
> Every day for you nice things I'm buying,
> And I'd like to see you smile, you know,
> Then she said, I know you are the dearest
> And the sweetest papa of them all,
> If you love me truly, you will tell me surely
> Who's the lady's picture on the wall?'

Prince had the attention of all of us. Even Peter turned to look at
him. He broke into the chorus with great confidence.

'There's another picture in my mamma's frame,
It's some other lady, her smile is not the same;
My mamma was sweeter, I think it is a shame,
There's another picture in my mamma's frame.'

Mrs Wilson wept quietly as Prince began the second verse.

'Yes, my darling, it's a pretty lady,
And she's going to be your new mamma,
She'll be good and kind to you, and, maybe,
You will love her, so 'twill please papa.'

Arthur drank two pannikins of beer while Prince was singing, and when Prince was finished he informed me darkly, 'Any man who marries twice wants his head read.'

I was tired and I fell asleep in the chair while the singing continued. When Peter woke me up the party was over.

'Arise,' he said in the tone of a Minister beginning a sermon. 'Arise, and come with me.'

We went out to the gig shelter where he had already prepared our beds. I snuggled into the chaff bags, but Peter stood holding on to one of the uprights and swaying. He suddenly raised his head and addressed the night.

'Between sky and water, the Clown came and caught her.
Our stirrups clashed loud as we lit.'

CHAPTER 29

Father wanted to know all that had happened to me on my trip with Peter. He questioned me closely about the men I met and asked me if I had talked to them.

When mother protested mildly against so many questions father quietened her with the rejoinder, 'I want to know whether he can put his shoulder to a man.'

He was pleased when I spoke excitedly about the staunchness of

the horses and of how they pulled the laden waggon home with
never a slackened trace.

'Ah! It's a good team,' he commented. 'Peter's got a great stamp
of a horse in that Marlo breed. They're never off the bit.' He
paused, then asked, 'Did he let you take the reins?'

He looked away when he asked me this, awaiting my answer
with his hands suddenly still on the table.

'Yes,' I told him.

He was pleased and nodded, smiling to himself. 'A pair of hands
is the thing . . .' he murmured, following a train of thought of his
own. 'A good pair of hands . . .'

He valued hands on a horse.

I remembered the feel of the horses' mouths on the taut reins. I
remembered the power of the horses that came through the reins,
the power they shared with me as they flattened in a heavy pull.

'The reins of straining horses take all the strength out of you,'
father had told me once, but I had found it otherwise.

'You never want to worry over not being able to ride,' he reminded me now. 'I like a good driver, myself.'

It was the first time for some years that he had mentioned my not
being able to ride. After I returned from the hospital I talked about
riding as if it were only a matter of weeks before I would be in the
saddle riding buckjumpers. It was a subject father did not
like discussing. He was always silent and uncomfortable when I
pleaded with him to lift me on a horse, but at last he must have felt
compelled to explain his attitude for he told me that I could never
ride – not until I was a man and could walk again.

He put his hand on my shoulder when he told me this, and he
spoke earnestly as if it were important that I should understand
him.

'When you ride,' he said, 'you grip the horse with your legs, see.
When you rise to the trot you take your weight on the stirrups. It's
not hard for a bloke with good legs. . . . He's got to have balance
too, of course. He goes with the horse. But your legs can't grip,
Alan. They're all right for getting you round but they're no good for
riding. So chuck the idea. I wanted you to be able to ride, so did
mum. But there you are. . . . There's often things a bloke wants to
do but can't. I'd like to be like you but I can't, and you want to ride
like me, and you can't. So both of us are crook on it.'

I listened to him in silence. I did not believe what he said was
true. I wondered that he believed it himself. He was always right;
now for the first time he was wrong.

I had made up my mind to ride, and even as he spoke it pleased

me to think how happy he would be when, one day, I galloped past
our house on some arched-necked horse reefing at the bit as it
fought my hold on the reins.

One of the boys at school rode an Arab pony called Starlight.
Starlight was a white pony with a thin, sweeping tail and a quick,
swinging walk. He had fine, sinewy fetlocks and trod the ground as
if to spare the earth his weight.

Starlight became a symbol of perfection to me. Other boys rode
ponies to school, but these ponies were not like Starlight. When the
boys raced, as they often did, I watched Starlight stride to the lead,
glorying in his superior speed, the eager spirit of him.

Bob Carlton, who owned him, was a thin boy with red hair. He
liked talking to me about his pony since my attitude encouraged his
boasting.

'I can leave all the other kids standing,' he would say, and I
would agree with him.

Each lunch time he rode Starlight down to the road-trough a
quarter of a mile away to give him a drink. It was a task that took
him away from the games in the school ground and he would have
avoided it if he had not been trained never to neglect his horse.

One day I offered to do it for him, an offer he quickly accepted.

'Goodo,' he said happily.

He always rode Starlight bareback down to the trough, but he
saddled him for me and legged me on to his back with instructions
to let him have his head and he would take me there and back even
if I never touched the reins.

I had already concluded that Starlight would do this and had
decided to cling to the pommel of the saddle with both hands and
not bother about the reins.

When I was seated in the saddle Bod shortened the stirrups and
I bent down and lifted my bad leg, thrusting the foot into the iron
as far as the instep where it rested, taking the weight of the useless
limb. I did the same for my good leg, but since it was not as badly
paralysed I found I could put some pressure on it.

I gathered the reins in my hands then grasped the pommel of the
saddle. I could not pull upon the reins or guide the pony, but I
could feel the tug of his mouth upon my hands and this gave me an
impression of control.

Starlight walked briskly through the gate then turned along the
track towards the trough. I did not feel as secure as I had thought I
would. My fingers began to ache from my grip on the pommel, but
I could not relax and sit loosely in the saddle, believing that, if I
did, I would fall, I felt ashamed of myself, but I was angry too —
angry with my body.

When we reached the trough, Starlight thrust his muzzle deep in the water. I looked down the steep incline of his neck dropping away from the pommel of the saddle and I drew back, placing one hand on his rump behind the saddle so that I could avoid looking down into the trough.

Starlight drank with a sucking sound, but in a minute he lifted his· muzzle just above the surface, with water running from his mouth, and gazed with pricked ears across the paddock behind the trough.

Everything he did was impressed upon me with a sharp vividness. I was sitting on a pony with no one to direct me and this was how a pony drank when you were on its back alone with it; this was how it felt to be riding.

I looked down at the ground, at the scattered stones against which a crutch would strike, at the mud around the trough in which a crutch would slip. They presented no problem to me here. I need never consider them when on a pony's back.

Long grass that clutched my crutches, steep rises that took my breath, rough uneven ground – I thought of them now with a detached, untroubled mind, feeling elated that they no longer could bring a momentary despair upon me.

Starlight began to drink again. I leant forward, bending down and touching the lower part of his neck where I could feel the pulsing passage of the water he swallowed. His flesh was firm and he was strong and fleet and had a great heart. I suddenly loved him with a passion and a fierce hunger.

When he had finished drinking he turned and I almost fell but now all fear of him had gone. I grasped the pommel and hung on while he walked back to the school. He walked beneath me without effort, without struggle, stepping on the ground as if his legs were my own.

Bob lifted me off.

'How did he go?' he asked.

'Good,' I said. 'I'll take him down again tomorrow.'

CHAPTER 30

Each day I took Starlight to water. I bridled and saddled him myself then led him round to Bob who legged me on and placed my crutches against the school wall.

In a few weeks I could ride him without concentrating on keeping my seat in the saddle. I could relax and did not retain so intense a grip on the pommel.

But I still had no control over the reins. I could not rein the pony in or direct him. When walking in the bush or riding in my chair I pondered over this problem. Before dropping off to sleep at night I designed saddles with sliding grips on them, with backs like chairs, with straps to bind my legs to the horse, but when on Starlight's back I realised these saddles would not help me. I had to learn to balance myself without the aid of my legs, to ride without holding on.

I began urging Starlight into a jog trot the last few yards to the trough, and gradually increased this distance till I was jogging over the last hundred yards.

It was not a pleasant gait. I bumped violently up and down on the saddle, unable to control my bouncing body by taking some of the shock with my legs.

The children watched me but were not critical of my riding. I had my own way of doing things and they accepted it. My seat in the saddle was precarious and suggested I would easily fall, but after observing this and noting that I showed no fear of falling they lost interest.

Those who rode to school often set off for home at a gallop. It surprised me that they seemed to ride so easily. I became impatient to improve. Surely what they could do, I could do too.

But my mind kept demanding results that my body was incapable of producing. Month after month I rode to the trough but my riding was not improving. I still had to hold on; I had never cantered; I could not guide the pony. For a year I had to be satisfied with walking and jog trotting to the trough, then I made up my mind to canter even if I did fall off.

I asked Bob was it easy to sit a canter.

'Cripes, yes!' he said, 'it's like sitting on a rocking horse. It's easier than trotting. You never leave the saddle when Starlight's cantering. He don't stride like a pony; he strides like a horse.'

'Will he break into a canter without trotting fast first?' I asked.

Bob assured me he would. 'Lean forward and lift him into it,' he instructed me. 'Clap him with your heels and he'll break into a canter straight off.'

I tried that day. There was a slight rise approaching the trough and when I reached it I leant forward quickly and touched him with the heel of my good foot. He broke into an easy canter and I found myself swinging along in curves of motion, with a new wind upon my face and an urge to shout within me. Starlight jogged to a stop at the trough and when he began drinking and I relaxed I found myself trembling.

After that I cantered each day until I felt secure, even when he turned sharply at the school gates.

But I was still clinging to the pommel of the saddle.

Two tracks converged at the trough. One led past the school but the other turned up a lane behind the school and joined the main road on the other side of the building. This lane was rarely used. Three winding depressions, made by the horses and waggons that were sometimes driven along it, wound through the grass between the enclosing fences.

One of these fences consisted of four strands of barbed wire stapled to the outside of each post. Following this fence was a pad made by the road cattle moving down to the trough to drink. Tufts of red hair clung to many of the barbs along the fence where the cattle had scraped their sides on the wire as they passed.

I had sometimes considered riding along this lane back to the school but since I had no means of guiding Starlight, I had to go along the track he favoured.

One winter day I touched him sharply with my heel as he turned from the trough and he broke into a swift canter, but instead of following the usual track to the school he turned up the lane.

I was pleased. I had rested in this lane many a time when walking back from the foot of Mt Turalla and I associated it with fatigue. Its tangly grass and ridgy tracks were not easy to walk upon, and now I looked down at them streaking swiftly beneath me, marvelling at the ease with which I passed above them. The troubling associations they always held for me did not now impress themselves upon my mind, and I looked at the rough earth with affection.

Starlight turned from the centre track and cantered along the cattle pad, a manoeuvre I had not anticipated. As he swung on to the pad I realised my danger and strained at the pommel of the saddle with my hands as if, in this way, I could turn him away from the fence with its waiting barbs.

But he kept on, and I looked down at my bad leg dangling helplessly in the stirrup and at the strands of barbed wire streaking past it a few inches away.

I was wearing long cotton stockings held up by garters above my knees. My bad leg was bandaged beneath the stocking that covered it, protection for the broken chilblains that, throughout the winter, never left me.

I looked ahead to where the pad moved closer to the posts and I knew that in a moment my leg would be tearing along the barbs. I was not afraid, but I felt resentful that I had to resign myself to this without being able to fight back.

For a moment I considered throwing myself off. I drew a breath and thought 'now', but I could not bring myself to do it. I saw myself with a broken arm, unable to walk on my crutches. I looked back at the fence.

When the first barbs struck the side of my leg they dragged it back towards the pony's flank then dropped it as the pad curved away again. It fell loosely, dangling free of the stirrup for a space before being snatched up and torn again. The barbs ripped through the stocking and the bandage and I felt the flow of blood on my leg.

My mind became still and quiet. I did not look at my leg again. I looked ahead to where the pad finally drew away from the fence at the end of the lane and resigned myself to a torn leg and to pain.

It seemed a long way to the end of the lane, and Starlight reached it without a falter in his swinging canter. He turned at the corner and came back to the school with eager head and pricked ears, but I was limp upon him.

Bob and Joe helped me off.

'Strewth! What's wrong?' asked Joe, bending and looking anxiously at my face.

'He went up the lane and dragged my leg against the barbed wire,' I told him.

'What did he do that for?' asked Bob incredulously, stooping to look at my leg. 'He never does that. Hell, your leg's bleeding. It's all cut. Your sock's all torn. What did he go up there for? You'll have to see a doctor or something. Cripes, your leg's crook!'

'Fix it up down the back before anyone sees you,' advised Joe quickly.

Joe understood me.

'I wonder who's got a handkerchief?' I asked Joe. 'I'll have to tie it up. What kid's got a handkerchief?'

'I'll ask Perce,' offered Bob. 'Perce'll have one.'

Perce was the siss of the school and was known to carry a handkerchief. Bob went to look for him and Joe and I went down to the back of the school, where I sat down and pulled my tattered stocking down round my ankle. I unwrapped the torn bandage and exposed the jagged cuts. They were not deep but there were several of them and they bled freely, the blood flowing sluggishly over the broken chilblains and the cold, bluish skin.

Joe and I looked at it in silence.

'Anyway, that leg was never any good to you,' Joe said at last, anxious to comfort me.

'Blast it!' I muttered savagely. 'Blast my leg. See if Bob's coming.'

Bob came down with a handkerchief he had taken almost by force from Perce, who had followed him up to learn what was to happen to it.

'You've got to bring it back tomorrow,' he warned me, his voice trailing off as he saw my leg. 'Oo, look!' he exclaimed.

With the aid of the handkerchief and the torn bandage I already had, I bound my leg firmly, then rose on my crutches while the three boys stood back and awaited my verdict.

'She'll do,' I said, after waiting a moment to see if its stinging would cease.

'She'll never bleed through all that rag,' Joe pronounced. 'No one will know.'

CHAPTER 31

Mother never knew I had torn my leg. I always attended to my chilblains myself after she had given me a dish of hot water, a clean bandage and wadding to put between my toes. Sometimes I thought I would have to tell her as the cuts refused to heal on the cold flesh, but when the warm weather came they healed.

I continued taking Starlight to the trough but now I never

cantered him till he was on the track to the school and the turn-off
to the lane was behind him.

I had often tried to ride with only one hand clinging to the
pommel of the saddle, but the curvature of my spine made me lean
to the left and one hand on the pommel did not prevent a tendency
for me to fall in that direction.

One day, while Starlight was walking, I began gripping the
saddle in various places, searching for a more secure position on
which to hold. My left hand, owing to my lean in that direction,
could reach far lower than my right while I was still relaxed. I
moved my seat a little to the right in the saddle then thrust my left
hand under the saddle flap beneath my leg. Here I could grasp the
surcingle just where it entered the flap after crossing the saddle. I
could bear down upon the inner saddle pad to counter a sway to the
right or pull on the surcingle to counter a sway to the left.

For the first time I felt completely safe. I crossed the reins,
gripping them with my right hand, clutched the surcingle and
urged Starlight into a canter. His swinging stride never moved me
in the saddle. I sat relaxed and balanced, rising and falling with the
movement of his body and experiencing a feeling of security and
confidence I had not know before.

Now I could guide him. With a twist of my hand I could turn
him to the right or the left and as he turned I could lean with him
and swing back again as he straightened to an even stride. My grip
on the surcingle braced me to the saddle, a brace that could
immediately adjust itself to a demand for a steadying push or pull.

I cantered Starlight for a little while then, on a sudden impulse, I
yelled him into greater speed. I felt his body flatten as he moved
from a canter into a gallop. The undulating swing gave way to a
smooth run and the quick tattoo of his pounding hooves came up to
me like music.

It was too magnificent an experience to repeat, to waste in a day.
I walked him back to the school humming a song. I did not wait for
Bob to leg me off; I slid off on my own and fell over on the ground. I
crawled to my crutches against the wall then stood up and led
Starlight to the pony yard. When I unsaddled him and let him go I
stood leaning on the fence just watching him till the bell rang.

I did not concentrate on my lessons that afternoon. I kept thinking about father and how pleased he would be when I could prove
to him I could ride. I wanted to ride Starlight down next day and
show him, but I knew the questions he would ask me, and I felt that
I could not truthfully say I could ride until I could mount and
dismount without help.

I would soon learn to get off, I reflected. If I got off beside my crutches I could cling to the saddle with one hand till I got hold of them and put them beneath my arms. But getting on was another matter. Strong legs were needed to rise from the ground with one foot in the stirrup. I would have to think of another way.

Sometimes when romping at home I would place one hand on top of our gate and one on the armpit rest of a crutch, then raise myself slowly till I was high above the gate. It was a feat of strength I often practised, and I decided to try it with Starlight in place of the gate. If he stood I could do it.

I tried it next day but Starlight kept moving and I fell several times. I got Joe to hold him, then placed one hand on the pommel and the other on the top of the two crutches standing together. I drew a breath, then swung myself up and on to the saddle with one heave. I slung the crutches on my right arm, deciding to carry them, but they frightened Starlight and I had to hand them to Joe.

Each day Joe held Starlight while I mounted but in a fortnight the pony became so used to me swinging on to the saddle in this fashion that he made no attempt to move till I was seated. I never asked Joe to hold him after that, but I still could not carry my crutches.

I showed Bob how I wanted to carry them, slung on my right arm, and asked him would he ride Starlight round while he carried my crutches in this fashion. He did it each afternoon after school was out and Starlight lost his fear of them. After that he let me carry them.

When cantering they clacked against his side and at a gallop they swung out, pointing backwards, but he was never afraid of them again.

Starlight was not tough in the mouth and I could easily control him with one hand on the reins. I rode with a short rein so that, by leaning back, I added the weight of my body to the strength of my arm. He responded to a twist of the hand when I wished him to turn and I soon began wheeling him like a stockpony. By thrusting against the saddle pad with the hand that held the surcingle I found I could rise to the trot, and my bumping days were over.

Starlight never shied. He kept a straight course and because of this I felt secure and was not afraid of being thrown. I did not realise that normal legs were needed to sit a sudden shy since I had never experienced one. I was confident that only a bucking horse could throw me and I began riding more recklessly than the boys at school.

I galloped over rough ground, meeting the challenge it presented to my crutches by spurning it with legs as strong as steel – Starlight's legs which now I felt were my own.

Where other boys avoided a mound or bank on their ponies, I went over them, yet when walking it was I who turned away and they who climbed them.

Now their experiences could be mine and I spent the school dinner hour in seeking out places in which I would have found difficulty in walking, so that in riding through or over them, I became the equal of my mates.

Yet I did not know that such was my reason. I rode in these places because it pleased me. That was my explanation.

Sometimes I galloped Starlight up the lane. The corner at the end was sharp and turned on'to a metal road. The Presbyterian Church was built on the opposite corner and it was known as the 'Church Corner'.

One day I came round this corner at a hard gallop. It was beginning to rain and I wanted to reach the school before I got wet. A woman walking along the pathway in front of the church suddenly put up her umbrella and Starlight swerved away from it in a sudden bound.

I felt myself falling and tried to will my bad leg to pull the foot from the stirrup. I had a horror of being dragged. Father had seen a man dragged with his foot caught in the stirrup and I could never forget his description of the galloping horse and the bouncing body.

When I hit the metal and knew I was free of the saddle I only felt relief. I lay there a moment wondering whether any bones were broken then sat up and felt my legs and arms which were painful from bruises. A lump was rising on my head and I had a gravel rash on my elbow.

Starlight had galloped back to the school and I knew that Bob and Joe would soon be along with my crutches. I sat there dusting my trousers when I noticed the woman who had opened the umbrella. She was running towards me with such an expression of alarm and concern upon her face that I looked quickly round to see if something terrible had occurred behind me, something of which I was not aware. But I was alone.

'Oh' she cried. 'Oh! You fell! I saw you. You poor boy! Are you hurt? Oh, I'll never forget it!'

I recognised her as Mrs Conlon whom mother knew and I thought, 'She'll tell mum I fell. I'll have to show dad I can ride tomorrow.'

Mrs Conlon hurriedly placed her parcels on the ground and put her hand on my shoulder, peering at me with her mouth slightly open.

'Are you hurt, Alan? Tell me. What will your poor mother say? Say something.'

'I'm all right, Mrs Conlon,' I assured her. 'I'm waiting for my crutches. Joe Carmichael will bring my crutches when he sees the pony.'

I had faith in Joe attending to things like that. Bob would come running down full of excitement, announcing an accident to the world; Joe would be running silently with my crutches, his mind busy on how to keep it quiet.

'You should never ride ponies, Alan,' Mrs Conlon went on while she dusted my shoulders. 'It'll be the death of you, see if it isn't.' Her voice took on a tender, kindly note and she knelt beside me and bent her head till her face was close to mine. She smiled gently at me. 'You're different from other boys. You never want to forget that. You can't do what they do. If your poor father and mother knew you were riding ponies it would break their hearts. Promise me you won't ride again. Come on, now.'

I saw with wonder that there were tears in her eyes and I wanted to comfort her, to tell her I was sorry for her. I wanted to give her a present, something that would make her smile and bring her happiness. I saw so much of this sadness in grown-ups who talked to me. No matter what I said I could not share my happiness with them. They clung to their sorrow. I could never see a reason for it.

Bob and Joe came running up and Joe was carrying my crutches. Mrs Conlon sighed and rose to her feet, looking at me with tragic eyes as Joe helped me up and thrust my crutches beneath my arms.

'What happened?' he demanded anxiously.

'He shied and tossed me,' I said, 'I'm all right.'

'Now we'll all shut up about this,' whispered Joe looking sideways at Mrs Conlon. 'Keep it under your hat or they'll never let you on a horse again.'

I said goodbye to Mrs Conlon who reminded me, 'Don't forget what I told you, Alan,' before she went away.

'There's one thing,' said Joe, looking me up and down as we set off for the school. 'There's no damage done; you're walking just as good as ever.'

CHAPTER 32

Next day I rode Starlight home during lunch hour. I did not hurry. I wanted to enjoy my picture of father seeing me ride. I thought it might worry mother but father would place his hand on my shoulder and look at me and say. 'I knew you could do it,' or something like that.

He was bending over a saddle lying on the ground near the chaff house door when I rode up to the gate. He did not see me. I stopped at the gate and watched him for a moment then called out, 'Hi!'

He did not straighten himself but turned his head and looked back towards the gate behind him. For a moment he held this position while I looked, smiling, at him, then he quietly stood erect and gazed at me for a moment.

'You, Alan!' he said, his tone restrained as if I were riding a horse a voice could frighten into bolting.

'Yes,' I called. 'Come and see me. You watch. Remember when you said I'd never ride? Now, you watch. Yahoo!' I gave the yell he sometimes gave when on a spirited horse and leant forward in the saddle with a quick lift and a sharp clap of my good heel on Starlight's side.

The white pony sprang forward with short, eager bounds, gathering himself until, balanced, he flattened into a run. I could see his knee below his shoulder flash out and back like a piston, feel the drive of him and the reach of his shoulders to every stride.

I followed our fence to the wattle clump then reefed him back and round, leaning with him as he propped and turned in a panel's length. Stones scattered as he finished the turn; his head rose and fell as he doubled himself to regain speed: then I was racing back again while father ran desperately towards the gate.

I passed him, my hand on the reins moving forward and back to the pull of Starlight's extended head. Round again and back to a skidding halt with Starlight's chest against the gate. He drew back dancing, tossing his head, his ribs pumping. The sound of his breath through his distended nostrils, the creak of the saddle, the jingle of the bit were the sounds I had longed to hear while sitting on the back of a prancing horse and now I was hearing them and smelling the sweat from a completed gallop

I looked down at father, noticing with sudden concern that he was pale. Mother had come out of the house and was hurrying towards us.

'What's wrong, dad?' I asked, quickly.

'Nothing,' he said. He kept looking at the ground and I could hear him breathing.

'You shouldn't have run like that to the gate,' I said. 'You winded yourself.'

He looked at me and smiled, then turned to mother who reached out her hand to him as she came up to the gate.

'I saw it,' she said.

They looked into each other's eyes a moment.

'He's you all over again,' mother said, then turning to me, 'You learned to ride yourself, Alan, did you?'

'Yes,' I said, leaning on Starlight's neck so that my head was closer to theirs. 'For years I've been learning. I've only had one buster; that was yesterday. Did you see me turn; dad?' I turned to father. 'Did you see me bring him round like a stockhorse? What do you think? Do you reckon I can ride?'

'Yes,' he said. 'You're good; you've got good hands and you sit him well. How do you hold on? Show me.'

I explained my grip on the surcingle, told him how I used to take Starlight to drink and how I could mount or dismount with the aid of my crutches.

'I've left my crutches at school or I'd show you,' I said.

'It's all right ... Another day ... You feel safe on his back?'

'Safe as a bank.'

'Your back doesn't hurt you, does it, Alan?' mother asked.

'No, not a bit,' I said.

'You'll always be very careful, won't you, Alan? I like seeing you riding but I wouldn't like to see you fall.'

'I'll be very careful,' I promised, then added, 'I must go back to school; I'll be late.'

'Listen, son,' father said, looking up at me with a serious face. 'We know you can ride now. You went past that gate like a bat out of hell. But you don't want to ride like that. If you do people will think you're a mug rider. They'll think you don't understand a horse. A good rider hasn't got to be rip-snorting about like a pup off the chain just to show he can ride. A good rider don't have to prove nothing. He studies his mount. You do that. Take it quietly. You can ride – all right, but don't be a show-off with it. A gallop's all right on a straight track but the way you're riding, you'll tear the guts out of a horse in no time. A horse is like a man; he's at his best when he gets a fair deal. Now, walk Starlight back to school and give him a rub down before you let him go.'

He paused, thinking for a moment, then added, 'You're a good bloke, Alan. I like you and I reckon you're a good rider.'

CHAPTER 33

Cars were appearing on the roads. With streamers of dust behind them they sped along highways designed for the iron-shod wheels of buggies. They wore corrugations in the metal, sent stinging pellets of gravel clattering against the dashboards of gigs they passed and honked their way through groups of road cattle, scattering them in fear. They had great brass lamps lit by acetylene gas, brass radiators and upright, dignified windscreens behind which men in dustcoats and goggles leant forward peering and clutching wheels they sometimes tugged at like reins.

Startled horses wheeled and plunged from the fumes and noise of their passing and angry drivers stood erect in buggies brought to a halt far out on the areas of grass that skirted the roadways, and cursed violently as they watched the receding dust.

Farmers left their paddock gates open so that frightened horses, fighting the reins, could be guided through into areas away from the road where they were held trembling and prancing till the cars had passed.

Peter Finlay was no longer a groom for Mrs Carruthers; he was her chauffeur and wore a peaked cap and a uniform and stood with his heels together when he opened the door to let her out.

'What do you hug the road for?' father demanded of him one day. 'Do you own the road? Everybody's got to get off on the grass when you come along.'

'You can't run a car off the road like a horse,' Peter explained to him. 'I've got to stay on the metal and there's only room for one.'

'Yes, and Mrs Carruthers is the one,' said father angrily. 'It's getting so I'm frightened to take a young horse out on the roads. If I could get a horse that would face that car I'd drive straight at you.'

After that Peter always stopped when father wanted to pass him with a young horse, but even then the horse went careering out on to the grass with father reefing on the reins and swearing.

He hated cars, but he told me they were here to stay.

'When you are as old as me, Alan,' he said, 'you'll have to go to the zoo to see a horse. The day of the horse is done.'

He was getting fewer horses to break in and prices were rising, yet he managed to save ten pounds for some jars of brown ointment which mother rubbed into my legs. It was an American treatment known as the Viavi System and the salesman who sold it to father guaranteed it would make me walk.

Month after month mother massaged my legs, using jar after jar of ointment till none was left.

Father had no faith in it from the beginning, 'but like a fool I hoped for a miracle,' he commented bitterly when mother told him the treatment was over.

He had prepared me for its failure and I was not disappointed.

'I'm not going to waste any more time on cures,' I told him. 'It holds me back.'

'That's what I think,' he replied.

I was now riding ponies he had quietened and was having frequent falls. Ponies, newly-broken, shied readily and I could never learn to sit a shier.

I was convinced that each fall I had would be my last, but father thought differently.

'We all say that, son. We say it after every fall. When a bloke has his last tumble he don't know it.'

But my falls troubled him. He was restless with indecision then, with sudden resolve, he began teaching me how to fall – relaxed and limp so that the blow from the ground was cushioned on yielding muscle.

'You can always beat a thing,' he impressed upon me. 'If not one way, then another.'

He was quick with solutions to the problems presented by my crutches, but what I was to do when I left school – this he could not answer.

It was only two months to the end of the year and my final day at school. Mr Simmons, the storekeeper at Turalla, had promised to give me five shillings a week to keep his books after I left school, but though it pleased me to think I would be earning money, I wanted work that would test me; that would demand the exercise of that part of my mind that was my possession alone.

'What do you want to be?' father asked me.

'I want to write books.'

'Well, that's all right,' he said. 'You can do that, but how are you going to earn your living?'

'Men make money writing books,' I argued.

'Yes, but only after years and years – and then you have to be well educated. Peter Finlay tells me writing a book is the hardest thing in the world – he's tried it. Mind you, I'm all for you writing a book; don't think I'm not, but you've got to learn first.'

He stood in silence thinking for a moment and when he spoke again it was as if he knew I was going to be a writer some day.

'When you write,' he said, 'be like Robert Blatchford. That's the bloke that wrote *Not Guilty* and it's a great book. It was written to help people.

'You see,' he went on, 'it's no good writing a book for money. I'd sooner break in horses. When you break in horses you make something good out of something that could be bad. It's easy to turn out an outlaw but it's hard to give a horse – well, sort of ... you know ... character, say – make him work with you instead of against you.

'When I first met Peter Finlay he gave me a book called *My Brilliant Career*. He reckons a woman wrote it but she calls herself Miles Franklin. It's the best book I've ever read. She never baulks a fence. She's game, got heart....

'I don't know ... writing's funny ... I don't think you see it right. You'd like to have a hell of a good time in a book you'd write. Now, that is ... maybe, when you've been tossed a few times you'll see it my way.'

We were sitting on the top rail of the horseyard looking at a colt he was mouthing. The horse champed at the heavy, mouthing bit. The corners of its mouth were red and raw.

'That colt's too long in the back,' he said suddenly, then went on, 'If a bloke gave you a hundred quid for a book you can bet your life it's his way, but if all the poor and suffering people raise their hats to you for writing it – that's different; it makes it worth while then. But you'll have to mix it with people first. You'll like them. We own this country and we'll make it a paradise. Men are equal here. Good luck to you, anyway,' he added, 'you write books. But take this job at Simmons' till you find your feet.'

Mr Simmons showed me an advertisement in the *Age* a few days later. A business college in Melbourne was offering a scholarship for training an Accountancy to those who could pass an examination in History, Geography, Arithmetic and English, the papers for which would be sent to the local schoolmaster on application.

I wrote away for these papers and a week later Mr Tucker told me they had arrived.

'You will notice, Marshall,' he told me severely, as if I had made an accusation against him, 'that the seal on these examination papers is intact. It is therefore impossible to tamper with the papers in any way. I have told William Foster about this examination and he will also be sitting for the scholarship. I'd like you to present yourself at the school at 10 a.m. sharp on Saturday morning. You may return to your seat.'

William Foster was Tucker's pet and his star pupil. He could name all the Victorian rivers without drawing a breath and could do mental arithmetic with both hands on his head to show he didn't count with his fingers.

He curved a concealing arm round his exercise book when working and he was hard to copy from, but I had often managed it by jabbing him in the ribs when I wanted his arm removed.

His mother was very proud of him and told my mother that, only for him, I would never get a sum right.

When I met him outside the school on the Saturday morning I suggested we sit together for the examination, but he had his Sunday suit on and it infected his attitude towards me. He was stiff and uncooperative and told me his mother had said not to let me sit near him.

This was a blow but I followed him into school and sat beside him despite his efforts to shake me off.

Mr Tucker observed my tactics and ordered me to the other end of the room where I sat looking through the window at Mt Turalla, green and vivid in the sunshine. I was thinking of Joe and what a great day it was for rabbiting when Mr Tucker rapped the desk and made an announcement.

'I am now about to break the seal securing the examination papers of Poulter's Business College,' he said. 'You will both note that the seal is intact.'

He then snapped the string and withdrew the papers from the wrapping, keeping his cruel eyes on me as he did so.

For the next twenty minutes he sat reading the papers, sometimes frowning, sometimes raising his head and looking approvingly at William Foster who lowered his head in acknowledgment of this assurance.

I would like to have punched Tucker fair in the eye, then dashed away to Joe.

I was busy explaining to Joe exactly how I did it when Tucker handed us our papers. He glanced at the clock as he did so and said crisply, 'It is now ten-thirty; you have till eleven-thirty to finish this paper.'

I looked at the printed yellow sheet in front of me.

'Work out the compound interest on . . .'

Huh, this was easy . . .

'If ten men took . . .'

Cripes, proportion! This was a soda.

'A piece containing four acres three roods two perches . . .

This was harder – hm!

I set to work while Tucker sat at his desk reading *The Field*, an English magazine with shiny pages.

I did not find the papers very hard, but when I compared my answers with William Foster after we left the schoolroom I concluded most of my answers were wrong, since they didn't agree with those given by William.

When I reached home I told father I had failed and he replied, 'Never mind. You had a crack at it; that's the main thing.'

A week before school broke up a long, brown envelope addressed to me came in the mail. It had been delivered to father and he was waiting in the kitchen with Mary and mother, for me to open it when I returned from school.

They gathered round me as I broke the flap and pulled out the folded paper.

Dear Sir,
    We take pleasure in announcing that you have been awarded a full scholarship . . .

'I've got it!' I exclaimed unbelievingly, looking at them as if for an explanation.

'Show me,' said father, taking the letter from my hands.

'He's got it all right!' he exclaimed excitedly when he finished the letter. 'Here, you read it,' He handed the letter to mother. 'Can you believe it! It says it all right. Fancy – a scholarship! Who would've thought as he'd've got a scholarship! I can't believe it.' He turned and clapped my back. 'Good on ya, son. You're a champion,' then to mother, 'What's the scholarship for, again? Let's look. What does it make him?'

'An accountant,' said Mary, who was looking at the letter from above mother's shoulders. 'An accountant has an office to himself and everything.'

'Who's an accountant round here?' asked father, seeking enlightenment. 'Would the bookkeeper in the big store at Balunga be an accountant, now?'

'No,' said mother decidedly. 'Of course not. He's a bookkeeper. Accountants have to be very clever.'

'Mr Bryan would be an accountant,' said Mary. 'He's the Secretary of the butter factory. Someone said he gets six pounds a week.'

'If he gets that someone's a liar,' said father decidedly. 'I don't think the manager gets that. I'll go up and find out from him what this accountant really is. It sounds like our troubles are over, anyway. If Alan ever makes six quid a week he needn't call the king his uncle.'

Father didn't waste any time. He saddled a horse and made for the factory. When he returned late in the afternoon he had further astounding news – William Foster had failed.

'It's right,' father exclaimed, unable to hide his excitement. 'I met Mrs Foster and she told me – as if it were wonderful, mind you – that she had got a letter saying William could sit for the examination next year. You should've seen her when I told her about Alan – hell!

'And I saw Bryan, too,' he went on. 'You're right, Mary, he's an accountant all right. And he told me that top-ranking accountants can get over six quid a week though, you never know, he might be talking through his hat. Anyway, they look after the books of big companies – oil companies and places like that. When they become accountants they have letters after their name – wait till I see. I wrote them down on a piece of paper.'

He fumbled in his pocket a moment then found the paper he was seeking. 'Just a minute now. I wrote it down while Bryan was telling me. Here it is – L.I.C.A. and that means – I've got it here – Licentiate of the Institute of Commonwealth Accountants, whatever that is. There's not many blokes got it, so Bryan says. According to him it seems an important thing to get, those letters. . . .'

He looked at me approvingly. 'I never thought I'd live to see the day that Alan has letters after his name.'

On a sudden impulse he lifted me in his arms, big as I was, and gave me a hug.

He got drunk that night and came whooping home when we were all in bed, and I heard mother ask anxiously, 'Any fights?'

'No,' said father, 'a couple of swings, that's all.'

For the next week he and mother sat up late at night, talking and working out figures on paper, and I knew they were discussing my future.

'Mum and I have decided that we all shift to Melbourne, Alan,' father told me one day. 'It'll take us a while to fix things up, but when we do we'll pack up our swags and beat it. Your future is down there, not here. I'll get work; that'll be easy enough. And you can take a job in an office while you're learning how to be an accountant. Any office'd rush you when they knew you got a scholarship. Anyway, I'm not doing so well here now. And it'll get worse, what with the number of cars you see getting round. I must have seen eight or nine today.' Then he added, 'How do you feel about leaving here?'

'Good,' I said. 'I'll learn to be a writer the same time as I learn to be an accountant. It'll be great, I reckon.'

'That's what I reckon,' he said.

But when, alone, I thought it over, I suddenly felt that I could never leave the bush from which, in some strange way, I gained my strength. I had never seen a city. Now I saw it as some vast complex machine attended by hosts of L.I.C.A.'s with their ledgers and sunless faces. The thought depressed me and I sought out Joe who was setting traps in the bush behind his house.

When I told him we would soon be going away to live in Melbourne he looked thoughtfully at the trap in his hand and said, 'You're a lucky cow; there's no doubt about it. But you always been lucky. Remember when you caught two rabbits in the one trap?'

'Yes,' I answered, pleased with the memory.

We sat down together on the grass and talked about Melbourne and the trams that were there and the thousands of people and of how I would earn six pounds a week.

'The best thing about it,' reflected Joe, 'is that you'll be able to go to the museum any time you want to. They tell me there's everything there.'

'I suppose so,' I said. 'I'll go there I suppose, but I want to write books. There's a big library in Melbourne. I'll go there, I reckon.'

'You'll have to give up riding,' said Joe. 'A horse'll come down in Melbourne quicker than anywhere.'

'Yes, that's the crook part about it,' I said, feeling depressed again. 'Anyway, trams take you where you want to go.'

'I wonder how you'll get on with your crutches down there?' Joe mused. 'The crowds an' that . . .?'

'Crutches!' I exclaimed, dismissing the inference contemptuously. 'Crutches are nothing . . .!'

KENNETH COOK
WAKE IN FRIGHT

May you dream of the Devil
and wake in fright

An old curse

CHAPTER 1

He sat at his desk, wearily watching the children file out of the room, reflecting that, this term at least, it was reasonable to assume that none of the girls was pregnant.

'Good-bye, sir,' said the last of the children to leave.

'Good-bye, Mason,' said the teacher, 'I'll see you next term,' and the small, shabby figure was lost in the glare of the doorway – the class was now no more than a babble of eager voices floating and fading in the heat.

The teacher looked around the empty room, which comprised the whole of the school, apart from some crude toilet facilities in the grounds. Twenty-two desks for twenty-eight pupils, boys and girls aged from five to seventeen. Twenty-eight pupils, twenty-seven at school only because the law insisted on their being educated until they were at least fifteen or because some desperate farmer, clawing a living from the clods of the great inland plains, thought that in education there might be for his child a little of the hope that he had abandoned.

And the twenty-eighth, young Mason – eleven years old, hungry to learn, eager, intelligent and inexplicably sensitive, but doomed to join the railway gangs as soon as he was legally old enough, because his father was a ganger.

The teacher stood up and flexed his shoulders to loosen the wet shirt from his body and began to close and lock the windows.

Through the glass he could see the plains stretching west, broken only by rare clumps of the hardy salt-bush that managed to draw sustenance even here where the earth had been innocent of any trace of moisture for months. Somehow people coaxed a living from the semi-desert, somehow they ran sheep and cattle – one head every ten acres – and kept them alive while they gained enough condition to bring a few pounds in the coastal markets of Australia; but the school-teacher could never understand how. Some people, owners of thousands of square miles, even made fortunes here by waiting for the occasional falls of rain, then bringing in herds to feed on the carpet of green grass that appeared overnight. But now there had been no rain for almost a year, the sun had withered every living thing except the salt-bush. The people had withered, their skins contracting and their eyes sinking as their stock became white bones. But they stayed in the wooden homes, because they believed the rain would fall some time.

The schoolteacher knew that somewhere not far out in the shimmering haze was the State border, marked by a broken fence, and that farther out in the heat was the silent centre of Australia, the Dead Heart. He looked through the windows almost with pleasure, because tonight he would be on his way to Bundanyabba; tomorrow morning he would board an aircraft; and tomorrow night he would be in Sydney, and on Sunday he would swim in the sea. For the schoolteacher was a coastal Australian, a native of the strip of continent lying between the Pacific Ocean and the Great Dividing Range, where Nature deposited the graces she so firmly withheld from the west.

The sea, twelve hundred miles to the east, had swelled and fallen in its tides, day in and day out for a year, and he had not seen it. For twelve months he had been master of the one-teacher school at Tiboonda, twelve months with only his leave pay to carry him through the term holidays. So he had spent them in Bundanyabba, the mining city of sixty thousand people which was the centre of life in the territory around the border. But to the schoolteacher it was just a larger variation of Tiboonda, and Tiboonda was a variation of hell.

But now the long Christmas vacation had arrived, six weeks' leave, with six weeks' pay. Two weeks' pay would cover his air fare to Sydney and back, and there would be four weeks' pay left, eked out by judicious visits to relatives. Six weeks by the sea, to just lie in the water and soak out the dust that had seeped into his being.

He finished with the windows and looked around, aware of the smell of the classroom which always seemed stronger when the children had gone. A chalky smell, an inky smell, a suggestion of body smells and stale sandwiches and brown apple cores, all mingled with the smell of the dust which, even in the room, stirred and eddied about his feet as he moved.

He picked up his brief-case and walked out into the sun. He always winced when the sun hit him. He could not pick up the trick the locals had of keeping their eyes perpetually screwed in a squint. He forced the wooden door into its sagging frame and turned the lock. Then he shook his head and fished out his sun-glasses. In a year in the west he had not been able to make up his mind whether the glasses were any use or not. The glare was white with them off and grey with them on, if glare can be grey, and the shafts of white came in at the side, like little pointed pieces of stone driving at his eyes.

He tried to keep his lids closed as much as possible as he walked across the school yard, past the fiction of a sapling fence that rose out of the white dust in futile protest against the possibility of stray cattle wandering into the playing area.

The road was distinguishable from the paddocks only by the deep tyre tracks in the dust, and the schoolteacher could feel his feet sinking in it as he walked.

One hundred yards from the school was the hotel, and near that the railway siding called Tiboonda Station. The three buildings made up the township of Tiboonda. All were timber and iron, all built in the monotonous, low box-form that characterizes western architecture; and all were riddled with white ants and dry-rot. They stood in the plain abjectly, as though they no longer made any serious claim to constitute a township.

The schoolteacher walked slowly, trying not to raise the dust. In all directions little white clouds showed where his pupils, on foot, bicycle, and horseback, were scattering to the railway camps, farmhouses and native shanties where they lived.

For them six weeks' holiday meant six weeks here where the creek bed was dry and cracked and the water to drink had to be brought from Bundanyabba by train, and all they could do was play in the dust, or perhaps tease the wild camels whose ancestors formed the inland transport system.

He reached the hotel and walked across the drooping veranda floor into the bar. It was shady there, but not cool. It was never cool in Tiboonda, except at night in deep winter when the cold bit into your bones. In the winter you wished for the summer, in the summer you wished for the winter, and all the time you wished to blazes you were a thousand miles from Tiboonda. But you had two years to fill in for the Education Department, and if you left before that, you forfeited the bond your uncle had put up for you when you were fool enough to think you wanted to take up teaching for a living. And so you'd stay here for another year, unless by the grace of God you could persuade the Department to move you east before that, and God probably didn't have that much grace to spare.

'Schooner, Charlie,' he said to the hotel-keeper, who emerged from his dark back room wearing, for some reason, a waistcoat over his drenched shirt.

Charlie pulled the beer.

In the remote towns of the west there are few of the amenities of civilization; there is no sewerage, there are no hospitals, rarely a doctor; the food is dreary and flavourless from long carrying, the water is bad; electricity is for a few who can afford their own plant, roads are mostly non-existent; there are no theatres, no picture shows and few dance halls; and the people are saved from stark insanity by the one strong principle of progress that is ingrained for a thousand miles, east, north, south and west of the Dead Heart – the beer is always cold.

The teacher let his fingers curl around the beaded glass, quelling the little spurt of bitterness that rose when he saw the size of the head of froth on the beer, because, after all, it didn't matter, and this poor devil of a hotel-keeper had to stay here and he was going east.

He drank quickly at first, swamping the dryness in his throat in a flood of beer; and then, when the glass was half empty, he drank slowly, letting the cold alcohol relax his body.

'Will you be wanting your room when you come back?' asked Charlie, scratching his belly through a tear in the shirt.

'Where else would I stay?'

'Fella before you stayed in a caravan, Jackie: thought you might want a change from the old pub too.'

The hotel-keeper was mocking him with the sneering irony that western people used on those who show no affection for their desolate territory.

'I'll be back here.'

'I'll try and keep your room for you.' The only permanent guests Charlie ever had were the masters of the Tiboonda school.

'Thanks.'

If by any chance the hotel were burned down would the Department have to close the school? Or would another small wooden box be hastily thrown up in the school grounds to provide the master with accommodation?

'Having another one, Jack?'

'Thanks.' He pushed the glass across the stained and grooved bar top and drew a packet of cigarettes from his pocket.

It was almost two hours since he had smoked at the afternoon recess, and the tingling satisfaction supplemented the beer; he looked almost kindly upon the hotel-keeper. But he had to look away soon.

Charlie had served the second glass of beer and was leaning against the shelves of bottles that served to bolster the illusion that there were those within fifty miles of Tiboonda who would think of drinking anything but beer. He was sucking on the disintegrating remains of a hand-made cigarette. Soon he spat the obscene object on to the floor.

'Going on the four-fifteen, Jack?'

'Yes.' He glanced at the hotel-keeper's fat and grimy hands and decided he did not want the rest of his beer.

'See you in six weeks, Charlie.'

'Sure, Jack. See you then.' Charlie grinned without humour or goodwill, as though he knew the schoolteacher's return to Tiboonda was something he did not want to think about.

'Good-bye, Charlie,' and good-bye to the stifling back room, the greasy meals prepared by Charlie's half-caste mistress in the filthy kitchen; good-bye to the sleepless nights and the arid dawns when the soft light gave false promise of a moment's release from the heat; good-bye to his twenty-eight pupils and their suspicious parents with shamed faces; good-bye Tiboonda, for six weeks at any rate.

He had his two suitcases packed and waiting in the bar, and he picked them up and walked across to the station. The single line swung out across the plain in a long curve, black against the dust. On the horizon he could see the small, dark cloud that could have been the first finger of a rain cloud. The cloud was almost imperceptibly running down the line, and in half an hour or so the four-fifteen would be in Tiboonda.

He wished he had stayed in the hotel a little longer because the lean-to shelter on the station offered no determined opposition to the direct beat of the sun; but it was doubtful whether the sun was worse than Charlie in any case.

He took out his wallet, and inspected his pay cheque again. One hundred and forty pounds, six weeks' wages and district allowance. There should be no trouble changing it to buy his ticket at the airways office, any bank would probably take a Departmental cheque once he established his identity.

There were twenty pound notes in his wallet as well, the savings from his wages for the past term. He had calculated on saving a hundred, but beer was expensive in Tiboonda, and a man felt he had either to drink or blow his brains out.

Still, he must take it a little more easily next term. 'Next term', the thought was like a nervous start, 'next term', six weeks away, another year in Tiboonda would begin again. Another year in this apology for a town, himself an outcast in a community of people who were at home in the bleak and frightening land that spread out

around him now, hot, dry and careless of itself and the people who
professed to own it.

Better not think about that. Better not think about anything,
except the sea, draw the image across his mind like a deep shadow
and pretend that it warded off the heat that seemed to thrust long,
hot fingers through his skull into the living, tender cells of his brain.

In its own good time the four-fifteen arrived at Tiboonda. Its
alternate name was the Friday Train, which distinguished it from
the Monday Train. The two were Tiboonda's only transport connection with the outside world, represented by Bundanyabba, apart
from the road, which could not be travelled when it rained because
of the mud, nor when it was dry because of the dust which would
bog cars just as hopelessly as mud would.

The Friday Train pulled a dozen freight cars and two passenger
carriages. The engine was the superb type of monster that can only
be found in the remoter sections of the Commonwealth, and which
always reminded the teacher of the sort of thing Indians chased in
American Western films.

Even before the train pulled into the siding, he could hear the
singing. On every slow train in the west they sing, the stockmen
and the miners, the general storekeepers and the drifting workers;
the aborigines and the half-castes shyly joining in on the outskirts.
And somebody always has a mouth-organ, and they sing with
desperate, tuneless gaiety the songs of the American hit parades
which filter through the networks of the Australian Broadcasting
Commission or from the static-ridden apparatus of the occasional
country radio station.

Out over the desert plains, behind the roar and grind of the
ancient engines, the dreary words and trite tunes of modern
America caused the dingoes to cock their ears in wonder, and
deepened measurably the sadness that permeates the outback of
Australia.

The singers had all congregated in the front carriage. The
schoolteacher boarded the rear carriage. He didn't want to sing. He
was alone except for a middle-aged aboriginal stockman with white
hair and the stubble of a white beard. He was a full-blood, with the
broad features of his people, and he stared constantly out of the
window as though there might be something in the plains he had
not seen before.

The schoolteacher had seen the plains, and he had made the trip
to Bundanyabba before, so he knew that, for the six-hour journey
ahead, the countryside would change so little there would be
almost nothing to indicate that the train had moved.

He put his bags on the luggage rack, opened a window, and stretched out on a seat, with his feet poised on an arm-rest.

'There is a heart that's made for you,' the singers were chanting,

> *A heart that needs your love divine,*
> *A heart that could be strong and true,*
> *If only you would say you're mine.*
> *If we should part my heart would break,*
> *Oh say that this will never be,*
> *Oh darling please, your promise make,*
> *That you'll belong to only me.*

And that, thought the schoolteacher, was the fate of a race of singers who had long since forgotten how to make songs.

He closed his eyes as the train began to move. The clatter of the wheels, the sound of the engine and the discordant cries of the singers formed a senseless rhythm as he drifted into the semi-coma of the train traveller.

The Friday Train swayed on across the plains and once every five miles or so there would be a decrepit homestead, and the train driver would sound his whistle. A ragged band of children would assemble and conscientiously wave and wave until the train was out of sight and there was no more train until Monday.

Eventually the sun relinquished its torturing hold and the plains became brown and purple and gold and then black as the sky was pierced by a million bursts of flickering light from dispassionate worlds unthinkable distances apart. The homesteads were just yellow patches of light in window-frames, but the train driver sounded his whistle just the same and, in the darkness, there were children waving just the same.

The schoolteacher shook himself into full consciousness as the train approached Bundanyabba. The city was a smatter of lights rather higher than the level of the plains, looking a little like the lights of a cluster of ships riding motionless on a still dark sea.

The teacher took off his sun-glasses and tucked them in his breast pocket. The singers had given up now and were presumably devoting themselves to gathering their luggage and shaking off the fug of an hour or so's dozing.

The Friday Train was rocking through the city and he looked out on the rows of weatherboard houses, built on tiny blocks of land as though there was a scarcity of space, or as though they had to huddle together to form a garrison against the loneliness of the outback.

The schoolteacher knew Bundanyabba fairly well from the two term holidays he had spent there. He had swum in the chlorinated swimming-pool, attended the picture theatres, drunk the heavily preserved beer that had to be railed from the coast, and thus had exhausted the pleasures offered. He wished there had been an aircraft flying eastwards that evening.

The train stopped with a relieved clatter as though glad it had arrived, and rather surprised that it had successfully traversed the plains once more. Grant carried his bags through the bustle on the station and handed the forward half of his return ticket to the collector. The other half he carefully stowed in his wallet against the time when he would pass through these gates again. He consciously ignored the torn scrap of cardboard's silent statement that he had not seen the last of Tiboonda.

Outside the station several taxi-drivers were waiting, touting for custom. The schoolteacher engaged one and gave him the address of the hotel to which he had written booking a room for the night.

'New to The Yabba?' said the taxi-driver as he drove through the wide streets, lined with buildings affecting awnings supported by poles which looked as though they suffered from rickets.

'Yes,' said the schoolteacher.

'Staying long?'

'Just tonight.'

'That's hard luck. You ought to see a bit more of The Yabba than that.'

One would have thought, reflected the teacher, that the driver was trying to sell a conducted tour, but he had noticed before that all the people of Bundanyabba seemed to be extremely patriotic.

'You think its worth seeing?' he said.

'I'll say I do. Everybody likes The Yabba. Best place in Australia.'

'So? Why?' He knew he was taking a risk, the determination of Bundanyabba people to deliver monologues on the virtues of the place required less encouragement than that. Still he was only committed to listen for the length of the taxi journey.

'Well,' the driver was saying, 'it's a free and easy place. Nobody cares who you are or where you come from; as long as you're a good bloke you're all right. Friendly place it is. I've been here eight years. Came out from Sydney because I had a bad chest. Chest cleared up in six months but I wouldn't think of leavin' The Yabba.'

The schoolteacher had also previously observed the friendly

habits of the people of Bundanyabba, and found them crude and embarrassing. As for the city's therapeutic qualities, the taxi-driver looked sallow and drawn, and distinctly in need of a change to the kinder climate of the coast.

'Try and stay a bit longer,' urged the taxi-driver as the school-teacher paid him.

The teacher fancied he had been overcharged, but he wasn't sure.

The girl behind the reception desk at the hotel was a faded facsimile of girls behind reception desks all over the world.

'Have you a room for John Grant? I made a booking by letter.'

The girl picked up a larger ledger without speaking and began turning over the pages. Grant put down his suitcases and stood waiting patiently enough. The girl found the page containing the night's bookings and slowly ran a finger down the column from the top. The finger stopped half-way down the page and she looked up.

'You only stopping the night?'

'That's all.'

'You'll have to pay now.'

'That will be all right.'

'Will you be wanting breakfast?'

'Yes, please.'

'Then it will be one pound ten.'

He took out two pound notes and gave them to her. She handed him in return a large piece of metal inscribed with the number seven and with two keys attached.

'One's for the front door and one's for your room,' said the girl in a monotone, as though she had said it many times before, which of course she had, 'there's ten shillings deposit on the keys. You'll get that back when you bring the keys back.'

'Good, thank you.'

She lost interest in him and returned to the vacuous contemplation practised by her kind.

'Could you tell me where room seven is, please?'

'Up-the-steps-and-down-the-corridor-to-the-right,' she said, as though it was all one word, without raising her eyes.

She at least was no apostle of the friendship doctrine of Bundanyabba, thought Grant.

Room number seven had an iron bedstead, an unpromising mattress, a small wardrobe, a chest of drawers and an unstable-looking table with a Bible and a jug of water on it. The Bible and the water-jug looked equally ancient and unused. Grant was thirsty, but Bundanyabba water, even when not contained in jugs like that, was so heavily chlorinated and so hard with natural chemicals that he had always found that drinking it was similar in effect to taking those harsh laxatives the newspaper advertisements were always warning about.

He dropped his suitcases on the bed and went out to find a café where he could get something to eat and drink. It was well after ten o'clock and the doors of the hotel bars were pulled to, although not quite shut, which was the Bundanyabba method of obeying the law that forbade the sale of liquor after ten o'clock at night and at any time on Sundays.

Grant passed a number of spotty milk-bar cafés which cropped up at fairly regular intervals, emitting uninviting odours of greasy chipped potatoes and milky coffee into the main street.

He began to feel that perhaps a couple of drinks were desirable before eating, and went into the first hotel he came to. It had bat-wing doors outside the main doors, like most of the hotels in Bundanyabba. These had to be pulled open and the main doors pushed open. Grant carefully pushed the main door to again, in deference to local usage.

It was hard to decide whether it was hotter inside the hotel or out in the street. The island bar was ringed with dense crowds of men and, inside, the hotel-keeper with heavy blue veins bulging from a reddened face, pulled beer with clumsy rapidity, at the same time urging two depressed and wispy barmaids to greater efforts.

'Men wanting a drink behind you there, Jean. Just a minute mate, and the girl will serve you. Two schooners? Right! Coming up. Four middies over here, Mary. All right, boys, just a minute and we'll get to you. Hello there, Jack, what're you having?' False good fellowship struggled with satisfied avarice to make up the expression on his hot, wet, mobile face; and it was even money which was the more successful.

The clang of the cash register rang steadily through the smoke-filled room above the clamour of fifty men all talking loudly and at once.

Knowing it was useless to hope that any of the dozens of hotels in Bundanyabba would be any less crowded, Grant threaded his way through to the bar and managed to obtain a beer from one of the women. He retreated to a corner, took out his cigarettes and found he had no matches. The effort of getting back to the bar to buy a box was too great, and he looked about for someone to ask for a light.

A uniformed policeman was leaning against the wall near him, drinking alone.

'Could I get a light from you?' said Grant.

'Sure,' said the policeman, dredging in his hip pocket. He came up with a large lighter fitted with an enormous wind-shield.

'New to The Yabba?' he asked, inevitably, holding a great stem of yellow flame to Grant's cigarette.

Grant concentrated on lighting the cigarette without singeing his nose before answering.

'Just dropped in for the night,' he said eventually, 'flying to Sydney in the morning.'

'Ah. Come from far?'

'Tiboonda ... I'm the schoolteacher out there.'

'Oh, the schoolteacher, eh? Let's see, then, your name would be ... ?'

Grant let him wait a little while then said, 'Grant.'

'That's right. You took over from old Murchison, didn't you?'

'McDonald his name was.'

'That's right, McDonald. Well what do you know ... my name's Jock Crawford.' He held out a large hand.

'John Grant,' he said. This sort of thing always happened in Bundanyabba. Still, it wouldn't matter just for that night. This time tomorrow night he would be in Sydney and Bundanyabba would be many miles and six weeks away.

'Will you have a drink, John?'

'Er – well yes, thanks.' It still distressed him a little when people, upon being introduced to him, immediately called him by his first name. Yet everybody he had ever met in the west did just that.

A lane through the crowd formed automatically for the police-man and he was served promptly by the hotel-keeper himself. He was back in less than two minutes.

'Do you like the Huntleigh beer, John?'

'Yes. It seems all right. Is it my imagination or is it a bit strong?' It was a worn subject, but one Bundanyabba people loved.

'It's got a hell of a kick. You want to watch it if you're not used to it. They have to put a lot of arsenic in it to preserve it on the way up here.'

Grant looked at the beer sceptically.

'Arsenic?'

'So they say.'

'Mmm. What time do the pubs close here?' He knew the answer, but he was curious about the police view of the trading hours.

'When the crowd goes home. Sometimes midnight, sometimes they don't close at all ... pay nights that is, mostly.'

'The police don't worry about it?'

'No. What's the use. Long as they keep the doors shut and don't make too much row we don't bother about them. If we did close 'em at ten there'd only be a lot of sly grog shops spring up.'

It struck Grant that this was a curious conversation to be having with a constable who was drinking in a hotel while in uniform. Fairly obviously the police were reasonably tolerant. There was nothing to be gained in labouring the point.

'Yes. Well. Um. Will you have another drink?'

'Yeah. Sure.'

Grant made to take the policeman's glass.

'Here, give us your dough. I'll get 'em quicker than you.'

Grant submissively handed over a ten-shilling note and the policeman was again back in two minutes with the beer. He gave Grant his change.

'You've finished work for the day?' said Grant.

'Just started. I'm on the hotel beat. Been on it all this week so far. It's pretty good, y'know; I don't pay for any of the beer I drink.'

Grant didn't quite know how to react, so he just said: 'Don't you?'

'I could get yours free too, but it'd be making it a bit thick, wouldn't it.'

'Yes ... yes of course.'

'We do the pubs a bit of good one way and another, y'know,' said the policeman, by way of justification, Grant presumed.

He felt himself beginning to expand under the influence of the beer. He hadn't eaten for ten hours. The heat in the bar was pressing less heavily upon him; the noise no longer crashed into his brain, but beat more remotely around him.

He looked into the raw, freckled face of the policeman.

'Been in The Yabba long, Jock?' he said, luxuriating a little in his faint irony.

'All m'life, John.'

'Ever think of leaving?'

'Leaving The Yabba? Not on your life. Best little town in the world this is.'

'Ever been anywhere else?'

'Did three months' training in the city. Didn't like it.'

Grant suddenly realized his private joke was not particularly good. He drained his glass.

'I'd better get along,' he said, 'haven't eaten yet.'

'Have another one before you go.'

'No thanks, I won't. It's a bit much on an empty stomach.'

'Go on, won't do you any harm.' The policeman winked heavily: 'It's on the house.'

Why not? thought Grant. It would be hard enough to sleep on that bed, anyway. He handed his glass to the policeman who again went through his crowd-penetrating routine.

'We'll just have this round here and we'll go along to the next pub. I've got to look in on them all tonight,' said the policeman when he came back.

Grant wondered what the incidence was of diseased liver among members of the Bundanyabba police force.

'I won't be drinking any more, thanks, Jock. I'll have to eat,' he said, realizing nevertheless that he had been put in the position of having to complete the round.

The policeman seemed content with that and addressed himself to his beer.

Soon he said: 'Where are you going to eat?'

'I don't know. Where's a good place?'

'The Two-up School's pretty good if you want a good steak.'

Grant, like every Australian, had heard of Two-up Schools. Every city has one and in the outback, miners, labourers, railway-men, anybody desperate for diversion, and that is almost every-body – will gather from a radius of a hundred miles to wager on the fall of the illegal pennies.

'They serve meals at the Two-up School, do they?' he asked.

'Best in town,' said the policeman, with the proprietorial pride which all Bundanyabba people evinced when they spoke of the city's excesses.

'Where is the place?'

'Just around the corner from the main street, I'll take you round there in a minute.'

Grant wondered whether free bets were allowed the police in Bundanyabba, but he did not raise the point with Crawford. He was beginning to like the policeman and, dimly, he was aware that this was a strong indication that he had drunk too much.

Crawford had finished his beer and was fiddling expectantly with the glass.

'A couple more?' said Grant, because he didn't know how to avoid it. He handed over the money and Crawford went for the beer. He took a little longer this time and when he came back he said, 'I slung your change to the girl . . . told her it was yours . . . do you a bit of good when you come in again.'

Grant could have pointed out that it was not at all likely that he would ever come in here again, and even less likely that the barmaid would remember him if he did; but he said nothing. He was smoking one cigarette after another now, as men do when they are drinking.

'Police have much to do in Bundanyabba?' he asked without really caring much whether they did or not.

'No, John, no; on the whole, no! We just keep an eye on things.' Crawford became a shade ponderous as he spoke in a semi-official capacity.

'Not much crime?'

'Almost none at all, John, nothing serious anyway. About the honestest town in Australia this is.'

'So?' Grant strove to look impressed.

Crawford rather spoiled the effect of his declaration by adding: ''Course no one's really game to try anything because we'd get 'em so quickly.'

'So?'

'It's so isolated, see? You can't get out of the place in a hurry without everybody knowing about it.'

'No. I suppose not. Then it's a pretty easy life for you?'

'It's pretty good,' said Crawford: ''Course we do have quite a few suicides ... they're a bit of trouble.'

Grant remembered having heard something of the suicide rate in Bundanyabba and the local custom of declaring the most blatant acts of self-destruction 'accidental death'. He asked the policeman why.

'Well,' said the policeman thoughtfully, 'I suppose it's because so many suicides give the place a bad name.'

Grant had heard another story about Bundanyabba to the effect that the local authorities kept the official thermometer on the lawn in front of the Town Hall. When the temperature rose above one hundred degrees in the shade, the lawn sprinklers were turned on to cool the thermometer down. In this way Bundanyabba's official maximum temperature seldom rose above one hundred degrees.

There was, reflected Grant, possibly some connection between the official attitudes towards suicide and high temperatures, although he was inclined to disbelieve the story about the thermometer.

Anyhow, the whole thing was far too complicated to pursue at this stage of the evening.

'I really must go and eat, I'm afraid,' he said.

'Have another before you go?'

'No. No really, I've had enough thanks; I'll pass out if I don't eat soon.'

'Easy seen you're not a Yabba-man, John,' said the policeman. 'Come and I'll take you round to the School.' The School, Grant realized, was another name for the Two-up game. More commonly still it was simply referred to as 'the Game'.

The noise of the bar dropped away as though they had shed something tangible when they stepped out into the main street. Grant tried to count the number of beers he had drunk, but found he couldn't. 'Fresh' would have been a gross misnomer for the air in the main street, but it was different from the air in the bar and Grant felt its effect.

He looked affectionately at Crawford. A character, that's what Crawford was, a fascinating chunk of local colour. He, John Grant, was savouring him to while away the time, making an erudite little study of Bundanyabba man. Grant stumbled slightly stepping from the footpath to the road.

Crawford led him a couple of blocks down the main street, talking at length on the features of life in Bundanyabba. Grant wondered whether Bundanyabba people talked as much among themselves as they did to strangers about the virtues of their city. He had the impression that they did, the city seemed to be an obsession with them. Yabba-Men – wasn't yabba aboriginal for talk? That seemed to be the basis for a pun, but he could not tie the threads of the thought together.

Crawford turned into one of the main cross-streets and a few yards down they entered a long dark lane. The lane ran parallel with the main street, and on one side Grant could see the backs of the business premises and shops silhouetted against the sky. On the other side were the tall paling fences bordering the backyards of people's homes.

There were no lights in the lane, and the buildings threw a dark shadow so that up to a foot or so above head level all was complete darkness. Grant became aware of many figures in the darkness. Twenty or so men were standing about in the lane, talking in low voices. Cigarettes glowed orange and then dimmed as men smoked, and often a match would flare briefly yellow. As his eyes became accustomed to the darkness, Grant saw that he and Crawford were attracting mild attention.

'How goes it, Jock?' a voice would drift from knots of men.

'Not bad, Jim, how's it?' Crawford would reply, identifying people by their voices as far as Grant could make out, because he could not distinguish the features on a single face.

They came to a gate where two men were standing with the
nonchalance only adopted by men standing guard.

'G'night, Jock,' they said, as Crawford and Grant drew near.
Grant could see they were looking at him as piercingly as one could
look piercing through almost complete darkness.

'This is a mate of mine, John Grant,' said Crawford. 'You can let
him in any time, he's all right.'

The two men grunted, and Grant and Crawford went through
the gate into what seemed to be a yard at the back of a shop-
building. Grant wondered why such care should be taken to guard
an establishment which was so obviously tolerated by the police.

As if answering him Crawford said: 'They won't let you in unless
they know you. They've had a lot of trouble with newspaper blokes.
They come out here every now and then and write the place up –
you know, sort of make a fuss about the gambling and the drinking.
Then we've got to shut the Game down for a while and make the
pubs close at ten.'

Crawford paused a moment, then added bitterly: 'They're a
bloody nuisance, I can tell you.'

They passed through the yard into a large room fitted with
wooden benches and plank seats. A number of men were sitting at
the benches eating. One side of the room was fitted out like a
hamburger stall. Two men in open-necked shirts were cooking
steaks on the stove.

Crawford went up to the counter and said: 'Fix a steak for me
mate, Joe.'

One of the men said: 'G'day, Jock,' and slapped another steak
down on the grilling plate.

'That'll cost you six bob,' said Crawford, 'and it'll be the best six
bob's worth you ever had.'

Grant wondered whether the organizers of the Game leased the
catering rights, or simply provided the restaurant as part of the
general organization. Crawford's enthusiam for the meals served
would have suggested that he had some interest in the business if
Grant had not known that Bundanyabba people were all proud of
the Game. Presumably this pride extended to the facilities.

Through a door at the other end of the room Grant could see
about a hundred men crowded around an open space in which two
men were conferring. That undoubtedly would be the famous
Game.

'Come and I'll show you inside while you're waiting,' said
Crawford.

The section where the Game was in progress had probably once been a large store-room. In the centre was a patch of green carpet about ten feet square. This was edged by a wooden bench about nine inches high, which was crowded with players.

Behind them, thrusting between their shoulders, squatting and standing, rising in tiers of humanity until they reached the side walls, were the rest of the players. Now that he could see the whole room Grant guessed there must have been about three hundred men in there. They were all dressed in belted trousers with open-neck shirts, except for a few with only singlets over their torsos. Grant felt a little conspicuous in his safari jacket.

In the centre of the carpet square were the two men whom Grant had seen conferring. They were both big, gaunt, rapacious-looking; quite obviously the controllers of the Game. With them was a small nondescript man holding a slip of wood in his hand. Grant saw him drop a bundle of notes to the ground at his feet.

'You know about the Game?' asked Crawford.

'Only vaguely,' said Grant.

'Well that bloke with the kip is the spinner.'

'Oh?' said Grant.

'He's dropped fifty quid in the centre. That's got to be covered before they'll let him spin.'

Various players around the square were throwing notes on to the carpet. The controllers were gathering them up. Then one called out: 'He's set!'

'That means the fifty quid in the centre's covered,' said Crawford. 'Now all the others can have their side-bets.'

Around the square, men were dropping little piles of notes and crying out: 'Ten quid tails,' or 'Five heads,' or 'Ten bob tails,' or 'Twenty quid tails,' according to their purses or ambitions.

As soon as the money hit the ground, other men dropped bundles the same size on top of it, declaring their intention to bet on the opposite side of the coins.

To Grant, who was none too clear-headed anyway, it seemed that money was being sprayed light-heartedly in all directions for no apparent reason. There must have been more than a thousand pounds on the carpet.

But there was nothing light-hearted about the faces of the players. There were intent, set, calculating. The whole business was transacted in terms of fairly subdued calls, except when some gambler, unable to get his stake covered, would shout to attract the attention of players on the other side of the ring.

Soon everybody setled down and a quiet fell on the room. One of the controllers said: 'All set?' and looked around. There were no objections, so he produced two pennies and placed them carefully on the slip of wood the nondescript man was holding.

The controller stood back.

'Right,' he said. 'Spin 'em!'

The man flipped the piece of wood and the coins spun up into the air above his head and dropped down onto the carpet.

There was silence.

The controllers went over and inspected the coins.

'Tails!'

Immediately activity burst out in the room as players dived at the pile of notes around the ring, extracting their winnings. Piles of perhaps two hundred pounds were rapidly divided by the simple process of each man taking what was due to him.

'Get the idea, John?' said Crawford.

'More or less – they just bet on whether the pennies will come down heads or tails, is that it?'

'That's it.'

'But what's all this business on the sides about?'

'Well, once the spinner's bet is covered anyone can have a bet on the side.'

'Then how does the School make a profit?'

'They take a cut from the spinner, and if any of the side blokes have a big win they're expected to sling a bit.'

The division of money was complete now and the School was settling down for the next spin.

'You'd think,' said Grant, 'that everybody'd be at each other's throats when they settle, it all seems pretty confused.'

'Hardly ever been a fight in the place. Everybody knows what he's got coming out of the ring, and he takes it – simple as that. 'Course it probably wouldn't work anywhere except in The Yabba. All these blokes know each other, y'know.'

The pennies were spinning in the air again.

'Tails!' and again the scramble for winnings. The man with the kip was stolidly surveying the mass of notes at his feet. He looked as though he was wading in money, thought Grant.

'When does he stop spinning?' he asked Crawford.

'When he likes, or when he throws heads – that means he loses the lot.'

'Does he have to leave all his money in?'

'No, he's only got to have a quid in the centre.'

The spinner threw tails again, and Grant calculated that he must now have four hundred pounds in front of him. Grant pushed forward, fascinated by the profusion of crumpled notes.

The coins flashed in the air once more.

Again the tails, and this time the spinner tossed down the kip and began to shovel the notes into his pockets. He had turned fifty pounds into eight hundred in less than a quarter of an hour. He picked up the last fistful of notes and thrust them into the hands of one of the controllers, walked out of the ring with unmoved countenance, pushed through the crowd and disappeared out of the door.

'That was Charlie Jones,' said Crawford. 'He comes in every pay day with fifty quid and throws until he has eight hundred quid or nothing.'

'Does he win or lose in the long run?'

'He pulls out the eight hundred about once every six weeks.' Crawford added as though in explanation: 'He's only got to throw four tails in a row to get that, y'know.'

'Very nice.'

Another player had taken the kip and laid out an investment of one pound.

Grant said: 'My steak's probably ready.'

'Yes, come on.'

They went back into the eating-room and collected Grant's steak.

'I'll have to be pushing off,' said Crawford, after paternally seeing Grant to a seat at one of the benches.

'All right, Jock, thanks for showing me around.' Grant was glad to see the end of the policeman now.

They shook hands and Crawford said: 'See you 'round,' and went out into the night.

The steak, Grant found, justified none of the claims Crawford had made for it. It was stringy and grossly overcooked, and Grant suspected that it would have tasted slightly 'off' if it had not tasted so overwhelmingly of burnt leather.

Nevertheless he felt much more clear-headed when he had eaten it, and the accompanying pile of soggy potato chips, and drunk the coffee which tasted, and looked, like milk which had been diluted with water, discoloured with some brown substance, and heated. The fare at the Two-up School was not, he decided, of the same standard as the entertainment, but probably was better than the average meal served in outback cafés.

He looked at his watch. It was eleven-thirty. His aircraft left for the east at eleven-thirty. He had twelve hours to fill in.

He made a pretence, for his own benefit, of considering what he would do now – go to bed, drink some more, go for a stroll. But he knew quite well that he intended to go back and watch the Game. He had been more interested in the spectacle than he cared to admit: moreover, an as yet bloodless phantom of intention was flitting about the darker recesses of his mind and he was pretending he could not see it.

In the playing-room yet another man in the ring had built an imposing collection of notes about his feet. He lost the lot in a moment when the pennies fell with tails to the carpet.

Grant stayed against one of the walls, watching intently the method of betting. His thoughts were running to the odds involved in heads or tails being thrown four times in succession, and he was very aware of the notes in his wallet.

Normally he seldom gambled, because opportunity seldom arose. But now he could feel in himself an emotion that was completely new to him – the strange passion that gamblers know.

'It would not matter a great deal,' he told himself, 'if I lost the seventeen pounds or so I have in cash – and I might win.' Deliberately he evoked the phantom, calling it into the light, recognized it as intention and gave it the authority of his will.

He took a five-pound note from his wallet.

The prospect of actually laying the bet produced a sense of diffidence, and he moved vaguely forward through the crowd with the note in his hand. Just in front of him, on the edge of the ring, a man had about a hundred pounds at his feet and was crying: 'Come on, another fifty wanted on tails. Anybody betting tails?'

Grant stood indecisively. He felt gauche among these confident gamblers and could not quite bring himself to lean forward and drop his five pounds on to the floor. Besides, he was not at all convinced of the infallibility of the system of distribution of winnings.

The note was snatched from his fingers.

'On tails, mate?' said a seedy-looking character who was standing directly behind the man calling for business.

Grant nodded because he could not think of anything else to do, and saw his five-pound note flutter to the floor.

Presently the controller called: 'All set?' and the coins were spun.

'Tails!' And Grant found himself pushed aside as players pressed forward to collect their winnings. He attempted to struggle forward himself, but could not summon the self-confidence required. Soon all was ready for the next spin, and Grant was crushed back against the wall, with no idea of the whereabouts of the man with whom he had laid his bet.

So much, he thought, for each man taking his due. He looked around angrily for someone from whom to claim his money, but with no real hope. Then he saw the seedy-looking character jumping up and down, trying to look over the heads of the crowd.

He was saying loudly: 'Anybody seen a tall bloke with a coat on? Anybody seen a tall fair sort of bloke with a coat on?'

Grant waved at him energetically and he came weaving through the players.

'There y'are, mate,' he said. 'Thought I'd lost ya.' He handed Grant two five-pound notes and began worming his way back to the ringside without waiting for an answer.

Grant looked ashamedly at the money and gestured remote thanks to the man who had rescued it. He was putting the money in his wallet when he experienced an entirely new emotion – the remorse of a gambler who has not put all his money on a successful wager.

He paused with the money half-way into his wallet. He had twenty-two pounds ten shillings. Twice that was fifty pounds. Twice fifty was a hundred. Twice a hundred . . .

Confident now, he thrust through the crown and even managed to squeeze himself on to the bench at the ringside. He took all his money from his wallet and held it in his hand, waiting for the completion of the present spin.

He gave no thought to whether he should bet heads or tails. He was out to win money on pure chance, and he knew that chance was not governed by whim.

When the time came he dropped his twenty-two pounds ten to the floor and called out: 'Twenty-two pounds ten on tails.' He chose tails simply because the man next to him was calling for bets on heads.

Immediately someone dropped a bundle of notes on to Grant's pile.

'Twenty-two ten on heads,' said a voice above him, adding conversationally: 'There's twenty-three there, mate.' Only then did Grant realize that the odd ten shillings was slightly out of place.

Again Grant's mood changed. He felt quite withdrawn. His bet had been made, in a few moments he would have fifty pounds or nothing. He could not change his mind now. Nevertheless he kept repeating to himself: 'It does not matter if you lose. It's a chance you're taking. It does not matter if you lose.' And by some instinct he could not analyse he kept his eyes tight shut with his head hanging low so that he might not be seen by the casual gambler whose money lay before him.

And his eyes were still shut when he heard the call of 'Tails'.

I have fifty pounds, thought Grant, and turned to give his

opponent his ten shillings change. But nobody behind him gave any indication of having had anything to do with the bet. A matter of ten shillings was of inconsiderable moment at the Game.

His money was still at his feet.

'Leaving all that on tails, mate?' said a voice above his head.

In one convolution of his mind he considered the matter, decided for it and said 'Yes.' In the next convolution of his mind he thought: Oh god, why didn't I take some of it out at least?

But the wad of notes had dropped swiftly from above and he had one hundred pounds before him.

Now he didn't give a damn what he looked like. His hands trembled grossly as he lit a cigarette and drew the smoke deep into his lungs with sucking breath.

He became terribly aware of the smoky room, the heat that gave the impression it could be shovelled away, the sweating tense faces of the gamblers, the insouciant greed of the controllers; and then the pennies were spinning, higher, higher, turning in a double arc, small brown discs of fortune; and down they plummeted.

'My God!' said Grant aloud: 'It's tails.'

He looked at his money, lying there all green and crumpled, and leaned forward to gather it up. And in the very act of leaning forward he experienced his third strange emotion that night – the mysticism of gamblers. He knew the pennies would fall tails again. He knew that as surely as he knew that he existed. All that was required was the will to act on his conviction and he summoned that very easily.

He sat upright again, leaving his money where it was and cried: 'One hundred pounds on tails!'

Three different gamblers contributed to cover Grant's money. He sat back on the bench and looked around while the other bets were made. He was not thinking; he was possessed with fore-knowledge, and while that strange devil spoke Grant would not even contemplate his own actions.

He almost felt doubt when the pennies described their arc and began to fall, but there was not time for doubt to crystallize before the controller called: 'And it's tails again!'

The reaction struck Grant hard in the stomach. For a moment he felt as though he would faint across his winnings. Then he leaned forward and began cramming the notes into his pockets.

He did not think of throwing a tip to the controllers, and they apparently had not noticed his win, for they demanded nothing. He pushed through the crowd, holding his hands on the money in his jacket pockets, almost staggered outside into the dining-room, the rear yard, the lane among the shadows of the loiterers, even more ghostly now that his eyes were unaccustomed to the dark, and then he was in the street.

His whole body sang with the exultation of his soul. He had won almost two hundred pounds. His seventeen pounds ten had become two hundred pounds.

The words 'two hundred pounds' kept on being repeated in his mind. 'Two hundred pounds. Two hundred pounds. TWO HUNDRED pounds. Unbelievable. TWO HUNDRED POUNDS!'

And he had his wages cheque intact in his pocket.

He had never had so much money in his life before, and now he could feel it swelling his pockets, making his clothes bulge, rustling when he walked.

He had to get somewhere where he could count it, look at it.

He never remembered the time he spent going back to his hotel room except for the moment when he fumbled for his key, and that was only because he had to rummage among the notes that jammed his pockets.

In his room he emptied the money out on to the floor and carefully counted it, laying the notes out on the floor in order of denomination. Then he took out his pay cheque and laid it alongside them.

Two hundred pounds in notes and a cheque for one hundred and forty pounds. Three hundred and forty pounds and tomorrow he would be in Sydney.

He looked into the mirror and saw his face, young and still taut, sweat-streaked; and his eyes glittering with the stimulus of winning money; his straight hair rumpled where he had been running his fingers through it.

'Grant,' he said to his image, 'you're a clever lad.'

He flung himself on his back on the bed, and stared at the ceiling, tingling with the joy of it all.

For the first time in a long while he thought about Robyn, and laughed at himself for supposing that two hundred pounds would make her any more accessible. Robyn of the long blonde hair, bound in plaits around her head. Robyn, confident and assured and remote. Robyn as he had last seen her a year ago, a week before he left for Tiboonda, standing at the gate in front of her home with the light behind her, making her hair shine.

Robyn, who had shown singularly little interest in John Grant. But, ah God! she was a lovely girl.

Could he not now, at this moment, put through a long-distance call to her, telling her he was coming home, that he was rich? But then Robyn was more used to money than he, and might not be so impressed at the idea of three hundred and forty pounds.

He laughed and leaped up and began to undress, and then stopped, stunned by the enormity of a thought.

If he had let his bet stand . . . and if tails had been thrown just once more . . . he would never have had to return to Tiboonda. He would have won four hundred pounds. Four hundred pounds and his wages cheque would have paid off the Education Department bond and leave him enough to live on while he sought work in Sydney.

One twist of the coins. Five seconds of time and he would have been saved a whole year in Tiboonda. Would have been . . . could still be . . .

He sat down on the bed and looked at the money. It was wonderful, but what did it offer apart from a few glorious weeks in Sydney. He could have that anyway, with his wages. And if he lost the whole two hundred pounds he would be no worse off than if he had lost the original twenty-two pounds ten.

But if he won, tomorrow he would be in Sydney to stay.

He argued with himself for several minutes, pointing out in exact terms why the risk was worth taking, and, in due course, he convinced himself.

He looked at his face in the mirror. The glitter had gone from his eyes, but the tautness of his skin had increased. Slowly he stood up, put his jacket on, packed the money into neat bundles and slipped them into his pocket, put the cheque back in his wallet, looked once more in the mirror and grinned briefly at his preoccupied face, and went back to the Two-up School.

They let him in at the gate without query and he went straight through into the betting-room. The crowd did not seem to have changed; if anything the room was hotter than before and the smoke heavier.

Grant felt more or less calm. He was no longer exhilarated by the idea of gambling. He knew that he had an even chance of getting what he wanted, and he was going to take that chance.

He spent about five minutes working his way back to the ring-side, and, as he pushed gently forward, he determined that he would bet on heads this time.

A space on the bench was vacated by a man who seemed to have won a fortune, and Grant sat down.

The controller walked over to the player next to Grant and offered him the kip. It was the custom in the Bundanyabba Game that the pennies should be spun in order of place by betters on the ringside bench.

The player shook his head, and the controller offered the kip to Grant.

For the rest of his life he was to remember the impulse that moved him to take it and follow the controller to the centre of the ring.

Normally he would have been embarrassed at being the centre of activity, but he knew the attention of everyone in the room was on the pennies and not on the spinner.

'How much?' said the controller.

Grant had no intention of prolonging his ordeal – a fifty-fifty chance was a fifty-fifty chance, and held as validly for one toss as for several.

'Two hundred,' he said, and drew the money from his pockets.

The controller counted it perfunctorily.

'Two hundred,' he called, and notes came in from around the ring.

Grant stood slackly with the kip in his hand.

'Centre's set,' said the controller, and the side-betting began.

Grant felt himself surrounded by money, but it all seemed a long way off except for the pile of four hundred pounds that he could touch with the toe of his shoe.

'All set?' called the controller.

The voices were quiet.

'Right! Spin 'em!'

Inexpertly, Grant jerked the coins into the air.

A moment of spiritual darkness.

Then the controller called: 'They're split!' and picked up the coins.

Grant did not know what this meant, and it was not until the controller was settling the coins on the kip again that he realized he had thrown one head and one tail, and that counted for nothing.

It occurred to him now that his decision to bet on heads had miscarried – as spinner he had to bet on tails. But he had no time to think about that because again the controller was ordering him to spin, and again he jerked the coins.

Two tails facing upwards from the floor – two tails – four hundred pounds; but like a harsh noise breaking through a pleasant dream the controller was saying: 'No throw! Bets off. No throw! Hold on to your money!'

The controller picked up the pennies and put them back on the kip in Grant's shaking hand.

'Throw 'em above your head, mate.'

Unnerved now, Grant jerked the pennies again. He tried to follow their flight, but lost them against the glare of the electric lamp.

Where were they?

There was a scramble at his feet, and the notes, the four hundred pounds had gone, and the controller had called heads and Grant was walking out of the ring and he hadn't even seen the pennies fall.

A humming numbness gripped his body and he was afraid that the other gamblers would see his deterioration. The muscles of his face were so taut he felt he must be grimacing wildly, and surely his cheeks were twitching. He leaned against a wall and smoked quickly, trying to laugh at himself, cursing himself, wishing he'd never come near the place, telling himself to get out of here now, because there was still danger. With that part of his mind that was independent of physical disturbance he repeated the words: It doesn't matter. You've only lost twenty-two pounds ten. You took the risk, and it didn't come off. You realized that before you took the risk. You are now no worse off than you would have been if you'd lost the twenty-odd pounds in the first place.

But he was not convinced. A minute before he had had two hundred pounds. Now he did not have two hundred pounds. Useless to say he had won it as quickly as he had lost it. He was dry, shaken, sickened by the anticlimax.

The absolute unconcern of those around him struck him as wantonly callous, but a little corner of humour left to him dispelled the twinge of self-pity, and he grinned as he thought of his lack of concern for the loser when he had won.

All right, Grant, he told himself, you've had your run. Go back to bed and forget it ever happened.

But he stayed leaning against the wall saturated in the atmosphere of money. It had been so easy to win. Just a flicker of two coins and money doubled itself, and doubled itself and doubled itself. God! but the hunger for money was a gnawing, tearing thing.

He barely recognized Crawford when he appeared and said: 'How's it, John, still here?'

Grant had no reserves left for social efforts.

'Will they cash a cheque here?' he said. No, he would not think about it, he would do it. He would do it. Act now and think about it later, but act now.

'Yes,' said Crawford, unsurprised. 'How much for?'

'One hundred and forty.' Grant took out the cheque and showed it to Crawford.

'That'll be all right, I'll fix it. You'd beter sign it.'

Grant endorsed the cheque with a pen supplied by Crawford, and the policeman made his way over to the controllers, who cashed the cheque without question, carelessly doling the notes out of their pockets.

Grant barely thanked Crawford when he brought him the money.

'Going to try the Game?' said Crawford, but Grant had forgotten him, and he was on his way to the ringside.

His lips were working in desperation. Somewhere in his mind the irrationality of his actions was clear to him; but he was like an automaton, dominated by an idea that was almost an instruction. He was being forced forward by a decision, made, it seemed now, forever ago.

Not for Grant the tedium of trying to build a bank from a small bet. He leaned over the line of players sitting on the benches, dropped his one hundred and forty pounds and called: 'One forty on tails.'

His voice sounded strange and removed, and despair was heavy on his shoulders, and dragging down on his stomach. He had no hope of winning, but he would not have recalled his bet even if there had been time before it was covered by showers of notes from half a dozen different directions.

Just three minutes after he had received the money for his cheque, he had lost it.

The cry of 'Heads!' had no effect on him; but a moment or two later there was the dull, bruising shock of realization. He watched blankly as the hands scraped away the money he had laid down. He kept on looking at the bare carpet where it had been, until suddenly another growth of notes flowered there, and the Game was going on.

He turned, staring, and walked out of the building, out into the night, walking rigidly, transfixed by the magnitude of his loss. What the loss meant to him was so grievous in import that he could not think about it. His mind had a small tight knot at the back, and around it whirled the destructive realization of what he had done, but until that knot unravelled, he need not think too deeply about what was to happen now.

He went back to the hotel, stripped off his clothes, fell naked on to the bed, and stared, hot-eyed, at the ceiling until suddenly he fell asleep with the light still burning.

CHAPTER 2

He thought of Robyn and the short white dress she wore at tennis; and the way a wave could curl in foam at the top and still maintain the deep, green sweep of its curving, moving shape: and then, Oh God! he was awake on an iron bed in a hotel in Bundanyabba and he had no money.

Grant rolled off the bed, looked hastily away from the grey face in the mirror and, still naked, walked to the window. He looked out without seeing the mean hotel yard and the paling fences of the backyards of the neighbouring shops. It was not long after dawn and already the smothering heat of the night had given way to the harsher, burning glare of the sun.

Grant turned and leaned his back against the paper-covered wooden wall, trying to draw an element of coolness from it. He took the jug of water from the table and poured a little on his head, letting it trickle, lukewarm, down his body.

'There is no point,' he said aloud, 'in being hopeless and helpless.'

But words did not help much to allay the mass of self-condemnation that was bursting inside him.

He sat down on the bed and looked at himself in the mirror. A dark spread of beard had appeared on his face; his hair was plastered down with water; a little sweat had already gathered on his chest and forehead.

He attempted a smile, and saw his lips respond; but his eyes remained dull and hollow.

'Life,' he said, again aloud, 'will appear brighter after breakfast.'

He lay back on the bed again, and almost succeeded in sleeping until a hotel bell indicated that it was time to shower, shave, and dress to present some sort of face to a world that had suddenly become unduly complicated.

Breakfast was surprisingly good, largely because somebody in the hotel had had the enterprise to include chilled paw-paw in the menu. That stayed thought a little, then a milky coffee and the first cigarette of the day.

The first cigarette, the first of eleven that were left in his last packet, and all that a search of his pockets had produced was two shillings and sevenpence. He felt he should eat all the hotel offered, because at best there seemed little chance that he would eat again that day, but the heat was dragging at his being and his mouth was raw from the constant smoking last night, so he ate only the paw-paw.

He ordered a second cup of coffee and began another cigarette because eleven would not last long anyway.

There were few people in the dining-room and he had a table to himself, so with the second cigarette there came the time when the situation had to be considered.

All right, now it had to be faced: what was he to do?

He had nobody he could borrow money from, certainly nobody to whom he could explain that he had lost all his money gambling.

And in any case, how much did he need to borrow? Just to stay alive until his next pay cheque was due would cost at least a hundred pounds.

If he got to Sydney there was just a chance that he could spend elongated periods with somewhat dim relatives, but what a chance with two and sevenpebce to spread over six weeks.

And in any case, how to get to Sydney? The train fare one way would be about ten pounds even if he felt like facing a forty-hour journey without any money for food. And when he arrived in Sydney would he walk with his suitcases to his uncle's home fifteen miles out in the suburbs?

Quite apart from which, it was all academic, because he did not have ten pounds.

Could he sell anything? Only his clothes, and there did not seem much of a market for secondhand clothes in Bundanyabba. His watch was battered and old and worth a few shillings at the most, and besides he knew of nothing that approached a pawnshop in the city.

The only possibility seemed to be to find some sort of work in Bundanyabba. If he could find a job in a shop, or an office, or labouring – anything to raise the fare to Sydney.

But where to stay in the meantime? He could not get work until Monday at the earliest, and he could not stay in the hotel because the bill would come to more than he would be paid.

The contrast between what lay before him now and what he had planned the night before swept across him with physical violence, but he jammed his thoughts back to the immediate problems.

Obviously he had to get out of the hotel at once. That at least

was a definite move. He went upstairs, collected his bags, glanced
once around the room to make sure that he had left nothing and
went downstairs again to the reception desk.

An odd sense of gratitude caught him when the girl gave him
back his ten shillings deposit on the keys. He had forgotten that.
And then he looked at the small, orange-tinted note and remembered the great wads of money he had lost last night. He thrust the
note into his pocket with the two and sevenpence and walked out
into the street with his suitcases.

It was nine o'clock on Saturday morning.

The sun hurt his eyes more than usually, and he put his sun-
glasses on. He turned into the main street and walked slowly down
the footpath under the dilapidated awnings, past the Town Hall
with its rare and nurtured patch of green grass on the front garden.

When he came to the corner by the Post Office he turned around
and walked back along the block again.

Where in the name of God was he to go?

He felt conspicuous, although there was no reason why anybody
in that busy street should think anything but that he was waiting
for a bus. He put his cases down by a bus-stop under the shade of
an awning and sat on one of them.

There must be an answer to this. He could not just wander up
and down until he collapsed. Although, of course, he could do just
that.

From where he was sitting he could see the great piles of mullock
and waste from the mines, artificial hills within a few hundred
yards of the centre of the city. When the wind blew, thick clouds of
dust drifted off the mullock and fell in a blinding cloud over the
streets.

Grant looked at the barren heaps of worked-out earth as possibly
being where he would spend the nights for the next six weeks.

Presumably there were soup kitchens in Bundanyabba, he
thought, a shade desperately.

He smoked another of his cigarettes while he sat there; then the
bus came and went and Grant, convinced now that he was drawing
attention, stood up again and walked the length of the shopping
centre with his suitcases.

By half past nine he could feel something like nervous hysteria
mounting in his throat. He had to find somewhere to put his
suitcases and think for a while.

The sun had raised the shade temperature to just on a hundred
degrees already, and the tar in the roadway was bubbling.

Grant felt himself exposed in no-man's-land. There was no

avenue of retreat and the enemy was invisible and unassailable. His supports had been dissipated, his arms were lost. He could not even burrow into the ground to hide.

A lone figure, not worth a burst of machine-gun fire, he seemed doomed to wander the desolate terrain until he just dropped into oblivion.

Damn it all! He couldn't just walk up and down the street for six mortal weeks.

He turned into the bar of the nearest hotel.

There were only about thirty men in the bar, taking their first drinks after breakfast, and Grant easily found a corner to stow his suitcases.

He ordered a pony of beer – the smallest amount sold. It cost him ninepence, but it bought respite from the street. He put it down on the bar untouched, determined it would serve as an excuse to stay in the bar as long as he liked.

Eight cigarettes left, and the one he was going to smoke now meant seven left. Strange that cigarettes should be so much more desirable when the supply was strictly limited.

He leaned on the brown bar top and looked up at the rows and rows of pennies and threepences stuck to the wooden skirting above his head. It was a local custom to wet small coins with beer and stick them to the woodwork. They amounted to several pounds before they filled all the available space above the bar. Then they were taken away and the whole process began again.

It was generally supposed that the publicans gave the money to charity, but Grant had never seen any evidence to support this supposition.

He estimated that there must have been ten or twelve pounds stuck up there, enough to get him to Sydney. However, there would no doubt be determined resistance to any move on his part to acquire the coins.

He sipped his beer prudently and rolled cigarette smoke around in his mouth, letting it trickle out slowly so that he could breathe it in again through his nose. Which, he pointed out to himself, was no advance at all towards the solution of his situation.

A little man with glasses came to the bar beside him and called for a middy of beer in what seemed to be the remnants of an Irish accent. He took off his panama hat, revealing a head almost completely bald except for small white tufts around the ears.

'Hot!' he said to Grant pleasantly, running a huge handkerchief over his glistening pate to support his statement.

'Hot,' agreed Grant, curtly.

The little man looked around the bar, but apparently saw no-body he knew and turned his attention back to Grant.

'New to The Yabba?'

Grant shrank a little – was everybody in Bundanyabba cast in the identical conversational mould?

'New to The Yabba,' he said so casually as to be rude, but rudeness of this type was unknown in Bundanyabba and the little man did not recognize it.

'Like the old place?'

At least, thought Grant, a new tack could be introduced at this point.

'No! I think it's bloody awful,' and that, he hoped would stifle any further approaches.

The little man paused with his beer half-way to his mouth.

'You don't like The Yabba?' This was the nearest thing to heresy he had heard in many a year and he did not quite know how to deal with it.

'No.'

The little man drank his middy without drawing breath and called for another. He seemed to ponder for a moment, then turned to Grant again and said:

'Will you have a drink?' It was as though Grant had done something unmentionable, but not quite sufficient to put him beyond the social pale.

'No. I'm just toying with this one, thanks.'

'Well drink it down and I'll buy you another.'

This had gone far enough. Grant had no desire to cultivate this balding *émigré*, despite the nostalgic lift in his voice.

'Look,' he said, 'I'm flat broke, and I can't afford to drink and I just want to drink this one slowly.'

But that was the wrong angle too.

'What's that got to do with it man? I said I'd buy you a drink, I don't want you to buy me one. Come on, drink it down now.'

The little man had begun to talk loudly and one or two other drinkers were looking at them, so Grant gave up, drained his tiny glass and put it on the bar.

'Make it two middies, miss,' said the little man, and soon Grant felt again in his palm the solacing curve of a ten-ounce glass full of cold beer.

'My name's John Grant,' he said unwillingly.

'Tim Hynes.' And Grant shook the proffered hand. It was hard, and for some reason quite cool. Probably from holding beer glasses, thought Grant, whose own hands were soggy with sweat.

'And how does a young fellow like you come to be broke?'

Oh God, these relentlessly friendly people whose sheer goodwill bordered on impertinence. Still, this was Bundanyabba and he was drinking the man's beer and, you never knew, Hynes might be able to help him find work.

'I lost my pay cheque and I've got to wait a few weeks until I can get another one.' That at any rate was literally true as far as it went.

'A few weeks?'

'I'm the schoolteacher out at Tiboonda, and I'd just got my Christmas holiday pay.'

But truth cannot be skirted indefinitely.

'How did you come to lose it?'

'I don't know. Just lost it. Might have burned it with some rubbish when I was packing.'

'And you've got no money?'

'A few shillings.'

'And how will you get your money?'

'Oh, I've written to the Department – they'll send me another cheque sooner or later, but they're pretty slow.'

'You'd come to The Yabba for your holidays had you, John?'

'Not on your life! I was on my way to Sydney.' Grant caught the slight discrepancy. 'I didn't realize I'd lost my cheque until this morning.'

'Well, and what are you going to do until your pay comes?'

'I haven't the faintest idea.' Now perhaps there might be some reward for his glib fabrication.

'Well you'd better have another beer at any rate. Two more middies, miss!'

'Look, thanks very much, but I don't like drinking your beer when I can't buy any ... I ...'

'Ah, think nothing of it, John. Think nothing of it. I been broke myself many a time.'

'I was thinking I might be able to get a job here for a couple of weeks.'

'You might too, John, you might too. Thanks, miss.' Hynes paid from a wallet fat with notes. He turned to Grant again.

'And how do you like teaching out in Tiboonda?'

Grant no longer wanted to get rid of Hynes, but he suffered a little sick self-loathing when he realized it.

'It's all right, a bit out of the way.'

'And you don't like The Yabba?'

'Well, I suppose I'm a bit browned off. It's probably all

right.' Hell's teeth! the things a man could say when he had
to.

Hynes leaned towards him and banged his glass for emphasis.

'Son,' he said intensely, 'it's the best little town in the world!'

Grand did his best to adopt an expression suitable to the occasion, but he could not for the life of him think what that expression
might be. He smiled non-committally.

'Everybody here certainly seems to like it,' he said.

''Course they do. Now, listen to me, John.'

Grant listened, and Hynes dropped his voice.

'Are you a Mason?'

'No.'

'You're in the Buffs?'

'In the what?'

'In the Buffs?'

'The Buffs?' Grant felt bemused.

'The Buffaloes.'

'The Buffaloes?' Could this go on much longer?

But Hynes was exasperated too.

'Are you a member of the Buffalo lodge?'

'No. Never heard of it.'

'Not a Mason and not a Buff,' Hynes was nonplussed; then, as if
in comprehension: 'You'd be a Roman Catholic then?'

'No, I'm not.'

'Not that that'd be much help to you, anyway. Well what are you
going to do?'

'I don't know.'

'And you're not a Buff?'

'No. I'm not a Buff.'

'Poor old John. Two more beers, miss!'

Grant did not bother to protest. He was beginning to feel withdrawn and his chagrin over his losses was turning to sadness. He
was not used to heavy drinking after a light breakfast of paw-paw.

He drank with Hynes throughout the morning and talked of
Bundanyabba, of Hynes's work – he had something to do with one
of the mines it appeared – of Hynes's two beautiful daughters, and,
later in the morning, of Hynes's wonderful wife.

At first Grant kept trying to bring the conversation around to his
chances of getting work in Bundanyabba, but that only set Hynes
off on the imponderability of Grant's not being a Buff, and Grant
couldn't stand it. So Grant, who soon didn't care much anyway,
just gave himself up to drinking.

And then, when Hynes was off buying some bottled beer to take home, Grant found himself leaning sombrely on the bar thinking of Robyn with deep melancholy.

Robyn spoke with a mellow, full voice and when she spoke her mouth moved a little shyly, a little boldly. Her eyes were grey and clear. There was a suggestion of oriental gravity in her fair, wide face, but the gravity disintegrated and crumbled away when she smiled. Her profile was calm and Grecian, her body soft and strong.

'We'd better be getting home for dinner.'

Grant realized he had been smiling gently at the bar, and he felt his thoughts falling and bumping against one another as he re-arranged them and turned to face Hynes, whose arms were full of bottled beer wrapped in brown paper.

'I can hardly land in on your wife for dinner.' Grant spoke slowly.

''Course you can. She's used to it.'

'Yes. But to be perfectly frank, old man, I've had a little too much to drink and I hardly like to visit a stranger's home ...'

'There's no strangers in The Yabba, man, come along now.'

It was almost one o'clock. They had been drinking for three hours and Hynes weaved as he led the way out of the bar. Grant walked straight, but slowly, very aware that he was holding himself together. Hynes opened the back door of a large Ford car and put the beer on the rear seat.

'Hop in,' he said to Grant and went around to the driver's side.

Grant fumbled with the door-handle, but got in all right.

The car had been standing in the sun for hours and the tempera-ture inside made him gasp.

But he had the drunkard's detachment and observed his own discomfort from afar.

Soon, he thought distantly, the future would have to be faced, but for the moment he was a man who lived life as he found it.

They drove to the outskirts of the city, past the Catholic Cathedral that looked too substantial and permanent for Bundanyabba.

Hynes's home was a low, wide weatherboard bungalow with an attempt at a front garden.

Hynes led the way across the wide front veranda, pushed open the front door and went into a dark hallway which gave a promise of coolness that was not fulfilled, because it wasn't cool anywhere in Bundanyabba in December.

'Go in and sit down,' he said to Grant, pushing him into a side room. 'I'll tell the wife we're here.'

Grant was in a darkened sitting-room, hung with heavy curtains, thickly carpeted.

The taste, he thought, is no doubt deplorable, but the comfort is enormous, and he sat down in a deep armchair, leather upholstery and wooden arms.

As his eyes became accustomed to the dimness he found himself doing small mental gymnastics, reluctantly abandoning his notion that the room must be over-furnished. It was quite pleasant.

He reached for a cigarette, found it was his last, and took one instead from an ornamental box on a coffee table.

He lit it and leaned back, inhaling. This at any rate was better than wandering up and down the streets, and when he felt a little more sober he would look seriously at the question of finding work.

After all, he was not completely ruined. He had only to find some way of getting a few pounds together and he might even yet manage a couple of weeks in Sydney. And if he didn't, well it was only another year in Tiboonda.

Another year in Tiboonda ... let that go anyway ... better not think too brainsickly just now.

A tall, solemn girl came into the room and said:

'Daddy will be in in a few minutes.'

Grant stood up suddenly, and, realizing as he did it that it was a shade too courtly, bowed slightly and said:

'How do you do?'

'Fine – how are you?' And Grant knew by the way she said it that she realized he was two-thirds drunk.

She sat down in a chair opposite him.

'I really must apologize for landing in on you like this. Your father more or less insisted.'

'He usually does.' And Grant felt that this had happened many times before, and he was just another shabby incident to be borne with tolerance.

She was very slim, but her body suggested a full roundness and the dark floral frock she was wearing clung to her as she moved. Her hair was long and dark, and her eyes were very big. So was her mouth, but not too big for her face. Grant had not known that there were girls like this in the west. They had all seemed lumpy, sweaty creatures with bad complexions.

He realized that he was standing staring at her and he sat down quickly, making a business of ashing his cigarette.

'My name's John Grant,' he said, regretting his boorishness as he spoke.

She smiled formally and let him wait a little before she said:

'I'm Janette Hynes.'

They both fell silent and the girl stretched back, resting her head on the upholstery of the chair and extending her arms until her fingertips rested on her knees. It was an expression of her reaction to the heat or the boredom of Grant's presence, or both.

Grant wished he was either more drunk or more sober, but as he was he just could not meet the situation, and he sat silent looking desperately at the cigarette he was smoking.

They remained like that for about three minutes and then Hynes came in with two large glasses of beer.

'A quick one before dinner,' he said.

Grant took the glass and again made some show of protesting against coming for a meal; but Hynes talked him down loudly, and while that was going on Janette quietly left the room.

Hynes recognized her departure in no way other than by sitting down in the chair she had left. He, too, was inclined to be silent, and Grant suspected that Mrs Hynes might not have been so docile as her husband had anticipated.

Grant wondered about the appearance of the woman, who, together with this odd little man, had produced Janette. She must have been a late child, unless Mrs Hynes were much younger than Hynes.

'Your daughter works in The Yabba, Tim?'

'She's a nurse.'

'She's your younger daughter, is she?'

'Yeah. The other girl's thirty.' Hynes did not seem as enthusiastic now about his daughter as he had been in the hotel.

Janette put her head around the door to say: 'Mother wants you to come to dinner now.'

Hynes and Grant finished their beer quickly and went out through the hall towards the back of the house.

In the dining-room Mrs Hynes was putting the last touches to the table and she looked up pleasantly enough as Hynes ushered Grant in. She was a square-shaped woman, younger than Hynes, but not much.

She brushed aside Grant's apologies and sat him down at the table where some quite good cutlery was arranged meticulously on a great expanse of white starched tablecloth.

Janette sat at one end of the table, her mother at the other, Hynes and Grant on either side. The other daughter was not in evidence.

Hynes talked continuously through dinner. Mrs Hynes laughed politely sometimes, said 'My, My!' at appropriate points and displayed absolutely no interest in either Grant or Hynes. Janette said nothing. Grant gained the impression that Hynes was recognized as the head of the family and that his wishes were more of less law, but that nobody thought much of him. He had encountered similar situations in other western families.

The meal was the standard outback dinner of steak and potatoes with unidentifiable tinned vegetables. But it was well prepared and Grant, his appetite inflamed by beer, ate it so readily that it was not until Mrs Hynes said 'Would you like some more, Mr Grant?' that he realized he was scraping up the gravy.

'No. No thank you. Quite an excellent dinner, thank you,' he muttered, avoiding looking at Janette.

They ate some sort of custard tart for dessert, and Hynes immediately took Grant back into the sitting-room with a couple of bottles of beer while Janette and her mother cleared away the table.

Grant felt more in possession of himself after the meal and determined not to drink any more. But he took one glass from Hynes, just to hold on to, and helped himself to another cigarette from the box on the table.

'Well,' he said to Hynes, 'I suppose I'd better be getting along soon.'

'Getting along? Where to?'

'Well I . . . well . . . I suppose I should be looking for work.'

'You won't find work on a Saturday.'

'No, probably not, but I . . . well . . .'

'Oh drink your beer, man, and enjoy yourself – why don't you?'

'Yes, but you see I've really got to do something.'

'We'll think about that later; now drink your beer, man, and stop worrying.'

The house vibrated as heavy feet thumped on the veranda. Hynes, his face brightening, called: 'Come in, men, come in!'

Two huge men, about thirty, in open-neck shirts, loomed in the doorway.

'G'day, Tim,' they said, and 'G'day, John,' when they were introduced to Grant.

Hynes went hurrying out to get more glasses, and Grant knew a few moments' awful anticipation until one of the men at last said: 'New to The Yabba, John?'

But Hynes came back before he had to go through it all again.

Hynes and his two friends fell to simultaneous speaking, exchanging the clumsy insults that pass for repartee in the west.

Apart from a few minor variations in feature, the newcomers

appeared almost identical, even to the patches of thick curly hair that appeared between their throats and their shirts.

One day, thought Grant, he would make a fortune by manufacturing those for sale, like dickies.

The two men were apparently miners who worked with Hynes. One was named Dick and the other Joe; and despite all appearances it seemed they were not brothers, nor even remotely related.

Whenever Grant had thought of miners at all he had thought of them as grimy people, who emerged from the ground like moles, except that they would blink and shake their heads, and who probably spoke with Welsh accents. These two were very well-scrubbed specimens, who spoke with the nasal twang developed by people unable to open their mouths too wide because of dust.

Grant found himself allowing his glass to be refilled, and then, surprised to find it empty, filled once more. Hynes seemed to have forgotten him and was engrossed in a conversation, largely incomprehensible to Grant, revolving around a pack of greyhounds the two miners owned jointly.

'Do you race the dogs?' Grant ventured once.

Dick looked at him as though surprised that he was still there.

'What else?' he said, and turned back to Hynes.

Grant gave his attention to his cigarette again, wondering, blearily now, how best to make his escape – and then where to escape to. But there was no real answer, so he just sat.

After a while he let his eyes close, and the voices became a constant unbroken drone. A warm drone, like bees, very big bees, on a hot, very hot, day.

Sinking, sinking, gently sinking, just enough awareness to know that it was pleasant to go down, down, blurry warmth, heavy heavy limbs at rest, the sense of flowing out, draining out, sinking slowly down without fear.

'You'll spill that beer if you don't sit up straight.'

Janette was sitting on a stool near his chair.

Grant shook his head and worked his jaw muscles, struggling to dissipate the fog that gripped his mind and body. It went slowly, reluctantly, painfully.

'I'm sorry,' he said, 'fell asleep.'

Hynes and his friends were still talking earnestly about dogs, and didn't seem to have noticed.

Grant took a huge swallow of beer from his glass and attempted a smile. It didn't work because his face wasn't responding properly.

But damn it all, there was a limit to the humiliation he could stand.

He pushed himself to his feet and said, a little too loudly: 'I'll be moving off, Tim, thanks for your hospitality.'

The three men broke off their conversation and looked at him. The young men's faces were blank, but Hynes's was perplexed, he didn't quite know what to do about Grant. Obviously he was tempted to let him go and forget about him. For a moment Grant thought he was going to do just that, and he began to wish he had not suggested it ... back to the streets of Bundanyabba.

'Where would you be going, man?'

The question was not answerable and Grant floundered, muttering inarticulately, knowing and glad that Hynes was going to insist that he stay.

Hynes advanced on him with a bottle of beer.

'You just hang around for a while,' he said, filling Grant's glass, 'we've got to see about fixing you up with a job.'

Grant was sure by now that Hynes had no means or intention of finding him work, but it was better really to shelve things for a while longer. There was no point in staggering off half drunk.

'Sit down and talk to Janette,' said Hynes. 'Can't you content yourself with a pretty girl for an hour or two?' Hynes went back to his friends, leaving the statement like a lump of something faintly distasteful between Grant and Janette, something not to be adverted to, but something of which both were unduly aware.

Or at least Grant thought they should both have been aware of it. In fact Janette smiled as he sat down again and said:

'What do you want to work for?'

'The usual reason, to get money.' He looked at his watch, it was almost half past five. How long had he sat there in a stupor?

Janette was looking at him inquiringly, and, was he wrong, or was there an element of warmth about her – a certain nuance in her manner that seemed to admit him to the circle of people she might be prepared to know.

Some further elaboration of his position was obviously required, so he gave her the same version of his plight as he had given her father.

'Still,' she said, 'you'll be all right as soon as the cheque comes, won't you?'

Grant found his glass empty every time he looked at it, and Hynes, still fretful and uncertain about his guest, kept coming across the room, filling his glass and assuring him that he would 'fix him up.'

Hynes was very drunk, and Grant could feel himself following down the pastel sprung corridors of inebriation; his voice echoing splendidly in his own ears; his frame larger than life, expanded and buoyant; and, he was sure, an ironic smile on his lips as he mocked life and his own predicament.

Grant was a fairly good drunk, and even though he was barely aware of what he was doing, he quite adroitly managed the salad and meat dish that was served him and the other men in the dining-room later that evening by a silent Mrs Hynes.

And he did not stagger as he made his way out of the room.

But there were gaps in the chain of happenings and he could not quite remember how he had moved from point to point.

His voice was full and rich and he spoke very slowly as he asked Janette why on earth she stayed in Bundanyabba.

He was out on the front veranda. Heaven only knew where the others were, but Janette was standing quite close to him, very close.

The western stars crammed the sky except where the moon blotted them out as it squandered its light in a stream cascading down to lend brief grace to the city of Bundanyabba.

Grant breathed deeply of the lukewarm air and gazed with majestic melancholy at the gleaming roof-tops of the city.

'The moonlight,' he said. 'Like snow upon the desert's dusty face.'

Janette didn't respond, so he added: 'You know, "lighting a little hour or two."'

Still she said nothing.

'That's from a poem,' he said, a little less grandly.

'I know.'

Was he making an ass of himself? Janette didn't seem to think so. Janette was talking to him now. He couldn't quite catch what she was saying, but it sounded pleasant. Janette's voice was low and soft, and Robyn was almost two thousand miles away, and in any case Robyn was a lost cause and Janette had a peculiar beauty of her own. Janette was lovely and lithe and solemn, and Janette was very close.

'Would you care to go for a stroll?' he said, smiling down at her, his face, he hoped, a mask of attractive suffering.

Somehow he got the impression that his suggestion was not so much an idea of his own as a statement of her intentions. Perhaps he was very drunk after all.

Then he was standing alongside Janette in the lounge room and Janette was saying:

'Daddy, John and I are going for a walk.'

The three men looked dully at them, and one of the miners seemed cross, but it didn't matter because soon they were walking

along the street, he was alone with Janette in the night and the
moon was making even the dust beautiful.

Somewhere in the whirling recesses of his mind he knew this was
all a little too easy. Janette had not been impressed with him earlier
in the day. He could not remember just when he had become
attached to her, but she didn't seem to have said anything much;
and there was an air of compliance now in the way she walked and
the way she had let him take her hand.

Why should she comply? Who was this tall, dark girl who was
walking with him now out past the limits of this barbaric city?

They turned off the road.

Who had initiated that movement? Grant held his mind hard
and looked at the girl beside him. She seemed purposeful; she
seemed ... what did she seem? ... why was she so quiet?

They were walking on hard dusty ground, wasteland between
one of the mines and the city, and they threw great long shadows in
the moonlight.

Grant looked again at the girl, but he felt his mind slip and his
thoughts shambled off on their drunken round again.

It was very quiet out there, there was not enough vegetation for
insects and their footsteps on the dust were the only sound. Grant
realized they had not spoken for five minutes or more.

'You're very... quiet,' he said.

'Am I?' Her voice was deeper, almost hoarse, and it disturbed
Grant.

She didn't say anything more and now she was walking with her
head very close to Grant's, and his eyes would not focus properly so
she had two profiles.

Her eyes were glazed and her mouth was open. She was looking
straight ahead, and walking quite quickly, leading him by the
hand.

Grant began to suspect a great deal, and knew for certain that he
ought not to be as drunk as he was. Something of the intensity that
gripped the girl was cutting through to Grant as she strained
forward, her body taut. She wasn't walking, she was going
somewhere.

Some instinct of caution moved him to say:

'Won't your father be worried if we stay out too long?' But it
sounded foolish even to his ears.

They came to a slight hollow in the ground in which a patch of
low scrub had grown like a hedge with a clear section in the middle.

Grant no longer merely suspected; he knew that Janette had
brought him here, and he knew why. Nobody could be that drunk.

She slipped through the scrub into the clear space and he followed her.

They stoped for a moment and stood together, two tall thin
figures in the moonlight between the mine and the city.

The urgency seemed to have left her and she sank down on to the
bare ground, and lay on her back, her hands clasped behind her
head. Grant stood above her briefly, feeling that something required
to be said, and then he sat down beside her.

Her eyes were closed and she was breathing deeply. Grant ran a
hand experimentally over her face. She moved her head so that her
open lips touched his fingers.

'You know you're very ... beautiful,' he said, but he didn't like
the sardonic smile that caught her lips as he said it. Perhaps no
words were required after all.

He took out his last cigarette and lit it, and found that somehow
Janette had moved so that her head was on his thigh.

He looked up at the sky and did his best to think with whatever
powers still survived the alcohol. It was obvious that he was being
tempted to seduce this girl, or allow himself to be seduced by her,
and he wanted things a little clearer than this. Besides, there were
certain technical difficulties ...

Still, she must know, so why not? He would. He would? Yes he
would, why not? Yes he would.

He still felt he ought to say something, but there didn't seem to
be anything to say, or anything that would be well received anyway.

There was Robyn, Robyn's hair was fair ... but Robyn wasn't
here. Robyn was a long way away. And what was Robyn to him,
anyway?

Suddenly he remembered that he had never had a woman before,
and he knew that if he were more sober he would have been startled
by the thought. But as it was, he just felt swept away by the
inevitability of it all. The time for retreat had passed.

He was too drunk to know the compulsions of passion, but the
anaesthetized impulses within him dictated his actions and he
stretched out beside her, crushing his cigarette in the dust, putting
an arm across her body.

They lay face to face. All Grant could see was a blur of cheeks,
hair, lips and great closed eyes. He pressed closer, raised himself on
an elbow and touched her throat with his hand.

They lay there for perhaps a minute, Janette breathing more and
more rapidly and never once opening her eyes.

Grant kissed her, a little clumsily; but then she responded and it
was strange how her lips seemed to caress his, and Ah! there at last

was a flicker of passion that seemed to strike through him to her,
but it didn't last long.

A fox yapped somewhere out behind the mine and the sound
served only to increase their immense isolation.

Sadness caught at Grant as he wondered what to do next. This
was not quite what he had planned for himself, and what if he
should sire a child out here in the barren land he hated? How the
girl's body quivered and shook. His own was passive now, and he
wished that he could lose himself in desire, but all he had was a
dreary certainty of his own intentions.

The fox yapped again, farther away now.

Grant lay there looking at Janette, bemusedly wondering at
himself and at her, and at the moonlight on the dust.

Slowly Janette moved her hand towards her throat and undid the
buttons of her dress. She drew the cloth aside and Grant saw she
wore nothing else.

She spread her arms out and let her head fall back, baring her
breasts to the moon.

Still Grant lay there, staring at her now, longing for the fierce
pleasure this should give him.

There was something more to all of it than just this, something
more surely, even in the way of simple pleasure.

The fox yapped again, so far away now it could barely be heard.

Janette reached out an arm and drew Grant down across her
body. Passion flickered again and he gave himself to the task in
hand.

But even as her arms closed around his neck nausea gripped him,
violently, incredibly.

He rolled off her body and knelt in the scrub and vomited and
vomited, painfully and noisily in abject humiliation.

Sick and ashamed he turned again at last to Janette. She was
standing outside the circle of scrub. Her dress was buttoned up.

Sorry,' said Grant, 'we'd better go back.'

Janette said nothing and they walked back on to the road and
now the moonlight was harsh and brittle.

Grant let his drunkenness take control; he sank into it as a man
will fall asleep to stop thinking.

Afterwards there were only patches of the rest of that night that
he ever remembered ...

– Janette brushing down his jacket before they reached the
house.

– The men singing inside. They looked at him when he came in
and someone had laughed.

– Janette being gone, lost somewhere between the front gate and the sitting-room where the men were singing.

– Another man at the party. 'This is Doc Tydon,' they had said. A sparse little man with a moustache.

– Beer being handed to him and his drinking it hurriedly, without pleasure, seeking only absence of thought and feeling.

– More beer and more beer.

– Then the beer had run out and there had been whisky ...

– Then the whisky had run out and there had been some kind of liqueur, sweet and sticky.

– 'How do you find The Yabba, John?' Who the devil had asked that?

– Angry words, but who was angry with whom?

Until at last oblivion came and Grant succeeded in annihilating himself utterly, for the time being at any rate.

CHAPTER 3

He was crouching in a corner of the schoolroom at Tiboonda, behind a desk and a man with a revolver was going to shoot him. The report of the revolver hurt his head and the flare of the explosion hurt his eyes.

And he was dead.

Pause.

Oblivion.

He was back in the corner, and the gunman was going to shoot him again and he knew it was for the second time. The pain in his head. The pain in his eyes. It was the fear more than anything. He was going to be killed and there was nothing he could do about it. The explosion. The flash.

And he was dead.

Pause.

Oblivion.

When he opened his eyes the light was unbearable and he shut them. But he had to open them again to see where he was.

He was lying on a stretcher. His clothes were saturated with sweat. Thirst was ploughing furrows in his throat. His head hurt and hurt and hurt.

Where the devil was he?

He stood up and swayed as pain swilled around inside his skull.

There was a door over there, and there was someone beyond that door. He could hear plates being moved.

Grant walked over and pulled open the door. It led to a sort of kitchen, and a man with his back to him was cooking something on a Primus stove.

The man turned around, sparse and little, with a moustache.

'G'day,' he said.

Grant had to try three times before he could form the greeting 'G'day.'

'I suppose you feel lousy?' said the man.

'Yes,' said Grant, who thought he was going to faint, or die.

'Like a drink?' said the man.

'Water,' said Grant.

'Beer,' said the man.

'Just water, thanks,' said Grant, who felt that he would scream if he had to speak again without drinking something.

'Yabba water's only good for cooking,' said the man. He went to a small kerosene refrigerator and took out a glass of beer.

'I let it go flat,' he said, 'it's better that way when you feel the way you do.'

Grant took the glass and thought he would vomit again when the sour smell of flat beer reached his nostrils. But he had to drink something and it wasn't bad once he was half-way through.

'I'm very sorry,' he said, 'but could you tell me who you are?'

'Tydon,' said the man, 'Doc Tydon – you met me last night at Hynes's place.'

Grant let that sink in. Hynes's place last night. Memory hit him a treacherous blow. He looked down at his clothes. They were unmistakably stained. O God, but at least the thought about that could wait until the pain had gone.

'You'd better sit down,' said Tydon, pushing a fruit box across.

Grant sat on it. Tydon took his glass and filled it from another one out of the refrigerator.

'I don't think I want another one, thanks,' said Grant.

'Two is what you want when you look like that. Then you'd better eat.'

Grant drank half the beer submissively.

'What am I doing here?'

'I brought you here last night. You were stung.'

'Stung?'

'Hit. Blotto, blind, inebriated – call it what you like.'

'Sorry. I'm not too clear about things yet. What happened?'

'You just drank yourself under the table after your little episode with Janette.'

Grant felt his face sagging at that.

'Don't get upset. We've all had little episodes with Janette.'

This would all take a great deal of thinking about when he felt better, but at the moment thinking was not a very practical proposition.

'Eat some of this,' said Tydon, pointing at a plate he had laid out heaped with a mash of meat and vegetables.

'Thanks very much, but I don't feel particularly like eating.'

'No, but you'd better eat just the same – come on.'

Grant could not argue. He pulled the box over to the table and began to eat the food with a spoon Tydon gave him. In fact, it did make him feel better. He ate it all.

Memory struck at him again – his suitcases, where were they?

He'd left them in a hotel. Which hotel? Dear God! He had no chance of finding them again. He felt tears in his eyes and fought them back. He'd lost money, honour, virtue and now his suitcases, and the suitcases seemed the most grievous loss of all.

But damn it! He couldn't break down and weep in front of this man Tydon.

'That must have been quite a party last night,' he said.

'It's always like that at Hynes's on the week-end.'

'What time did we finish?'

'About dawn.'

'What's the time now?' His own watch had stopped.

'About four o'clock.'

'Hell!' Grant did his best to stand up briskly. 'Well, thanks for your hospitality. I'd better be getting along.' He'd said that somewhere before recently ... of course ... at Hynes's.

'You've got nowhere to go, so you might as well stay here.'

'But I can't stay here indefinitely.' He felt a need to explain himself. 'You see I'm a schoolteacher at Tiboonda and I lost my ...'

'Yes. I heard all that crap last night. I don't believe a word of it.'

'You don't?'

'No.' Tydon was carelessly contemptuous.

'But ... why not?'

'I saw you at the Game on Friday night.'

'Ah ...'

'What did you want to lie about it for?'

'Well, a man feels a bit of a fool ...'

'Better men than you have been made fools of at the Game.'

Grant could see and hear Tydon clearly for the first time now and he didn't like him much. He had very bad teeth.

'No doubt. But in any case I can't stay in your ... cabin indefinitely, can I ?'

'It's not my cabin. Belongs to the mines. I've just been living in it for five years.'

'Yes, well anyway ...'

'You might as well stay here as try to sponge on men like Tim Hynes.'

There was not much to say to that, so Grant sat there and looked out of the small window of the kitchen. The plain dwindling away to dancing heat-haze made him turn his head hurriedly.

He had to say something to Tydon, he supposed, so he said:

'You've lived here for five years?'

Tydon reacted as though he had been waiting for the question.

'If it will satisfy your curiosity about me,' he said, although Grant was not aware of having expressed any particular curiosity about him, 'I am a doctor of medicine and an alcoholic.'

Grant did not care, and could not see what that had to do with the length of time he had been living in the hut, but Tydon went on:

'I came to Bundanyabba seven years ago because it is probably the only place in Australia where I could practise medicine without the fact that I was an alcoholic preventing people coming to me.

'I discovered in one month flat that I could live and drink as much as I liked without working at anything, provided I remained what the locals term a "character".'

Grant said 'Hmm', and hoped the monologue had come to an end. It hadn't.

'I remained a character. I live in this hut. I obtain all my meals free from my many friends who also provide me with my requirements in beer, which, with some self-control, is the only alcohol I allow myself.'

That was probably all a lie, including the part about being a doctor, thought Grant, but what the hell? Who was he to worry about people lying, anyway? Just the same, he did not like Tydon.

Tydon was again drinking flat beer, and Grant suspected now that it was flat because it was the remnants of open bottles from the night before which Tydon had scavenged.

'And you get along without money altogether?' he asked, because Tydon obviously expected some reaction to his self-revelation.

'Not quite – I have a couple of pounds from a war pension; but it's possible to live in The Yabba without money, provided you conform.'

Was this wretched man suggesting that he, John Grant, should 'conform', should adopt the same wretched life as Tydon?

At that, it might be the solution to the next six weeks.

But not here, not in this oven of a hut. And damn it, he had to get out of Bundanyabba after that episode last night, apart from anything else.

Tydon opened the refrigerator to get more beer and Grant saw a number of partly empty bottles on the lower shelf.

The pain in his head had settled down to a gnawing ache that he did not think he could stand for long.

'You wouldn't have an A.P.C., would you?' he asked.

'No,' said Tydon, 'but I've got something a lot better.'

He pulled a tin out of his pocket, opened it and took out one of a number of large white pills.

'This'll fix your headache and pep you up a bit.'

Grant took the pill from Tydon reluctantly. He fully shared the rest of Australia's distrust of alcoholic doctors.

'Wash it down with beer, it's better that way,' said Tydon, filling Grant's glass.

'I ... I find a lot of drugs upset me ... perhaps I'll ...'

'There's nothing in that will hurt you,' said Tydon with authority, 'swallow it.'

There were few things Grant would not do rather than suffer embarrassment, and he swallowed the pill in a gulp of beer.

It had no immediate harmful effect.

Tydon rolled a cigarette from a pouch of tobacco and handed the pouch across to Grant. Grant's mouth felt as though it was coated with soft cement but his being yearned for a cigarette, and with fumbling and slightly trembling fingers he rolled one.

If he could get through today and just take a few drinks to soothe his sick body, he would think hard tomorrow about getting work or getting to Sydney.

And for the meantime, why not stay here? But about his clothes ...

'I've left my suitcases in a pub somewhere, I'd better try to find them, I think,' he said.

'I wouldn't worry,' said Tydon, 'they'll be there tomorrow and you've got an appointment in half an hour.'

'I have?'

'Forgotten that too? You're going 'roo shooting with Dick and Joe.'

'Dick and Joe?'

'The two miners at Hynes's last night,' Tydon added conversationally. 'You were lucky Joe didn't beat you to a pulp.'

'What did I do?'

'Janette.'

'Oh . . . I see. Actually you know, nothing happened between me and her.' He didn't know why he bothered to tell that to Tydon.

'No?'

Grant didn't feel like pursuing the point. After all it had not been his fault, or Janette's, that nothing had happened.

'Janette,' said Tydon, determined to discuss her, 'is a very interesting biological case.'

'So?'

'If she were a man she'd have been jailed for rape two years ago.'

'Go on. What's all this about kangaroo shooting?'

'You arranged to go shooting, that's all.'

'With a man who was going to beat me to a pulp last night?'

'Yes, But you'll be safe enough while Janette's not around. Now if I ever married, Janette is just the sort of girl I'd marry. She likes sex, she likes to experiment and she likes variety.'

Grant listened in despair; he was in no condition to listen to the prurient speculations of this wretched man.

'And she's an intelligent girl, she's got a good body and a pretty enough face.'

Grant thought of Janette's face as he had seen it, sharp against the moonlight and, later, blurred and close to his. Oh Robyn, Robyn of the cool white skirts.

'Moreover, like most of the other men who've met her, I know what she's like in bed; and she's good, damned good.'

That did not ring true to Grant. Tydon seemed to him a nasty little psychopath who had neither been a doctor nor gone to bed with Janette, even assuming that bed was a euphemism for that bare patch in the circle of scrub between the city and the mine.

'I thought about marrying her once,' Tydon spoke savagely all the time, as though contemptuously quelling somebody in a bitter argument, 'but I couldn't live with any woman for long. Just the same I think I'll bring her out here for a while again soon.'

Great, thought Grant, wonderful; but what did he do? Get up and stalk out into the sun? Stalk over the hot dust to the city? and then stalk up and down the streets until he dropped dead from heat prostration?

No, he would sit here and let Tydon tell him about his sex life, or

supposed sex life, or rather supposed life – it was certainly sexy . . .
he lost the train of the thought.

Tydon was still talking.

'But what's wrong with a woman taking a man when she feels
like one?'

'I . . . don't really know.'

'You don't know because there's nothing wrong with it, nothing.
It's a damned sensible, civilized way to behave.

'And yet you'd find people who'd call Janette a slut – women
who'd like to act like her, and men she hasn't given a tumble.'

'Are you coming shooting?'

'Yes. Sex is just like eating, or sleeping or eliminating. It's a
thing you do because you have to or because you want to. Have
another drink. And yet it's been surrounded by all the mystery and
ballyhoo of centuries for God knows what reason.'

'Thanks.' But that must be the last drink for today.

Tydon was sitting hunched on his box, making spasmodic little
movements with his haunches as he talked so that he seemed to be
twitching in pain.

Grant noticed that the ache in his head had been replaced by a
sensation which was, if anything, worse – a sort of humming
vibration which seemed to start at the top of his spine and spread to
the top of his skull and back down again into his body.

That, he thought, was doubtless the 'pepping-up' that Tydon
had promised.

He wished he had not taken that pill.

Tydon, twitching all the time, went on and went on about
Janette, his face slipping a little each time he mentioned her name,
about sex hygiene, about social disease, about conception and
miscarriage and abortion and homosexuality (a lot of nonsense was
talked about homosexuality, there was nothing wrong with it,
although he didn't practise it himself) and about genital organs and
the effects of their size on cohabitation and about Janette and about
Janette and about Janette.

Grant felt as though he had been released from dank and noisome
captivity when a car drew up outside, a horn sounded, a dog barked
and a voice shouted: 'Come on, Doc!'

Tydon went to the door.

Grant flinched at the block of light that fell into the room.

'Come in, be ready in a minute.'

There was some disturbance outside as the men got out of the car
and resisted the efforts of the dog to follow them. Then they were in
the hut, big, boisterous, booming, showing no effects at all of the

previous night's debauch. But then they probably hadn't debauched as much as Grant had.

'Hi, John!' they said, 'feeling lousy, eh?' and 'Take a hair of the dog, boy, a hair of the dog,' and 'Come on, Doc, shake a leg.'

Tydon had opened a home-made cupboard and taken out a very efficient-looking rifle.

'We've got a gun for you, John,' said the miners. 'It hasn't been used in five years so it might blow your head off.'

'Ha. Ha.'

'Come on, Doc, let's get out of here.'

And they were out of the hut, climbing into a big American car. Most of the population of Bundanyabba seemed to affect big American cars, of varying vintage.

Opening the rear door Grant found himself looking into the face of an enormous greyhound. It filled most of the back of the car and its legs overflowed into the front and out of the window. Its great slobbering tongue was everywhere, and it dribbled.

But Grant rather liked the yellow and fawn beast – it was the first living thing he had seen in Bundanyabba that seemed reasonably uncomplicated and was certain not to talk to him.

He pushed into the bony and yielding tangle of dog and found himself room on the back seat. Joe, or Dick, he wasn't sure which, pushed in beside him. Tydon got in the front and the other miner took the wheel.

They were on their way, four men and a dog, stewing together.

When you travel by road in the west you travel with a cohort of dust which streams up from your tyres and rolls away in a dis-integrating funnel, defining the currents of air your vehicle sets in motion. And somehow a lot of dust comes in the windows and settles in your hair and your clothes and most of all in your eyes and throat.

And the heat is unthinkable, no matter how widely the windows are open, and the sweat streams off your body and into your socks, and if there are a number of people in the car their body stenches mingle disagreeably.

So it was with Grant and Tydon and Joe and Dick and the yellow and fawn dog, except that the dog did not sweat, but its mouth gaped hideously and it panted stertorously and its tongue lolled out and it dribbled and it smelt; Lord how it smelt!

The miner drove fast on the rudimentary road, bouncing high on the ruts and slewing fiercely in the drifts of soft dust.

The western roads are cut with causeways built in the hope of channelling whatever rain falls into some useful direction. These cannot be seen in the flat country until you're almost on them. And if you're travelling at sixty miles an hour you don't have time to slow down before you hit them and the front wheels of your car shoot briefly into the air and the car lands with a crash two feet down, then shoots up the other side and crashes on to the level of the road again.

It plays hell with the springs and Grant thought he was going to die every time it happened and every time the big dog's body bounced limply to the roof of the car and flopped down again, mostly on Grant.

A dim acceptance of the fact that this whole situation was near farce was no consolation as he shrank into the seat between the dog and the miner.

He felt himself in the impossible position of a man with an overwhelming problem to solve, but lacking the neural energy even to make an attempt to solve it. Some time he had to think about getting to Sydney, or doing something, but not now, not just now.

'We'd better have a drink at Yindee,' said the miner driving the car.

'It'll be dark if we do, Dick,' said the miner sitting beside Grant, from which Grant deduced that he must be Joe.

'So what?'

'So we want to have a go with the dog.'

'We'll see something before we hit Yindee.'

'All right.'

Grant felt obliged to add something to the conversation.

'Where,' he said, 'is Yindee?'

'About sixty miles out of The Yabba,' said Joe.

Grant wondered whether it was Joe or Dick he had upset by his interlude with Janette last night. Tydon had named one of them, hadn't he? Anyhow, neither seemed at all put out today.

'How do you feel after last night?' said Joe, startling Grant a little.

'Bloody.'

'Hit it a bit hard, eh?'

'Much too hard.'

'Cheer up, a few drinks'll put you on your feet.'

Grant looked forward cheerlessly to the few drinks at Yindee. Even one round would have his capital resources, two would pauperize him.

He should not have come on this trip, but he could hardly have stayed in the hut. Tydon seemed to expect him to stay there indefinitely, but he hadn't put it in so many words.

Dear God, the air in this car was foul.

Abruptly the car stopped dead and the funnel of dust which had been trailing behind caught up and enveloped it.

'Down there,' said Dick, and pointed.

The country slid away a little to the left, forming a minutely shallow valley about a mile wide which, in a gentler land, might have been split by a stream. Running parallel with the road about a quarter of a mile away a low line of scrub formed a swathe across the otherwise bare earth.

On the other side of the scrub Grant could see a mob of about twenty kangaroos.

The dog had seen them too, or smelt them, and was slavering around the window, thrusting its hindquarters into Grant's face, lashing him with its tail.

Joe reached across and opened the door.

The dog vaulted from the car and hurtled towards the kangaroos, moving in unbelievably long bounds, floating, touching the ground, bouncing up, floating ... its formerly ungainly limbs coordinated into a magnificent motivating principle.

The kangaroos watched it impassively until it was about two hundred yards from them. Then they turned and leaped away, stiffly erect, propelling themselves with thrusts of their giant hind legs so that they looked like so many mechanical toys except that at the height of their leap their tails streamed out behind them and their bodies leaned forward so that they speared through the air like abstractions of flight.

Grant forgot even his hangover as he watched the hunter springing after the kangaroos as they crossed the plain like the shadows of aircraft.

The mob rose in a wave over one of the occasional fences that appear inexplicably in the plain country, but two baulked and turned along the fence towards the road.

Immediately the motor of the car roared, the gear slammed in and Dick drove diagonally off the road, cutting across the flight of the two kangaroos.

There was not much difference between the road and the open country, but there were boulders on the plain and Dick performed mighty deeds with the car, keeping it at fifty miles an hour, swerving hard when he reached the fence and driving straight down to the kangaroos.

The dog anticipated the manoeuvre and turned diagonally out from the fence.

The kangaroos sighted the car and they too turned out from the fence, heading back to the patch of scrub. And now the kangaroos and the dog were travelling in two lines which would soon meet.

Tydon had his rifle out now and was firing through the window. Joe was trying to aim across Grant's shoulder, and still the car bounced over the ground at fifty miles an hour.

The men were shouting, the motor was roaring, the sharp smell of gunpowder drowned all the other smells in the car.

The dog pulled down one of the kangaroos in a tangled heap about fifty yards from the fence. The other kangaroo paused for a moment when its mate fell and Grant could see it watching the slaughter, immobile, expressionless. Then it streaked back towards the fence again.

But the car was between it and the fence.

Dick, yelling madly now, drove straight at the kangaroo, pressing down the accelerator, driving as no sane man would do, crashing over stones, through low scrub, wrecking the mudguards on the remnants of trees, and still the kangaroo came on, unharmed by the fusillade of bullets which Tydon was pumping out the window.

Grant clung to the seat, fascinated, watching through the windscreen the fluctuating approach of the kangaroo. Up it went and down, then up, up, and down, a wild grey figure bearing down on them as though in passionless attack.

It turned ten yards from the car, but Dick, quite mad now, pulled the car around and ran the animal down.

It disappeared quite suddenly under the bonnet.

A thud, the car lifted, skidded, rocketed almost over on to its side, righted itself and stopped.

Grant looked out of the rear window as the others tumbled out. A grey bundle was flopping about in the dust behind the car.

Following the others over the broken mess, Grant saw Dick draw a long-bladed knife from a sheath at his side, kneel down, and cut the animal's throat. It died then.

'It's not worth cutting up,' said Dick. The kangaroo had split open and trailed entrails for a dozen yards. Its body was so shattered that bones stood out from the skin every few inches, white and glistening.

Joe and Dick started off to look at the damage to the car, but Tydon lingered, took out his own knife and neatly castrated the carcass.

Grant watched the incident blankly and Joe said: 'Doc eats 'em, reckons they're the best part of the 'roo.'

Grant thought wanly of the hash that Tydon had given him that afternoon.

Tydon, meanwhile, slipped the scrotum into his pocket and they all walked over to the car then.

The radiator grille was dented slightly and there was a fairly deep curve in the bumper bar. Underneath they could see grey patches on the gearbox.

They all got back in and Dick drove across to where the greyhound was worrying the other carcass.

'He's a dead loss too,' said Joe.

The kangaroo had apparently had some disease, its hindquarters and belly were a mass of black scabs.

Joe dragged the dog away and bundled it into the car. Now it smelt of blood and dead kangaroo.

It snuggled against Grant.

The vibrations in his head that Grant had noticed back in the hut had become a fierce drumming that pervaded his whole body. He felt unnaturally alert, as though he had constantly the physical reaction of having just been made aware of danger.

'What was in the pill you gave me?' he asked Tydon as they drove off.

'Benzedrine and stuff,' said Tydon, 'want another?'

'No thanks.'

One thing was certain now, thought Grant, once this hunting episode was over he would not return to Tydon's hut.

The sexual mania he could bear; the heat had to be borne anyway; Tydon's breath was noxious, but not impossible; the man's conversation was appalling, but probably sufferable for a time; but a diet of kangaroo's testicles was altogether too much. He would set out to walk back to Sydney before he would stay with Tydon.

Joe rummaged on the floor of the car and came up with a twenty-two rifle.

'This is yours,' he said to Grant.

'Oh, thanks.' It seemed quite a reasonable weapon, a single shot with a much scarred stock, but apparently unmarked barrel.

Joe gave him a large handful of cartridges.

'Plenty more here if you want them. Know how to use that?'

'Yes, thanks.' Grant worked the loading mechanism.

'Done a bit of shooting?'

'Oh, on the coast, a few rabbits now and then.'

The car shuddered and the dog rose to the roof and came down, banging its jaw on the barrel of the rifle.

'Are all the roads around here like this?'

'This isn't bad. You ought to go out to Mundameer.'

'Where are we going now?'

'Place out from Yindee we know. We'll get a lot of 'roos there.'

'Do we shoot in the dark?'

'Spotlight. We've got a beaut.'

The sun was setting, dropping down below a cloudless horizon, glowing red through the dust haze low to the ground. To the east the plain melted into mauve and black.

The township of Yindee popped out of the darkening country quite suddenly. It was one lone, long, low hotel.

They pulled up right at the door, clumped over the inevitable wooden veranda and Dick called for four beers.

'There's a fox,' said Joe.

In the fading light about fifty yards down the road they could see it, padding along on the dust, looking as though it was going somewhere.

Elaborately casual, Tydon, Joe and Dick walked back to the car. Grant followed them.

They took out their rifles. Grant took out his. Three rifles cracked. Grant was still loading his.

The fox swung around and lolloped back down the road. Dust flicked up around it as the bullets landed. It turned at right-angles and began to run across the road, and then it dropped its neck, slid a little way, kicked and lay still.

The greyhound was by now hysterical, but they did not let it out of the car.

It had been an extremely good, or lucky, shot that had brought down the fox in that light. Grant, who had got in one shot, and rather thought he might have hit the fox, wanted to go and get it; but the others wouldn't hear of it.

'Mangy brute,' said Joe, 'not worth skinning. They never are out here.'

So the fox was left on the road and they all went into the bar where the publican, unmoved by the fusillade at his front door, had set up the beer.

Grant, who had been thinking a great deal about the paying for this beer, took out his ten-shilling note at the prompting of a furtive and unadmitted instinct, and tossed it on the bar.

Joe picked it up and handed it back to him.

'No one who's broke buys beer in The Yabba, mate,' he said; and, as that was what Grant had half expected or hoped would happen, he took back the note after suitable protest.

But he avoided looking at Tydon, who had begun to drink his beer already.

He must not drink too much, thought Grant, just enough, and
then if he found somewhere to sleep tonight he would be in fit shape
to find work, or something, tomorrow.

But how much was just enough? One beer was wonderful, so
cool, so wet, so much desired by the dusty throat.

Two beers slowed down the benzedrine-inspired drumming in
his body.

Three beers and his head was clearing, and then came the need
for a cigarette.

'Anybody got a cigarette?'

'Sorry, I don't smoke,' said Joe.

'Nor do I,' said Dick.

Tydon took out his pouch and handed it to Grant.

Grant wished he hadn't raised the question; he would give up
smoking rather than ask Tydon for another cigarette, or anything
else. He hated Tydon, he realized, with a clear, hard hatred.

Still, the tobacco was good.

Joe said to the publican: 'Give us a packet of Craven A, mate.'

The publican handed the cigarettes to Joe and Joe slapped them
on the bar in front of Grant.

'Here y'are, mate. I used to smoke, I know what it's like to be
without 'em.'

'Look, really – thanks very much, but ... I mean ...' Grant
laughed foolishly.

'Take 'em, John. Go on, mate, a few bob's nothing to me.'

'But I ...' but what could he do? 'Well, thanks very much.'

'Forget it.'

Tydon did not make any attempt to buy beer, and it did not seem
to enter the miners' heads that he should. They took it in turns to
order the rounds of four.

Four beers and a man's troubles appear not as grave as they did
before he had one beer. But a man could still rather regret that he
had no money, and a man could feel sick at being given a packet of
cigarettes.

Grant made a fairly serious attempt to buy the fifth round, but
Joe, helped by Dick this time, brushed him aside.

'Well, I'll tell you what – as soon as I get some money you
must let me take you on a bash.' That sounded banal even as he
said it.

'That's all right, John, don't worry about it.'

Five beers and a man begins to rather like his companions,
except for Tydon. Tydon was a rat of the first water. It was
remarkable that two men like the miners would associate with him.

With all their faults they were men, and Tydon was a twisted, revolting creature.

'Have you always been a miner, Joe?'

'No, John, only since the war. Me and Dick drifted in here together and liked it, so we stuck.'

'What did you do before the war?'

'Boxed.'

'Boxed?'

'Yeah, boxed.'

'You mean fought professionally?'

'Yeah. Can't you see our noses been broken?'

'No. I hadn't noticed.'

'Well they have, both of them.'

Joe and Dick were so alike to Grant that he kept confusing them. They corrected him gently and good-humouredly.

'No, I'm Dick.'

'No, he's Joe.'

'You know, I used to do a bit of boxing.'

'Did you, eh, John? Pro?'

'Oh no, just amateur.'

'What class?'

'Welter – it was a few years ago, mind you.'

'We were light-heavy. It's a mug's game though, bein' a pro.'

Seven or eight or nine beers and a man is in control of himself and his destiny, no matter how bad a hangover he had when he woke up.

To round things off Joe and Dick and Tydon had a double whisky followed quickly by another beer. Grant baulked at this, but he had a final beer, to keep them company.

Then Joe – or was it Dick? – bought a couple of dozen bottles of beer and two bottles of whisky.

'We might need a drink before we finish.'

And so they went out into the night to shoot.

It was quite dark now and there was no moon yet.

About ten miles east of Yindee they pulled off the road along a fairly well-defined track. They were in amongst one of the large patches of scrub and scrawny trees that appear every now and then in the plain country in apparent defiance of the laws of nature.

Joe reached up and drew back a panel in the roof of the car. Then, from beneath the seat, he took out a lamp with leads attached and screwed into a fixture, installed for the purpose, in the roof. He pushed down a switch and a wide, bright beam of light poked forward far into the black night.

All the time Dick drove at a steady forty miles an hour. He seemed to know the route quite well.

Grant could see in the beam of light pairs of coloured spots, yellow spots, blue spots, orange spots; glinting suddenly and fixedly, then flicking out. These were the eyes of the animals of the scrub, 'possums, sheep, foxes, dingoes, cattle, kangaroos, rabbits, rats, emus, wild-cats, bandicoots, all turning their eyes into the giant white beam that pointed its way through their bush, catching a little of it and sending it back, coloured. Then they would turn their heads and bolt away and the colours would flick out.

Grant was caught in a rush of visual effects – black shadows, coloured spots, the great white beam, the cigarette of the man in the front seat, strange little glints from shiny leaves, the heavy darkness of the scrub, all held and contained by the hovering curve of the black, black, purple black sky which only the stars could penetrate.

The stars, the western stars, so many, so bright, so close, so clean, so clear; splitting the sky in remorseless frigidity; pure stars, unemotional stars; stars in command of the night and themselves; undemanding and unforgiving; excelling in their being and forming God's incontrovertible argument against the charge of error in creating the west.

The car stopped and Dick opened a bottle of beer with his teeth.

Grant had never seen it done before and Dick explained that the technique involved pressing down with the top teeth and levering with the lower teeth.

'You don't want to try it,' he said, 'if you've got false teeth.'

Grant's teeth were his own and in excellent condition, but he did not want to open bottles with them.

Tydon had a drink, Dick had a drink, Joe had a drink and Grant had a drink, so the bottle was empty and they drove on.

Grant was feeling relaxed and sure of himself now and he opened the breech of his rifle to load it. There was already a shell in place. That was odd. He must have reloaded after firing at the fox. He didn't remember. That could have been dangerous. He closed the breech again and leaned forward in the wildly bumping car to see what the spotlight revealed.

'Stand up and put your head out the top,' said Joe.

Grant cautiously raised his head through the trap in the roof of the car and pulled the rifle through after him. With the night rushing past he leaned forward with his elbows on the roof and raised the rifle to cover the area lit by the spotlight. The car was rocking and bumping continuously and he could not keep the barrel pointed at the light, much less take a sight.

A hare broke in front of the car and ran forwards in the light.

Grant cocked the rifle and after several attempts to level it at the hare tried a wavering shot. There was nothing to indicate that the bullet landed anywhere near the hare and soon it veered off into the night.

Grant heard Joe's voice rising from the darkness below in the car: 'You'll never hit anything but a 'roo while we're moving, son.'

'No, I suppose not.'

It was very pleasant and refreshing up there, protruding from the vehicle like the commander of a tank. His companions seemed distant and he felt nearer to being alone than he had since he came to Bundanyabba.

Something was digging into his hip. He put his hand down and felt it. Round, cool and smooth, a sharp excrescence on one side. It was the end of a rifle barrel. He pushed it aside and it fell back against his hip.

Grant bent sideways so that his head was level with the roof of the car.

'Joe,' he said, 'your rifle's more or less pointing at me.'

'Yeah.' Joe was polite, but not concerned.

'You're sure it's not loaded?'

'Yeah, it's loaded.'

'Well – ah – isn't it a little dicey?'

'No, it's got a safety catch.'

'Oh.'

Grant stood upright and looked once more along the beam of light. But he did not feel so alone now.

He tried to arrange his body so that the rifle was not pointed in a line that would pass through his entrails, his chest and his head; but he could not manage it.

He stayed there until he was confident that nobody would connect his sitting down with the fact that he was nervous of the rifle, then he came back into the car and sat down.

The greyhound had taken up his part of the seat and he had to push it aside.

'You needn't worry about my rifle,' said Joe, 'It's safe enough.'

'No, I didn't. I just thought I'd come in for a bit.'

The dog was protesting amiably against being shifted and it licked his hands.

He wished they would open some more beer.

The car swung sharply to the left and stopped. The dog thrust its head out of the window and began to growl and scrabble with its back feet. Joe stood up, thrusting his head out through the trap. Tydon and Dick craned out of the windows, levelling their rifles.

Grant, who had not seen anything yet, squeezed up through the trap beside Joe, drawing his rifle after him.

They were on the edge of a small clearing. On the other side, about a hundred feet away, five kangaroos were standing poised, watching, waiting.

'Right!' said Joe, and fired.

Everybody fired.

The kangaroos began hopping backwards and forwards, fretful, keeping their heads turned towards the car, their eyes orange in the spotlight.

The rifles exploded irregularly, the fast staccato of the automatic Tydon was using; the slower rhythmic beat of Joe's repeater broken with little clashes of metal as he worked the ejector; the spasmodic cracks from the single-shot weapons Grant and Dick were firing as fast as they could reload.

All the rifles were point 22s and one of the small slugs was seldom sufficient to bring down a kangaroo.

But the range was so short it was impossible to miss, and as Grant's eager fingers worked to reload he could hear the tearing thump of bullets made as they hit flesh.

And presently the kangaroos began to fall down, even in the act of dying keeping their heads turned to the great mass of light that had burst from the bush to become the last thing they would see,

Soon they were all down except one, and it, breaking at last from the hypnotic light, hopped crookedly away into the scrub.

The night seemed wonderfully silent in the moment after the firing stopped, before the motor started, while the still air was yet heavy with the smoke of gunpowder.

They drove across the clearing and all climbed out to examine the kill. The dog had to be forcibly kept in the car.

'Couldn't he get the one that was wounded?' asked Grant.

'No, we'd never get him back if we let him go in the dark,' said Dick.

Three of the kangaroos were dead. One had its leg broken and looked at them with undisturbed eyes.

Joe smashed its head in with a branch he broke off a dead tree.

Grant was surprised that he did not feel particularly upset at the mass carnage. They were, after all, only kangaroos.

Joe and Dick each took a carcass, ripped open the belly, spilled out the intestines and sawed off the hindquarters, complete with the long muscular tails.

Grant had never seen anything quite so sudden. In one moment the kangaroos had been quite respectable corpses; in the next they were horrible bits of animals trailing their insides.

Tydon meanwhile had his own business with the carcasses, but Grant could not look at that.

The miners dumped the quarters in a large box they had built into the car in place of the boot.

Soon they were driving off again, and the grieving night closed in on the grotesque half-carcasses protruding from the heaps of entrails, waiting for the dingoes and the foxes and the crows and the ants; tomorrow they would be only bones.

'Why only the hindquarters?' said Grant.

'That's all that's got any meat, that and the tail,' said Joe.

'What do you do with it?'

'It's for the dogs, didn't you know?'

Grant remembered that the miners kept racing greyhounds.

'Does this fellow race?'

'Gawd no! He's just a hunger. Wouldn't bring the runners out here, wreck 'em.'

'How many 'roos do you want?'

'Many as we can carry. What we don't use the other blokes will.'

'You don't eat any of the meat yourselves – the tails, I mean?'

'Sometimes get the old woman to make soup out of 'em. Don't like it much myself, too gamey.'

Grant saw a big grey kangaroo standing by the track.

He had his rifle cocked and levelled as the car slowed down.

The kangaroo was only twenty feet away, quite still, just outside the main glare of the light, facing out into the darkness for some reason.

It didn't seem to even notice the car, thought Grant in the moment that the car stopped, and then with fumbling haste he fired.

The bullet went home with a thud so distinct that Grant felt as though he had thrust something into the animal with his hands.

It went down suddenly, merging into the patch of scrub in which it stood.

The patch was isolated and there was no other cover for twenty yards. Grant waited to see whether the kangaroo would break out.

A horrible noise came from the scrub, a hoarse, sucking, raucous breathing.

'Good shot,' said Joe.

But Grant was caught, horrified by the breathing. It bubbled and choked, and it was so loud, so very loud.

'He won't move now,' said Joe, 'I'll get him.'

Grant still did not speak. He was frightened of what was in the patch of scrub and he didn't know why.

As Joe walked across, the breathing stopped. It did not die away, or fade, or splutter out. It just stopped.

Joe reached the patch of scrub and halted.

Grant heard him say: 'Well I'll be damned.' Then he walked through the patch, it was only about six feet square.

He walked through it twice, then turned back to the car.

Grant knew what he was going to say, but he didn't think he could bear to hear it.

'There's nothing there,' said Joe, and even his voice was subdued.

'Rubbish,' said Dick, 'it couldn't have got out. Go and get it.'

'I tell you it's not there!'

Grant stood erect staring, his eyes stinging, his lips trembling, a strange prickle on his skin. He knew the kangaroo wasn't there. He didn't know how he knew, nor why it wasn't there! but he knew it wasn't there. Oh God! why wasn't it there?

Tydon and Dick went over to look, but they couldn't find the kangaroo either.

Grant would not leave the car.

'Funny,' said Dick, at last.

'Bloody funny,' said Joe.

Grant felt his nerves tearing.

'You saw it go down, didn't you?' He wondered whether his voice was breaking.

'Yeah. Still ... things look funny in the bush at night.' Dick spoke slowly.

'Did you hear the noise it made?'

'Yeah. Funny noise.'

'Ah well!'

'Ah well!'

Dick opened some more beer then; and because the effects of his earlier drinking were wearing off, he took a swig of whisky.

Grant refused the beer, but he took a mouthful of whisky from the bottle. He could not drink whisky neat when he was quite sober, but he had no trouble with it now. It was quite pleasant really, and very reassuring.

As they drove on, they kept passing the whisky round, because everybody felt in need of it.

Grant hunddled back in his seat, drinking whisky when

it was offered to him, wondering about the kangaroo he had shot.

It didn't matter much now, in the car; but back there, in the night, under the stars ... Oh God, he wished he was not drunk again.

They came across another mob of kangaroos quite soon. There were ten or twelve with one huge animal which just stood upright and looked steadfastly at the light.

One by one in answer to the demands of the cracking rifles the kangaroos dropped to the ground, or hopped lamely off into the night; all except the big one, which never moved.

'He's the leader of the mob,' said Joe, as he and Grant, side by side in the trap, pumped bullets at the kangaroo. 'He's hit all right too.'

Dick started the car and drove over to the kangaroo. Still it stood there.

'Don't waste any more bullets,' called Dick, 'I'll fix him!'

The kangaroo had two red stains on the white fur of its chest. One of its arms hung loose, shattered at the shoulder joint.

Dick advanced on it, his knife in his hand.

The kangaroo turned calmly to face him.

Dick made a casual movement with his knife towards its head. It swayed back slightly, resting on its tail, but made no other movement.

Joe chuckled.

'Y'see,' he said, 'the 'roo's trying to draw him on, rip his guts out with its hind legs if he goes in close.'

The man and the kangaroo surveyed each other in the glare of the spotlight.

The miner was grinning, amused.

The kangaroo was indifferent.

This, thought Grant, was the type of situation that titillated the Romans when they matched men against exotic beasts in the arenas.

The kangaroo was taller than the man who was now so close that it was looking down at him.

Dick jumped to one side and the kangaroo shifted ground to face him. He dodged the other way, and for a moment the tip of the kangaroo's tail came within his reach. He grabbed it, lifting it high into the air.

Unbalanced, the kangaroo flopped about, unable to control its movements, its head bent forward, helpless, without dignity.

Still holding the tail with one hand Dick leaned forward and with his knife cut deeply into the kangaroo's leg beneath the crutch. Then he cut the other leg, and dropped the tail.

Hamstrung, the kangaroo stood motionless, its back to the light, not moving its head.

Dick grabbed it by the snout and hacked open its throat. It shuddered and sank to the ground. Dick ripped it open, turned out the entrails, cut off the hindquarters and bore them back to the car, leaving half the kangaroo lying on the spot where it had stood and faced him a minute before.

Everybody slapped Dick on the back and they quartered the other carcasses, and all drank some more beer and drove on again, leaving the night to cover the things they left behind them.

'Isn't that sort of thing dangerous?' Grant found he was speaking slowly and ponderously again.

'No, John,' said Joe, 'not if you know what you're doing.'

'Have you ever done it?'

'Yeah, often, nothing to it really.'

'I'd like to have a go.'

'Would you now?' He leaned forward. 'Eh! Dick, John here reckons he wants to have a go at a 'roo with a knife. Will we let him?'

'Why not?'

Tydon had turned around. Grant could not see his face; his head was a black shape against the light in front. Grant thought he was grinning.

'Why not?' said Tydon.

And 'Why not?' said Grant. On they went, plunging through the night.

They flushed the next mob by the side of the track, and the night rang with rifle fire and the biting fumes filled the car. The kangaroos died or limped away, but there was one that hopped brokenly for a few yards then stopped among the trees, clearly visible from the car.

'That's for you, John,' said Joe, handing Grant his knife.

Grant took the knife and clambered out through the trap to avoid struggling with the greyhound, jumped to the ground from the roof of the car and lunged towards the kangaroo standing limply in the spotlight as though it was looking into the darkness so close at hand.

Grant could hear the men in the car cheering. A rifle went off. He didn't know where the bullet went. He was crashing through the undergrowth, tripping, stumbling.

He might have fallen on the knife, so he held it out in front of his body, like a bayonet at charge. But that felt foolish so he pointed it towards the ground.

The kangaroo did not move.

It was not until he had almost reached it that he realized it was a very small kangaroo, no more than four feet high. It was badly wounded, and just stood, looking into the darkness beyond the spotlight's glare.

Grant reached it, and if he had not known the men in the car were watching he would have turned back for his rifle. He stood behind the animal, wishing it would move. Then he put a hand on its shoulder. It was furry and warm. Its chest was heaving. When he was that close the animal had two heads,. Janette had had two profiles the other night.

Grant leaned back and struck at the kangaroo with his knife. The blade slit a deep gash down its back and the blood came out, a thin line on the fur, black in the spotlight. Still the kangaroo did not move.

Oh God! what was he, John Grant, schoolteacher and lover doing out here under the contemptuous stars butchering this warm grey beast?

He leaned forward and drove the knife into the white fur on the kangaroo's chest. The blade went in easily, deeply, but the kangaroo would not die.

Its flesh closed hard around the blade and Grant had to drag it out.

Sobbing, he drove the knife into its chest and its back again and again, and it stood there, mute, unprotesting, but it would not die.

Grant stood away for a moment, drew his hands across his eyes and heard the yells of encouragement from the car.

He put his left arm across the kangaroo's shoulder and pulled its head back and began hacking away at its throat. In time the blood gushed out, warm on his hands, and he could feel the head pulling farther and farther back until at last the kangaroo shuddered terribly and fell to the ground.

Grant grabbed it by the tail and began hauling it back to the car.

And as he stumbled in front of his load he pulled down the shutters in his mind and just walked and dragged and drew the blanket of drunkenness over his being again.

Being drunk is warm and soft and there is no pain and it does not really matter about kangaroos that are shot and breathe horribly and disappear in the night, or about little kangaroos that you cut to pieces before they die.

Grant killed many kangaroos that night and once even made a

disastrous attempt to eviscerate one before he was sure it was dead; and it flopped about with its entrails spilling.

Everybody laughed, and they laughed again because Grant was covered in blood and they drank all the whisky and all the beer and their shooting became wilder.

Someone fired a bullet through the roof of the car and someone else fired one through the windscreen, and everybody laughed again.

Their shouts and their laughter and their bottles and their bullets and the roar of the car's engine and the crashing of its wheels through the scrub were their contribution to the sounds of the night. The box at the rear of the car filled and overflowed with hindquarters; scattered in an erratic pattern of their progress were the half-carcasses; and in dark glades and dry creek-beds kangaroos stood with bullets in their bodies waiting to die without comment.

Dear God, but man was a powerful thing and another drink would make him feel a lot better. Grant was leaning heavily on the greyhound. It didn't mind.

Soon after all the liquor had gone Dick turned the car back, and weaving a little, drove to the road. It did not take long because they had been driving around in a circle most of the time.

The hotel at Yindee had anticipated their return and was still open. Hotels seldom close in the west.

They all went in and drank beer, and Grant did not know who paid, or cared. Everything that had happened to him that night was being re-created in his brain in spasms, little bursts of imagined action, one after the other, very quickly; the shooting, the killing, the driving, the running, the drinking; bright images, coloured images; they said you could not think in colour. They were wrong. There's a time when your mind flashes colour, green, orange and fire. No, that was wrong too. That was the dawn. Incredible colours on the low horizon.

The car must be moving. Now there was another hotel.

He could not see much any more, but he was aware of people and things. They were terribly far away, near the outside of him. But he had retreated far inside, so far inside that a great margin of blackness lay between himself and the outside of his head.

But he was there, a little bright flashing light, that was the core; the darkness was the flesh and the shell was his face and the top of his head and the back of his head.

They were moving, and then he had arrived and he stayed.

Nothing for a time.

Then, Oh God! The light was bright and this could not be.

Tydon. But the light went out. Then he went out. That was terrible. It should not have happened.

Nothing for a time.

Oh God! The light was bright and this could not be, again. It was all to do with being drunk because this could not, did not, happen to John Grant, schoolteacher and something. Tydon was a foul thing. But so was John Grant. Oh God, that light! But it was going out. And it went out. But what had happened before was terrible. It should not have happened. It could not have happened. It had happened twice. And then nothing for a long time.

When he awoke he did not know where he was or when it was; he knew only that if he moved again the pain would start.

For a time he lay secure in the calm that precedes the agonies of a hangover.

Then the tortures began to happen to him, approaching stealthily, penetrating deeply and swelling.

He was sick.

Memory struggled within him and deliberately he subdued it. But it came back.

Slowly he raised his head. He was back in Tydon's hut. That was not really a surprise. He could see bloodstains on his arms.

Last night's orgy flitted back to him in hideous little cameos. But he was too sick to know remorse yet.

That bare, whitish, heaving thing there? It was his chest. He raised his head a little more. He was naked. He turned his head. His clothes were in a heap on the floor. Tydon was lying on another stretcher, asleep, covered by a sheet of some sort.

Grant let his head fall back. He had so many things to regret and so little strength to regret with. Perhaps he could sleep?

But now the arid wakefulness that comes to the drunkard was upon him and he knew he had to face a day of living.

Suddenly – what about those spasms of light in the night?

An awful sickness washed over him. What had happened to him in the night? Something appalling had happened to him, but what was it?

Driving thought and memory back, Grant sat up quickly. And the pain started flooding his mind in blinding waves.

Never mind, while his head hurt he could not think. But get out of here. Get out of here now.

He rolled his legs off the stretcher and stood up. He felt as though small leaden weights had been sewn to his intestines, his eyes, his nerve-ends. Oh God! the pain in his head.

Slowly, but not caring whether he woke Tydon, Grant dressed. His clothes were stiff with blood and they smelt. What had happened to that kangaroo that had disappeared after he had shot it? Things half remembered and terribly feared, shrieked at him; tears of mystic terror rimmed his eyes. And that blasted, damnable, bloody light in the night. What had that been? What had happened?

Careful, Grant, careful, he didn't really want to remember.

Tydon woke up as he was lacing his shoes.

'Going?'

'Yes.' The word seemed to come from a long way away.

'Where?'

'Sydney.' The thought formed in his mind as he answered the question.

'How?'

His jaws did not seem to be working properly and he did not answer; in any case he didn't know.

He was not looking at Tydon, but he knew Tydon was smiling at him.

'Want a drink before you go?'

Grant shook his head, slowly.

'Food?'

'No.'

He could not see very clearly and it took him a long time to tie his shoe-laces.

At last he stood up and looked about him for the door of the hut.

'Don't forget your gun,' said Tydon.

Grant turned and looked at him, confused. He thought Tydon looked like an emaciated rat thrusting his face out from under the sheet. Dear God, what had he done last night?

'What gun?'

'The boys made you a present of the gun.' Tydon nodded towards the rifle lying on the floor near Grant's feet.

Grant eased himself down and grasped the rifle.

Tydon was saying something else, but Grant could not understand and didn't listen. He walked to the door, shut his eyes, opened the door and stepped out into the full light of day.

He stood outside the hut and let the door close behind him; stood with his eyes shut waiting for the first feverish attack of the heat to subside to the dull, bruising blast that would not cease until dusk.

He half opened his eyes, looked around until he found the direction of the city and began to walk, head down, doggedly, grasping the rifle in one hand, not thinking.

It was only about half a mile to the first houses, and it did not

take as long as Grant thought it did for him to walk there. Not once
did he look back to Tydon's hut.

He plodded down the street, between the houses, not caring
whether anyone thought his appearance strange.

A slight breeze was blowing, and the dust from the waste heaps
beside the mines swirled knee-deep along the streets, like a drifting,
shifting low-lying cloud.

Grant's face was taut and dry. People never seem to sweat while
they're in the sun of the west; the beads of moisture dry up as they
ooze through the skin.

The dust caked on Grant's lips. His mouth was an arid gap in his
head. Once he almost thought of Robyn, but she did not really exist
any more; there was nothing but his pain and the heat and the dust
eddying around his knees and the necessity to get to Sydney.

He stopped, transferred the rifle to his left hand and felt in the
fob pocket of his trousers. Slowly he drew out his money; the
crinkled ten-shilling note, the two-shilling piece, the sixpence and
the penny.

Clutching the money in his hand he began to walk again.

In the main street people looked at him, unshaven, befouled, his
clothes darkened with blood. People shifted about him almost on
the outskirts of his consciousness. He walked straight along the
footpath and people melted away in front of him.

Then one did not melt away.

Grant stopped, his nose almost against a uniform shirt. He raised
his eyes. There was a face under a peaked cap. It was a policeman.

'Look here, John, you can't go carrying a rifle through the street
like that.'

The policeman seemed to know him.

He brought his eyes to bear on the face. Yes. He knew the
policeman too. It was the one he had met the first night in Bundanyabba, so long ago.

He tried to say something, but he only croaked.

'Here, show us it, son.' The rifle was plucked from his hands.
The policeman was doing something to it. Then he pressed it back
into Grant's hands in two pieces, the stock and the barrel.

'There, that's all right now, put this in your pocket.' The policeman gave Grant something small and hard. He looked at it. It was
the rifle bolt.

'What's the matter with you, John?'

Grant reached down into himself and brought out: 'Been shooting.'

That made everything clear to the policeman.

'Ah! Bit hung over, eh?'

Grant allowed his head to drop, then raised it again. Surely the policeman knew that meant 'yes'. He didn't have to speak, did he?

'You need a hair of the dog, mate – come on.'

The furtive cunning that Grant now knew in himself turned in the void of his mind and he managed to almost grin as he said: 'Sorry, mate, but I'm out of cash at the moment.'

'What's that got to do with it?' said the policeman, as Grant had known he would. 'Come on.'

There's nowhere in Bundanyabba that's far from a hotel, and Grant just had time to slip his money back into his fob pocket before he was leaning on a bar, his foot rising automatically, feeling for the footrail.

The relief he knew he would find in beer stimulated him in prospect and he tried to drag the policeman's name out of his memory. Not that it mattered much: 'mate' would do.

'Couple of schooners, Joyce,' said the policeman, 'me mate's in a bad way.'

'He looks it,' said Joyce, whom Grant could not see because he did not turn his eyes from the bar.

The policeman said something then that seemed to require an answer; but Grant could not absorb it.

'Sorry, mate,' he said, 'I'm feeling a bit crook. I don't get you.'

The policeman laughed.

'You must have done a lot of shooting.'

The beer came. Nausea and thirst warred briefly in Grant; and thirst won, thirst and the need for something that would make his body something he could bear to be with.

His fingers were shaking as he curled them around the cold wet glass. He brought it to his face and breathed the coldness from the froth-crowned liquid.

Then he absorbed the beer into his racked frame, quickly to kill the nausea, then slowly to feel it caressing through his body, sending soft broken waves of coolness out from his stomach. Then it was all gone.

'Better?' said the policeman.

'Better,' said Grant. 'Thanks ... Jock.'

'Have another?'

'Oh ... I don't really like to ... I ...'

'Ah bulsh, you can buy me a few next time you see me. Two more thanks, Joyce.'

Grant felt terribly weak standing waiting for the next beer. It was probably quite some time since he had eaten; he could not remember when. He was not too sure what day it was, but

he thought it was Monday. He didn't much care what time
it was.

'I thought you were pulling out of The Yabba on Saturday?'

'Yes. I was.' But that had been in another world, another life.

'What went wrong?'

'Oh, I ... got involved.' He wasn't up to talking yet, nor to
thinking, and if that beer did not come quickly he would probably
fall at the policeman's feet.

It came and Grant drank it quickly, without pausing. There was
no pleasure in this; this was for sheer survival.

The policeman said something to him again, but he did not know
what it was.

'Jock, you've damn near saved my life. How about completing
the job by giving me a cigarette?'

While he was rolling the cigarette Joyce came up and said 'Same
again, boys?' and Grant absent-mindedly ignored her so the two
schooners reappeared filled. The policeman was getting it free,
anyway.

Half the third schooner, then Grant got a light from the policeman and let the smoke roll around his mouth, up behind his nose,
then took it down into his lungs. It made him feel a little ill, but a
man's metabolism could be balanced by beer and tobacco whether
he liked them much or not.

Clarity descended upon Grant, but he knew that it would not last
an hour unless he became drunk, and he would not become drunk.

'Jock, where could I get a shower?'

'Well ... at your pub, I suppose.'

'I'm not in a pub.'

'Wherever you're staying then.'

'I'm not staying anywhere.'

'I don't get you, mate.'

'Look, Jock, I'm in a mess. I'm broke. I want to get back to
Sydney, and before I go I want to have a shower and clean myself
up a bit. Can you help me?'

The policeman looked at him, wondering, then said, 'Ah, yes, I
can help you, John. Hey, Joyce!' And when Joyce came up: 'Can
my mate here have a shower upstairs?'

Joyce looked at Grant a moment, doubtfully, but then, because
the policeman had asked, 'Oh, yes. That's all right, I suppose.
Long as he doesn't mess the place up.'

'I won't.' Grant looked away from the barmaid's face and saw
his suitcases standing against the wall.

'Oh!' he said, 'they're mine.'

Joyce and the policeman looked at the suitcases, then at each other, then at Grant.

'Are they?' said Joyce.

'Yes. I must have left them here yesterday . . . no, not yesterday . . . the other day.'

'They've been here since Saturday.'

God! what day was it?

'That's it. I was in here drinking with a man. Tim, his name was. Do you know Tim?'

The barmaid looked at the policeman.

'I don't know any Tim,' she said. 'Anyway, I wasn't on, on Saturday.'

The policeman said: 'Anyhow, if John here says they're his, they're his. What's in them, John?'

'Books in that one and clothes in the other.'

The policeman went over and tried the lock on one of the cases. It came open.

'Books,' said the policeman, re-locked the case and came back to the bar. 'Didn't doubt you, of course, John.'

Grant did not care. He finished his beer.

'Thanks a lot, Jock. I'll get up and take that shower now. Be seeing you.'

He picked up the cases and the dismantled rifle and walked towards the door leading to what seemed to be the residential section of the hotel. He stopped and looked back. The policeman and the barmaid were both looking at him.

'Where are the bathrooms?' he said.

'Out the door, up the stairs and turn left.' Joyce was obviously regretting having given Grant permission to use the bathroom. She turned inquiringly to the policeman as Grant left the bar.

In the bathroom he stripped off his clothes and turned his head in disgust at the smell of his own body.

The hot-water tap gave him a drizzle of lukewarm water, and he stood under it, scraping his skin with a fragment of soap he found on the side of the bath. It was hard to raise a lather with the water that came from the Bundanyabba mains.

He turned on the cold tap, and the temperature of the water lowered very slightly, but he stood under it for several minutes, hoping for some refreshment from it.

He did not have a towel so he shaved standing naked in front of the mirror allowing the water to drain off his body. He cut himself three times with the razor and almost cried when he saw the blood, not with pain, with helplessness.

Then he dressed himself in clean underclothes, socks, shirt, trousers, shoes and even added a tie. His other clothes he jammed in a bundle in a corner of his suitcase. His money he put in his fob pockct.

He combed his hair and looked at himself. He was all right except for his face,; it was bloated and grey and his lips were trembling. Tears seemed to be forming in his eyes.

'My God, Grant, you're in a bad way.'

The policeman had left the bar when Grant came back with his suitcases and his rifle, and the barmaid looked at him without speaking.

'If I follow the main road out I get on to the eastern road, don't I?' said Grant.

'The eastern road?'

'The road that leads to the east, to the coast.' Every word was a job of work.

Grant walked out of the hotel. The footpath was still almost hidden by the drifting dust. He looked along the glaring length of the street and his resolution evaporated. He went back into the hotel.

'Is there a bus that goes out that way?'

'Which way?'

'Out to the eastern road.'

'The 416 goes out there.' She spoke as though that were something any fool would know.

'Where do I get it?'

'At the bus stop.'

Oh God, this dreary woman.

'Yes, but where is the bus stop?'

'Just outside the door.'

Did she have to speak as though he were an idiot or worse; still, he was, wasn't he?

'Thanks. Could I have six boxes of matches please?'

'It'll cost a shilling.'

'That's all right.'

Grant thought he heard her mutter: 'I thought you were broke,' as she turned away to get the matches.

She held out her hand for the money before she gave him the matches.

'And a bottle of beer please.'

The beer cost three and sixpence. He had eight and a penny left.

In a shop near the hotel he bought a meat pie for a shilling and packed it, in its brown-paper bag, in the case with his clothes along with the beer and the matches.

He still felt frail and leaden in one, but the change of clothes had removed some of his sense of degradation. And as yet he did not have to try very hard to stop his mind prying back into what had happened over the past few days.

The bus took him to the outskirts of the city on the western side, near the sewerage treatment works. The fare was one and sixpence.

He paid the driver and stepped down from the bus on to the road and found that the glare had almost gone; dusk was setting in. That meant it must have been about seven o'clock. Where was his watch, anyway?

He waited on the roadside until the bus had turned round and headed back to the city, trying to remember what his intention had been. It had seemed fairly clear back in the hotel.

The sewerage treatment works was the only building near, and he couldn't see any people about. A ditch had been dug along the side of the road for some purpose or another and a sort of rampart of earth had been thrown up. Grant clambered over it with his cases and his rifle and slid down into the ditch.

From a suitcase he took a travelling rug which someone had given him once and he'd never used before. He spread it on the ground and sat down.

Taking the bottle of beer out of the case he looked at it, and wondered how to open it. Hadn't he seen someone opening bottles with their teeth? He couldn't do that. He took out his penny and worked on the top with it, levering it off a piece at a time. It took a long while and once or twice he thought he was going to cry with the sheer effort. But it came off at last.

He drank half the beer fairly quickly, it was already warm, and then unwrapped the pie and took a bite. The pastry was yellow and dry and the meat was a glutinous brown mess. He chewed on the mouthful but could not swallow it and eventually spat it out, wrapped the remains in the brown-paper bag, drank the rest of the beer and lay down.

It was almost quite dark and the stars were breaking through the purple of the sky, building up into an immense curved blanket that lay over him, quite intimately.

He wondered whether he would be able to sleep. He could feel nerves throughout his body twitching and pulling and every few moments he would start as though he had been frightened.

Strange, he thought, that he did not particularly want a cigarette. Cigarettes were round and white and they made your mouth taste foul if you smoked too many. His mouth tasted foul now. Robyn had a wonderfully-shaped mouth. She wore a white skirt at tennis. He was about to serve and he stood poised on the base line. He tossed the ball into the air, swung his racket in a perfect movement and sent the ball sizzling over the net in an unplayable shot to win the game. His opponent did not even have time to move. A great big man, he must have been thirty feet tall and terribly broad, was towering over the nets. He was dressed in tennis shorts and a fawn sleeveless pullover. Was it fawn or yellow? You didn't dream in colour.

And then he was completely asleep and the stars moved across the sky on their prescribed courses and the little animals of the night snuffled around him and then scuttled away, alarmed at his heavy breathing and restless movements.

Grant woke at dawn feeling wonderfully refreshed, until he moved. Then he realized that he was very weak and shaky. Still it was so much better than yesterday.

He was enormously hungry and when he unfolded the meat pie he found it was not so bad after all. But the yellow pastry was hard to take without something to drink. He was shockingly thirsty.

He finished the pie, packed the rug in the suitcase and forced the pieces of rifle in too. He picked up the empty beer bottle, rummaged around until he found the top and clambered up on to the road.

It must have been about half past five and the sun was tossing hot waves on the the plain, preparing the way for the full tide of heat which would rise with the day.

Grant left his cases by the side of the ditch and went over to the sewerage treatment works with his beer bottle. There did not seem to be anybody about, so he filled the bottle from a water tap, took a long drink, filled it again and jammed the top on.

The first car to come past was a big black Buick, and it rushed by spraying him with dust, his hand lifted foolishly.

Ten minutes later a utility came along and drew up as he gestured towards the east.

'I'm only gong to Yindee, mate,' said the driver, a thin, stringy man with a very brown face and a much chewed cigarette butt attached to his lower lip.

'That would be a help, thanks.'

'Throw your bags in the back.'

Grant took his water-bottle with him into the cabin of the utility because he was not too sure about the top. He sat with it between his knees as the utility jerked forward and began bouncing through the mist of dust which still hung around the road to mark the passing of the Buick.

'Where are you heading, mate?' asked the driver.

'Going to Sydney.'

The driver said nothing for a time, his eyes squinting against the white glare of the road.

'That's a long way, mate,' he said at length. 'Gonna hitch all the way?'

'I hope so.'

'You'll have your work cut out once you get out from Yelonda. Still, I suppose you'll make it. There's always a truck or two goes past in a week. You might be lucky and get a run through to the coast.'

'I hope so.'

They were silent, the driver with his thoughts on whatever the smaller farmers of the west think about, and Grant trying hard not to remember the last time he came along this road.

A truck or two a week the driver had said. And this was Tuesday, he supposed. He was fairly sure it was Tuesday, but he didn't like to ask.

The driver spat the stained cigarette butt out of the window and with considerable dexterity rolled another cigarette, keeping the car steadily on the road the while. He passed the pouch to Grant.

'Smoke?'

'Thanks.' Grant had been trying to forget the dry brittle ache in the mouth and throat that a heavy smoker experiences when deprived of tobacco for any period.

He rolled a generous cigarette and lit it.

The smoke made him feel a little dizzy and sick but he took it down deep into his lungs and let it out slowly.

The sweat was running freely down his face now and his clothes were damp. He felt distinctly more healthy than he had since he had first met Tim Hynes, except that he seemed terribly nervous. His body was constantly taut and he found himself taking deep breaths, trying to relax, but not succeeding.

He was quite clear-headed, but his thoughts came very quickly, in little repetitive bursts.

And he didn't like himself.

'Your best bet,' said the driver, 'would be to hang around the pubs at Yelonda. You'll probably find a truck going through from there.'

'Thanks, I'll try that.' The devil he'd try that. He'd wait on the road and if necessary die on the blasted road before he'd go into a pub again.

'How come you're hitch-hiking to Sydney?'

'Broke,' said Grant.

'But it only costs a few quid in the train, mate.'

'I'm broker than that.'

A pause. The utility swayed in the soft dust of the road. The sun was high now and the pastel colours of morning had dried up; there was just white glare.

'Haven't you got any money at all?'

'About five bob,' said Grant, cheerfully. Now that he was definitely on his way to Sydney the fact that he had no money did not seem to be quite such a tragedy.

The driver looked at him long enough to endanger the utility. He swerved back on to the road.

'How far you come?'

'Just from The Yabba.'

Another pause. The driver contemplated the white road intently.

'You're gonna be mighty hungry before you get to Sydney.'

'I don't know. I've got a rifle. I'll pick up some game.'

'Hmm.'

The driver did not speak again until they were pulling up at the Yindee Hotel. Then he said: 'I'll be dropping you a mile up the road. Come, and I'll buy you a drink.'

'No thanks,' said Grant, too abruptly.

'My shout,' said the driver.

'No thanks, I'm off it,' said Grant.

'Well I'm going to have one,' said the driver, a little annoyed, and stopped the utility outside the hotel.

By the time Grant had hauled his bags out of the back of the vehicle the driver's spate of ill-humour had dissipated.

'Come on,' he said, 'I'll buy you a drink. You'll need it.'

'Thanks all the same,' said Grant, 'but I'm off it. Thanks for the ride.'

He picked up his cases and began walking east.

The driver looked after him as though he thought he was insane.

'And to bloody hell with you,' he said, and went into the hotel for his drink.

Grant, wilting under the sun, walked a couple of hundred yards up the road until he came to a dessiccated gum tree which offered a pretence of shade.

He sat down on one of his cases and looked westward along the road. There was no suggestion of the tight swirl of dust which would have meant a vehicle, only the drifting cloud the utility had raised, settling gently back on the plain.

He prised the top off his bottle and drank some of the warm water. It was probably about noon, and he wondered again what had happened to his watch.

Off to the right was a line of scrub indicating the course of a creek. It would undoubtedly be dry, but he might pick up a rabbit there. Food was an absolute necessity, so he had better take the risk of losing a lift and see what he could find.

He carried his cases a few yards away from the road and took out the pieces of the rifle. The mechanism puzzled him briefly then he laid the barrel in the butt groove and screwed in the holding pin. Then he slipped the bolt into the breech, cocked it and heard it click home when he pulled the trigger.

There were plenty of cartridges in the pockets of his safari jacket. He took out a handful, shuddering at the feel of the blood-stiffened cloth, and placed one in the breech, leaving the rifle uncocked.

The creek bed was only a hundred yards or so away and he walked quickly across, his feet breaking the sparse and brittle blades of dead grass.

This was not wise, walking out here in the sun; God send he saw a rabbit or some sort of game reasonably soon.

He saw one almost immediately on the opposite side of the creek, sitting up looking at him, its ears erect and quivering.

Dropping to one knee Grant cocked the rifle and raised it to his shoulder. One eye closed, the other squinting against the glare, he tried to line the rabbit up in the sights, but they swayed and jumped and he realized he could not keep his hands still enough.

He lay down and the grass stalks pricked his body through his clothes, but he could hold the rabbit in the rifle sights. It was still bolt upright, its ears moving gently.

Holding his breath, he squeezed the trigger.

The report was slight, lost in the echoless plains, and the rabbit leaped high in the air and fell over backwards.

Grant stood up quickly; and blackness swamped out of his chest towards his head, but stopped and receded. He had better keep out of the sun, he thought; he should have a hat of some sort.

The creek-bed was dirty, as he had supposed, and quite shallow, and he crossed it to pick up his rabbit.

It was rotten with myxomatosis.

He held it, wondering whether he could salvage anything from the carcass, then threw it away with a twinge of disgust.

He could feel his confidence draining away as he looked along the creek-bed, red on the sides where the underlying clay had been exposed and white with thick dust on the bottom.

But having come so far he might as well walk a few yards more, and he jumped down and began to follow the path of dust which traced out the course the water took when it ran for a week once a year, if times were good.

His feet made no sound in the dust and he came upon a second rabbit around the first bend. It was only twenty feet away and seemed too surprised to move.

Even with his shaking hands he could not miss and he raised the rifle to his shoulder, lined up on the rabbit's head and squeezed the trigger.

The bolt clicked home, but there was no report. He had forgotten to reload.

Grant had done quite a deal of shooting, and he stood motionless for a moment, then slowly lowered the rifle, drew back the bolt, ejected the spent cartridge, inserted a live one, cocked the rifle, and raised it again, all without startling the rabbit.

Then he shot it through the head.

It was lean, but had no visible trace of disease about its body. Grant carried it by the back legs across to his suitcases and then moved under the tree again.

There was still no sign of a vehicle on the road; the utility had gone from in front of the hotel now. He must have missed hearing it while he was in the creek-bed.

He took his razor from the suitcase and extracted the blade. Holding the rabbit on the ground he slit the skin around the neck and peeled it off the body like a glove. Another slit and he emptied the entrails on to the ground.

Immediately swarms of blowflies descended and Grant moved a few yards away to hack off the rabbit's head. But the leaden beat of the sun sent him back under the scant shade of the tree so he tossed a few handfuls of dust over the skin and the entrails to discourage the blowflies and flung the head well away.

He had no trouble lighting a fire because the tree bark, dead grass and a few dead branches had long since been emptied of any vestige of moisture.

As the fire died down he dropped the rabbit into the centre of it. He did not expect to enjoy it, anyway. All he wanted was food with at least the semblance of being cooked.

When it began to char he pulled it out of the fire and broke it in half. One half he wrapped in an old shirt and stuffed into his suitcase. The other he began to gnaw, squatting by the empty road.

The meat was still half raw, lean and stringy and would have been unpalatable even if it had been allowed to hang. But he chewed through it, wishing only that he had thought to provide himself with salt. That would not have cost much. He might buy some in the next town since he proposed to live like this for some time.

Some time – how long was some time? There was really nothing to indicate that he would ever stop living like this, except that he would eventually run out of bullets.

He cleaned the bones of the rabbit conscientiously and sat down with his back against the trunk of the tree looking down the road towards Bundanyabba.

Despair settled on him like a fog as the day wore on and the colours that aborigines like to paint appeared on the plains when the sun sank down towards the horizon.

He sat there, longing for a cigarette, trying to stave off the nagging hopeless anxiety of the hysteric; desperately trying not to think of the past or the future.

Several times he took swigs from the bottle of now almost hot water. He thought of going back to the hotel to fill it, but he was afraid he might buy cigarettes if he saw them in front of him, or beer.

He'd come forty miles in one day and he had hundreds of miles to go. He would take a month on the journey if he maintained this rate. A month on the road with five or six shillings in his pocket. And it might be longer.

And when he got to Sydney? But he would not think about that. Anything that happened there must of necessity be better than being in Bundanyabba.

A spiral of dust arose in the purple dimness underlying the flaring orange of the sunset, and he began to take the rifle apart. It wouldn't do to beg a ride brandishing a rifle. He packed the pieces in a suitcase along with the now empty bottle and waited, wondering whether the car, truck, utility, whatever it was, would turn off on some improbably excuse for a side-road and disappear, a fading swirl of dust in the gathering darkness.

In any case it was almost certain to stop at the hotel. He doubted whether there was a driver within five hundred miles of Bundanyabba who could navigate his vehicle past a hotel without stopping.

Soon he could see that it was a truck, bouncing fast along the pitted road. The fact that it was a truck meant nothing. Many of the small landholders kept quite large trucks to take their produce to Bundanyabba and they used them as cars at other times. The only vehicles that would be going any great distance would probably be semi-trailers. Still, another fifty miles would be something.

From the time he first saw it, twenty minutes passed before the truck reached the hotel. It didn't stop there.

Grant started flagging it when it was still fifty yards away. The driver slowed down and Grant could see him peering out at him. Even in the west a man gives a little thought to whether or not he should pick up a stranger by the road at nightall. But Grant looked all right and the driver stopped.

Grant walked over and put his head up to the offside window of the driver's cabin.

'Could I get a lift as far as you're going?' he said.

'Where are you going, mate?' said the driver, a round-faced, unshaven man of about thirty-five.

'Sydney, eventually,' said Grant, apologetically.

'I'm only going as far as Yelonda, mate.'

'That'd be a help.'

Again the driver pondered, keeping his eyes steadily on Grant. Then, apparently reaching some conclusion: 'All right, hop in.'

The driver switched on his lights as they moved off, for the darkness was almost complete.

The sound of the engine and the feel of the broken leather of the seat soothed Grant after the long hours under the tree hearing only the inexplicable rustlings in the dead grass and the occasional unpleasing cry of a crow.

'Where you travelling from?' said the driver.

'The Yabba.'

'Been on the road long?'

'Only started today.'

'In trouble?'

'I beg your pardon?'

'In trouble with the cops?'

'No. Not at all. Why should you think that?'

'City feller like yourself, carrying bags, wearing those clothes. Stands to reason you ain't travelling this way because you like it.' Then, conspiratorially: 'They watch the trains and aeroplanes, don't they?'

'Possibly. I wouldn't know. But I assure you I'm not in trouble with the police.'

'You say you're not. I believe you. It's your business, anyway. Shouldn't have asked. Sorry.'

Grant could feel an unaccountable sensation of utter guilt.

'No really, I'm just thumbing my way to Sydney because I'm broke.'

'Sure, all right; you say it, I believe you.'

Both fell silent, Grant dumbfounded, the driver sceptical.

Not that it mattered, thought Grant, in fact it was rather amusing. Some day it would make part of a good story he could tell about his adventures in the west. But no, perhaps it would not do to tell a story about his adventures in the west.

He realized then that for a time his mind had stopped making determined darts back into the events of the past few days, but now it was searching, delving, remembering; and there were little things that had better not be remembered. He felt a little sick clutch of fear – the noise of the kangaroo that disappeared. Strange the way he kept thinking about that. It could be explained quite easily, probably. But then there had been those bursts of light that night and ... *No!* He would not think back.

'How far is it to Yelonda?' he said suddenly.

''Bout forty miles, I'd say. Take us about two hours.'

'What do you reckon my chances are of getting a lift through to the coast from there?'

'Fair, I'd say. Just fair. Your best bet would be to hang around the pubs. You'll find somebody going through eventually.'

Yelonda duly appeared as a dusting of lights on the plain ahead. It had been a town which flourished when paddle-steamers had run up and down the Harden River, almost halfway across the continent when there was water in the riverbed. But the paddle-steamers had not run for forty years and Yelonda had died thirty-nine years ago. Was it forty years ago the paddle-steamers had stopped? He must check that in case one of his pupils ever asked him. Dear God, his pupils. It was strange the way he could forget things, and then they would leap into his thoughts so violently as to almost hurt ... and before he saw his pupils again?

But at the moment the truck was stopping in Yelonda and the immediate problem was how to continue the journey to Sydney.

Yelonda was just a few broken-down houses interspersed with hotels. Half the people wandering around the dim streets were either aborigines or half-castes.

The Harden River wound its way past the edge of the town, dark, narrow and deep by the standard of western rivers. Grant resolved to go downstream a little in the morning to bathe and shave.

The driver stood by while Grant pulled his suitcases out of the back of the truck, then: 'Come and have a drink,' more as a statement than an invitation.

'No thanks,' said Grant, 'I'm off it.'

'Off it? You mean you don't drink?'

'I'm just not drinking for the moment.'

'I can see that; what I said was, let's go and have one.'

'Thanks, mate,' said Grant patiently, 'but I've given up drinking for a while.'

'Well, I'll be b—,' said the driver; 'you mean you won't have a drink with a man after he's given you a ride for fifty bloody miles?'

Convinced now that poverty was no bar to drinking in the west. Grant did not raise the point. He shrugged in some embarrassment and murmured: 'Sorry, mate, but I'm just not drinking.'

'Well you can bloody well go and get —,' in tones of complete contempt, and he turned and was lost behind the batwing doors of a hotel.

Peculiar trait of the western people, thought Grant, that you could sleep with their wives, despoil their daughters, sponge on them, defraud them, do almost anything that would mean at least ostracism in normal society, and they would barely seem to notice it. But refuse to drink with them and you immediately became a mortal enemy. What the hell? He didn't even want to think about the west or its people and their peculiarities. Let them be. Once he was in Sydney, who knew, he might never come back.

He was walking towards the river with his suitcases. Tonight he would camp under the bridge, bathe early in the morning and walk out on to the road a way to try to pick up some more game, then wait for a lift again. By the time he had walked a hundred yards he was saturated with sweat and he put his cases down to rest.

Across the way was the Yelonda picture theatre, a comparatively vivid patch of light in the dull street. People milled around outside or dived across the street for a few drinks during the interval.

A poster glued to the front of the wooden hall which passed for a theatre advertised some obscure movie that Grant seemed to recall as a product of the war years.

He stood looking at the picture crowd and wondered why the celluloid image of American culture should have penetrated so far into this desolate land. Strange it was that these withered and weathered people of the west should be fascinated by some American director's concept of war; that they should pay to come from their wooden homes to sit in discomfort for hours, dripping sweat, to watch a badly scratched film of purely formal heroics.

Still, let them be, let them be. City people went to B class movies too, so what the hell? He turned to pick up his cases and was suddenly obsessed by the word 'Sydney'.

Sydney.

SYDNEY, in large capital letters.

He shook his head and realized he was reading the word.

It was on the door of the cabin of a semi-trailer parked in the main street of Yelonda.

It was the last line in a block of printing on the door. Grant stood back.

J. CARRINGTON
Haulier
7 HODEN STREET
WYTON
SYDNEY

A road transport might well go through to the city in less than four days. Four days: dear God, he could go without food for that long, and anyway what money he had would carry him through. Four days, say at the most five.

Grant chewed his lower lip, trying to control the hope he realized depended entirely on the driver of the semi-trailer for fulfilment.

Where was the driver?

He looked around. The nearest hotel to the vehicle was the one across from the picture theatre. It was reasonably certain that the driver would be in there. But if he were not and Grant was in there looking for him he might come back and drive off. On the other hand he might be spending the night in the hotel and Grant would face many hours of waiting by the roadside.

He decided to try the hotel. He could keep an eye on the road in case the driver came back.

Leaving his cases where they were he hurried across to the hotel. It was crowded now with people from the theatre, but they would all leave in a few moments when the interval ended.

In fact, as Grant pushed through the batwing doors into the yellow, smoky light of the bar, he heard a handbell ringing outside, and the men began to drink their beer at a gulp and make for the doors. Soon there were only about twenty left in the bar and Grant peered at each, trying to decide which would be a professional transport driver.

He stood in a corner where he could see the semi-trailer and several of the drinkers turned and stared at him. Strangers were not all that common in Yelonda.

To Grant all the men in the bar seemed alike, sun-blasted with blank eyes. He could see nothing about any of them that suggested a transport driver.

He went across to the bar and when the bartender was down at his end asked: 'Any idea who owns that semi-trailer across the road?'

The bartender, a short man in a waistcoat who looked as though he might own the hotel, stared at Grant. Then he turned and bellowed to the bar in general: 'Gent here wants to know who owns the semi-trailer across the road,' and went on with the business of pulling beer.

Everybody in the bar turned and looked at the 'gent', then a heavily built man of about fifty detached himself from the wall he had been leaning against, drinking alone, and advanced on Grant.

Grant felt his hopes subsiding as the man came nearer. His face was gross and heavy and he had small pig-eyes. He stood in front of Grant and looked at him inquiringly, but said nothing.

'You ... you own the semi-trailer?' said Grant at length, conscious that everyone in the bar was still staring, and listening.

'What of it?' The voice seemed to come from somewhere down in the man's stomach rather than his throat.

'Nothing ... just that I ... I wanted to see if I could get a lift.'

The man looked at him blankly, presumably thinking, but giving no indication of it, then: 'Where you going?'

'Right through ... to the city I mean ... I'm trying to hitch-hike ... you see I ... well ...' Grant petered out miserably.

Again the man looked at him ruminatively.

'What's it worth?'

Dear God, he'd met probably the one man in the west who would demand money for a ride.

'I'm afraid I'm broke. That's why I'm begging rides.'

And that probably settled it. The man would be afraid he'd have to feed him, and it seemed too bloody foolish to say that he intended to shoot his food. Shoot! Perhaps ...

But the man was speaking: 'It should be worth a couple of quid.'

'It would be,' said Grant, 'but I'm really flat broke – look ...'

'Tell you what, make it a quid and it's a deal.'

'I'm sorry, but I've only got six bob, but I'll tell you what, I've got a rifle ... I'll give you that if you'll take me through.'

'What sort of rifle?'

If only he could spit in this man's face and walk out.

'Twenty-two. Quite a good one ... and about a hundred rounds of ammunition.'

'Where's the rifle?'

'Over in my case, near your truck. I'll get it.'

'All right.'

God curse the man's swinish face, thought Grant, as he hurried

over to his cases. The loss of the rifle didn't worry him, but having
to travel with an animal like that did. Still, to make the trip in one
run was worth a great deal. He wrapped the pieces of the rifle in an
old plastic raincoat because he felt he was already drawing enough
attention in the bar.

The man was draining a glass as Grant arrived back. He took the
rifle without comment and examined it.

Then he said: 'What about the ammo?'

Grant took the rounds from his pockets.

'Sorry I haven't got a box.'

The man took them and dropped them into his own pockets. Did
that mean the deal was made?

'There's not a hundred there,' said the man.

'I'm sorry. I thought there probably was. That's all I've got.'

'All right. I'll take you. But you ride in the back.'

'O.K. Thanks.' Grant couldn't work out why he had to ride in
the back; probably the man hoped to sell the front seat to somebody
else. In any case he was grateful because that meant he might be
able to sleep.

'Let's have a drink,' said the man, and a cold hand spread
around Grant's stomach. The devil and blast it! Was this the stock
conversation of everybody west of the Great Dividing Range? Of
course it was. He knew that already. But ... ah well, he could not
afford to quarrel with this man as he had with the other two
drivers.

'Surely,' he said, 'but it'll have to be my last for the trip, a couple
of rounds'll clean me out.'

'It'll be the last for the trip, I'm going straight through.'

'Going straight through.' The grateful words consoled Grant for
the three shillings he paid for the two glasses of beer – it was even
more expensive at Yelonda than at Bundanyabba.

His companion almost immediately turned his back on him and
began a mirthless conversation with a man alongside him with
whom he apparently had some business dealings.

Grant drank his beer without pleasure. The taste nauseated him
and his empty stomach rebelled. Still, it soothed his parched mouth
and throat. He must remember to fill his water-bottle.

'Going straight through' – that meant he might well by in Sydney
before the Sunday.

When the beer was finished the man ordered two more without
looking at Grant and made no move to pay for them. Grant waited
as long as possible but it was obvious that he was expected to pay.
So he did. And that left him with seven-pence.

He stood sipping his beer in utter humiliation, aware that he would accept any sort of treatment from this fat-faced swine rather than lose the lift through to Sydney.

The beer drunk, the fat man waved again at the bartender, and Grant interrupted nervously: 'I'm afraid that cleans me out. Would it be all right if I waited in the truck?'

The man turned to him, his face expressionless.

'Cleans you out? You mean you got no more money?'

'I told you I'm broke,' said Grant, pleadingly. 'I'm sorry, but that's the way it is.' Couldn't the bloody fool understand English?

The man looked at him for a while.

'All right,' he said, 'you wait in the truck. I'm gonna have a few more.'

'Thanks,' said Grant wretchedly, and turned away.

'Here,' said the fat man, 'if you're really broke I don't want to take this off you.' He held out the rifle.

Grant looked at him, stupefied.

'Take the bloody thing.'

'But I . . .'

'Take it.' There was nothing gracious in the man's manner. Grant took it.

'Thanks,' he said, utterly routed.

'Here. I'll buy you a bloody beer.'

'No. No thanks. I'd really rather wait in the truck if it's all right with you. Thanks very much all the same.'

'Just as you like,' and the man turned to his business friend.

Grant went blindly back to the semi-trailer, shaking with humiliation. Bad enough to beg, but to be treated with that blasted, disinterested contempt, God damn it all! He sat down on a suitcase, trembling bodily.

Then, after a moment, what did it matter? This was all the price to be paid for folly, and it wouldn't last for ever.

He explored under the canvas of the trailer and found plenty of space alongside rows of crates piled one on top of the other. Packing the rifle back in one suitcase, he pushed the two of them under the canvas and climbed in after them.

Inside he pulled out some of his older clothes and fashioned a pillow, then stretched out on the wooden floor.

It was very hot and stuffy, but he was past caring.

A mildly sick pain in his stomach reminded him that he had not eaten for several hours and he sat up again to ferret the half-rabbit out of the suitcase.

The smell assailed him as he unwrapped it; meat spoiled quickly in that climate, and being wrapped in a shirt in a suitcase had not helped stay the processes of decay.

He gnawed at it a little, but it was too sickening and finally he ejected it under the flap of the canvas.

Could a man live for four or five days without food? He had better try to buy half a loaf of bread with his remaining sevenpence.

He seemed to be lying there for hours, listening to the steady noise made by the men drinking in the half a dozen hotels within earshot, the mechanical voices and constant gunshots from the theatre, the thud of horses' hooves on the road outside, the growl and clatter of the occasional car or truck, the disembodied voices of people walking, scraps of conversation, flat and removed from their context, and then at last the sound of the door of the semi-trailer opening and shutting.

A voice, slightly slurred: 'Are you in there?'

'Yes, thanks,' called Grant.

Nothing more.

The engine clanked into life, the gear engaged, the vehicle shuddered and they were on the road.

At first the movement was soothing, then uncomfortable, and within an hour every jolt jarred against his bones; but he was moving, moving east towards the sea, towards Sydney and perhaps even towards Robyn. But Robyn was a fleeting thought he did not feel qualified to entertain.

After much experimenting he found that the best way to lie was on the flat of his back with his hands clasped behind his head. He wondered how long it would be before the driver stopped to sleep. He knew that transport drivers performed prodigious feats of endurance to cover vast distances with only snatches of sleep. This man had probably only come from Bundanyabba that afternoon and he might travel another three or four hundred miles before stopping. The semi-trailer seemed to be moving extremely quickly for so cumbersome a vehicle.

Now that the problem of getting to Sydney had been satisfactorily overcome he had better think about what he would do when he got there.

It wasn't all that hopeless really, he supposed. The semi-trailer was based at Wyton, so it might well go straight there. He could leave his cases somewhere and walk to a friend's place at Double Bay where he could quite decently borrow a pound or two. Then he would go to his uncle and explain that he was in difficulties; there would be no need to be strictly accurate after all. His uncle would give him food and lodging temporarily and he could get some sort of work. Perhaps there might even be pleasure left for him in his vacation.

If only he didn't feel so damned sick. And there were so many things. He felt stained; he needed to rid himself of something that had penetrated since he had gone to Bundanyabba. He wanted something like the confessional that Roman Catholics had.

Still, that would pass. He had achieved his escape from Bundanyabba. He was on his way to Sydney, and a bath and a good night's sleep and a decent meal would make things a lot simpler, probably.

Wouldn't it have been wonderful if he had never gone near the Two-up School; or better if he had not gone back the second time? He might have been with Robyn now, walking somewhere, somewhere cool, by the sea.

Sleep advanced on Grant with many and fearsome dreams which made him start upright, knocking his head on the crates. But gradually he settled down into a sort of fitful coma from which he burst occasionally, oppressed by an awful sense of despair.

And finally he slipped into a glittering, bright dream that was not about anything much except that it all seemed very clean and sunny, just a great area of innocent light.

And through that light a voice from a long way off, then closer and closer:

'All right. You're here! Hey, inside there! You're here!'

Grant awoke to the darkness, confused. An urgent need to understand the voice conflicted with his inability to orientate himself. Then as his thoughts settled into order, despairing fear set in.

Frantically he clawed aside the canvas. The man was standing in front of him. God! get out of the way, where was he?

It was a wide street.

With street lamps.

And shops, many shops on either side.

Grant stared and stared and knew he must go mad.

He was in the main street of Bundanyabba.

CHAPTER 4

From a great emptiness that seemed to have engulfed him Grant heard his own voice saying, very gently: 'You know, I thought you were going to Sydney.'

'Dunno why.'

Grant pointed to the sign on the door of the driving cabin.

'That was where I bought it, never took it off. I run between 'Londa and The Yabba.'

'But you said you were going to Sydney. Why did you say you were going to Sydney?' What did it matter, anyway?

'I never said anything about Sydney,' said the driver, climbing back into the cabin, 'you said you wanted to go through to the city – well, this is a city isn't it, mate?'

The door of the cabin closed.

'Anyway,' added the driver, as he started the engine, 'the trip didn't cost you anything.'

'That's not exactly the point,' said Grant softly as the truck pulled away leaving him standing beside his suitcases in the middle of Bundanyabba.

He watched the truck until it turned around a corner, vaguely surprised that he was not so much upset as utterly devoid of any sensation apart from this impression of emptiness.

After all, this was the end. Perhaps there was nothing more to fear.

With no idea of where he was going he picked up his suitcases and began walking once more down the street.

It was very late and the only activity was around the hotels.

Thoughts came to Grant now as a series of stunning impossibilities. He could not go on walking for ever. But there was nowhere for him to stop. He could not stay in Bundanyabba for five weeks. He could not leave Bundanyabba without any money or supplies, not even ammunition for the rifle. The whole thing was just a morass of hopelessness. There was nothing he could do.

He just walked and walked until sheer fatigue made him stop. He was somewhere near the eastern end of the main street, opposite some sort of park.

The park offered escape from the street, so he turned and went into it, walking over the dried roots of grass until he came to a tree. Then he put his cases down and sat with his back against the tree and looked at the stars. For a long while he sat with his head back, looking at the stars wondering at their remoteness, marvelling that they, unchanged, should still be part of his world, which was shattered.

And then after a long time his mind went back to the things that had happened to him, and he almost smiled at the enormous absurdity of it all.

But what was so fantastic was that there had been no element of necessity about it all. It was as though he had deliberately set about destroying himself; and yet one thing had seemed to lead to the next.

But he needn't have done any of it.

He shook his head, then let it fall back against the rough bark of the tree and closed his eyes to the stars.

He needn't have done any of it. He hadn't had to play Two-up. And when he had won, nothing forced him to go back. He need not have got drunk with Tim Hynes; there had not even been any point in that. And even though he had been drunk he had decided of his own volition to seduce Janette Hynes – to try to seduce Janette Hynes.

He need not have gone shooting with the miners, not that there had been anything in that as such; but there was no reason why he should have got drunk again and gone on the orgy of killing. And if he had not done that there would not be the echo of horror in his mind about what followed.

Strange, now, he did not mind thinking about anything. Perhaps because nothing mattered, now; it was all finished, there was nothing he could do.

Of course there had come a point where decision was not involved. The business of bursts of light in the night and the foulness he suspected went with them had not had much to do with his decisions, except that what he had done earlier had led to them.

Everything had led to something else. There had been no necessity about any of it, but each had carried within it the seed of the next.

Chance had played some part, that ridiculous business with the semi-trailer had hardly been a matter of his choosing; and yet even that would not have happened had he not been wrecked by drink.

At almost every stage of his personal little tragedy he could remember a point of decision where he could have made it otherwise.

And now here he was, with sevenpence, a rifle and no ammunition, and several boxes of matches. And he was sick and weak and would have been in despair if any emotion could have penetrated the cloud of emptiness or nothingness that surrounded him.

And all he was going to do was sit here and wait, and if nothing happened he would probably die, and so what?

He put his hands in his pockets and let himself slide down until he was lying almost flat.

Then his right hand encountered a small cylindrical object, hard and cool. He felt around it. It was a cartridge, he must have missed it when he gave the others to the driver in the hotel. He took it out and sat up to examine it. He had one cartridge.

It looked a harmless little piece of metal in the light of the stars, but it could be used to kill.

Why not to kill John Grant?

Other people killed themselves. It had been done.

It would be a solution to the immediate problem and would intercept any problems he might have in the future.

Why not?

He looked at the cartridge and rolled it around in his fingers. It was very small.

Why not?

Anyway, he would think about it for a while, get out the rifle and load it, see how the proposition looked then.

The precise operation of assembling the rifle was comforting in a way. He put the cartridge into the breech and pushed the bolt home.

With the loaded weapon across his knees he thought: this could be used to remove John Grant from Bundanyabba and Tiboonda and himself for ever.

All he had to do was point it at his head and pull the trigger.

He reversed the rifle and put the muzzle against his forehead. It was quite cool, cool and hard.

But he could not reach the trigger comfortably this way. He experimented with his finger. He would have to push the trigger, not pull it.

Many suicides – suicides, the word had a chilling quality – put the muzzle in their mouth. He tried it that way. The taste of gunmetal was quite distinct. But this way the bullet would tear up through his palate, burning and gouging. He took the muzzle out of his mouth.

Through the heart? He tried pointing the rifle at his body, but it was almost impossible to reach the trigger that way.

In any case, it seemed better in some way to shoot himself through the head, more necessarily final.

And his head did not seem so vulnerable.

That was a foolish thought.

He cradled the rifle in his arms. It was held by some that suicide was an evil thing. Catholics argued that it meant damnation. What precisely did they mean by damnation? He preferred the pantheistic 'now he is part of the loveliness which once he made more lovely.' Was that how it went? Anyway he had not made anything more lovely. Quite the reverse.

Chesterton used to say that the geat wrong in suicide was that it destroyed one's whole world. All right, he didn't mind destroying the whole world, not at all.

Even Robyn?

But Robyn was a dream, a white-skirted dream. Whether he killed himself or not, Robyn was in another world.

Another world? Supposing he precipitated himself into some other life. But the cold stars assured him there was no other life.

The fact was he could either kill himself or not kill himself. He simply had to make the decision.

There was another point of decision. He could either do it or not do it, and from that decision would flow the consequences. But there would be no consequences if he killed himself. There would be nothing.

Probably there would be nothing. A lot of people had argued that there was something after death. And what if that something were unpleasant for suicides? But since he had never believed it to be wrong to commit suicide how could he suffer for it?

This was nonsense. Where had the suggestion of suffering come from? Suffering was here and now. If he killed himself he would be dead and that was an end to it.

But the question of decision? Was this the one act that absolved man from all the consequences and responsibilities of his own decisions? Of course it was. If he killed himself he would be dead, and that was an end to it.

He drew back the bolt of the rifle until he heard the double click which meant it was cocked.

Now it needed only the slightest pressure of his finger and John Grant would come to an end and his troubles would be over.

It was strange that he was so reluctant to kill himself. It was quite a good idea really. There would be no pain, just oblivion, for ever, he supposed. It would be quite reasonable to kill oneself just to find out what happened then. So it must be all the more reasonable to kill oneself to solve a problem.

He seemed to be advancing arguments to himself to justify suiciding. Well, it didn't hurt to think about it awhile.

But damn it all! there was nothing else to do; tomorrow offered no hope.

Was the problem sufficiently grave to warrant this? Tomorrow and tomorrow and tomorrow for five weeks in the heat of Bundanyabba with no money and no food and nowhere to go, and then a year in Tiboonda . . . yes, it was grave. And besides, the John Grant he had once been was a soiled miserable creature now.

He rested the muzzle against his head, holding the barrel in both hands, the butt on the ground.

He was really sick to death of himself, he wanted to be rid of John Grant.

And why should John Grant not be got rid of?

To hell with it! If it suited him he would suicide.

And it did suit him. His hands clenched on the barrel. Get it over with! Do it! Make the decision! Push the bloody trigger!

But first, just one moment to wish it were otherwise, that he might have been a little more like the man he once thought he was. And just one moment to think of Robyn and the sea.

The emptiness evaporated and pain flooded around. He felt the tears burning his eyes and spilling down his cheeks and he did not know whether he meant to do it or not, but Oh God life was a mess and, sobbing, he reached out and pushed the trigger.

THE IMPACT WAS DREADFUL

and then just nothing.

CHAPTER 5

In the night the train rocked along the single track, over the plain, under the stars, past the yellow squares of light in the windows of homesteads. It rocked and swayed and rattled and set up a lulling rhythm of sound and motion which the singers caught and blended with the rhythm of their song.

They sang; for a song, once learned, takes a long time to die in the west:

> There is a heart that's made for you,
> A heart that needs your love divine,
> A heart that could be strong and true,
> If only you would say you're mine.
> If we should part my heart would break,
> Oh say that this will never be.
> Oh darling please, your promise make,
> That you'll belong to only me.

The floors of the train were littered with scraps of paper and food, and every now and then a bottle shot out of a window, kept pace with the train for a few seconds, then dropped unbroken on to the dust of the plain.

For reasons known only to himself the driver would sound the steam whistle and the melancholy wail would stretch out over the darkened land, and kangaroos and cattle and foxes and dingoes would raise their heads inquiringly before going about their business.

John Grant sat, travelling backwards, in a window-seat, looking out into the night.

He was smoking, and every now and then he would take the cigarette from his mouth and raise his hand to his forehead feeling a fresh scar in his closely-cropped hair.

He looked with satisfaction at the glass in the window. Lately he had developed a deep affection for the normal, simple trappings of being alive. Wood, and paint, and smells, and the feel of cloth, and the taste of food, and the comfort of cigarettes, and glass – now glass was a wonderful thing . . .

. . . Glass was the first thing he had seen when he recovered consciousness in hospital. A glass syringe, a huge glass syringe in the hand of a nurse. And he was on a sort of trolley in a white room without any windows.

The nurse pushed him so that he rolled over and his buttocks were exposed – he seemed to be wearing something like a white nightgown which stretched only to his waist, no, it had been rolled up.

The nurse plunged the needle of the syringe into his buttock and pushed the plunger. Grant saw about a quarter of a pint of clear fluid expressed from the syringe into his flesh.

'What's that?' he said.

'Oh, you're awake,' said the nurse. She was about thirty and rather plain.

'What is that stuff?'

'Anti-gangrene gas.'

Suddenly Grant was aware that a huge pain surrounded his head. It had been there all the time but it had been so great he had not noticed it. It was a shocking pain.

And he wasn't dead at all.

He lay his head back.

'How bad am I?' he said.

'I couldn't say,' said the nurse. 'You'd better ask the doctor. Not very bad I'd say; a bit of concussion.'

Grant raised his hand to his head and encountered a bandage.

'How did it happen?' asked the nurse.

Was it possible she did not know? Was it possible that no one knew he was now that most ludicrous of all beings, the unsuccessful suicide?

'I'm not sure,' said Grant, and the nurse seemed satisfied with that.

She pushed the trolley out of the room into a corridor, into a lift, into another corridor and into a smaller room. Gently she tumbled him off the trolley on to a bed. The room was quite bare apart from the bed and a small wooden chest.

She pulled a sheet over him and asked: 'Would you like something to eat?'

'Yes, please. I think so, and something to drink, and, nurse? I have the most frightful pain in my head.'

'Well, what do you expect?'

She went out and shut the door after her. He heard the lock turn. He braced his head against the pain and looked around the room: only one small window, high on the rear wall.

So they knew it was attempted suicide after all.... Now, sitting in the train, listening almost with affection to the singers, it seemed incredible that he had tried to shatter his own brains. But it had been different back there under the tree that night.

One of the men opposite mutely offered him a swig from a whisky bottle he had almost emptied in the past half-hour. Grant shook his head and said: 'No thanks.' The man scowled at him and drank the whisky himself.

That shirt the fellow was wearing looked like part of a police uniform ...

... The last time he had seen a shirt like that was in the hospital. The doctor had just seen him. A tall, well-dressed fellow, the doctor had been, wearing a white flower in his buttonhole.

'How are you feeling?' he asked in a pleasant, rich voice.

'Not bad. I've got a hell of a pain in my head. Are you the doctor?'

'Yes, one of them.'

'What happened?'

'I think you'd know that better than I would.'

Grant realized he should have been embarrassed at that, but he didn't care much.

'No, I mean where did the bullet hit me?'

'Top of the forehead. It cut a chunk out of your skull. You've got a dose of concussion, but you'll be all right.'

'Have I had an operation?'

'No, I just cleaned you up.'

'How did I get here?'

'The police brought you here.'

'How long will I be here?'

'That depends – where do you live?'

'Sydney.'

'Well you won't be able to travel for a month, maybe longer.'

'Oh.' Still that was not so bad. In fact, it more or less solved things for him. That was funny really, the bullet had not been utterly misspent.

'There's a policeman outside to see you. Do you feel up to talking to him?'

'Oh yes, I suppose I'll have to.'

'You don't have to immediately, you know. I can put him off for a while.' The doctor was really a kind man.

'Thanks very much, but it doesn't matter. I might as well get it over with.'

'I wouldn't worry too much. They're pretty tolerant of this sort of thing in Bundanyabba. I'll send him in.'

Grant knew the policeman would be Crawford. It was.

'Hello, John,' he said, looking rather foolish.

'Greetings,' said Grant, and waited.

'Don't like to bother you, John, but there's a kind of formality when a gunshot wound is admitted to the hospital, you understand.'

'Surely,' said Grant. 'Don't worry, go ahead and ask what you want.'

'Well,' said Crawford, almost shaking with embarrassment, 'it's like this: I thought, so as not to tire you like, I'd write out a statement of what probably happened and you could sign it like, if it was all right. How's that?'

'Fine by me.' What happened to people convicted of attempting suicide. Weren't they sent to lunatic asylums?

Crawford pulled a sheet of paper out of his pocket and handed it to Grant.

With some effort he held it up with one hand and read: 'The gunshot wound to my head was the result of an accident. I was returning from a shooting trip and carrying my point 22 rifle. I stopped to rest in a park off Randon Street, and believing the rifle to be unloaded I dropped it to the ground butt first. It exploded and that is all I remember.'

Grant looked up at Crawford and smiled.

'That'd be about it wouldn't it, John?' said Crawford, looking at his feet.

'Sure, that's about it. Thanks, mate.'

'Could you manage to sign it, do you think, John?'

Grant signed the paper with Crawford's pen.

'Thanks, John. We won't need to bother you any more. Be seeing you around.' And Crawford left as hurriedly as possible . . .

. . . The temperature inside the carriage rose steadily as the journey progressed, and the sweat rolled down the passengers' faces in drops, flickering and shaking with the motion of the train.

Grant lit another cigarette and blew the smoke out of the window to be whipped to nothing by the rushing air. The heat was making him ill, he'd become unaccustomed to it while he was in hospital. Hospitalization had proved not unpleasant as it had happened, lying there in the coolness induced by air-conditioning, on clean sheets, with the clean aseptic pain in his head eliminating subjective thought. It had been quite pleasant really, a period to be looked back on as one of non-disturbance, except for one day, when he had been there about a fortnight ...

... They would not let him out of bed, and his room was always kept locked. He supposed that was because they thought he might try to commit suicide again. It did not matter, he was quite content to just lie there.

An electric bell with a push-button in the wall just to the right of his head enabled him to summon a nurse when necessary.

One push meant he needed a urine bottle, two meant a bedpan, three meant a general call to be answered when convenient and four meant an emergency call.

Grant had suffered a great deal with the first two in his early days in hospital but he became resigned.

On this day, reconciled after some debate to the necessity, he pushed the button twice.

The nurses were quite prompt and it was only a couple of minutes before he heard the lock turn in the door. A nurse came in carrying the detested vessel decently shrouded in a white cloth.

Grant pulled himself into a sitting position, his face the careful blank he employed on these occasions.

Then he looked at the nurse's face.

It was Janette Hynes.

For one second his soul shrieked at the impossibility of this, the last humiliation, but then he realized that that was only the way he thought he ought to feel. In fact, it didn't matter, it was only happening to John Grant.

Just the same, he would if necessary, suffer internal injury rather than use that particular pan.

Janette said: 'Hullo, I heard you were here.'

'Yes,' said Grant, 'I'm here.'

She stood by the bed, still holding the pan, probably as embarrassed as he was, thought Grant, but she didn't show it.

There didn't seem much to say that could be said, but somebody had to say something.

'Sorry about that call,' said Grant, 'I meant to push three times. Just wanted some more water whenever anybody was passing.'

Janette looked at the water-jug by his bed. Grant looked at it. It was almost full.

Janette put the pan on the bed.

'It's all right,' she said, 'I'm only a nurse here.' And she went out.

Grant used the pan eventually, there was nothing else he could do. And Janette came back and took it away....

... The sadness of the plains at night was for some reason much more apparent from the inside of a moving train, thought Grant. Perhaps it was because of the people singing; the thread of melancholy which rang through even the most boisterous of their songs was something that was part of them, possibly born of this very sadness of the plains. All his memories of Bundanyabba and the people he had met there were tinged now with this plaintive, suppressed misery.

They had all been sad; Crawford, the policeman, the people at the Two-up Game, Tim Hynes and his daughter, Tydon and the miners, the people who had given him lifts.

Even the almoner at the hospital had left him with an impression of sadness, he didn't know why ...

... They had given him back his suitcases and taken him to the almoner's office where he had been presented with a bill for twenty-four pounds.

'I can't possibly pay this for a while,' Grant said.

'I couldn't care less,' said the almoner amiably. 'Whenever you can manage it.'

'Thanks,' said Grant, 'I'll pay it in about two months.'

'You're a schoolteacher, aren't you?' said the almoner. 'Sit down for a moment, why don't you?'

Grant sat down.

'Cigarette?'

Now that was a thought. There had been no real hope of cigarettes in the hospital and he had almost forgotten about them.

'Thanks.' The first intake of smoke was delicious, but it made him dizzy.

'This is a damn silly question,' said the almoner, 'but you're feeling quite all right now, aren't you?'

'Yes. Quite all right, thanks.'

'I mean ...'

'Oh, I see.' Of course it would be the almoner's job to see that Grant did not immediately go and undo all the hospital's work by successfully blowing his brains out.

'Quite all right in that line, thanks. I was just broke and feeling sorry for myself. It's all over now.'

'Quite sure?'

Grant thought a moment.

'Reasonably sure. As sure as one can be about these things.' He smiled.

The almoner smiled back.

'All right,' she said. 'What are your plans now?'

'I haven't got any.'

'Got any money?'

'No.' How many conversations of this sort did the almoner go through with frustrated suicides?

'We've got a sort of fund here to deal with things like this, you know,' said the almoner, 'I could let you have a loan of twenty pounds.'

'That's an extraordinary thing, surely?'

'Not really. The Rotary Club keeps it up. There's quite a need for it. Could you use the loan?'

Grant wondered whether the offer was extended to any indigent patient of the hospital, or only to would-be suicides.

'Yes. I could, thanks.'

The almoner gave him the money, and he signed a form promising to pay it back within six months if he could.

'That's fixed that,' said the almoner, 'I'll let you get away....'

... The train stopped, as western trains will do, miles from anywhere, for some reason known only to the driver. The sudden ending of motion and the violent drop in the noise level had a curious lulling effect. Even the singers were quiet and everybody looked out into the silent night. Grant recognized it as one of those moments he would always be able to recall. Another one had been when he walked out of the hospital earlier that day ...

Leaving the air-conditioning and meeting the heat once more was very much like starting life all over again. He stood on the hospital steps realizing how suspended and unreal his life had been in hospital. With nothing to do, with people bringing him his food, making his bed, even attending to his bathing, he had entered into that trance-like state that comes to people removed from any serious independent action, like prisoners in jail or 'other ranks' in the armed services.

But the first waves of heat which rolled up at him from the blistering road and beat down from the glaring haze of the sky dried up his trance and he became once more John Grant, responsible for himself.

Which is not, he thought, such a gravely important matter as one might suppose....

... The train had started again and was rocking through the night with renewed intensity as though anxious to make up for its lapse in stopping.

The singing began again; but there had been a change of mood now, and somebody had started playing a mouth-organ, and as

though shyly admitting for once the west's great burden of un-
happiness, they sang:

> *But hark there's the wail of a dingo,*
> *Watchful and weird; I must go,*
> *For it tolls the death knell of a stockman*
> *From the gloom of the scrub down below.*

Grant moved his body on the seat and plucked at his sweat-
sodden clothes to detach them from his skin. He wondered how
long he would be able to maintain this sense of satisfaction at being
able to feel anything, even minor discomfort. Not for long, he
thought, probably not for much longer than it would take the hair
to completely cover the scar on his head so that he would not be
constantly reminded how near he had come to never feeling anything again. . . .

. . . He had been very conscious of that scar while he was in the
hotel earlier that day, waiting for the train that was due in an
hour's time.

He leaned on the bar with his left elbow so that he could feel the
scar by resting his head on his hand. In his right hand he held a
glass of beer. The babble of voices formed a cocoon of sound
around him and he felt isolated, which was how he wanted to feel
just then.

He was absorbed in the taste of tobacco, the feel of the glass in
his hand, the prosaic wonder of the solidity of the floorboards
beneath his feet.

'I will never, never get drunk again,' he said softly, and added,
'except in good company.'

He looked around at the drinking men, and the sweating barmaid in the smoky fug of the bar.

A vivid joyousness quickened in him simply at being there,
alive. . . .

. . . The train stopped again and Grant stepped out on to the
railway siding called Tiboonda Station.

He was the only passenger to alight and he waited on the platform until the train pulled away again. As it went he could hear the
fading voices of the singers, still voicing the lament of the stockman:

> *Wrap me up in my stockwhip and blanket*
> *And bury me deep down below,*
> *Where the dingoes and crows won't*
> *   molest me,*
> *In the shade where the coolibahs grow.*

And soon Grant was standing alone under the stars, the train a silent line of yellow squares growing smaller.

He stood looking up, dazed and exhilarated by the brilliant, wild placidity, the riotous order of the stars.

Then he thought, almost aloud:

I can see quite clearly the ingenuity whereby a man may be made mean or great by exactly the same circumstances.

I can see quite clearly that even if he chooses meanness the things he brings about can even then be welded into a pattern of sanity for him to take advantage of if he wishes.

'What I can't altogether see' – he turned his eyes from the stars to the blackness of the plains and back to the stars again – 'what I can't altogether see is why I should be permitted to be alive, and to know these things. . . .'

He picked up his suitcases and began walking towards the patch of light where he knew Charlie the publican would be waiting, his curiosity about to be excited by the scar on Grant's forehead.

'. . . But I feel that I will probably find out sometime.'

NENE GARE
THE FRINGE DWELLERS

CHAPTER 1

Trilby paused to look back at the mission. The box-like buildings straggling either side of the wide roadway were ugly, utilitarian, and the only graceful note was lent by the tall wide-reaching gums which shaded them. At this distance the children's voices sounded like the carolling of birds, echoing and re-echoing as they laughed and called to each other.

Trilby stuck a long leg over the boundary fence, lifting her skirt high above the line of barbed wire at the top. Safely over, she bent her head against the wind and continued her walk. Outside the fence the slender-leaved wattles spread circular skirts to break the force of the southerly. In this dry red land of North-Western Australia the southerly blew all summer long, strong and straight. It blew Trilby's hair back from her face and down her faded cotton skirt between her legs. It inclined her figure at an angle and only her down-bent gaze shielded her eyes from the flying red dust.

Soon the mission was just a block of indistinct outlines, and the bell-like voices were truly those of the birds. A line of river-gums appeared and as they grew more distinct Trilby speeded her steps. Under the trees was the river-bed, dry and sandy now, but still cool beneath the low trailing branches of the ghost gums. Trilby stopped to look wistfully at a mud-bottomed hollow that some-times, when there had been good rains farther north, held water all through the long dry summer; but the rains had been sparse this year and the pool was dry. She stooped to brush a scurrying line of big black ants from a sandy spot beneath one of the trees, then she settled herself down, her back against its trunk. Here, where the force of the wind was broken, there were small bush flies by the hundred. They settled on the girl's face and arms and legs and lost themselves in her hair. She leaned over to pick a frond of leaves to use as a fly-switch.

Trilby was classified as a half-caste. For years now she had lived at the mission. There were four of the Comeaways there – Trilby's older sister Noonah, and the young ones, ten-year-old Bartie and the baby Stella, who was six. Trilby had always hated the life, though the active rebellion of her first year or so had dwindled to a dreary acceptance, lighted only by wild plans for the life she would lead when she was free. She dreamed of excitement and gaiety and laughter and joyous adventure, but these things did not belong to mission life, and until now there had always been the cold awakening to this fact. Not today, though. Today she could dream as much as she liked. Only one more night at the mission for herself and Noonah. One more night between herself and the wonder of pleasing herself what she did. Her mouth curled upward in ecstasy.

With her face turned to the clear strong light, it seemed that most of the dark blood in this girl had drained into hands and feet, leaving the skin of her face a glowing amber, highlighted with gold. There were stripes of gold in her hair too, over dark honey. But her eyes were her most outstanding feature. Between curving black lashes they glinted like silver.

Trilby's grandfathers, both of them, had been white. The cold arrogance of one had been centred in the narrow grey eyes that Trilby had inherited. From him, too, she had her slim height and her high-held head. And perhaps her stubborn rebellious spirit. Back at the mission she was considered a spitfire, cheeky and almost unmanageable. The other kids teased her about her strange light eyes, but Trilby was only acting when she bit back at them. At fifteen she was not yet brave enough to tell them she liked to be different. And that she liked most to be different from coloured people. The lovely velvet-brown eyes of most of the other children went unadmired, She preferred her own long secretive eyes.

She flung a careless arm across the tree and leant her soft cheek against its hard satin trunk. The sprays of delicate pointed leaves dipped and danced about her face. Across from her, in the very centre of the dry river-bed, a tortured gum grew almost parallel with the earth but its foliage strained towards the sky, lifting and rippling as the wind drove it ever downward. The coarse white sand rose in clouds, the wind went flying through the leaves, and presently Trilby, in tune with her surroundings, flung straining arms tightly round her tree. Happiness leapt in her heart like a living thing so that laughter was caught in her throat and strangled there. The hardness of the wood crushed her chest but she only pressed closer to it, as if this were life itself she held in her arms. But at last there were tears as well as laughter, and the tears slipped down her cheeks and were bitter and salt on her tongue.

There were two who sat on the steps of the schoolhouse in the late afternoon, and the faces of both were bleak and still. All the comfort

Noonah had to give had been given, and the boy Bartie was not comforted. Sitting on the step below her he pressed himself against her legs, empty eyes watching the antics of a group of small boys rolling over and over in the red-dusted sand. Tomorrow Noonah would be gone. There was no thought more important than that. And so it was for Noonah. Tomorrow she must leave Bartie and Stella behind to get on as well as they could without her. And the more she thought of the little things she had done for them, which nobody but an older-sister-turned-mother would ever think of doing, much less have time to do in this crowded and busy mission, the more desolate grew her thoughts. They would miss her so! And how cruel that she, who loved them, should be forced to withdraw herself from them and leave them alone. She slipped an arm over Bartie's shoulders and when the boy looked up at her inquiringly she smiled at him – the unutterably tender and reassuring smile of a mother for her child. Bartie questioned her with his eyes, and the girl searched swiftly for words that had not been said before.

'What you have to remember is that it isn't going to be for long, see? I'll ask them as soon as I get down there and tell them you and Stella have to come down too. And if there isn't any room where they are, I'll make them shift somewhere or build another little place just for you and Stella. See?' But ten is not a looking-forward age. Nothing the future held had power enough to drag Bartie's mind off the present. Mourning, Noonah watched his dark eyes fill and brim until the boy dropped his head in shame and she could see only the curling black hair. Unable to bear his misery she scrambled to her feet. 'Bartie, I have to say good night to Stella again. I want to see her just once more before – ' she stopped. 'Come with me,' she begged, 'before the bell goes for you too.'

Bartie nodded, blinking his eyes. The two walked off, and as they walked their hands brushed and would have clung. But not here. Not until they had left these others behind them.

'Mrs Gordon cut our hair, mine and Trilby's, and she let us use some of her shampoo,' Noonah said cheerfully. 'It smelt nice, too.'

Bartie cast a brief look at Noonah's hair, swinging like a bell over her thin shoulders and cut in a thick fringe across her forehead. Every hair glinted with lights that had nothing to do with its rich black. The glow of the setting sun was on her face, too, ripening the amber skin that belonged to all of these Comeaways.

'You look pretty,' Bartie discovered shyly, his eyes lingering.

'Go on!' Noonah's oblique glanced mocked him.

They were approaching the large central building where they ate and sometimes played if it was wet, and where they gathered

together to sing in their clear sweet voices. There was always one
mission employee to grow enthusiastic about the way these coloured
children sang, and to coach them in hymns and old-time favourites,
and to bring them on as a star turn on the occasion of important
visitors.

A few of the bigger boys and girls came clattering down the steps
as they passed. The fly-wire door crashed behind them and there
was Trilby, long slim legs dancing; her hair, fresh-washed, springing alive and springing round her face. She caught sight of Noonah
and Bartie straightway and came over to them. There were no
doubts about these three and their relationship to each other. Wide
low brows, broad and slightly flattened cheek-bones, strongly
modelled noses with flaring nostrils and then the clear sweet curve
of lips that parted on square white teeth. Only Trilby had those
strange light eyes. The others' were warm brown with jetty depths,
the whole of the iris showing between wide-open lids. Only Trilby's
hair had that sun-struck look. The others had hair the colour of
coal, coarse hair that curled softly round their faces.

'Still grizzling?' Trilby questioned, teasing Bartie with a glance.

Before Noonah could answer a man in a pair of knee-length
khaki shorts appeared, brushing the palm of one hand rhythmically
across his fat thigh with each brisk step. This was Mr Norton, the
superintendent of the mission. He bent an attentive look on the
girls. 'One more night for you two, hey? Well, early to bed so you'll
be fresh for the trip. It's a long trip, mind you, down to where
you're going.'

'Yes,' the girls murmured submissively.

The man nodded approvingly, switched his attention to a boy
who lounged indolently against a veranda post. 'Better give that
kikuyi grass another sprinkle tonight, George. Can't have it dying
on us, eh?'

The boy gathered up his languid body and moved away, unresponsive but obedient.

Trilby curled her lip after the man. 'Always so damn cheerful,'
she muttered. 'Treating everyone like they were children. Gee, I'll
be glad to get away from this place.'

'It isn't too bad,' frowned Noonah, reminding her sister of Bartie's
presence. 'Lots of kids like it better than where they come from.'

'Like to know where they've come from, if they like this dump,'
Trilby said shortly.

'All you kids are going out in the ute tomorrow, aren't you?'
Noonah asked Bartie. 'Into town, Mrs Gordon said.'

Bartie nodded lifelessly.

'Now don't start howling,' Trilby warned him. 'You gotta stay here if you like it or not. We had to when we were your age. And we were younger when we came, too.

Bartie tried a valiant sniff but a few tears chased each other down his cheeks. A couple of boys around his age stopped to stare.

'Lookatim cry,' the bigger one jeered. 'Ole Cry-baby Comeaway.'

Trilby turned on them furiously. 'Get, you kids. Go on! And don't forget Bartie isn't the only one around here cries. What about you two an the way you cried when your mummy come up to see you. Thought she wasn't ever going to get away from you, I bet.'

Her grey eyes sparked as the two children made sulkily off. 'Never can let anyone alone,' she fumed. 'Always someone around to stick their noses in someone else's business.' She swung round on Bartie. 'An you! You make me ashamed you're my brother. You're the big one, aren't you? That has to take care of Stella. Don't you understand that?'

'Shut up!' Noonah spoke sharply. 'Bartie's coming down with me to see Stella. He'll be all right if you just leave him alone and don't bully him.'

'Us two are leaving early tomorrow morning,' Trilby said gruffly to her brother. 'If you want to say good-bye you'd better do it now.' She bent towards the boy and gave him a hug. Her thin fingers with their oval nails and perfect moons, like delicate shells against the dark skin, slid into the black curly hair. She gave it a tug, a rallying gesture to him to keep his emotion out of sight. Nobody ever saw Trilby in tears. Her world was peopled with enemies waiting to pounce on any such weakness and turn it to their own account, and every observation she made confirmed this fact more fully in her mind.

'Come on, Bartie,' Noonah said gently. Trilby looked after them, undecided about accompanying them, then she shrugged and turned in the opposite direction, chin high and eyes narrowed.

Bartie had caught some of his sister's fierceness. 'I am not a cry-baby. I hardly ever cry, do I, Noonah?'

'You're all right,' Noonah said affectionately. 'Trilby just said that because she felt like crying herself. She was all worked up, and she doesn't know half what's she's talking about when she gets worked up.'

'About once a year, that's all,' Bartie still smarted, and his cheeks were still a bit wet.

A woman in a canvas deck-chair looked up in surprise as the two approached her. She was accustomed to Noonah's nightly visits, but the girl had already tucked her small sister into bed and kissed her good night.

'Can we have just one more look?' Noonah begged. 'I'm going tomorrow and I just thought – Bartie and I thought –.'

'They're all asleep in there,' the woman said doubtfully. 'You'll have to be very quiet. One wakes the lot sometimes.'

'We won't make any noise at all,' Noonah promised.

'Go on then,' the woman said. 'But no noise remember! My feet are killing me today.'

Noonah pulled her brother after her into the children's nursery. Usually, only the children under five slept here, but Stella was small and delicate, prone to chesty colds and barking coughs, so she slept in here with the babies where supervision was night-long. Noonah went over to the far corner of the room where she knew her sister slept. The little girl had tossed off her sheet, and her night-gown was twisted round her waist so that her small round bottom and relaxed limbs showed dark against the white cotton sheets. One small hand dropped over the side of the bed; the other cradled her head. She was breathing lightly and evenly, her soft mouth parted.

Forgetting Bartie for a second, Noonah kneeled. She took up the tiny relaxed hand and pressed it gently to her cheek. Beside her, the boy bent his head to look at his small sister. His mouth curved upward. Hands on knees, his breathing carefully controlled, he continued to gaze. Then brother and sister exchanged a long look. Bartie nodded slightly, his eyes shy.

When they were well clear of the nursery, Noonah spoke. 'You couldn't come with me and leave her behind, Bartie, could you? She's so little, and she loves you.'

She walked Bartie to the dormitory occupied by the smaller boys. Before he passed through the doorway he stopped and turned back to her. 'Remember,' he said expressionlessly, 'you promised.'

The door closed behind him, and it was Noonah's turn to blink.

They were in the train at last and Trilby was almost out of her mind with excitement, terribly afraid that it was all a dream. But the train gathered pace and the familiar things outside the window continued to pass from her sight one after the other. No dream sister could look as real as Noonah on the opposite seat, or the man and woman across the carriage from them. She could read the notices, too, that told her not to pull the communication cord and not to expectorate on the floor. She could even make out the inscriptions under the dusty looking pictures of tall timber. Convinced, she sat back in her seat and looked out the window again. It was all bush now. Miles and miles of wattles and drooping river gums vanished behind the line of the frame. She tried to stay their progress by fixing her eyes on one special tree but the train flew too fast. She gave up trying and fixed candid curious eyes on the other passengers.

Noonah did not take her eyes off the view outside her window. For a long time she watched it unseeing, but gradually her brow grew lighter and her mourning mouth took an upward turn. The thing was done, the separation complete, and she was still too young to distrust the future.

By and by the little train grew weary and its first fine burst of speed slackened considerably. It picked its way more carefully now and sometimes, though still between stations, it stopped completely. On the track, men walked up and down, intent and busy, and the passengers in the carriages rushed to watch them pass. Some complained, irritably and angrily. Others craned their necks and narrowed their eyes against the sun and passed low-voiced comments to their companions. The lucky ones were those at whose carriage the mechanics halted to leer and poke and get down on hands and knees to examine wheels more closely. Trilby and Noonah, politely flattened against the backs of their seats to make room for the watchers, waited patiently and trustfully for the wrong to be righted, and in the meantime they took the opportunity to observe unobserved.

Trilby knew of only two types of white people. Those who did not care one way or the other about you, and the others who, like the white children on the school bus, waited wet-lipped and bright-eyed for your reactions to taunts dealing mostly with the colour of your skin. Towards the end, the mission had been given school-rooms of its own and government teachers had come to teach in them, but in the beginning the mission children had attended the town school along with the white children. A school bus came out to pick them up and Trilby remembered well the twice-daily trips in and out. The mission children preferred to sit together but that wasn't always possible and then they might have to share a seat with a white child. Pinched legs and hair-pullings Trilby could deal with and she did, very effectively. Remarks such as 'Pooh! What's the stink around here?' and 'Wonder if she et up all her nice lizards this morning?' resulted in a win for the white children, most of them needle–sharp at detecting evidence of victory whether it were wet eyes and vulnerable soft mouths closing over sobs or the angry snarls and hating looks they got from some of the bigger mission children. Nearly always there were bumps and bruises and torn shirts and frocks. Half-smiling Trilby remembered the dreadful

satisfaction of hearing a pocket tear away from the material it had
been anchored to.

Once, a girl sharing a seat with Trilby had cried, 'Why, that's
my old dress you're wearing.' Warmth and happiness had flooded
over her. She had turned to smile at her neighbour because she had
thought, knowing no better at that stage, that here among her
enemies was a friend. And then the girl had laughed, and in her
eyes there was no friendliness at all – just a look that Trilby could
not remember even now without feeling ashamed. The girl had
turned to the others in the bus and told them, 'The kid's wearing
one of my old dresses. My mum must have given it to her because
it's all worn out. See?' She had pointed to a patch on the skirt, and
those nearest had left their seats to examine the patch. So Trilby
had learned.

There were other things. Waiting at the side of the road for the
school bus, hoping this would be a good day, when the mission
children could sit together. Bracing herself, just in case. Not joining
in with the chatter of the others because she had been too busy
cautioning herself against showing those tell-tale signs of a bull's-
eye for which her enemies waited.

Trilby turned a narrow-eyed gaze on the wispy-haired woman
who over-flowed the seat in the corner diagonally opposite. From
the safety of today she took a cool look at the days of her first brush
with education. She and Noonah had been with their parents then,
living temporarily in a camp on the outskirts of a small northern
town. Dad, Trilby remembered, sometimes let her and Noonah go
with him to help burn off the great yellow stumps of the gum trees.
Often they had camped alongside a glowing log all night, and the
red glow would still be there under the pale silvery ashes when they
woke next morning.

At this particular town Mrs Comeaway had been seized with the
idea of sending the two girls to the town school. She had had a little
mission training herself, but in her case the training had been
confined to kitchen chores, with an hour or two in the classroom
whenever it was felt she could be spared. Maybe she would not
have had the courage to break the ice, but there were other camps
round about and other coloured children attending the school in
the little township.

The girls had fallen in with her plan for different reasons,
Noonah because she was an even-tempered child who usually did
as she was told and Trilby because she was curious.

Trilby leaned her head back against the carriage seat. It had not
been much of a school. A few little tables and chairs in a draughty

old timbered hall. A square blackboard on three yellow legs with a shelf to take chalk and the yellow felt pad used for cleaning off writing. And a woman schoolteacher with wispy dry red hair that stood up in peaks, and peaky eyelids to match. From narrow shoulders her body had flowed down to enormous hips and the black shiny stuff of her apron had given off a smell of bitter peaches. There had not been enough of the little chairs and tables to seat the coloured children, so they had sat on the floor at the side of the classroom. One of them was expected to keep the blackboard clean. Trilby had hated the choking white dust.

The teacher directed most of her attention to her white pupils, but she always knew if one of the coloured children wasn't listening to what she said. A ruler across the knuckles or a stinging smack on the leg was her answer to that. Every day one of their number was sent home for any one of a variety or reasons. Too loud sniffing if a child had a cold but no handkerchief, torn clothes, dirty clothes, unwashed hands or hair, inability to answer a sharply-put question. Some of the cloured children, Trilby knew, committed any and all of these offences on purpose, wanting to be sent home, but she had not seen things this way. When her nose was wet she wiped it on the skirt of her frock, if she had overlooked her skimpy morning wash she sat on her hands, and because she listened with stony attentiveness to all that the teacher said, she was able to give satisfactory answers to the questions. Because it was so much nicer to play around the camp or to accompany her father to the paddock to help with the burning-off, Trilby had never quite understood why something in her rebelled at being sent away from the school-room. Even Noonah did not mind. They had all been sent away in the end. A policeman had come out to the camps and talked to the parents, and Tribly had learned, after sneaking close to him and listening, that some of the white mothers and fathers did not want their children to sit alongside coloured children because they had too many colds and they scratched their heads too much.

When the policeman had gone Trilby heard her mother grumbling to her father. Mr Comeaway had only laughed, but her mother had been crabby for days. There had been painful scrapings of their scalps with a fine-toothed comb, and slatherings of kerosene and even dark suspicions directed at the other camps. That had been the beginning of the ending of the girls' wanderings with their parents. The bug of education had established itself firmly in Mrs Comeaway's head and, a few weeks after that, Trilby and Noonah had been dumped at the mission. 'Where yous lucky to be at,' was her final and firm admonition to them both.

The long years that had followed! Half a dozen times since then the girls had seen their parents; the last time had been when Bartie and Stella had been brought to join them. Trilby glanced over at the corner seat. The woman sitting there was staring at her. Trilby remembered that same look in the eyes of her long-ago teacher. Curiosity with no warmth in it. If she had only known, that teacher. The distaste she had felt for the coloured children and shown so clearly had been equalled by the fearful shrinking they had felt for her and her white-rimmed eyes with their peaky lids. And her face which was the colour of the underside of a sleepy lizard.

'Ugh!' Trilby shivered, and the woman turned her head away.

CHAPTER 2

Just before they reached the last station, the cheerful guard came to tell them to put all their things together so that nothing should be lost. He dug in his pocket and bent over them. 'An here's something for yous to spend on lollies,' he whispered. 'You been good kids.'

To each girl he handed a shilling.

Noonah took her coin shyly, with whispered thanks. Trilby looked from her shilling to the guard and back again. Then she flashed a look of such pure gratitude at him that the man's expression of easy benevolence changed to one of surprise. 'It's only a bob, ya know,' he chuckled at her. 'Won't buy yous much these days.' And he hurried off on other duties.

Trilby followed his progress down the corridor, still smiling. 'I don't mind him,' she said softly to Noonah. 'He's nice.'

'Yes,' agreed her sister. She was busy with parcels and cases. 'Trilby, where's the little bag with the soap in it?'

'Sitting on it,' Trilby said, after a search. 'Here you are.'

'I promised Bartie I'd ask about him and Stella coming back as soon as we get there,' Noonah worried.

'Let it go for a while,' Trilby frowned. 'Gee, *we* had to stay there, didn't we?'

'Praps I won't mention it the first day. But soon!' Noonah's cares were beginning to settle around her shoulders again. What would it be like, living with her mother and father? Would they be nice to her? Would they want to get the others back? How could she convince them that Bartie *must* come back? That she had promised.

'Can't you listen?' Trilby said impatiently. 'I said let's get up early tomorrow morning and go straight in to the town.'

'I'll see the hospital,' Noonah said, her expression clearing again. 'I want to see the hospital first of all. I'm going to train there, to be a nurse.'

'And no more school,' Trilby said, making a firm line of her lips.

'You told Mrs Gordon you'd go back until you got your Junior,' Noonah reminded her sister.

'She'd have gone on and on if I hadn't. I'm not going back but.' Her brows drew together, narrowing her eyes. 'I'm going to look at the shops first of all and get some new bathers and I'm going to swim and have some fun, and later on, if I feel like it, I'll get a job somewhere. Serving in a milk-bar, I think. With a pink uniform like those others had at the Rainbow Milk-Bar. You think I'd be all right for a job like that, Noonah?'

'Anyone could do that,' Noonah said.

'I don't mean that,' Trilby frowned.

'What did you mean well?'

'Ah, never mind! You go and train to be a nurse, and I'll do things my own way.' But Noonah was not listening. Her soft cheek was pressed against the glass as her eyes strained ahead. 'Look at all the lights, Trilby. We must be nearly there.'

There were a good many lights. The station looked big and important. On another line a big black engine puffed past, trailing carriages after it in a neat orderly line. There was clamour outside the carriage and bustling busyness inside it as the other passengers cleared the luggage rack and gathered their cases and coats together in tidy piles. Guards called directions, friends shouted greetings, people's faces flowed past the window like an animated mural, and a sharp stuffy smell seeped into the carriage.

'How will we find them?' Noonah panicked, slim dark hands clutching the edges of her seat. There was a last jerk, a gentle shaking, and their train was still. The girls stayed in their seats until everyone had left the carriage then walked out with their own cases. There was the business of stacking everything on the station platform, neatly, so that coats did not get dirty, and after that nothing but to stand and wait. Uneasily, darting questioning looks at each other.

'Here they is,' said a remembered voice, and the girls turned with brightening faces. Mrs Comeaway's hair was greyer than they remembered it, overhanging the collar of her coat. She was fatter, too, so that the hand holding the folds of coat had much ado to prevent them from flying free. But her wide dark face was alight with pleasure and her voice excited as she called back over her shoulder to the man behind her. Mr Comeaway came up grinning. His wet hair had been sleeked back from his good-humoured face, his clean white shirt was open at the neck to show the curly grey hairs on his chest, his cuffs neatly buttoned at the wrist.

'So big!' Mrs Comeaway said wonderingly, admiringly. 'You two big now, eh?'

'Outside we gotta taxi,' Mr Comeaway told them. 'For all this stuff ya got. You bring im along an that taximan take care of that lot.' He waited politely for the girls to pick up their cases, then he led the way, nodding encouragingly. Mrs Comeaway escorted the girls from the other side, beaming and panting. 'We gotta nice place right by Green's. An a bed each for ya. New beds straight fum shops. How ya like that, eh? Eh, I didn't even kiss yous yet.' She stopped the procession to deliver two resounding kisses. 'Gee, you girls got big.' Her plump face creased in folds of firm and shining dark flesh as she laughed. Outside the station, the waiting taximan took their cases and slung them into the boot. The elder Comeaways climbed into the back seat and sat forward, smiling broadly. 'Come on!' they beckoned.

Trilby and Noonah climbed in too. The girls sat very straight whilst their father and mother looked them over from the tips of their toes to the tops of their heads, smiling all the while, nodding approvingly, nudging each other.

And the girls' prevailing feeling was one of warm pleasure. It was nice to have a mother and father waiting for you at the end of a long trip. It was a good feeling to see them acting so pleased just because you were there, it was by far the most satisfying of the day's experiences. They belonged again.

In between exchanging smiles with her parents, Noonah took fleeting looks at the scene beyond the taxi window. Perhaps they might pass the hospital.

'Was it nice on the train?' Mrs Comeaway inquired. 'Did you get looked after good? Them mission people writ us a letter and they said we wasn't to worry about ya because you was gunna be looked after.'

'These two didn't see a place this big before,' Mr Comeaway chuckled. 'Not a word outa them.'

'Can we swim?' Trilby asked.

'You can swim,' Mrs Comeaway told her. 'They give ya that for nothing here.' She laughed uproariously and her husband joined her.

'Will we go past thc hospital?' Noonah inquired.

'You the one's gunna be a nurse, eh? You look out there now. That big place with all them trees. See?

Noonah peered through the window excitedly. There was nothing to be seen but a tallness of lights, but her heart leapt. There! Inside that tallness was the matron who already knew about Noonah Comeaway and how she was coming down from the mission to learn to be a nurse. She was expected there. Maybe even now the matron was saying to someone, 'Wonder when that girl's coming?'

'Gee!' she sighed ecstatically.

'An here's ole Heartbreak Hill,' Mrs Comeaway said luxuriously. 'An we don't walk up *him* tonight. Ya gotta walk up this damn hill ta know what it's like. Gunna get arkattack fum that hill one a these days. There, up we go an round the top. An over an down an up again.' She sat waiting for the dips and turns, enjoying them as would a child. 'An this is it.'

'We get out here,' Mr Comeaway explained kindly, letting himself out through his door. His wife eased herself out after him. The taxi driver opened the girls' door and stood grinning at them. From the road they could see nothing but the dim whiteness and a rise. The man got their cases from the boot and deposited them at the side of the road. 'That'll be four shillings,' he said impersonally.

There was a short wait.

'Go on!' Mrs Comeaway said firmly. 'Give the man is money.'

'Didn't you have the money?' Mr Comeaway asked in injured tones.

'I did not,' Mrs Comeaway said even more firmly. 'An why would I seein ya didn't give me none.'

'Ah well!' Mr Comeaway shook his head at the taxi driver, sorrowing for him. 'I better come down tomorrow and fix you up.'

'Making it as near a pound as don't make any difference,' the man said. 'Okay! See you tomorrow.' He got back into the taxi and turned it expertly. The Comeaway family stood there in the dark, watching the tail-light disappear over the hill.

'Well, up we go,' Mrs Comeaway sighed. 'Come on!'

Mr Comeaway had already started.

'Come back here, you,' Mrs Comeaway called sternly. 'Just you grab them girls' cases, first time they home.'

'Gee, all right,' Mr Comeaway said, coming back to the road on a small slide of sand. 'Jus thought I'd get a light goin for yous, that's all.'

'Yes, you did,' Mrs Comeaway withered him. 'Now come on, you two, an follow me. Then ya won't fall over nothin.'

Trilby and Noonah groped for each other's hands. Their sides were heaving with their efforts to giggle soundlessly. Their mother plunged up the sandy hill and they followed her closely. The blackness was lit by a dim yellow glow to the right. 'That ain't it,' Mrs Comeaway panted, ploughing on past the smudge. 'That's where the ole lady lives. We're a bit further back. You kids is gunna like the ole lady. Real nice woman. Lets us use everything she got, dub an all.'

Another patch of yellow sprang out of the darkness ahead. It shone through between sheets of galvanized iron and spilled over a doorway. 'Don't you get too far over that side,' Mrs Comeaway warned, 'or you'll be goin arse over tip down the hill.' She giggled. 'On top a Billy Grey's roof, maybe. Is camp just down there.'

In the lighted doorway, the girls stood blinking and smiling and looking around them. This was home. They walked into it thankfully.

The room they were in measured about twelve by twelve. A hurricane-lamp stood on top of a heavy home-carpentered table, and a black-handled frying-pan, some crockery, a milk-tin full of dripping and a couple of empty brown bottles crowded it for room. Against each outside wall was a small iron bed topped with a mattress and several folded army blankets. The floor of the room was of earth stamped hard. A black iron stove bulked large across one end, its top cluttered with dim objects. Wooden uprights supported an assortment of clothes crowned with hats and bags, and across another aperture at the back of the room hung a man's thick brown coat, presumably acting as a curtain. Trilby's gaze was caught and held by a single brown chop in the frying-pan. It was frozen in a pool of brown fat, but her mouth watered for it.

'Fixin that catch on the door certainly kep them dogs out,' Mr Comeaway said, picking the chop out of its fat and tearing off a piece. 'Didn't even finish me dinner,' he told the girls, 'the ole lady was so anxious ta get down that station.' He waved a casual hand. 'Hadda leave everything an rush.'

'These here are the beds,' Mrs Comeaway said proudly, bouncing happily. 'Good new beds these. I put a coupla rugs each for yous. Look in that tin on the table, you kids. Might be some biscuits left.'

Mr Comeaway took the lid from the tin himself. He searched through the crackling debris of half a dozen old biscuit wrappings and finally found a few crumby biscuits. He proffered them graciously.

'You kids look wore out,' Mrs Comeaway said sympathetically. 'An likewise us. So I tell you what we gunna do. We all gunna get some sleep, an in the morning you can tell us bout everything. What ya think, eh?'

'Ya hungry?' Mr Comeaway asked, a bit anxiously. 'I shoulda arst before I et me chop.'

'I give em a good big feed tomorrow,' Mrs Comeaway said, clearing her conscience and her mind in one swoop.

'Yeah, that's right,' Mr Comeaway nodded. He gave the girls a big smile. 'I better get out now, an let ya get ta bed.' He hesitated, slightly embarrassed. 'G'night!' He mooched into the next room, ducking his head beneath the army overcoat.

'An you leave all that stuff till tomorrow, too,' Mrs Comeaway said, waving her hand at the cases. Her pleased eyes sought the beds again. 'You gunna be real comforble in them beds. Now!' She moved over to her daughters and hugged each in turn. 'Inta bed with ya.' She moved off after her husband and disappeared behind the coat, returning, however, almost immediately. In a loud whisper she told them, 'If ya wanta use the dub it's round the side. Take the lamp so ya won't trip over nothing.' The coat swung back into place and the girls were alone in their bedroom.

Noonah perched herself on one of the beds. Trilby's eyes still brimmed with laughter, but neither girl spoke, aware of the two in the other room. Their ears pricked to the strange thuds and groaning sighs as their parents prepared for bed. Trilby caught Noonah's eye and gestured over her shoulder with a thumb. Noonah nodded. They took the lantern by its wire handle and crept outside. It was a while before they found the toilet crouching drunkenly beneath a tree.

'You think it's going to be all right?' Trilby said softly, on the way back.

Noonah nodded vigorously. 'I like them. Don't you?'

Trilby spluttered suddenly. 'Why do you think they made that hole square?'

Noonah choked. 'Shut *up*!' she begged. 'They'll hear.'

'And I'm so hungry,' Trilby wailed softly. 'That lovely chop!'

'I was just going to ask if I could have it,' Noonah giggled.

'We'll have a drink instead,' Trilby said, waving the lantern round. 'Where's the tap?' But there was nothing that looked like a tap. Inside again, she poked round on the stove for the kettle, but there was no kettle there.

Noonah thought longingly of washing her face, which felt dry and dirty, then she shrugged her shoulders. Tomorrow would do. She fished in her case for pyjamas and undressed as quietly as possible. Trilby did the same, removing one of the hats and hanging her clothes over the things that already hung from a nail. The arranging of the beds came next. Trilby's extravagant miming when she looked in vain for a pillow nearly set Noonah off again. The girls climbed at last between the grey woollen blankets, using their arms as head-rests. Noonah reached for the hurricane-lamp and blew out the flame.

'Good night, Trilby,' she whispered.

'Night,' Trilby whispered back. 'We'll get up early tomorrow morning and have a look round, shall we?'

CHAPTER 3

Trilby was the first to wake, her face barred with sunlight that slipped through the inadequate walls of the humpy. She smiled almost as soon as she opened her eyes. This was the real beginning of freedom. She looked across the room at the still sleeping Noonah and smiled again, remembering the night before. There was no sound from the inner room. She swung her legs over the side of the bed and sat considering. Then she reached for her clothes and stripped off her pyjamas. A few minutes later she crept out through the doorway, breathing quickly through parted lips, her silver-grey eyes shining.

Ten feet away tall sunflowers grew together in a great golden mass. Already bees were climbing clumsily over the pollen-dusted black centres. Behind the sunflowers the ground dropped away steeply. Tribly walked to the edge and looked down on a wattle-studded valley, tenderly, brightly green. The smoke from a couple of camp-fires rose thinly on the quiet air. Trilby counted a dozen roof-tops sheltering beneath the green; galvanized iron painted white, the grey of weathered tarpaulin and the rust-streaked glimmer of scrap-iron.

She turned to examine her own domain. The humpy was as she had imagined it to be, a ramshackle arrangement of tarpaulins and scrap-iron nailed to bush timber. A bough shelter projected from one end and beneath it stood another rough table and two cane chairs very much the worse for having been sat on. Suspended by a string from a nearby wattle swung a wire safe, its door hanging open, its shelves bare. The ground beneath her feet was pure beach sand, but along one side of the humpy grew several tomato plants. Trilby lifted the drab green leaves, but the tiny red tomatoes were holed and uneatable. She picked one and threw it high over the valley, watching the red speck until it disappeared into the wattles.

Back from the humpy was a weathered house, its roof sagging and broken, its timbers silver grey and splintery. At its side a blackened copper stood on some red bricks, and a wooden stand held wash-tubs. A few elderly stocks grew in a line along the wall, and dusty-leaved honeysuckle clung to the rail of the front veranda. But a big old gum flung sheltering boughs over the entire structure and the effect was one of peaceful homeliness. Along the line of the fence, where now not more than a dozen palings stood, peppermint trees trailed dim green leaves and clusters of rose-pink berries. The house was set on the flat top of a hill which stood like an inverted pudding-bowl, dominating the rise to the left and the wide stretch of plain that lay behind it. Scattered over the flatness were tiny box-like houses set in fenced paddocks of gold and green. The sun turned their roofs to squares of colour from a child's paint-box. Towards the township a grey fortress-like tank squatted solidly into the gentle slope of a hill which half obscured it, and far beyond that Trilby saw the line of the sea, slashed with foam, its slaty-blue merging into the softness of the summer sky.

She stood relaxed and still, looking into the distance, content with a new feeling of peace and happiness. And as she stood, the miscellany of tiny bush sounds smoothed themselves into a vibrant silence.

Three silvery notes broke the spell. Trilby watched smiling as a grey dot of a bird pretended to lose its balance on a bough over her head.

A group of children straggled forth from the grey weather-board house. And Noonah's voice sounded behind her. 'Why didn't you wake me up?'

The children came closer, staring at the strangers with wide almost black eyes, their scrutiny both competent and impersonal.

'Hello!' Noonah greeted them companionably.

The faces melted into grins. A bigger girl bent to pick up a small night-gowned figure and settle it over one hip. Two boys stood their ground, alert and sure of themselves. Another small girl maintained precarious balance whilst she scraped with one foot at the back of a leg. 'Mrs Green's,' Trilby said.

'That's our Gramma,' the little girl said. Noonah bent to look into her face and to pat her cheek.

'We stay with Gramma an go to school,' the older one volunteered.

'You don't go to school yet, do you?' Noonah smiled at the little girl.

'Her mother lets her stay here when she goes away working,' the same older girl said. 'She's Bonny, and this is her sister,' looking down at the very smallest one on her hip.

'Let me take her,' Noonah offered. She took the baby girl and smoothed her hair back from her face.

Trilby grinned. Noonah would be busy for an hour now if she knew anything about her sister. 'Look, I'm going to get washed,' she told Noonah. 'I've found a tap.'

Noonah only nodded, already engrossed with the children.

Trilby went back to the humpy and searched quietly for something to wash in. She found a basin underneath the table. A skinny grey washer hung over its side. Trilby wrinkled her nose and used it to wipe out the inside of the grey-rimmed basin. Then she took her new washer and soap from her flowered sponge-bag.

When she had washed herself she took the basin to the side of the hill and flung its contents in a silvery sweep over the hillside. A river of rusting tins and trash already littered the slope, and under a wattle just over the brow glinted a stack of amber bottles.

Down in the valley there were signs of life. Voices floated up – the high clear voices of children and the rounder, deeper notes of adults.

She replaced the basin and went into the humpy to change her frock. She was tying the laces in her shoes when sounds of vast yawnings and luxurious stretchings came from the inner room. 'You girls awake yet?' called her mother.

Trilby stepped uncertainly towards the coat-veiled aperture. 'We've been up for ages.'

'Come on in then,' chuckled her mother. 'Nobody in here gunna bite ya.' So Trilby stepped past the coat.

The inner room was thick with gloom. The only opening in its walls was covered by a heavy jute sugar-bag. Occasionally this lifted a little with the breeze and a breath of fresh morning air stirred the atmosphere. In this room a thin strip of linoleum had been laid at the side of the big double bed that took up most of the room. Head and foot of the bed were festooned with garments, and from its sagging middle Mrs Comeaway rose to greet her daughter. Mr Comeaway was still asleep, and as his wife sat up in bed his head rolled down the slope to her back. Mrs Comeaway, using her husband's chest as a back-rest, looked with pleased interest at her daughter. 'Aaah! Nnnh! You all dressed up, eh?'

Trilby ducked her head and smoothed the skirt of her frock.

'Come an sit on the bed a minute while I get me circulation goin,' Mrs Comeaway invited

Trilby sat on the end of the bed and looked curiously round the room. Across one corner stood a high, old chest of drawers, its cream paint striped with scratches. The inevitable clothing littered its top and scattered through the debris were two tins of talcum, a brush stuck with a hairy black comb, a xylonite tray from which flashed an assortment of jewellery, and two large white plaster-of-Paris rabbits with pink-lined ears.

'Ya think ya gunna like it with us?' Mrs Comeaway asked, wringing a groan from Mr Comeaway as her elbow slipped into his neck.

'It's going to be lovely,' Trilby said, with warmth.

Mrs Comeaway looked pleased. 'Course, it ain't much of a place,' she said complacently, 'it does us but. Keeps the wet out.'

Trilby doubted that, but she did not care overmuch.

'Can I have a look at that stuff up there?' she asked, pointing at the brooches and ear-rings.

'Me jools?' Mrs Comeaway said, with a grin. 'Go ahead.'

While Trilby examined the array, she slipped from the bed and pushed her feet into a pair of black patent court shoes with alarmingly slanted heels. She waddled, lurching a little, to the chest of drawers, selecting a few articles of clothing from its top. When she had donned these over and under the petticoat she had worn to bed, she took down a tin of carnation talcum. Pulling out the neck of her frock, she shook some of the powder down over her chest and with one hand smoothed it across and under each armpit.

'Take what you want,' she told Trilby. 'Never can remember to use it meself. Woulda give it to the kids long ago except it comes in handy if ya run short a money.'

'How?' Trilby stopped in the act of screwing on a pair of bright red ear-rings.

'Playin cards, you can use anything,' Mrs Comeaway said matter-of-factly. 'Played for nails before this.' She unstuck the comb and wrenched it through her hair. 'Now,' she grunted contentedly, smoothing the dress against her hips, 'we better get you girls somethin ta eat. Where you say that Noonah was? My word, you look real nice, Trilby. Come on outside so I can see ya proper.' She took the girl by the arm and then clapped her hand to her head.

'The old man,' she murmured. 'Did e or did e not say e was gunna go down the wharf this morning? Hey, you!' She walked purposefully over to the bed, and in one business-like gesture swiped two blankets and an old overcoat from her husband's peaceful form. Trilby stepped back giggling as her father's night atire was revealed in all its scantiness.

'Come on, you!' Mrs Comeaway said firmly.

Mr Comeaway kept his eyes tight shut. 'Not *this* morning, he said thickly, his hand groping for and finding the covers. 'What about them girls? Gotta show em the place, ain't we?'

'Didn't you say today?'

'Tomorrow just as good.'

Mrs Comeaway raised her shoulders high and let them fall again. 'E never did like work,' she told her daughter philosophically, leading the way out to the other room. 'Now then!' She swayed over to the black stove in the corner and opened the oven door. 'Not a bloody crust,' she said disgustedly. 'I tell ya what, Trilby. You just nip over an tell Mrs Green we got damn all ta eat an will she let ya have something till we go down town. Ask er fa what ya want yaself, weeties or something. She'll have it. Has to with all them kids. An say does she want anything down town.'

Trilby was horrified. 'Gee, Mummy, I don't like to.'

Mrs Comeaway straightened. 'Why doncha? She's a nice ole woman, Mrs Green. Wouldn't hurt a flea.'

'You come too.'

'Yeah well, I suppose I could,' Mrs Comeaway said, as if she had been presented with some novel idea. 'Come along then.' She lumbered ahead, her tremendous bottom hoisting her over the ground with a sailor-like roll. She began hoo-hooing immediately, keeping it up with a sort of absent-minded persistence until they were inside the house. 'Hoo-hoo,' she called through another doorway. 'Anyone around in here? You home, Mrs Green? I'm outa tucker.'

Trilby followed her across the earth-floored porch, and stood behind her sniffing a warm, wonderful smell of food cooking. The inner room was gloomy, but a good big fire burned in the shining black stove and on top of it sizzled a huge frying-pan-full of eggs and sliced tomatoes. This much Trilby saw before she closed her eyes and made a brief wish.

A woman holding a bunch of cutlery in her hand looked over and smiled. 'This is the other one, eh?' She had a rich full voice with velvety overtones. Trilby smiled back at her, hopefully.

She saw Noonah, sitting at one end of a big table with a child on her lap. The other children were either already seated or busy dragging chairs out for themselves. The place looked like a home, and the centre of it, Trilby knew, was this elderly woman with the sparse grey hair whose voice sounded so much younger than she could be. Mrs Comeaway was talking to her and, under cover of the conversation, Trilby studied Mrs Green curiously, a little hesitantly, before she switched her gaze to the room and its occupants.

Against one wall was a horsehair sofa upholstered in shiny black, split a little here and there, showing deep hollows where springs were missing or broken. At the end of the sofa sat an old, old man. He did not look up at the newcomers because he was busy steadying a steaming cup of tea. Trilby felt an urge to go over and steady it for him before he spilt it on his thin shanks. The woman, Mrs Green, followed her gaze. 'That's Skippy,' she said. 'Don't you worry about him. He's all right.'

'How old is he?' Trilby said respectfully. The old man's eyes peered from beneath folded lids. His hands on his cup looked like dark brown claws, and his face was wrinkled and shrunken. He looked across at her as she spoke, growling in his throat, his eyes two wicked pin-points of light.

'I – I just thought you must be pretty old,' Trilby repeated.

'Mumblin away,' the old man grunted pettishly. 'An damn kids everywhere shoutin their heads off.'

'Drink up that tea,' Mrs Green said pleasantly, 'or you'll be grizzling because it's cold.'

'Too damn hot,' Skippy grumbled. 'Nemind bout ole man, givim tea still bilin hot.'

Mrs Green smiled over at Trilby. 'You sit down with your mummy an have a cup too.'

'If ya got some ta spare well.' Mrs Comeaway lifted the nearest child from his chair and sat down with him in her lap. 'You take Martin on ya knee or get yaself another chair,' she told Trilby.

'Go on!' Mrs Green nodded. 'In the room at the back.'

So Trilby picked her way carefully past the old man and went doubtingly along the passage.

'Don't take any notice of Honay,' Mrs Green called after her.

As well as a suite of dining-room furniture in dark oak, the further room held a rickety-looking wooden bed and a woman occupant almost as old as Skippy. Trilby darted one look at the woman's face, grim even in sleep, and snatched up a chair, returning with it to the warm dark kitchen.

'Honay still the star boarder?' Mrs Comeaway inquired, with a twinkle. 'Her and Skippy,' Mrs Green smiled.

'How'd the ole devil get on yesterday?' Mrs Comeaway asked.

Trilby placed her chair next to Noonah's and sat down. Mrs Green pushed a cup of tea across to her and laughed. 'How d'you think?'

'I dunno how e does it,' Mrs Comeaway marvelled. 'Seems e's got them mon-arch just where e wants em.'

Mrs Green looked at the two girls. 'Skippy got picked up for receiving. They caught him with a bottle of conto,' she explained. 'He got off all right, but he's still mad about sleeping down the jail. Said he got cold.' She turned to Mrs Comeaway. 'Wouldn't mind betting he goes to see the sergeant about that.'

'What happened down the court?' Mrs Comeaway's eyes were crinkled with amused anticipation.

'Let me tell, Gramma.' A young girl came into the room holding a baby in her arms. Noonah's eyes went straight to the baby, but Trilby's mouth opened in surprise. Gramma Green's roof seemed elastic.

'You go on then, Lee,' Mrs Green said comfortably, 'an I'll just dish up this stuff.' She bent to take some plates from the oven where they had been heating.

The newcomer smoothed her long curling hair with one hand and smiled a greeting at Noonah and Trilby. 'Ya here, are ya? Ya mummy certainly made a fuss bout you two.' She went over to the sofa with her baby and lay back with it against her breast. 'The crowd of us went up to the court,' she said gaily, 'an we was lucky we didn't get put out. Ya not supposed to make any noise up there,' she told the sisters, 'but we was all gigglin. Couldn't *help* gigglin. First of all the magistrate says to Skippy, "Now I want the whole truth, Skippy, in ya own words." Skippy gives them cops a look, then e says e picked up this bottle off the street an before he's even opened it ta see what's inside, e gets picked up. So the boss looks down at is papers and then e says, "But that ain't the way ya told it to the police last night, Skippy." An Skippy says to im, "Ah, I tell them pleece anything. I wait till I see the boss before I tell how I got that bottle." So the magistrate scratches his head and ya can see he's trying not ta laugh, an then e says, "That's the truth then, is it?" And when Skippy says that's the truth, e dismissin the case. Skippy gets off. An ya know the first thing e says ta them monarch? E turns round on em an yelps, "An now ya can just gimme back that bottle."

Mrs Comeaway choked on her tea. 'Gawd! Wait till I tell me ole man,' she crowed. 'There's a man for ya, eh?' She looked admiringly over at the old man. At the end of the sofa, Skippy had been listening approvingly, nodding and shaking his head, his wicked black gaze flicking on and off like a snake's. He was half blinded with trachoma, his ears were so full of wax he only bothered to listen when it pleased him, he was older than anyone could remember, including the department, and both legs had been lamed early in life. But he was known and respected as a fighter for miles around. For his rights, that is. Nobody could stick up for Skippy the way he stuck up for himself.

'Nobody knows how he does it,' Mrs Green told the girls, with a shrug and a smile. 'He just does, that's all.'

'Them pleece put there in that horfice ta do things for us fellers,' Skippy said belligerently, 'an not go bossin us fellers round.'

'Skippy!' Mrs Green shook her head helplessly.

'They guvmint, ain't they?' he demanded.

Mrs Comeaway tittered. 'Lissen to im. Ya can't make im understand.'

'Look, now you're here, you'd better stay an have breakfast,' Mrs Green said, her glance taking in the three Comeaways.

'Okay!' Mrs Comeaway answered for them all. 'That suit yous girls?' Noonah and Trilby nodded.

Mrs Green began serving up the food already cooked. The tomatoes drowned in their own gravy and the eggs were edged with brown lace. Noonah and Trilby exchanged looks and felt their mouths moisten.

'Went up and seen that partment feller yesdy,' Skippy said in his cracked old voice.

'Eh! You think that partment man ain't got enough ta do thout ole rascal like you wastin is time?' Mrs Comeaway mock-scolded.

'E take care a me fum long way back,' Skippy said complacently. 'I got card up that office. All things bout me. Yesdy I showim new boots. You see im?' With difficulty he pulled up his trouser leg and shoved out his foot.

'More new trousers too,' Mrs Comeaway said, truly scandalized.

'An still none to fit him,' Mrs Green added wryly. 'We had to turn those cuffs up three times before he stopped tripping over them.'

'These good pants,' Skippy said indignantly.

'Yeah, good pants,' Mrs Green soothed. 'And you were probably lucky to get them with that young Mona and Lee here waiting about to give you a bit of soft soap.' She looked over at Lee, her mouth firming, but a twinkle at the back of her eyes. 'Pension day Skippy's that popular he doesn't know himself. Thinks he must be getting young again, eh, Skippy?'

'I didn't ask him for nothing.' Lee's eyes were innocent.

'Ah, young girls all the same,' Mrs Comeaway said tolerantly. 'Do the same meself if I thought I could get away with it. Pity YOU don't put the nippers in fer a few bob but,' she accused Mrs Green. 'Him sittin round here week after week fillin is belly up.'

'No good tucker down ere,' Skippy snarled before Mrs Green could answer. 'Gotta go out in the bush fa good tucker.'

'Seen a big fat goanna round here yesterday,' Mrs Comeaway laughed at him.

'You girls full of plans, I suppose,' Mrs Green asked Trilby and Noonah.

'Noonah's gunna be a nurse,' Mrs Comeaway answered for her. 'Trilby don't know yet what she gunna do.'

'What sort of jobs can a girl get down here?' Trilby asked casually.

'Jobs?' Mrs Comeaway considered. 'Lee had a job minding someone's kids a while back.'

'No kids,' Trilby said promptly, 'or housework.'

On the sofa, Lee sat up straight, her face full of interest. Over the table, the older women's eyes met in a quiet look.

'You wouldn't like to be a nurse like Noonah?' Mrs Green suggested.

'Nup! What about those milk-bars. Don't they have girls there?'

'I wouldn't set me heart on anything like that,' Mrs Comeaway said uneasily.

Trilby's hands were quiet in her lap. 'You mean they wouldn't have me?'

Lee laughed scornfully, 'Ya don't think they want *our* hands poisonin their drinks.'

Trilby looked at her, her young face hard, and there was a little silence. Mrs Green entered into the breach, her eyes on the frying-pan she was scraping. 'What are you, Trilby? Fifteen? Sixteen?'

'Fifteen, an her sister two years older. Ain't that right?' Mrs Comeaway appealed to Noonah. Noonah nodded, serious-eyed.

'It's smart, these times, to get some education,' Mrs Green said pleasantly. 'What about going back to High School for a while, till you think things over?'

'Yeah, you could do that easy,' Mrs Comeaway said eagerly.

The girl's face stayed as quiet as her hands.

'Don't let Gramma talk you inta goin back to school,' Lee scorned. 'She tried ta talk *me* inta that.'

'I reckon Gramma's right,' Mrs Comeaway defended. 'Wisht I

hadda got more schoolin. Can't get the sense a them comics sometimes.'

'You girls like some more to eat?' Mrs Green asked.

'No thank you!' Noonah refused. Trilby had not heard.

Mrs Comeaway eased the little boy to the floor and slapped the back of his pants. 'Spose we better get goin,' she sighed. 'Make a cuppa tea fa me ole man.' She rose cumbersomely. 'An if ya want somethin down town, you send one a the kids over before we go.'

The girls picked their way through the kitchen and waited at the door. Mrs Green measured sugar and tea into a glass jar and handed it to Mrs Comeaway. 'That'll see you through this morning,' she murmured, 'and I'll just butter a bit of bread while I'm at it.' She buttered two thickslices and wrapped them in newspaper.

'Ta!' Mrs Comeaway said casually. 'See ya later. You girls say thank you fa ya breakfast?' she enquired. 'Then we be off.'

Noonah smiled her good-byes. Trilby's mouth smiled, but her eyes were still thoughtfully cool. They walked one each side of their mother away from Mrs Green's home.

'An now ya fed,' Mrs Comeaway said comfortably, as if some mammoth task had been satisfactorily completed.

The thoughtful look disappeared from Trilby's eyes. 'Gee, isn't it *lovely* to be away from that mission?' she asked Noonah.

'Isn't Mrs Green nice, Mummy?' Noonah said, affectionately slipping a hand through her mother's arm. 'She speaks sort of nice too, doesn't she? Different from' – she hesitated – 'us.'

'Been most of her life up on one a them big stations,' Mrs Comeaway said. 'Yeah, I always like ta hear her talkin. No rough stuff about er.'

'Yes, I like *her*,' Trilby added, a note of decision in her voice.

A lot of people liked Mrs Green. Coming of a people to whom hospitality came naturally, there was a gentle kindliness mixed with Mrs Green's that set it a little higher. There were never less than a dozen of her friends and relations under her roof; some of them part-paying guests, some of them just 'staying' with Gramma until some better job turned up than the one they had left. And there were the children of school age, who represented a cross-section of Gramma's children's broods, whose parents took it for granted that the old lady would see that they got their education. Under the shaky, boy-trodden roof there were three outside rooms, built on and added to by visitors who were used to providing their own shelter, and four main rooms, the biggest of which was the kitchen. The two top rooms were labelled sitting-room and dining-room, and occasionally, on some special occasion like someone's wedding, they were used as such. Mostly, the genoa velvet suite and the dining-room table were pushed aside to make room for beds. Not seldom, the bumpy old lounge served as an extra bed. Only two spots in the house were sacred to Mrs Green – her tiny bedroom that opened off the kitchen, and the oven-side of the kitchen table which she needed because nearly all her chores involved the use of both. There on the top of the stove her washing-water heated in a kerosene-tin, her irons grew hot, her big black kettle boiled, and her savoury stews and fries sent mouth-watering smells throughout the kitchen.

There was one hard and fast rule. No young males over the age of sixteen. They didn't mean to, but they always made trouble, specially with the teenage girls. The high-spirited youths went down to the big camp in the wattle-studded valley, the reserve set aside for coloured people, where there was plenty of space for them to fight and rough-house each other without endangering their surroundings.

Mrs Green was old-fashioned about swearing. She had accustomed herself to the men's easy oaths, but she was quick to correct the children and the young girls, so the children and the girls hardly ever swore when Gramma was round to hear. Mrs Green thought fighting and swearing gave you a bad name with the neighbours. Her own neighbours were a couple of hundred yards away on each side, but the old lady kept on the politest of terms with them. It was never the neighbours who complained about the kids playing on the road in front of the house. It was the townsfolk and the visitors who did that. They never failed to yell angrily from the car window when they had swerved to miss a child, though Mrs Green could have told them there was not much to worry about. The children were quick as race-horse goannas, and mostly they ran the gauntlet of the road just to see what the driver of the car would do and say.

Mrs Green had acquired citizenship years before – before, in fact, she and her late husband had known or cared about such things. The owner of the station where she had spent most of her life had attended to the details for them. Mr Scott had talked of citizenship rights as something rather valuable, but it was not until Mr Green had died and Mrs Green had moved to the house on the hill, nearer to town, that she had appreciated to the full the distinction and convenience of possessing them. She rarely abused her privilege of buying grog, and when she did it was to benefit her friends and not her pocket. Mrs Green did not trust easy money, and she knew of more than one citizenship-rights holder who had spent a month or two in jail because his pals had split on him.

Mrs Green's own children had married well. One of her sons assisted with the management of a small station. Another owned a farm. Mrs Green went visiting whenever she felt like it, and her children and their families were always overjoyed to have her. They even arranged for transport, paying her fare on the train if they could not pick up a lift for her.

Mrs Green had a plan for living and she stuck to it. First you went to school and stayed there until some of the teachers' learning came off on you. And you didn't wag it from school because you'd rather go swimming or fishing or tramping over the sand-hills that bordered the beach. Mrs Green had a special deterrent for the wagsters under her control. She treated them as if she felt sorry for them for not understanding better. Somehow, it worked. Mrs Green was philosophical when it didn't. She had quite a few successes to look back on. Little Nancy was a fully trained typist now, working in the department's office down in Perth. Joe was apprenticed to a signwriter, and his two brothers had gone into the army. The others were good boys and girls, even if they did come back every so often from their jobs on stations, as musterers and shearers' assistants and childrens' nurses, filled with complaints about their bosses and their bosses' wives and the dullness of life lived miles from anywhere. And wanting, as Mrs Green very well knew, just a bit of a holiday with the other youngsters before they took another job on some other station, mustering someone else's sheep and minding someone else's children.

More than a few romances had blossomed from Mrs Green's house. There were always a few young bloods down at the camp. Some romances ended well. Some didn't. You couldn't blame a boy who came down from a station ready for a bit of fun, and the girl more than willing, even if it meant having the girl on your hands for months before the baby was born. Besides, after the baby had arrived, the young started to take things, and each other, a lot more seriously. And if they didn't, well, a baby was as good a way as any to teach a girl that she had to carry it in other ways than in her arms.

Mrs Green loved babies, anyhow.

'She didn't act a bit as if we were nuisances,' Trilby said slowly.

'Why should she?' Mrs Comeaway asked mildly. 'She's me neighbour, ain't she?'

CHAPTER 4

The girls sat with their backs against trees and watched the smoke-blackened kettle resting against a burning log. The stove inside the humpy functioned only as an extra hold-all. 'Smoke everywhere,' Mrs Comeaway had explained cheerfully. 'And outside just as good. Maybe the ole feller fix im up one day.'

Trilby agreed with her mother. It was fun to cook outside and there wasn't much wrong with sitting here looking down over the valley while you drank your second lot of tea for the morning.

'That big camp down there,' Mrs Comeaway pointed, following Trilby's gaze, 'that's the government place. Anyone come ta town an don't have some place to stop at, they go there. Can do washin if ya like. Them little places down there, they take their washin up the big camp. Have a shower – anything they like.'

Mr Comeaway came through the doorway yawning and yanking at his pants. He smiled amiably at the girls and sat down between them. Mrs Comeaway took him an enamel mug of tea, steaming hot and strong. 'This packet's fa you. Mrs Green give it to me for ya.'

Mr Comeaway took his bread and butter. 'You girls like this place?'

'It's so pretty here,' Noonah said warmly. 'Mummy!'

'Watcha want?'

'I told Bartie I was going to ask you could he and Stella come back,' Noonah said diffidently. 'They want to. They don't like being left behind.'

'The young'un, eh?' Mr Comeaway said, with pleased interest. 'How's e goin, up there?'

'Nnnh!' Mrs Comeaway cocked an eye at her husband, frowning. 'I dunno bout that, Noonah. That mission a good place fa kids. All right ta come back when they been there a while an got some education. When they bigger.'

'Not Bartie,' Noonah said. 'Bartie's different from the others and they laugh at him. He draws, Mummy. You should see the things he draws. And he says funny things all the time, not like other kids his age. He NEEDS to come back.'

Mrs Comeaway's lower lip was pendulous, her smoth brow puckered. She kept her gaze on Mr Comeaway's face as if it acted in lieu of a hand over his mouth.

'It's like this here,' she said at last. 'You kids don't understand proper. I made up me mind ta send my kids to a mission a long while back. Up there, theys all the same, nothing ta choose between em. Nobody don't call em names just because they coloured. An even if they don't like it for a little while ... '

'I hated it,' Trilby burst forth. 'All the time I was there I hated it.'

Mrs Comeaway's face was wounded. 'Ya never said well.'

'You didn't come up much,' Trilby said indifferently.

'We knew yous was all right but,' Mrs Comeaway said a little anxiously.

'The little bloke – he don't like it up there,' Mr Comeaway brooded.

'Now don't you start on about it,' Mrs Comeaway said angrily. 'There wouldn't be no place for em ta come, not like they got up there. I *seen* them little houses,' she half accused Trilby. 'Little beds with covers over em. A place ta go to school. Plenty a fruit an tucker. They just gotta stay there like yous two, and come down when they bigger. That's all about it.'

'If we got a place to live like Mrs Green's got?' Noonah questioned, her eyes wide and brown and sad.

'None ta get,' Mrs Comeaway said briefly. A deriding expression on her face changed to pity when she saw tears fill Noonah's eyes.

'Stop worrying about Bartie and spoiling everything,' Trilby said, her voice irritable. 'It won't kill the kids to stay up at the mission, will it?'

Mrs Comeaway bent to the kettle again. Her voice was more cheerful. 'Nah! Not gunna kill them littlies. Kids – they soon get over things.' She straightened, and with the steaming kettle in her hand, looked over at Noonah. 'I got ambitions for my childrens, just like Mrs Green.' She stumbled over her explanation. 'I put my kids up there in that place cause I think that a good place for coloured kids to be all together, see?'

'I promised!' Noonah was humble in defence. 'And it wouldn't matter, Mummy, except he seems different from the others. I *know* he won't be happy now.'

'I know those things ya mean,' Mr Comeaway said unexpectedly. 'That Bartie. He a funny kid all right. All those questions he asks a

feller. Does leaves like blowin around in the wind? About how
heavy's a cloud? An drags a man out of a good sleep to show im a
bit a water with some oil on top of it. Pretty, too, them colours in it.
Yeah, I know! Always comin out with something that sort of
catches ya up because ya ain't expectin it. I tell ya something else. I
miss that damn kid.'

'Don't you get worryin, Noonah. E gunna be all right.' Mrs
Comeaway's back was to her daughter. There was a sombre note in
her voice.

Noonah looked at her mother, at the uneven hem of her frock, at
the run-over black patent shoes, at the strong arm lifting the heavy
kettle from the fire.

'It's all right, Mum,' she said, as if it were her mother who must
be comforted. 'It's all right.'

'Where do you wash the cups?' Trilby said practically when Mr
Comeaway had had his fill of tea and bread and butter.

'Just take em over to the tap an give em a rinse,' Mrs Comeaway
told her. 'Sure ya had enough?'

'Oh yes, haven't we, Trilby?'

'I want to hurry and go down and see things,' Trilby said gaily.
'I can hardly wait.'

Mrs Comeaway laughed indulgently. 'Course we'll hurry.'

She watched the girls as they went off with the cups. 'What ya
think of em, eh?' she asked her husband.

Coupla nice kids,' Mr Comeaway approved. 'Smart, too.'

'Didn't do them too much harm,' Mrs Comeaway half-questioned.
'Gee, when that Noonah starts talkin about young Bartie. As if I
don't know. Terrible hard job it was ta leave im, that time I took
the two littlies up. Had me cryin too.'

'The ole lady seems ta manage all right.' Mr Comeaway nodded
in the direction of Mrs Green's house.

Mrs Comeaway looked stubborn. 'She got her ideas. I got mine.'

She set to work damping down the fire wth the tea-leaves. In a
little while her habitual expression of cheerful good will returned to
her face. She hummed a bar or two of a song as she waited for the
girls to come back.

Trilby was dancing with impatience.

'All right!' Mrs Comeaway humoured her. 'I gotta change me
frock first. Get meself dolled up to match yous two.'

She walked through to the inner room and went over to one of
the hanging wardrobes. From the drapes she picked out a blue silk
frock she had once picked up at a jumble-sale. Mrs Comeaway
went to all the jumble-sales, though she rarely kept what she

bought. She looked on sales as a quick and easy way to boost her income. The dresses and overcoats and other odd items she bought always brought four times what they had cost – friends and acquaintances down for a holiday snapped them up quickly, if Mrs Comeaway got in early before their holiday pay had been gambled away or borrowed. This particular blue silk, though, she had marked out as her own. It was a bit tight, but good looking and almost new except for the split under the arm. She smoothed the dress down over the pendulous bosom that rested on her high, proud stomach. She kicked off her run-over shoes and felt round under the bed for the suitcase that contained all the things she couldn't hang from nails. Another pair of shoes appeared from the case and she sat heavily on the bed to pull them on. And that was a hard enough job. She winced as she stood upright and tried to wiggle her toes, but the toes were caught, squashed, imprisoned against the hard toe-caps.

Giving up, she teetered across to the chest of drawers. The drawers of this piece of furniture were never used. The slats for the drawers were broken and they were almost impossible to open. There was another swift flurry of Carnation talcum powder down the neck of her frock. And a careful application of oil to her hair.

'Someone bring me that flannel hanging out there,' she called.

Noonah, who had been taking a quick wash, came hurrying in with the blue-striped washer.

'Gettin flash,' Mrs Comeaway admired. She scrubbed the wet washer over her face and ears and handed it daintily back. Then she took up a vast black purse and scrabbled through its contents. Face intent and serious, she hid the dusty purple of her wide mouth behind a swathe of pale pink. With her index finger she smoothed the gummy mess into her lips.

'Now!' she said, with satisfaction. 'All yous ready out there?'

Noonah had changed her dress for a clean one. The two girls stood before their mother, young, slim, bright-eyed with excitement. Mr Comeaway's white shirt was on him again, wrist-bands buttoned. His hair had been wetted and sleeked down. Mrs Comeaway looked them over with approval.

'Come on!' Mr Comeaway pleaded from the doorway. 'Anyone'd think we was gunna see the Queen.'

The girls laughed.

They started off down the slope to the road, waving to Mrs Green, who sat with a child on her lap on the veranda of her house.

'Not too fast now,' Mrs Comeaway warned. 'I gotta remember

my feet. These damn heels likely to send me over if I don't take
things quiet.'

The other three slowed their pace down the dark blue road. Mrs
Comeaway walked with bent head, her mouth pursed with dis-
comfort, her eyes searching the road ahead for the smoothest path.
From one hand dangled the overstuffed black purse.

Down the road a bit a sandy track curled off into the bush. Mrs
Comeaway stopped her stomping. 'I wonder,' she said, 'if we better
not stop an see Hannie and Charlie a while. They lations, an I tell
them bout these two comin down. They got two girls round your
age,' she told the sisters. 'Nice girls, they are.'

Everyone changed direction. Mrs Comeaway stopped again as
soon as she stepped off the hard road and into the softer track. 'An
now I'll just take these damn shoes off a while,' she said with
satisfaction. 'Gawd! That's good. Felt like I had me feet in a coupla
traps.'

The girls followed the sandy track, their shoes sinking ankle-deep
with each step. Pleasing itself where it went, the path turned and
twisted like the bed of a creek. The bush crowded close. Branches of
green wattle and wild hibiscus brushed the girls' clothes and stung
their faces and legs. Cream blossoms covered the wild hibiscus, the
smell of them wildly sweet. The ground beneath them was sown
with patches of colour, amethyst, blazing yellow, deep bright pink –
each star-like flower upturned to the sun. A delirious chirping filled
the air.

Mrs Comeaway walked with a sprightly step, freed from her
shoes. Mr Comeaway rolled himself a cigarette and smoked contentedly. Noonah, her mind on Bartie, stepped off the path to
exclaim at the vivid blue of a trailing creeper. 'An what ya think a
this?' Mr Comeaway grinned, pulling free a spray of white flowers
with delicate green stamens. Noonah smiled happily. Today she
would buy paper and pencils and a big black box of water-colour
paints. There was tenderness in her smile. And a doll for Stella,
with eyes that closed and opened.

Trilby looked ruefully down at her shoes. Their bright polish was
lost under a layer of dust. The black sand had seeped inside them,
making her feet feel hot and tight. She looked ahead at her mother
and envied her.

Around the next bend they heard voices. The girls sighed thankfully. Ahead of them they saw a camp like their own, though here
there were only two side-walls – both ends being open to the air.
Sheltering beneath was a double bed with long thin legs of iron. A
second shelter projected from the first, its roof a tattered travelling-

rug. A length of wire tied between two wattles supported a line of still-dripping washing, the barbs acting as pegs. At the back of the camp, a sight which drew both girls' eyes, a man's bicycle hung in lonely state from the branches of a tree.

The chattering of the group had died away. Four people, an older man and a woman, and two girls, sat in watchful silence waiting the approach of the Comeaways. The older man and woman relaxed first. They grinned a welcome.

Noonah saw a fat baby kicking and gurgling in the middle of the sagging bed. With an exclamation of pleasure, she went to it, but Trilby remained, shy and strange, a little behind her parents.

'This is them,' Mr Comeaway beamed. 'Come last night. What ya think of em, eh? You, Noonah over there, an Trilby! This your Auntie Hannie an Uncle Charlie; an these over here is Blanchie an Audrena. You say hello now and make good friends. That's Blanchie's baby, Noonah. Good big one, eh? How old now, Blanchie?'

Blanchie rose, grinning with embarrassment. She sidled closer to Noonah. Blanchie's hair hung lankly to her shoulders. The dress she wore was old and shapeless, hanging almost to her ankles. She and her cousin showed square white teeth in shy smiles.

Uncle Charlie's gaze flicked back and forth between his own girls and his brother's children. 'They smart all right,' he admired.

Mrs Comeaway turned her prideful look on Auntie Hannie. 'Noonah's gunna be a nurse down that hospital, if ya don't mind. Nurse young Tommy next time e goes in, eh?'

'Thought you was goin down the wharf this morning,' Uncle Charlie addressed Mr Comeaway. 'I was goin down too. Didn't turn out that way but. Got a bit tired last night when all them peoples was here.'

'Feller needs a holiday,' Mr Comeaway allowed. 'Sides, we gotta show the girls round a bit today.'

'Take my tip an don't go fa that road work,' Uncle Charlie said seriously. 'Did that a coupla days last week. Gettin a bit old fa that stuff. Better on the wharf. Easier on ya back.'

'Gotta work hard sometimes,' Mr Comeaway said judicially. 'Keep ya wits about ya too. Knew a bloke got loaded inta one a them ship's holds right along with the wheat one time. That manganese ain't a picnic either.'

Trilby and Audrena took each other's measure. Unsmilingly.

'You live here too?' Trilby asked curiously, turning to look at the shoddy camp.

'We got a mattress under that ole blanket,' Audrena said. 'Young Tommy sleeps in with Mum and Dad if it's cold. This is only

tempry but. Dad's savin up the deposit fa one a them houses down
the Wild-Oat Patch. Then me an Blanchie's gunna have new beds.
No use wastin good stuff in this dump. Might get wet.'

Trilby was impressed. 'You mean you're going to have a new
house?'

'Course it takes a while ta save up that deposit,' Audrena said
wisely. She grinned. 'Specially when the old man gets on the plonk
an keeps rattin what we got. Make ya laugh. It's im wants the
house. Mummy don't care all that much.'

'Don't you want it yourself?' Trilby kept her eyes politely away
from the present dwelling.

'Be beaut!' Audrena said simply. 'Sometimes the rain gets on
Blanchie an me.' She gloomed at the thin-legged bed. 'Four's really
too many fa one bed. All legs, it seems like.'

Trilby turned over the remark wonderingly. Her thoughts returned more gratefully to the two new beds that had been bought
for her and Noonah.

'Let's sit down,' she said, collapsing on some grass. 'And you tell
me what it's like in this town. Do you do any work?'

'Used to,' Audrena said laconically. 'Had a job once up at a
station, lookin after a coupla kids. It was beaut ta start off with.
Had a room to meself and everything. Got sick of it but. Nothing ta
do at night. I wasn't supposed to have nothin ta do with the station
mob, y'see. The missus said they wasn't good company for me. So I
used ta sneak out down the camp when she thought I was asleep.
Then one night I get caught an that was the end a that. I spose she
thought I was gunna stay up there fa the rest a me life never havin
any fun.' She sat in silence for a while, brooding. Then her face
brightened. 'Gee, there was a beaut chap up there. I had fun with
him all right.' She giggled and looked away from Trilby's candidly
curious grey eyes.

'Don't you have fun down here?'

'Not if the ole man can help it.'

'No one's going to start ordering me about,' Trilby stated definitely. 'Come on, Audrena. Tell me some of the things you do.'

Audrena was flattered. The girls' heads moved closer.

Noonah sat with the baby on her lap. He was rounded, cuddle-
some, good-tempered – the sort of baby to draw your heart out of
your body with love for him. His skin was cocoa-coloured, satin-
soft. Noonah felt her hands too large and clumsy to handle him but,
quite obviously, he liked to be cuddled. She gathered him up and
pressed her cheek into the silk of his black curls.

'You really gunna work at that nursing?' Blanchie asked. 'That's pretty hard work I know, because I done it. Not proper nursing like. In the hospital but. An I hadda wear a cap. The things they make ya do.' She shuddered. 'Real dirty stuff like emptyin pots and helpin ta wash people. Wait till ya strike them old men up there. Little bottles, they got. An some a the nurses is that crabby. I left after a while. Didn't like it.'

'I won't mind,' Noonah said with all the assurance of no experience.

'An it gets on ya pip, all this washin and boilin things. Ya gotta be that damn particular. Every day – stuff that useta look all right ta me – all gotta be cleaned up again. An floors polished that nobody's hardly stepped on.'

'That's because of germs,' Noonah said earnestly. 'Mrs Gordon up at the mission, she got me some little books, and it's all in them, the things I have to learn.'

'Ya gotta have ya Junior. Ya know that?'

'I've got that,' Noonah told her cousin.

'I went ta the High School down here meself,' Blanchie offered. 'Got sick of it though. Couldn't be bothered goin on years more.'

Noonah opened her mouth and firmly shut it again. And anyhow, what did education matter to someone who was married already?

'Aren't you afraid Tommy will roll off the bed,' she questioned.

'Did a coupla times,' Blanchie said. 'Course, it's soft ground here. Doesn't hurt im – just gives im a fright like.'

The older women got up and went over to the line of clothes. Mrs Comeaway straightened a dress that was hanging by one barb. 'Ya wanta take care a that dress,' she told her sister-in-law. 'I coulda got ten bob fa that if I hadn't just thought a you.'

They came over to where Noonah nursed the baby. 'Ya like kids, Noonah, eh?'

Noonah nodded. Auntie Hannie's face mooned round and fat from her stringy dark hair. There were many gaps where there should have been teeth in her nervously smiling mouth, but her dark eyes were shy as well as kindly. Noonah smiled reassuringly up at her.

'I'm used to kids. I helped round the nursery up at the mission.'

'That mission – a good place?'

'Yes, not bad.'

'You look all right. Smarter than Blanchie an Audrena.' There was no envy in her voice.

'Can't we go down town now?' Trilby asked plaintively, behind her mother, and Mrs Comeaway turned to chuckle. 'Okay, we better get goin,' she told her assembled relations. 'Less she goes an leaves us behind.'

'I just can't wait to see everything.' Trilby begged forgiveness.

'We don't get no peace till this girl's been down the town, I can see that,' Mr Comeaway said.

There was a chorus of good-byes as the Comeaways made their way back down the path. 'Don't forget about the beach,' Audrena screeched. 'Might see ya down the wharf tomorrow,' Uncle Charlie called after his brother.

'Monday fa sure,' Mr Comeaway called back.

'I see now you might make a real good nurse,' Mrs Comeaway said approvingly to Noonah. 'Had that baby eatin outa ya hand in no time. Just the same, ya better get a bit a fun in as well. That Blanchie, she thinkin a gettin married soon. Gunna get married in a church. Maybe we have some sorta party after.'

'Blanchie is the one with the baby?' Noonah asked.

'She didn't count on havin im,' Mrs Comeaway commented philosophically, 'but she's got im just the same.'

'What a fool she must be,' Trilby said.

'She ain't a fool,' Mrs Comeaway said with mild surprise. 'She's a real nice girl, that. Bit slow, but nice. Her an that young feller that comes down, you know the one, Tim. Hannie tells me they thinkin a gettin married.'

'Is it his baby?' Noonah pursued. She was trying to set these facts inside the framwork of the mission-teaching.

'Gawd no, that's not is,' Mrs Comeaway replied. 'That baby's a quadroon. Didn't you see the colour of it? Father's a white man. Blanche hadda go down ta the partment bout that baby. Fix up about is maintenance. They made er sign papers an Gawd knows what all. After a while, they find out she's said the wrong name. Course it wasn't er fault. All she knows is the man's name is Popping an it happens there's two Poppings up in this place. They arst er which one, Neil or Billy, and she says what with them up in the office there starin at er she got real nervous an said Neil thout thinkin it might be the wrong one. An then this Neil sends a picture down the partment ta prove it ain't im and Blanchie looks at it an she's never seen im before in er life. She thinks now it musta been Billy, so she tells em that an everything's held up while they get on ta the bloke that really done it. She was lookin forward ta that money too, poor kid.'

The girls exchanged a quick look which was the undoing of both.

'I said something funny?' queried their mother, quite startled. Then she began to laugh herself. 'Eh, Joe!' she called. 'You ever think a that bloke's face up there when the pleece got on to im bout Blanchie's baby?' She slapped her chest and her laughter ended in a fit of coughing.

After a while they went on again, the four of them welded together by amusement, anticipation and newly-found affection for each other.

'What if it isn't the other one either?' Trilby giggled.

'Gawd, don't say that,' her mother said, sobered. 'If it ain't one it's gotta be the other, isn't it?'

'Can't think how that lot get emselves in so many damn mix-ups,' Mr Comeaway mused. 'Take Charlie now. Just thumbin imself a ride landed Charlie in jail a while back.'

'Tell us, Dad,' Trilby begged, still alight with laughter.

'E's comin back ta town see?' Mrs Comeaway took over after a pause. 'An e's tired, so e waits on the side a the road for a car ta come along. When one does e yells out for a lift. So the ute stops an ole Charlie climbs in the back an, believe it or not, a pleeceman gets outa the drivin seat an walks round to where Charlie's makin imself comfortable an the first thing e wants ta know is what's in the bag. An ya know what's in that bag?'

The girls waited, deliciously apprehensive.

'Three chooks, that's what e's got.'

'And where did he get them from?'

'Pinched em, a course,' Mrs Comeaway said promptly. 'I don't mean e went in someone's place. E told us after, they was jus walkin down the road, these chooks, so e wrung their necks for em, looked round fa something ta put em in, an was gunna bring em home to me an Hannie.'

'Only Charlie,' Mr Comeaway shook his head, 'would pick out a pleece ute. Got a gift fa doin the wrong thing, ole Charlie.'

'An I was gunna get one,' Mrs Comeaway said regretfully. 'The ole fool.'

CHAPTER 5

From the house, the greater part of the township had been hidden behind circling hills. Now, at the top of a steep rise, the girls saw it spread out beneath them, and stopped short in surprise and pleasure. The houses, and the street that bisected them, the tallness of pointed pines, the grand columns of a rose-coloured building standing proud on a rise, the cathedral, golden in sunlight, a red and white striped lighthouse guarding the distance, every detail stood out delicate and pure in the crystal-clear air. Away on the outskirts, white combers broke on a curving coastline. Two ships, like visiting majesty, rode at anchor inside a piled-stone breakwater. To the two girls, used to one wide main street and a scatter of grimy houses, the town looked breathtakingly big.

'Well, there she is,' Mr Comeaway said modestly, vastly pleased at their reaction.

'Bit bigger'n what you been used to,' Mrs Comeaway commented, coming to a panting standstill behind them. 'So's this hill we gotta climb down. Look at it, will ya? Should cut the top off it before they started buildin all over it. All right fa them that's got cars an them that takes taxis. Gawd, I'm beginnin ta wish I hadn't wore these shoes.'

The two elder Comeaways went cautiously on down the hill that curved into the township, leaving their daughters still ecstatic at the top.

'Wonder if there's pictures,' Trilby breathed.

'Which way did we come last night?' Noonah wondered. 'Where's the hospital from here?'

'You and your old hospital,' Trilby laughed, skipping off down the hill like a young foal.

They reached the main street through another road that meandered past shops and business premises and shabby little old-fashioned houses built close to the footpath. Now that they were in the centre of the town, the girls edged closer to their mother. Mr Comeaway had sloughed himself at the very first corner, claiming important private business. Mrs Comeaway, now that the hill had been safely negotiated, was smugly conscious of her good blue silk frock and her two fresh pretty daughters. The slowness of her pace was calculated to allow everyone a good long look at them. In return, her friends and acquaintances received gracious nods, bestowed with the dignity of a queen.

'My bathers, Mum,' Trilby whispered. 'Can I have some to go swimming with Audrena?'

'Don't tell me!' Mrs Comeaway's promenade stopped short. 'If I didn't clean forget about money.' Her face cleared suddenly. 'That's where e went. Ta get some. You'll have ya bathers,' she promised her daughter. 'We'll pick up with ya dad again and get some money for em before e spends it all. 'Where's he getting it from?' Noonah asked.

'Round about,' Mrs Comeaway said largely. 'Someone'll be owin im some. Or e'll borrow some. E knows I gotta pick up some tucker, anyhow. Can't do that thout money.'

'Can we go inside one of these shops and have a look round?' Trilby begged.

'I dunno!' Mrs Comeaway was uneasy.

'We can look, can't we?'

Trilby moved determinedly off through the doorway of a dress shop. Noonah and Mrs Comeaway followed.

'Can't move a step in these places,' Mrs Comeaway whispered stealthily, 'thout one a them tarts comin up. Give anyone the willies.'

Delightedly, the girls whirled through the dresses on a circular steel display stand. Mrs Comeaway, her back to her charges, a worried frown on her face, stood guard. But at the approach of a slim smiling salesgirl, her courage evaporated. 'Come on,' she ordered, 'we gettin outa here.'

Trilby's face was discontented. 'We'll go inta Coles,' Mrs Comeaway placated her. 'That's a real nice shop an nobody don't bother ya.'

'I don't see why ...,' Trilby began rebelliously, but Noonah intervened. 'Come on, Trilby, we can go back to that other place tomorrow.'

At the entrance to the chain store a toddler, escaped from his pushchair, stumbled across their path. Instantly, Noonah had him on the crook of her arm. She was about to return him to his small jail when he was snatched from her arms. 'That's my baby,' a young woman said frowningly. 'I'll take care of him, thanks.'

The smile faded from Noonah's face. More than her arms felt empty.

'What did she think ... ?' she began helplessly, but Trilby cut her short. 'You're a nigger. Remember?' For the space of a second, the sisters' eyes met. Noonah forgot her own hurt in a flooding of sympathy for Trilby, who in some way had suffered a deeper wound. But she controlled a desire to express her sympathy. Trilby did not care for stuff like that.

Mrs Comeaway's expression spoke volumes but she too kept her mouth closed.

The chain store was fascinating. The glittering jewellery counter held both girls in thrall. Even the bored-looking girl behind the counter was moved by Trilby's unashamed wonder.

'I'm going to have lots of these,' Trilby said excitedly. 'Look, Mummy, ear-rings and necklaces to match.'

'Yeah! Yeah!' Mrs Comeaway exchanged a shy smile with the counter girl. 'She's not used ta stuff like this.'

'Well,' the girl was moved to be gracious. 'I wear it myself sometimes.'

'Do you have paints? And little sleeping dolls?' Noonah inquired.

'Two counters up,' the girl replied, and the Comeaway party moved reluctantly away from the bright display.

'That should keep em happy a while,' Mrs Comeaway said comfortably when Noonah had completed her purchases. 'That was a real good idea, Noonah. An lucky ya had some money ta pay for em.'

'Mrs Gordon gave me a pound for helping her,' Noonah said. Most of the pound had vanished. Mrs Comeaway, and Trilby too, had chosen gifts to add to Noonah's original selection. The whole transaction had been completely satisfying to them all.

'I could stay here all day long,' Trilby sighed, when they at last made their way out. 'Those bathers with the red spots, Mummy. Are you sure Dad will let me have them?'

'Course e will,' Mrs Comeaway reassured her. 'E's going ta work tomorrow. An this time I'll make sure e goes.'

Tribly's brow was unclouded again, her grey eyes shining with happiness. She stopped before a milk-bar, resplendently pink and white, a counter replacing the usual glass front. 'Oh, a milk-bar. Mummy, can we ... ?'

'Better not,' Mrs Comeaway said quickly, out of her depth again. 'Besides,' she remembered gratefully, 'we ain't seen the ole man yet, ta get some money off a him.'

'It'll be all right,' Noonah said, as dazzled as Trilby. 'I've got some money left.'

Mrs Comeaway stood her ground. 'Not fa me,' she declared firmly.

Trilby's eyes flared again, a danger signal Mrs Comeaway was beginning to know. Shoulders back, chin high, the girl marched into the shop. Noonah looked doubtfully at her mother, then followed. They waited behind a group of people who stood at the inside counter. Gradually, the group melted away until only the two girls were left waiting. The attendant looked them over, coolly casually. 'Shop at the top of the street serves you people,' he said. 'Go on! Beat it!' Whilst he spoke his eyes kept darting to his customers.

'Come on,' Noonah whispered, her face hot.

With the handle of a silver teaspoon the attendant began a quick tattooing on the marble-topped counter.

'Two vanillas, please,' Trilby ordered in a high clear voice. She kept her blazing eyes full on the man's watchful face.

Several customers looked over curiously.

'Look ... I ... all right!' the boy capitulated suddenly. He began spooning ingredients into two silver containers. 'Just drink em at the counter, will ya?' He shoved the tall containers beneath two electric mixers, watching the rest of the shop from a mirror that backed a display of chocolates.

Noonah placed a two-shilling piece on the counter as he slid the foaming malted milks over to them.

'You'll get the brush-off in here,' he warned them in a low voice, 'and don't say I didn't tell ya.'

Trilby's face was grey. Deliberately, she lifted her container from the counter and walked to a table. Helplessly, Noonah followed and heard an anguished 'Gawd!' behind her.

The table Trilby chose already had one occupant – a middleaged man drinking a cup of coffee. He looked up when the girls sat down and for a moment his face retained its pleasant good humoured expression. Then his features froze. He shot a look full of irritation at the boy behind the counter. When he lifted his coffee cup again, it was to drain the contents at a gulp preparatory to leaving.

Just as he was about to rise, however, a voice came from the next table. 'It's to be hoped they use some sort of disinfectant on these glasses.'

The man resumed his seat. He looked again at the lowered heads of his table companions, as if he wanted them to look up at him. Then he turned and addressed the young girl who had spoken.

'That was a damned rude remark,' he said roughly. 'If you were my daughter, I'd take you over my knee.'

Grey eyes and brown looked up at him. Shy and startled. It was Trilby who caught his attention. He smiled uncertainly at her as he rose again. And Trilby smiled back at him, the brilliant dazzling smile whose effect Noonah knew well.

The girl at the next table had her back to them again, stiff, straight and offended. 'Trilby, do you feel all right?' Noonah whispered. 'Your hands are shaking.'

'I don't want this drink,' Trilby said distastefully.

'Leave it,' Noonah begged, 'and we'll just walk out.'

Trilby flung a quick look at the occupants of the milk bar. Nearly all of them were watching openly. Only the offended girl kept her back to them.

'Wonder if Mum's still out there,' Noonah said.

'I can see her,' Trilby said through stiff lips. 'She looks scared stiff.'

Noonah thrust back her chair. Trilby was forced to follow suit. They walked slowly and with dignity out of the shop. The attendant whistled softly as they passed. He was smiling, but they would not meet his glance.

Mrs Comeaway bustled over to them. 'Wonder they even served ya in there,' she scolded. 'I keep telling ya. Little places like that, ya gotta be careful. Them people got their places. We got ours.' She marched grimly along the street. 'An I tell ya something else. We like it that way, see?'

Their shopping was done. The presents had been posted to the mission, and a string-bag filled with groceries and meat dangled heavily between Trilby and Noonah.

Somewhere or other, Mr Comeaway had come across some money, and held carefully under Trilby's arm was a parcel containing two pairs of bathers, for herself and Noonah.

'I been thinkin,' Mrs Comeaway said. 'Spose we walk down an take a little look at them houses in the Wild-Oat Patch. You know, Joe. The ones like the Maybes live in. The ones Charlie keeps yappin about.'

Despite their load, the girls agreed happily. Mrs Comeaway considered her swollen feet and decided they might hold out if she walked real slow.

'Them houses are goin up special fa coloured folk,' she told the sisters. 'All scattered about, too, not in a heap like we was rubbish. That's what they call discrimination.'

Mr Comeaway laughed. 'Ya got that arse about,' he told his wife. '*Ass*-imulation, that's what you mean. An I ain't never heard what the nobs think of it. You seen the Maybes lately, Molly? How they getting along with them neighbours a theirs?'

'All right!' Mrs Comeaway said drily. 'They don't come out an beat em off with sticks. The trouble, I think, is with them Maybes. Stuck-up lot, them *an* their kids.'

'One wrong thing that partment did,' Mr Comeaway said pensively, 'they made our places different from those others. Seems ta me they shoulda all been the same.'

'Ours looks bigger,' Mrs Comeaway defended.

'Thinkin a the kids we gotta bed down,' Mr Comeaway commented. 'Beats me bout these white folks. Never seem ta have many kids. I reckon they got the money and we got the kids, eh?' He chuckled.

They had reached a part of the town where the streets were narrow and crooked, where mean little houses peered distrustfully through dusty windows, their untidy side-yards over-grown with weeds, only an occasional glory of sunflowers lighting their drabness.

Towards the centre of the town the level of the houses rose. They were bigger here and set well back from the road, freshly painted, steeply roofed, their cold polished eyes glaring arrogantly or hidden deep in the dimness of cool verandas. They had smooth green lawns and gardens where frangipane, flame trees and apple-blossom hibiscus took the place of the vulgar sunflowers. Along the next street, huge well-proportioned Moreton Bay fig trees threw thick shade on a dusty footpath, and when these had been passed the town gave up the struggle and allowed its streets to meet and mingle where they would.

Another steep rise led them to a second attempt at planning. Here, the streets stretched tidily away at right angles to each other, each lined with houses so neat they might have been coloured drawings or children's models. Most of them were built of asbestos. Some were of timber, freshly painted in bright glowing colours, each just a little different from its neighbour. The whole area seemed treeless. The little tiled roofs could be seen stretching away and away into the distance, geometrically planned, efficiently finished. This was the Wild-Oat Patch which the town council had bulldozed out from undulating sandhills and sown quickly with the seed of the wild oat for protection from the wild southerly winds which swept in off the sea.

Along the outskirts of the area, several houses were in the process of being built. 'We been here seven years,' Mrs Comeaway mar-

velled, 'an all that time they been buildin these houses. Gawd
knows where the peoples come from ta fill em up. Praps them
emigrants come up ere. Ever hear em jabberin away, Joe? Wonder
ta me they understand what they talkin about.'

'Everyone's got their own language,' Mr Comeaway said patiently.
'Same as us.'

'Sounds funny just the same,' Mrs Comeaway was obdurate.
'What's more they teach it ta their kids stead of learnin em ta speak
proper. Little bits a kids talkin a lot a damn nonsense nobody can't
understand.'

'Cept their mothers an fathers,' Mr Comeaway grinned. He
turned to Trilby and Noonah. 'Look there! That looks like one a
ours. Nice big place, ain't it?'

'Daddy! Mummy!' Noonah's voice had a breathless note. Her
eyes were luminous and pleading. 'Why can't we have a house
down here?'

The four stopped in their tracks and looked at each other in
silence.

Trilby smiled her dazzling smile. 'Gee!' she said. 'Gee! could
we?'

Mr Comeaway looked at his wife. 'I suppose we could,' he said
wonderingly. 'I suppose we damn well could. If we wanted to.'

'And get Bartie and Stella down?' Noonah breathed joyously.
'Could we?'

Mrs Comeaway kept looking from the half-built house to her
husband and back again, as if she needed to see material symbols
before she could begin to grasp the potential.

'Nothin ta stop us,' Mr Comeaway said recklessly.

'The money,' Mrs Comeaway said in a rush. 'We got no money.'

'Forty pound,' Mr Comeaway said grandly. 'Charlie told me.'

'We could save it up,' Trilby planned.

Mr Comeaway looked thoughtful. 'Now that forty pounds is the
deposit, an ya gotta pay that much before they let ya in the place.
An Charlie says after that ya got forty year ta pay the rest. That's a
good long time, ain't it?'

Mrs Comeaway beamed. She saw herself opening her front door
and inviting her friends in. Plenty of room for everyone in a place
that size. Bartie and baby Stella. They could all come – she could
have friends staying with her as often as she liked and no crowding
either.

Mr Comeaway's thought ran parallel with his wife's. He saw
himself leaning on his own front gate, smoking, talking to his
neighbours. He saw himself host to his friends. He was conscious of

mild surprise that he had not thought of something like this before. Still, he'd thought of it now and he'd see that department man first chance he got and arrange everything properly. Tomorrow, maybe. Some time this week, for certain.

Trilby was off and away, climbing all over the half-built house, counting up rooms, comparing them for size, deciding which one should be her own, determining to have it to herself, planning the furnishing right down to the colour of the frilly net curtains she had seen in magazines.

Noonah's eyes were on her parents, loving them, thanking them. She saw herself meeting Stella and Bartie at the station, the way she and Trilby had been met. Already, in her mind, she was wording the letter they would write to the superintendent of the mission, telling him that Bartie and Stella could come home. Home!

'Ain't nothin' ta cry bout, that I can see,' Mr Comeaway rallied her, but Noonah's mother said nothing, only moving closer to the girl's side to pat her shoulder and to smile at her.

CHAPTER 6

On the corner of the main street stood an hotel and at the back of the hotel was a square yard marked off from the lane behind it by an old stone wall. In summer, the wind blasted in straight off the ocean, carrying clouds of sand from the beach that backed the shops. In the winter, the wind was less boisterous but it was keen and cold, cutting through clothing and chilling the spines of those who loitered.

Winter and summer, there was always a little group who sheltered in the lane at the back of the hotel, in the lee of the good solid stone wall. For it was here that Horace held court. Here that he untangled quarrels and deliberated and passed judgement and, incidentally, kept himself informed. Horace's position was not unique. For every group there is one who leads. Horace was the leader of the coloured community and the only time he absented himself from his duties was when he was locked up in the town jail.

And no one of his friends felt less than uneasy until he was back at the helm again.

On his way up to his present eminence, Horace's nose had been knocked sideways, his ears had been as badly treated as a tom-cat's, he had lost three or four of his splendid white teeth, and the tear duct of one eye had been damaged. There had been talk of an operation to repair this last bit of damage, but as a certain party said, 'It's like this. The operation is going to be very expensive. And it's not as though Horace has ever been what you might call a "handsome" man.' The operation had been deferred, a most happy decision, for Horace's tears only added to his sympathetic and benign expression.

Mr Comeaway was one of Horace's friends and admirers. He admired Horace's strength especially. Many a time he had watched Horace being bundled down the street shouting and swearing, his foot slipping slyly out to trip an adversary, his iron fists flailing and, with all the commotion, looking as if he were having the time of his life. One bottle of port royal did a lot for Horace. Three gave him the strength of a giant.

When all was over, and Horace had had a good rest on his jail cot, he was a different man entirely, gentle and well-behaved, shocked and unbelieving of his doings of the night before, changing to remorseful amusement as his memory was refreshed by the monarch. In fact, such was the undivided attention Horace bestowed on those who refreshed his memory, so many were the grave shakings of his battle-scarred head, the officers of the police force quite often grew confused; feeling that they placed a case before a kindly but impartial judge.

True to the promise he had made his family, Mr Comeaway was on his way down to see the department man. But first he wished to have a word about the matter with Horace. It was not that his mind was not firmly made up. Perhaps it was an urge to astonish his old friend and, at the same time, to receive what undoubtedly would be Horace's stamp of approval on the venture.

Horace nodded affably. Mr Comeaway rolled two cigarettes and courteously left his friend's unlicked. Then he selected a good place to lean. They smoked a while in companionable and comfortable silence.

'Calling in by the partment chap today,' Mr Comeaway said at last, very casually.

Nothing about Horace betrayed that his attention had been instantly engaged. Being a semi-official employee of the department, he frequently called there himself. There was his weekly ration to pick up; there was his pound note to collect once a month; his buckets and brooms and mops wore out and had to be replaced, and when he was quite certain that evil-doers were well off and away, he reported breakages of equipment on the government reserve which was his sacred charge.

Moreover, being such a regular visitor, he was in a position to advise would-be visitors of their correct behaviour, particularly if such advice might be needed to smooth out mistakes and misunderstandings.

'Bout one a them houses down the Wild-Oat Patch,' Mr Comeaway said, eyeing the shaggy end of his cigarette.

Horace remained silent a while, after which he cleared his throat and spat.

Mr Comeaway waited. And then he became impatient. 'What ya think a the idea?'

Horace took out his own tobacco and cigarette papers and rolled another cigarette. When it was lit he fixed his back against the wall and squinted through smoke at a group of men emerging from a doorway on the other side of the street.

'Well!' Mr Comeaway said. His bottom lip jutted a trifle. 'Ya think something's wrong bout getting a house?'

Horace turned right round. 'Ya gunna regret it, boy. I think ya gunna regret it.'

Aggrieved and disappointed, Mr Comeaway threw his new cigarette down and ground it out half-smoked as it was. Regret it?

'You all right where ya are, ain't ya? Nice little place up on the hill? Mrs Green – an there's a nice ole lady – livin right near an handy so ya ole woman don't get running round fa someone ta talk to? And ya wanta shift out there? An pay rent an stuff?'

A sweet wash of relief cooled Mr Comeaway's injured feelings. If that was all!

'We got that worked out,' he said simply. 'I just keep goin down that wharf every day not missin out. We can pay that rent all right.'

The glint in Horace's eye could easily have been warm interest, and only Horace knew for sure that it came from a lack of illusions. Horace forgave because he understood. Now he settled himself into another more comfortable position and examined the sky.

'Rent days has a habit of comin up pretty regular,' he gave of his wisdom. 'Can upset a man's whole day, sposin e's been working out some different sort a plan fa spending is money.'

Mr Comeaway grappled with this in silence for a while, deciding finally on another tack. 'This ain't no new thing,' he said earnestly. 'Mus be two weeks now we went down an had a look at them

houses. Showin the kids the town like. An we had a look at one just
goin up, an Noonah – that's the one's gunna be a nurse – she said
why didn't we just get one a them houses an live down there. So
that's how we done it but we saved a bit a money first – that's for
the deposit – to show im we was good peoples to let get a house.' He
dragged a tobacco-tin out of his pocket and fiddled with the tight-
fitting lid. 'That's what I got here. An that ain't all,' he continued,
a little uncertain now. 'After we been there a while I been thinkin
we might get our rights.'

Horace showed his shock. A look almost of unfriendliness passed
over his face, though this was the only sign he gave that his friend
had stubbed, with his big clumsy tongue, right at Horace's single
sensitive spot. Citizenship had been in Horace's mind for many a
long day, but so far it had remained out of reach, advancing and
retreating in line with his periods of freedom and his periods of
confinement to a jail cell. He had tried often to bring it within
grasping distance, but when the time was ripe, which is to say,
when his unbending determination was beginning to melt into a
mere resolve to keep out of trouble if he could and when this first
coincided with one of his many friends arriving at the camp with a
big shearing cheque, then, as surely as a punch in the nose brings
close arrest, Horace got himself picked up.

It was the strength in him that did it. All that strength that a few
bottles of conto lent him. A man couldn't use it all up in talk and it
had to be got rid of somehow. Horace could never fathom his
reason for seeking out uniforms but it always happened that way
and he had never yet met the monarch who was as forgiving as a
friend might have been.

These slips between cup and lip constituted the only infelicity in
Horace's otherwise happy adjustment to life, and nobody who ever
followed his sage counsel to stay citizenshipless ever suspected that
the grapes were sour.

He now wagged a stern finger under Mr Comeaway's nose. 'Get
that house if ya like, but leave them damn rights alone.'

'Why?'

A tear or two ran down Horace's left cheek. 'Because,' he said
heavily, 'I'll tell ya for why. Me boy,' another long pause whilst
Horace searched the street for advancing friends and inspiration,
'ya don't know what ya might be running yaself into.'

Horace was genuinely at a loss how to proceed from here. Only a
week or so back he could have used his most potent argument – no
more hand-outs from the department – but some busybody had
changed all that now, and a man only needed a teaspoonful of

blackfeller blood in his veins to be eligible for departmental aid.

'Ya know all them questions ya gotta answer?' Horace asked gravely, seeing his tack at last.

'What about them then?'

'Peerin and pokin round ya private life?'

Mr Comeaway's face took on a wary look.

'Ain't even sure they might want ya to confess.'

'What's that?'

'Things ya done,' Horace said airily. 'Any little thing ya mighta done. Robbin a bank, things like that.'

Mr Comeaway was definitely uneasy now.

'An I tell ya something else. Everyone say you good man, Joe boy. So why would ya go an think ya was better than other peoples, you tell me that?' Horace was convincing himself as well now. His heart overflowed with compassion for his friend. If *he* had been deemed unable to manage citizenship rights, how much less able was Joe Comeaway? Clearly, he must save his friend from all that worry and responsibility.

'Ever see the Maybes?' he asked quietly.

'Not too often.'

Horace nodded, his expression stern. 'That ole man wouldn't give ya one drop a conto, not if ya lay dyin. One time I arst im. Too good now. Think us fellers unrespectable, think trouble might come spose they look at a feller. An that ole woman a his, marchin round with er string-bag and that black hat on er head, telling the childrens ta come on an stop talkin when I know them kids since they was born. Lations a mine even. Arrk!' Horace spat disgustedly.

'It was them girls,' Mr Comeaway said humbly. 'They said about it.'

'I'm tellin ya well,' Horace said sternly. 'You leave them rights fa the foolish ones. Nother thing, I can get ya a bottle a conto when ya want it – cheap,' he weighed Mr Comeaway's possibilities, 'seven bob? Eight bob? Real good stuff fa nine or ten bob. An that's without you landin yaself in no trouble.'

'Them Maybes,' Mr Comeaway allowed, 'act sometimes like they wouldn't spit on ya.'

Horace's nostrils flared. 'An nor us on them,' he declared vehemently. 'Don't you be forgettin that.' He snorted. 'Im with is wouldn't wanta get in no trouble. For a bit of a drink for a bloke that's been a friend to im *and* er.' His brown eyes twinkled. '*And* her,' he repeated.

Mr Comeaway's mind had wandered. 'By gee, I could *do* with a drink. Two or three.' He took out his tobacco tin again and carefully extracted two pound notes.

They melted beneath Horace's big dark hand. Horace smiled sweetly. 'That feller that gets me the stuff, lets me have it fa ten bob now. Cause e knows I don't tell where I get it spose I get picked up. Get yaself a name like I got boy an ya right.'

'An fa Gawd's sake don't drop the bag comin up the hill,' Mr Comeaway begged.

'I ad a haccident,' Horace said primly, 'that time.'

Mr Comeaway looked as if he might be about to comment, but he changed his mind. If Horace knew he had had a look about, just a squint, round the place where Horace had said he had had his accident, because he thought maybe the sugar-bag might have cushioned just one bottle's fall, and that he had found nothing at all at the said site, not even a bit of broken glass or a sugar-bag ... Mr Comeaway's instinct and his long undisturbed friendship with Horace sealed his lips. He nodded understandingly.

'Bloody rock on the road,' Horace said, and again Mr Comeaway nodded.

'Jus fa Christ's sake be bloody careful,' he begged. 'I'm puttin me neck out just givin ya the money, ya wanta know. All the whole lot of em's talkin bout nothing but this damn house.'

It was Horace's turn to nod understandingly, but his eyes were on his next lot of visitors. He welcomed them with a smile. Careless but proprietorial, he moved a step away from the wall.

Mr Comeaway went on his way meditating, concluding with some relief that no matter what, it was a good thing for a man to have a friend who would take up his troubles, sort them through and return them to him all straightened out.

'Where's the girls?' Mr Comeaway asked later that afternoon, dumping a parcel of meat on the table.

'The skies'll fall,' Mrs Comeaway said, eyeing the bloodsoaked package. 'What's come over *you*, bringin meat home thout even askin?'

'Ya need it don't ya?' There was an irascible note in his voice. Bad enough lugging the stuff home without being eased out of the rôle of benefactor.

'Course I do,' Mrs Comeaway admitted. 'Didn't need enough ta feed a flock a elephants but. Have ta give some ta Mrs Green I spose. Save it goin bad.' She sat down on one of the beds, leaving the meat where it lay on the table.

'Naggin womans,' Mr Comeaway confided to the ceiling, having lowered his weary body on to Noonah's bed. 'Where's the girls, I arst?'

'Trilby's around somewhere. Noonah's gone down to see that hospital woman,' Mrs Comeaway answered. 'Ain't she been talking bout it for a fortnight?'

'Yeah! That's right! Wonder if she'll be all right.'

'Course she will. Somethin wrong if she don't.'

'Where ya think I been?'

'Standin outside the pub talking ta ole Horace,' Mrs Comeaway said promptly.

'Well I ain't,' her spouse said, shooting out his bottom lip at this second piece of obtuseness. 'I been down to the partment an seen that man. Told you I was going this week,' he added, glumly reproachful now that he had Mrs Comeaway's full attention.

'Bout the house?'

'Yeah!' Mr Comeaway said triumphantly.

Trilby skipped through the swinging door of the humpy.

'Guess where ya father's been,' Mrs Comeaway said instantly, swinging round to face her.

Trilby's eyes went to her father. 'Where?'

'Been down ta see bout the house, that's what,' Mrs Comeaway said, simmering excitement in her voice. She turned back to her husband. 'Now! What happened? We get one?'

'Well,' Mr Comeaway said portentously, removing some obstructions at the foot of Noonah's bed simply by kicking them off, 'I'll just tell ya.'

'Did you ask if we could have one with red paint and little steps and a veranda on the side?' Trilby asked eagerly.

Mr Comeaway puffed out his cheeks. 'First,' he announced, 'we gotta save up another eighteen pound. That's the first thing we gotta do. Twenty-six pound the deposit is.'

'Wait,' Mrs Comeaway said, doing a little figuring in her head, 'we already got ten, ain't we?'

'Eight,' Mr Comeaway said smoothly. 'Horace is gunna bring a few bottles up tonight ta celebrate.' He kept a stern eye on his wife until he saw that she accepted this fact.

'Then, when we *got* this eighteen pound, we shift down there.'

Trilby hugged herself and hopped about on one foot. Mrs Comeaway beamed.

'Then when we *get* into the house,' Mr Comeaway continued, 'we gotta pay rent an we don't have ta get behind with it. That gotta be paid every week regular like a clock. I told im then bout me workin down that wharf an that rent business don't worry us. Told im few other things, too. Like how we keep the place clean an got Noonah goin ta be a nurse an all that. So he knows we's a good family an got nice childrens.'

'And what about the colour?' Trilby demanded. 'Can we have a painted house?'

Mr Comeaway shook his head. 'We gotta do all that.'

'I think they're just being mean,' Trilby said furiously. 'I wanted a painted house. Now everyone'll know it's just a nigger's place.'

Mr and Mrs Comeaway gazed at their daughter in frowning bafflement.

'Why, you just a young hussy, sayin things like that bout ya own people,' Mrs Comeaway said, raising to stand threateningly over her daughter. 'What you say a thing like that for eh?'

'It's not me – it's them,' Trilby said, angry tears choking her voice. 'They spoil everything for us. They try every way they can to make us feel mean and little. Even down at the post office they try. We've got a name, haven't we? So why do they have to lump us all under "Natives". What's so different about us? They're beasts. I hate the lot of them.'

'I oughta give ya a good clip over the ear,' her mother said, still frowning. But there was more worry than anger in her face now. She flung a look of appeal at her husband.

'Let er alone,' Mr Comeaway said, himself perturbed at the outburst. 'She's jumpin out of er skin with excitement. Ain't that the trouble, Trilby?'

Trilby forced herself to be calm, despising herself for her weakness. It didn't pay to lose your temper. It never had in the past. It never would. Her mother cuffed her gently on the side of the head. 'All right! You remember what I said, though, an don't go callin us peoples niggers.'

'Ya know what?' Mr Comeaway ruminated. 'We sposed ta keep this house only to ourselves. No lations, no peoples comin down for a holiday like. E says tell em we don't have no beds for em.'

'They ain't partickler bout beds,' Mrs Comeaway said dubiously.

Neither saw much sense in the advice. A good roof meant shelter, and the number of those who sheltered could only be limited by the size of the roof. To the Comeaways, twenty–six sounded a likelier figure than six.

'E showed me a thing e called a blue-print,' Mr Comeaway said at last, dismissing the matter. 'So I could see everything. Got little rooms an one big room fa livin in, got a stove an a sink fa washing up cups, an all the clothes get washed inside this house, an there's troughs to wash em in.'

'I seen them sinks,' Mrs Comeaway nodded. 'Stainless steel. That's gunna be a jump up, eh Trilby?'

'Are we allowed to paint it any colour we like?' Trilby asked.

'It's our house, ain't it?' grinned Mr Comeaway.

'Not yet it ain't,' Mrs Comeaway was more practical. 'We gotta save up more money yet.'

'The partment man's gunna do that,' her husband said comfortably. 'All we gotta do, we take im our spare money, and e puts it away somewhere and lets us know when we got enough.'

'Sounds safer than that ole tobacco tin,' Mrs Comeaway chuckled. 'Remember that time we was gunna save up and go an see the kids up the mission.'

'Always rememberin some damn thing happened years ago,' Mr Comeaway said irritably.

Mrs Comeaway chuckled again. 'An I got plenty a things ta pick from.' Seeing a storm gathering in her husband's eyes she relented. 'Good things, too. Spose I remember back far enough.'

Trilby giggled. Then she bent a persuasive look on her mother.

'Can I have a room all to myself where I can put things and not have people touching them? Can I please, Mummy?' Her grey eyes were limpid pools and did not disclose that on this point she had already made up her mind. The front room of the humpy had become, with the addition of the two beds, a comfortable sitting-room. Often, the girls had to wait wearily for visitors to depart before they could claim their beds. Oftener still, being healthy young animals whose activities took place during the hours of daylight, they tired of waiting and curled themselves up on the big bed in the back room. Sometimes the visitors would still be there when they woke next morning, and they would find their mother stretched out alongside them and their father sleeping on a pile of old clothes on the floor.

Trilby hated this disorderliness and tried to alter it, but she might just as well have saved her energy.

'They living way over in the bush,' Mrs Comeaway would say vaguely. 'Mighta missed their way in all that dark.'

'They should have left when it was light enough to see well,' Trilby would snap.

'Yeah! That's right,' Mrs Comeaway would agree cheerfully. 'An they meant to. They was going ta do that! It was just we got talkin an then someone wanted a game an there ya are.' An expressive shrug of the soulders disclaimed responsibility.

'I don't want anyone to sleep in my bed but me,' Trilby pursued.

Her father chuckled. 'I would say the same.'

'Well!' Mrs Comeaway soothed. 'I should think ya can have a room to yaself. You an Noonah.'

Trilby considered. 'And nobody else, not even if they're cousins.'

Mrs Comeaway looked over at her husband. 'You sure that man meant real lations like Hannie an Charlie an them girls?'

'I hope he did,' Trilby said spitefully.

Noonah came through the door and stood there, hot, perspiring and happy. 'It's all right! I can be a nurse.'

'And we're getting the house,' Trilby said triumphantly.

CHAPTER 7

Mr and Mrs Comeaway and Trilby sat listening to all that Noonah had to tell them. Mrs Comeaway's face showed surprised respect at the long medical terms which tripped so easily off her daughter's tongue. Mr Comeaway blanketed equal respect under a lavish display of casualness. Fortunately, he could leave all questioning to his wife, because Mrs Comeaway was willing to admit to any shameful degree of ignorance in order to find out what she wanted to know.

'An what would that thing be, that thing you said?'

'Vocational Guidance Test? That's to show if I'm going to be all right at nursing.'

'You *wanta* be one don't ya?' Mrs Comeaway said with simple faith. 'An what comes after that?'

'I have to go away for ten weeks to a training school in Perth. If I pass my examination when that's over I can start training at the hospital here.'

'Perth, eh?' Mr Comeaway said. 'My daughter,' he would say later, to selected friends, 'has to go to Perth. The government wants her to go to Perth for a while.'

'I get about six pound a week to start off with.'

His eyes widened. He had never looked on his children as potential money makers but the thought was not unpleasant.

'Two pound fifteen is taken out every week for board and stuff,' Noonah said.

Mr Comeaway did some mental arithmetic. Even after two pound fifteen had been taken out there was still a wad of money left over.

'Of course I'll have to buy a lot of text-books to start off with,' Noonah went on, 'and there's deductions for uniforms and insurance ... '

Mr Comeaway gave up his mental arithmetic and philosophically went back to just listening.

'Now tell us about nursing,' Mrs Comeaway begged, settling herself more comfortably. 'What sorta jobs ya have ta do. I was in a hospital once. Fa bein ill, I mean. Always wakin ya up ta wash ya an if they not doing that they dosin ya up with medicine. Wake ya up when it's still *dark* just ta wash ya. I tole em not ta bother bout me, seein they had so much else ta see to. Didn't do no good. I hadda be washed just the same.'

'Me too, that time I broke my arm,' Mr Comeaway said feelingly. 'Made me feel real shamed, the things they done ta me. Didn't like ta say nothing, but by crikey, I dunno. Don't seem ta act like ordinary womans, them nurses. And will I forget the day I come in. Damn near took the skin offa me, they did. "Fair go," I told em, "a man's gotta have some sort a cover fa the meat on is bones."'

Noonah giggled. Trilby, who had been listening in scornful silence, joined in. Obligingly, their parents followed suit.

Recovering, Noonah said, 'The scrubbing is to get all the germs off you, so they won't infect you with something.'

'Thought germs was little things you could hardly see,' Mr Comeaway said whimsically. 'Not stuff ya have ta take a great mop to.'

'That's one of the subjects I have to take in Perth,' Noonah said, her eyes alight. 'Hygiene, asepsis.'

'Come again!'

'I think we'll be taken to see the sewerage places and the water department and things like that.'

'I see,' said Mrs Comeaway, who could see no connection.

'Listen to these,' Noonah said, reading from a prospectus. 'Anatomy, Physiology, Theory and Practice of Nursing, Personal and Communal Health, and First Aid.'

'I know what that First Aid is,' Mr Comeway said quickly, grateful in his knowledge. 'People faintin and all like that.'

'I haven't learned much about it yet,' Noonah said tactfully.

'So you'll be goin off ta Perth just when I'm gettin used ta having ya round,' Mrs Comeaway said, but without reproach.

'And when I come back I have to live at the hospital,' Noonah said anxiously. 'You knew that, didn't you? I'm allowed home praps three nights in two weeks. I'm not sure. Anyhow, I get some time off and I'll come straight home.'

'Oh well,' Mr Comeaway said, 'Love ya an leave ya.'

'Mummy, you can have all the money that's left over,' Noonah said earnestly. 'And that'll help you when the kids get back.'

'I spose we better start thinkin bout beds fa everyone,' Mrs Comeaway said.

'Gee, I nearly forgot,' Mr Comeaway took her up. 'We can get beds all right. Might be a bit left over fa some other doo-dahs too. That partment man says we get forty quid ta spend on furniture, soon as we move inta that house. An that's fa nothin.'

Mrs Comeaway looked as if the entrance to her mind was getting choked up again. 'Beds!' she murmured. 'Fa six of us. An we got three already.' She gazed intently at the two new beds.

Trilby said nothing. There was plenty of time to take action. But her bed cover and frilly curtains seemed a certainty, now.

'How old would Bartie be?' Mr Comeaway mused. 'Nine? Ten?'

'Ten. And wait until you see his drawings.'

'Bartie's nuts,' Trilby said tersely.

'He is not,' Noonah flashed. 'He's going to be an artist.'

'If he's let,' Mrs Comeaway had been sitting very still. A minute or two passed before she said, with a sort of compassion, 'You think it can all be settled just movin into a house, buyin a coupla beds, don't ya, Noonah? You think I sent you all away when there wasn't no real need, eh? You come here an look.' She took Noonah's hand and pressed the fingers against an inch-long scar running through one eyebrow.

'I didn't want my kids hurt,' she said quietly. 'An called names. They might get that, Bartie an Stella, at this new school.'

Mr Comeaway growled deep in his throat. 'Gawd! Ya don't wanta talk like that roun these kids. That little bit of a thing. That ain't nothin.'

Trilby laughed suddenly. 'You think it doesn't happen now?' she asked her father. She turned empty eyes on her mother. 'You think your precious children are safe up at the mission? We're not safe anywhere, you fools. There's always someone around to make us feel we're dirty – not fit to touch. They wouldn't even serve me an Noonah with a drink – until I made them.'

'That man wanted to be nice to us,' Noonah reminded her sister. 'They're not all horrible.'

'Yes they are,' Trilby repudiated roughly. 'All of them. Some let you get closer than others, that's all. They still keep a line between us and them. And when you look at the way we live,' her eyes swept over the room scornfully, like grey lightning, 'you can't blame them, can you? Pigs live better than we do. I tell you I hate white people because they lump us all together and never give one of us a chance to leave all this behind. And I hate coloured people more, because most of them don't *want* a chance. They *like* living like pigs, damn them.' She jumped up, wild-eyed and defiant, and ran from the room.

Mr Comeaway glowered after her. 'Gettin a bit cheeky, ain't she?'

'If she feels like that,' Mrs Comeaway said distressfully, 'what's she wanta live right in among white people for?'

'Wasn't like what she said, up at that mission?' Mr Comeaway asked Noonah, underlip out. Noonah hesitated.

'I thought you was all happy up there,' Mrs Comeaway said reproachfully.

'Mummy,' Noonah said impetuously, 'happiness isn't just food and a bed and clothes. Not for children. At the mission, they teach you to go into your class-room at the right time, and they feed you and teach you to brush your teeth and they give you a bed in a proper room, but they could never teach us to stop wanting our own mothers and fathers and our own homes. And it doesn't matter if the home isn't a very good one – it's where we want to be. It's like being sick all the time. Not in your stomach, but up here.' She placed her thin hand against her heart. 'The little kids pretend Mrs Gordon is their mother. Whenever she walks round they crowd up against her and hold on to her hands or her frock and make her bend down so they can hug her. I know they're pretending she's their mother, because I used to pretend myself. And I used to want to smack the other kids and pull their hair – anything to make them go away from her so I could have her all to myself. And sometimes when I saw kids walking along with their mothers and holding on to their hands I used to wish and wish it could be me, back with you.'

Mr Comeaway's eyes had kindled. 'Ain't that what I said?' he accused his wife. 'Didn't I tell ya the kids should stay with us?'

In her mind Noonah was back at the mission, remembering the babies who had come to them from time to time. Infants of two and three or even younger. And one little chap who had drooped his softly-curled ungainly head that had seemed too large for the stem-like neck. He had sat on the floor silent, indifferent to cajolery, something stony and dead about him which had frightened her.

She had picked him up and looked into his dark eyes and seen there something she could not forget. Not endurance, nor hopelessness, nor pain. It was as if this baby she held in her arms had travelled far beyond these things and only the shadow of them remained to quiet his mouth and dull his eyes. She had wanted passionately to undo the wrong that had been done to him, to wipe the remembrance of it from his heavy eyes. And something in her had known that she was helpless, that the hurt had gone too deep and that the shadow of it would remain, perhaps for ever.

Mrs Comeaway shook her head. 'Don't like what you said, Noonah. Bout them kids hangin on some woman's skirts. Not fa my kids I don't.' She straightened her shoulders. 'Looks like we better get them beds quick an lively.'

'An about time,' Mr Comeaway said needlessly.

'You!' His wife withered him with a look. 'Only reason *you* didn't want em ta be in that place was all the fuss an bother it was ta get em there. Men!' She sniffed.

'Ere!'

'An I'm talkin the truth,' Mrs Comeaway said belligerently. 'If ya hadda sat still in one place I mighta done different. Fine time they'd a had, shiftin bout from pillar ta post, never knowin when they was gunna sleep under a decent roof, an no sooner gettin set somewhere than you up an talkin bout goin somewhere else. Ya known damn well ya didn't think bout them kids no more than if they was a lotta billy-goats.'

'I'm gettin outa this,' Mr Comeaway said, heaving himself off his bed. 'Man only gotta open is mouth an ya jumpin down is throat. No good ta me.'

'That's right! Get out when the goin gets rough,' Mrs Comeaway taunted, malevolent-eyed. 'Jus like a man.'

'It's not that they didn't try to be nice to us, up there,' Noonah said nervously.

Mrs Comeaway patted her shoulder. 'That's all right. I'm glad ya told us what ya did. But ya don't think I'm gunna let that one get the laugh on me, do ya?'

CHAPTER 8

Mrs Comeaway hoped that Mrs Green would be alone, though she knew it was as well to be philosophical about this. People went to Horace for advice on problems. They called in Mrs Green when they needed to have all their fears and anxieties resolved into one easy-to-deal-with problem. Mrs Comeaway was vaguely troubled about Trilby. Sometimes she was all brightness and cheek. She had her father twisted round her little finger – could wheedle him into letting her do or have anything she set her mind on. But the things she said – right in front of people. Things that made people feel uncomfortable. Walking towards Mrs Green's open doorway, Mrs Comeaway stopped to shake her head and frown, and ponder.

People coming in for a little visit. Trilby acted as if that was something bad, though where the badness lay – again Mrs Comeaway shook her head. You didn't push your pals off just because it was time to eat. And all this walking round town. Mrs Comeaway had a corn on her little toe that was giving her gyp. Trilby said if they stayed home someone was sure to come, so they'd go out. And out they went, dragging up and down that damn street, never stopped to talk to anyone because Trilby wouldn't let her – or else they went down to the Wild-Oat Patch and picked out the house with the prettiest paint because, Trilby kept saying, just as if her father hadn't already agreed, *their* house was going to be painted the minute they got into it.

There wasn't really much to worry about. Trilby was good company and the food bills were certainly a lot lighter. Mrs Comeaway paused to hope piously that she wouldn't need to cadge a meal for a while yet. The truth was, she missed her friends and her way of life. After all, she'd lived it a good few years,

Mrs Green met her at the back door, coming out with an armful of steaming clothes.

'Not out today?' Mrs Green twinkled, as Mrs Comeaway trudged back to the clothes-line with her.

'She's off out with Blanchie and Audrena,' Mrs Comeaway said, without her usual grin.

'Finding her feet,' Mrs Green said sympathetically, pegging out a faded pink frock.

'She's worn mine off up to the ankles,' Mrs Comeaway said gloomily.

'We'll have a cup of tea,' Mrs Green said comfortably, 'just as soon as I get this lot out.'

'Anyone around?'

'Polly's out there under the trees,' Mrs Green gestured with her head. 'Having a sleep.'

They went back into the kitchen. The big black kettle dozed at the side of the stove. Mrs Green moved it to where it would get more heat. 'Those girls, Audrena and Blanchie, they know their way about, don't they?'

'Bet that Audrena does. I like Blanchie better.'

Mrs Green frowned slightly.

'Ya think they might lead er inta mischief?' Mrs Comeaway said bluntly. 'Ya don't need ta worry bout that. Trilby's the one'll do the leadin. An not inta mischief. Just down ta the Wild-Oat Patch ta have a look at the houses.' She rubbed her foot with tender fingers.

'I just thought,' Mrs Green said delicately. 'Trilby isn't used to going round with a gang of girls and boys. And you know what these boys are like. Specially the ones down for a bit of a holiday.'

'Ya mean last Monday night,' Mrs Comeaway said. 'She would go. So I tole Blanchie. "Now you get that girl home early cause er father ain't gunna like it she comes home late." And I said for em to keep away from that wharf down there, with all them men off boats like. An they was all promises an big eyes. Dunno what time they got in.'

'You ask her next morning?' Mrs Green asked innocently.

'No, I didn't. An what woulda been the use? She'd a told me a lotta lies,' Mrs Comeaway smiled a little. 'Same as I'd a done at er age.'

'She's so young an pretty,' Mrs Green murmured, searching for words to fit what her heart knew without the need for them. 'Pity not ta keep your hands on the reins a bit longer. You let kids gallop off where they like and pretty soon they're going to think it doesn't matter where they go.'

'Gawd! You tellin me a wild one like Trilby's gunna take notice a me?'

Mrs Green poured some tea-leaves in the pot and lifted the

boiling kettle. 'I had 'em like her before,' she said softly. 'Like a young brumby, you know? That you have to handle gently.' Her mind went back into the tender memories of the past, and she noddcd her head. 'Yes. Those little wild ones with their eyes rolling and their long thin legs a bit shaky with fright. And you don't go near, but just stand there and talk to them and you keep on talking. They gallop off to start with, but you hold on to your patience, and every day you're there at the same place and after a while they stay and listen to you. And their eyes don't roll any more and their ears don't lay back on their heads, but perk up real straight. Trying to hear if you mean all that soft talk you're giving em. Patience? You hurry those little wild ones and you've lost em for good. They have to trust you. And there's nothing like a little wild brumby for finding out the ones it can trust.'

Mrs Comeaway nodded impatiently. This was way out of her depth. 'What I thought – I came over ta arst ya – couldn't you tell Trilby some a them things you tell ya own kids, like about education an stuff, an getting a good job. She likes you. She'd listen to you.'

Mrs Green set out the cups. And, as though summoned, two figures blanked out the light in the doorway.

'Look who's ere,' Mrs Comeaway said, brightening a little. 'What you two doin back ere? Thought you was lookin fa better company.'

'Mary!' The woman's voice was peremptory. 'We got no tucker.'

'Sit down,' Mrs Green said, reaching for more cups.

'Thought you was well on the way ta Carnarvon,' Mrs Comeaway rallied.

'You better let me an Enry sleep in that ole bed a mine,' Honay snapped. 'Till we think somethin out.' Each word left her mouth neatly clipped from its predecessor. She sucked in her bottom lip and waited.

'What about – you know?' Mrs Green looked meaningly at the silent Enry.

'We gunna start when we leave ere,' Honay said.

'You gunna let em stay here?' Mrs Comeaway asked, amused. 'Don't tell me.'

Honay shot her a vindictive look. She and outspoken Mrs Comeaway had had many an argument during the time Honay had stayed with Mrs Green waiting for the release of her Enry from jail.

'Go on!' Mrs Comeaway was baiting her now. 'Didn't you tell Mrs Green you wasn't gunna sociate with niggers? Didn't you say Enry said you was ta keep away from us after e come out? What you doing back ere again then? After Mrs Green kept you in tucker all the time ya ole man was in jail. Gawd!' Her uproarious laughter filled the kitchen.

Honay stood shaking with rage. 'This one,' she told Mrs Green furiously, 'she's a no-good nigger. No good ta Enry or me. I tole you before.'

'Eh!' Mrs Comeaway's mirth dried up as suddenly as it had begun. 'Oo ya think you callin nigger.'

'Honay!' The silent Enry spoke. His voice was reproving. 'Honay!'

'I'll give er Honay!' Mrs Comeaway snorted with indignation, though amusement was not yet dimmed in her eyes.

'Honay,' Mrs Green said. 'You and Enry better sit down and have a cuppa now I got it made. And I suppose you can sleep in that bed a night or two. If it holds together. But you did tell me yesterday Enry didn't want you to associate with coloured people any more.'

Honay tossed her head. 'We don't even got no blanket,' she accused. 'You want me an Enry ta sleep thout no blanket?'

Mrs Green sighed. 'I got one I can lend you. But remember, I have to have it back. I need all my blankets.'

'We givim back,' Enry spoke softly. 'Soon!'

'I hope,' Mrs Green said feelingly.

'We have cuppa tea now,' Honay bossed. 'Sit down, Enry.'

'And if Skippy comes back while you're here,' Mrs Green begged, pouring tea, 'don't you two start fighting, Honay.' She looked over at Mrs Comeaway. 'I thought I was all through with their fighting. The way they act they're not much better than the kids.'

Honay wiggled her nose from side to side, slid a finger over one nostril, and blew the contents of the other over the floor. She looked quickly and defiantly at Mrs Green.

'Honay!' Mrs Green's tone was exasperated. 'Don't *do* that. You go outside now and get a rag and wipe that up. You dirty old woman. Go on!' She withheld Honay's cup of tea.

Honay rose from the table without a word, walked outside to where a wet rag hung on a nail and returned with it. Sulkily, she got to work.

'And Enry!' Enry looked up obediently from his tea. 'You and Honay can stay a night or two, but you've got to see that old woman of yours behaves.'

Enry nodded. 'You git me bottle, missus. I give er smack on the side of the ead she don't behave.'

Mrs Comeaway leaned over and clapped the old man on the back with such force that the tea held to his mouth slopped over the side of the cup. 'Good on ya, Enry, ole man,' she said.

'Damned if I don't go out and get that bottle for ya meself.'

Honay looked down her long nose, pursed her lips, and sniffed.

Trilby's new bathing-suit was a deep vivid green. In the sunlight
her skin had a dusky shimmer to it and her long, free-swinging
stride only emphasized the delicious youthfulness of her body. She
stopped to dig her foot deep into the hot sand, letting it trickle
smoothly back through her toes. When Blanchie and Audrena
caught up with her she moved off again, completely happy. It was
good to have the late morning sun burning into her flesh, good to
know that any moment she chose she could dash into the sea, fling
herself into it and feel its coolness against her.

There was peace to be found along the lonely little stretch of
beach too. The ageless and immutable peace that belongs to everything in which man has taken no part. A little way out from the
shore, moulded green waves shattered to white froth over submerged reefs. Overhead, seagulls swooped and screamed and described their flights against a background of soft blue.

The girls were walking along the less frequented part of the
beach. The tide had climbed high in a curving line, leaving the
sand wet and firm. Where the girls walked, their footsteps followed
after them, delicately perfect. Between the beach and the road grew
thickets of grey-green salt-bush, scored through with a hundred
paths leading down to the sea. The noise of traffic was muted with
distance, no more disturbing than the wash of the waves or the soft
chatter of the girls. Unheard in their ears, the deep strong pull of
the ocean went on for ever.

'School for you soon,' Audrena said, looking pityingly at Trilby.

Trilby gave her cousin a long look. 'I can always get a headache.'

Audrena laughed.

'Wasn't you gunna get a job?' Blanche asked. 'Serving or
something?'

Trillby looked sullenly ahead. At one time or another she had
been into every shop in the town. Foreigners she had found, some
golden-skinned, some dark, a few of them hardly able to make
themselves understood, but there had been none like herself. Trilby
bit her bottom lip savagely. On one point her mind was firmly
made up. There would be no housework for her, nor minding of
kids. For another year she would go back to school. By that time
she would know more about this town and then she would see.

She forced a casual air. 'I'm going to get my Junior first,' she told
her cousins. 'So I can get a better job. In an office or somewhere.'

Blanchie stared admiringly at her not doubting for a moment

Trilby would get what she wanted. Blanchie did not mind taking second place to her glamorous cousin. She found it exciting to be with her, swimming when Trilby decided to swim, looking in shop windows, sitting at the far end of the Esplanade at night with a crowd of young ones, laughing, gossiping, wandering home late at night with a few fellers to keep them company.

Audrena fell in with most of Trilby's plans, too, but sour envy made up a good proportion of her feelings towards her cousin. Even Trilby's untouched body was a source of annoyance to Audrena. It was as though she set a price on herself. Audrena had to admit that Trilby had had her opportunities. The fellers hung round her like ants after jam. It beat Audrena to know why, when there was herself with all her experience and none of this stupid hanging back from something that was bound to happen to a girl some time or other.

Audrena was always watching for a chance to get under Trilby's guard. Her tongue shot venom wherever she knew it would sting most.

'Better not set ya heart on no office job,' she said now. 'You could be the best typewriter in the world an not get a job here.'

'Typiste!' Trilby flicked back.

'All I'm saying, ya want one a them jobs you'll have ta go some other place where they don't know ya got colour in ya.' Her glance went spitefully to Trilby's dark gold skin.

'That's what I'm going to do,' Trilby said proudly. And in that second decided to do just this. Of course! She should have thought of it for herself. What she must do must be to leave everyone behind her; begin a new fresh life of her own. The thought of it excited her. With a sudden uprush of spirits she sprinted up the beach, turned a somersault and landed laughing and breathless in the odoriferous scratchy seaweed where a group of boys waited for them.

She had chosen this spot herself, because it was far from the popular beaches and usually deserted. Nearly every morning a crowd of youngsters swam and played about on the beach. There were dozens of tight-packed seaweed balls to throw at each other. Sometimes they formed a circle and played a regular game. The boys wrestled and fought and showed off their strength, and when everyone was tired they could lie on the warm, wet seaweed and talk, with the suffocating smell of it deep in their nostrils. When the sun became too hot there was the sea.

This morning they made straight for the water. Audrena and Blanchie shrieked with pleasure, dived deep and came up with seaweed in their hair. Trilby swam out a little way and turned on her back. Through half-shut eyes she watched Phyllix follow her. She smiled, satisfied. She waited until he was within a couple of feet of her then dived cleanly beneath him. The two raced for the beach.

Argosy Bell and his brother Nipper, who were staying with the Beemans, threw themselves enthusiastically amongst the laughing girls, upsetting them, grabbing their ankles, ducking them unmercifully. Two more young girls who ran down to the water's edge and stood there pretending fear were seized and dragged in by their feet. Like young animals they kicked and fought, giggled and splashed; smooth-skinned, lithe, their eyelashes sticking together in wet points, their round pink tongues showing between their square white teeth.

Phyllix fitted his hands to Trilby's waist and pulled her slowly, deliciously, through the coolness. In the water the feel of someone's hands on your body was nothing. It was when Phyllix stopped pulling and let Trilby's body drift close to his, when he bent his head so that his cheek brushed wetly against hers, when she felt the intimate warmth of his breath, that Trilby was suddenly shaken. Her own breath caught in her throat. She liked the feeling even as she grew wary. But those golden eyes so near her own – under their level look Trilby found she had no power to drop her own gaze. Each gazed deep, and there was no holding back.

Blanchie called, and obediently they left the water for the warmth of the piled seaweed.

'You nearly broke my leg.' Audrena pouted, watching Nipper from the corner of her eye whilst she stroked and smoothed her outstretched leg.

'Want me ta do that?' Nipper said slyly, reaching out a hand.

Audrena whisked the leg beneath her haunches. 'No, I do not. See?'

Nipper slid his hand further towards her leg. 'I can fix that leg easy.'

Audrena threw her head back and her voice husked over with sweetness. 'You'd like to, wouldn't ya? If I let ya.'

Seated a few feet away Trilby watched the little scene with calm eyes. This was a sort of play-acting to which she was new. Nipper was a great one for touching – running his hand over your leg, slipping an arm high up round your waist. With other girls – not with her. Trilby could not let him. His hands were hot and wet, his breath smelled bad and sometimes his body smelled bad too, as if it were never washed clean.

This was one of the things about which Audrena teased her most; what Audrena called her stupid hands-off attitude to boys. But

Audrena could inflict no hurt here. Never, never would she let anyone touch her if the touch brought her no pleasure but only loathing. Not for any amount of experience. Yet she was curious. If it were only half so good as the girls said ... She turned her head away from the goings-on, caught Phyllix's gaze fixed squarely upon her and was again unable to look away.

'I'm going ta sleep,' Blanchie yawned, burrowing her head into her arms. 'I'm tired.'

'Out late last night?' Albany teased. 'With Tom?'

'Not Tom,' Blanchie said innocently, and was just as innocently surprised at the laughter this brought forth from the boys.

Trilby clasped her hands tightly round her knees and let her own head droop forward. Behind the screen of her gold-tipped hair she watched Phyllix and tried to understand her feeling for him.

She liked him, but why? He was not so good to look upon as most of the others. He had a thin delicate frame. When he walked there was a touch of the stalker in him. A soft-footed easy lope. His features were not well formed. The gravity of his expression was carried to sternness by the dark thick slant of his eyebrows and his wide, thin-lipped, unsmiling mouth. His eyes were like the eyes of a cat, tilted at the corners, tawny, the pupils mere pin-points. Perhaps it was those strange eyes that drew her. Phyllix did not laugh easily, or play the fool like the others. He seemed a little apart from them always. Almost, Trilby thought irritably, as if he would not bother himself with their foolishness.

Nobody knew who was his father, least of all Phyllix's mother. Older folk remembered much about his mother. A happy one, that. Certainly not the kind to sit on the outskirts if there was any fun to be had. It was likely that Phyllix's father had been a sailor or a deck-hand off a boat. Enough of them berthed here. His thin nose with its narrow nostrils was more Indian than aboriginal. But there was his skin, the smooth brownness of it blotched with tawny freckles.

He was still watching her, Trilby saw through her hair. She lay back, pretending to sleep, and was conscious of a sudden deep wish that these others would go away, all of them, and leave her alone with Phyllix.

Egoline Barclay squealed. Someone had thrown a seaweed ball at her. She picked it up, ready to throw it back. There was a scatter of sand and seaweed. Someone tripped over Blanchie's hot sunburned body, and she came to her feet with a yell of anguish. She caught Nipper by an ankle as he rose and he went sprawling. Instantly, he was upon her, manhandling her into the water, seizing his chance to lay hands on a female body. And the game was on.

Trilby looked after them, pretending absorption in their flying figures, conscious only of Phyllix.

Blanchie screamed madly until water closed her mouth.

Trilby knew when Phyllix changed his position. She peeped through her lashes and the yellow eyes looked straight into hers.

'You coming down town tonight?' Phyllix asked softly.

'What d'you want to know for?'

'You and me might go for a bit of a walk. It's nice walking along the beach at night. Nobody about.'

'What do I want to go for a walk with you for?'

She dragged a ribbon of seaweed from the tangled mass of it. It was almost the colour of Phyllix's eyes.

'All right!' she answered his demanding silence. 'I'll come down for a little while.'

'People fishing,' Blanchie called breathlessly. 'Come and see, you two.'

The beach was not deserted any more. Looking along it, Trilby saw the figures of three people, a woman and two men, busy about a net.

'Let's come and see how many they get,' Audrena said eagerly. 'Might give us a few if they can't carry them all.' She laughed wildly and fled up the beach.

The rest trailed after her. They might as well have a look. Nobody could stop you from looking. The net was half out now. The men were completing a half circle with it, their steps slowed, the pull of its weight showing in their down-bent heads and straining backs.

'They won't get anything, Phyllix murmured. 'Too early! When the sun goes down, that's the time.'

But they had caught something. Trilby saw. There was a sudden threshing in the net. The men waded faster, hurrying to reach the beach before their catch escaped. The woman there waited, tense and excited, her clenched fists beneath her chin, her back to the coloured youngsters. Audrena grinned, made a wicked gesture, and walked over to her. She was close behind the woman before she asked: 'D'you think I an my friends could have some of your fish if you catch a lot?'

The woman's back stiffened. She did not turn her head. 'I don't know, I'm sure.'

'We'd pay for them, if you wanted to sell some.'

'You'll have to speak to my husband about that.'

Audrena made a face, then swaggered grinning back to the others. 'Says we'll have to ask her ole man,' she called loudly.

'Silly damn fool,' Phyllix said coolly, though there was heat in his eyes. Some of the others laughed. There was a long wait, whilst the net was dragged up on to the beach. Then everyone ran to see the black threshing body it held. They saw a giant stingray, the curved tail long and forked at the end. A vicious tail it was, trying desperately to attack. The hooded eyes of the stingray rose and fell with its breathing. The big black body heaved helplessly in the meshes of the net and the black seal-smooth skin rippled like water.

'Damn!' one of the men said ruefully. 'I thought we had a good haul there.'

'What are you going to do with it? Throw it back, or leave it here?' the woman asked nervously.

'Better kill it. That's a dangerous beast there. And it's too close to the beach where the kiddies swim,' the man answered. He took out a knife. The other man hooked the slippery tail. Once, twice, three times the man with the knife slashed before he cut right through it.

'That's the sting gone,' he said with satisfaction, as he hacked at it.

Trilby's eyes were large. How did this Thing feel without its tail? Both portions of the body twisted in agony. The eyes sank despairingly down, only to rise again in a frenzy.

'Perhaps if you push that stick through the eyes ... ,' the man suggested.

A heavy stick was thrust down through the rubbery mass of the creature's eyes. But life was still there, and now blood poured from the cut portions of its body, gushing quicker with every flailing movement.

'Oh!' the woman cried, clasping her mouth with both hands. 'Oh!'

The man stabbed again and again. More blood poured out from the mutilated parts. The eyes continued to labour up and down, up and down, despite their wounds.

The woman looked furiously at the group of coloured youngsters, and her eyes were hard and hurt. 'These niggers,' she shrilled, 'you can never get away from them.'

Trilby did not even hear her. She had had enough. She wheeled and skimmed off down the beach. She flung herself down on the seaweed again, hid her face in her arms and saw again the anguished eyes rising and falling, the blood gushing out to stain the white sand with red.

The others drifted back and sank down beside her.

'What ya want to run away for, old softie?' Audrena asked, amusement in her voice.

'If they leave that tail behind,' Phyllix mused, 'I might pick it up. Good meat in that – like whiting.'

Trilby jerked upright. 'No!' she said tautly. 'No!' And her eyes, too, were hard and hurt.

CHAPTER 9

A moon the colour of water sailed frigidly through the tenebrous sky, shedding no beam of light on the beach nor on the black moving water lapping insistently at the line of the shore.

'You all right?' Phyllix asked.

'Yes!' Trilby said shortly. She was finding no magic in the night. Instead, she felt like a fool. To be stalking along this beach alone with Phyllix, on guard against being caught up into something she might not want.

Phyllix reached out and caught her hand. His own was warm and dry, and its grip was firm. After a while he slid his hand around so that his thumb was on her palm.

Trilby's loose thoughts, like dropped stitches, were knitted up into a single thrilling awareness of his touch.

Gently and rhythmically, Phyllix stroked her palm. 'Nice bein quiet for a change, isn't it?'

Like steel to a magnet, Trilby swayed closer to him. Here was the magic! It had been waiting, ready to leap to life at the touch of his hand. Yet there was shyness in her now. Wantonly, she dissipated the sweetness with words.

'Did you take the tail of the stingray, Phyllix?'

'You told me not to, didn't you?'

She sensed that he was smiling. 'I thought they were awful, those people. I *hate* to see anything helpless. Specially something like that stingray that was so big and strong. They should have put it back in the water.'

'Why?'

'They don't hurt anything – stingrays.'

'Why do you think about it?'

'I won't, any more.' For a moment she was lonely because he had not shared her pain. 'Where are we going?'

'Along here a way. Don't you like walking?'

'I don't mind walking with you.' The words came out unwillingly. Her shyness was back again.

'You never gone for a walk with a feller before?'

'Not just me.'

'I think you never been with a feller – any way at all. Have you?' His face was turned towards her, and though they kept on walking it was as if everything stood still, like a moment out of the wholeness of time to stay forever fixed in their memories.

'No!' Trilby breathed. 'I never wanted to.'

'I could tell,' Phyllix said expressionlessly. 'You can always tell.'

Trilby thought of Audrena. A small surge of triumph gave her face gaiety. After tonight she would know all that Audrena knew. She need no longer feel like a silly kid when Audrena talked of fellers the way she did. Nor try to carry off her ignorance with a high hand. She dwelt with a little wonder on Blanchie. Even Blanchie knew what this was all about.

Noonah came into her mind as well. And with Noonah came more uncertainty. At the mission, there had been strict supervision of the elder boys and girls. At night they had been locked into their dormitories, and there had always been someone from the staff to keep an eye on them. Even so, things had happened. There was that time, her thoughts roved back, when a lot of them had gone for a walk and come across a swimming-hole. First a boy had disappeared and emerged into view splashing and laughing, leaving his clothes on the muddy bank, and that had started them off. One by one the fellers and the girls had flung aside their clothes and gone slipping and sliding down into the pool. And that was where Mr Gordon had found them all – or nearly all. A couple had disappeared. And another couple had been about to sneak off when the panting and fuming superintendent of the mission had caught up with them. Crikey, what a row! And what fun it had been! But afterwards, she and Noonah had agreed that the two girls had been stupid fools to go off like that, getting themselves into all that fuss and bother, having to submit to being punished like kids. And Trilby had thought contemptuously that all that sort of thing could very well wait until there was no danger of someone tailing you up and making a fool of you in front of everyone.

Well, and here it was, and she supposed she had a right to please

herself what she did now she was home. She flicked the thought of
Noonah from her mind. She felt as superior to Noonah as she had
felt towards those two girls who had gone into this thing so greedily
and unthinkingly. There was a time, and this was it.

'I bet *you* have,' she teased Phyllix, sure of herself now, feeling
superior even to Phyllix.

'Have what?'

'Gone with girls.'

'It's different,' Phyllix frowned, 'for fellers.' He looked down at
her again. 'Wish I hadn't, sometimes.'

There was magic again. Their feet slowed. In an opening up of
warmth and wonder, Trilby claimed the night as her own. The
moon, ripening slowly to pale gold. The blackness of the water,
changing now to rippling velvet. The white beach lit by the pale
moonlight. It was all for her, and it was all hers.

To their left as they walked were the mounding bushes, etching
themselves grey against the sky. 'Let's sit here for a while,' Trilby
begged, and pulled Phyllix over to their shelter.

'This is good,' Phyllix said, with a sigh, stretching himself out on
the cool hard sand.

Trilby sat alongside him, her ankles crossed, her chin in her
hands, dreamily content. The air moved clean and tangy, gently
cool against her hot face.

'You like to be away from the others?' Phyllix asked softly.

'I like to be with the crowd better,' Trilby teased him.

'They talk too much,' Phyllix said disinterestedly. 'Noise – that's
all.'

'Why do you go round with them if you don't like them?'

Phyllix moved his shoulders. 'Have to have someone to go round
with, I suppose. Besides, you're there.'

'What's different about me?' Trilby fished.

'You don't yap.' Trilby laughed delightedly. 'And besides ... '

'Besides – what?'

'You damn well know. You've got em all beat. That Audrena,
she's jealous. They're all a bit jealous.'

Trilby's heart lifted. Of course she knew it, but it was good to
have Phyllix say it.

A dark figure appeared, strolling close to the water's edge on the
hard wet sand. Trilby put out a hand, pressed Phyllix's shoulder,
warning him to be silent.

It was fun to sit there, themselves unseen, and to watch as this
man walked by. Everything was fun.

Phyllix reached for her hand and held it, and she knew he was sharing something of what she felt. They watched the man out of sight.

Suddenly Trilby was restless. Something more was needed. She thought of the cool rapture of water against her skin. Remembered the first tingling shock of its touch and the calmness as it rose higher and higer.

She rose in a lovely fluid movement. Phyllix sighed and prepared to rise too, but she pushed him back. Behind some bushes she stripped off her clothes and walked to the edge of the water. She felt the splash of a tiny wave at her feet and walked through it. When she was far enough out she began to swim. And the water was as she remembered it, like the touch of hands.

She heard Phyllix's call. 'Trilby, where are you?'

She stopped swimming and floated on her back. She would not exert herself to call. Phyllix must come to her. She closed her eyes and waited, and opened them to find Phyllix swimming close.

'Take my hands now,' she said when they both were tired from swimming. 'Pull me in. Please!' But Phyllix placed his hands instead over her breasts and drew her smoothly ghrough the water. Until the water became shallow. And then he picked her up and carried her over the beach to the bushes.

Trilby learned that that was how it was. Peace flowing through every limb, and languorous weariness. She turned to her lover and sighed, the smallest fluttering breath. At her side Phyllix breathed deeply and quietly.

The air was like a kiss on their bodies.

But not all of Trilby's vitality had been used up by the walking and the swimming and what had come after. When she had rested a while she felt a desire to talk with Phyllix and question him a little. She wanted to hear him murmur again the things he had murmured against her ear.

'I'm glad it was you,' she whispered.

After a while she raised her head and stared down at him because he had not answered. She put her face close to his. 'Phyllix! Phyllix!'

Still there was no answer. Phyllix slept deeply.

Trilby was conscious of shock. How could he sleep, when she was so near?

She rolled over, took his shoulders in her two hands and shook him. 'Phyllix!'

She put her mouth to his and waited for the response. There was none. Sitting, she gazed unbelievingly down on him. He could lie there and snore after saying those things. After . . .

She sprang to her feet, her hands on her hips, her mouth thin with temper. Viciously she kicked him in the ribs, but Phyllix only moaned and curled himself tighter.

Now – she would teach him a lesson, this snoring fool. But first to cleanse herself from every trace of her foolishness. Like a shadow she slipped into the water again, swimming far out, diving deep, threshing furiously at the water with strong young arms and legs. She had to search for her clothes when she came out at last, and her clothes were covered with sand. Uncaring she pulled them on over her wet body, intent only on her outrage. She would leave him sleeping, and he would wake to find her gone. That would teach him that Trilby Comeaway was not – in the act of tying her sash, she froze.

Would that be a punishment? Would he care if she went or stayed? Now?

She began to run, but her thought kept up with her and it was not her exertion that made her feel hot. Her hair streamed away from her face and the sand flew from her feet, but the waves of shame kept coursing through her body. She had thought to use a man and he had used her instead.

And he must surely have known, Phyllix, that this was the way of it.

She was gasping for breath when at last she slowed her pace to a staggering walk. But the needles of agony in her side did not hurt half so much as the humiliation in her heart or the tears that stung her eyes.

Overhead the moon hid its cool loveliness behind a trail of clouds. And the beach grew dark.

CHAPTER 10

'I dunno! Seems like an awful waste,' Mrs Comeaway said doubtfully, surveying the humpy. 'We've kept adding bits and now we
got it real comfortable. I went an promised Charlie e could have it,
too. Till they get their own money saved up. An after that I thought
the Thomases. They got all them kids an nothin but a bit a canvas
to keep em dry when it rains. Mrs Green wouldn't mind. She and
Mrs Thomas been friends a good while now.'

'Nup!' Mr Comeaway shook his head. 'The partment man says
e's gotta come down less other peoples moves in. Says e don't want
that.'

'No time ta pull im down now well,' Mrs Comeaway said practically. 'You'll just ave ta come up some other time, when we get set
down there in the Wild-Oat Patch.' She looked at Mr Comeaway
with limpid eyes. 'Spose they ain't no harm in Charlie livin here till
we get the time, isn't it?'

'Ya want wood ta burn, don't ya?' Mr Comeaway pointed out
what had been craftily pointed out to him. 'Ain't no bush stuff
round the Patch. All been bulldozed. You take them up-rights now.
Good wood there.'

'Yeah! Yeah! Well, we ain't got the time, I tell ya. I gotta get this
stuff sorted out.' Mrs Comeaway destroyed nothing and threw
nothing away.

'What ya gunna take?' Mr Comeaway asked. 'Tim an me better
get busy.'

'There isn't much worth taking.' Trilby said contemptuously.
'Why don't we just take the new beds and chuck the rest of that
junk away?'

'Don't tell!' Mrs Comeaway said, shocked. 'Ya think I'm gunna
leave me good safe an me chester draws and them chairs? I like my
ole bed. Fits me. Wouldn't sleep so good in no other now.' She
ruminated a while, kneading her chin with one hand. 'Joe!' she
called. 'Best thing you can do – bring everything out an I'll look it
over. Go on, now. An you come ere with me, Trilby.'

Trilby followed her parents into the humpy. She was sulking. She did not care much now if they went or stayed. The thought of the new house no longer enticed her.

Mr Comeaway made a great business out of heaving the table through the entrance. At one end of the precious bed, Mrs Comeaway heaved and pulled and hammered until the rusted spring came free. 'Get on one end, Trilby,' she ordered, 'and we'll get it outside.'

They stood the mattress against a tree and Mrs Comeaway bent to peer at it. 'Been gettin bites some nights,' she said critically. 'Maybe fleas, or else it's them sand-flies.' She chuckled suddenly, diverted. 'That Annie. She tole me a man came out ta the place where they was livin in Perth an bought a jar of fleas offa one a her lations. Paid a pound a hundred for em. This man trained them fleas, so he said.'

'Ugh!' Trilby said disgustedly. 'Where did she get them from?'

Mrs Comeaway shrugged. 'Offa the dogs, offa the blankets, out of er ead. She said the man liked yuman fleas the best. Smarter! Easier to train.'

'They make me sick,' Trilby snapped. She looked suspiciously at her mother's hair. 'Why don't you give your hair a good comb? You'll be getting fleas in your own head if you're not careful.'

'Not me,' Mrs Comeaway disclaimed.

'How do you know?' Trilby sneered.

'I don't itch,' Mrs Comeaway said cheerfully.

'This bed looks awful,' Trilby frowned. 'All broken. Why don't you get another one with the money the department gave you?'

'We are gunna,' Mrs Comeaway said. 'Fa Stella and Bartie. Gee, I bet them kids is gettin excited bout comin down.' She straightened to beam at her daughter. Everything was turning out most happily. There were drawbacks. So-called friends who accused her of getting too uppity, guessed she would be too proud to speak to them when she had gone into her new house. At one state – when it was pointed out to her that she would be a far walk from a yarn or a game of cards – she had almost been ready to back out of the deal. But Joe seemed real set on it, and she hardly liked to think what the girls would say, particularly Trilby. Besides, there were always taxis.

Her only regret now was that all her friends and relations were not moving down to the Wild-Oat Patch with her, though this had been partly solved by generously distributed invitations to come down and visit.

'Young Tim should be here by now,' she pondered aloud. 'Bet

something's gone wrong with that ute.' Tim was Blanchie's 'boy', whose offer to move their furniture had been sought and accepted.

'Ya don't wanta worry bout Tim.' Mr Comeaway sat down to rest from his labours. 'That one can make a engine go with more parts out than in. Last time I seen that ute e'd ripped the engine cover off. Said it kept fallin on is ead when e was working on it like.' He brooded for a while. 'I tole im but, you bring one a ya pals along ta do ya windin for ya. I ain't takin any more chances with that handle. Damn thing about knocked me out last time. Needs a expert at the game.'

'When do they get married, him and Blanchie?' Trilby enquired, with the faintest show of interest.

'They was talking bout it last time I seen em,' Mrs Comeaway said. 'Pity him an Blanchie can't get into a house like we got. Could start off all nice.'

'They won't get married,' Trilby said tightly.

'May not! If they change their minds. An there ain't no hurry for a girl ta get married, that I can see.'

Trilby shot her mother an irritable look.

Mrs Comeaway was examining the food-safe. 'Ya know, ya might be right bout this safe. E seems to ave broke it up a bit getting it out, clumsy great elephant. Ya think it might do Charlie and Hannie?'

'It stinks. Burn it.'

'I'll take it,' Mrs Comeaway decided. 'I can still *put* things in it. An ya never know.'

Tim and his mate appeared, ploughing their way through the sand.

'There they are,' Mr Comeaway said unnecessarily. 'Tole you they'd come.'

'We ain't half sorted out here yet, Timmie,' Mrs Comeaway said. 'You come right in the nick a time ta help us get these things out an look em over.'

Tim chuckled. 'Reckon I'd a come in the nick a time if I'd left it another week.' He grinned at the recumbent Mr Comeaway.

'Im! Gawd, yes. E ain't much help.' Mrs Comeaway did not even glance at her husband. 'Thing is, we dunno what ta take and what ta leave, eh, Trilby?'

'Ain't seen ya round lately,' Tim ventured to Trilby. 'Whatsa matter? You too busy learnin books down that school?'

Trilby walked back into the humpy without replying. Most of her resentment was directed at Phyllix, but there was enough of it to cover the rest of the boys who had formed part of the group.

'What's bit her?' Tim enquired of her mother.

'Dunno! Gits like that. Doesn't do ta ask questions but. Comes down on ya like a ton a bricks. What ya think a this safe, Timmie? Ya think I should leave it now its legs is broke off?'

'Take anything ya like,' Tim said generously. 'Plenty a room on the back.'

'Ya want me ta give ya a hand?' Mr Comeaway asked anxiously.

'You make im help ya,' Mrs Comeaway said strongly. 'Don't tell me! Ow e gets on down that wharf I dunno. Hides isself behind the stuff, I suppose. Get up there! You get that safe on ya shoulders an be off down that hill. An don't do it no more damage either.'

'I offered,' Mr Comeaway said, with dignity. 'Anyone think I didn't offer.'

Trilby came out with some cups on her fingers. 'No school today?' Tim asked, passing her.

'I'm home to help,' Trilby said coolly.

'Don't ya like swimming no more?' This was from his mate, Albany Bell.

'Just don't get the time,' Trilby said loftily. 'I'm taking my exams end of this year.'

'Whadda ya know well,' Albany grinned, nudging Tim.

'*You* wouldn't know *anything*,' Trilby flared, glaring at him.

'I know some things pretty good,' Albany grinned again. 'You ask Audrena.'

Mrs Comeaway had trundled off down the hill with some things, and Trilby was glad. Perhaps both these boys knew. Perhaps Phyllix had told them.

'Don't see Phyllix no more now, neither,' Tim said casually. 'Think e musta went off ta Meekatharra with a shearin team.'

Trilby felt weak with relief.

Mrs Comeaway returned with Mrs Green in tow. She struck an attitude before the humpy, hands on hips, mouth turned inward. 'You see any sense in it?' she asked of her friend.

'Well I could use it myself, for the overflow like,' Mrs Green said, feeling her way delicately, 'but I think I see what he's getting at.'

'See a damn sight more than I do well,' Mrs Comeaway said sturdily. 'Place like this wouldn't go beggin long. Them Thompsons – got six kids parked under that ole bit of tarp.'

'Mrs Green might not want a lot of kids here,' Trilby interrupted angrily.

'She don't mind kids,' Mrs Comeaway said. 'Don't be silly.'

'I hear they're putting up some more of those little places down the camp,' Mrs Green said gently.

'That's the lot fa this trip,' Albany called, passing them with the table balanced on his head. 'Anyone comin down?'

'What about you comin down?' Mrs Comeaway urged Mrs Green. 'See the house. These boys gotta come back ta pick up the rest a the junk.'

Mrs Green looked pleased. 'You sure there's room for me?'

'Plenty,' Mrs Comeaway said magnificently. 'An there's no need runnin back an changin ya dress. No one's gunna see ya.'

'I'll wait here,' Trilby said coldly.

'Please yaself,' Mrs Comeaway said. The two women went over the sandhill and down to the road.

'Well!' Mrs Comeaway said admiringly. 'We got more stuff than I thought.'

'It ain't too secure,' Tim warned. 'Didn't have enough ropes. You two better sit in front with me an the other two on top a the load ta keep a eye on things. You think ya can climb up there?' he asked Mr Comeaway, grinning.

Mr Comeaway eyed the load. He placed a foot on the running board, steadied himself on a chair and worked his way carefully to the top of the load. Two saucepans, insecurely balanced, crashed noisily to the road.

'Look what ya doin,' Mrs Comeaway said indignantly. 'Them's new from the second-hand shop.' She picked up the saucepans and dusted them off. 'Here, ya better hold em,' she ordered, handing them up to her crouching husband.

Mr Comeaway moved slightly but inadvisedly. The already damaged safe collapsed with gentle cracks and enveloped him.

'E meant ta do that,' Mrs Comeaway said with conviction. 'E had it in is mind ta do that all along.'

Albany leaped with agile grace to restore the threshing limbs.

'Ya wouldn't know *why*,' Mrs Comeaway said sarcastically, pushing Mrs Green ahead of her into the front seat.

'Will it start?' Mrs Green asked, her eyes on the naked engine.

'She got up here,' Tim said. 'You two just hang on while I get er goin. Ignition's on, I think.' He went round to examine the engine.

'Don't blow us allup,' Mrs Comeaway giggled. 'Don't strike no matches around here,' she called to the two at the top of the load.

A car or two passed while Tim worked. The occupants peered curiously, especially at the assorted furniture. The car engine started up with a powerful deep-noted roar and the whole load swayed backward as it jerked off in top gear.

'Always like a hill ta start off on,' Tim grunted contentedly, after he had landed with a crash in the driving seat.

There was another crash from behind. 'Them chairs wasn't tied on proper,' Mr Comeaway yelled.

'Can't stop for em now,' Tim yelled. 'That all right, Mrs Comeaway? Pick em up on the way back.'

'Less they gets run over,' Mrs Comeaway said dubiously. 'Never mind, Timmy. We just gotta take the risk.'

'Hang on up there,' Tim warned as they breasted the second hill and dived down the curving road to the township.

'Take it easy fa Gawd's sake,' Mr Comeaway wailed. 'It ain't safe up ere.'

Mrs Comeaway turned a threatening glare on her husband. 'Shut that big mouth a yours an stop worryin Timmy. E's busy.'

The utility took a corner dangerously wide, and there was a sharp crack at the back. Mrs Comeaway's irritation got the better of her. 'You broke something *else*? What's got inta the man?' she inquired of nobody.

Mr Comeaway, with Albany's help, regained an upright position. He looked as irritable as Mrs Comeaway.

'We'll fix it,' Tim comforted Mrs Comeaway. 'Ya lucky the ole man didn't fall off.'

'Would be just like im,' Mrs Comeaway snapped. 'Right in the middle a movin. Don't you go fallin off now,' she warned her husband.

Mr Comeaway grinned. 'I'm trying hard *not* ta.'

'This here's the house, ain't it?' Tim asked. 'Come on, stop, you ole bastard.' He pumped at the brake, and the utility drew to a reluctant halt, only three houses past the right one.

'Gotta get them brakes relined,' Timmie murmured, leaping out. 'Don't seem ta grip good any more.'

'We're here!' Mrs Green said.

'You men can bring all the stuff in,' Mrs Comeaway directed, 'while me and Mrs Green has a look round.'

They climbed out of the utility and walked up the footpath. Mr Comeaway, slapping his pants, followed them.

'You get back an help them boys,' Mrs Comeaway said sternly, when she was opening the gate. Mr Comeaway went sulkily back.

The two women stood for a while admiring the house. Then they walked up the wooden steps and Mrs Comeaway unlocked the front door. She preceded her friend into the living-room.

'This here's the sink,' she said, walking over to it and running her hand admiringly over its glittering surface. 'It's stainless steel. What ya think a that, eh?'

Mrs Green touched it, also admiring. She turned on the tap over it and there was water. 'That'll save your legs.'

'What ya think a this stove?' Mrs Comeaway asked, leaving the sink for the green enamelled stove that was set midway between the walls. 'Nice an clean, eh? New, that's why.' She pried the iron circles off the top. 'See? Never been used.'

She walked over to the louvres. 'See these here? You want some air you put em like this. It's cold, ya shut em up.'

'Yes, I like these,' Mrs Green said raising and lowering the blades. Her face was full of pleasure.

'Now come out an see the rest,' Mrs Comeaway ordered, again preceding Mrs Green. 'This here's the place where I wash, an there's a tub fa baths. Anyone can have a bath that likes,' she said proudly. 'Get the water hot in the copper.'

Mrs Green amused herself turning on the taps. They all worked. Both women watched in a kind of trance as the water spattered in a strong stream against the cement.

On the other side of the veranda were the bedrooms, two long rooms with a connecting door, louvred on one side.

'And that other door on the front veranda leads to another room,' Mrs Comeaway said. 'Three places ta sleep, not countin the big middle room. We gunna keep that room fa eatin in.'

The men came in and out, piling furniture in the centre of the main room. Mrs Comeaway extricated two chairs and she and Mrs Green sat in them.

'You reckon Trilby'll like it down here?' Mrs Comeaway asked, a little anxious note in her voice.

There was a scuffle at the back door, and both women glanced over. Round the frame of the door appeared the head of a child. It withdrew and another took its place. Mrs Comeaway rose in surprise and the sound of the stifled giggles gave away to the sound of scampering feet.

'Young devils,' she exclaimed, smiling as she again lowered her bulk to the chair.

For a moment, both women watched the door, their faces amused.

The next sound came from the roof. And at the same instant a childish treble of voices called, from a little way off, 'Nigger!'

'They threw a stone,' Mrs Comeaway said slowly. The expression of amusement had faded. Her bulk melted. She looked smaller than she had.

'I think,' Mrs Green said, and her voice was firm, 'I think Trilby will *love* it here in this nice house.'

'What about – that?' Mrs Comeaway said after a while. She waited with a sort of polite interest for Mrs Green's answer.

It was not long in coming.

'I can't see anyone saying that to *her*,' Mrs Green said with composure. 'Not twice.'

CHAPTER 11

Bartie was happy. He liked the new house, and with his freedom restored, his world opened up for him again. At the mission the days had been neatly sectioned off – meal times, school times, bed times, Sunday services – the little patches of leisure time had never lasted long enough for him to lose his feeling of being hurried – of having to get things done quickly or not at all. He had been lucky only in that he had never been bored as most of the others had. The overworked staff had little time for organizing games or any other pleasurable pursuits. The feeling was that the least the children could do in return for all they were getting was to amuse themselves.

Mostly, the children proved ungrateful. Instead of organizing themselves they stood around picking their noses or they crouched over the ground and poked holes in it with a stick, or they gawped and giggled and followed, with their round brown eyes, the perambulating excursions of visiting patrons. But whereas the bored ones had also a sturdy endurance, Bartie was never free of a panicky fear that this state of things would go on for ever.

Sometimes, now that he was home, he would remember the emptiness of the days after Noonah had gone. If it was night-time, he would hold his breath and listen anxiously for the gentle re-assuring snores of his mother and the heavy regular breathing of his father that told him he was back again, part of the warmth of living that make up a family.

Here, every day brought possibilities of joy. Of long expanses of time which he could fill as he wished. Even school could be escaped if he went the right away about it. Just keeping out of the way until it was too late worked most times. With so many people about the house his mother could not be blamed for overlooking one small boy in the morning's sorting out.

At the mission he had slept in one of a long line of beds. Another line faced him from the opposite wall. He preferred the big sagging bed in which he and Stella slept together. It was not even necessary for him to make his bed. Mrs Comeaway might remember to smooth the big grey blankets. More often than not he crept straight into the nest he had made for himself the night before.

At home the state of his teeth and his hair and his finger-nails was a matter which concerned only himself. Noonah, when she had leave from the hospital, might make a laughing, joyful matter of a big steaming-hot bath for him and Stella. Less often, his mother might regret that little use was being made of the fine big tub in the laundry – and do something about it. He might clean his teeth and smooth a little water over his face if Noonah were due home. At other times, only his hands caused him much concern. Dirty hands left marks on the drawing paper with which Noonah kept him plentifully supplied.

There were other things he liked about living at home. The food was different – nicer. Sometimes there was a big plate of fried meat with onion rings festooning its rich brownness. Or he might be handed a twist of newspaper containing crackly fried fish and a handful of crisp chips. There was always spongy new bread to spread thickly with jam and often a whole packet of biscuits sandwiched together with cream. Fruit in tins was not the luxury it had been at the mission; nor was the fizzing drink in bottles. And at home he was allowed to collect the bottles and sell them back to the shop.

Some mornings when he left for school, his mother gave him two whole shillings to buy his lunch with – and that meant the warm steamy interior of Colour Mary's shop with its pyramids of buns and stacks of sandwiches and soup in little bowls and the hot penetrating breath of pies and pasties. For two shillings he could buy a pasty and two buns and a bottle of orangeade. Or six buns and a Coke. and often Colour Mary slipped a banana or an apple into his bag before she handed it to him. She called him her 'good boy'.

All the children knew either from experience or from having been thankfully-innocent bystanders that Colour Mary would not hesitate to come out from behind the counter to the children who were *not* good.

Outside the shop and away from her hearing, some of the children complained resentfully of discrimination and occasionally forced some of the fruits of it from unwilling hands, but there was no other shop near the school, and the township was out of bounds, so Colour Mary's shop continued to be well patronised.

School, with the exception that there were more teachers, was much the same. But there was after-school to look forward to and Bartie rarely went straight home. He went often to the beach at the back of the town. That was his favourite place. He had come upon it by accident one day when he had felt a longing to follow up his thoughts undisturbed. A curling road, following faithfully the curling line of the beach, had enticed him on. He had walked much farther than he had intended.

Bordering the beach was the grey-green salt-bush, and to his left were spreading acres of it – stiff, small, unyielding cushions. A lighthouse, remotely tall, shot from their midst. Beyond the border on his right sparkled the sea, restless, fretting at the reefs, which guarded the shore, surging triumphantly at last to the base of the sandhills that formed a second barricade.

The wind swept round and past him, carrying the tops of the waves that stood in its path, spreading them in a mist over the road and the grey-green salt-bush. It swished sand from the beach and sent the particles flying in a whirlwind dance and they struck against Bartie's face and tried to find his eyes. He licked his lips and tasted salt and he raised his face to the still-hot sun and felt the coldness of the wind rob the rays of their warmth.

He walked on past the lighthouse, slowly, his school-books under his arm. Around the next curve he stopped, a small boy spellbound into stillness. His greedy eyes absorbed the sight before it could vanish.

The sea rolled lazily in from the horizon – the palest clearest lime-green streaked with soft dark sapphire where banks of seaweed floated just beneath the surface. Towards the shore-line two streams slapped lazily together and spilled in transparent green circlets on the clean slope of the beach. Wet seaweed clung to wet rocks, darkly richly red. And nothing Bartie had seen was so free-flowing and graceful as the sandhills that swept through the sea in a long sweeping curve.

Bartie came to this place often. There were days when the water deepened to jade; when the foam cresting the waves matched the snow-white sandhills, and he saw the sandhills when the setting sun touched them to warm, cream, beckoning curves.

There were stormy days, when tossed seaweed turned the whole bay to turquoise, when waves smashed angrily up the steeply-sloping beach and reached with lacy fingers for the purple pigface that grew high beyond their reach. Each time he came, Bartie worshipped.

'Where you been, eh?' Mrs Comeaway would demand sometimes, if Bartie came within her orbit. But she did not stop for an answer, nor would Bartie have given her anything but his wide and secret smile if she had. Yet he loved her for letting him alone and because she laughed with him.

For Bartie, there was something irresistibly appealing yet humorous in the sight of his mother laboriously spelling out some of the words in his school-books. He had a child's sense of achievement in knowing something still hidden from his elders, even though at these times, in some unaccountable way, he felt more love for her welling up into his heart.

'Aaah!' Mrs Comeaway would say, half-vexed, half in amusement. 'Once I knew how to read a little bit. Now no good, eh? An you think you clever, isn't it? More clever than ole Mum?'

Bartie was never deceived by her vexation. He knew she liked it that he could read so much better than she could.

'Read out some for me,' she would demand sometimes, when she found him with his nose in a book. 'Learn ya ole mummy something fa a change.'

Obediently, Bartie would read a few sentences to her, but sooner or later she would stop him, a look of scandalized unbelief on her face.

'You take your mummy for ole fool, eh? You think I believe in this little boy so big only as a thumb-nail? An he got arms an legs an a head still? That book so damn good, only tell lies.'

If Bartie giggled, her suspicion of him would increase. 'You tellin me that all writ down there in that book? Or you jokin? You tell me.'

Bartie, choking with laughter, would roll over and bury his head in his arms, and Mrs Comeaway, giving him up as a bad job, would stand over him with the nearest thing to a scowl she could ever call up on her smooth and shining face. There were times when she doubted the wisdom of education. To her it was cloudy with mystery. Real things that you could see or feel, people, trees, the sun and the rain, good food and the comfortably distended belly that resulted from eating, the miserable gnawing feeling of hunger – all these she understood, they were part of the life she lived. Bartie's primers – the glimpse he gave her of their contents – often there was unease in her spreading breast. Sometimes it was hard to throw off. More often, pleasanter things entered her mind, and she forgot it.

Bartie began to trust his mother. Noonah was at home for only two days in a fortnight. When he had drawn or painted something he felt was good, he needed to test it through another's eyes. He showed his things to Mrs Comeaway and here she was on firmer ground. These things were real and, in gratitude for this quality, she gave them her whole attention, dropping whatever it was she happened to be doing, taking up the drawing or the painting and retiring with it to where the light was better.

'Aaah!' delightedly. 'That sea, eh?' Or 'Nice big tree that is. Pretty, too! You did that good, Bartie.'

Her praise was not discriminating. She liked everything he showed her. Nevertheless, she sent him back to his work with a smile on his lips and warmth in his heart.

There was a day when he ran home from school, jumping the little fence in his hurry. He went straight in to where his mother sat narrowing her eyes against the heat of her tea. He flung skinny arms round her comfortable waist and dug his hard little bullet head into her chest. And Mrs Comeaway's cup of tea went back on the table quickly so that she could throw her protecting arms about her boy.

She waited a while, smoothing his head, then she pushed him away from her. 'You tell me now, eh?'

'The kids blamed me. And it wasn't my fault at all.' Bartie shivered, wrestling to get close to her again. 'I didn't even know she was going to do it.'

'An who did what?' Mrs Comeaway asked patiently.

'It was Trilby,' Bartie said, quieter now. 'I was in the play-yard at lunch-time and she went past and I waved to her and she came over to talk to me a bit. Then, when she was just going out the gate another girl came along, a white one. She was holding her nose and Trilby stopped an started yelling at her. She called the girl a white-faced bitch. An she smacked her across the face, all the time yelling. An then she rushed out.' Bartie's breath sobbed in his throat.

'An what happened then?' Mrs Comeaway asked dully.

'An then a teacher come up, and the white girl's nose was bleeding, and she said she was sneezing and was just trying to stop it by holding her finger against her nose. She said Trilby went and hit her before she knew it.'

'She said Trilby's name?' Mrs Comeaway asked gently. 'She knew who it was?'

'She said "a coloured girl", that's all.'

'An did they do anything to ya?'

'Not the teacher, but the kids. The teacher took this girl away because her nose was still bleeding, and then the other kids started on me an called me a dirty black nigger. None of them liked me any more Mum an I didn't do anything. Even Joe Wheeler that I was playing with, he wouldn't come near me any more.'

Mrs Comeaway's voice was heavy. 'There ain't anything I can do, Bartie. That girl, the one that said about sneezin, she mighta been, or she mighta been holding er nose like some do when they pass ya, some a these cheeky bits a kids.... I dunno! Trilby shouldn't a hit er. She shouldn't a took no notice. That's just somethin they do – Gawd knows why. To make people laugh or something, that's all.'

'Why?' Bartie's expression was confused and beaten. 'Why?'

'I dunno,' Mrs Comeaway said tightly. 'Now what about I get ya a cuppa an we sit ere an drink it up an you don't go back ta school fa today, eh?'

'I'll sit on your lap if you like, Mum.' Bartie said carefully.

Mrs Comeaway's laugh hit the ceiling. But in her eyes was all that Bartie needed to see.

They sat there in the dim cool room a long time. And Mrs Comeaway talked to him. For Bartie, she recalled the days of her own girlhood, when she had been as young and younger than Bartie. She told him how she had ridden on the back of a camel from one sheep or cattle station to the next, with her own father and mother, and how they had carried everything they owned on the backs of their two camels.

They had stopped wherever there was work to be had, staying a week, two weeks, up to a month. And then they would pack up their things and she would take her place behind her mother on the camel called Daisy, who was so lazy she had to be switched often.

'An often enough it was me got a good smack instead a Daisy,' Mrs Comeaway finished feelingly, 'when Mummy didn't get er judgement right.'

One look at Trilby's closed face decided her mother to say nothing of the matter to her. She could understand the grief of a hurt child who ran to her for comfort. She was not brave enough to risk one of Trilby's hurting and puzzling rebuffs.

For her part, Trilby could not have told her mother of the sick dread that stopped her breath and weighted her legs when she walked through the gate to the High School next morning.

She waited throughout the day for a summons to the room of the head teacher. More than once she was reprimanded for not paying attention. And then the head teacher actually came into the room.

Trilby's mind as well as her fingers, froze. She could not look up whilst her own teacher and the head teacher talked together.

Her teacher's voice brought feeling and movement back to her. 'Trilby Comeaway? Please?'

Trilby stood, somehow pushed herself down the aisle towards the front of the classroom.

She could not force herself to hardness. She felt only fear.

Outside the classroom, following the head teacher down the wide echoing passage she felt better. A wind cooled her face and calmed her thoughts. Her head went back and her chin up.

In his study, the head teacher slid into his chair, leaned his elbow on his desk, and looked quizzically up at her as she stood before him.

Then he smiled. 'I brought you in here, Trilby, because I've a word of advice for you.'

Trilby did not return his smile.

'You smacked a girl across the nose yesterday,' the head stated. 'I wanted to tell you that the girl's mother wrote a note to the Primary School headmaster this morning.'

Trilby waited. The thing she had been dreading was happening – and the feeling was much better than the one that had preceded it. She felt able to manage anything in the way of anger or abuse which this man might pile on her.

The head teacher reached for his pipe. 'I think she must be quite an understanding woman,' he said almost casually. 'She wants the thing dropped. She doesn't want anything done about it. No punishment for you . . .,' he looked up under his lashes. 'You think that was a pretty nice gesture for her to make, Trilby?'

'Yes, sir,' Trilby said woodenly, a shade sulkily.

'Okay! Skip off,' the head said briskly, turning himself about to face his desk, beginning at once to riffle through some papers upon it.

Trilby's mouth opened and so did the narrowed grey eyes. She stayed where she was.

'Well!' the head said, looking up again, clear-eyed and polite.

'Yes, sir,' Trilby said gladly.

Only later she was ashamed. Not because of the hurt she had inflicted nor because the girl's mother had acted so generously in the matter, but because this was the way any ignorant coloured girl might behave, to lash out with tongue and hands, to lose control. Never, she vowed, would she let that most despised half of her get the upper hand again.

CHAPTER 12

A termagant wind beat at the glass louvres and scattered fine white sand over every object in the room.

The object upon the wide double bed moaned fretfully and tucked its untidy grey head beneath a prune-coloured arm. The hips moved mountainously, in slow revolt against the dry, devitalised air. Hot it might have been in the little back room of the humpy – but dark and quiet, squealing wind and stinging sand defeated by the windowless walls.

And no loneliness! Ten yards to the liveness and laughter of other people. Big cups of tea, hot sweet and strong. And more tea-leaves in the pot when the first lot was done.

Tea! She could taste the first hot draught of it in her dry mouth, loosening her swollen tongue, washing deliciously down to her waiting stomach.

Mrs Comeaway sighed deeply, remembering her carelessly emptied tea packet and the distance to the nearest shop.

The doorbell rang, and she raised her head in surprise. Too early yet for Bartie and Stella to be home and nobody else played with the bell – not with the front door standing hospitably open to all her friends.

It rang again.

Mrs Comeaway smoothed back her hair with one hand and stumbled stiffly over to the door of her bedroom. Caught unawares, because she had been peering into every corner of the big living-room, Mrs Comeaway's visitor swivelled nervously.

'Them kids,' Mrs Comeaway thought swiftly. 'She's seen them kids swingin on her fence an pullin up her flowers.'

'You're Mrs Comeaway, aren't you?' the woman asked, whilst Mrs Comeaway took mild note of the fact that the eyes and the mouth of this woman showed quite different expressions.

'Yeah! An if I've tole them kids once I've tole em a dozen times,' she rushed to defend herself. 'I knew you could see em out your window. I'll get to em the minute they get home fum school and I'll

say you been in here an gunna get the pleece to em if they don't
stop.' She stopped herself mainly from lack of breath.

'Get the – oh! Yes, I did see the children but never mind about
that now.' The visitor stopped to compose a suitable expression.
'Mrs Comeaway, I've come to welcome you to our little community.
As a member of my church! I thought perhaps we could have a cup
of tea together and get acquainted. We ladies of the Guild hope and
believe that if we – if you – I mean . . .,' her voice trailed away. She
searched for simpler words which might convey her meaning more
surely.

'I knew you was in a stink about em,' Mrs Comeaway apologized. 'Specially that big pink one. But ya know what kids is. Don't
take no notice however I yell at em. When they know you been over
they might do different.'

'Don't you worry your head about a few flowers.' A little irrita-
bility here because of these flowers which would keep complicating
things. 'I'm sure the children didn't realize – anyhow, as I was
saying, I thought it might be nice if we. . . .'

'You mean you wasn't in a stink after all?'

'Not the least little bit. Now, what about . . .?'

'That's all right then well,' Mrs Comeaway said happily.

'I made some hot scones on purpose,' the visitor said with a tiny
quiver in her voice. She banished the quiver. 'The tea's all ready
too. You will come, I hope.'

Mrs Comeaway's happiness shattered. She looked down at her
feet, and they were bare. From her own feet she shifted her glance
to her visitor's feet, shod neatly in black shining leather. There
was something intimidating about the way those feet stood there,
planted so firmly on the wood of the veranda.

'I should go in there –?' Mrs Comeaway's eyes turned fearfully
on her neighbour's house, noting the open door and the speckless
highly-polished boards of the veranda, the daunting neatness of
green lawns and bright flower-beds.

An indulgent smile. Mrs Henwood recovering herself completely.
'Of course!'

'Comb me hair. Put me shoes on. Been having a lay down. I
dunno! Didn't bother bout gettin dressed proper yet like.'

'That's all right!' Mrs Henwood said inexorably. 'I'll wait here
for you.'

Mrs Comeaway moved back into a bedroom that seemed even
less of a sanctuary than before.

*   *   *

'Now just don't bother about that,' Mrs Henwood said, just past the doorway of her house. 'My fault! I had no business putting a vase on that table. Come right through here to the kitchen and sit down and I'll get a cloth and mop up that water. Won't take me a jiffy.'

Mrs Comeaway moved with slow caution into the kitchen. As a butterfly alighting on a flower, she lowered herself on to a chair, sat with her body forward, her hands interlaced, her black patent courts pressed primly together. There was a tiny red pot of geraniums on the window-sill behind her. Oppressively close. She could feel its impact between her shoulders. She rose and inched her chair away from the danger zone.

Mrs Henwood came back, a little flustered. 'And now we can have our tea, can't we?'

Mrs Comeaway allowed herself one brief and comprehensive look at her surroundings. Everything was pretty. Bright colours everywhere. Shining things. White cups and plates on a checked tablecloth. Her hostess handed to her a plate with a tiny red check handkerchief on it. And here was bewilderment.

'What's this ever?'

Mrs Henwood laughed gently. 'That's a serviette. A little napkin. For you to wipe your hands on.'

Mrs Comeaway shook out the square of material and wiped her fingers carefully, one after the other. When she had finished she crushed the material nervously, got rid of it into her pocket.

The tea was hot and strong, the way she liked it, but the cup was small and held about two good swallows. She sat with it in her lap while the woman nattered. How she liked living down here in the Wild-Oat Patch. How Mrs Comeaway would like it – after she got used to everything. How much nicer it was than those terrible camps at the back of the town.

'And you'll find very little *colour* prejudice,' Mrs Henwood said gravely. '*You*, Mrs Comeaway, can help stamp it out where it *does* exist.' Her eyes held Mrs Comeaway's. Mrs Comeaway tried to remember what they reminded her of.

She knew damn well she'd seen eyes like that somewhere or other.

'We all of us realize,' Mrs Henwood continued, still grave and solemn, 'that you have a lot to learn about our white way of life and that you probably need help. We are prepared to *give* you that help, Mrs Comeaway.'

'Yeah!' Mrs Comeaway said, her thoughts on the woollen-covered teapot.

'Let me fill your cup. And please, do try one of my scones.'

After that it was better for a while. They were very good scones. Mrs Comeaway enjoyed them.

'Tell me,' Mrs Henwood settled back. 'What was your life like up there in those camps?'

'Awright!'

'No, but –,' Mrs Henwood coaxed delicately, 'do tell me. I've often wondered what really happens in those places.' She leaned forward, eyes bright and still.

'Galahs!' Mrs Comeaway thought. 'They got eyes like that.' Aloud she said, 'Didn't have so much damn wind, that's one thing certain.'

'Oh!' It was snipped off, as though she had used scissors. Mrs Comeaway rattled her tea cup in its saucer, not very much.

'There are *some* people around here,' Mrs Henwood said with relish as she poured more tea, 'who might just give you trouble.'

'Had enough a that,' Mrs Comeaway said stolidly, as she might have refused another scone, if there had been another scone.

Mrs Henwood softened. 'If you've had experience of this type of thing, I only hope you have not let it harden you, Mrs Comeaway. You must not let yourself get bitter. Though nobody could blame you. Nobody!'

The moisture in the round hard eyes disturbed Mrs Comeaway momentarily, then Mrs Henwood blinked rapidly and the moisture was gone.

'Drunk that tea down too quick,' Mrs Comeaway guessed, relieved.

She began on the cake, just to be polite, though she felt uncomfortably full already. And when the cakes were finished she sat, comatose and languid, waiting for them to digest.

'Just to start you off,' Mrs Henwood said later, 'I have a little creeper in a pot. And I'm sure my husband would take cuttings for you if you wanted them. Shall I ask him?'

'Yeah!' Mrs Comeaway said obligingly. It was a word she had said a good many times that afternoon.

'I'll just run down and get your little pot now,' Mrs Henwood said excitedly. 'You sit here and wait. I won't be long.'

Mrs Comeaway waited obediently. Mrs Henwood pattered down the back steps. Mrs Comeaway reflected that now would have been a good time to slip a few cakes into her pocket for Stella, if she had only foreseen the opportunity and left some of the cakes.

'There!' Mrs Henwood said, thrusting a small pot into Mrs Comeaway's hands.

Mrs Comeaway examined her plant. She thought it was a funny-looking plant and a bit withered.

'It's a sweet thing, isn't it? Mrs Henwood encouraged.

'Yeah!' Mrs Comeaway said, taking another look at the pale-green tendrils dripping over the side of the pot. She wondered uneasily if Mrs Henwood really meant her to keep it. Should she hand it back? She made a motion with the pot.

'No, you can keep it,' Mrs Henwood said gaily. 'You go home and pick out a good spot for it. I'll walk to the gate with you, shall I?'

Mrs Comeaway brightened, like a child hearing the school bell. The two women walked down the front steps and along the little green cement path to the front gate. Leaning on it, Mrs Henwood said, 'As Kipling says, Mrs Comeaway, we are sisters under the skin.'

Mrs Comeaway was knocked clean off her pins. She stood there, grappling silently, and everything else Mrs Henwood said floated right past her.

She walked three or four steps in the direction of her own front gate before the first question resolved itself. She stopped. 'Eh? she called to her neighbour, 'You come fum up Mullewa?'

Mrs Henwood, who had not heard the question, nodded pleasantly. After a moment, Mrs Comeaway went on.

Bartie and Stella had arrived home from school. They had dragged a chair over to the safe and they were searching for something to eat.

'Gee, I'm hungry, Mummy,' Stella wailed.

Mrs Comeaway stood in the doorway, smiling with relief, well content to be back in her own home. She went over to the safe and reached into it for the bread and the tin of jam.

'What ya got in ya pocket, Mum?' Stella asked, pulling out the little red-checked square. 'Can I have it for my doll?'

Mrs Comeaway looked at the square without interest. 'Ave it if ya like. Do for a shawl, eh?'

She spread two thick pieces of bread with jam and, as she spread, a second question posed itself in her mind. She dismissed it impatiently. 'Never even *met* the bloke, far's I know.'

'Whose pot plant?' Trilby asked later.

Mrs Comeaway frowned. 'Her next door,' she said reluctantly. 'Comin over ta plant it too, so she says.'

'You mean she just came over here and gave you this plant?' Trilby was surprised.

'She didn't give it to me over here. She gave it to me over there,' Mrs Comeaway nodded in the direction of her neighbour's house.

'Did you go over there?'

'I didn't *go* over there,' Mrs Comeaway said coldly. 'I was took. She come over an took me.'

'What for, Mum?'

'She just come over here an arst me to go over there an have a cuppa tea with er,' Mrs Comeaway said, irritably for her. 'Don't ask me why, because I dunno why.'

'Afternoon tea, that was,' Trilby pronounced. 'She asked you over for afternoon tea. Don't you even know that? Up at the mission we used to have lots of people coming to visit us and have afternoon tea.'

'No need ta carry on,' Mrs Comeaway said. 'Course I know bout afternoon tea. Didn't think they done it in places like this but.'

'Is she nice?'

'Er? All right!'

'That's her husband, that runs the garage up in town,' Trilby said. 'I bet her house is nice inside. What's it like?'

'Ad a damn fool table just inside er front door,' Mrs Comeaway remembered indignantly. 'Right bang inside er front door waiting for people ta trip theirselves up on it an might be get a leg broke.'

'Mum you didn't knock her table over, did you?' Trilby asked, shocked.

'I didn't arst ta go over, did I? An what if I did? Shouldn'ta had that mat there. Serve er right, ask me.'

'Gee, I bet she was mad,' Trilby said gloomily. 'Why couldn't you be more careful? Now she'll never have you over again, most likely.'

'An a good thing too,' Mrs Comeaway's retort had spirit in it. 'Ya wrong fa once but. She behaved the way she should, puttin mats round fa people ta slip up on.'

'What did you do after you tripped over the mat?'

Mrs Comeaway did not like that. It made her sound like a clumsy fool. 'I ad me tea an come ome,' she said shortly.

'Come on, Mummy, tell me some more. How did her house look?' Trilby sat on the kitchen table and swung her legs. When her face was alive, as it was now, there were no doubts about her beauty. Mrs Comeaway thawed under the sweet conciliation in the long grey eyes.

'She ad another little pot a flowers on er winder-sill, an she ad a check cloth on er table, an before she gave me me tea she made me wipe me hands on some bit of a hanky. Anyone think I didn't wash meself proper.'

'That was a serviette,' Trilby frowned. 'Are you sure she said you had to wipe your hands on it before you could have your tea? Like her damn cheek if she did.'

'If ya don't believe me ya can have a look an see where I wiped em,' Mrs Comeaway said stoutly. 'Stella, just gimme that little bit of a hanky I givé ya. Let Trilby look at it an ya can ave it straight back.'

'Mum, you didn't bring it home,' Trilby said on a great wail. She rushed at Stella and grabbed the napkin from her. She held the piece of material up before her. 'You'll just have to pretend you forgot about it,' she said at last. 'I'll take it back and tell her you put it in your pocket by accident. She'll think you don't know *anything*, Mum.'

'What's all the carryin on about?' Mrs Comeaway asked, mightily surprised. 'She gave it to me didn't she? Same as she gave me that pot over there. An ya wrong bout it bein a serve yet. I ironed enough a them damn things in me time. Ya got things all mixed up.'

'She *lent* you this *serviette*,' Trilby said passionately. 'There's little ones as well as big ones. And you don't wipe your hands on it before you have your tea. You wipe your hands on it *after*, and even then you only pretend to. If you want to know how people do it, they just pretend to mop up their mouths and then they crush it up a bit – not hard like you did –and then they put it back on their plate. That's so it can be folded up again and put back in the drawer. Except you don't do that till everyone's gone. What you're supposed to do, you're supposed to wash it after every time it's used but if people only crush it up a little bit you don't have to. What's the use of talking to you though?' she finished scornfully. 'You just don't understand.'

'Seems a lot a fuss ta make bout a bit of a hanky,' Mrs Comeaway said, resignedly. 'All right! Take it back. I'm sure I don't want nothin I'm not supposed ta have. Take it back now if ya like.'

Stella's round brown eyes filled with tears. 'You said I could have it for my doll.'

'You can't then,' Trilby snapped. 'I'm going to take it back straightaway.'

'Let er have it, let er have it,' Mrs Comeaway soothed. 'I'll find somethin else for ya. You just come in the bedroom an I'll hunt somethin up.'

'Ole horrible thing,' Stella whimpered. 'I hate Trilby, Mummy.'
Trilby made a sound of disgust.

At the back of the house Bartie sat with his back against the
veranda post. One hand smoothed the stiff red coat of a sprawling
cat. The other held a beginner's book on water-colour painting. But
the angry voices that came from inside the house kept tearing at the
edges of his concentration, forcing him to spell out a sentence two
or three times before he got the sense of it.

He felt no urge to investigate. Rows like this one could catch a
boy up if he so much as put his head inside the door to see what it
was all about. Better by far to push the cat aside and get out of
range. Behind the patch of low-growing wattles at the end of the
yard he would be out of sight, and the back fence was as good a
place to lean against as the veranda post.

He gathered up his things and retreated quietly. At the bottom of
the yard he sat down again and opened his book. Red Cat, who had
followed him, stepped daintily round the wattles, her nose twitching nerviously, her pale-green eyes perturbed. Already reading,
Bartie raised his hand, palm flattened. Patiently, he waited for her
to push her head beneath it. But first she must satisfy herself that
no danger lurked. Stiff, straight, watchful, she stood at his side, her
tail twitching gently. In a little while she relaxed her tautness,
poured herself out upon the ground like a pool of honey. Her wide-
open eyes slept as his hand began its rhythmic soothing.

At this distance from the house the voices blended into a background of other noises – car engines, the hard sound of iron-shod
wheels and hooves, a mowing machine and overlaying all that the
lazy buzz of flies round Mrs Comeaway's uncovered refuse bin.

Bartie read steadily on. Here and there he came across some
fragment of knowledge which was already his and the excitement of
recognition was almost too great to be borne. Then, both hands
were needed to hold the book and the cat must wake and wait with
regal displeasure for the caressing to begin again.

Until now Bartie's preoccupation had been colour – the velvety
softness of petals, the luminous grey pearl of the little sandy-cows
with their delicate black tracery of legs, the rainbow sparkles in a
handful of sand, even the ruby sheen on the back of a cockroach.
And there was the mystery of what made Trilby's eyes so brilliant
and Noonah's so soft. The world was full of colour, and you could
not rest until you had tried to capture some of them. For the deep
glow of Trilby's skin he had mixed purple and sienna and yellow

and the result had been dull and lifeless, not the tender lustre he had aimed at.

His teacher, Miss Simmins, had found some of his attempts inside the cover of an exercise book.

'But what do they represent?' she had inquired.

'You see that?' Bartie had pointed out, shyly. For once, he knew he had come near to success; had almost captured the glowing gold that burned on the edges of the clouds for one long and lovely minute after the sun sank into the sea.

'Yes!' Miss Simmins had said thoughtfully, after he had explained. 'Yes!'

It had been strange, Bartie remembered, to see this lively little woman so lost in thought.

She had not let the matter rest there. After school she had beckoned him and questioned him further. Her bright brown eyes had held his steadily, and her questioning had cut through to his innermost desires and thoughts. She had tried to explain form to him – and to tell him that this way of life would be hard, especially for him. Already Bartie had forgotten most of what she had told him. The words had been too big and strange for him to hold in his memory. But he wanted passionately to please her. Miss Simmins was not young, nor even very pretty. She did her soft greying black hair in a funny old-fashioned way, loose about her head and confined in a tiny bun near the top of it. But her voice fell pleasantly on his ears, and her words were strong words which lifted him from his dreams and set him face to face with facts.

There had been other men like himself, who had succeeded. Among them one called Albert Namatjira, who had painted the Australian bush and the rocky outcrops and the trembling blue of the skies, and people had paid him much money. But he had had to work hard at his painting.

Bartie smiled. Work? How could anyone call this work when it was the reason he woke each morning.

CHAPTER 13

Trilby and Noonah sat, each on her own bed, and looked at the heap of clothes on the end of Trilby's bed. They were part of a great heap with which Trilby had staggered back from Mrs Henwood's house, after her visit to return the 'hanky'.

Trilby was annoyed. 'You should have seen her,' she told Noonah. 'The more I kept saying "No", the more things she kept pulling out of her wardrobe and throwing over my arm. She said she'd had them hanging there for years and she never wore them because some were too tight and some she didn't like any more. I don't know why I took them. If I'd had any sense I'd have chucked them straight back at her.'

'Some of them will look nice on you, Trilby, if you pull them in a bit at the waist.' Noonah got up to examine a blue-flowered summer frock with a gathered skirt.

'The stink,' Trilby scorned, giving the dress in question the merest glance. 'And talk about pleased with herself. The more she threw at me the more pleased she got. Grinning all over her face.'

'You could wash them,' Noonah said. 'They'd be as good as new, some of them.'

'Wear her frocks?' Trilby frowned. 'Catch me! D'you know what I'm going to do with them? I'm going to give em away to anyone who wants them. That Carter woman, the dirty old one who looks as if she sleeps under a bush. She can have some, and Blanchie and Audrena can have the rest.' She propped herself up on her bed. 'And I wish,' she said viciously, 'I could see that old dame's face when she sees someone else wearing her dirty smelly old dresses.'

'I don't see why you want to do that.' Noonah stopped her inspection to gaze in perplexity at her younger sister.

'Because she's got a nerve, that's why,' Trilby burst out. 'You think *she'd* wear someone else's clothing? Course she wouldn't. New ones for her. So why give the things to me? I'll tell you why. Because she thinks someone like me should be grateful. See?'

'Gee, your mind works a funny way,' Noonah said wonderingly. 'I thought it was real nice of her.'

Trilby flounced into a sitting position. 'I've had enough of other people's clothes,' she said angrily. 'Up at the mission. And I'm never, never going to wear anything that isn't new from now on. Even if I have only one dress it's going to be new, bought for me, and nobody else worn it before.' She cast a look of loathing at the frocks on the end of her bed. 'Look there under the arms. Making them stink just like she does. D'you think I'm going to have her sweaty armholes touching me?' She kicked the clothes on to the floor. 'And the ones I don't give away,' she said violently, 'I'm going to tear up and use washing the floor.'

'Trilby,' Noonah said disapprovingly.

Trilby turned her scorn on her sister. 'You're just a fool, Noonah. And you always will be. Didn't I say how pleased she was to be giving them to me?'

'What's that got to do with it?'

'You can't see?' Trilby was yelling with rage. 'It made her feel big, that's what. She wasn't giving something to me. She was giving something to herself. Oh!' Full of unbearable irritation, Trilby sprang off the bed, kicked once more at the clothes, and flung herself out of the room, slamming the door shut with a crack like thunder.

'What's the matter with you?' Mrs Comeaway said mildly. She had squeezed herself into one of the garments that had been given to Trilby – a shabby faded blue cotton cardigan with most of the buttons missing. The sleeves moulded her massive arms into sausages and her bosom sprang, unchecked, from the gaping front.

'You're going to wear that cardigan,' Trilby half-questioned, half-stated, breathing hard through dilated nostrils. 'I might have known it.' She stood with her hands on her hips. 'Encouraging them.'

'Now what?' asked the harassed Mrs Comeaway, 'Encourage who?'

'People like that, to give us their old cast-offs,' Trilby spat out.

'Ya want er ta give us er new ones?' Mrs Comeaway commented reasonably. 'I like this coat. Got nice big pockets. An you know I like a big pocket ta hold me money in when I ave a gamble.' She chuckled. 'When I *got* any money.'

'Ah, you make me sick,' Trilby said disgustedly.

'Ere, you shut ya guts,' Mrs Comeaway said, injured. 'Wasn't even me took em. Ya brought em back ya own self.'

'I didn't intend to *wear* them.'

'What, well! Eat em?'

'I was going to.... Oh, what's the use of explaining to anyone. You never understand anything. I don't know how you can *be* like you are. If someone came up and asked you to lie down in the mud so they could walk over you, would you do that too?'

Mrs Comeaway, brow ridged, clutched for understanding. 'I ain't never laid down in no mud yet, an just you stop that shriekin at me, my girl, or I'll stop it for ya.' She advanced threateningly.

Noonah appeared in the doorway. 'Trilby, stop it!'

'You *won't* wear them, I'll see to that,' Trilby cried wildly. She snatched at the clothes on the table and ran into the other bedroom, where she scrabbled at the clothes on the floor and heaped them over her arm.

Noonah and her mother followed, to be thrust aside as Trilby passed them on her way out again. Mrs Comeaway received a sharp elbow in the softest and most pliable part of her anatomy which caused her to clutch and gasp.

'What's she gunna do now?' she muttered as she moved in her daughter's furious wake.

Trilby fled down the back steps and across to the rubbish bin. She thrust all the clothes deep down into the mess that was already there, then she raced back into the house again. Mrs Comeaway, having been shoved once, made haste to flatten herself against the railing, and in a flash, Trilby was back carrying a bottle of kerosene and a box of matches.

She threw kerosene on to the clothes and started striking matches. But she was clumsy in her hurry, and at least half a dozen matches broke off in her hand before she succeeded in lighting one. In that time, Mrs Comeaway had come alive to her daughter's purpose, had crossed the yard in a couple of bounds, and had reached one hand into the rubbish bin to rescue some of the clothes. The match ignited the kerosene at the exact moment that Mrs Comeaway's hand disappeared into the soft materials. There was a roar of flame and Mrs Comeaway leapt back from the conflagration with a shriek of pain that could have been heard half-way up the street. Her yowl continued even after Noonah, who had come to the rescue, had assured her that the cotton sleeve had saved her arm and that her hand was only slightly scorched.

Trilby watched her mother, narrow-eyed and tight-lipped, not even moving to examine the burn. With Noonah's arm round her waist as far as it would go, the upset woman moaned her way across to the steps.

Just as they reached the bottom step, while the fire in the bin was burning fiercely, a head appeared over the dividing fence. 'What's the matter over here?' Mrs Henwood called urgently.

'Burnt all the clothes ya give er,' Mrs Comeaway said dramatically. 'An tried ta burn me up as well, er own mummy. Me hand woulda went easy.'

'Mummy,' Noonah whispered distressfully. 'Come inside, quick.'

Mrs Comeaway turned one more shocked look on Trilby, began moaning afresh and, with Noonah supporting her, ascended the steps.

'An that'll show you what I think of your rotten old frocks,' Trilby said harshly to the face at the fence.

The face, scarlet and bulging-eyed, disappeared. After a while, when the flames had died down, Trilby went too.

'I spose ya wouldn't ave a bit a money in ya bag would ya, Noonah?' Mrs Comeaway said delicately. 'Ya father doesn't seem ta be getting much work down that wharf lately.'

She was sitting at the kitchen table drinking tea which Noonah had made for her. Her scorched hand was bandaged neatly and it lay in prominence before her on the table.

'You can have all I've got,' Noonah said cheerfully. 'But I don't think it's much. I had to buy some more stuff for Bartie, and then there was a kid in the children's Ward – he's pretty sick – and I saw these little koala bears in a window so I bought two. You go an look in Trilby's room, Stella, and see what's there.'

With the exception of Trilby, who was reading comics in a corner, the whole family followed Stella as she ran, shrieking with excitement, into the girls' bedroom.

'Ain't that nice now?' Mrs Comeaway smiled.

'Gee, it's soft, isn't it?' Bartie admired.

'It's mine,' Stella said importantly. 'Noonah bought it for me, didn't you, Noonah?'

'See how much ya got, will ya, Noonah?' Mrs Comeaway said casually.

Noonah took some money from her bag and handed it to her mother. 'That enough, Mummy?'

'Hafta be, won't it?'

'I mean I can give you ten shillings more if you really want it.'

'This'll do,' Mrs Comeaway said comfortably. 'Now you come ere Bartie an find me one a them pencils an I'll just write down a couple things I want.'

'Can I have a Coke?' Stella whined. 'An a packet of chewy, Mummy?'

'I spose.'

Slowly and laboriously, in a heavy childish hand, Mrs Comeaway wrote out a list. Trilby came over to read it. She laughed. 'Gee, just look at the spelling, will you? I'll get it, if you let me get those white beads I want.'

'Ya don't deserve nothing,' Mrs Comeaway said strongly. 'Burning me hand like that.'

'I'm sorry I burnt your hand. I told you. But I'm not a bit sorry I burnt those clothes,' Trilby said impetuously. 'I *couldn't* keep them, Mummy. Don't you understand that?'

Mrs Comeaway gave up. 'Jus the same ya did a foolish thing there. If ya didn't want em yaself, I coulda got a pound or two for em. Why didn't ya think a that?'

Trilby looked helplessly at Noonah, then shook her head and laughed. 'Let me get the beads and we'll be even,' she teased.

'Get em. Get em,' Mrs Comeaway said with an ineffectual flap of her hands. 'Won't get no peace till ya do, I spose.'

'We're coming too,' Stella told Trilby threateningly. 'Me an Bartie's getting Cokes.'

Noonah laughed and sat down at the table. 'Wait till they go and we'll have another cup of tea, Mummy.'

'Does Trilby like school?' she asked her mother, when the trio had gone.

'It's a nice big school, ain't it?' her mother said. 'Never said she *didn't* like it. She's a hard one ta understand though, Noonah. Don't tell me!' She rolled up her eyes.

'Praps she hasn't settled down yet,' Noonah pacified. 'She seems a bit jumpy.'

'A bit jumpy,' Mrs Comeaway said, heavily ironical. 'More'n a bit, ask me.'

Mr Comeaway came through the back door smelling strongly of shaving soap. His thick black hair was slicked wetly back and his shirt was clean. When Noonah was home, he always shaved.

'One thing, ya got a good excuse fa not doin ya work,' he chuckled, eyeing the white-bandaged hand. 'Ya think it'll be all right, Noonah? Won't need ta get it cut off?'

Noonah smiled affectionately at him. Mrs Comeaway tucked a ten-shilling note into an old tobacco-tin and placed it on a shelf behind some plates. 'An don't you think ya gunna get that,' she warned her husband.

'What I want with ya ole money?' Mr Comeaway said offendedly. 'Keep it, all I care.'

'Tea!' Noonah said firmly.

'What's been happening?' she said, when the three of them were drinking their tea.

'Them Berrings in trouble again, that's one thing,' Mr Comeaway said.

'Yeah!' Mrs Comeaway chuckled, 'I think they musta been pinchin people's chooks an ducks, fum what I hear. Now them white people's worryin the guvmint ta make em go back further yet. They been moved back once already, few years ago, so's them white ones can build there houses out there, but now they're up to em, an they wanta build more houses. That's what they say. Ask me, I think the chooks an things done it. An them carryin on night-times, yellin and kicking up rows.'

'Wasn't one thing it'd be another,' Mr Comeaway said philosophically. 'Them Berrings is in bad everywhere. Always was. Always will be.'

'Got their rights, too. Think they a cut above us peoples,' Mrs Comeaway added. 'Funny, ain't it?'

'Don't see much of em, them livin out the opposite way,' Mr Comeaway said thoughtfully, 'but the things ya hear ya gotta laugh. Cheeky devils. Hardly a time one of em ain't in jail. An got enough kids between em ta fill a mission on their own. One thing but. They stick together. An they reckon they ain't gunna shift back no more'n what they have. I reckon them white people'd been better off buildin their houses way from there.'

'What's been happening up that hospital,' Mrs Comeaway asked Noonah.

The Comeaways liked to know about the hospital. Especially Mr Comeaway, who liked, in turn, to talk about it with Horace. Yet none of the tales Noonah told them ever quite convinced him that she was not speaking about quite different people from those that were familiar to him: gangling Dr Graham, who had trouble fitting his long legs into his tiny black car; frowning impatient Dr Bentley, who had once stabbed him with a needle before he properly knew what it was all about; stately pigeon-toed Mr Meagher, who looked at people over the tops of his spectacles, more as if they were a lot of ants rather than people. They bore the same names, yes, but this lot that Noonah talked about acted like ordinary human beings, and ordinary human beings was one thing Mr Comeaway knew they were not.

He followed attentively when Noonah chattered hospital lore, and rolled T.P.R.'s and four hourly backs round on his tongue for the sheer pleasure of knowing what these things meant.

He had been in hospital once himself, afraid to move for fear of creasing his bedcover, asking for bed-pans only when discomfort became greater than the embarrassment he felt at using them.

'The old ones, they like a lot of fuss made of them,' Noonah smiled. 'One old chap first chucks his pillows out of bed, then he falls on them just so we'll all come running. Makes sure he doesn't hurt himself but.

'And some like to help. They get sick of staying in bed and they're glad to be doing something. Last week I gave a man a tray of dirty crockery to put in the service hatch, and instead of waiting for it to come up he just dropped them – crash! I was near enough, so I heard a voice come up the chute, "Jesus, who the hell did that?"'

The Comeaways roared with laughter.

A sudden thought struck Noonah, 'Mummy, the sister-in-charge told me some coloured mothers won't call for their children when they're well again. The hospital sends them a letter to tell them to pick their children up and they just don't come, some of them. Why?'

Mrs Comeaway sat stolidly on her chair, not answering for a moment. At length she moved restlessly. 'Look, Noonah. S'pose ya got no place ta bring that kid back and ya know it needs somewhere decent. Better for it ta stay in the hospital, ain't it? No good bringin it back somewhere it's gunna get sick again, isn't it?'

'Someone should *do* something,' Noonah said pitifully, not quite knowing what. 'Why do they let their children get things like enteritis and burns and malnutrition even?'

Mrs Comeaway pricked up her ears. 'That thing! That nutrition! I know bout that. Had some woman on me back one time when young Stella was a baby. You give em plenty a good tucker, I tole er, an never mind bout all this nutrition.' She sniffed. 'An I was right, seems. The damn thing's puttin kids in hospital now.'

Noonah spluttered, 'Malnutrition, Mummy.'

'That's somethin quite different see?' added Mr Comeaway, taking the cue from his daughter.

'Nobody's gunna tell me that little Tommy's got what you said,' Mrs Comeaway said doggedly. 'I seen im with me own eyes put away enough tucker ta stuff a elephant. Coupla packets a biscuits, jam slapped a inch thick on is bread – yet that's what they say e got all right. An been in an out that hospital three or four times now.'

'Gutsache, that's what,' Mr Comeaway grinned before Noonah could speak.

'They do say you have to have protein as well,' she got in when the two had stopped laughing. 'And vitamins, too.'

'Yes, ya ole fool,' Mr Comeaway teased his wife.

'I like ta know who *you* callin ole fool,' Mrs Comeaway said, half rising from her chair. 'An if ya think I'm gunna start feedin ya all them things Noonah says, ya make a big mistake.'

'But . . .,' Noonah said, laughing.

Mr Comeaway held up one hand. 'Let er go,' he said peaceably. 'I managed this long on the stuff she slaps together. I dessay I can go it a bit longer.'

'Ere's ole Skippy,' Mrs Comeaway said, looking over their heads. 'Just look at im, will ya?'

'Think it was a walkin heap a clothes,' Mr Comeaway guffawed, 'if ya didn't know ole Skippy was inside of em.' He got up and walked to the doorway. 'Someone tole me e was in hospital one time an they discharged im as being a uncurable. Been uncurable ever since an likely ta see the lot of us out, ask me.'

Noonah joined her father, watching the old man affectionately. All his clothes looked too big for him. His boots clopped loosely on the pavement, his trouser legs, even though folded over and over at the bottoms, still concertinaed round his boots, and the sleeves of his coat obscured his hands. Like the rest of his clothes, his hat, a wide-brimmed felt, was too big for his shrunken head, and at this moment it was sideways on. Every now and then Skippy gave it an impatient jab and it did a little jig on his head before sliding down again over his forehead.

He stopped inside the gate and looked towards the veranda. His dim old eyes peered anxiously from beneath the brim of his hat and his black cavity of a mouth hung open. He looked like an old prehistoric bird. His face brightened when he saw Noonah standing with her father. Noonah was kind to him, and gentle. He liked her.

'You've come down at last,' Noonah said, as she helped him up the steps.

'Gettin a house meself soon,' Skippy cackled. 'I come down ta see what this one like.' He fixed her with a stern eye. 'Ya got ya water on yet?'

'Water?' Noonah said, puzzled.

Mrs Comeaway laughed. 'I know what e means,' she told Noonah. 'Now fa Gawd's sake get im inside an let im sit down. Poor old bugger must be wore out traipsin down here.'

'Like a mug?' Mr Comeaway said loudly, waving a cup in front of the old man's face.

Skippy refused to be seated. Instead he rolled across to the sink. 'Let im go,' he commanded, looking at the tap.

Mrs Comeaway smiled into Noonah's mystified face. She gave

the tap a twist and let the water stream down into the sink. 'Hunhh!' Skippy grunted, and rolled back to his chair. For a while he just sat, recovering the breath he had lost in his climb up the steps.

'What's that about the water, Mummy?' Noonah whispered.

'Some of is pals, up the road a bit. They get theirselves a house, an because they was in such a hurry ta move in the water didn't get put on till a while after. Skippy was stayin with em, see? An nobody couldn't make im understand that that water was comin just as soon as the waterworks people got around to it. You know what I tell ya bout him thinkin the pleece do everything. So what he does, he takes his pension book up ta the station an throws it down on the counter an roars that the pleece can keep their damn pension if they ain't gunna put water on his lations' house. Went ta town on em, e did, an the pleece no more able ta make im understand they got nothin ta do with it than the Mungos ad been.'

Noonah laughed and sent a compassionate look at Skippy. 'So what happened then?'

Mrs Comeaway's bulk was shaking. 'The water gets put on the very next day. Don't ask me if the pleece done something bout it because I dunno. An don't try ta tell ole Skippy they didn't, either. E thinks that water got put on because he ticked off them pleecemen.'

'And what about his pension book?'

'Ah, they made im take it back. Gawd, that little ole bastard.' Mrs Comeaway looked admiringly at Skippy. 'Makin everyone crawl to im. Dried up little runt like im.'

'Ya hear?' Skippy asked Mr Comeaway. 'I tell ya I gunna get me place. I been arstin fa this ouse long time now. Long time. Now I get im.'

'Where's e gunna be built?' Mr Comeaway roared.

'I gotta place,' the old man tittered. 'Gettin old now. Time I go back, eh? I borned up there, ya know that? Now I go back. An my friend e build me ouse.'

'Who's his friend?' Noonah asked in an undertone.

'That's the partment man,' Mrs Comeaway said. 'No wonder e's buildin im a house. Glad to get rid a the ole bastard I s'pose.'

'Im friend,' Skippy said indignantly. 'My friend.'

'There y'are,' Mrs Comeaway said, amused. 'One minute deaf as a post. Next minute bitin ya head off cause ya said somethin e don't oughta heard.'

'Give im a cuppa tea,' Mr Comeaway said. 'Settle im down.'

'Hope e's got it right,' Mrs Comeaway said dubiously. 'Don't e

come from up the Kimberleys? Seems funny ta me, sendin someone
up all that way ta build im a house.'

Skippy mumbled happily over his tea. 'Git pretty colour on *my*
floor now.'

Mr Comeaway grinned. 'You get new wife now you got new
house?'

Skippy nodded amiably. 'For work. For cook,' he squeaked. 'Git
plenty kangaroo tail now awright.'

'Puttin ideas in is ead,' Mrs Comeaway said disgustedly. 'Gawd
elp im if one a them young ones gets old of his pension book.'

Mr Comeaway rose and stretched himself. 'Gunna take a little
walk. See what's doin.'

'Ya gunna take im with ya?' Mrs Comeaway nodded at the
drowsy old man.

'He's nearly asleep, poor old thing,' Noonah said sympathetically.
'Let him stay for a while.'

Mr Comeaway looked at his wife. 'What about a couple, eh?' He
moved nearer the shelf on which Mrs Comeaway had placed the
tobacco-tin.

Mrs Comeaway hesitated. 'Ah, go on then,' she said weakly. 'Be
careful but. No gettin us in trouble.'

'Doesn't Dad still work on the wharf?' Noonah asked her mother
when Mr Comeaway had gone and Skippy's old head was resting
on his arms.

Mrs Comeaway shrugged. 'E goes down sometimes. I dunno!
P'raps there ain't been so much loadin lately.'

'How do you manage well?' There was a little frown on Noonah's
forehead.

'I get me little bit a dowment comin in now – fa young Bartie an
Stella. All helps. You bring a bit home. Get a bit at cards. Tick up a
bit down the corner shop.'

'What about rent?'

'Now don't you go worryin ya head bout us,' Mrs Comeaway
soothed.

Noonah ran a hand over the knicked table-top, feeling its grooves
and bumps. 'Audrena came up to see me this week. Auntie Hannie
and Blanchie came up a couple of days after.'

'Money?' Mrs Comeaway enquired swiftly.

Noonah nodded. 'I don't mind, Mummy. But I get in trouble if I
have too many visitors when I'm on duty. We're not supposed to.'

Mrs Comeaway sat stiff and angry. 'Ya don't have ta tell me.
They on to ya now. They know they can go up an bite ya fa a bit

every now and then, the cows. I like ta knock their blocks off, comin round gettin you in trouble. I'm gunna tell em ta keep away fum you.'

'Gee, Mummy, I don't suppose it matters as much as all that.' Noonah was a bit perturbed. 'It's just that I'm not supposed to leave the ward when I'm on duty, and I have to, to get my money.'

'You wouldn't be the only one,' Mrs Comeaway said, still grim. 'Anyone knows ya got a bit, they on ta ya like a lotta seagulls. Even me an my bit a dowment.' She rested firmly fleshed arms on the table. An indrawn breath flared her nostrils and curved her mouth into a line of irony. 'Not that ya can blame the poor bastards, I s'pose.'

'An awful lot don't work, and they don't seem to want to,' Noonah said diffidently. 'Why, Mummy?'

'Don't you go measurin us up against white folk, Noonah,' Mrs Comeaway warned. 'The men works, they get the rough stuff to do. They get tired a that. Many a time I helped Joe do the burnin off on properties round about ere. An that's a picnic longside a some other jobs e's had.'

Swift sympathy softened Noonah's face.

Mrs Comeaway was encouraged to continue, 'Can't really blame em, wantin ta take a bit of a holiday like, every now an then. Would meself, I hadda do half what the men do. Sides,' she chuckled suddenly. 'It's all in. Ya bite someone one day, ya gotta expect ta be bit back when it's your turn. Ain't that right?'

'Gawd, Noonah,' she said a moment later. 'I ever tell ya bout that time ole Bung Arrer's pension come through?' She settled back in her chair and swished her pink tongue round her smiling lips. 'It's like this, see? The ole bloke's been bummin round on folk long as I been here. And then someone sees bout a pension for im. E goes round tellin everyone e's gunna get this big lotta money that's been buildin up since e's reached the age where they give out pensions, see? And the day e gets it, there they are, all of em. Seventeen! For a bit a fun I counted eads. All watin outside the post office fa ole Bung Arrer.' She put her head back and held on to the rippling folds of her stomach until her laughter had spent itself. Noonah laughed too, but there was compassion in her laughter.

'It's all right,' Mrs Comeaway gasped. 'Some a them seen the funny side an they left im a bit ta get on with.'

'And what were you doing there?' Noonah teased, relieved at this not too unhappy ending.

Her mother was unabashed. 'Waitin ta bite im, a course.'

'You're awful,' Noonah giggled, but there was affection in the look she gave her mother. Despite their undercurrent of tragedy, these were the tales she loved to hear when she came home. These were her people. She would not have had them much different.

Skippy woke with a start. He pulled his lax old limbs and his bird-like head in, towards his skinny body, as though he must concentrate his strength.

'Come down ere fa a good cuppa tea,' he announced, an evil twinkle in his hooded eyes.

'Ya just had a cuppa tea,' Mrs Comeaway roared indignantly.

The twinkle vanished. 'Nice thing, ole man can't git a cuppa tea when e needs it. Nice thing that is.'

'All right!' Mrs Comeaway moaned. 'All right! Put the kettle on, Noonah.'

CHAPTER 14

One of the things Mr Comeaway liked to do on these hot nights was to sit on the top step of the front veranda and from there to survey his new kingdom – neat, small houses behind them – little white picket fences marking off each quarter-acre block, and now that dusk was falling, the sweet and heady scent of Mrs Henwood's stocks to delight his nostrils.

'Them plants her-next-door put in, they growin?' he enquired of his wife, who was seated in a cane chair just behind him.

'Dunno!' Mrs Comeaway said. 'Ain't seen er for a week or more.'

'Thought ya said she was gunna come over an see to em.'

'She ain't and I ain't,' Mrs Comeaway said, kismet fashion. 'Tell ya the truth, I clean forgot about em.' She leaned forward to peer over the veranda. 'Don't see em now, do you?'

Mr Comeaway heaved himself up and clumped down the steps to investigate. 'Nup! Nothin there.' He straightened and sighed. 'Woulda been nice, avin a few flowers.'

Mrs Comeaway shook her head in commiseration. 'Musta been somethin wrong with that pot-plant she gave me, too. Went brown an all the leaves come off.'

'Don't matter,' Mr Comeaway said nobly, climbing the steps again. After a while he said thoughtfully: 'Praps if you was to tell er them plants she put in went an died, praps she might put in some more.'

'An take better care next time,' Mrs Comeaway disapproved. 'After all, it ain't me that's the gardner. She was the one seemed set on a garden.'

Trilby listened without interest, leaning her head languidly against the wall of the sleepout. Bartie and Stella whispered and giggled together and dragged themselves round the veranda on their stomachs.

'Wouldn't mind a few peoples round tonight,' Mr Comeaway offered.

'An it looks as if ya gunna have em' Mrs Comeaway told him. 'Here's a taxi comin now.'

The Comeaways peered hopefully through the dusk. Few of their friends owned cars. Most of them were forced to use taxis, unless, of course, they preferred to walk, and few of the Comeaways' friends preferred to walk.

The taxi stopped before the Comeaway house, and everyone on the veranda waited expectantly. Dark figures detached themselves from the cab and on the still air there sounded the sharp clink of bottle against bottle.

Mr Comeaway smiled gently, and contentment flooded his soul.

'Couldn't let ole Nipper go back thout comin down ta see yous an ya new house,' Charlie said jovially. 'Gee, we ad some times since e's been down. Goin back tomorrow.'

'Ole Nipper, eh?' Mr Comeaway's voice was full of welcome. 'Whadda ya know? An young Stoney Broke an Phyllix, ain't it?'

'An Hannie,' Mrs Comeaway said of the sad silhouette that followed the men. 'Come in then.'

Behind her mother. Trilby stood stiffly against the wall, her body pin-pointing with shock.

'An be gee, we gotta remember the time that train goes tomorrow,' Nipper grinned in warning. 'They short anded. Boss only let me come down ta get me back fixed. Thinkin a takin young Phyllix back ta help out, seein is own team's finishing up.'

'What's a coupla days between friends,' Mr Comeaway said hospitably. 'Should park yaselves down ere with us a while. Got plenty a room.'

'I'll say,' Stoney remarked, looking round admiringly. 'Trouble is, it wasn't zactly like the boy ere says it was. Boss didn't *let* us come. We just tole im we was comin. Cause a Nipper's back.'

'An bicrikey, was e mad!' Nipper chuckled. 'Thing was, we was just startin a shed, an me ole pal Stoney wasn't gunna let a bloke come down by hisself.' He winked. 'Not havin this bad back like.'

'E stacked on a turn,' Stoney grinned. 'Said if we went we didn't need ta come back because e'd get someone else in ta do the job.'

'So ya see ow it is, boy,' Nipper finished. 'We miss that damn train tomorrow, e just might *git* someone else ta do the job. An Mirrabilli's all right. Not real bad. What you think, Stoney?' He raised an eyebrow at his pal.

'Ah, e's not a bad ole bugger,' Stoney agreed tolerantly. 'Now – what about a drop a grog.' He reached into the sack and withdrew a bottle of wine.

'Don't think the young bloke's taken to me,' Hannie mourned, taking Stella up on her lap. 'Makes off soon as e sees me comin.'

Mrs Comeaway gave a great laugh. 'I know where that one'll be. Run off to is bed. Always does, minute anyone comes. We hadda put Maudie Mungo in is bed one night, couldn't very well let er lay out on the veranda fa the neighbours ta see in the morning. E didn't like it but. Said she kep im awake snorin. An took up all the bed. Course e's a bit shy, ya know. Give im time ta get used to ya, Hannie. Ya takes some gettin used to, you ave ta admit that. Eh, Charlie?' And her great laugh roared out again.

'I was just thinkin,' Mr Comeaway said, watching Stoney pour the conto into come cups, 'didn't I say to ya, Mollie, I could do with a bit a company aroun?'

Nobody noticed that neither Phyllix nor Trilby had followed them into the living-room. The two stood together on the veranda, Trilby striving for calmness.

Phyllix took her hand and pulled her gently away from the oblong of light. 'I been lookin for you since I came back.'

Trilby flashed him a sideways look.

'Didn't see ya on the beach or nowhere.'

'I wasn't there, I suppose.'

'Why?'

Trilby tried to achieve crispness. 'I have to study. I'm takin my Junior the end of this year.'

'You got ya back up still,' Phyllix accused. 'Bout that night on the beach.' His tone gentled. 'You didn't have to, Trilby. I wouldn't of made ya.'

Trilby's chin went up as her temper sparked. 'You didn't make me. Nobody makes me do things.'

'We could get married, the two of us,' Phyllix's eyes held hers steadily. 'If you wanted it.'

Trilby's grey eyes widened, then she jerked herself away from him. 'What makes you think I'd marry you? I would be a fool.' There was resentfulness as well as bitterness in her voice.

Phyllix's heavy brows met over his nose. 'What's wrong with me? You think you're too good?'

Trilby's self-assurance grew. She liked the feeling of having hurt him. She wanted to hurt him yet more. 'Marry you and live in a camp like the others up there on the hill? You must fancy yourself if you think I'd go back to that just because you asked me to.'

'I haven't asked you ta do that, Trilby.'

Trilby would not soften to the pleading in his voice. She would have liked to fight him physically, as well as with words. There would be satisfaction in tearing at his face with her finger-nails. For weeks the thought of him had disturbed her. Why must he come back just when she had succeeded in putting him out of her mind?

Dismayingly, she felt her thoughts falter, her body lose some of its tautness, as Phyllix moved closer to her. He slipped an arm about her waist and pulled her towards him so that once again she felt his hard maleness. Her defiance crumbled. She felt the warm wetness of tears in her eyes before her head drooped to rest on his shoulder.

'Where can we go?' Phyllix muttered, and his warm breath was on her neck.

'No!' Trilby's voice was hardly audible.

'Come on,' Phyllix said urgently. And there was sweetness as well as shame at following him.

In amongst the grey-green salt-bushes they lay close together. Trilby had waited to pay her debt of remorse and self-loathing, but this time there had been no payment to make. Instead, knowledge had come to her that Phyllix had taken from her no more than she had taken from him. And with this knowledge had come tenderness for him, and a pity which included herself.

'Better I tell Nipper I don't go with him on that train tomorrow,' Phyllix whispered.

Trilby made no sound. There was a peace about them that she would not disturb.

'You know, I had girls before,' Phyllix said dreamily. 'Not like you, Trilby. You get in a chap's head, keep him remembering.' She felt his intensity as he struggled for words. 'That's why I think we better get married. I want you with me always. All the time.'

'I will marry you,' Trilby said vehemently. And she knew she spoke so because what she said was not the truth. She did want to be with him always. In one short hour he had become dearer to her than anyone had ever been – his strong hard body to which her own had submitted so joyfully, his warm dry hands which were so gentle, the rough feel of his hair – he was her own. Sadness was deep within her because she knew she would let him go, *must* let him go, or she could not fulfil the promise she had made to herself.

'You could come with me,' Phyllix told her. 'They got good quarters on Mirrabilli.'

Trilby was glad of the dark. 'No! Not yet.'

'Not me neither well,' she knew he was smiling. She kept herself still so that he would not rouse to kiss her. So that she could think.

'Phyllix, you know I don't want to live like they do in those awful humpies. I want a house, a good house. And stuff to put in it.'

'You got a house. Room fa one more, isn't there?'

'Not there.' Trilby was patient. 'I want my own place. Like other people.'

'You want to live like white people live, that it?'

Trilby was ready to stiffen in case he should laugh, but Phyllix did not laugh.

'And I want a garden with roses and things in it.' Trilby's voice was vehement.

Phyllix did laugh then, but tenderly. 'You got some funny ideas in ya head, haven't ya?'

'They're not funny.'

'Ya want a whole house to yaself?'

'Yes.'

'I dunno! I suppose I could save me cheques. Work a few more sheds if I wanted to.' He turned suddenly, caught her hands and pressed them down, one each side of her head. His face was close and she could imagine the golden eyes holding her own. 'You better be here when I get back,' he told her, his voice thickening again. 'An don't you let no one else touch ya, see?'

Trilby's lips parted. Relief mingled with shame. It had been too easy to fool him into believing she would wait for him. She knew coldly that she would not.

Mr Comeaway leaned his arms on the table-top and focused his benevolent gaze on his friends. It had been a good night, and he was mellowed through and through with good will towards men.

'You still thinkin a comin down ere, Charlie?' he enquired with kindly condescension.

'Yeah, we still thinkin,' his brother returned comfortably. 'Only thing, that damn money pretty hard ta get. That deposit ya gotta pay.'

Mr Comeaway turned out his bottom lip, nodded understandingly.

'The truth bein,' Charlie added in a burst of frankness. 'We gone an spent the damn lot. Gunna start again soon's I get a week or two down the wharf.'

Mr Comeaway's expression was sphinx-like. He wanted to express his good will in some magnificent and overwhelming manner. Because he liked old Charlie as well as he liked anyone, he decided his brother might as well be the one to benefit.

'Charlie,' he said, banging a fist on the table. 'You can put that money right out ya head. I got a better idea.'

'Yeah?'

Mr Comeaway took a breath. 'Ya can come down ere an live in *this* house.'

Charlie took him up swiftly. 'Ya mean the lot of us? The whole four an the kid too?'

Only for a second did caution overtake Mr Comeaway's generosity. Then his fine independent spirit took charge. 'My place, ain't it?' he asked, with a hint of belligerence. 'Anyone say it ain't my place? You lot can come ere soons's ya ready. Eh, Mollie, I jus said Charlie an is mob can come down ere an live stead a wastin a lotta money. Ya think that's all right?'

'Wouldn't mind stayin ere meself, ya say the word,' Stoney Broke grinned. 'She ain't a bad sorta camp.'

Mrs Comeaway had been nurturing a little good will on her own account. Her hesitation was even more fleeting that Mr Comeaway's had been. Trilby's objections, Noonah's, Bartie's – she dismissed them in the moment of considering them. Another woman right on tap, even though it was only Hannie, would do away with those long lonely periods when for some reason or other she was unable to get into town or up to the camps at the back of the hill.

'Plenty a room,' she declared. 'Plenty. Dunno why we didn't think of it before.'

'Trilby don't seem ta like peoples much,' Hannie contributed nervously.

'Ah, she won't mind,' Mrs Comeaway said largely. 'Long as nobody pokes their nose in er room.'

'Gawd!' Hannie disclaimed, even more nervously. 'Ya think I want ta go in there, with er waitin ta pounce? Not me!'

'Fixed it all up erself,' Mrs Comeaway told the others. 'Cover-ups fa the beds, curtains, stuff on the floor. Cleans it out erself, too. Looks real nice.'

Mr Comeaway chuckled. 'Where is she, anyhow? An young Phyllix, too? They musta gone off somewhere.'

'They was out on the veranda,' Mrs Comeaway told him.

'Down the Fun Fair, likely,' Nipper said easily. 'Ringin ashtrays an jugs. The lot of us went there last night.'

He had no sooner spoken than the two were at the door.

'Where you two been?' Mrs Comeaway asked, looking from one face to the other.

'I'm tired. I'm going to bed.' Trilby moved away from the doorway, and Phyllix stepped into the room.

'Ow many ash-trays tonight?' Stoney asked, grinning. 'This is the boy to ring em,' he told the Comeaways. 'They was chasin im away last night. Woulda went broke if e'd stayed much longer.'

'Eh, Trilby!' Mrs Comeaway called. 'Come back in ere. We gotta nice surprise for ya.'

Trilby came slowly back to stand alongside Phyllix. She looked sulky.

'How would ya like it if Blanchie and Audrena come down ta stay for a bit?' Mrs Comeaway asked, over-heartily.

Trilby gave her mother a straight glance from her silver-grey eyes. She did not speak.

Mrs Comeaway stuck doggedly to heartiness. 'Ya father an me, we thought it might be a good idea ta have Charlie an Hannie an the girls come down ere.'

'I don't call that a nice surprise,' Trilby spoke clearly. She swept the group with a look which scorned them, then she swung round. They heard her bedroom door bang shut behind her.

Phyllix leant against the wall, his face expressionless.

Mrs Comeaway looked round uneasily. 'Nice sorta thing ta say,' she said weakly.

'Some bark, eh?' Stoney was impressed.

Hannie quivered in her chair. 'If it's all the same ta yous, I think we stop up there by Mrs Green. It pretty comforable – an quiet like. We come down ere, I dunno – that Trilby, she just as well might break out on us.'

Mr Comeaway sat back in his chair and roared with laughter.

From the doorway Phyllix echoed it.

'Be gee,' Mr Comeaway gasped, casting a look of appreciation at the only member of the party to share his amusement. 'Look at em all, will ya? An that Trilby! Ain't any pleasin er. An she got ole Hannie shakin in er shoes thout even comin near er. Don't you take too much notice a that one, Hannie. We gotta big chain jus outside that door. After you an Charlie get down ere, we gunna chain that Trilby up, like a dog.' He roared again.

'Better we stay where we was,' Hannie said primly, 'then we ain't under no compliments ta nobody.'

'What gets into er, eh?' Mr Comeaway asked Phyllix as one intimate to another. 'Tramps over people like they was muck under her feet.'

Phyllix grinned. 'Ah! I dunno!' He slid one hand higher up to door jamb, rested the other on a slim hip. 'Maybe she thinks different than the rest of us round here.' There was a glow in the depths of the yellow eyes.

'She's a young huzzy,' her mother said, with an unwilling smile.

CHAPTER 15

With hardly a discussion, the Comeaways dropped, for the time being, the idea of inviting their relatives to share their home. There had been no misunderstanding Trilby's views on the matter, and neither of her parents felt strongly enough about it to risk their daughter's continued disapproval. Mrs Comeaway, in particular, in the few short months since her daughter had arrived back from the mission, had found that falling in with Trilby's ideas paid off in a more or less peaceful atmosphere. Besides, Trilby always won in the end. Her mother was the first to admit that her daughter had a way with her, when she wanted something.

Right from the start, Trilby had done all of her own washing. And she spent hours pressing her cotton frocks and her school tunic with Mrs Comeaway's old flat irons heated on top of the stove.

There was a strong bond between Trilby and her father. Mr Comeaway saw nothing wrong in Trilby's pertness or her sometimes cruel criticism of her bewildered and harassed mother. What other girls at school had, Trilby must have too. Whoever or whatever went short in consequence was no concern of hers.

Not that she did not help with the rest of the house. Over weekends especially she was ruthless about what she called 'rubbish', and many a time Mrs Comeaway was forced to sneak out to the rubbish bin to retrieve something she cherished. In lots of small ways, Mrs Comeaway's life had become more complicated, but her pride in her smart daughter most often outweighed any resentment she felt.

There were her other children, too, with whom to relax, and her friends who lived in the humpies at the back of the town.

Only Noonah worried about things like rent. On Saturday mornings off she would bath both children and dress them in clean clothes, settle her mother into her blue silk frock and comb her greying hair back from her smooth cocoa forehead, cajole her father for money, when he had it, and start off for town with them all.

That was the happy time that Noonah remembered most often in the years that followed. For a short time the Comeaways prospered. After harvest, the town was always busy, and wharf-work was easy to come by. In fact, if you were a wharfie you reported regularly if you knew what was good for you. The big boats must not be held up. Every hand was needed to fill the holds with wheat.

Mrs Comeaway had her eye on an oak dining-room suite she had seen in a second-hand shop. Noonah thought it would be nice for her mother to have a really big cupboard for the kitchen. Bartie wanted genuine camel-hair brushes for his painting, Stella wanted a bride-doll, and Trilby found something else she needed every time she went to town.

Noonah was business manager. Occasionally some need more pressing than mere signatures on tiny scraps of paper bobbed up and her calculations went astray but it was so good to be home she could never worry overmuch about rent. In town on Saturdays, it was milk-shakes and chocolates and cool drinks for the kids, and a whole heap of stuff from the grocer who delivered, and agreeable little gossips with Mrs Comeaway's friends and perhaps a taxi trip up the hill to see Gramma Green.

With the utmost good nature, the Comeaway family had exhausted Mrs Henwood's attempts at rehabilitation, and the only contact they now had was when Mr Comeaway caught sight of her and strolled over to the dividing fence to advise her on her activities in her garden.

In a secret corner of her mind Mrs Comeaway still cherished the idea of getting Charlie and Hannie down to live in the Wild-Oat Patch, but for the present she vanquished the bogey of loneliness by spending most of her day in the township where there was always a group of friends to join; at the corner by the barber-shop, sitting on hard garden seats outside the bank, or sheltering from the wind behind the stone wall where Horace held court.

During the evening, if there were no visitors, she fed her husband the morsels of gossip she heard.

'Knew well as anything ole Skippy'd got is talk of getting a house all mucked up,' she told him one night. 'Mattie up the camp tole me.'

'An Horace tole me,' Mr Comeaway added, 'they gettin a lot a little houses up the camp stead a them camps. An Horace, he gunna be first gettin one.'

'An that's where ole Skippy's house is gunna be built,' Mrs Comeaway said. 'course it is.'

'They all been trying ta make Skippy understand proper, but e sticks to it e's gunna have is house built special, up where e comes from.'

'Poor ole chap.' Mrs Comeaway was sympathetic. 'Gawd, what a time someone's gunna have, gettin it çlear to im.'

'Should do something bout it. Someone should,' Mr Comeaway said vaguely.

'Maybe cost too much.'

'Still, ole chap like e is. Wouldn't hurt em.'

'Nnnh!' Mrs Comeaway sighed.

There was no longer any doubt that a baby was coming. The knowledge overwhelmed Trilby at first. If he had been near, Trilby would have sought Phyllix out, flung hysterical accusations at him. All her resentment of him was back, multiplied into hatred. But he was gone from the town, and the only thing left to do was to try to hide her burning humiliating suffering from every eye. She hated herself, too. She, with her wonderful plans, to be such a fool. To know she had gone into this thing with her eyes wide open.

In bed at night she beat her belly with clenched fists, hating the thing it enclosed.

She told nobody because nobody could help her. She sickened when she thought of the future. Soon she would grow big, and everyone would know and laugh. She guessed how they would laugh, how glad her mother's friends would be to see her beaten. The thought of their gladness drove her mad. She would not bear it.

At school she stayed aloof from everyone, took a day off as often as she could without causing too much comment. Day-time was worst. Other people forever about, any one of them likely at any time to guess her secret. She had no clear plan except to meet each day and endure it until darkness came.

During the evening she left the house to wander round the

curving road that followed the line of the beach. Alone, she penetrated deep into the acres of marshy salt-bush, sought out deliberately, once, the place where she had lain with Phyllix – and departed
from there with the ache of tears in her throat.

Sometimes the older Comeaways would still be up when she
reached her home. There would be lights glaring from the windows
and the noise of voices and laughter on the air. Nobody noticed
when she came in because she went straight to her room. Her room,
which she would share with nobody, was her one blessing.

On other nights the house would be dark and silent, every
occupant in bed and asleep. Trilby walked for miles, but rarely
enough to tire herself so that she slept straightaway. There were
always the hot, lumpy pillow, the tangled sheets – and weary half-
closed eyes.

She felt an overpowering need to confide in someone – her
mother, or Noonah – and this feeling had to be fought and subdued,
not once, but often. Mrs Comeaway would have been astonished
and unbelieving if she could have known that there were days when
Trilby would have given much to be in Bartie's place, or little
Stella's, when Mrs Comeaway sat on the top step with a careless
arm round each, or told them, with the object of keeping them
amused and happy, some tale of her childhood, or, more rarely,
when she gave each a quick hug or a kiss or a playful smack on the
behind. Sometimes Trilby resented her mother simply because
Mrs Comeaway did not guess her daughter's need of her.

The temptation to tell Noonah was even harder to resist, and
Trilby did not truly understand why she kept silent, unless it was
that she wanted her sister's regard for her to remain unaltered, not
tinged with sympathy. When, in the long night hours, she worked
things out, she knew she wanted sympathy from nobody – not even
from her mother.

One night, prowling along a back street, the glass window of a fire
alarm caught her eye. She walked over to it, idly, not too interested,
and bent to read the instructions. The thought came into her head
that this glass must have been broken often, perhaps not always
because there was a fire in its neighbourhood. There were boys –
mischievous, unafraid of the consequences.

And a girl!

Glass shattered round her feet. She looked with unbelieving eyes
at the stone she held in her hand. Her heart almost stopped beating
as she dropped it and pressed hard against the bell in the little
saucer-shaped container. She drew her finger away sharply, but the

little bell remained depressed and Trilby knew why. In the fire station at the other end of the town, an alarm was sounding, right this minute. And it would continue to sound until someone switched off the mechanism. Any time now the fire-fighting truck would come clanging and shrilling down the street, waking everyone as it passed.

Like a shadow, and as quietly, Trilby slipped down the dark length of the street. Her heart thumped and beat in her throat so that she felt choked. Why had she done such a thing? Could someone have been watching her? What happened to a girl who broke the glass of a fire alarm when there was no fire?

Quietly – quietly, she crept into her bed that night, and lay trembling beneath her blankets.

But that night she did not lie awake in bed, thinking. It was morning before she knew it. And nothing had happened to her.

At the end of a week Trilby felt safe from consequences, but it was longer than a fortnight before she dared revisit the fire alarm. She hardly questioned that she *must* see it again.

It had been mended. A new glass shone in the moonlight.

Trilby looked to right and left this time, to make sure she was not being watched. Then she picked up a stone and hurled it satisfyingly straight at the little glass window. The tinkling of the glass as it fell was like music. Music that exhilarated and excited her. Her heart beat and thumped as she held her finger to the bell. She laughed. And suddenly, the future appeared free of worry. The suffering burning ache that had been with her since she had guessed about the baby – it was gone. Where it had been there was left only a tingling and fusing of all her senses.

This time she could not tear herself away from the scene. More! She must have more! What happened when a fire alarm was set off? If she hid, she would know. The Moreton Bay fig tree, its branches hidden beneath big sheltering leaves! If she climbed up into it, hid herself in its darkest part, she would see and hear everything.

Trilby heard the truck approach, watched it stop, gloated as the men fanned out to look for the fire then converged once more on the truck. She heard them talk, heard every word they said. The exhilaration remained. It was like being born again. She saw and heard everything and herself remained safely hidden.

'Same one did it before, I'll take a bet on that.'

'Might be around still, too.'

A man with authority in his voice spoke last. 'Two of you men stay here. Have a good look round, everywhere, and I'll go down to the station and fetch a policeman.'

Trilby's heart gave a great lurch. She kept very still, almost too afraid to breathe in case she made her presence known. The two men angled out from each other, searching the dark doorways of shops, penetrating the night-filled lane across the street from the fire alarm. Trilby knew she must drop from the tree and take a chance on escaping, but she waited too long. The men came back. Trilby's fear grew. She wanted to believe that she was dreaming and that she would wake from this horror safe in her bed. Sweating, shaking still, but safe! It could not be she who perched in this tree while two men below searched only for her. It *must* be a dream.

A third man came. Trilby recognised his uniform. This was the policeman the other man had called. Despite herself, a sob of terror forced its way through her lips. The branch of the tree shook and a dead leaf detached itself and fell scuttering to the ground.

The officer was quick. This was something in which he had been trained, this lightning-quick note of detail. In a second he was underneath the tree, peering up through the branches.

He called: 'I see you! Come on down, whoever you are.'

Trilby clutched the branch tighter but did not answer. There was a chance that he was gammoning. How could he see her, through so many thick dark leaves.

He had a torch out. The beam was directed up into the tree. It moved slowly across and across, thoroughly exhausting the potentialities of one spot before moving on to the next. Trilby closed her eyes, endured the torture of waiting. Then she felt the beam of the torchlight strong on her eyelids.

'Hah!' There was satisfaction in his voice. 'Got you!' The fire-brigade officers followed the line of light, saw the material of Trilby's skirt and her dangling dark legs and her clutching hands.

'A girl!'

'You coming down or am I coming up to fetch you?' the police-officer called.

A wild rage surged through Trilby. 'No!' she yelled, lashing out viciously with her foot. 'And if you come near me, I'll kick you, you hear?'

'You will, will you?' The policeman grinned. 'I'm coming up just the same, young miss. Unless you change your mind and come down.'

'Go away!' Trilby shrieked. 'Go away! If you come near me, you bastard, I'll push you down. I'll make you fall. You'll get hurt.'

'Tut! Mustn't threaten police-officers. Mustn't swear, either.'

'I think you'd better come down, girlie.' There was a kindly note in the voice of the fire-brigade man. 'Can't stay up there all night, you know.'

'I won't come down, I won't. Go away, all of you.'

'Looks like I'll have to go up,' the policeman said. He moved over to the great round trunk of the tree, searched with experienced eyes for a foothold. Trilby saw him come up the tree with the agility of a small boy.

She froze with fear. He must not be allowed to touch her. She would not let him. She closed her eyes and her mouth opened in a grimace. Letting go her hold on the branch she jumped forward just before the man reached forward to stop her. A broken bough caught her skirt when she was half-way to the ground. She hung for a second, then the branch broke with a tortured crack and she fell the rest of the five or six feet to the ground.

She was up like a shot. Off and away! But the fire-brigade officers were too quick for her. She felt her shoulder grasped. She rammed her head into one man's stomach, putting all her force behind it. When he lost his balance and detached his hand from her shoulder she made off again, but the other one had her this time.

'I got her,' he called breathlessly to his mates, 'but you better come and help me. She's as strong as a young lion.'

The policeman dropped from the tree and came over to them.

'All right! All right! Break it up,' he told the terrified and struggling girl.

There were three of them. And they had caught her.

Trilby stopped fighting, relapsed into fatigue and hopelessness. She was in terrible trouble, another sort this time.

Between two of them she walked, docile enough now, to the police-station. She did not even hear the men when they spoke to her. She only heard their footsteps echoing along the empty dark street, saw only the dull gleam of glass in shop windows.

Inside the station, terror seized her stomach so that it knotted. She kept her head bent, knowing there was only one weapon left to her, silence.

'Look, don't you understand? All we want from you is your name, and your age and a couple of other things, and then you can go and have a sleep.' The young police-sergeant was getting impatient.

Each time he asked, Trilby's alertness increased. She felt danger ahead if she answered so much as a single question.

'Find out, if you want to know,' she snapped once, and when one of the officers had moved closer to her she had lashed out at him with her foot and caught him a crack on his ankle. He kept his distance after that.

'I've got an idea she's one of those Comeaway girls that just came down from some mission,' one officer said after a while.

'Your father Joe Comeaway?' the sergeant asked sternly.

Trilby maintained her sulky silence.

'Take her away, Ted,' the sergeant said at last. 'Lock her up until she's in a better frame of mind.'

Lock her up? Trilby marshalled all her strength for one last attempt to get away. Before any of the men knew what she was about she had darted back to the doorway.

She was nearly out into the street before one of them grabbed her arm and held it fast. She was jerked inside again, kicking and struggling. The man was strong. She felt herself shoved through a doorway, then a door slammed. She looked up. A light shone feebly through a barred space at the top of the doorway, illuminating a few objects. She picked out a bed against one wall. A chair stood alongside it. She swung it up and crashed it against the door and her wrists jarred painfully. Once more she lifted it and smashed it against the locked door. Across her mind raced the words: 'Lock her up'.

Only when her strength was gone did she pause in her efforts to break down the stout wooden door.

'Bet she's broken that damn chair,' said a voice. 'Gee, some temper.'

Another sterner voice floated through to her. 'If you don't behave yourself you'll be made to behave. Get on that bed and lie down. Now!'

'I will not!' Trilby shrieked. She made a jab at the hole with one of the chair legs. There was a scuffling noise and a yell of pain. Trilby felt fiercely triumphant.

She looked round the room to see what else it held in the way of missiles. On a table in a corner of the room stood a glass jug of water with a tumbler alongside it. She swooped on it, crept with it to the door, standing to one side so that she should not be seen.

'Is she in bed yet?' someone asked softly. 'Have a look!'

Trilby let fly with the jug of water. From further sounds of snuffling and gasping she knew she had scored one more victory. Her upper lip was curled back from her teeth and her eyes caught the glow of the light.

Footsteps receded down the passage and there was silence. Like a cat, Trilby prowled round the room. Her thoughts darted here and there, seeking a way to escape. She had to get out – she had to put an end to this suffocating feeling of being locked up like a dangerous animal. There was no hope of escape through the door. There was equally small chance of squeezing her body through the narrow barred window. The walls were of crumbling stone and cement. The jail was old. The walls had been built by convict labour. Trilby did not know that. In one of circuits of the room she stopped to lean against the old stone wall. Her hand reached out idly to crumble a little more of the loose cement. Others had been at work on the stones beneath her hand. It was almost free of the wall. A tug showed her that it was still too firmly embedded to be dislodged. But she could do it! She darted over to where the broken chair lay on the floor and took up one of the pieces of splintered wood. With it as her tool she worked doggedly away at the deep furrow surrounding the stones. Action – any sort of action was preferable to waiting and thinking.

At first she worked carelessly, but as her spirit quieted caution came and she knew that any loud noise would bring an officer up the passage seeking the cause. Every now and then she stopped to listen. Once she heard footsteps approach. Like lightning she made for the bed and dived under the blanket on top of it. And none too soon. The beam from the torch shone on the bed. Trilby closed her eyes and lay still. The light was switched off and the footsteps retreated. As soon as she was sure it was safe, Trilby was out of the bed again.

Soon the stone was almost free of the wall, and a gentle tug was all that was needed to move it. Pausing only to place it on the floor at her feet she started on the next one. Before the grey of coming day appeared like smoke in the square of the window, Trilby had removed three stones from the wall. She had not expected to tunnel her way through. The arduous work was meant only to occupy her mind and her strength, and to fend off the quivering madness that had overwhelmed her when she had been flung into this room and imprisoned there. It meant, too, that she was not submitting tamely. If she could fight, she could hope to beat them.

CHAPTER 16

When the grey was tinged with blue she curled up on the bed. At her side were the stones she had patiently chipped from the wall.

Later, when footsteps came near, she folded the blanket so that they could not be seen – and waited. The top half of a man's face appeared at the square hole in the door. Trilby gave stare for stare, her eyes shining silver-grey between swollen lids.

'Going to behave yourself this morning?' the police-officer asked banteringly.

Trilby did not reply. Her hand closed hard over one of the stones.

'I've got some tea and toast here for you,' the man said, and she heard a key grate in the lock of the door.

She was ready with her stone the moment the door opened and the officer, taken completely by surprise, dropped his little tray with a crash and stood for a second holding his shoulder whilst he gazed at her with shocked eyes. Trilby had time to throw another of her stones before he was on her, holding her down on the bed by the shoulders.

'Why, you young devil. You might have killed me,' he said when he had her thin young wrists in a bone-crushing grip.

'Let me alone,' Trilby said between her teeth. With her head she tried to butt him in the stomach. With her feet she kicked wildly at him.

'Hey! Les! Come here,' the young officer yelled, but another man had already entered the cell.

'See if there's any more stones in that bed,' Trilby's captor said. 'And if there are, grab them.'

'Gee!' The man gaped as he searched under the blanket and found the cache of stones. He took them over and dumped them outside the room in the passage. 'Where the hell did she get them from?' he marvelled.

Trilby screamed. She was flung back on the bed and the door banged shut again. One round-eyed face shoved another round-

eyed face from the hole at the top of the door. Then both officers
went back down the passage.

Trilby ran to the door as soon as they had gone. She banged on it
with both fists. She screamed through it. She hurled names up the
length of the passage. Names which she had heard but which she
had never used in her life before. Nobody came near, and she went
on screaming. It wasn't really herself screaming. A little calm spot
in her brain told her that. The screaming came from a Thing inside
herself, that squirmed, terrified and beaten, and used her voice.
Her whole body shook. The bones in her legs turned to jelly. Just
above her eyes and back of them was a place that was stabbed with
knife-like pains each time her body tensed itself to scream. After a
while she stumbled to the bed and lay face down. She let the bed
take the whole tremendous weight of the pain. She sank down and
down so that the bed absorbed her. She was part of it. Not a girl at
all but a rusty iron bed with a tossed blanket on top of it. And
nothing would ever happen to her again.

'Ahoy there! Someone to see you.'

Unwillingly, Trilby came out from the twilight of peace. She
heard a door closing. And that meant it must have been opened
again. She tried to raise herself so that she could see but she could
not care enough to make such an effort. She felt a weight settle itself
alongside her. She waited wearily for the next thing to happen. And
was unprepared for the sound of her mother's voice.

'Trilby! Wake up!'

'Too late now,' Trilby's thoughts formed themselves, slowly,
achingly.

'Trilby, you look real sick. What they done to ya, love? Sit up an
tell ya ole mummy, will ya? Ya daddy said fa me to tell ya e's comin
later if ya wanted im to. Noonah's comin too, and Bartie. Don't
worry, Trilby.' The heaviness at the side of her removed itself and
her mother's voice spoke near her ear.

Trilby wanted to respond – to pour out the whole wretched story,
beginning with someone called Phyllix. But things were all tangled
up in her head. She dragged herself away from her mother, her
stomach knotting at the movement. What was the use of words?
Especially with someone like her mother. With anyone! Nobody
would understand why she was here if she must fit the things she
had done to words.

When her mother placed a timid hand on her shoulder she
moved restlessly and it fell away.

'Dearie!' Her mother must be crying. Her words were choked.

'They want to know, outside, why you done it. Be a good girl and tell Mum why you broke their old glass, come on.'

Trilby wanted to laugh but she had no energy. A broken glass! As if a broken glass mattered. That was the end, not the beginning.

'Go away!' she muttered. 'I don't want anyone. Not anyone.'

'They're waitin,' Mrs Comeaway said in a frightened whisper. 'Ya got to tell em something, Trilby. They might keep ya here if ya don't.'

Why couldn't they just leave her here on the bed, Trilby thought desperately. She twitched away again as her mother moved closer to her. And to blot out the sound of Mrs Comeaway's pleading whispers she buried her head in the blanket.

After a while the bed creaked and her mother's weight was gone again. There were more voices – her mother's and some more. Then the door opened and shut and she was alone.

She had brought this aloneness on herself, but that did not stop the bitterness flowing from her aching throat into every part of her body. She pressed her hands over her eyes and tried to clear her mind.

She was taken from her cell to another little room behind the court and left to wait. She had but one dreary victory to contemplate. With everyone who had questioned her she had maintained a stony silence. The police, the man from the department, a woman welfare worker, her mother and Noonah – she might have talked with her sister if she had not suspected that Noonah would take the tale straight back to the police and the others who wanted to pry into her affairs. And Trilby had decided recklessly that she would rather stay at the jail for ever than give strangers the right to shake their heads over her.

She paced the tiny room restlessly, her impatience growing as the minutes passed. After a half-hour spent entirely alone she felt urged to one more act of revolt against those who held her a prisoner. A chair had served her before. It should serve her now. She snatched up the one she had been sitting on and swung it over her head. The crash of wood against wood broke the numbing silence. Breathing quickly, her grey eyes slits beneath her frowning brows, she waited.

The door of the little room opened. A strange startled face peered round the edge of it. 'Hello! What's going on in here?'

'Mind your own business, stickybeak,' Trilby snarled, and the face, looking even more startled, withdrew. Trilby did not recognize the man. She did not care who he was. But her act of violence calmed her a little. When finally she was led into court by one of the officers, she felt almost cheerful. The sight of her mother and her father sitting at the back of the courtroom added to this. She gave them her brilliant dazzling smile and watched their expression change from tired bewilderment to glad recognition.

Her part of the business was over quickly. She was a minor; it was her first offence and, moreover, the magistrate was favourably impressed by her slim uprightness and the smile that had given such beauty to her face. In justice, she could not be entirely spared, but the seven days she had already spent in the little jail was considered sufficient. She was free to go home with her parents.

Mr and Mrs Comeaway did not come off so well. Both were brought to stand before the clear-eyed magistrate and listen to his sternly-delivered homily. They were too confused and embarrassed to understand more than that this whole sorry affair might have been avoided if they had taken better care of their daughter. Neither was disposed to argue, and apparently the magistrate was satisfied to accept their wondering silence as agreement. With a curt nod he dismissed them. They were free to collect Trilby and to take her home.

'Your hands, Trilby,' Noonah cried when once they were home. The hands that Trilby had taken such care to keep out of sight were examined with compassion. Perturbed and impatient, Trilby saw that Noonah was crying.

She dragged her hands away and put them behind her back. 'That's nothing! I did it getting the stones out of the wall. I suppose they told you that.'

More tears waited to fall. 'Trilby, I hate them too. I know you didn't deserve to be put in jail. Those policemen were beastly. I hated them. And they'll never get you again.'

Trilby remembered her first night in jail and smiled wryly. 'Don't be a fool. I broke that glass, didn't I?'

'Never mind,' Noonah said passionately. 'They were horrible and Dad went mad.'

'He didn't get me out,' Trilby observed drily.

'He helped,' Noonah said swiftly. 'He called in at the office nearly every day, just to tell them about you and how you weren't a bad girl at all.'

Trilby smiled. Her eyes watched her sister narrowly. She wondered if now would be a good time.

'You know what's wrong with me, don't you?' she said roughly. 'I'm going to have a baby.'

With a sort of sour pleasure, she watched the shock in Noonah's face. And admired unwillingly when she saw that Noonah instantly conquered her shock and allowed only her affection to show in her eyes.

'Does Mummy know?'

Trilby shrugged. 'They soon will.'

'Do you want me to tell them? Trilby,' she reached for her sister with impulsive hands. 'Trilby, I'm sorry if you don't want it. What about your – the man. . . . Does he . . .'

'He doesn't know and he's not here,' Trilby said shortly. 'He won't be back for a long time – and I don't want him back. See?'

'Yes.' Noonah's eyes were puzzled.

'And when it's over I'm going off somewhere,' Trilby said defiantly. 'The baby can go to a mission. It isn't mine really. I didn't want it. I don't even want to see it. Another six months of *this*,' she finished savagely, looking down at her still flat stomach. 'I'm sick – nothing I eat tastes good. I hate this baby before it's even born. And there's still six months to go.'

'Trilby, you shouldn't talk like that. You can't hate babies. It's not the baby's fault. Can't you see . . .'

Trilby interrupted her sister. 'You don't understand anything.'

'You can give it to us if you don't want it,' Noonah said childishly. 'We'll have it.'

Trilby gave her sister a long straight look. 'It's my baby and it's going to a mission.'

Noonah's bottom lip trembled. 'Don't, Trilby. Don't let's talk about it yet.'

'All right! I don't want to talk about it.'

'I'll get you some books from the hospital. You can read them.'

'Okay!' Trilby picked up a comic, lay back on her bed pretending to read it. She had just remembered school. Of course she could not go back now. She'd made a muck of things. Behind the comic the long grey eyes stared blindly.

'What'll er father say?' Mrs Comeaway moaned, when she knew about the baby. 'Blame me as usual, I spose. An I kept telling er not to go gallivantin about, specially night-times. Warned er bout them sailors too. Dunno what more e expecks. Gawd, no wonder she run amuck, always bein full of erself and what she was gunna do after she took this exam. Poor kid! You listen ta me, Noonah, an don't you go getting yaself in no fix like that. It's always the girl's left ta look after the babies when they come.' She flashed a look of inquiry at Noonah. 'She tell you who done it?'

'Just that he's gone away and she doesn't want him back. I don't think she likes him, Mum.'

'Musta liked im one time,' Mrs Comeaway said with weary worldliness. 'You can't tell em but. Think ya just an ole fool tryin ta spoil their bit a fun.'

Noonah went over to the stove and pushed another piece of wood under the kettle.

'Yeah, that's right,' Mrs Comeaway said gratefully. 'We'll make a nice cuppa tea.'

'I wish it had been me,' Noonah told her mother fiercely. 'I'd love a baby.'

'Gawd, don't you start,' Mrs Comeaway said comically. 'Let's get this one over first. An you oughtn'ta talk like that anyway, girl. Ya might bring something down on yaself.'

'You don't have to worry about me,' Noonah said bleakly. 'All the boys I see round act as if they're frightened of me.'

'An a good thing too,' Mrs Comeaway pronounced.

Noonah was not so sure. If training to be a nurse cut you off from other youngsters, she was not so sure she wanted to be one.

Mr Comeaway reacted with a flood of anger that covered every inmate of the house, except the cause of it. 'I tole you,' he said furiously, 'ta keep a good eye on er. She's just a bit of a kid and doesn't know what goes on. That damn fool Hannie oughta keep er two away fum ours, gettin Trilby mixed up with their bunch. Ya know the tricks they get up to, careerin round them sandhills, stayin out all night fa all that silly fool Hannie cares.'

'Don't you come that bullyin with me,' Mrs Comeaway defended herself, standing like a battleship before him. 'After all it's ony nacheral, ain't it? Happened ta plenty before Trilby. Gunna happen ta plenty more.'

'Who done it?' Mr Comeaway demanded.

'Ain't no father,' Mrs Comeaway said shortly. 'She don't want no father for it.'

'Ya mean she don't *know?*'

'He went away, Dad,' Noonah said nervously. Apart from the nights when her father grew uproariously argumentative after a night on the conto, this was the first time she had heard him in a rage.

'Bicrikey, if I get me hands on im,' he smouldered. 'Why wouldn't she tell ya who the bastard was? Dunno what everyone's gunna think. First jail, an now this.'

'All *your* pals is too busy thinkin bout their own mistakes ta bother much bout other peoples,' Mrs Comeaway informed him. 'An now shutup. I ad enough. I'm gunna drink me tea.'

'An you'll be next, I spose,' Mr Comeaway said unhappily, at Noonah.

'I just tole er,' Mrs Comeaway said imperturbably. 'Not till we get this one over. An not then less she likes ta make a fool of erself. Come on girl, stop starin an sit down. An call that Trilby out. Won't do er no arm ta get a cuppa tea inside erself.'

Noonah's face felt hot. She got a few cups down from the sink and set them out on the table.

'You don't know bout things like that do ya?' Mr Comeaway's face was unhappy. His eyes had a wounded look.

'Keep ya big mouth closed,' Mrs Comeaway said sharply. 'She don't wanta learn fum you, anyway.'

Trilby would not come out. Noonah took her tea into the bedroom, then she returned to the living-room to have hers with her mother and her father. The three of them sat round the kitchen table holding the heavy cups, sipping the steaming brew.

'Saw Mrs Green today,' Mrs Comeaway said in a normal conversational tone. 'Know what ole Skippy bought isself last pension day? If e didn't turn up in one a them furry ats. An a feather in it, believe it or not. Said at last e's gotta at what don't fall down over is eyes. Real pleased with isself.'

Mr Comeaway broke into delighted laughter. 'I seen im hoppin down the main street,' he said. 'An later on I seen im goin ell fa leather up that hill. Dunno ow e does it with them legs a his.'

'Mrs Green says e's always yappin bout is house. What e isn't gunna do when e gets it. An ain't no one been able ta make im understand it's gunna be built up the camp.'

'Someone oughta go in an tell that partment man,' Mr Comeaway brooded. 'Ole man like im buildin up is hopes.'

Mrs Comeaway stared at her husband in derision. 'Ya think that man ain't in the same boat as us? Don't tell me.'

Mr Comeaway chuckled again.

Mrs Comeaway pushed her cup across the table to Noonah. 'Ya know, I miss that ole place we had, up there with Mrs Green. Ya feel a bit out of it down ere.'

'Trilby will be company for you,' Noonah reminded her mother.

Mrs Comeaway looked uneasily at the wall that divided the living-room from the girls' bedroom. 'She's me own daughter, an I wouldn't say a word against er, but I tell ya what. I ain't lookin forward ta that. Not the way she's feelin.' Her face brightened a little. 'Wonder what it'll be. Girl babies is nice – easy ta have, too. I always liked a little girl. Bet young Stella will too. Like another doll ta that one.' She stopped suddenly, looked at Noonah and at her husband in turn, and began to laugh.

'What's a matter with you?' Mr Comeaway asked heavily, looking up from his tea.

Mrs Comeaway lowered her voice to a whisper. 'Just thought of it. She's gunna make something on the deal. What about that dowment?'

Noonah looked worried. 'Mummy, she's going to send the baby away as soon as it's born. To a mission.'

'Send it away soon as it's born?' Mrs Comeaway was scandalized. 'She ain't gunna do no such thing. Bit later, if she wants to. Not while it's little.'

'I knew you'd say that, Mum.' Noonah's voice was jubilant.

'What's she comin at, sendin a baby off ta some mission?' Mr Comeaway wanted to know. 'Can't she look after it erself?'

'I spose I can help me own daughter raise er baby.' Mrs Comeaway bridled.

'She doesn't want it.' Noonah shruged her shoulders.

'Lotta rubbish,' declared Mrs Comeaway. 'We gotta good house, ain't we? Plenty a room?'

'Got some idea in er head,' Mr Comeaway said darkly. 'Fum that Audrena, most likely.'

'You wait,' Mrs Comeaway told them. 'She won't wanta send that baby away once she's seen it. Look at young Blanchie. She was the same way, wasn't she? You try an get that baby away from er but.'

'I remember,' Mr Comeaway's face wore an embarrassed grin. 'Babies is funny all right, but when they belong to ya – I dunno. Something different bout em then. Remember when we was worried bout young Bartie, eh?'

'That was when e had the stummick trouble,' Mrs Comeaway said. 'Didn't think we was gunna keep im. An that woulda been the third boy I lost in a row, just because round that time, after we had you two girls, we was wantin one. Joe was, anyway, wasn't ya, Joe?'

'I spose.' Mr Comeaway was still embarrassed.

'How did you lose them, Mummy?'

'Stummick trouble mostly,' Mrs Comeaway said matter-of-factly. 'Ain't much ya can do bout that once they get real bad.'

Noonah nodded. She had seen many children hospitalized because of stomach trouble. 'Enteritis,' she told her mother. 'It's caused through. . . .'

'Damn thing,' Mrs Comeaway pondered. 'Seems ta hop fum one

to the other, too. There's seasons for it I spose, just like ya get colds
when it's wet and blowy. Nothin you can do bout it.'

Noonah compressed her lips, and vowed silently that the new
baby wouldn't get enteritis, not if she could help it.

'Ya don't bring any of ya friends down fum the hospital,' Mr
Comeaway said suddenly. 'Why don't ya do that, Noonah?'

Mrs Comeaway threw an uneasy glance in the direction of the
house next door. 'Ah, ya either got em stickin to ya like feathers ta
honey, or they lookin down their noses at ya like you was dirt.'

'I don't want them down here anyhow,' Noonah said indifferently. 'I see enough of them all day long.'

'Eyein ya like you was a dog with two tails,' Mrs Comeaway
grumbled softly. 'Mind,' she told her daughter, 'you wanta have
some girl down ere, you can have er. You just let me know, an I'll
be off out fa the day.'

Noonah laughed. 'Well you can just stay home, because I'm not
asking anyone.'

'Not ta speak of them serve yets, which I ain't got any.'

Noonah was giggling. The atmosphere was clearing again.
Trilby's baby wasn't nearly as big a piece of trouble as she had
imagined it might be. Her mother would handle that as she
handled everything else. Comfortably, with no fuss and bother.

'I just thought,' Mr Comeaway brooded over his second cup of
tea. 'I just thought.'

CHAPTER 17

The last drop of bitterness in Trilby's cup was in having her
Aunt Hannie and the rest of Hannie's family move in to the
house in the Wild-Oat Patch. She thought the invasion had
come about because her mother, no less than her aunt, now
considered her no better and her opinions no more important
than anyone else's.

In fact, Mrs Comeaway had felt an urgent need for company
more cheerful than Trilby's promised to be during the next few
months, and Hannie, never a strong opposer of other people's

wishes, had at last allowed herself to be persuaded that life in a real house held luxury and ease far beyond her imaginings.

As far as the elder Comeaways were concerned, the enlargement of their *ménage* had been entirely successful. Mr Comeaway found that company right in the house was a fine and handy thing to have. It made unnecessary the long walk into the town and the longer and more arduous walk up Heartbreak Hill. He and his brother spent companionable hours discussing the things most important to them, and as the long summer days shrank to the cooler ones of winter they settled into a pleasant routine. In the mornings they sat on the back steps, and in the afternoon, when the sun moved over, they sat on the front steps.

Often, they planned to go down to the wharf and get themselves a job. Several times, they actually hitched their pants higher round their waists and set off, just a little too late to be among the men picked to work on the ships that day. They could always blame the women for their late start and even before they left the house they were openly pessimistic about their chances and self-righteously indignant that they had not been woken earlier.

When they found their pessimism most gratifyingly justified they walked on into the town, seeing they were this far already, and if they did not see anyone they cared for on the main street they most times took the bit between their teeth and bolted up Heartbreak Hill to the humpies and temporary camps scattered in the bush behind it.

Back home again some time in the late afternoon or evening, depending on hospitality offered, they shook their heads regretfully over their inability to get jobs. 'Never could expect to,' Mr Comeaway would say reproachfully, 'not *that* time in the morning.' And according to whether Mrs Comeaway herself had enjoyed her day, she either accepted the implied reproof in the proper spirit or counter-accused.

Not that there was any need for real worry about jobs for the men. Noonah's money came in regularly and so did the child endowment. And there were plenty of extras like relatives and friends arriving for a holiday with two or three months' pay in their pockets. Mr Comeaway thoroughly enjoyed acting as host, differentiating not a whit between friends and relatives with money and friends and relatives without. The main thing was having company.

It followed naturally, too, that the Comeaways' fame as hosts spread and there were weeks when the house seemed never to be free of guests.

In between times, Mrs Comeaway felt she could have done with a little more of liveliness in her chosen companion, but on the whole the two women managed to live together in the same house remarkably well, with an immense tolerance and good humour on the part of Mrs Comeaway and a noteworthy capacity for listening on the part of Hannie. Hannie never argued nor put forth her opinions. She was perfectly happy with Mrs Comeaway's even when these changed from day to day and sometimes from minute to minute.

'Better than the damn cat,' Mrs Comeaway told her husband. 'Even if she don't talk much ya know she understands ya lanwidge.'

On the other hand, her aunt irritated Trilby to the point of frenzy, and the girl would spend hours of her time in her own room rather than be forced to look at her aunt slip-slopping about the house in her draggle-tailed dresses, her hair hanging like greasy black snakes on her greasy fat neck, her shoes, when she wore them, too loose on her large awkward feet. Work, to Hannie, was a trap into which only the unwary fell, but in a household where the accent was on comfort rather than on spotless cleanliness she annoyed nobody but Trilby with this deep-rooted dislike of exertion.

Blanchie's baby was the pet of the entire household, apt to find himself swung up from the floor and soundly hugged by whoever tripped over him. Since one of Blanchie's friends had just lately rolled over on her own baby one night and suffocated it, Tommy slept on a couple of chairs alongside his mother's bed, safe from this danger if not from falling through or over the edge of the chairs.

Audrena went into the double bed with Stella and Bartie, and with this bed wedged tightly against the wall, room had thus been made for the tall double bed which belonged to Charlie and Hannie.

Trilby had refused indignantly to share her room with anyone but Noonah, so Blanchie had to make do with the living-room, but as everyone who used the living-room made do with her bed as a sort of settee, the arrangement was really quite satisfactory. And it still left plenty of floor-space for the accommodation of out-of-town holday-makers and casual droppers-in.

One of these out-of-town friends had recently embroiled the whole family in a lot of trouble. The Comeaways had had much difficulty proving to the police that they had had nothing to do with a certain robbery involving the premises of a golf club. Nothing, that is, apart from innocently partaking of the spoils.

The true culprit was eventually forced to take full responsibility, but on the day of his trial Mrs Comeaway still smarted. 'Ain't nothin ta say ya can't cook a few chops if someone brings ya some,' she said indignantly, sweeping the back veranda with unusual vigour.

The line of men dangling their legs over the edge turned their heads away from the clouds of dust. 'Lucky fa young Willie it's gettin to the end a summer,' one of them ruminated. 'That jail gets awful hot some of them summer days.'

'Bicrikey, you was lucky ta get outa that, Joe,' Dusty Dodd said, shaking his head. Dusty had just come back from a trip to Perth to see his wife who was in hospital. Three hundred and fifty miles by taxi had chewed quite a hole in his pay packet, but there was still some money left, and Dusty was staying with the Comeaways until it had been spent.

'Ask me, that Willie's a real bad one,' Charlie said heavily. Charlie was remembering that his commands to Audrena to get off to bed had had no effect alongside Willie's invitation to her to go for a walk along the beach.

'Gee, it's got some kick, that stuff,' Mr Comeaway said approvingly. 'I ain't never tasted that whisky before. Jus as well them pleece didn't show up an start askin their questions after ole Horace got a taste of it. Woulda landed someone sure. I just knew e was ripe for a bit of a do.'

'You too,' Mrs Comeaway stopped to berate him. 'You'd a got us all in trouble if I hadn't kep pokin ya with me elbow. Talk bout Horace. You was lookin fa trouble two days after. An ya know them monarch have ya up soon as look at ya. That's the way they get ta be sergeants, pinchin people.'

'Not me,' Mr Comeaway said comfortably. 'They wouldn't pinch me. They know I don't go round makin trouble.'

'Dunno so much bout that,' Mrs Comeaway said acidly. 'Ya pretty free with ya fists when ya had a few.'

Hannie appeared in the doorway.

'That meat smells like it might be burning,' she said mildly.

'Fa Gawd's sake put a bit more water in it well,' Mrs Comeaway told her.

Hannie nodded amiably and disappeared.

'Better do it meself,' Mrs Comeaway said resignedly, following her. She grabbed for the saucepan whilst Hannie stood meditating before a shelf of crockery.

Mighty snarlings and cracklings filled the air as Mrs Comeaway held the saucepan under the cold water tap.

'Was just lookin for somethin ta get the water in,' Hannie said apologetically.

'I fixed it now. Ya can go back an sit down.'

The hint of worry disappeared from Hannie's brow. She settled herself gratefully on her chair before the stove.

'Never can make out what goes on in your head,' Mrs Comeaway said good-naturedly, stirring the contents of the saucepan. 'Always sittin about thinkin. Ya don't seem ta know alf what's goin on.'.

'Dunno that you'd call it thinkin,' Hannie disparaged. 'I just like ta sit where it's warm.'

Mrs Comeaway chuckled. 'One thing, ya don't do much harm jus sittin. It's when ya up an about ya get in me way.'

Hannie listened attentively. Now that the move had been made, she had settled down into contentment again. She would have been equally content in the humpy or back in the bush camp.

Trilby spent more and more time in her room. She hated anyone, especially men, to see her in her present condition, and the house seemed always full of visitors. Most of them she had never seen before, and she liked their rough good humour no more than she liked their curious glances.

The visits of the police had reawakened the nightmare of her own stay in jail: heightened the feeling she had of being caught in a trap. So far she had found no way out.

Examining her face in the mirror she brooded over the shape of her features and the colour of her skin. She was lighter-skinned than many of the others. She had seen white girls with deeper toning. Perhaps, down in Perth, she might be accepted as a white person. Would her flattish nose give her away, or the short square white teeth? Fretfully, anxiously, she would peer at herself in the mirror; colour her lips with red to hide the tint of dusty purple that she hated; try out a trace of pink on her cheek-bones, varnish her shell-pink nails the same bright red as her lips.

She practised walking, holding herself high and proud. A lot of the girls she knew walked like old women, shoulders forward, knees bent, in a kind of shamed shamble.

Sometimes she would rise from the bed sick with herself, seeing herself besmirched with the colour and the features of the aborigine, certain that nothing but frustration lay ahead of her.

It was during one of the latter periods that she first accompanied Bartie on one of his rambling walks. She had followed him on a swift impulse, and when he sat a short distance from a tree that had blown almost horizontal with the ground and proceeded to draw it, she thought him quite mad. Bartie acknowledged her presence with a shy grin, presently losing himself in his work, so that he forgot she was there. Trilby drew closer, watched the wind-swept tree appear again on paper, and was interested in spite of herself.

After that first time she went with him often, and a sort of comradeship grew up between them. Gregarious by nature, Trilby craved company even whilst she shunned it. Bartie asked no questions. He was quite simply uninterested in anything outside his drawing and painting. He had to be quicker than lightning to catch the curl of a wave before it broke. And he needed all his concentration to get down on paper what that wave meant to do. Trilby's interest grew, and whilst she was with Bartie she shared, in some strange way, his inner peace and his quiet happiness.

At home she rebuffed every attempt at friendliness. She could endure neither her mother's frank comments on her changing shape, nor Audrena's sly eyes that always slid to her belly. Once, in answer to a sneer, she rushed at her cousin with a hot flat-iron, but her mother grabbed her wrist and made her drop the awful weapon. She fled from Mrs Comeaway's impatient and irritable scolding, though if she had stayed she would have heard a second being delivered to Audrena. There were no flies on Mrs Comeaway, and she had not missed any of Audrena's attempts to upset Trilby's hard-won control.

Towards Noonah, Trilby felt an impatient and grudging gratitude. With gentle consideration, Noonah skipped side issues and concerned herself only with present problems. She informed her sister of all that lay ahead of her, what she could expect in physical changes and sensations, and she anxiously minimized the pain of the actual delivery. Trilby was interested in spite of herself in a book Noonah gave her about methods of painless child-delivery.

Noonah gave her other things, too. Small-scale clothing for the new arrival, half a dozen napkins, a dainty pink and white frock. Trilby was not interested in these things. She stuffed them away in her drawer, out of sight.

Sometimes, lying on her bed in the dark, hearing Noonah's quiet breathing alongside her, Trilby fought out a private war inside herself. In the hiding dark she wanted to pour out all her doubts and fears – tell her sister exactly what had happened – question Noonah, why? Sometimes she had to bite her lips to keep back the flood. She would not give in. She would not allow anyone to see the weakness in her.

Allow Noonah to know that she had gone into this thing with eyes only half open, like any stupid, ignorant black-nigger girl? No! And again, no! It was the stupidity Trilby could not forgive in herself. Badness, wickedness, anything was excusable except plain downright stupidity.

In her own bed, Noonah was always conscious of Trilby's tenseness. She thought it was because Trilby hated to share her room and, though this was no fault of hers, she tried to make amends. She told her sister amusing things that had happened at the hospital, coaxed Trilby to tell her what went on at home. Once she was started, Trilby could keep Noonah amused and entertained for a couple of hours. It took only a description of Hannie sitting in her chair nodding her head and agreeing with everything Mrs Comeaway said for Noonah to have to stifle her giggles in her pillow.

'And lazy!' Trilby said one night on a breath of scorn. 'You know everywhere she's been by the stuff she leaves behind her. She doesn't even pull the chain in the lav. If she puts on a dress and it's inside out she just leaves it that way. She's always wrapping up little parcels of rubbish and leaving them on the sink so she won't have to go outside to the bin. And Mum is always coming across them and stuffing them away in the food safe. I found three lots of tea-leaves there yesterday. Mum seems to like her but I think she's crackers. She falls off her chair asleep every time she has a bit of conto, she lets people cheat her at cards, she just smiles when Uncle Charlie yells terrible things to her, and one day she let Stella eat a whole tin of condensed milk so that she was sick. Mum says her trouble is she's too good-natured. I think her whole trouble is in her head.'

'She IS kind,' Noonah decided. 'What's Blanchie like?'

'Blanchie's like a young Auntie Hannie. Tommy nearly choked the other day on something she gave him to play with, and Mum had to pick him up and bang him on the back to make him cough it up. Blanchie just stood there giggling.'

'She was nervous,' Noonah said, with quick sympathy. 'I think she really loves Tommy.'

'Mum does,' Trilby told her sister. 'Every time she goes out she buys something for him. Every time she's got money, that is. There isn't much around here except when you come home. God knows how we eat.'

'Doesn't Dad work at all?' Noonah asked, troubled.

'Doesn't want work, if you ask me,' Trilby said shortly. 'He keeps saying he's going to get up early and go down to the wharf, but he never does. That's since Uncle Charlie came. They don't do anything but sit around on the veranda or take little walks up to the town. Dad wins some money at cards sometimes. They gamble just about every night. If they don't have money they use matches or razor-blades or even their clothes. Dad lost his good trousers the other night, and he would have lost that big coat too if Mum hadn't hidden it. Not that she doesn't go mad about cards too. She's as bad as the rest. She just likes that coat to put over feet at night.'

'Does Dad lose often?'

'You've seen him,' Trilby said indifferently. 'All depends who he's playing with. Dad plays so fast I can't follow him, and sometimes I think he wins because nobody else can follow him either. When they've been at it a while you wouldn't disturb them if you dropped a cart-load of bricks alongside the table. The only time they talk is when someone's brought a few bottles. Then they start arguing and won't always pay up if someone else wins. I always go to bed, but I can hear them through the wall. If there's an argument I lock the door. One night some woman came wandering in looking for a mirror. She woke me up when she put the light on. She had her eyes all bunged up and her nose was bleeding. Mum told me her husband gave her a thrashing because she tried to take his cards.'

'What did she want a mirror for?' Noonah wondered.

Trilby sniffed. 'Said she had to breathe on it so she'd know she was alive. Told me she read it in some book she got hold of.'

Noonah let out a delighted giggle then she sobered. 'Do they wander into the kids' room too?'

'Mum keeps them out of there,' Trilby said significantly. 'A man went in one night and woke them up. They were playing for pennies that night and he'd been winning.' She smiled unwillingly. 'He said he had too many and they were too heavy to carry, so he was going to give some to the kids. Stella got frightened and yelled, and Mum rushed out and told him off, and then Dad came out and there was nearly a fight. I was scared stiff with all the noise and shouting. I thought the police might come because the whole street must have heard them.'

'Dad had a right to keep him out of the kids' room but.'

'Dad shouldn't have encouraged him to come here,' Trilby gloomed. 'We have some awful people here sometimes. You should have seen some we had last week. All the women bring their kids, and so they'll get some peace they open up their blouses and let those kids feed from their chests right in front of everyone.' She shuddered. 'They make me feel sick.'

'It shouldn't,' Noonah said mildly. 'That's the best food most of those babies get.'

'These aren't babies,' Trilby said scornfully. 'They're up to three and four and five, and they sit on the edge of the table and hold those women's tits up to their mouths and suck and drool – I can't *help* feeling sick.'

Noonah was silent. In the dark, her hand went to her own small, firm breast. She wondered, with a little shamed thrill, how long it would be before she felt the warm mouth of a baby drawing its nourishment from her.

'Mum told me about a little boy who'd turned six and still wanted his mummy's tit. But even she thought he was too old, so she stopped him by painting a big black face on her chest. When she undid her buttons and dragged it out he got such a fright he ran screaming.' Noonah heard the distaste in her sister's voice and was glad Trilby could not see her own highly-amused expression.

'Noonah!'

'Yes?'

'I liked being home at first, and still can't help liking Mum and Dad – you know the way they are – we have fun sometimes still. And Bartie's not a bad kid, or Stella either. But I hate all those people who come round.'

'Mrs Green has a lot of people at her place, too. She says they just come, and how can she send them away.'

'Some of them look so rough and awful,' Trilby brooded. 'And they tell me they're my "lations".' She mimicked one of them. '"I'm your lation, gal. Ya mummy's my lation an so's you." Some of them want to give me money. A few have such big rolls of notes after they get their cheques changed at the bank. I suppose some of them aren't too bad.' Her voice was reluctant. 'I must say they make the place a bit more cheerful, the nice ones. But one old woman frightened the life out of me. She would keep talking about "hairy men". She said I must never go outside at night if I heard birds calling or whistling because likely they were "hairy men" waiting to catch me. She said you can always tell. She said she threw a stone at an emu once and the emu ducked, and that's how she knew it was a "hairy man" because emus are too stupid to duck stones. She said it chased her.'

'Gee!' Noonah said, impressed.

'She was so dirty, too. Even Auntie Hannie looked clean and tidy alongside her. She used to follow me about and get me to listen to these terrible stories that I just don't believe. She said she was staying at a camp once when there'd been a drought and there wasn't much food about, and she saw a man drag a baby away from its mother and throw it straight on the fire. And after – he ate it. That wouldn't be true, would it, Noonah?'

'That's silly,' Noonah said stoutly. 'You ask Mum. I bet if you'd told Mum what she was talking about Mum would have got her out of here.'

'Don't be silly,' Trilby derided. 'She frightened Mum just as much as she frightened me. And Mum believed her, specially about the "hairy men". She said she didn't, but I knew she did.'

'I don't.'

'And she told me the way to get rid of a baby is to put dirt in its mouth as soon as it's born, or chew up some bread until it's soft and mix it up with tobacco and let the baby suck it. And I could have killed her for the way she looked at me, as if she thought I might do the same. But she's gone, thank goodness. She must have started on Dad one day because he got wild and called her a dirty black nigger. She looked at him just as if next minute she was going to spring at him, then she went down the path yelling back at us and swearing every other word. And she shook her fist at Dad. I think it was what he called her that made her get in such a rage. She was just a fool!'

'A fool?'

'Yes, every time she talked about herself she called herself a black nigger, but because Dad said the same thing she went crazy at him. I thought she was going to have a fit. Right here. Her eyes ... ,' Trilby hesitated, 'and her mouth with white spit all round it as if she'd sucked soap. You know what, Noonah? I hated her then, but I was sorry for her too.'

'Why ever?'

Trilby's barriers were down. What she was saying now was coming from inside her, from the sore hurting spot that questioned and could not accept that a coloured skin made you different – and inferior to white people.

'Because I knew how she felt. I even know why she could call herself a black nigger. She had to keep saying it, to try and fool people into thinking she didn't care, and that it didn't matter to her if she was black or white or any other colour. And that was so they wouldn't call her that if they wanted to hurt her. I don't think she'd have cared what else Dad called her, so long as it wasn't that. Black nigger! Imagine, Noonah! Even a poor, dirty, skinny old witch like she is still doesn't want to be called a nigger.' Trilby sat up in bed and her voice was fierce. 'If anyone called me that I'd *kill* them.'

'I just hope she never comes back,' Noonah said worriedly. Her thoughts were occupied with Bartie and Stella. She had hardly heard Trilby's last words.

Trilby was instantly hurt and furious. 'Don't you ever think about the colour you are?' she demanded passionately.

Noonah was getting drowsy and was not so sensitive to Trilby's change of mood as she might otherwise have been.

'What's the use?' she yawned.

Trilby let herself trembling down on to her pillow. For a long moment she was bathed in humiliation. Again, her own fault. What was the use, as Noonah had just said? Of anything! Especially telling anyone the way you felt. She tried to stiffen herself to resentment, but a forlorn sense of betrayal brought a rush of tears to her eyes. Behind her closed lids they forced a way out, ran endlessly down her cheeks to her pillow. And Noonah slept.

CHAPTER 18

It was midweek, and Mr Comeaway was alternately yawning and wishing that the rain would stop long enough for him and his brother to take a walk down to the town. If he did get down there he was darned if he wouldn't go into that Employment Agency and try to get himself a job somewhere. A man got tired of sitting about the house, specially on a rainy day. Mrs Comeaway had kept the children home from school: Blanchie's Tommy was crawling around on the floor, Blanchie and Audrena were sprawled on the settee-bed reading magazines and comics, the women were sitting as close as they could get to the stove, and Charlie was taking a rest on his bed under a pile of old clothes . Besides not being able to take a step without falling over someone – Bartie was lying right in the centre of the floor – Mr Comeaway did not care for the company. He felt alert and restless, not in the least like taking a nap, and he was conscious of active resentment towards Charlie for leaving him alone with a lot of women and children.

He cast a hot, angry look about the room. Mag, mag, mag. Yap, yap, yap. And nobody else getting any warmth out of the stove with those two sitting almost on top of it. He hesitated, toying with the idea of pushing his chair between the two Mrs Comeaway and Hannie occupied, disturbing them from their seeming content. Then he grunted, rose and stamped over to the doorway, where he stood looking gloomily out at the slicing silver rain. And then a figure sloped up the street and turned in at the gate.

Mr Comeaway's face brightened. It was a man, anyway. And who? The figure reached the shelter of the porch and lifted its head.

'Phyllix Barclay!' Mr Comeaway welcomed warmly. 'Fa Gawd's sake come in an dry yaself off a bit.'

Phyllix moved over the veranda, smiling and shaking water from the coat he was taking off. 'Trilby home?' he asked eagerly. 'Thought I'd come down an see her for a bit.'

'Trilby?' Mr Comeaway said vaguely. 'Trilby's here, of course. Too wet ta be anywhere else, ain't it?'

'Course she's here.' Mrs Comeaway came over to the door and examined the visitor curiously. 'Bit wet, ain't ya? Better come in an dry off a bit.'

'Where's Trilby?' Phyllix asked, looking round the room.

'Layin on er bed readin, I spose,' Mrs Comeaway told him. She raised her voice: 'You in there, Trilby?'

'What's wrong?' Trilby called back. The door of her room opened and she stood peering out. Moving over to the doorway of the living-room she caught sight of Phyllix and her face went ash-grey. Phyllix started towards her, but Trilby backed quickly, slamming the door shut in his face.

He stood there for a second stupidly then turned back to the wondering Comeaways. 'What's the matter with her?'

'Don't take no notice a that,' Mrs Comeaway shrugged. 'She's actin funny lately. Gunna have a baby; that's why, I spose. Maybe she feel sick today.'

'Maybe all you women might get up off ya behinds an make a man a cuppa tea or somethin,' Mr Comeaway said testily. 'Shiverin cold e is, an ya don't do nothin but stand there an mag.' He winked at Phyllix. 'Get on ya ruddy pip, these old womans. Always having ta keep em up ta the mark, a man is.' He swept a clutter of clothes from a chair-seat and swung the chair over to the stove. 'There y'are.'

'There goes ya good coat,' Mrs Comeaway told Hannie, glaring at her husband.

Hannie looked hazily over at her daughters. 'Jus pick up me coat, will ya?' she asked. Blanchie reached down to the floor and yanked at the coat. She settled it round her feet and went on with her reading. Audrena sat back on her heels and looked boldly over at Phyllix, but Phyllix was unnoticing. 'Trilby married?' he said hoarsely.

Mr Comeaway looked back at him, surprised at his tone. 'Not yet she ain't.'

'You mind if I go in her room? I gotta message for her. Friend a hers told me ta be sure.' Each sentence was jerky.

'Won't get no change outa that one,' Mrs Comeaway said practically. 'Go in if ya like.'

Shining-eyed, moist-lipped, Audrena watched Phyllix as he went quickly back on to the veranda. She swung her feet over the side of the bed as if to follow him.

'No ya don't,' Mrs Comeaway ordered. 'You stay outa her room. Ya know she don't like ya in there.'

'What's e want, anyway?' Mr Comeaway asked of nobody in particular. 'Ain't e actin a bit queer?'

'An you keep ya nose out things to,' Mrs Comeaway said firmly. 'She don't want im in there, she don't ave ta ave im. You leave that to er.'

'If she don't want im in there, e's gunna come out with a flea in is ear,' Audrena snickered.

Mrs Comeaway swept the girl with a look of dislike and irritation, but she said no more.

There was something going on here which she did not entirely understand, but she was not going to buy into it until she had to.

Phyllix tried a soft knock at Trilby's door but this brought no response, so he quietly turned the handle.

Trilby was lying across the bed with an opened magazine before her. She looked up at him, and for a moment eyed him with a steady gaze. Then she bent her head to the magazine again.

Phyllix moved farther into the room. 'They said ya gunna have a baby,' he said slowly.

Trilby's body stiffened, but she would not speak.

'Trilby, what's wrong? What's the matter with ya?'

'I suppose I can lay on my bed if I want to, can't I?'

'Trilby, is it – was it me?'

Trilby raised her head again. There was scornful detachment in her face and a jeering at the back of her eyes. Whether directed at Phyllix or at herself even Trilby did not fully know.

'Not you,' she said carelessly. She laughed and leaned back on one elbow. 'What made you think it might be you? You're not the only pebble on the beach, are you?'

Phyllix's face was different now. He took Trilby by the shoulders and shook her. 'Who was it?' he asked softly. 'Who was it?'

Trilby tried to free herself. 'Leave me go,' she demanded indignantly. 'How do I know who it was? It wasn't you, that's all I know. You think I'd have a baby of yours? You get straight out of my room, you hear?'

'You been muckin round with other fellers,' Phyllix said, still in that quiet voice. 'Been muckin round with anyone liked to ask?' His fingers dug deep into the soft skin of her upper arms. He shook her again.

'Get out,' Trilby screamed. 'Mum! Dad! Come quick, he's hurting me.'

Phyllix slapped her across the face, not once, but several times. The pain of the slaps shocked Trilby into violence. Springing off the bed she went for him, kicking, biting, scratching, sobbing and screaming in turn. 'Don't you dare to touch me, you beast. I hate you, see? And I'll do it with whoever I like, but never, never you.' Like a cat, and as quickly, she avoided the hands that tried to pinion her and stood with her back against the wall, panting and fierce-eyed.

Her father, with the rest of the family solidly behind him, stopped open-mouthed on the threshold of the room, then he dived at Phyllix. 'For Gawd's sake,' he said, 'what's goin on in here?' He gripped Phyllix and swung the boy away from Trilby. The three were panting now. 'Whatya wanta do a thing like that for?' Mr Comeaway asked again, a mighty puzzlement outweighing all other emotions.

Phyllix switched his attention to Mr Comeaway. 'Who done it?'

'Who done what?' Mr Comeaway said irritably.

'Ya mean the baby?' Audrena said slyly from behind him. 'Why, we thought it was you, Phyllix. We all thought it was you.'

Trilby uttered a choked cry. Her face was grey again. She made for Audrena with upraised, clawing hands. Audrena yelped shrilly, with Trilby's hands twined tightly in her skimpy hair.

'You liar! You liar!' Trilby kept saying in a thin scream, and with each word whe wrenched at Audrena's hair. Audrena recovered her wits, drew her finger-nails down each side of Trilby's face, leaving stripes of blood behind.

Phyllix's eyes went mad. He tried to get at Audrena. Mr Comeaway warded him off with one hand whilst he tried vainly to separate the two girls. 'You – get – out – of – my room,' Trilby said wildly, her fisted hands beating at her cousin's face. 'Dad, make her get out of my *room.*'

Mr Comeaway, comprehending no reason for the uproar, was out of his depths entirely, but his wife bounded into the fight with a wild cry, pulling Audrena off Trilby by main force. Trilby staggered, and Phyllix tried to steady her, but she flung him off.

In the background Hannie set up a wild caterwauling of her own.

'Fa Gawd's sake,' Mr Comeaway begged. 'Will everyone stop it.'

'*Charlie,*' he called desperately, '*Charlie!* Come in ere an give me a hand. *Charlie!*'

Charlie, wakened from a sound sleep, made Trilby's room in four jumps, pulled up sharp in the doorway and stood there pop-eyed with amazement.

'Don't just stand there,' Mr Comeaway puffed testily. 'Get that lot a yours quieted down, will ya?' He was having his work cut out holding Audrena back from a second attempt at Trilby. Phyllix was holding Trilby's struggling figure. Hannie had dropped her voice to a lower range and was yowling like a tired tom cat, and Mrs Comeaway was issuing orders to everyone in sight.

Bartie watched fascinated from behind a veranda post. Stella stood alongside him, holding two dolls by their legs. Blanchie had grabbed up Tommy and fled with him into the backyard.

Against the dividing fence, Mrs Henwood stood craning her neck, her mouth pursed and disapproving, her eyes, naked of their heavy lids, showing pleasure and awe.

It was a good ten minutes before Mr Comeaway and Charlie between them shouted the others into silence.

At the end of it all, Trilby was drooping with exhaustion, her wrists gripped in Phyllix's strong hands. From behind Mrs Comeaway Audrena still glared hatred at her cousin, her nostrils quivering, her hair a tangled whirl. Blanchie, with Tommy on her hip, ventured to peer round the doorway of the living-room. Hannie stood against a wall and examined with puzzled interest a foot that somebody had stamped upon.

'Now!' Mr Comeaway said. 'What was all *that* about, if ya don't mind?'

A utility with a monkey-cage at the back of it came to a standstill outside the front gate, and the atmosphere around the group changed to wary watchfulness. A policeman jumped out of the cab and came with business-like tread up the front path. 'Anything going on here?' he enquired menacingly as he approached. 'Neighbours rang to say you've been creating a disturbance. You better break it up or you can all come back to the station with me. Plenty of room in the cage.'

Mr Comeaway stepped forward, his smile conciliatory, his manner polite and deferential. 'No disturbance here. Just a bit of a quarrel between the family like.'

The officer glared disgustedly round at the dishevelled 'family'. He narrowed his gaze to the self-appointed leader. 'Saw you last week, didn't I? Weren't you connected with that breaking-and-entering up at the club?'

'We didn't have nothing ta do with that,' Mr Comeaway said with dignity. 'Not us.'

'H'm!' The man's eyes were sceptical. He gave the group another threatening look. 'Come on, now. Out with it. What was all this shindig about?'

Mrs Comeaway stood blank and frozen behind her husband. Charlie was as much in the dark as the officer and could only wet his lips and shuffle his feet. Audrena and Blanchie took slow steps backward, and Hannie took this new complication as one more mystery to be added to the rest. Trilby and Phyllix were half-hidden behind Mr and Mrs Comeaway.

Mr Comeaway took a deep breath. 'Ya don't want ta take no notice a the neighbours,' he said heartily. 'Gee, that wasn't nothin. Sort of a disagreement, that's all that was. We worked it out a while back.'

The officer took his heavy foot off the bottom step and placed it alongside its fellow. He seemed disinclined to relax any part of his monitory attitude. As if, now he had their undivided attention, his job was to hammer home his point so that they should never forget it. He grunted and swayed backward, still, however, holding them with a frosty blue eye.

The Comeaways held their breath and hoped.

'Look!' Mr Comeaway inclined his head with even more deference. 'I'll let it go this once, see?'

No one spoke a word.

'But no more rows, see? You kick up any more fuss around here and you'll end up at the station, the lot of you.'

'Yes, sir,' Mr Comeaway said meekly. He waited for a moment to allow his meekness to sink in before he added: 'Only this wasn't a *real* row, if ya get what I mean.'

'Real enough to have someone lay a complaint against you,' the officer said grimly. 'All right now! You lot keep the peace, understand?'

He flicked each face with his cutting look, swung round and stamped back down the path. The Comeaways waited like statues until the utility had pulled out from the kerb and gone off down the street. Then they relaxed.

'There y'are, y'see.' Mr Comeaway swept his group with a disgusted eye. 'Nearly got us all in trouble.'

'How the hell did e get ere?' Charlie said, this last problem troubling him more than all the rest.

'That was er,' Mrs Comeaway said sagely, nodding her head in the direction of the Henwoods' neat house. 'Er an er pot plants,' she added scornfully. She moved to the edge of the veranda and darted a piercing look at the curtains that swayed gently behind Mrs Henwood's lounge windows. She took a deep breath, but

before she could expel it in vituperation Mr Comeaway's black
hand reached forth and plucked her back.

'You ain't had enough trouble?' he enquired fiercely. 'You wanta
bring that monarch back?'

'None a her business,' Mrs Comeaway fumed, sailing majestic-
ally past her husband and into the living-room. 'An you keep them
hands a yours off me.'

'All you women get inside an stay there,' Mr Comeaway ordered
roughly. He turned back to Trilby's room and stood just outside,
addressing himself to Phyllix and Trilby. 'An you two behave
yaselves, see? Gawd!' he added to the attentive Charlie. 'I'm gettin
outa this for a while.' He turned back to the two in the bedroom.
'An when I come back I don't wanta find no rows going on
neether.'

A minute later, with Charlie in tow, he disappeared down the
street, his old grey felt hat clapped on his head to keep off the last of
the softly-falling rain.

Left alone, Trilby turned smouldering eyes on Phyllix. 'Well!
You going to stay here all day long?'

Phyllix eyed the girl reflectively. 'You ain't been going out with
other fellers. Why did ya tell me you had?'

Tears of weakness spurted into Trilby's eyes, but she blinked
them back. Audrena's spitefulness had been a stab in the dark, she
was sure of that. But she was equally certain that Phyllix would
never believe, now, that the baby was not his. He could stand there
and eye her with satisfaction and know that it was he who had done
this to her – set a limit to what she could do, forced her to play a
waiting game when she was so madly impatient for action.

She looked at him through a haze of nausea, and Phyllix stood
there and, most hatefully, smiled at her.

With the quick dart of a lizard, Trilby spat in his face. 'You think
I'd have a baby from you?' she asked, her eyes sick.

Phyllix wiped his cheek with his sleeve. 'I'm going now,' he said
evenly. 'I'll be back when you've cooled off a bit.'

Trilby compelled her trembling legs to support her until he had
gone, then she dropped on the bed. As she had done once before,
she let the soft depths of it absorb her weight of misery.

'Ya think it mighta been him, that Phyllix?' Mr Comeaway asked
his wife that night in the double bed.

Mrs Comeaway frowned into the darkness. 'Ya can bet ya boots
I didn't arsk,' she said emphatically.

'What's gone wrong with er?' Mr Comeaway worried, 'ta carry

on the way she did today? What's she got against that young bloke? Ain't e a nice enough feller?'

A thought flashed through Mrs Comeaway's mind, surprising her with the simple solution it offered to all Trilby's queernesses.

'She didn't want im. That might be it. E made er do it an she didn't want im to. Praps e hurt er. Gave er a fright. An then this baby started comin an frightened er worse.' She sat up in bed, half-inclined to go to her daughter with this newfound knowledge. 'Men!' she said, with tired disgust. 'Like animals the whole lot.' And as her husband muttered defensively, she added: 'I know. Ya can't tell me.' She still sat up. Her instinct was to gather up Trilby the way she would have gathered up any one of the others if they had been hurt. But Trilby was different. She frowned again in doubt of her ability to handle this thing. You never knew what was the right thing with Trilby. Might just snap at her.

How about if she had a word with Mrs Green and got the old lady to talk to Trilby?

As she sat there hesitating an icy wind blew through a broken louvre. That decided the issue. Mrs Comeaway lay down again and pulled the bed-clothes high up around her shoulders.

Alongside her Mr Comeaway was deep in thought.

'Ya know, ya might be right bout that,' he said at last. 'Seems ta me that stuff oughta be done the way it used ta be. Ole fellers takin the girls off inta the bush for a few days an gettin them used ta things slow an easy, so when they come back they know what ta expec.' He chuckled wickedly. 'Those times was here now I mighta got a few a them jobs meself, eh? Learnin the young ones round the camps.'

Mrs Comeaway gave her spouse a good poke. 'Ah, you!' she derided. 'Smoke stick better'n ugly ole bastard like you.'

CHAPTER 19

The house in the Wild-Oat Patch was locked back and front, and the silence surrounding it hit mournfully against Noonah's ears. The thing she loved most about her home was its cheerful clamour. A memory lit her eyes with laughter. Last time her family had gone off on a trip to a neighbouring town they had left Red Cat asleep on one of the beds and he had broken a louvre trying to squeeze his way out. She reached on top of the fuse-box for the big key, opened the front door and searched through the house for forgotten animals. She found a jug of souring milk in the food safe and poured it into a saucer and carried it outside to the veranda for Red Cat.

Then she locked the doors again and picked up her little case. She did not feel injured. She knew that her parents never missed a country show if they could help it. They liked to meet up with old pals, and at shows the card-playing was likely to be brisk and accompanied by real money.

Probably Bartie and Trilby would be waiting for her up at Mrs Green's. This would not be the first time Noonah had spent her days off with the old lady. The house on the hill was a second home to them all.

Walking along the crooked streets Noonah found time to ponder on her sister. Phyllix was almost one of the family now, though nobody, not even Audrena, dared to connect his presence with Trilby's baby. He had simply been absorbed in the same manner as other long-staying visitors.

Yet Trilby had certainly altered since he had come back. She was more cheerful and she took more care of her appearance. And she did not keep to her room so much as she had. She did not encourage Phyllix in any way that Noonah could see. Rather the opposite. Peremptorily, she made use of his services, ordering him to do this and that about the place, but rarely talking with him.

Phyllix showed no resentment. He had money, that was certain. The financial outlook of the Comeaway family had brightened considerably. Noonah wondered how long the money would last, what would happen when it was all gone. If Phyllix would go on another shearing trip to get more. And if he did, would Trilby's new cheerfulness disappear?

It had surprised Noonah to find good fellowship developing between Bartie and Phyllix. Phyllix was so quiet. Yet Bartie had told her he knew all about the aboriginal artists his Miss Simmins had spoken of. And Bartie seemed charmed to find that Phyllix shared his feeling for colour and the shapes of things. Noonah had been amused as well as a little hurt to have her opinions of Bartie's latest sketches brushed aside if they did not coincide with Phyllix's.

Noonah herself liked Phyllix. Gratefully, she had found a strength in him to add to her own. She felt that whilst he lived with her family nothing very bad could happen to them. Alone of the Comeaways, she doubted that the powers would allow them all to go on living in the house in the Wild-Oat Patch for much longer unless they paid more rent. Her thoughts swerved away from how much must be owing by now.

And there was no doubt about Phyllix's feelings for Trilby. Sometimes, watching his eyes as they rested on her sister, Noonah wondered how it would feel to have someone look at her like that. Her step had a different spring to it as she pursued the thought. How good to know you were important to someone, some man. And then she sighed. None of the boys she met ever looked at her except with wariness and distrust, as if she might bite them if they came closer. What was wrong with her?

Again she turned her thoughts from such unrewarding channels. A nurse's training was harder than she had thought. And she knew the reason for that. She could not concentrate as the others did. Stray thoughts of Bartie, her mother and father, Trilby, Trilby's baby, a particular patient in the hospital, the girls with whom she was training, even a patch of blue sky with the lightness of clouds on it, any one of these things was enough to detach her mind from her work. She was good at practical nursing. She knew the reason for that also. She liked handling patients, making them comfortable in their hot and wrinkled beds, setting the pillows the way they wanted them, cheering them when they were miserable. It brought real happiness to her to know that many of them were getting well under her care.

And guiltily, she knew that they appreciated her small departures from routine, the fact that she could be persuaded to pass over an early morning wash, skip a detail of diet, quickly rid their ashtrays of too many cigarette ends. She liked the other trainees, too. She was continually grateful to them because they got her out of trouble. One or two of them had even lied for her on the times when she had felt urgently that she must sleep at home instead of in her room at the hospital. She would have done the same for them, most willingly.

Nobody could save her from examination time though, she thought ruefully. That was coming, even though it was a long way off yet. Her step brisked again. She smiled with relief. Examination time was a long way off.

Bartie was waiting for her at the bottom of Heartbreak Hill. 'Nobody home,' she said cheerfully. 'Thought you must all be dead.'

'They went in the ute,' Bartie chuckled. 'And when they all got in there was hardly any room left for Horace. And it was him borrowed the ute. There's a show over at Marytown, Noonah, and Mum's gunna bring me back something from it.'

'Nice,' Noonah said as they struggled up the first steep rise. 'Mrs Green know I'm coming?'

'Yeah! I think she's glad. Her leg's bad. She's been in bed and all us kids hadda get our own breakfast. Trilby made the tea and let me make some toast by the fire.'

Noonah's pace quickened. 'Ah, poor old thing.'

Mrs Green was sitting on the front veranda in an old cane basket chair; Gramma's chair everyone called it, the chair nobody ever sat in because whilst it was empty there was always the chance that Gramma might come out on the veranda for a minute and sit down and maybe stay a bit longer than she had intended, watching them while they played, looking mightily surprised at their cleverness, encouraging the more timid, settling small fights, telling them the games she had played in her own childhood. And any game, if Gramma was there looking on, was more exciting.

'A touch of the screws,' she deprecated as Noonah climbed the sandy drive and sank down on the wooden step. 'Thought I'd just sit out here in the sun an wait for you.'

'You've got that wool wrapped round your leg?' Noonah asked anxiously. She had bought the wool herself.

Mrs Green gave her skirts a twirl. 'So much wool wrapped round me I feel as if it's shearing-time,' she declared.

Noonah laughed.

'Bartie tell you about the trip?' Mrs Green asked, amused glints in her eyes. 'You should've gone. Might've got yourself a nice young feller up there. All come down for these shows, they do, from the stations roundabout.'

'I wouldn't get one,' Noonah said frankly. 'They are different when I'm around.'

Wisdom was in the old lady's face, and a little sadness mixed up with it.

Noonah leaned against a veranda post and watched Bartie playing with the other kids. 'Gramma,' she asked, a small frown between her eyes. 'Why would a boy sling off at me because I'm training? Isn't it all right to train to be a nurse?'

Mrs Green thought before she spoke. 'It's different,' she said at last. 'That's about the only thing wrong with it.'

Noonah looked her enquiry.

'The different ones gotta pay a bit just to BE different,' Mrs Green said.

'Why?' Noonah resented.

Mrs Green settled herself back with a sigh. 'I don't know how to make it plain, girl. It's just something I know. You go off and do something different from what the mob does, they don't understand. An what they don't understand they don't like. That's a thing that's true all round. You don't understand something, you don't trust it and you don't like it.'

Noonah rubbed with a forefinger at the splintered grey boards of the veranda. 'When people-,' she gave Mrs Green a swift upward look before she went on, 'and it isn't only the boys, Gramma – when people sling off at me for wanting to be a nurse, I feel the same way I used to feel with the white children on the school bus. As if I should be ashamed. As if I've done something terrible. On the bus it was because I wasn't the same colour as the white kids. Now it's because I'm doing my training. And there's no sense in it, is there?' Her eyes met the old lady's. 'Is there, Gramma?'

'You've got to be strong enough to get above em,' Mrs Green said steadily. 'And not let em hurt you. They don't *want* to hurt you, not really. It's just – they don't understand. Praps, I don't know, they might feel you're going over on the other side. Going against *them*. That might be it.'

'I want to be like the other girls but,' Noonah said a little forlornly. 'They don't *see* me, up at the hospital. When I come home, why can't they forget all about me being a nurse?'

Mrs Green shook her head helplessly. 'Don't ask me. An don't blame them neither, Noonah, not too much. A lot of it's jealousy. You've had chances. They haven't.' Her eyes went to the group of children playing in the front yard. 'All these kids – I want them to get their chances too. That's why I stay here. Why I *have* stayed here.'

The slight emphasis was lost on Noonah whose thoughts were following another path. 'What would you think of the boy in the butcher's shop, grabbing hold of my hand when he gave me my change?' she enquired unexpectedly.

Mrs Green's eyes came alert. 'I'd say you better keep your wits about you an count that change,' she said drily.

'I've seen him up the street a few times. Once he walked a little way with me,' she told the old lady, her eyes round with questioning again.

Mrs Green's shoulders slumped a little in her chair. 'Noonah, I can tell you only one thing. I had a girl here once, like you. She wanted to be a nurse, too. Started doing her training up at that hospital, got on real well for a while.'

'What happened to her?'

'She had a baby,' Mrs Green said heavily. 'Like Trilby out there. But it was a white man's baby. After it was born, you could see that all right. I knew, anyhow, because she told me. This white chap but, he wasn't like Phyllix is. This girl told him about the baby an you know what he said?'

Noonah did not move.

'He told her to go an find some other father to pin the blame on,' Mrs Green said. 'Went away about then, too. She couldn't find out where.'

Noonah's eyes were wounded. So was her mouth. She had the feeling of being punished for something she had not done, had not even contemplated doing.

'I didn't say . . . ,' she began, her full bottom lip trembling.

'I know you didn't say,' Mrs Green told her, and there was kindliness and a great depth of understanding in her voice now. 'There's a lot of things a girl doesn't have to say, Noonah, to someone that's as old as me. The trouble is, there's so many ways a girl can take that's wrong, and that won't turn out the way she thinks. Trilby took one way. That girl I just told you about, she took another way. That's two you know about, an there's plenty more. What you want to be, my girl, is careful. Think what you're doing. An if you think real hard, maybe you don't do it.'

She leaned forward to stroke Noonah's hair back from her broad low forehead. Noonah caught the old hand in hers. 'I shouldn't have worried you,' she said remorsefully. 'I won't any more.' She jumped up. 'I'll cook the dinner instead.'

They went down the passage together. 'Where's Trilby?' Noonah asked.

'Down the yard with a pile of comics. Ruthie an Betty went out somewhere. Couldn't get her to go with them, of course.'

'Sit there by the stove, so your leg will keep warm,' Noonah ordered. 'And tell me what you're going to cook.'

She pushed a chair nearer to the still glowing fire in the big black stove. 'I should get up here more often,' she said, 'and I would if there wasn't so much to do always, when I get home.'

'You like being home, don't you?' Mrs Green twinkled.

'Too right!'

Mrs Green laughed.

'Go on now,' Noonah ordered. 'Tell me what you want done. What you really should do is get to bed, and I think I'll make you, too.'

'I'm fine just sitting,' Mrs Green declared, and when the girl was busy slicing vegetables into a big blue saucepan she added: 'Soon I'll have nothing to do but sit.'

Noonah glanced at her over the saucepan.

Mrs Green nodded. 'I'm getting old, Noonah, and I get a bit tired.'

'Ah!' Noonah threw back affectionately. 'Getting old now, eh?'

Mrs Green stopped to regard with whimsical amusement this slim youngster who was such a stranger to old age that she could not even understand it in another person. And it would come to her too, the old lady thought, so surprisingly fast, as it came to everyone. One day your thoughts filled only with the future and the next knowing that only this present day meant anything to you.

'Or maybe,' Mrs Green said aloud, 'It's just the pain in my leg that's troubling me.'

'Of course that must be it.' Noonah was perfectly happy with this explanation, Mrs Green could see.

'Gramma, why would a girl act the way Trilby acts with Phyllix, and still get herself up nice for him?'

Mrs Green smiled. 'She wants – she must have right now – something that Phyllix has got for her. That's why she dresses up for him. She doesn't want him herself, any more than a billy-goat, but she doesn't want anyone else to have him neither.'

'If she knew the way he looks at her,' Noonah said, cutting meat into thin slices.

'She does,' the old lady chuckled. 'Don't you make any mistake about that. Funny thing about Trilby. I've looked at those two many a time, and I thought a couple of times. ...'

'What?'

'He went the wrong way about things,' Mrs Green said seriously, as if Noonah was of her own generation. 'For a girl like Trilby he missed the mark by a mile. Easy an gentle does it with that one. You remember what I said about trusting, out there on the veranda? Wouldn't mind betting if he could get her to trust him – even now – !'

'Go on!'

'Ah, never mind,' Mrs Green smiled. 'Look, Noonah, I got something to tell you. I'm going away.'

'Why?' Noonah asked in consternation, dropping her work to gaze at Gramma Green.

'Partly the government,' the old lady went on. 'They came up the other day. Said I couldn't go on living here less I got that roof fixed.'

'Gramma!'

'One other thing they said. Seems this is a real good block of land this house is built on. Nice view and everything. They thought I wouldn't have much trouble selling the place.'

'They can't make you,' Noonah said indignantly.

'One of em happened to be looking for a block right now.' Gramma smiled a little. 'Wanted to fix up a deal there and then. I said I'd think it over and let him know. And now I've thought. I'm going to write to Robby and tell him he's got a buyer for his house and he can let it go because I want to go back home.'

'The kids! And their education,' Noonah appealed to what she knew Gramma held almost sacred.

'I don't know, Noonah.' There was a quality in the old lady's voice that made Noonah regard her more closely. She went swiftly over to the chair, took Mrs Green's head in her hands and pushed it gently into the crook of her shoulder. 'Yes,' she crooned. 'You want to go back to where you were born, don't you? Mummy's told me all the things you told her. She knows you love the north better than here. And the kids will be all right. Someone else will look after them. You don't have to worry about anything, Gramma.'

Mrs Green reached up and squeezed Noonah's forearm. 'I thought you'd understand without a lot of talking.'

Noonah patted her shoulder and went back behind the long kitchen table.

'I even had a white kid here for a while,' Mrs Green meditated. 'For a year or two.'

'You did?'

'The mother asked me to mind it for a day – and there were some thought she'd never come back and I'd have that kid for always. I knew she'd come back. She loved that kid of hers. Pretty, it was. Had a lot of red hair – same colour as a little pony I had once when

I was a kid myself. I got real fond of that little girl, the time she was here.'

'She reminded you of your pony?'

'Ah!' Mrs Green laughed.

'And what did the woman say when she came to get her?' Noonah had finished making her stew and she came to sit alongside Gramma.

'Don't remember,' the old lady said, her smile tantalizing. 'Lot of silly things. Even wanted to pay me.'

'Didn't she say why she'd gone off and left it with you?'

Mrs Green looked surprised. 'Where else did she have to leave it?'

'Gramma!' Noonah slipped off the table. She turned to the door as Bartie came flying in. 'What do *you* want? Getting hungry?'

'What about you and me going for a walk – you know.' Bartie gestured towards the valley and Noonah nodded.

'All right!' She wiped her hands on the side of her frock and carried the big saucepan over to the stove.

'How's your leg now, Gramma?' she asked, whilst Bartie danced with impatience in the background.

'I'm going to sit here and think,' Gramma said. 'About the sun all hot on me, getting right through to my bones, and how I'm going to soak it up and let it get rid of every pain in every part.'

'We'll miss you but,' Noonah told her. 'It'll be terrible with no Gramma Green to stay with.'

'Off an go for your walk,' Mrs Green said briskly, 'before Bartie drags your arm off.'

CHAPTER 20

Bartie had a friend of his own age. A real friend who liked him better than she liked anyone else. And she lived in the valley below Mrs Green's house.

Diane was the same age as Bartie, but she was a class below him at school. In contrast, Diane was all cheek and cheerful laughter and she had a disregard for authority that stunned Bartie into

lasting admiration. She arrived late at school nearly every day, her
stiff curly hair bouncing in two bunches on either side of her round
shining black face. Diane was much darker than anyone else Bartie
knew, and that was because she was part negro. Diane was nearly
always in trouble, both at home and at school. The man who
taught her class was an emigrant under the teacher-training
scheme. His nationality was a source of continual conjecture for the
children he taught, and sometimes the conjecture became ribald,
especially if Diane was implicated. Mr Jenzen was extremely slow-
spoken and he had a passion for discipline. Once or twice a day
he took Diane through her misdeeds and endeavoured, without
success, to find out why she had erred.

'You know that school begins at nine?' His face was turned
slightly, for this first question, his pale blue eyes fixed askance on
Diane's lively little face.

'Yes,' Diane would nod.

'Then why,' with the air of one springing a trap, 'are you late?'

Diane's answer was always a shrug, with perhaps a beguiling
little smile to soften it.

'You know you must be punished when you are late?'

'Yes!' The big brown eyes opened wide in innocence.

A quick lift of the heavy chin and the broad face with its high
cheek-bones would come full-face, pale blue eyes glowing beneath
down-drooping lids on which grew scant white eyelashes. 'You
fetch me my stick, please?'

This was the period the waiting children enjoyed most. Only
Diane could pretend such concern and distress over the whereabouts of the stick. The diligent eyes searched in every corner
where she knew it was not.

And there was the rising impatience of Mr Jenzen as he stood
next to his table drumming a soft tattoo with the tips of his fingers.
And finally, most exciting moment of all, the leap of anger to his
face; the long stride to the cupboard inside which, suspended by its
strap, hung his stick.

And there was the extra force with which he lashed at the small
pale palm held out obediently in answer to his curt instruction.

To Diane it was all worth while, even the pain in her hand,
because afterwards, during the lunch-hour, she could take aside a
crew of selected friends and ape Mr Jenzen so perfectly that even
her lively little face took on for the time being the dour cast of her
teacher's.

Diane's mother was big and tall and calm, almost as slow-spoken
as Diane's teacher, but whereas Mr Jenzen's voice was scratchy

and ragged, words dropping from his mouth with a sound as of shell grit, Mrs Mongo's voice had the far-off sound of poured treacle, and it lingered on each word caressingly, as though reluctant to pass on to the next. Diane was the eldest of a brood of six, and Mrs Mongo had lately begun to think that the size of her family had got beyond a joke.

But it was well known that she would suffer no infringement of the rights of either herself or her children. She came often to talk with Diane's teacher, her soft brown heavily-lidded eyes gazing gravely into his. She begged the teacher to remember that he, too, had once been young. She spoke without emotion of the day when it had taken four grown teachers to hold her down because they had considered she needed punishment. Mr Jenzen, if he had troubled to inspect her tall strength, must have been under no illusions about what she could do to four grown teachers at her present stage of development. And finally, she reminded Mr Jenzen that her daughter attended the school in order to be educated and that she, and not Mr Jenzen, was the one who must deal out punishment to her own.

The wicked Diane always contrived to be within earshot at these interviews, with the result that her select band was treated to yet another comic representation of what had transpired.

Noonah had heard much of Diane. Now she and Bartie were on their way down the hillside so that Noonah could actually see the girl.

They walked through the wattle-studded valley until they came to the Mongo camp. It was a fair-sized camp, this, to cope not only with the Mongo small fry, but with Mrs Mongo's old mother, her sister who had three children of her own, and Denzyl, who was currently acting father to her sister's children.

Mrs Mongo's mother sat on a chair in the doorway of the main erection, exchanging gossip with her daughter who had just finished washing and was now spiking clothes on the barbed-wire clothes-line. Diane rose from the midst of a squirming mass of children and came dancing to meet them.

Mrs Mongo stopped hanging up clothes long enough to shake her head at Noonah.

'If e took my tip,' she said in her lazy melodious drawl, 'e'd keep well away from that one. Mischief she's in all the time – an no one knowing what she's gunna be upta next. They tole you bout last week-end?' She raised black scimitars of eyebrows over her calm brown eyes.

'Nekked – no cloes,' cried the old lady in the doorway, rocking

energetically and darting quick little looks at her daughter, at
Noonah, at the children playing in the dust, and at Bartie and
Diane.

'They hadda come back through the bush,' Mrs Mongo said, 'an
wait till after it was dark, too. Couldn't think where she'd got to.'

'What happened?' Noonah said, curious.

'Ah, clothes is silly,' Diane said scornfully. 'You ever been
swimmin without clothes? That water feels like little hands strokin.'

'These two's always goin fa walks,' Mrs Mongo said. 'Long that
beach at the back where all them nasty men live. Talkin doesn't
stop that Diane. Beltin don't neither. An Gawd knows where she
left er good school frock.'

'I told you,' Diane said breezily. 'I put it under a bush in the
sand-hills, but we forgot to mark the place, so we couldn't find it
again. Let's go down now, Bartie, an have another look. Bartie, did
your mother go mad at you too?'

Bartie grinned and the grin slid over to include Noonah. 'She
didn't know,' he said simply. 'I just crept in to where I sleep and
got into bed.'

'We ran along the beach,' Diane told Noonah. 'As hard as we
could, and I beat Bartie, didn't I? And sometimes we went in the
water. And we went nearly to the end of the sand-hills.'

'An them ole pensioners livin just the other side,' Mrs Mongo
said, her eyes meeting Noonah's. 'All sorts goes on down there.'
She shrugged. 'I tole er. Serves er right if they get er, some time.'

'Wouldn't get ME,' Diane said, with decision. 'We climbed up
the top of one sand-hill and we seen em. They got little places just
like ours. We seen em, didn't we, Bartie?'

'An a good job nobody see you,' the old lady grumbled. 'Kids
thout cloes.'

'Yes, you've *gotta*,' Diane said suddenly, pulling at Bartie's hand.
'Come on!'

Bartie looked at Noonah, who nodded. The two were off and
away like rabbits, out of sight in an instant.

'They didn't mean the beach but, did they?' Noonah remembered, in a little alarm. 'That's not where they've gone, is it?'

'She found something. Forgot what it is, but she been talkin bout
showing it to young Bartie. Guess they've gone where she found it,'
Mrs Mongo said, draping more clothes over her homemade line.

Bartie went out of Noonah's head when she looked round to see
Phyllix and old Skippy. As usual, Phyllix did not waste time on
words when there was someone with him to do the talking. Noonah
could see that Skippy was upset. His old voice shook with rage and

the tone was so high it occasionally slid over the edge into a raspy croak.

'A full-blood, that's what I am,' he yelled, eyeing the group belligerently. 'And im down there in the town want me ta live up ere with all them arf-carse no-goods. Me live with fellers like that – carryin on – fightin all over the place. I tell im I'm a full-blood an wanta go back long my place. Nother thing,' his jaw shot out and back, 'who's gunna do me cookin up there, eh?'

Noonah gestured to the old man to sit on the kerosene-tin where she had been sitting herself. Skippy gave the tin a contemptuous kick with his heavy loose boot and stood breathing fire on everyone present.

'Praps they think you're too old to live too far away from everyone,' Noonah shrieked into his ear. 'What about up there. Anyone to do your cooking up there?' With her hand she waved vaguely towards the north.

'Yeah, an e said I couldn't ave me bike,' Skippy snarled, his thoughts turning to fresh injury. 'I got the money, ain't I?'

Noonah turned a look of enquiry on Phyllix. But Mrs Mongo answered for Phyllix. 'E went into a shop in town when he found e just gotta take this ouse up the camp or go without,' she said, amusement making her voice even richer, 'and blow me down if e didn't order isself a bike, so's e could ride back up north. With them legs a his.'

'Shopman rings up this partment bloke,' the old lady continued, 'an this ole man don't get is bike.'

Skippy glared round, half comprehending. 'Up outa this,' he ordered Phyllix. 'I want me tea. Fellers like this,' he glared at Mrs Mongo and then at her mother, 'no good ta be roun. Like them others up there in the camp.'

'Keep ya wool on,' Mrs Mongo said good-naturedly. 'Ya can live where ya like, as far's I'm concerned an,' she eyed her fighting brood, 'take some a these with ya ta keep ya company.'

Skippy stamped off, ploughing an uncertain path up the hill to Mrs Green's house, but Phyllix stayed behind.

'Been lookin at them new ouses?' Mrs Mongo inquired.

Phyllix nodded. 'Seen them?' he asked Noonah. 'If you haven't, come on back and have a look.'

Noonah smiled a good-bye to the Mongos, and Mrs Mongo looked with kindly interest from her to Phyllix. 'Don't see ya sister round no more. Someone tole me she's wild bout gettin a baby. Won't do no good now, I spose, but I could tell er a few things after she's ad it, if she wants ta know. I found out a few things.'

'I'll tell her,' Noonah said, feeling hot.

'Tell er I got all the dope in some book someone give me,' Mrs Mongo called after her as Phyllix led her back along the path he had taken.

Noonah peeped at Phyllix, but he was looking woodenly ahead of him.

The big camping area was soft with fresh green grass threaded through with bright wild flowers. Six or seven newly-built small houses sat in a prim circle in the middle of it.

'Not bad, eh?' Phyllix asked.

This was Noonah's first visit to the government reserve. She stared about her curiously, noting a bigger building at the back obviously intended as a laundry, with two smaller rooms each end.

'That's the showers, and so on,' Phyllix told her. 'That's for everyone.'

'It's nice,' Noonah said, more for something to say.

'Not a bad lot of people up here now either. Not much drinking and fighting goes on. A lot of young people, too.'

'Yes,' Noonah said, wondering.

'This was gunna be Skippy's joint,' Phyllix said, stopping at one of the little empty houses. 'One room, with a stove in it, and a bit of a veranda. All new, too.'

Noonah peeped through the glass louvres, admired the new wood stove inside the tiny room.

'You think Trilby'd like to live here?' Phyllix said abruptly. 'When it's all over?'

Noonah's face was pitiful. Mrs Green had mentioned something about Phyllix not knowing the right way to go about things with Trilby. How far out he was, she thought, if he meant to ask Trilby to live on the reserve with him.

'She wouldn't do it,' she told him. 'Trilby hates reserves. She thinks they're terrible places to live. You wouldn't get her on one if you built a castle for her.'

Phyllix looked away from her. 'It's all right. Just something I thought up when I heard old Skippy going hot and strong about not wanting the place. It'd be a start, is all I thought.' He kicked a stone at his feet. 'But I spose I knew she'd never come to a place like this.'

They turned away from the little house and moved down the track that led to it. 'Pity it isn't bigger,' Phyllix said. 'Mighta done for ya Mum and Dad and the kids.'

Noonah smiled, not really considering the idea. 'We've lived in places smaller than that.'

'Trouble here is they won't let ya,' Phyllix said. 'Skippy's place is for a couple at the most. No more. If ya Mum and Dad came here they'd have ta send the kids back to the mission.'

'No,' Noonah said in horror. 'They wouldn't do that.'

Phyllix shrugged. 'Just thought if they got kicked out down there. Because of the rent.' He went on in silence for a while, then added: 'Course they wouldn't have to worry bout Trilby. I could look out for her, if . . . ,' he frowned, 'if she'd damn well let me.'

Noonah's mounting fear for the welfare of Bartie and Stella was drowned in a gush of sympathy for Phyllix. She touched his hand. 'It'll be all right,' she told him. 'You just wait. It'll be all right later on, between you and Trilby.'

'I got a feeling,' Phyllix said tensely, 'things aren't ever going right for Trilby and me.' He stopped to break two fly switches from a wattle, one of which he handed to Noonah. She took it gratefully and used it to beat off the horde of tiny bush flies that had come with the greening grass. 'I've tried. Done everything I could think of. She won't have a bar of me.'

'Phyllix,' Noonah said impulsively, after they had walked a while in silence. 'Why do you – you know?'

'Hang around,' Phyllix said hardly, giving her a brief look. 'Ever since I was a kid I wanted not to be kicked around when I grew up. You know how it is. Some a these white people don't seem ta think ya got any feelings at all. Just because ya dark. Talk right in front of ya face as if ya couldn't hear, or as if it didn't matter if ya did hear. Even the pleece. Ya gotta keep on the right side of em. Get in any sort of a mix-up an ya sure to be the one that collects. I wasn't sixteen when I had my first barney with the pleece. I was up for takin a drink a conto. Didn't even like the damn stuff. Did it for a joke sort of. But Trilby,' his head came up, 'nobody's gunna tell *her* what ta do. Not even the pleece. She makes all the others look like a lot of dead-heads.' His mouth curled in a grin. 'Even snappin an snippy the way she is, I still rather have her than any other one. Trouble is, she don't seem ta feel the same way bout me.'

Noonah's mouth smiled back at him, but her eyes were wistful. She wanted some feller to feel that way about her. Why should Trilby be the only lucky one?

'I tell ya what,' Phyllix said restlessly, 'I'm goin away again. For a while.'

CHAPTER 21

The man who was keeping nit leaned easily against a tree, his heavy-lidded incurious gaze fixed steadily on the two men who approached him. Mr Comeaway stopped in order to hand over the pound note he had in readiness, and before the nit-keeper stuffed it carelessly into his pocket he jerked his head towards the gloom of the bush. Mr Comeaway nodded, and he and Charlie marched off in the direction indicated.

A quarter of a mile into the bush and past a clump of wattles, a bright yellow glare chased the night away. A burning pyramid of old motor-car tyres bellied flames and smoke both upward and over a sprawling group of people who sat close enough to breathe in the pungent odour and to peer through watering eyes at the cards in their hands and at the five that lay face up on a piece of old grey blanket thrown down in their midst.

'Manila,' thought Mr Comeaway pleasurably. He nudged Charlie's hip, and the two exchanged grins. Nothing like a game of Manila for excitement. Two cards dealt to each player and you made what you could of the cards in your hand and any three of those five in the centre.

Plenty of players tonight, Mr Comeaway noted approvingly. Old Mattie, her wide, flattish features and craggy brow outlined against the glow of the fire, her crutches placed carefully at her side so that she could get at them to aid her in rising or to lay about her if trouble threatened. Horace, sitting there quiet and dignified; Billy Gumnut and his shyly giggling bush black, quiet and subdued now as she listened to the betting; and more than a dozen others, all quiet and tense.

Mr Comeaway and Charlie sank to their haunches and waited patiently. When the dealing started again Mr Comeaway moved forward to the circle.

In his pocket, resting gently against his hip, were the ten pound notes Marty had lent him. The surprise and warm pleasure of watching Marty count out that money had not yet left Mr

Comeaway. His lucky day all right, bumping into the young chap just, it must have been, after he had cashed his cheque at the bank and before anyone else had had a chance to get at him. Nice young bloke, that. Probably could have asked for twice what he did and got it. For a second Mr Comeaway's thoughts were tinged with regret. But no, a fair thing was a fair thing. You wouldn't want to clean a feller out on his first day, and what Marty had would go soon enough once he started flashing his money about.

'Hope the feller has a bit of fun before they all get on to im,' Mr Comeaway thought with expanding generosity. 'Damn well deserves it after doin that string a sheds.'

The next hand was dealt, and Mr Comeaway's palms were suddenly wet. The sweat sprang out across his upper lip and under his arms too. Yet his body pricked with coldness. Two aces in his hand. Two aces! And in the centre, a couple of kings, an eight of clubs – and two more aces.

The betting started, rapping from person to person as quick as the crackles of a bush fire. The hand in the middle was a dandy to bring up the betting. The peace that settled over Mr Comeaway told him that all would be well. He clamped down on himself. No flicker of excitement must show on his face – no smallest quaver of it in his voice. And it was him to bet. 'Ten pounds,' he said, allowing exactly the right amount of time for deliberation.

There were a few sharply-indrawn breaths. No one else bet now until it was the turn of the man opposite him. A stranger, this one. Big mean-looking chap with bunchy shoulders. He might need watching. The man's voice was a squeaky whisper. He had to clear his throat and start again, and this time he grunted deep. 'Ten pounds – and thirty pound better.'

People sat still like statues now and the only sound came from the subdued roar of the flaming tyres. Nobody bet until it was Mr Comeaway's turn again. He hesitated just a bit longer this time. 'Thirty pound back twenty-five pound.'

The brightness of dark brown eyes was fixed in unwavering attention, weighing up, giving value to the slightest flicker to pass over the faces of the two men.

The big man cleared his throat again. 'Twenty-five pound back to another fifty.' Fifty? A sigh went round the table. Old Mattie clutched her wooden crutches tighter and eased her skinny haunches into a more comfortable position.

'Fifty pound,' Mr Comeaway said indomitably, 'Back fifty pound.'

'Give us a look at ya cards,' said the dealer.

Mr Comeaway had been waiting for just that. An examination of his cards by the dealer meant that no examination would be made of his pockets. He handed them over, and the dealer scrutinized them through narrowed eyes and returned them. Now the dealer's face looked smooth and secret.

The big man shot the dealer a look of anger. His mouth formed a line of disgust. He threw fifty pounds in notes on the table, and whilst the dealer counted them he snarled: 'See ya.' But the flicker at the back of his eyes and the bad-tempered look of his mouth meant defeat, and everyone around the circle knew it.

Mr Comeaway, his mouth still under control, though not his eyes, threw down his two aces with a modest flourish. And the quiet was shattered. Laughter, jeers for the big angry man, shrill squealing from Mattie, back-slapping and more roars of laughter, and over the top of it all the big man's voice as he lurched to his feet and leaned over to accuse: '*Wunmulla jinagubby* Mt Magnet bastard.'

'Ya right,' Mr Comeaway grinned, and the laughter in his eyes leapt out to pile coals on the heat of the other's anger. While the babble went on and on the stranger tore more money from his pocket and threw it down on the old grey blanket. One hundred and eighty pounds in all. One hundred and eighty pounds!

It was months since there had been such a downright victory. The sight of the money stirred the whole crowd.

Mr Comeaway gathered it up and stuffed it deep into the pockets of his trousers. And he laughed and roared with the rest of them, feeling light-headed and almost sick.

A woman plunked herself down on his lap and held his head to her redolent bosom, and Mr Comeaway felt the good warmth of her soft thighs with outspread hand. She was plucked from his lap as suddenly as she had arrived, and an anguished squawk from the rear followed her disappearance. Mr Comeaway watched indulgently as she was cuffed into order.

He could have gone home right away. Nobody would have stopped him. But he stayed. He needed a few minutes more to gain control of the trembling in his legs. He played again, and again after that. And the last time he played he won more money with a full hand king high.

It was as he was gathering up his further winnings that the mopoke in the tree ten feet away gave voice to its lugubrious and mournful 'Morepawk'.

He concluded, afterwards, that it was Mattie who had started the commotion, but if this were so then she had but a split-second start on the rest. However it began, the tearing screams that followed the initial rending of the quiet night almost lifted the scalp from his head. People leapt to their feet and vanished. Almost between one breath and the next Mr Comeaway saw someone snatch the bird from the tree, chop it into small pieces with a knife, and stuff it into a hole clawed deep by frantic fingers.

'Bastard's after someone,' the man gasped, and then he was away himself, following the shrieks into the black of the bush.

The stamping crowd had gained a start on him, but Mr Comeaway pushed doggedly on, his eyes popping with exertion, his powerful legs flailing and, with all the excitement, both hands holding tight to the notes that bulked in his back pockets. Past wailing Mattie, whose legs had forgotten the need for crutches, past the big angry man and the little dealer of cards, past others who crowed for breath and those who still had sufficient for screaming. And at last he was running ahead of everyone, with Horace on one side and Charlie on the other, and the three of them caught up with the exhilaration of it all, wanting most to stop in their tracks and roar out their mirth now that that first panic had left them.

And at last they did. 'My Gawd!' Charlie wheezed and panted and chuckled. 'They got me in, with at damn yellin an carryin on.'

'Bicrickey,' Mr Comeaway agreed.

But it was left to Horace to nod his head in wisdom and thought and point out: 'Jus the same. Ya never know bout them things. Just as well we came away fum there.

'Ya mean ya believe in all that?' Charlie scorned, still panting.

'All I'm saying,' Horace warned. 'Ya never know.'

And so they walked on.

After a while the thought of the money took precedence.

'Wouldn't mind spreadin that money out all over the table an havin a good look at it,' Charlie said.

'Yeah! No wakin up the ole lady but, spose she's asleep,' Mr Comeaway warned. 'We gotta think this thing out careful first.'

'Can't never trust womans,' Horace agreed, his thoughts playing lovingly with possibilities.

Near the outskirts of the town a taxi cruised past. Mr Comeaway hailed it with a peremptory gesture and all three climbed in.

'An if we call up the camp,' Horace said graciously, sinking into his soft leather seat, 'I might just find I had a bottle or two hid away.'

'If ya got the money ta pay for it,' the taxi-driver offered, 'I can get as much as youse three'll want.'

'Could do with a drink,' Charlie said wistfully.

'Yeah boy,' Mr Comeaway enthused. 'We might do that.'

But after all, the caution that made them stop the taxi a hundred

yards away from the house in the Wild-Oat Patch was wasted. The
night was younger than they had thought, and the women were still
out of bed. There was nothing for it but the grand gesture, and Mr
Comeaway made it not unwillingly. The pound notes, the fivers,
the ten shillings, the silver, all fluttered and chinked and rolled and
were caught and clutched and stared at by the dazed and delighted
Hannie and Mrs Comeaway.

'An it don't mean trouble,' Mr Comeaway answered the look
Mrs Comeaway shot at him. 'All come by honest. Ain't that right,
Horace?' Horace nodded gravely. 'I dunno what ta do first,' Mrs
Comeaway said, sinking down on a chair.

'Pork chops,' Hannie said tentatively. 'Wouldn't mind a pork
chop meself.'

'Gotta nother letter fum that man bout the rent today. Least, I
think it'll be bout rent. Didn't open it yet.'

'We can pay that,' Mr Comeaway said grandly. 'The whole
damn lot.'

'An that sour-face butcher,' Mrs Comeaway added. 'An the
grocer man an a coupla others. An what about we take a big heap a
stuff up Mrs Green's an cook it up there an let's have a good feed,
eh?'

'Where would a heap a money like that come fum?' Hannie said
reverently.

Horace opened one of his bottles and poured the contents into
cups. 'Seein it's early,' he said pleasantly, 'we might jus as well sit
in to another little game while we drink this stuff.'

'Only first,' Mrs Comeaway said firmly, 'we put all this money
away somewhere where it ain't gunna blow away.' She picked up
Stella's little school case off the floor by the table and stacked all the
money inside it, leaving out only a little of the silver. Poker-faced,
Horace watched her.

Mr Comeaway took a good long swallow of his conto. 'Count
ME out,' he said lazily. 'I rather just sit ere an think,' He smiled a
beatific smile round the circle of faces and closed his eyes.

Horace said nothing.

The news of the win spread quickly. Auntie Milly arrived down
from Mullewa for a little visit with her relations and two months
later, when her husband got picked up for supplying, she decided
she might as well fill in the time he would be away where she was.
Neither Mr nor Mrs Comeaway was entirely happy about this
arrangement because Auntie Milly was bossy and interfering and
wanted to run the roost. Mrs Comeaway managed to put up with

the old lady by living one day at a time which was all right with old Milly since that way her welcome lost nothing of its freshness. Mr Comeaway ignored her and slipped free of entanglement by pretending not to hear her when she spoke to him.

She was good with the kids, though, and could always be relied on to keep them quiet by some means or another, even if she had to frighten six months' growth out of them.

'You kids jus better be quiet,' she would warn, blazing eyes turned on the darkness outside the window. 'Wijari round here tonight. You see em dancin over that window – quick – up down, up down.' Her shoulders would rise towards her ears, and the children's fascinated eyes would follow her gaze to watch moonlight flickering among the shadows.

Having quietened them until their hearts beat fast with fear, she would lie down alongside them and comfort them with her presence. She believed what she said, too.

'Wijari after *me*' she told Mrs Comeaway indignantly, one afternoon.

'Yeah!' Mrs Comeaway scoffed, whilst Hannie watched wide-eyed and nervous from her chair by the stove.

'They after me true. Sitting round in them wattles. I did see em, dancin backwards. Wijara them was. My Word! An after ole woman like me.'

Mrs Comeaway straightened, half-believing. 'H'nnn!'

There were other visitors, too, to whom news of the win came like an unexpected dividend. Nobody could be accused of cadging who had visited only in the spirit of friendliness like Dora Dicker, because she was convinced she was dying.

Dora Dicker was a pest and a menace. Even Hannie was gently sceptical.

Only Mrs Comeaway's generous heart was touched. 'Ah, winyarn,' she murmured, when Trilby told her scornfully that Dora was just putting on an act.

'All that screaming and going stiff and putting her hand to her heart,' Trilby scowled. 'There's nothing wrong with HER.'

'Anyone can get sick,' Mrs Comeaway said firmly. 'Might happen ta me one day.'

So Dora was humoured and pampered, and while there was a bit of money about she had special food and Blanchie's bed while Mr Comeaway fought valiantly all night against the threshing limbs of his two youngest.

'I'm gunna die,' Dora moaned one day. 'I can feel it. Here!' She rolled big agonized eyes. The skin on her face was wet.

'You gunna be all right. Ain't she?' Mrs Comeaway appealed to Auntie Milly, to the dumb and uncomprehending Auntie Hannie.

She tried to roll Dora down on the settee. 'No good,' Dora yelled. 'You gotta get the littlies down so I can see em before I die.'

Now this was a thing Dora mentioned often, and Mrs Comeaway would have complied long ago if it had not been for Mr Comeaway and Trilby and old Auntie Milly and even Noonah, who all believed that the limit of accommodation had been reached with thirteen people already under the roof more or less permanently. But there was only old Auntie Milly to defy today, so Mrs Comeaway took the bull by the horns and promised to get Dora's children down.

'The doctors say there ain't nothing wrong with er, don't they?' Mr Comeaway said irascibly, when told. 'Then that settles it, don't it?' She can stay ere a while longer, turning the whole place into a madhouse, then she can get back where she belongs, an a damn good riddance.'

'I said she could have em down,' Mrs Comeaway said firmly, though wearily. 'Fa Gawd's sake let's get em jus so's she'll shut up bout em.'

'You go an send one a them tellygrams ta their gramma,' she ordered a reluctant Trilby.

'Don't know as I like so much womans bout a house,' Auntie Milly sniffed and tossed her head at the look she saw in her niece's eye.

The children arrived with their gramma on the following day, the children tired and cranky from their long trip down by train and the walk that had proved so long and wearisome, from the station to the house in the Wild-Oat Patch.

Dora was languidly pleased to see them, and the children were hysterically pleased to see their mother. Mrs Comeaway's heart was touched. Even Hannie and Auntie Milly nodded approvingly, though the problem of sleeping everyone was still to be solved. It was a piece of good luck that Mrs Comeaway and the newly-arrived gramma liked each other and were pals of old. It helped lighten the atmosphere.

At night it was Hannie and Auntie Milly who complained least. Hannie wandered round until she found a spot that would take her bulk, and Auntie Milly was happiest sleeping in front of the dying fire anyway. Bartie and Stella slept in Noonah's bed, monitored by a vigilant-eyed and sharp-spoken Trilby, while Mrs Comeaway harboured the girls in hers. Mr Comeaway and Charlie made their own arrangements, sometimes not bothering to come home at all for their nightly rest, though there was one night when Mr Comeaway's loud-voiced complaints might have been taken to indicate that he had come to the end of his endurance.

Having got themselves into a game that had lasted most of the night both he and Charlie had decided that the long walk home to the Wild-Oat Patch was not worth the effort. They had bedded themselves down on the floor under a couple of old blankets that had been thrown to them.

'An I dunno what was in them blankets,' Mr Comeaway complained, 'but whatever it was, they had a bite on em like a alligator.' He scratched vigorously. 'Got bit allover.'

'E did,' Charlie said. 'I couldn't feel much.'

'No,' Mr Comeaway glared at his brother. 'They was all on my side, seemingly. An there's Charlie tellin me ta keep quiet an lie still an when I did, that's when the buggers *really* started bitin. Gawd, no more a that fa me.'

Dora's children were sufficient only for a week or so. After that she felt she was getting worse and should have her husband with her to comfort her in her dying hours. Dora's husband had a good job with the Railways Department, a good permanent job at which he collected regular weekly wages, and it might have been this fact which helped Mrs Comeaway make up her mind to send for him. No win, however big, could long stand the strain of keeping a dozen or so stomachs comfortably filled every day.

She made a good decision. Dora's husband, already gloomy on the subject of his wife's health, immediately handed in his notice, collected back pay and holiday pay and arrived down by taxi to pick up Dora and take her down to Perth for further examinations. They left in the same taxi, with all the Comeaways except Trilby waving fond farewell from the front fence.

Mr Comeaway looked over the inmates of his house with a certain brooding dissatisfaction when he trailed them back again. There seemed a good big crowd of them and it sort of unsettled a man when he couldn't even count on a bed at night. Two or three pals, that was one thing. This great heap of womans, that was another thing altogether, specially when there were the kids as well.

He showed displeasure first by roaring at the startled children, who were quite unused to anything but kindliness and indulgence from the head of this house. When he had thoroughly disconcerted the children he turned his attention on old Auntie Milly, who had merely been sitting about meditating and minding her own business. Auntil Milly was so incensed she took Mrs Comeaway to task for marrying such a man.

'Ah, I dunno! He's all right,' Mrs Comeaway said wearily.

'You *good* woman, Molly,' old Milly said emphatically. 'That Joe there,' she darted a vindictive look in the direction of the bedroom where Mr Comeaway lay at rest, 'he a wijari hisself which I know.'

CHAPTER 22

Mr Comeaway left the house quite early the following day. Soon after Charlie followed him. With both men and the ailing Dora out of the way, Mrs Comeaway felt easier. She made a swift decision to get out of the house herself, even if it meant taking everyone with her. Bartie and Stella went off to school. The visiting children went with them. And Mrs Comeaway made a pot of tea.

It was a comfortable fit round the table now, and everyone felt happier. 'I still got a bad feelin but,' old Gramma Dicker said, over her first cup of tea.

'Ya mean what?' Mrs Comeaway said, her mind set comfortably on the thought of staying round here until the children got out of school, then getting out and walking up the hill to Mrs Green's and maybe staying on there for a meal. If they did that they would only need to put all the kids to bed when they came home and there wouldn't be any need to bother with food. 'What was ya sayin?' she asked Gramma Dicker, absent-mindedly.

'That time I wanted someone else,' said Gramma surprisingly. 'Didn't even get im neither. I was sposed to meet im at the corner, but all e give me were a bash in the face an I hadda go back ta me ole man after all.'

Old Milly sat up straight and cupped a hand round her ear.

'Worried me a bit till I'd got it off me chest ta the ole priest.'

'What'd ya say?' Mrs Comeaway settled herself to hear another of Gramma Dicker's tales.

'Just told im all bout it, Molly. How after thirty years or more I gotta have that other man. An after all them children too. Jack's children. So after that I gotta say fifty Hail Marys – I forgot em a course – an something else. I hadda give em some money.'

'How much?'

'Ah,' Gramma winked. 'I tole that ole man I gotta pay some accounts. E lets me off at two bob a week fa five weeks.'

Mrs Comeaway laughed, as Gramma sighed, 'I still feel bad but.'

Auntie Milly lifted her cup and took a long drink, her dry old lips spread flat. 'Ya got outa that all right, didn't ya?'

Gramma sipped too, narrowing her eyes against the steaming tea. Then she looked across her cup at the attentive faces. 'It's me conscience,' she told them sadly.

'Go on,' Mrs Comeaway rallied. 'A change is as good as a holiday, ain't it?'

The wrinkled eyelids lifted in surprise as Gramma considered. She set her cup down suddenly. 'I think I ruther have that holiday.'

Even Auntie Milly's face was blank for a minute. Then everyone laughed. Mrs Comeaway's stomach rolled and bounced and hurt her until she held it. 'She rather have a holiday,' she gasped at the others. 'An ya know what? So'd I.'

Trilby came out of her room to see what was going on. 'We all goin up the hill when the kids come home,' Mrs Comeaway told her daughter. 'Ya wanta come with us?'

'I'll stay home and get a bit of peace,' Trilby said sourly. 'You don't get much around here.'

'Suit yaself,' Mrs Comeaway said easily. 'There's some bread in the cupboard an a new tin of jam. We gunna have tea out, with a bit of luck.

They started the minute the children came home from school, all but Audrena, who had already left the house on a mission of her own. Blanchie carried fat little Tommy on her hip and when she got tired Mrs Comeaway gave her a hand. But before they got to Mrs Green's there were some others to look in on. Mrs Comeaway hadn't left the house for a fortnight and she wanted to see all her friends.

They came across Addie and Johnny Bean, just down from Carnarvon and busy building themselves a shelter alongside the Dowies'. They had found some good pieces of iron down on the dump, enough to make another little shelter after they finished the first one.

'Spose we got visitors,' Mrs Bean explained, 'it'll do to keep the wind offa them.'

Addie was peering into a big pot when Mrs Comeaway and her little band appeared. She acted annoyed and even though there were friends she had not seen for a time the scowl stayed on her face as she greeted them.

'Them dogs it is,' she declared indignantly. 'Come an et all the meat outa the pot.'

Mrs Comeaway examined the evidence – a pot scraped dry with only a few crumbs of bread adhering to the bottom. 'That two-legged dog,' she chuckled, 'ta scrape up all the juice as well.'

Johnny Bean, huge and majestic, frowned and scratched his head. 'Musta been when we was down the dump.' He looked along the rise to where the Dowies camped. 'That Tinker! E come along ere an eat my tucker, e find imself on the end a this. Im an is big dawgs always sneakin around.'

'Whyn't ya build ya place a bit farther away?' Mrs Comeaway asked. 'Ya know what them's like over there. Never got nothin an always hungry.'

'Ah gee, is done now,' Johnny said ruefully.

A tall skinny woman came climbing up the hill towards them, pushing a way through the stunted wattles. Her feet flapped, her brow was corded and in her arms she carried a loaf of bread.

She ignored Mrs Comeaway and the others and slopped her way over to Addie. 'Ya bread,' she said, handing over the loaf.

'That'll be somethin fa us ta eat,' Addie snapped, 'seein the meat's gone. You see any a that meat, Polly?'

Polly smiled ingratiatingly. 'An now we jus run outa potatoes,' she said. 'Ya wouldn't have none, would ya?'

Addie hesitated, considered and shook her head, and Polly looked with disappointment at the loaf of bread she had handed over. Addie followed the look. Her eyes swerved to where a couple of tins of meat lay beneath a fold of tarpaulin. 'Ah, take ya bread,' she said ungraciously, shoving it back.

Polly took it eagerly. She turned to greet Mrs Comeaway. 'How are ya sister? Ain't seen ya for a long time.' Her gap-toothed grin widened to include them all, then she began slapping back the way she had come.

Addie's mouth was thin. 'Needn't think she's gunna live offa us jus because we neighbours. Hey!' With her hand to her mouth she sent a call after the retreating Polly. When the woman stopped and looked back she yelled: 'I *guv* ya that bread and when I give ya thing I don't want em back. But if I borry things, then I *do* want em back. Ya hear that?'

'Awright!' Polly bellowed amicably. 'I remember, sister.'

'Ah, ya always was a bit snippy,' Mrs Comeaway said affectionately, when Polly had disappeared, 'but ya not a bad ole bastard an it's nice ta have ya back.'

Addie did not unbend, but a pack of cards appeared in her hand. 'Ya got the time?' she queried.

Mrs Comeaway looked uncertainly at the others. Auntie Milly was already settling herself on a patch of grass. Hannie waited patiently for orders. The children were chasing a lizard down the dusty road.

'Hafta be fa matches but,' she weakened, 'if ya got some.'

They all had cups of tea, too, at Hannie's camp. And a little game of cards hurt nobody, specially when it was only matches they played for. It was nearly dark by the time they got to Mrs Green's.

There was no light showing from the old house and that was strange because the Greens were connected up with the electric power and it only needed a finger to push down a switch.

'Hoo oo!' Mrs Comeaway called cheerily into the dusk. 'Hoo oo!'

They walked over to the side door that had hung apart from its hinges ever since Mrs Comeaway had first settled into her humpy at the top of the yard. The door was closed. Somehow someone had managed to pull it tight shut, and as well as being closed, it had been stapled and a big padlock hitched through the staples.

'What is it?' Mrs Comeaway asked blankly, looking at the silvery shining padlock as if it had been a snake. 'What'd she put a big lock on er door for?'

'Gee, I forgot,' Blanchie said suddenly. 'She went, Auntie Molly. She doesn't live ere any more.'

Mrs Comeaway turned slowly away from the door. 'Yeah!' she said flatly. 'Ya right. Noonah came an tole me an it went clean outa me head.' She stood for a while silently, her shoulders sloping sadly. Around her, the other women stood in a protecting group, waiting.

'I woulda liked,' Mrs Comeaway said at last, 'ta say goodbye ta the ole lady. She was a nice old lady, that one.' And she led the way back down the sandy slope and up on to the road.

Mrs Comeaway only wanted to get back home now. The heart had gone out of her as far as visiting went. She wanted to tell Joe about how they had all walked up to Mrs Green's and how she had thought it was funny that there had been no light and how she had remembered, after seeing the lock on the side door, that the old lady had been going and must have gone and not a good-bye or kiss me foot from the one who had been as close to her as if she had been a mother and not just a friend.

Mrs Comeaway ached everywhere and most of all in her heart.

'Ya just missed Joe,' Charlie said from Hannie's chair alongside the stove, when they arrived home.

'Jus missed im?' Mrs Comeaway said, puzzled. 'Where's e gone off to now?'

'E said for me ta tell ya,' Charlie began, and he wasn't comfortable about this telling, a blind man could have seen that. 'E said e was gunna write an tell ya soon as e got settled in somewhere. An ya wasn't ta worry bout him because e wouldn't be gone long. Just ta get a job like, an get a bit a money together.'

Mrs Comeaway just stood there, looking at him with dull eyes.

'An after that come straight back,' Charlie murmured. He got up from Hannie's chair. 'Time ya got a bit a tucker ready, ain't it?' he said roughly to Hannie. And then, finding that anger hid much of his discomfort from these others, he indulged it more fully. 'Get a move on, can't ya?' he snarled. 'Bout time ya got up off ya fat arse, ain't it, and did a bit round ere?'

'Leave er alone, Charlie,' Mrs Comeaway said absently. 'Leave er alone.' And without another look at anyone, she walked with her ache into her bedroom.

On the edge of the big double bed she sat staring before her, hoping that if she just sat still long enough, her thoughts would become clear again, and manageable.

Bartie came quietly through the door and sat close up against her. He took up her hand and held it in both small paws. 'Mum,' he whispered, 'Mummy.'

Mrs Comeaway did not stir.

'I'll help ya Mummy,' Bartie said, loving her. 'I'll help ya.'

She was herself again next morning, maybe because she had slept soundly and sweetly with Bartie and Stella curled up alongside her.

'Didn't come back I see,' she said, as she made the first pot of tea for the day. 'Thought e mighta changed his mind.'

'E say anything?' Auntie Milly asked.

'Said nothing,' Mrs Comeaway said shortly. 'Jus have ta wait an see I spose.'

'I reckon e mighta gone off up ta Carnarvon,' Charlie volunteered. 'E been thinkin there's lots a work up that way.'

Mrs Comeaway considered. 'Might be. Yeah, ya might be right, Charlie . An I spose we could do with the money e'll get.'

'Auntie Milly could help Gramma Dicker with the kids on the way back to Mullewa,' Trilby said calmly. 'They're a bit of a handful just for you, aren't they Gramma?'

'First I would hafta get some money fa me fares,' Gramma

pondered. 'Didn't we see Willis yesterday? If he would still be here I might get it offa him.'

'I'll see if he's still round,' Trilby said coldly, pushing her point.

'A course ya don't need ta hurry,' Mrs Comeaway said, her eyes unhappy.

'I got me own fares,' Auntie Milly said proudly. 'Ya don't need go roun the town askin fa money fa me, I can tell ya that.' Her faded brown eyes that looked as if the colour had washed out of them and into the whites, glared angrily. 'I can take a int, too, if ya like ta know.'

'If it's a big enough one,' Trilby said, too low for Auntie Milly to catch what she said. She cut herself some bread and spread it with jam, poured a cup of tea and went with them into her bedroom.

'Takes after er father, that one,' Auntie Milly said sourly. 'What was that last thing she said Molly?'

'I dunno,' Mrs Comeaway said, stolid and determined.

From the chair by the stove Hannie said gently, 'Would ya like me ta run in an ask?'

Mrs Comeaway's mouth went broad in a grin.

'Er too,' Auntie Milly snapped. 'Mumblin so peoples can't ear.'

CHAPTER 23

'No,' Mrs Comeaway said with determination. 'I'm gunna stick ta me ole man. E's been all right ta me, an you kids too. If you think I'm gunna make a big fool outa him your makin a mistake.'

'One thing, wouldn't cost anything,' Hannie put in, pouring what she imagined to be oil on troubled waters. 'An Joe isn't gunna mind gettin a bit of a letter, is e?'

Her comment was ignored.

'He's been away three months now,' Trilby said scornfully, 'and Horace told us he had a job. He can't just have forgotten about us. Look, all you have to do is write a letter and ask for maintenance like that man said, and if he doesn't send you anything you can get money from the government.'

'Yeah, an land me ole man in jail at the same time,' Mrs

Comeaway said, still stubborn. 'I tell ya, ya don't ave to be worry-ing bout money all the time. E'll be back soon, when e feels like comin back, an then there'll be plenty fa everyone.'

'What about those letters from the Housing people?' Trilby said angrily. 'They won't wait, will they?'

'You ad no right ta go pokin round in my letters,' Mrs Come-away said resentfully. 'They was mine, an sent ta me.'

'Someone had to read them,' Trilby said irritably. 'And you didn't.'

'An what would've been the use? No good reading things like them when ya can't do nothin bout em.'

'He had no right to run away,' Trilby said, 'and leave us all.'

'Ain't e done all right for ya so far? Gettin us all set up in a nice house an that.'

'A house we can't pay any rent for,' Trilby sneered.

'There's pounds an pounds gone off in rent,' Mrs Comeaway said hotly. 'I wouldn't mind a bob in me hand fa every pound e's ad ta give the damn guvment fa this house. An if you think I'm gunna put me ole man in jail ... We ad enough trouble with them pleece already. We don't want any more.'

'That's right,' Trilby said bitterly. 'Sling off at me every chance you get.'

'You started, didn't ya? I didn't want any argufyin.'

'Ah, you make me sick,' Trilby said, moving her heavy body through the kitchen. As she passed Audrena, head bent over a comic, she shot out a hand and gave the head a push.

Audrena glared. 'Who you think you're pushing now, Miss High an Mighty?'

'Shutup, all of ya,' Mrs Comeaway said strongly, 'or I'll make ya.'

She was tired. Things had been this way for the last fortnight; everyone snapping and snarling at each other – everyone, it seemed, going out of his or her way to make more bother. And these everlasting rows about rent. Why was rent so important? The grocery man waited, didn't he? Mrs Comeaway's thoughts came to a halt and lingered uncertainly round the grocery man. Even him! Getting more difficult every day to get an order. What was the matter with the man? People had to eat. And a lot of good his stuff would do him sitting there on shelves.

'I just don't see how there could be so much owing,' Noonah said, fingering one of the worrying letters.

'I thought I'd burned those damn letters under the copper,' Mrs

Comeaway said, giving the one Noonah held a fierce look. 'They just ain't added up right, that's all. An ya don't need ta worry. Ya father'll be back soon, and everything'll be fixed up.'

'This one came yesterday, Trilby says,' Noonah said slowly.

'Ho! Did it? An she couldn't wait ta show it to ya,' Mrs Comeaway said irritably.

'This is an eviction notice but,' Noonah frowned. 'You don't want to move out of here, do you?'

Mrs Comeaway gazed carelessly round her kitchen. 'Ah, I dunno. Course, it's bigger here. If Charlie hadda gone up ta Mrs Green's an picked up all that good iron an stuff, there woulda been no trouble. We coulda put up a nice place back fum the camp, like Mongo's. Ya can't get im up off is backside but, lazy ole devil.'

'Like the other one?' Noonah pursued, her eyes worried.

'It was nice,' Mrs Comeaway said, 'livin down here. But ya miss seein peoples ya know.'

Noonah giggled. 'Don't tell me you ever get lonely.'

Mrs Comeaway chuckled. 'Yeah, I know.' She pulled a chair round and sank into it. 'You got any money, Noonah?'

'Course I have. Nearly all of it.' Noonah reached into her pocket and pulled out a fat purse. Mrs Comeaway took it and sighed with relief. 'Just about have ta pay cash fa everything nowadays,' she said simply. 'Terrible inconvenient sometimes too.'

'Where's everyone?' Noonah asked.

'Went down the beach gettin that driftwood,' Mrs Comeaway said. 'We might get a quiet cuppa tea before they come back.'

'I see Skippy,' Noonah said, looking over her mother's shoulder. 'Hello,' she called, as the old man came rolling up the path.

He saved his breath until he reached the top, then he hung to the veranda post for a while, his open mouth like a dark hole in his shrunken face.

'I'm orf,' he greeted them, one eye obscured behind his hat, the other glinting wickedly. 'Orf on Mondy. E tells me give it a try and I give it a try. An it ain't no place fer a full-blood, that damn camp. Where's Joe?' He bent forward to peer into corners.

'Gone away,' Mrs Comeaway shouted, pointing north. 'I tole you already. Up there!'

'What?' Skippy was indignant. 'Where's e gorn?'

'Gawd,' Mrs Comeaway said helplessly. 'You tell im, Noonah. I tried to a hundred times.'

Noonah smiled at the old man and steered him into a chair. 'Dad went away. Coming back soon,' she said into his ear.

'Build nother house up there, where I come fum,' Skippy said.

Noonah knelt to tie the laces of Skippy's boots. 'You'll be falling over,' she scolded him.

Skippy jerked his feet away. 'Don't have ta deafen a feller. Like me boots comforble, so I can walk in em. Don't you go puttin a lotta knots in them laces,' He looked round the table. 'Cuppa tea?'

'Ya know, if e really is goin,' Mrs Comeaway said, pouring tea, 'it mightn't be a bad idea ta try an get that house a his.'

'You can't,' Noonah said tragically. 'Too many of you.'

Mrs Comeaway flashed her a look. 'I could fix that easy. Could say it's jus fa me an Joe when e gets back.'

'An what about Bartie and Stella?'

'I could say I was sendin em back ta the mission,' Mrs Comeaway said triumphantly.

'You wouldn't though, would you Mum?'

Mrs Comeaway shrugged. 'You think it's turned out so good down ere?'

'They love it. And there's Auntie Hannie too.'

'Ya, Auntie Hannie! She'd be just as happy sittin on a perch,' Mrs Comeaway said with finality. 'Just so long as she's sittin.'

'Eddication,' Skippy said suddenly. 'That's it, you gel there. You get eddication an you all right.'

Blanchie came in from the bedroom where she had been taking a nap along with Tommy. Noonah reached for him and Blanchie gave him up, laughing. At eighteen months, Tommy's eyes were black and clear and his eyelashes touched his feathery baby eyebrows. He suffered from no lack of food because someone was always feeding him something and his fat firm cheeks compressed his mouth into a wet rosebud. He was a good-tempered child, playing contentedly about under people's feet, sleeping soundly, though the house might be rocking with noise. Noonah adored him and brought him a new toy every time she came home. This week it was a yellow rubber puppy. Even Skippy was an interested observer as Tommy stared at the toy with big round eyes before trying it for taste. And whilst he played Blanchie watched him, her body curved towards him, her eyes and her mouth soft with love. When he dug into the soft rubber with a tiny forefinger, then looked up at her with his little pearl-like teeth showing between his pursed red lips, she snatched him up and buried her face in his fine black curls, gently biting the sweet soft curve of his neck.

'You two girls walk home with Skippy a way,' Mrs Comeaway said, when Skippy had finished his third cup of tea. 'No good a ole feller like him being out after it gets dark.'

'Tell Joe bout me ouse,' Skippy ordered, as the girls waited watchfully for his skittering feet to reach the bottom step. 'Where's e gorn, anyway?'

'Ave a good time up there,' Mrs Comeaway roared from the living-room. 'Don't do nothin I wouldn't do.'

Later, as the girls walked back from the end of the road, Noonah eyed her cousin thoughtfully. 'Blanchie,' she said abruptly, 'are you still going to marry Tim?'

Blanchie's eyes were innocent. 'What'd you do if you was me? Would you go up ta where Tim's workin an stay round them camps – or wait'll e gets a job down ere in town. E's always promisin e'll leave that place where e is now an come down ere. It's Tommy I'm thinkin about,' she said artlessly. 'If e got sick or something.'

'You could look after him.'

'It's easier down here than up there in them camps.'

'What camps?'

'Not camps exactly. Little sort of huts. An ya sposed to stay round there an not go near the homestead. Ya gotta stick round with all that mob that's hardly had any education ever. I never been used to living with people like that, always living round the town like. An spose I don't like it! After all, I got money comin in regular down ere. Me allotment an what that feller sends – when e sends it.' Blanchie's sideways look at Noonah was swift and sly.

'What about a job? Minding children, praps, or something like that.'

'Can't!' Blanchie said flatly. 'I already tried to get a job like that but they don't want Tommy. An Tim don't like me goin off an leaving im.'

'Does Tim send you money too, Blanchie?'

'E gives me some, when e comes down. E don't send me none because e knows bout that other.'

Noonah sighed. 'What about Audrena? Couldn't she take the job you nearly got?'

'Mrs Milton won't ave er. Audrena's a bit cheeky, an she don't like workin too hard neither. What's more, she says nobody's gunna make her stay in every night when she wants ta go out. The woman doesn't like that. She only lets ya go out once or twice a week an even then ya gotta be home early. Not like Audrena.'

'Where would she go every night?' Noonah wondered. 'What's there to do?'

Blanchie shot her another look, opened her mouth to speak then closed it again. She shrugged.

'I might try and talk to her,' Noonah frowned. 'We need girls like her up at the hospital, taking round trays and things like that. She'd get good pay, too.'

'You could try,' Blanchie said indifferently. 'Wouldn't waste me breath if I was you. That Audrena – she gets all she wants thout workin for it.'

Noonah felt burdened with care. But at home she forgot it. Trilby was in labour.

Outwardly calm, Trilby kept her eyes on the little wristwatch Noonah was using to time her pain. They came at ten-minute intervals now, and as each one surged like a giant comber throughout the length of her body Trilby relaxed like a sawdust-filled doll and let the pain take possession of her.

Everyone was looking to Noonah, their own first-hand experience considered a trifle when set alongside the booklore that was in Noonah's head. Trilby heard Noonah issue orders – Blanchie to go for a taxi, Hannie to finish packing to two battered old cases she would take to hospital with her. Trilby looked once at her mother's anxious face then rested her heavy head against her folded arms. She was drenchingly glad that Noonah was here to look after her.

'You'll stay with me all the time, Noonah?' Her voice was a thin thread. She had to strain to make it more than a whisper.

'Yes,' Noonah said briefly.

Trilby lifted her head to smile. She was afraid, but she hoped nobody would know just how much. It was not the pain. She could bear that, grindingly slow and exhausting though it was. It was the thought of Phyllix and what he might do – after the baby came. Trilby was blaming herself bitterly for having let him hang around her while she was pregnant. She should have snapped that tie – driven him off from her by some means or another. She could have done it – somehow.

She thought of the days when she would have to stay at the hospital. It would be like jail again. And outside, Phyllix might go ahead with his plans. Noonah and her mother might help him. They would try to stop her from going away and leaving them.

On the hard high bed in the labour ward, her head turned restlessly from side to side. She determined to rid herself of the baby the moment she left the hospital. And not only the baby. She would rid herself of the whole family, even Noonah. Step out of this life like she would step out of a dirty dress. In Perth everything would be different. It must be! And she would go soon. Neither Phyllix nor anyone else should stop her.

A nurse gave her an injection. After a while it was difficult for her to think clearly. She strove to identify herself with the fierceness of her desire, but her body was soft and weak. A while longer and not even the pain was real. She knew that Noonah's warm comforting hands held her own tightly and for that she was overwhelmingly grateful. Someone else was pushing down on her stomach with relentless urging strength, helping her weary body to push forth the weight inside it. How kind! How wonderfully, surprisingly kind.

'Here it comes now. Push! Push hard, that's the girl.'

Trilby put the last ounce of her strength into the straining muscles of her belly. She did it gladly, uplifted to the heights from sheer love of those kindly, helping hands.

CHAPTER 24

Again, surprising her, she found herself back in a perfectly ordinary world. She looked from her sister to the nurse, half-embarrassed, wondering if she had behaved like a fool – if these two would presently laugh at her.

Noonah was smiling. And the little nurse took up something and held it before her eyes. A white-wrapped bundle with a red wrinkled face at the top of it. An almost featureless face capped with damp, black curls.

It was Trilby who laughed.

When she woke again she lay in bed in a ward, of which she appeared to be the only occupant. There were two more beds, and their fresh virgin white, the neat and wonderful angles of their quilts enticed her to look again and again. It was enough, for a while, to see those beds or to watch the thin voile curtains blow in the soft breeze. It was happiness to move a slow hand over the flatness of her stomach and know that she belonged only to herself again.

Later, while she was still under the spell of the blowing curtains, the neat white beds and her own flat stomach, her mother came into the room. She disturbed its peace, breathing loudly, glancing nervously at the doorway behind her, whispering enquiries. But she

did not stay long and Trilby watched her vanishing form with pale
and complete satisfaction.

Noonah came, to lean over her and kiss her, and to tell her she
had had a daughter and that it looked exactly like her. 'I bet you
feel happy now, don't you?' Noonah added. 'Now it's all over?'

That last remark roused Trilby's dreaming mind as nothing else
could have done. When Noonah went she was alert again and on
guard. Phyllix would come soon. She must be ready for him.

She never doubted that he would come, even though he had
taken a job twenty or thirty miles out.

The baby was brought to her and she was made to suckle it.

'And what are you going to call her?' the nurse asked pleasantly,
showing Trilby how to feed her baby.

Trilby looked down at the minute head, at the unbelievably silky
black curls and the little mouth fastening so knowingly on her
nipple. She laughed, and the nurse laughed with her.

'You'll have to find a really pretty name for such a dear little
baby,' she said in her cheerful friendly fashion.

Trilby's face was hidden by her hair, but the nurse saw the quick
movement of rejection. The baby, losing the comfort of its mother's
breast, moved its head blindly, mewed protestingly.

'Did she hurt you? Are you tender? I hope you're not going to
have trouble with your breasts,' the nurse said anxiously, bending
down to guide the baby's mouth once more to the nipple. This time
the child fastened small hands in the softness of Trilby's swelling
breast, kneading it, thought its amused mother, as a kitten might
knead the belly of a mother-cat.

She felt detached, as if it were almost an imposition for this small
creature to expect nourishment from her. And she was relieved
when she could cover herself once more.

The regular visits of her baby brought nothing but a slight
embarassment until one day the baby refused to feed. It lay against
her, sleepy and uninterested. Again and again its tiny mouth slipped
unheeding from her breast. The nurse murmured vexedly, one
hand cupping Trilby's full bosom, the forefinger of the other parting the baby's lips by pressing downward on its small chin.

To Trilby it seemed obvious that the baby was not hungry. She
could not understand why the nurse persisted in her efforts to make
it drink.

Suddenly the nurse gave her baby's leg a slap. The child woke
and sobbed, and at the sound Trilby hugged it to her and swung it
away from the nurse. 'Why did you do that?' she asked, her eyebrows almost meeting over her narrowed grey eyes.

'Here, let's try her again before she goes off to sleep,' the nurse said, trying to get at the baby's head.

'Don't you touch my baby,' Trilby quivered. 'Go away! Go on! I'll feed her myself.'

The nurse straightened and laughed.

'Good gracious, that didn't hurt her,' she scoffed, 'a little bit of a smack like that. That's what we have to do to wake them. They must be fed regularly, you know.'

'This is *my* baby,' Trilby scowled. 'She *won't* be smacked.'

'Okay.' The nurse gave up, her pleasantness undiminished. 'See she gets enough though, won't you?'

Trilby watched her walk from the room, and only then did her cradling arms relax. She looked at the bundle as though she were seeing it for the first time. And before the nurse came to take it back to the nursery, she had unwrapped it and taken off all its clothes and examined it minutely. She handed it to the girl with the greatest reluctance, and when she lay back against her pillows the mother in her was dominant over the girl. Her thoughts were of her baby.

She sensed danger in her changed attitude. She would need all her strength and energy to stand up to Phyllix and her family. She must not allow this tiny scrap to pull her from her purpose.

She tried to woo back her old attitude of detachment but despite her reasoning looked forward eagerly to the times when the baby would be brought to her. And the baby looked up into her eyes with boundless trust and contorted its small face into grimaces which should have been hideous and were not, and the last of her clearseeingness retreated before the ever-growing tide of her love for it.

Nobody could have had a baby like this before. So perfect! Why was it hers when she had not even wanted it? Why could she not have had an ugly baby – or one deformed in some way? Here was no difficulty which she had overcome and left behind her. Here was a living breathing baby whose demands on her were increasingly hard to ignore.

Phyllix came and brought her near to nervous collapse. He was harder to deal with than she could ever have imagined.

'You want us to get married now?' he asked, his eyes begging.

Trilby would not let herself respond, not even in anger.

'No. I'm going away. I don't want to stay here any more.'

'You taking our kid?'

'I'll put her in a mission. She'll be all right.' The contractions of Trilby's heart did not show on her face.

'That's my kid, too,' Phyllix said stolidly, resolutely.

'I haven't ever said that,' Trilby reminded him, feeling the great thump of her heart lifting her bosom.

Through stiff lips she told him: 'I don't know whose she is. There were others besides you.'

'There was only me. I know that.'

'You're a fool,' Trilby said tearingly. 'If I say so, there *were* others. How would you know?'

'I know,' Phyllix repeated obstinately. 'And I don't want my kid in a mission. A father gotta sign them papers too, remember.'

'I don't believe you,' Trilby panted. 'You're just making that up to frighten me.'

'I seen that department man about us. Told him we was gunna be married. Trilby!' There was pain in his cry. 'Couldn't you just think about it a while, Trilby?'

'Go away!' Trilby said desperately. 'I won't marry you. Nobody can make me do that. Nobody! And I hate you. Do you understand now? Dumb idiot. I hate you, and if you don't let me send the baby to a mission I'll run away from you, anyhow. I'll run away now. Now!' She thrust her legs from the bed and stood up, shaking with fury.

Phyllix was shocked. This was a situation he had no idea how to handle. In a flash he saw Trilby sick and ill, hurt badly perhaps because he had so excited and upset her. And perhaps, through her, the baby would get sick, too. He tried gently to force her back into the bed.

Trilby flung him off, her grey eyes big in her ashy face.

'I better go,' he said at last, helplessly. 'I'm sorry. Trilby. Sorry I made you angry. I won't come back in here again.' He dug into his pocket and dragged out two pound notes. 'That's all I got left,' he told her. 'I can get more if you want it but. For the kid or something.'

'I won't have it,' Trilby cried in a fresh panic. 'You want everyone to think it's your baby. That's why you're giving me that. You just take it back. I won't have it, see?' She threw the money back at him.

Phyllix ignored the notes. His look was both puzzled and sad. He went quietly out of the room.

And when he had gone Trilby dug her head into the pillow and wept tiredly because she wanted peace so badly – and could find none.

CHAPTER 25

Her sister's behaviour was deeply troubling to Noonah. She had put up with Trilby's moods of rebellion during her pregnancy, trusting that everything would come right after the baby was born. And here was her sister just as jumpy and irritable as ever – at one time showering her baby with loving attention, at another thrusting it into Noonah's or the nurse's arms as if it were something to be feared and disliked.

If Noonah talked of the future, however lightly, sullenness swept Trilby's face like a grey mist. She had not yet chosen a name for her daughter, and flared out at her sister in tempestuous rage when Noonah suggested names.

Noonah was not the only one who was perplexed.

Never had Mrs Comeaway tried so hard to please someone – and failed so dismally. Her bewilderment was the kind Bartie's school books aroused in her. She supposed – pathetically – she was too far behind her different-thinking children. Just an old fool. Annoying instead of pleasing with her tremendous efforts to understand.

'What sort of a girl,' she asked Noonah indignantly, 'not even to give the littlie a name yet. We gotta cal it "she" still, same as if it was a damn cat.'

'Trilby'll be all right soon,' Noonah reassured, as worried as her mother.

'She got over them idears of ers yet?' Mrs Comeaway probed. 'Sendin that baby off ta some mission an trackin down ta Perth erself?'

'I don't know,' Noonah said helplessly. 'She won't talk about anything like that.'

Mrs Comeaway regarded her daughter in a rich silence then, inevitably, went to the stove to fix a pot of tea.

There was only one way out of the mess she had got herself into. Trilby could not recall when first the chilling thought had struck her, but each time the baby was brought to her – so small, so helpless – it leapt again to ugly life. No matter if she tried to crowd out this thought with others – if she withdrew in shuddering horror – it stayed in the deepness of her mind, festering with possibilities.

To cover the baby's tiny face with a pillow until it suffocated, to roll a pellet of bread and stuff it into the open pink mouth, to unclose her arms and allow it to fall; this last would at least be quick and she would not have to watch it as it struggled for air, or choked on something too big for it to swallow.

Often Trilby lay with her eyes closed, the wind ice-cold against her damp and perspiring body, her hands clenching and unclenching in her anquish. Or she would gather up her child and stare into its face, her eyes tortured and wild.

For the better part of the day and night she was alone with her thoughts. Noonah could not visit every day. Her mother had concluded and dumbly accepted that Trilby was better left alone. Nothing she said or did seemed to please the girl. Trilby snapped her up as if she were being purposely annoying.

So in solitude the battle went on. With all that she knew herself to be, must she go back to the life she so hated Because of this tie between herself and her baby which, despite the darkness of her thoughts, grew stronger every day?

She saw nothing good in a return, just a further sinking, a giving up of the fight before it had fairly begun.

For Trilby, the only good lay in this other life she would make for herself. Only when she had it firmly in her grasp could she walk proudly, consider herself the equal of anyone. She was so tired of fighting. With her whole heart she wanted to live in the certain knowledge that she was accepted completely.

There was no room in her mind to consider her family. She recognised no kindliness in them, no warmth of good fellowship, no loyalty nor generosity, not even gaiety. Her pity was all for herself. She blamed them for the feeling of desperate loneliness which was with her every waking minute of the day, promised herself that soon, after she had escaped from them, it would vanish.

The day was hot, with a careening wind picking up the dust from the streets and whirling it in through windows and down passageways. The baby had been fed and, whilst she had fed her, Trilby had drained her water-jug. Yet she was thirsty still and the skin on her face felt taut with dried perspiration.

No nurse came to take the baby away. Trilby looked at its sleeping face, deliberating between setting it down on the bed and taking it with her to the bathroom whilst she refilled her jug. She was frighteningly aware of the thought so firmly established in her mind, and to reassure herself was doubly careful of the safety of her baby, as if by examining safety-pins, loosening too tight clothing, touching the child with gentle hands, speaking to it in a voice that was low and sweet – she could ignore evil and cause it to vanish.

She made up her mind and, with the baby on her arm, took up her jug and left the room.

The bathroom was two doors down the passage. Trilby pushed the heavy glass door and let it swing shut behind her. And then she found she would need two hands to fill her jug.

She knelt and placed the jug at her side whilst she rearranged the baby blanket to alow a thick fold for the baby's head.

She filled her jug at the tap, feeling its weight grow heavier. Carefully, she balanced it in one hand whilst she bent to pick up the baby with the other. And in the act of picking it up the thought flashed across her mind that here was the time – and the place.

The shock of revulsion that raced through her body hastened her movements. The white rug, already disarranged, unwound itself. There was a soft crack as the baby hit the floor head first. And Trilby, staring down at it in fear and horror.

There was a crash and tinkle of glass and a great splash of water as the jug, too, fell from her nerveless hand.

Trilby reacted swiftly, in terror now of authority. To wrap the baby again in its rug, to hold it tightly, not daring to examine it for hurt – to wait with her heart in her mouth for the sound of running feet.

After a while she knew that the crash had gone unheeded. The nurses must be busy. Moving slowly and awkwardly, she picked up the pieces of glass and dropped them in the lidded tin behind the bathroom door. With the towel from the roller, she mopped the water from the floor as well as she could. She threw the soaking wet towel into a hand-basin and, on shaking legs, made her way back to her room. With the last of her strength she sank down on the bed, her clutching arms holding the baby tightly to her breast.

She could not look at it. She told herself that it would be all right, and that nothing could have happened to it. Mothers had dropped babies before. She had seen them. Seen Blanchie drop Tommy – and not only once. It had always been possible to charm away the bruise – or the cut – with a teaspoon of sugar or a suck at a finger coated with condensed milk. Why should her own baby suffer more than a bruise – or a cut?

All this she told herself while she waited with endless patience for the nurse to take her baby. And when the baby had been lifted from her arms she waited still, because she knew that what had happened to those other babies had nothing to do with this, and that her own baby would not have lain so quietly in her arms if she had not been hurt badly.

The nurse came back, as Trilby had known she would. Refuge was to be found only in silence.

The matron bustled in too, worried, perturbed, deeply shocked. 'Your baby is ill. Seriously ill. The doctor is with her now and he wants to know what happened. You must tell us.'

She waited for a reply, anger growing in her. Then she looked more closely at Trilby before turning to the little nurse behind her. 'Tell the doctor to come quickly. Here!'

So Trilby's breaking mind grew quiet under anaesthetics and the gleaming slits of her eyes saw nothing but blackness.

Noonah was there when Trilby woke. A Noonah who sat straightly on her straight-backed chair and whose knuckles showed pale on clamped hands.

This was it, Noonah thought painfully. This was the thing she had feared before it had happened, only the thing itself was so much more dreadful. She could not have imagined anything so dreadful as this. How could she, or her mother, or Trilby or even Phyllix, overcome something so big and full of trouble?

When she saw the dark lashes lift over the dreaming grey eyes she tried to smile and though questions sprang to her lips she fought them back, waiting until Trilby should be fully awake.

After a while she leaned over the bed. 'What happened, Trilby?'

Trilby's eyes opened wide and a wave of thankfulness passed over Noonah. Her sister's eyes were clear, not shuttered, as they had been at the jail. But the look in them shattered Noonah's composure and her tears would not be held back. She felt she could not bear that naked defenceless plea for help. That was the way Bartie had looked at her back at the mission the night before she left it. She dropped on her knees beside the bed.

'Trilby, tell me.'

'I didn't do it on purpose, Noonah, but. ... '

'But what?' Noonah urged desperately.

'You'll hate me. You'll go away.'

'Oh!' If Trilby only knew how far out she was, Noonah thought. At that moment she would have sacrificed anything, and gladly, to help her sister. 'I won't go away,' she promised steadily.

'I'd been thinking about it. It was in my mind all the time – that I could easily drop her and pretend it was an accident.'

'Yes.' Noonah kept her voice gentle.

'And now I'll have it to think about for the rest of my life. That I wanted her to die. So she wouldn't be a nuisance to me.'

'Trilby, tell me the way it happened,' Noonah implored, and she took her sister's hands in hers and held them tightly to stop their trembling.

'I thought I'd end up like Blanchie – and those others,' Trilby whispered. 'And I couldn't see that it was fair when – I *wasn't* like them – not ever.'

'I know.'

Two tears showed between Trilby's closed lids. 'Blanchie's still got Tommy,' she said and her mouth twisted.

'Tell me,' Noonah begged. 'Just tell me, Trilby.'

'I told you,' Trilby wept, and her weeping was tired and hopeless. 'I wanted her to die and she died.'

'You didn't do anything to her?'

'I couldn't – it was the baby blanket – it slipped and she just rolled out and her little head . . . Noonah, I can still hear the sound of it – her little head on that hard floor. Her hair was always so soft and warm, Noonah, against my neck.'

'They let me see her,' Noonah said after a while, her voice dragging.

Trilby's eyes were wide open, imploring. 'And. . . .)

'Her eyes,' Noonah said pitifully. 'They're crossed somehow. And she won't take any food. They think she'll die.'

Trilby went limp again. 'I won't see her any more. Not ever. And I love her so much – now. I always tried not to, but I couldn't help it. Noonah, this is all Phyllix's fault. Why didn't he stay away from me – leave me alone?'

'Was the baby – is Phyllix . . . ?' Noonah stumbled on the words.

Trilby turned her face away. 'There was only him,' she answered her sister's question.

A nurse came, quick-stepping and business-like, her expression grave and remote. 'Matron would like to see you before you go,' she told Noonah.

Noonah was home, trying to quiet Mrs Comeaway's boundless fears when her own worry clouded her every thought.

'She's dead,' Mrs Comeaway crooned to herself, and her eyes were unbelieving. 'The littlie dead already, before I even seen er close up. Noonah, did Trilby say – ya think maybe she went crazy?'

'It was an accident, Mummy. She told me.' She told her mother what Trilby had said. 'But I had to see the matron after, and she said there's bound to be a bit of trouble about it. Something they have when people die in accidents. An inquest.'

Mrs Comeaway's voice was full of melancholy. Her eyes darted, seeking comfort from familiars. 'So much trouble ta come on us. It seem all the time trouble come after I get yous back. An now ya father away an nobody ta tell me anything what ta do. What we do, Noonah? What we do?'

Noonah's shock began to tell on her. She could give no comfort. She needed it so badly herself. With a little sob she sank to the floor at her mother's feet and pressed her head into that warm and comforting lap. And her mother's face cleared of its worry. This was something she could do; run her hands over her daughter's hair, murmur soothingly, lift the hem of her frock and wipe away Noonah's tears. The future, as always, must take care of itself.

The sun rose as usual – they ate, slept and woke – the children went off to school and returned – in all of these unchanging things lay reassurance, and the thought of Trilby's baby's death began to hold less horror for them.

Other things – visits from the department man and from the police, the questionings and their own reiterated answers, the quenched looks and quiet voices of Charlie and his wife and his children – had to be borne patiently until some decision arriving from unquestionable sources told them of change – for Trilby perhaps. Perhaps for all of them! Not even Noonah was entirely clear about what was going on.

But, from Mrs Comeaway down to little Stella, each felt that his neglect of some fact must have contributed.

'I just wisht I hadn't of gone in an upset her,' Phyllix said miserably to Noonah.

'If you tell,' Noonah warned, 'they might think she did it on purpose.

'I don't tell nothing,' Phyllix said, his face hard. 'I might say something wrong, so I don't say nothing. Not to anyone. Except you.'

'And it's no use worrying about anything. Not now,' Noonah said sadly.

On the day of the inquest, put off until Trilby had been declared fit, it was the girl's attitude, so aloof and unco-operative, which delayed the verdict for so long.

The coroner was puzzled. He had thought it a clear case of accidental death, but surely a girl would not act as Trilby acted if

she had just lost her baby. She seemed utterly indifferent to all that
was going on.

For the first time since they had come down from the mission,
Noonah was seeing her sister defeated, without the fire of rebellion.
Here again was a hurt that had driven deep and that would not be
easily forgotten.

And for a fleeting moment, as the enquiry dragged on, Trilby
thought of the girl she had been – the unknowing and happy
dreamer who had leaned against a tree and planned for her future.

'An ya don't wanta worry bout what e said at the end,' Mrs
Comeaway braced. 'Main thing is, ya got off all right.'

'I thought the matron at the hospital was so nice,' Noonah said
diffidently. 'Saying all that about us loving our children and making
more fuss of them than white people, and about you getting cross
with that nurse for smacking the baby.'

'The doctor seemed a nice understandable sort of a feller too,'
Mrs Comeaway added.

Trilby looked round at her assorted family, and for a second her
old impatient spirit seemed about to leap out at them. Then her
shoulders slumped. Without a word she walked away from them
all, towards her room. Her door closed softly and definitely behind
her.

CHAPTER 26

The affair of the eviction notice had been shelved, not forgotten.
Noonah was at home on the day Mrs Comeaway received her
curtly-worded reminder. She urged her mother to visit the department man and find out if she could have the little house Skippy had
scorned.

Mrs Comeaway applied to Horace for help, and Horace did not
fail her. She returned from her visit to the department man with
official permission to move straight on to the reserve.

'Wouldn't hear of Charlie and Hannie stringin a tarp from the
side but,' Mrs Comeaway commented, 'so I spose they better move

in with the Dickers till they find some place a their own. This place
a one unit place, y'see.' She grinned at her daughter. 'I tole im we'd
fit in smaller places an that an got on all right.

'What did he say about the children?'

'I said we was gunna send em back to the mission after Christmas.
By that time e mighta forgot about em.'

'I don't know,' Noonah worried. 'He'll probably write it down
somewhere. Gee, I wish you could have got one of the big places.'

'Don't get worryin bout us,' Mrs Comeaway soothed.

'And there's Daddy,' Noonah revived. 'When he comes back
he'll have enough money maybe to take another place for rent, and
Bartie and Stella can stay down here.'

'That's right, too,' Mrs Comeaway beamed. 'We'll jus put one
over on that bloke – an serves im right fa takin back all that stuff e
give us.'

'What stuff?'

'Them beds an things we got with that forty pound,' Mrs
Comeaway said, with indignation. 'Don't you remember e said it
was a present from the partment? An now every single thing gotta
go back. Beat that, if ya like.'

'Oh well,' Noonah soothed, 'you wouldn't have room for it up in
the camp. Not in one room. And you've still got the big bed and the
two stretchers.'

'Ain't that. It's the principle of the thing,' Mrs Comeaway said
severely. 'Wastin our time goin an pickin it out an all the time it
ain't really ours.'

'Only if we'd stayed here,' Noonah pointed out. 'Look, Mum,
what say I help you get packed up before I go back?'

Charlie and Hannie and the girls and young Tommy had been
accepted philosophically into the shelter of the Dickers' big camp,
but they were not far from the reserve and Hannie spent most of her
time hovering over Mrs Comeaway's stove – a good thing, as it
happened, because never before in her life had Mrs Comeaway had
so much need of some living thing to talk at.

Trilby was difficult and moody. She had been hard to get along
with before. She was even harder to understand now that she had
to share her mother's bed during the night and either put up with
Auntie Hannie or lose herself in the bush for the better part of the
day. She would have nothing to do with the other young girls
around the camp, and even kept apart from Bartie and Noonah.
Her appetite was easily satisfied with a piece of bread and jam and
a cup of tea, and she grew thinner.

She was jerked finally into more awareness by little Stella. She felt she could hardly bear the child's endless qustionings. Stella had been looking forward to having a real little new baby as part and parcel of her family life. Aggrieved when this delightful thing had not come to pass she wanted to know the reason, and she asked not once a day but every time a fresh sense of her injury overcame her. Trilby began to think once again about leaving. And this time, she vowed to herself, nothing should stop her.

Bartie had suffered not a pang at his removal from the Wild-Oat Patch. He saw much more of Diane now, and for the first time in his life he was learning the meaning of a completely satisfying friendship. Noonah was on another plane. He almost worshipped his sister. Diane dipped round and about his own level, laughing, enticing, mischievous and strangely, perfectly tolerant of his curious hobby. So long as she could see herself in finished drawings and paintings, she would not pester him, using her time as model for the brewing up of fresh plans for mischief.

Mrs Comeaway was just beginning to find peace when Stella took sick. She complained and whined and drooped about the house, spending whole nights in coughing even after Mrs Comeaway brought her in from the cold little veranda and warmed her in her own bed. And it was something more than bad temper which caused Stella to refuse bottles of cool drink, cream-filled biscuits and the little bags of lollies which Mrs Comeaway would send Bartie to buy. After a night when the child had exhausted herself in fit after fit of painful coughing, Mrs Comeaway dressed herself and set off for the hospital and Noonah.

Noonah came, anxious-faced, to met them.

'It's Stella here,' Mrs Comeaway said in a whisper, her surroundings affecting her as they always did with their cold cleanness and the echoing quality of the walls. 'She ain't been eatin good for a week now. I dunno! Maybe I been a bit worried bout other things an didn't take much notice. But now it's cough, cough, jus on all night. I thought maybe you could get a bit a medicine for er.'

Noonah dropped on one knee, her own conscience a bit uneasy. She took Stella's hot little face between her hands, and the child's dry skin burned her fingers. Bronchitis? she wondered uncertainly. Pneumonia? hearing the rales crackling in the little chest.

'Mummy, you'd better take her to the doctor straightaway,' she said, rising. 'He'll probably put her in hospital for a while. I'll ask Matron if I can take care of her. And don't worry, Mummy. She'll be all right here with me. Just take her to the doctor straightaway though.'

'If that's what you think, Noonah,' Mrs Comeaway said, with relieved obedience. 'Gee, I'm glad you're a nurse an all like that. Always get a bit scared less I know somethin's real bad. Them doctors don't like it if ya waste their time.'

'Off you go then,' Noonah said, infusing a note of cheerfulness into her voice for Stella's sake. She bent to kiss the woebegone little face. 'You're going to stay here with me tonight, Stella. Won't that be nice?'

She gave her mother a quick hug, then stood to watch the two walk away down the drive, her mother self-conscious and dignified, with her old black hat pulled firmly down on her curly greying hair. And not until she was back in the ward helping with the afternoon sponges did she recall, with a throb of anger at herself, that she had forgotten just how far away from the hospital the doctor was, and how her mother and little Stella must already have been tired from their walk down Heartbreak Hill.

Why hadn't she given her mother the money for a taxi? And what change had been brought about in her mother that Mrs Comeaway had not, in her usually cheerful forthright fashion, asked for it?

Stella was admitted to the hospital that same day. Slipping into the children's ward as soon as she got the opportunity, Noonah was cut to the heart. On Stella's face as she lay quietly in bed was the same patient look she had seen on the face of Trilby's baby.

This time, she swore, it would end differently.

'We're going to start her on oxygen straightaway,' the little nurse said sympathetically. 'But it all depends on her resistance. She's not a very big child, is she?'

Noonah thought back to the week-ends she had spent at home and blamed herself for being unwilling to disturb the happiness she had always found there. 'I should have told her Stella is too thin. I should have told her what to do,' she thought in wretchedness. 'It's right there in my books and I didn't tell her.' She remembered the grocery orders, and the biscuits and cool drinks and pasties.

'This is my fault,' she thought, her eyes frozen in misery.

Noonah was not permitted to nurse her sister and, while she rebelled, she knew she could not have forced her little Stella to do the things she must do in order to get better.

However, no order could stop her from visiting. At night she had to be pushed out by the sister-in-charge so that she herself could get some rest before going on duty again. But because she was Noonah's sister, and because Noonah had made a place for herself in this great hospital, every little nurse who had anything to do with Stella's care put extra effort into her work. And of course the child took comfort from her sister's presence. Nothing could hurt her whilst Noonah was near. When Noonah nodded, Stella knew it was all right to submit to the prick of a needle or the paraphernalia of the oxygen-tent. Her docility under treatment endeared her still further with all the little nurses.

She did not, though, improve as everyone had hoped. She had too little resistance.

Occasionally Mrs Comeaway tiptoed in to pay a visit. More often she applied directly to Noonah for news, her awe of her surroundings making any contact with the nursing staff a thing to be dreaded. If Noonah had not been here she would have overcome her dread and perhaps obstructed the nursing with her suspicions and doubts. That had happened before where coloured children were concerned. But Noonah was here. Mrs Comeaway had perfect confidence in her daughter, if not in medical practitioners.

Each time she came she brought little parcels of food – big stripey all-day suckers, round hard rainbow balls, a package of chocolate cream biscuits or little bottles of Coca-Cola. There were quick visits from Hannie and Blanchie and even from Audrena. Bartie sent with his mother all the things most precious to him – a water-colour of waves, his game of snakes and ladders, a tiny dressed doll in a box, bought with money intended for an easel. And, behind the stone wall at the back of the hotel, Horace dispensed first-hand news to all who sought it. It took more than a nursing staff to awe Horace.

Only Trilby did not come. Still sunk in depression, she was miserably sure that nobody would believe in her concern for her small sister. The blame for this was hers, she knew that. She had never had much time for Stella when the child was well. It was too much to expect that Stella would want her now that she was ill.

Yet Stella did want her sister. The baby that Trilby had been going to bring home was still in her thoughts. Neither Trilby nor anyone else had given her enough of an explanation to satisfy her. She wanted to know. She asked in her thready little voice for Trilby, who must surely know what had happened to the baby.

So one day Trilby, too, visited Stella.

'Don't upset her,' the nurse warned. 'She has to be kept very quiet so that she won't waste any of her energy.'

Trilby promised.

The first heart-rending came when she saw how thin the little girl had become, and how big her brown eyes looked in her dry-

skinned shrunken little face. Her heart was stormed completely at
Stella's question.

'Tell me what happened to the baby. Please, Trilby.'

As soon as the tears filled her eyes, Trilby remembered the
nurse's warning. She blinked them back and forced herself into
calmness. She knelt by Stella's bed and put her head close to her
sister's. As gently as she could she told Stella of the accident and
how the baby had died. She told her more. Of the soft warm hair
and the delicate and perfect limbs. 'Her hand was only half as big
as my thumb,' she said, her eyes remembering.

'And she used to wave them about when I took her shawl off –
and kick her legs, too.'

Stella's fathomless eyes held her sister's. These were the things
she wanted to hear. After a while she sighed, so long and deep that
her small chest moved the sheet above it.

'I wish you could have another one,' she said wistfully. 'Will you,
Trilby, and let me play with it?'

Trilby took a deep breath. 'Yes,' she said steadily. 'I'll have
another one for you, Stella, if you promise to get well.'

'Of course I'll get well,' Stella said in amusement. 'Silly!'

The crisis came and was past. It was certain now that Stella would
get better. But it was weeks before Noonah took her sister home.
Careful nursing and Trilby's visit had played their part in the
graver issue. The nursing had to continue even more devotedly
before Stella's health was completely restored. But at last she was
allowed to go home.

Such happiness!

Noonah hired a taxi. The child was painfully thin still, her
lengthening legs like sticks. And at home there was more happiness. There, at the door of the one-roomed house, his face a vast
and welcoming grin, stood Mr Comeaway.

CHAPTER 27

'Dad!' screamed Stella, scrambling from Noonah's grasp. 'My Dad!' Illness forgotten, she went leaping over the grass to her father, and Mr Comeaway waited to catch her and seat her on his shoulder.

Noonah followed, her eyes damp, herself surprised at the surge of love she felt for this returned traveller.

Mr Comeaway flicked a grin at the taxi-man and put one arm round Noonah's waist. Inside the small room Mrs Comeaway and Bartie laughed at the success of their surprise.

'Yeah, I'm home,' Mr Comeaway said. 'Took a lift all the way up to Wyndham an damn well hadda stay there for a bit. An what's all this stuff they been tellin me? Don't anyone know how ta behave their selves when a man goes off on a little trip? Get down here an I find I don't even live in the same place no more. Fine fool I looked, walkin in that front door an paractically landin on ole Mrs Mingo's lap.'

Noonah laughed and her eyes danced. She did not care how long her father had been away. Now that he was back, with his cheerfulness and optimism and unfailing good humour, everything would be all right again.

Mrs Comeaway was bustling importantly round the stove. She looked a different woman. The whole place, Noonah thought with satisfaction, felt like a home again.

'An where's a man like me gunna fit in here night-times?' Mr Comeaway enquired. 'Bit small after the other one, ain't it?'

'Stella'll come in ere with us,' Mrs Comeaway planned, 'an Noonah'll sleep out on the veranda with Bartie, eh, Bartie?'

Bartie nodded delightedly.

'Where's Trilby?' Noonah asked, looking round.

Mrs Comeaway sobered. 'I got somethin ta tell ya. Young Trilby's knicked off.'

'I seen er too,' Mr Comeaway said, a frown between his eyes. 'But the mob was round me an I couldn't get ridda them ta see what she's doin with a big case in er and. Anyway, when I got round ta findin out, she's gone. Never been back all day.'

'You got any idea where she coulda went?' Mrs Comeaway asked Noonah.

'She'd had her case packed a long time,' Bartie said, wide-eyed. 'But she just told me to mind my own business when I asked her what was in it. It was locked,' he added ingenuously.

'She couldn't have had any money,' Noonah said distressedly, her thoughts going straightaway to what Trilby had said about going to Perth. 'Would she try to get a lift to Perth?'

'What she wanta go ta Perth for?'

'The young devil,' Mr Comeaway said admiringly. 'Always told us she was goin. Probably half-way there by this.'

'I dunno,' Mrs Comeaway sounded dashed. 'That ole Mrs Green, she always said Trilby was gunna be hard ta handle. I wonder if young Lila – she's goin down by bus tomorrow – would she keep a bit of an eye out for er. What you think Noonah?'

'You could ask her,' Noonah said doubtfully.

'Or I could go in an see that partment chap,' Mrs Comeaway frowned.

Noonah frowned too. 'Trilby would hate that, Mum.'

Mr Comeaway moved on to the bed. 'Ah, she's gone. Bring er back an she'll be off again, soon as she gets the chance.'

'I wish Phyllix was here,' Noonah said, feeling depressed. He'd know what to do.'

'She never even spoke to im, when e come up here,' Mrs Comeaway said definitely. 'Acted as if e wasn't around.'

'Let er go,' Mr Comeaway insisted. 'She'll come back when she wants to, soon as she gets tired of bein away.' His face lightened in a grin. 'Like er ole man, eh?'

Mrs Comeaway smiled. 'Laugh on the other side a ya face if ya got put inside,' she said threateningly. 'Running out like that. An I can tell ya I damn near signed that paper bout maintenance. Close as a stick of chewie, I was. Spose *I* go off when I like an have a holiday. Nice if I went off like you do, eh?'

'There she goes again,' Mr Comeaway said, still grinning. 'Nag at a man soon's e gets back.'

'Kettle's boiling,' Noonah said diplomatically. 'Shall I make tea, Mummy?'

'This girl,' Mrs Comeaway told her husband, 'she's been real good ta us. Brung all er money home. An she the only one didn't get herself in no trouble.'

'What about me?' Bartie said, from the floor.

'You!' his mother said scornfully. 'You and that Diane. Less said bout you two the better.' She bent to take a good grasp of his hair, giving it a tug which made the boy yelp.

Noonah thrust this new trouble to the back of her mind. There was a thing she wanted to know.

'Daddy, did you do much work? Did you bring home some money?'

A look passed between her parents.

'Did you, Dad?'

'Well,' Mr Comeaway was uneasy. 'Off an on I did a bit. Off an on.' He picked up Stella and held her on his lap. 'An how's my girl, eh?'

Stella snuggled into his arms and Mrs Comeaway came over to look searchingly into her daughter's face. Stella's eyes were bright and clear now and there was no sign of listlessness. 'She'll do,' she said at last. 'They took good care of er up that hospital. You shoulda seen this one the day she went in, Joe. But er sister nursed er better.'

Noonah sat down alongside her father, disturbing a brown paper-wrapped parcel covered lightly with a blanket. A clinking came from the parcel.

'I thought,' she said carefully, 'we might be able to get a bigger place after you came back, Daddy. Did Mummy tell you about this being just for one or two people? The man at the department said you could only keep the kids here a little while.'

'Ah, ya don't wanta go huntin trouble,' Mrs Comeaway said, embarrassed. 'E's not a bad bloke, that partment feller. E'll let us stay here. You wait an see.'

Mr Comeaway rubbed his chin, And his brother chose this moment to join the family group.

Mr Comeaway greeted Charlie with relief. 'I was just startin ta tell Noonah what I been tellin you, Charlie me boy.' He turned to Noonah. 'It was all right, Noonah, but there wasn't all that much work about. Most a the money I got I hadda spend ta keep meself in between jobs, see? An then when I got stuck up at Wyndham an couldn't get a lift back I hadda pay out a good bit fa the taxi that took me down the next town. I got a few weeks' shearin there an thought I better come back while I still ad me pay. I got that bit, or most of it, but that ain't much. Still,' his voice grew hearty, 'now I'm back home me an Charlie's gunna go down the wharf again an pick up a bit down there.'

Noonah nodded, but she could not force a smile in answer to her father.

'Pity you couldn't a hung on ta that house down the Wild-Oat Patch,' Mr Comeaway brooded. 'Got a real shock when ya mother tole me bout that rent. An I wouldn't be surprised if them blokes down that office didn't go an make a mistake in their addin up. I could see the partment chap about that. What you think, Noonah? You think I should go in, maybe, an have a bit of a talk with im?'

Noonah swallowed the lump in her throat.

'I suppose you could do that,' she agreed.

Noonah and Bartie were sitting on the beach. Bartie's favourite beach, where the green waves swelled smoothly until they broke in lace-edged scallops on the sand.

Bartie had a silky-smooth piece of driftwood in his hand. After a while he used it to make patterns on a strip of wet sand.

'Bartie,' Noonah said. 'Would you mind going back to the mission very much?'

'Do I have to? Why? Don't Mummy and Dad want us down here any more?'

'Bartie, of course they do,' Noonah said warmly, hugging the boy close to her. 'But it's a pretty small place where they are now. They're not supposed to have you two kids there at all. And if they keep you with them they might have to shift out. That means another camp in the bush just like the others. You wouldn't like that, Bartie, would you?'

'Wouldn't mind,' Bartie said easily. 'Have beaut fun in a camp. Diane lives in one.'

That had been a stupid thing to say. Noonah tried another approach.

'When I was up at the mission Mrs Gordon used to wish she had someone even partly trained like I am, to help her look after the kids when they got sick. I thought I might write to her and ask her if I could have the job. What about that? Would you like to go if I was there too?'

Bartie considered. 'I like it down here better,' he said at last, 'but not without you. Why would you want to go back, Noonah?'

She did not, Noonah thought. But she had an aching longing for peace. There were still troubles ahead. If she went back to the mission and took the two children with her, that would settle a few of them. She sighed. Life didn't seem to be a matter of making up your mind and going ahead. Things happened, all sorts of things. Other people's lives got mixed up with yours and your thinking altered. And there was that other business she had talked about with Mrs Green, though with nobody else. Your own people got sulky with you if you didn't do everything the way they did it. Even training to be a nurse made them act differently towards you, as though they couldn't trust you any more. Why? She sighed again. And against her shoulder Bartie's head moved.

'Why didn't you answer me? What are you thinking about? You look as if you're crying, Noonah.' His hand touched her face. 'Without tears.'

Noonah laughed and held him closer. 'You wouldn't mind, if Stella and I were there too, would you?'

Bartie sagged. 'I spose I wouldn't mind as much, If you wanta go, Noonah, I'll go with you.'

The case was not large, but Trilby had been carrying it for hours. Now her shoulders felt as if they were being dragged from their sockets and the palms of her hands were sore. Plenty of cars had passed, but so far Trilby's nerve had crumpled as each one approached and she had hidden herself behind the wattles that edged the road. She had had little experience in dealing with strangers and her worry over the right approach made her unwilling to begin. As well, she remembered hearing tales of girls being brought back home by the police after attempting to escape, as she was doing. Her father might have asked the department man to search for her. She shuddered at the mere thought of it, but for all she knew the very next car might contain her pursuers.

Her plans, after she reached Perth, were non-existent. She would take a look at the place and something would suggest itself. The main thing was to get there.

She had had nothing to eat since breakfast nor had she brought any food with her. Her only thought after her father had arrived had been to escape before he subjected her to questioning. The hurts that had taken so long to heal could not bear a fresh scraping-over. She would talk to no one about them. She had had enough.

She trudged on with her head bent, resolved to wait round the very next bend. Wait, and not fly like a coward the moment she heard an engine. This time she would walk out on to the road and hold up her hand.

She stopped and set down the case, intending to sit on it. But the case was very old. It sank inwards beneath her weight, so she got up and thumped it back into shape, then sat on the road at its side. She concentrated her gaze on the highway in the direction from which she had come. So intent was she that she failed to notice the noise of a car coming from the other direction. She was alarmed when it pulled to a stop opposite her.

Phyllix swung open the car door and jumped to the ground.

Instantly, Trilby's heart fluttered, but she was not afraid. At least this was someone she knew. She looked at the car from which he had jumped, and smiled. It was almost as decrepit as Blanchie's Tim's car. The driver of the car, a big stolid boy Trilby remembered from her days at the beach, sat staring at her with cool curiosity.

'Where are you off to?' Phyllix asked softly.

'I told you,' Trilby lifted her chin. 'I told you I was going to Perth.'

'You walking all the way?'

'I'm getting a lift with the next car that comes along.'

'Anybody stopped yet?'

'Didn't want them to. I thought I'd wait a bit.'

Phyllix nodded. 'You know you gotta be careful?'

'You mean the police?'

Phyllix hesitated. 'Praps. You're only a kid. The police might chase you up. I was thinkin of other things. Some men ain't too particular. Specially with a coloured girl.'

Trilby just stared at him. Her heart began to thump with alarm.

Phyllix shrugged. 'You want a lift, ya gotta take a chance. You gotta think of all things like that. Sposing you're miles from anywhere, who's gunna hear you if ya call out? And who's gunna believe you if ya tell about it?'

Trilby bent her head to hide frightened tears. She hated herself because she was afraid. She hated even more the idea of asking Phyllix's help.

'We're going into town,' Phyllix said smoothly. 'Tonight I'll be seein a man who might take you ta Perth if ya want. Praps tomorrow. You wanta come along?'

Trilby's feet dragged as she followed Phyllix over to the car. He flung her case on to the back seat. Then he motioned to the front seat and after she was in climbed in alongside her. The driver grunted and put the rattly old machine in motion.

'You want to come with me or go home?' Phyllix asked under cover of the noise it made.

Trilby hesitated. Of the two alternatives, Phyllix's company would offer most reward. 'Where are you going?' she queried.

'Tonight I reckon we'll be stayin up with the Berrings,' Phyllix said. 'We're on our way there now.'

'I'll come with you,' Trilby said. 'But I mustn't get in any trouble, understand?'

'You won't get in no trouble with us,' Phyllix assured her. 'They might have a few bottles up there, but you don't need to have any.'

He said nothing further and when Trilby stole a glance at him from time to time she saw only his profile. The yellow eyes were fixed on the road ahead and a slight smile lifted the corner of his mouth. Trilby wondered what he could be thinking about. A bitter little smile appeared on her own mouth. Whatever these Berrings were like – and she had heard plenty about them from her mother – she felt confident to handle Phyllix.

CHAPTER 28

It was late afternoon when the old car churned its way up Heartbreak Hill. It turned into the bush track along which Trilby remembered walking on the morning her mother had taken them to visit Charlie and Hannie. The track was firmer now after the winter rains, but the car made heavy going of it. Trilby was bounced and bumped, flung first against Phyllix and then against the driver. Without a word, Phyllix took her arm and tucked it firmly beneath his and Trilby was grateful. A mile down the track the driver pulled into a sort of clearing. Trilby slipped from her seat and stood at the side of the road, staring curiously at the half-dozen humpies which made up the Berrings' camp. They were clustered on the outside edge of a half-circle of bare brown earth and behind them, shielding them from the wind, grew bushy stunted wattles.

The humpies were of wood and rusty iron reinforced with rotting grey canvas, and none of them looked large enough to contain any more than two small rooms. From each humpy projected the inevitable bough shelter which also served as a kitchen. Rickety tables fashioned from bush timber held frying-pans and saucepans and washing-bowls, and grouped around the shelters were receptacles to catch the rainwater which was directed into them by makeshift arrangements of guttering.

A thin acid smell pervaded the atmosphere around the campsite, mixing with the sweeter smell of the surrounding bush. Following Phyllix, Trilby made her way to the first of the erections, picking her way carefully over the litter round the doorway.

The air inside the place was warm and full-bodied with a dozen separate smells. Burned cooking-fat, perspiration, the thick heavy smell of old clothes and, stronger now, the thin penetrating acid smell.

The gloom of the windowless room was offset by a hurricane-lamp swinging from a hook of wire which depended from a heavy piece of bush-timber beaming. Trilby recognised the woman inside. She was big, with a curling mop of black hair and in her bright black eyes was an alertness that turned to curiosity when she caught sight of Trilby.

'Trilby Comeaway,' Phyllix introduced them briefly. 'This is May Berring, Trilby.'

'I know er,' May said. 'Ain't she the one that killed the baby?' There was no trace of censure in her tone, merely pleased recognition.

'She dropped it. I told you that,' Phyllix said roughly, and the woman shot a surprised look in his direction.

'All right! All right!' she grinned. 'Keep ya shirt on. I was only askin.'

'I told Trilby she could stay the night here,' Phyllix said. 'That all right with you, May?'

'Why, fa sure,' May said with exaggerated politeness. She winked at Trilby. 'Any pal a yours, I'm sure.'

'I gotta go out again,' Phyllix said with an unsmiling look at Trilby. 'Be back later.'

'Come in then,' May told Trilby. 'Might as well sit down now ya here. On the bed'll do.' She moved up along the bed on which she herself was sitting and the movement disclosed the sleeping figures of two children, a small boy and a girl. The boy lay on his back, his mouth slightly open. The little girl lay on her side, pressed close to him, one fat hand cuddling her round chin.

'Will I wake them up?' Trilby asked nervously. Now that it was dark she was conscious of a deepening gratitude to Phyllix. At least she would not have to spend the night in the bush or, worse still, with one of the fellows he had told her about. She looked over her shoulder for another reassuring glimpse of him, but he had gone.

'He'll be back,' May said, amused. 'Ain't nobody gunna hurt ya here. Sit down, will ya?'

Trilby perched on the side of the bed. She took a quick look round the room. A cupboard made from wooden boxes stood uneasily alongside one bulging wall. Some food stood on its shelves – butter still in its wrapping paper, a knife interred in its yellow heart, jam in a tin, another tin labelled powdered milk, a saucepan with rich brown gravy set in cold rivulets down its side, a loaf of bread on a wooden platter and below, along the bottom shelf, an assortment of cups, saucers and cracked brown plates. A shoe box at the end of the shelf held cutlery.

At the sight of the food, Trilby's mouth watered. She sped her gaze in another direction and caught the brilliant green of a set of canisters.

'They're pretty, aren't they?' she said, nodding.

'Jack won em down the Amusement Park. He's pretty good on them games. Yeah, they're pretty all right. Real handy ta put things in too, specially if I want a hidin place.' May laughed.

'Are these your children?' Trilby asked mechanically, looking down at the occupants of the bed.

'Yeah,' the woman said a bit impatiently, as if children were a poor choice of topic. 'You gunna stay with that Phyllix now?'

Trilby felt a fine perspiration break out on her upper lip and beneath her arms. 'I – I don't know,' she said weakly.

'Why'n't ya have a bit a fun first?' May advised. 'Once ya get running round with only one bloke ya fixed before ya know it. Seem ta think ya married to em or something. Take me. I been with Jack three years now. Dunno what started me off but I'm getting a bit tired of just stayin round here. I might go back home for a while, with me father. Me and me sisters used ta have fun up there.'

'Where does your father live?'

'Half-way up the road,' May said ambiguously. 'Hundred – hundred and fifty mile up. We got a big camp there. I got two sisters and we used ta have fellers stayin, helpin with the fencin. Us girls useta dig the holes, an the men come along behind puttin in the posts an stringin em together. We was the best team a fencers they ever had, some a the bosses said.' There was pride in May's voice. 'Could always get plenty a contracts. My ole man, everyone knows im up there, e useta do musterin too, us helpin. Gawd, we ad some fun. I miss them times. Satdy nights the fellers useta go inta the town and pick up a few bottles an we'd go on all night long sometimes. Nobody there ta kick up a fuss. Different ere.' The tone was moody now. 'Kickin up fusses all the bloody time. An now they wanta push us further back yet.' The black eyes sparkled. 'Jack says we moved all we gunna move. We stay put now. They can all just damn well move themselves, them white bastards. I'm gettin a bit sick of it but. Too many rows up ere, with the monarch comin out every time we make a bit a noise an stickin someone inside. I tell ya what. I might even take Jack with me. Dad can always do with fellers ta help an Jack's strong all right. Damn near killed me once when e ad a bit in. Took the axe offa me like no one's business and chucked it over in the bush there. Nobody ever found that axe yet. I spose I was lucky e didn't use it on me.'

Trilby's eyes were wide and fascinated. She hid her fear and distaste behind a tremulous smile. 'It's cold, isn't it? Do you think the kids are warm enough?'

'Them two?' May said off-handedly. 'They're all right. If ya like ya can help me shift em inta the nex room. No use wakin em up fa tucker now. They can make it up in the mornin. An the men'll be here soon. Once these kids is awake they just make a nuisance a themselves.' She rose from the bed and bent across Trilby to look at the children. Trilby got a whiff of rose-scented hair oil.

'Young devils,' May said fondly, stripping a thready grey rug from the children's bodies. 'Get ya in trouble soon as look at ya. That man they send out fum the school, e's got is knife inta me because they don't turn up ta school some days. I send em off. Glad ta get rid of em. Gawd knows where they get to after that. Off down the beach I spose. Ere, you take Elvie an I'll take young Albert.'

Trilby picked the little girl up as gently as she could, trying not to wake her, but the long curling eyelashes lifted and Trilby looked down into sleepy brown eyes.

'Come on you,' May said god-naturedly to the little boy. She swung him up in her strong arms and led the way into the next room. 'Jus dump em on top of everything and I'll throw this blanket over em,' May ordered, and Trilby did as she was told.

Two single black iron beds pushed close together and further cemented by a dirty black and white ticking-covered double mattress took up a good deal of the space. The children settled into each other's warmth almost without stirring, and May flung over them the tattered rug.

'Hope they don't wet me mattress again,' their mother said. 'Buggers fa wetting the bed these two are. Jack's always sayin e'll get em sent away if they don't learn to behave emselves. That's because they ain't his but. E gets a bit jealous sometimes, an takes it out on the kids.' She laughed. 'E don't really mean it but. An I'd like ta see im try, anyway.'

The small room was chilly. Trilby cast a last look at the children on the bed and felt relieved that they still wore their clothes. She followed May back into the other room and as she did so another woman entered.

The new arrival straightened herself with a hand to her back and surveyed Trilby in silence, completely ignoring May.

'You're one a them Comeaways, ain't ya?' she said at last.

'The one that's baby died,' May said significantly before Trilby could answer.

'I know.' The newcomer nodded a bit impatiently.

'I been down ta your place plenty a times, playin cards. But ya always shot through an shut yaself up in ya bedroom. What's the matter with ya? Don't like ta play cards?'

'No,' Trilby said flatly.

'Or ya think yaself too good to sociate with us fellers,' the woman asked, though there was no annoyance in her tone, only amusement.

'I don't like all the arguing,' Trilby said stiffly.

'Ah, ya don't wanta worry bout a bit of argument,' the woman laughed. 'Sides, we behaved ourselves real nice down your place.' She turned to May. 'She oughta been up ere last night, eh?'

May laughed. The newcomer took a seat on a chair, swivelling it to face Trilby.

'What'd ya say if ya man got hold a ya arm an twists an twists till it breaks?' she asked, wickedness flickering in her eyes.

Trilby only stared.

'I'm Rene Riley,' the woman said. 'Ya heard a me, ain't ya?'

Trilby nodded. Of course she had heard of Rene Riley. In the last months the tale of Rene Riley had unreeled itself like a serial story. Not only Mrs Comeaway, but all the people who lived in the big camp and the others who tucked themselves away under wattles and rotting tarpaulins round the outskirts of the town, knew and discussed with varying degrees of admiration and envy, but always with absorbed interest, the doings of Rene Riley.

Rene was a Perth woman, and the story went that she had left a good house down there to follow her man up to Wilga, where he had a contract to fence. But Fred Riley's estimate had been low and the family had ended up in debt to the fellows he had employed to help him. Fred had taken the easy way out, doing a bit of supplying, but he had been caught and his son Robbie had tried to break into a small store to get some money to pay his father's find and he had been caught too. A real old mix-up it had been, and through it all Rene Riley had moved with majestic force – speaking her mind to police and department alike – defying a threat of being charged herself, for contempt of court, by some means or other wresting her son from the clutches of the law and, finally, settling them all in a camp which sat on a small rise overlooking the town. And before the Riley family had been in the camp a month the town council had approved her request to have water piped up to her from the town supply.

Trilby had heard about the camp, its cleanliness, spaciousness, the garden that was bounded by dark bottles, the trees she had planted herself – there was more than curiosity in Trilby's grey eyes as she looked at the woman. A hint of admiration was there too.

It was rumoured, too, that this woman read all the books she could get her hands on, newspapers too, though, from the look of her, with her shapeless spreading body in its faded frock and heavy pocketed coat, her feet thrust into run-over slippers and her hair a frizzle of tiny grey curls, the reading had done nothing more than encourage a certain glint in her watchful eyes.

She made no secret of hating this town, but her husband had landed himself a respectable job as caretaker for an oil company and he refused to leave. Neither of the Rileys drank, preferring to gamble instead. It was generally agreed that what Fred lost on the horses, Rene picked up on the cards. It was certain that she was lucky at cards. Many a time she had played a man's hand for a stake in his winnings, if she happened to be broke.

Many more tales circulated. Kindness was never mentioned in the same breath as her name, but it was a fact that if a child shivered, Rene would find a warm garment for it and if a family had no food, they could always find a feed at the Rileys' camp. Rene was a good talker and whatever gathering she chose to join was never dull. She exchanged gossip with everyone and knew more of what was going on around the town than anyone except perhaps Horace. And what went in her ears came out her mouth, for the entertainment of anyone who cared to listen. She suppressed no incident that might accelerate the enjoyment of her audience, everything and everyone she talked about was stripped down to its bare bones, yet no one had ever heard her condemn anyone. She seemed to get her own enjoyment merely from contemplation and it was perhaps because of this fact that she rarely received just appreciation for favours bestowed. Though they were entertained, most people were a little afraid of Rene and her tongue, never knowing when they themselves might be found fitting subjects.

'What about a cuppa?' she said now, persuasively, to May, settling herself on the other end of the bed.

'Make it yaself,' May said. 'Ya know where the tea is.'

'Everything looks better after a cuppa,' Rene said calmly, getting up to poke at the sticks beneath the big black kettle. 'You got that big cup yet May, or ya broke it?'

May laughed. 'Ya lucky, Rene. I threw it at me ole man last night an only the handle came off. There tis, under the bed still.'

Interest was flickering in Trilby. There was something likeable about this woman Rene. If May had not been there in the room with them, she might have asked Rene about Perth and the things a girl like herself could do down there.

Rene had no such scruples about audiences.

'You on ya way somewhere?' she questioned later, pouring tea into three cups. Tea without milk or sugar, so that Trilby looked round, embarrassed, for a least a little sugar.

'Where's ya sugar?' Rene asked May. 'Don't take it meself. Makes things simpler,' she told Trilby. 'Now, where was we?'

You going off some place all by yaself?'

'Phyllix brought er,' May said, sipping. 'E'll be back soon.'

'Seems ta me,' Rene said, watching Trilby with intent dark eyes, 'ya wasn't keen ta have im round, a bit back.'

'I just met him on the road,' Trilby defended.

'What road?'

'I'm going to Perth.' Trilby lifted her chin.

'Nnnh!' Rene relished. 'Perth, eh?' She took a swallow of boiling hot tea. 'An what ya gunna do down there?'

Trilby opened her mouth, then hesitated. How could she tell this woman in two or three sentences what she intended to do? And, for that matter, why should she tell anyone anything? She withdrew, as if from a trap, and took up her cup.

'Ya got plans?' Rene said softly.

Trilby nodded.

'An I can tell ya what they are without ya even sayin a word,' Rene told her. 'Tell just by lookin at ya.' She shook her head. 'Don't you go, sweetie-pie. Won't do ya no good.'

Trilby frowned, but would not give significance to what this woman said by answering her.

Rene looked deeply into her cup. 'Ya look a sensible girl, that'd probably take some notice of a bit of advice I can give ya. I wonder now ... ,' she threw at Trilby a glance that was both mischievous and chiding. 'Ya gunna listen to me?'

Trilby nodded ungraciously.

'Use em,' Rene said promptly. 'That's it. Use em an don't let em use you. That's the only way you'll come out on top. But you try an break loose from these fellers an all you'll get's a kick in the face.' She looked squarely at Trilby. 'Not only from those white bastards. You'll get it there all right. But when ya come crawlin back, these fellers'll be waiting ta pick up the ball. See?' She held Trilby's gaze for a second, then dropped her own and shook her head. 'No, ya don't see. I mighta known. Too young! Too young!'

'I was just tellin er to have a bit a fun while she got the chance,'

May broke in. 'You know. Before ya got a string a kids round ya all gettin sick or gettin in trouble somewhere, spoilin ya fun. An people comin sticky-beakin round wantin ta know how ya feed em an if they got beds an snatchin em off ya ta send up some mission if ya don't look out.'

'Kids gotta be looked after,' Rene said practically. 'Polly's kids got took because Polly an er ole man both got picked up the same night an the ole woman they left them kids with couldn't hardly look after erself let alone a couple babies.'

'Wouldn't mind bettin you had something ta do with that,' May said darkly.

'Wouldn't ya now,' Rene said equably.

'Ya always down that office,' brooded May. 'See ya comin outa there plenty a times. An ya been too bossy with me sometimes, too.'

Rene flashed a smile at Trilby, completely ignoring this further comment from May. 'What I mean by usin em, them white folks, I got two a my kids already in that place the partment's got in Perth. They go ta school from there. Get all their books, nice uniforms, hot bath every day if they like, nice little rooms ta sleep in.' She chuckled and looked sidelong at Trilby. 'Look after my kids all right, don't you make no mistake bout that. Them kids can be what they like when they bigger. Go a long way further'n I ever went, with all me brains, that's a bit more than some silly buggers got,' she finished with a grin at May.

Trilby looked at Rene with a good deal more attention.

'My sister . . . ,' she began hesitantly. Rene's head was slightly tilted. There was kindliness in the depths of the dark eyes. Trilby felt the words being drawn out of her. 'Mrs Riley, wouldn't there be some place in Perth where I could get a decent job?' So I could live better than people do up here? I want to.'

'Course there's nice people,' Rene said calmly. 'But your not gunna come up against em. You'll be beat before ya get that far. The ones your gunna meet, spose ya go ta Perth like ya seem set on, they gunna be the small fry, the mean ones that likes ta have someone ta treat like dirt. Makes em feel bigger. Or ya'll maybe get friends with some white man that doesn't mind comin ta camps like this.'

'What was it like – where you lived in Perth?'

'Them!' Rene was scornful. 'They was a good lot, they was.' Her eyes were on Trilby, weighing, measuring. 'Kicked up a fuss before we even moved inta the place, before they even seen us. An it took a couple big dogs ta keep em fum pesterin the life outa us after we was there.' She laughed suddenly and then mirth took her over entirely, shaking her in its grip until her whole body bounced merrily, until May had been infected and even Trilby was forced to smile. 'Gawd! Will I ever forget that monarch flyin down the path with a bit outa his pants an then screechin at me over the gate. An me pretendin not ta understand.'

'Didn't you make any friends?' Trilby asked.

'If ya could call em friends,' Rene said. 'I minded plenty a kids for people that wanted a night out on the tiles. I didn't ask em to mind mine. An there was the ones like I said made em feel big havin someone ta look down on. Gave me all their ole clothes, too, that wasn't good enough for em no more. But we was all square there. Did a bit a tradin with me pals, an a bit a cash always come in handy. Nup! We didn't have em in our place, an they didn't have us in theirs. That way no bones got broke.'

Trilby stared ahead of her, her tea cold in its cup.

'I found out who me pals were – when I needed a bit of a help,' Rene continued softly. 'We wasn't let ta starve, up in Wilga. Always got a handout from the camps round about, an no questions asked. That's something ya gunna find out fa yaself, Trilby, ain't it? Ya not gunna let me tell ya. Don't think I don't know that, an Gawd knows why I been wastin me time talkin to ya. Eh, May, any more tea left in that pot?' She reached for the teapot and felt its weight.

'Gawd, she can drink tea,' May said with much amusement. 'Good job it ain't conto.' 'An that reminds me,' Rene said, apropos of nothing. 'Fred got my bit a money fa some horse e fancied. If ya got five bob, May, it'll do ta start me off tonight if I can get in a game.'

'Dunno why ya always come down on me,' May complained, reaching reluctantly for an oversize brown handbag and raking through its depths.

The canvas cover gave to the push of a hand. Phyllix walked in followed by a white man. The white man's dirty sweat-stained shirt billowed almost to his thighs before being confined in the skin-tight jeans that showed every curve of his fat swaggering body. In one hand he carried a sugar-bag that was full of clanking bottles. This he lowered gently to the table.

'Well!' he said, planting his pudgy hands on his hips, fixing his small piggy eyes on Trilby. 'So this is the gel that wants a lift down ta Perth. An me going down that way meself tomorrow. What ya think a that, eh? Like ta come with me?' He leered.

Trilby's eyes flew to Phyllix. His gaze met hers unblinkingly and she read the meaning in his eyes. If she wanted a lift to Perth this was the sort of man she would travel with.

CHAPTER 29

'I can't go to Perth,' Trilby thought wretchedly. 'Phyllix will have to take me home again.' Questioning by her father seemed infinitely preferable to continuing with a plan which might end with her having to accept favours at the hands of such a man. She actually shuddered at the thought.

She moved towards Phyllix, but the white man cut across her path. Taking two bottles from the sack he waved them at May. 'What about a drink to warm ourselves up? These two's yours, May. That treacly muck you like.' He moved closer to Trilby. 'What's your name, gel? You can call me Teddy – or Bill – or anything else you like. I don't mind.' He laughed uproariously at the expression on Trilby's face, slapping his obscene hips.

'His name's George,' Phyllix said levelly, going to the make-shift cupboard and selecting some cracked cups and a couple of peanut butter jars. 'You wanta drink, Trilby?'

'Course she wants a drink,' May sniggered, while Rene looked disapproving. 'Looks as if she could do with a drink, that one. Go on, Phyllix, give us all one.'

Phyllix filled the cups. George lowered his bulk on to the sagging bed between May and Rene and put an arm about each. Rene shrugged him off irritably, but May giggled and widened her beautiful dark eyes at him. 'Now, you,' George admonished, 'Don't you go puttin on a turn. I don't want to get in no trouble with *your* ole man. I had enough a that last time I was here. I'm gunna do a line with the little gel that wants to go to Perth with me.' He reached forward a paw and gave Trilby's waist a squeeze. His breath was already strong with alcohol and, as well, through the loose and flabby lips came the odour of decaying teeth. Phyllix cleared his throat and when Trilby looked over at him he gave her the smallest of beckoning nods. She went to him gladly and stood quietly at his side, her flesh remembering the hot clutch of the pudgy hand.

'You wanta drink?' Phyllix motioned towards the filled cups.

Trilby hesitated, then picked up one of the glasses. It was uncomfortably full and took some balancing.

Before anyone could drink another man came into the room. Trilby had seen him around town. He had a broad good-humoured face and his flat widely-spaced brown eyes were rayed about with laughter-lines. He was grinning now and his smile disclosed an even row of square white teeth. Only for an instant, as his gaze fell on George, did his face lose its glow of good fellowship. But George exerted himself to be affable.

'Brought up a bit of the doings, Willis. Sit down an have one, man.'

'We got another visitor too,' May simpered, moving primly away from George. 'Look who's here, Willis. Young Trilby Comeaway. She's doin a bunk ta Perth tomorrer. With George.' She laughed shrilly.

Willis turned to Trilby. 'You the one that's just had ya baby die on ya?' he inquired with rough friendliness. 'Ne'mind, sister. You'll have more.' He grinned at Phyllix. 'If the young bloke has any say in the matter, eh, Phyllix?'

Trilby drank from her glass to hide her confusion. Phyllix bent to whisper. 'Ya don't have ta drink it. Just hold it.'

'I'm hungry,' Trilby whispered back. 'Is there anything to eat?'

Phyllix moved quietly over to the shelves and fossicked round among the tins. He came back with a few biscuits, soggy and smelling of mildew. Trilby pushed them into her mouth, grateful even for them. Her stomach ached with emptiness.

'What say we light a fire outside?' May said brightly. 'Then we can all sit round an get a bit warm. An Billy can come over an play is mouth-organ. C'mon.' She stood up, smiling secretly down on George, then turning wide innocent eyes on her big husband.

'An you jus behave yaself see?' Willis rumbled, his uncertain gaze on George.

'Don't you go lookin at me,' George said heartily. 'Come on, Willis. You and me'll hunt up some wood. I don't go muckin round with no one else's woman. Not when the bloke's as big as you, anyhow.' He clapped an arm round Willis's shoulder and the two went out.

Trilby and Phyllix exchanged glances, then they too tried to sidle unobtrusively out through the doorway.

'Gunna play handies,' May's bright-eyed gaze followed them. 'You better look out fa that George, Trilby. I think e's got is eye on you.' She laughed again, and Trilby felt a flash of anger. She turned to give it vent, but Phyllix gave her a little push. She swallowed her anger and passed through the doorway before him.

'She don't mean any harm' Phyllix said gruffly. 'Ya don't want to take any notice, that's all.'

'She's just stupid,' Trilby said proudly. 'As if I'd let a man like that touch me.'

'I've got a blanket,' Phyllix said. 'Here it is. We can sit on it.'

The two men had already lit a fire. In ten minutes it was a blaze of warmth. Trilby and Phyllix sat near a wattle, watching it. Trilby had placed her glass of wine on the ground nearby, but Phyllix held his and sipped at it.

Trilby was tired and her shoulders drooped. Perth seemed as far away as ever it had been. She thought of Rene and the things Rene had said. She lifted her gaze to George as he stood to pour himself another drink. As surely as ever, she knew what she wanted, but there were so many things in between. For the first time, there were miserable doubts in her mind. Above all, weariness both of mind and body. Behind her was Phyllix's shoulder. She felt she must keep away from it.

'Drink up your wine before it's spilt,' Phyllix whispered in her ear. 'One glass won't hurt you.'

Recklessly, Trilby picked up the glass and drained it. And having done that she resisted no more the impulse to lean against Phyllix. As her eyelids drooped and her lips parted on a soft sigh, Phyllix slid his hand round her waist, moving so that he was steady beneath her weight. For an instant before she slept, Trilby felt warmly safe.

It was quite dark when she woke. The fire still burned high and someone was singing. Lazily through half-closed eyes, Trilby watched the lit figures of women and men, and as she did so there was a scuffle on the other side of the fire. One of the big Berring men was holding a smaller man by the scruff of his neck. It looked so funny that Trilby laughed. A woman raised her voice in indignation. 'Only jokin, that's all e was doin. Put the pore bastard down. If ole Nosy Parker May over there hadn't told ya. ... '

'Did e or did e not ask ya?' the big man demanded.

'If ya wanta know e did and I said I would, like hell, with you around.'

'Ah! You!' The big man shook the smaller one as if he had been a toy. 'If you was half a man. ... 'He shook him again, disgustedly. 'Go on, you just get.'

Strong legs set wide apart, hands on hips, he stood watching as the man scurried out of sight into the surounding bush. Then he began, with calm unconcern, to upend a bottle over an enamel mug.

From the bush came a plaintive protest, 'Always pickin on me.'

A roar of laughter went up from the circle as the big man strode forward a few steps, bent forward from the waist and emitted a most realistic roar of rage which was answered by a frightened squeak and more frantic scufflings.

'That'll be the end a him fa tonight,' he came back grinning. 'The sawed off young runt.'

'Woke up at last,' Phyllix said, as Trilby laughed with the rest. 'You've been sleeping a couple of hours.'

'The little gel want something ta drink?' George said amiably, staggering a little as he plastered himself alongside Trilby.

Trilby stopped laughing abruptly and moved away.

'Come on. Less fill up ya glass,' George leered into her face.

'No, thank you,' Trilby said politely.

George snatched at her glass and poured from his bottle until the glass brimmed and spilled on her lap and her legs. Then he pushed it into her hand, spilling more of the strong-smelling stuff as he did so.

'Drink it down,' he ordered, 'an I'll come back an give ya some more.'

'That's right,' May yelled from her position against a man's shoulder. 'Drink it up girl, or there won't be none left for ya to drink.

George leaned over and pressed her arm. 'I'll be back, kid. You wait here and George'll take care of ya.'

Phyllix followed George with his eyes. 'You still want that lift ta Perth?' he murmured and Trilby shuddered.

Another argument had started up opposite them, between the same couple.

'Ah, shut ya guts,' the big man said tiredly. 'Give a man a bit a peace. If ya gunna yap all night ya might as well go after im.'

'Awright well, I will,' the woman snapped, staggering to her feet with difficulty. 'Ya don't treat me like no bloody dog an get away with it.' She tried to draw herself up proudly but she had had just a little too much conto. The big man gave her a careless shove and she fell forward on her face. Again the group brayed with laughter. It was too much for the woman. On her back, she lashed out at the big man with both feet, catching him on the side of the head with her high-heeled shoes.

Phyllix rose swiftly, blocking out the sight of the fracas which followed from Trilby's horrified gaze. 'Come on,' he said quietly. 'We're getting.' With one hand under her arm he pulled her to her feet. Trilby was shaking from the cold and from fear. With the whole camp now in an uproar, she clung desperately to Phyllix's hand as he dragged her after him.

She took one last look at the firelit scene as they plunged into the bush, one shocked and unbelieving look. These were the kind who had befriended Rene when she needed help? These fighting yelling madmen and women?

Into the chilly darkness Phyllix led her, far beyond the light of the fire and the raised and angry voices. Wattles stung their faces and the ground beneath felt soft and springy. When the silence of the bush was all about them Phyllix stopped and spread out the rug. Trilby sank down on her haunches and rested her weight on her hands. Phyllix would have pulled her close, but she resisted. 'I'm tired. Can't we just sleep?'

'No!' There was pent anger in the short sound. Phyllix moved so that his face was between her and the grey of the bush and sky. 'We're gunna have this out properly – now, if ya never listened to nobody before, ya gunna listen to me now. Ya saw that crowd back there? You go to Perth by yaself and that's the kind of people ya gunna end up with. An men like that George. Their own kind won't have a bar of em so they buy their way inta camps like the Berrings' with a bagful of cheap wine. You won't find nothing ya want in Perth. I'm telling ya.' His voice changed. 'Trilby, why won't ya stick with me? What's changed between us two? You said we was gunna be married when I come back from the bush that time.'

'I never meant it. I said it to get rid of you.' Trilby flung the truth at him impatiently and in the long silence that followed she was only relieved to have found so quick a way of ending the talk between them.

She was all the more startled and angry, therefore, when she found her shoulders gripped by strong fingers. Jerking upright, she saw bared teeth and a glitter of eyes before her head was shaken back and forth in a quick and relentless rhythm. The strong fingers bit even deeper into her forearms. A scream that rose to her throat was choked before she could utter it. Then her head hit the ground with a thud as the boy flung her from him.

Dazed and afraid, she rolled herself into a ball and covered her face with her hands. Her breathing was tangled with deep wrenching sobs. She heard Phyllix say, 'All right! We're finished.' And there was such a note of scorn in his voice she shrank as though she had been slapped. She felt him withdrawing from her and instantly an insanity of fear possessed her. This was like the time when her mother had sat on the end of her prison bed and pleaded with her.

And had risen and gone away because she would not answer. There was the same feeling of terrible loneliness, the same desperate need for something strong and unchanging to which she could cling. And in the moment of his withdrawal, Phyllix became that which she sought.

Like an agile cat, she grasped at his belt and hung on to it.

'Don't go, Phyllix. Stay with me.'

Phyllix did not move.

'Let me tell you,' Trilby wept. 'You don't understand, Phyllix.'

Slowly the boy slipped back to the rug. For a while he listened to the girl's tearing sobs, then, with her hand still clutching his belt, he moved her with his arms until her head rested on his shoulder.

'Tell me,' he said, and his voice was gentle again. With one hand he smoothed the side of her head, the warm soft skin of her face and the springing curling hair. He crooned over her and held her until at last she was quiet. They rested for a while in silence. Trilby's eyes were closed, and over her head Phyllix looked unseeing into the grey and misty bush.

'I'd stay with you,' Trilby said at last, haltingly. 'You don't know how easy that'd be. But it's not only me, Phyllix. It's something I live with, here,' her clenched fist struck her heart as though she would hurt the thing that lived in her breast. 'It keeps telling me I'll end up like that old woman if I don't get away from you all.'

'What old woman?'

Trilby stared away into the bush, seeing again the witch-like body, the black eyes spitting sparks, the rim of foam that crusted the curled and snaking lips. 'Dad had to kick her out. And he called her an old black nigger. She hated him then. She would have killed him, killed him some awful way that would have made him suffer as much as possible. And I knew why too. I know she was filthy and old and horible to look at, but she'd got so that she didn't mind all those things. She didn't mind anything but being called a nigger. Don't you see, Phyllix? She was as young as me once, maybe just like me, wanting all the things I want, and now – all she wants is not to be called a nigger. All the things she used to be afraid would happen, like I am, they've all happened. She's only got one thing left to be afraid of.'

'Go on,' Phyllix said quietly.

'If I stay with you, the things that happened to her will happen to me,' Trilby said pleadingly. 'I want a proper house to live in and I'll get a humpy. I want nice things to wear, my own things, not other people's cast-offs. And I'll end up with one single dress. If I have children I want them to be clean and pretty, not running

round with dirty noses and no pants on because it's too much
trouble to wash them. But after a while there'll be so many kids I
won't care how they look so long as they don't bother me. I won't
care about anything but gambling and winning at cards and sitting
round talking with all the other women. And if we want to drink,
we'll have to sneak it and drink it quickly, so the monarch won't
catch us, and you'll get drunk and come after me with a bottle or
break my arm on purpose like one of the Berring men did once.
And we'll quarrel all the time and I'll end up like that old woman,
not caring about anything so long as I'm not called a nigger.' She
straightened a little in his grasp. 'Phyllis, I hate that name as much
as she did. I could kill someone, too, if they called me by it.'

Phyllix drew a deep breath of the cool clean night air. His
shoulders straightened.

'You don't have to stay, Trilby. I won't make you. I'll even help
you get away and give you some money so you can stay somewhere
decent. Just remember but, I'm waiting back here for ya when you
want me.'

Trilby only looked at him, unable for a moment to take in what
he had said.

Phyllix gave her a little shake. 'It's all right,' he told her.

Sudden tears wet Trilby's face again. 'What if I don't come
back?'

Phyllix sighed. 'You might get tired of fighting, Trilby. An even
places like the Berrings look good when ya tired.'

'Rene said that,' Trilby said slowly.

'One other thing,' Phyllix said, his hands firm again on her
forearms. 'Don't you go thinking it would be like you said – with us.
That's not what I want neither, that drinkin an gamblin stuff.
That's why I always wanted you, Trilby.'

Because Trilby could see over Phyllix's shoulder she was the first
to see the stumbling figure of George.

'Found ya,' he said triumphantly, weaving towards them. 'Come
on, boy. I told ya. My turn now with the little gel.'

Trilby screamed in fear but Phyllix was up in a flash, between
her and George. He snarled in his fury like an animal, his body
crouching, his elbows crooked. Then the two figures merged and
Trilby was alone, edging herself along the ground, her frightened
eyes trying to distinguish between the two locked figures, the hard
crack of blows on bare flesh making her wince.

The fight did not last long. One of the figures fell with a heavy
crash and Trilby knew that it was George. Phyllix stood above him,

still crouching, waiting to see if he should rise. But George only groaned and then lay still.

Trilby looked towards Phyllix, needing him near her still. She rose trembling to her feet, and the boy moved over towards her.

'It's all right,' he told her as she nestled against him.

Trilby drew his head down to her and closed her eyes, exulting in the hard firmness of his body, pressing so close to him that she could feel the pounding of his heart as if it were her own.

'Trilby, will you stay – for a while?' Phyllix said at last, his need as great as her own.

Trilby nodded. Phyllix found her mouth and tasted salt from the tears that once again were seeping through her closed lids. She wanted to tell Phyllix what she knew he most wanted to hear – that she would stay not for a while, but for always. And she could not. The thing that lived in her heart would not let her. So long as she had youth and strength and pride, so long would she seek to escape this life.

KIT DENTON
THE BREAKER

It took patience, hard work, understanding, love and much sympathy to write this book. I showed very little of any of them, therefore this is for my wife LE who showed them all.

Before you begin ...

There *was* a Breaker Morant. He lived his life in the times and company of many of the people mentioned in this story, and he went through much of the action in these pages. I had hoped to write a true history of the events and the people concerned, but the obduracy of the British Government in refusing to release a number of essential documents has made this impossible. Nonetheless, this book has in it many of the historical facts and I've departed from history only when the facts weren't discoverable or when I felt it was necessary in the interest of a good story. Morant lived, wrote, fought and died pretty much the way I've pictured it.

For various kinds of assistance with the book I'm indebted to the Australian Council for the Arts; Trevor Beacroft of the Bank of New South Wales; Jim MacDougall of the Sydney *Daily Mirror*; Mrs Ira Quinlan of South West Rocks; Tony Mays of Canberra; Peter Scasighini; Qantas, and their Public Information Officer, John Ford; Mrs Cook of the library at Victoria Barracks in Sydney; Lieutenant-Colonel Gentles, Assistant Director, Legal Services in the Australian Army; my sister Stella and her husband Allan and Lieutenant-Colonel Tim Swifte, Assistant Director, Army Public Relations, who's been my friend for sixteen years and never more so than during the writing of this book. My thanks to him and to everyone else who got me to this point.

K.D.

AUSTRALIA

November 1901

The corner of the small paddock collected the bars of sunlight sliding through the sapling fence, stretching them in white-gold lines across the green shadows which were almost black. Paddy leaned on the gate, looking into the corner, squinting against the clean hurt of the morning sun, seeing only the light and shadow contrasts. The whistle was sharp and brief, his

tongue hard against the back of his teeth, and then more teeth
showing as his mouth widened in a grin. There, in there in the
barred darkness, Harlequin lifted his head to the sound, his
ears pricking forward and his lip lifting in a quiet answering
whicker. Then he stepped out, the movement showing him for
the first time, a graceful zebra for a moment, for a moment a
pale green unicorn, touched with gold, then a golden horse
walking dainty-hooved onto the plate of gold that was the
short grass between the trees and the gate.

Whenever it happened, as often as it happened, Paddy
sucked in a breath, shaking his head a little in admiration,
thinking, No wonder Harry wanted him.

Harlequin saw the man at the gate and flicked his head to
one side, the mane sliding like black silk across the golden arch
of his neck, the black tail moving with it, and he came out
easily in a trot, half circling, playing his morning game.

'Hey, there, Harlequin.' It wasn't a call, just a low-voiced
greeting, part of the whole ritual, part of the months behind
them both, alone on the property.

'Hey, horse. Come on over here, then.'

The man was big across the chest and shoulders, looked big
in the way some stocky men do, and the face was a quarry
where the years and the weather had dug. The voice was a low
rumble and Harlequin heard and felt the affection in the lilt of
it, checking on the turn and pausing, his hooves close, his body
balanced. Then, head a little lower, he walked with delicacy
towards the gate, towards the half-opened hand with the little
heap of browny sugar in it. A yard from it the horse spun
about and the ritual began again, both of them enjoying it,
both knowing exactly how long it should last, both conscious
of the admiration and the love that inspired it. When it ended,
Harlequin edged his flank against the gatepost, rubbing it
gently for the comfort of the rough timber, and his muzzle
went down to the sugar, silk lips cool against Paddy's palm.
Paddy looped an arm onto the horse's neck, tugging gently at
the mane, rubbing knuckles into the crest between the ears
and talking.

'Ye're a fine feller, so y'are. And ye know it too, don't ye?
Ah, ye do so. Ye're a lovely liddle horse an' ye miss yer master,
don't ye?' He wiped his damp and empty palm against the side
of his trousers and ran it over the soft muzzle, Harlequin
leaning his head in, a small grunting noise in his throat.

'Ah, well, feller, the both of us misses him, that's the God's

truth of it. But he'll be back one of these times, boy, and slap a
saddle on that goldy back of yours and ye'll be off like the
wind, ye will.'

Paddy wondered how many times he'd said that, how many
times he and Harlequin had stood here like this, or over there
in the shed when the weather was bad, half leaning on one
another, the man and the horse each remembering – he was
sure the horse remembered – each seeing in his mind the
pictures of Harry. Outside the Barracks on that going-away
night, up at Renmark in the rum-sweat of the breaking-in, on
the track down over the hills to Adelaide. All the months since.

'That's it, then, me son.' He pushed Harlequin gently away,
the flat of his hand on the long neck muscles, and the horse
rubbed his nose against Paddy's jacket, seeming to nod. Then
he was away, moving into a short step then a long stride,
across the diagonal of the paddock, mane and tail glittering
back in the sun's glare.

Paddy watched him run, seeing him and not seeing him,
seeing again the start of it all.

The heat outside had been a flat, bright thing, crisping a man in his
own natural juices. Inside, it was the heat of an old stale oven,
reeking with ancient odours. The man stood in the doorway, the
blue-bronze daylight behind him, his shadow stretching down the
shaft of light and across into the dimness in the corners of the broad
room. No one stopped drinking or talking, none of the fourteen or
fifteen men in that dull hotbox. No one stopped drinking or slapping damp cards down. But as the man walked to the trestle bar he
knew that everyone there was watching him, considering him,
lifting eyebrows one to another. The barman was fat and grey and
moist. He just stood as the man dropped his bag and took off the
blue cap, black-blue with sweat, and slapped the dust away from it
on the edge of the bar top.

'Good afternoon. May I have a rum, please?'

The voice was low and tired, but the intonations carried and the
courtesy did what the man's entrance had not done. It stopped the
talk. In the little silence the barman moved only far enough to pour
from a green bottle into a thick glass and to push a battered jug of
water alongside the drink. One hand held onto the glass, the other
lay palm up, fingers curling. The man looked evenly at him and
fumbled a few coins from a pocket, dropping one into the ready
hand. The glass came free and the man took it and drank the rum
down, little drops of moisture spattering from his head as he jerked

it back. The barman put small coins down and the man slid them
back towards him, watching as the bottle tilted again, this time
adding water and sipping as his elbows came down onto the bar
and his back relaxed. The silence had lasted twenty seconds, and
he spoke into it.

'I wonder whether you know of any work in this neighbourhood?'

The fireplace in the far wall was a dead hole, part-filled with the
readiness of next winter's warmth, topped up with rubbish. From
the half-dozen men round it there was a giggle. The wet mouth in
the barman's face moved.

'What kinda work?'

The giggle came again, a voice growing out of it.

'Elocution teacher, mate!'

The others round the fireplace laughed now and one of them
punched the speaker appreciatively on the upper arm. The man at
the bar ignored them.

'I don't mind, as long as it's something I can do. I'm not much of
a farmer, I'm afraid.'

The giggler spat into the crackle-dry logs in the fireplace and
moved forward, the others moving with him. 'Ya don't look to be
much of anythin', mate.'

From a corner, Magee watched what was happening, listened to
the laughter swell again, saw the card hands slow and stop. He
stood up, leaving his empty glass on the table.

The man at the bar glanced round at the grinning men, the
barman's voice turning him back again. 'Only thing I know is I c'd
use a yardman – swabbin' down an' cleanin' out an' that. Y'talk a
bit fancy f'r a yardman, son.'

The group from the fireside had reached the bar, clustering near
the man. The giggler picked up the blue cap, fingering the leather
peak. 'He's not a yardman, Dick – he's a porter fa the railways.
See!' He tossed the hat to one of his cronies and it began to move
from hand to hand, the way small boys will toss a friend's ball
around to tease him into trying to grab at it. The man at the bar
made no move, except to turn his head to the giggler.

'Why don't *you* take the yardman's job, my friend? You look as
though you're used to dirty work.'

There was a snap of silence before the laughter came again,
everyone joining in this time, one of them jeering, ''E got ya there,
Sims. Right in the guts.'

The giggler, Sims, face flushing, scowling. 'I c'd clean *you* up
right enough, fancy boy –'

The man turned his back. Near him Magee had the cap, squinting down at it curiously, then handing it back. The man nodded his thanks. Sims' hand on his shoulder was hard and sudden and it spun him fast, so that his back joggled the bar top and his drink slopped.

'How'd ya like it if I was ta knock that bloody great plum outa yer mouth, eh?'

'Stop behaving like a schoolboy.'

The hand stabbed out again, the heel jarring against the man's shoulder. Behind the bar, the moist man shifted bottles and glasses and laid a truncheon on the bar top with care. The man reached up and knocked Sims' arm aside. His voice was still low, still tired.

'Look here, you're dirty and you smell and your manners are appalling. But I've no wish to start a brawl with you or anyone else. Go and finish getting drunk, there's a good chap.'

Before he could turn his back again, Sims' fist caught him high on the chest, staggering him. The barman took up the truncheon and rapped with it.

''Nough, Sims. No fightin' in here, right?'

Around Sims, his friends were pushing at the man, urging.

'Go on, fancy. Take 'im on, why don't ya?'

'Ya not gonna let ol' Simsy knock ya like that, surely!'

'Give 'im a scrap, matey.'

The truncheon beat loudly on the bar top, then waved before them. Magee moved closer to the man whose eyes had not left Sims. Magee spoke low, into the man's ear.

'C'mon now, me son. You don't want to be fightin' with anyone –'

The press of men round them pushed him away. Sims was grinning.

'Well, me pretty little porter, ya comin' outside?'

In a swell of sound everyone was shoving towards the door, Sims already rolling his sleeves up, the man caught in the movement, letting himself be taken along. Magee edged close to him as they came out into the lowering sun's blaze, his voice pitched above the excitement.

'Aw, c'mon now boys – it's too hot fer fightin'!'

No one listened, but the man swung a little to look at Magee.

'He's a bad devil, that Sims. Y'll get kilt, y'will.'

The man's voice was crisper now. 'I think I can take care of myself, thank you.'

And then they were all in the street, in a rough ring in the dust, and the silent and sleeping shanties sent out others to make them a crowd. One or two women stood in doorways and the gaps in the crowd's legs filled with boys and yipping dogs. Sims stood, braces hanging over a wide belt, sleeves well up, grinning, waiting.

On the other side of the ring, Paddy Magee spread his elbows to dig himself room at the front and look across at Sims. The stranger stood just to one side of Paddy, carefully folding the long blue coat. Paddy reached a hand to it. 'I'll hold yer clobber for ye, boyo.'

'That's kind of you.'

'Ah, it would be a damn sight kinder if I was to hit ye over the head with a bit of wood. Quicker, annyway.'

'I *have* been taught something about boxing.' The man seemed unperturbed as he folded back the cuffs of his shirt to just below the elbow. Paddy thought, Them's good strong wrists he has there, that's true enough. And he stands nice and easy. Maybe . . .

Across the shifting circle of dust Sims stood now with his shirt off, a grey-dirty woollen vest holding in the thick bulges of his shoulders and the swell of his belly.

'That Sims, he's very big, son. But ye'll see he's got a fair piece of a belly there, 'n' if ye was to catch him a knock in it ye'd do him some damage. Not the head, now – it's like a barrel of sand, so it is.'

Sims' cronies had been calling across to the man and now Sims raised his voice. 'Are ya comin', then? Or do I haveta come an' get ya?'

The man moved forward into the centre, to where Sims was waiting, hands hanging loose at his sides, sweat-stains black on the wool of his vest. There was a second of silence, then the crowd exploded in a crack of laughter, jeers rising out of it. The stranger had placed himself directly in front of the grinning Sims, left toe forward, left arm half extended, right arm cocked high, back straight. Paddy sucked in hard.

'Holy Christ Jesus, he's a Marquess of Queensberry man! He'll be murdered!'

Moving lightly enough, the man stepped a foot closer and jabbed high on Sims' cheek with the left. Sims took the tap, stepped back and kicked the man in the crutch.

The roar of applause drowned the man's gasping grunt of anguish, but Paddy saw the mouth jerk open and the eyes close, saw the sudden tears in the dust on the man's face as he went over, his hands clutching at the tearing pain. Sims walked in flat-footed and clubbed his fist onto the back of the lowered head, and again as the man went crookedly to his knees. The crowd was shouting encouragement and Sims grinned round at them before turning back to the crouched and retching stranger, again going close then jerking a savage knee into the man's cheekbone, watching as he toppled sideways into the dust still doubled round the hands holding his groin.

'The boot, Simsy, give 'im the boot, mate!'

The smile now was a tighter thing, curling the edge of Sims' mouth and slitting his eyes. He measured his distance carefully and swung his foot with deliberation into the bent body in the dirt, the toecap of the heavy boot sinking into the side of the man's gut once and once again. A flood of bile and vomit shot from the man's mouth, opened in speechless pain, and Sims shifted his stance to avoid it, lining himself up for a final kick to the head. As his foot came forward, the man heaved again and the kick took him where his neck and shoulder joined. Sims stirred him with his foot and walked away into the crowd, accepting the backslaps and congratulations and holding his cheek in mock agony for the extra laugh.

Paddy stooped to look down at the unconscious man. 'Ye wouldn't be told now, would ye! C'mon – up ye come!'

He dragged the man upright, hitching him like a sick old sheep over his shoulders, and walked heavily to where the tired horse slept standing by the trough.

The man groaned when he was humped across the saddle, groaned and half-opened his eyes. Paddy took the hessian headband off the horse and used it to pass a lashing across the man's back, through his belt and onto the saddle. He tucked the coat and hat into the blanket-roll and went back into the pub, into the smoky dullness and the noise, Sims and his mates still shouting with laughter. Only the barman noticed Paddy and, without speaking, he bent behind his bar, straightened and passed the stranger's bag around the end. Paddy took it out, slung it to his own saddle, took the other horse's reins as he swung up and led off down the dusty afternoon street.

One side of the sleeping man's face was lit by the leaning flames from the fire, yellow-orange and sideways with the early night breeze pushing at them. The thin moonlight on the other side showed a dark patch where his open shirt had pulled away from his neck, a patch darker than the shadows where the skin and the bone beneath were deeply bruised. The billy, propped on a couple of stones, boiled over, hissing into the hot wood-ash and the man stirred, opening unfocused eyes on the fire and the blackness behind it. When he moved his head his face creased in sudden pain and he groaned quietly, not quietly enough for the sound to escape Paddy, dozing with his back against a tree. He rolled upright, moved the billy a little, put another dry branch across the edge of the fire and stooped by the man under the horse-blanket.

The man concentrated on Paddy's face, his forehead skin wrinkling down with the effort. 'I've seen you before –'

'Ye have that. It was me tried to stop ye gettin' yerself kilt. D'ye remember that?'

Again the deep frown, then the eyes cleared. 'I do indeed.' He tried to prop on to an elbow and the pain snatched at him again, stopping him halfway. And he grinned, though it was more of a grimace. 'And obviously I *was* killed.'

Paddy's laugh crackled into the night. 'Ye come close enough to it, and that's the God's truth! Here now – take a sip at this, will ye.'

With Paddy's arm behind his shoulders the man managed to get high enough to reach the pannikin of tea that had been stewing by the billy, and he sipped and sank back again. Paddy looked down at the sweat the effort had brought out.

'Ye're not much of a complainin' man, I'll give ye that. I've some food for ye here. Can ye handle yerself up to it?'

Lips tight, the other man edged and worked himself half up in the blankets and Paddy moved a saddle and a bag of feed behind him then spooned some thick stew from the billy onto a tin plate and passed it. The man rested it on his legs, watching as Paddy tipped a rum bottle over the pannikin. Paddy glanced across at him.

'D'ye not want the stew, then? Ye need some food in yer belly, son – it'll put the stength back in ye.'

'I don't normally dine with people I haven't met.' The man's voice was shaky with pain, but controlled. 'My name's Morant. Harry Morant.'

Paddy lowered the bottle and beamed. 'I *knew* there'd have to be some of the Irish in ye! Morant, eh? No one but an Irishman'd be daft enough to try and fight that devil Sims like a gentleman! I'm a Magee meself. Patrick, naturally, and Paddy just as naturally.' He reached a hand.

Morant's hand in his was hot and dry and very firm. 'Well, I'm bloody grateful to you, Paddy. Where the hell are we?'

'Oh, just a bit of a camp I've been keepin' for a day or two now. You wouldn't remember ridin' out here, hung across yer own saddle like a dead corpse?' Morant shook his head. 'Ah, ye'll be right enough be the time ye've had a sleep.'

'I'm glad one of us believes that!'

Paddy watched him as he spooned up the stew, noticing how fast the hot food was reviving him. He swigged from the bottle of rum and spoke with an almost complacent certainty. 'Ye're a gentleman of course.'

Morant let the spoon drop onto the empty plate and slumped back. 'Am I? There are plenty of people who'd argue with you.'

'Ah, no – ye've the stink of privilege all over you. Ye've been used to livin' with tablecloths and servants and all the doodads an' there's no way ye can hide it, boyo.' He was pushing tobacco into the bowl of a black, short-stemmed pipe. 'Did ye run, Harry, or did they chuck ye out to Australia?'

'That's none of your damned business,' said Harry Morant.

'Ye're right,' said Magee. 'It's not.'

November 1901

Sixteen, seventeen years back. Always on a horse, it seemed, in those times. Young Harry Morant up in the saddle out on Sand Flats the first time they'd worked together with cattle. The fight with Sims was seventy miles and a week behind them, although the word of it had got to the Flats first and the stock-foreman had looked at Harry and said, 'It's no job f'r a bloody boxer, Morant, y'know that don't ya?' And Harry had looked straight back at him, the bruises on him going that dull yellow colour by then, and he'd said, 'That's quite understood, Mr Downes – I'm retired from the ring. Temporarily, at any rate.' And that flash of a smile had come out and Downes had grinned back and asked him if he could ride at all? Paddy heard Harry's voice again, a touch of sarcasm in it, just the littlest touch, saying, 'Yes, a bit. Haven't had anything to do with cattle, I'm afraid, but I can sit a horse after a fashion.' Downes had waved a hand round at the small holding paddock and told Harry to find himself something to hang a saddle on, told him all he had to do was what Downes said and he'd be right enough.

He'd watched then as Harry walked in among the working stock, seen him run a hand down a leg here, across a neck there, talking to the horses as he shoved them aside and looked them over, curling a hand into the mane of a tall five-year-old roan gelding and leading it out to where an old saddle was waiting over the top rail of the fence.

Harry was no stockman then. It was several months before he really began to look as though he knew what to do with a

mob of cattle ... but it was only a couple of days before
Downes and the other men were aware that his statement
about being able to ride 'a bit' was somewhere well below the
truth. Downes had put it into words for them all, hunched over
his pipe by the fire one evening while the cook's offsider edged
up in and out collecting tea-mugs and the men turned to warm
the side the night-frost was beginning to reach. Old Bull
Downes sucked on his pipe and the words came out in blue
puffs. 'You told me you could sit a horse. Y'never told me you
was a professional horse-sitter. If it wasn't f'r yer weight I'd
put y'down as a bloody jockey, son. You was brought up with
a saddle stitched inside y'trousis 'less I'm mistaken.'

Harry, leaning back on an elbow now, face poker-stiff, spoke
back across the fire. 'Yes, well I *have* been riding for a year or
two, you see. No point in making a great halloo about it
though.' Downes had looked hard at him. 'I s'pose y'drink a
little bit too, eh? Just a bit, like?' Harry had agreed, 'Just a bit,
as you say.' He caught the half-bottle Downes threw across to
him and held it up to the firelight inquiringly. 'Rum?' Downes
shook his head. 'No – brandy.' Harry shrugged that kind of No
Difference shrug, tossed the cork into the darkness behind him
and dragged at the neck of the bottle. Then he threw the
empty back to Downes while the drovers and drifters and
rouseabouts roared their laughter into the night. ...

Paddy pushed himself off the gate and walked back into the
big shed, walked back in the years as he did.

The saddles were on pegs in the back corner alongside
Harlequin's stall ... the working saddle, high in front, high
behind, smooth as beach-stones and dull-glossy under the
dubbin, and the racing saddle that Harry had won that time in
Orange, the English saddle made of nearly nothing that he'd
used so many times in so many races for so many prizes.
Including the women.

Not that first year, though. That had been a working year,
begod! hard yakker right through. That mob of cattle they'd
drafted for Bull Downes had taken them as far down as Dubbo
where they'd hung about for nearly a fortnight, eating at the
Chow's, sleeping late in what seemed like the luxury of the
falling-down hotel, drinking, playing cards. That still face of
Harry's had helped there, that and the fact that he seemed to
know every variety of card game ever invented and every trick
ever dreamed up for each of them, and they'd won in ten days
more than they'd earned in the previous month. By unspoken

agreement, Paddy looked after the money, stitching half of it into an old canvas belly-band against a rough time.

Like the sick three weeks on the Victorian side, up in the edge of the high country where Paddy had begun to sneeze and eye-water and Harry had told the boss they were going to stay put till he was well again. The boss had shrugged and given them their pay till then and some supplies and gone on with the sheep they were moving down out of the winter snow, and Harry had made a bough hut and got Paddy into it, weak and sweat-shivering by then. None of it was clear to Paddy for a while, except the chest-pains and the way the coughing seemed to break his bones, but when he came out of it, calf-wobbly and thin, the shelter had been flanked by piles of chopped wood and there was a windbreak of wood and saddles and scrub in front of it. Beyond, there was already a couple of inches of sunny snow, crackled with frost ... He could smell the rabbit-stew Harry had made for them.

The long days of convalescence brought talk with them – Harry's talk mostly. Paddy's quietness in the snug hut had kept Harry's voice low and reminiscent and he'd talked for the first time about his sister Helen and his mother and the admiral, his father. And about himself as he had been, Lieutenant Harry Harbord Morant, begod! of Her Majesty's Royal Navy! Till he gambled and drank his way out of it in disgrace.

God, but they'd covered some ground that year – cattle and sheep and fences and even a shearing shed where Harry seemed to draw blood with every blow of the clippers till the ringer had given him an ultimatum and a broom. It looked there for a moment as if Harry was going to put those clippers into the ringer's gut hard enough to show his wrist on the other side. And then he'd grinned and taken the broom and finished that week keeping the floor clean of tailings. Ah, he'd changed that year. Fined down a lot. Hardened up a lot. Picked up his bush-name, too.

They worked to the front of the crowd as the man hit the ground, hard on his shoulder and upper arm, and even the shouting couldn't hide the dull cracking noise as the collar-bone went. Half a dozen men darted in and dragged the yelling man clear and the grubby-looking horse with the Roman nose lashed heels at them, then stood red-eyed watching around him.

Paddy saw Henry, the shopkeeper, and elbowed his way next to him. 'Hey, Henry y're losin' trade, d'ye know that? Harry and me need some tucker and things. And what the hell's goin' on, anyway?'

'G'day, Paddy. It's that brumby. One of Dickson's abos brought him in and Dickson reckons he's no use till he's broke an' there's no one can break 'im, see?'

Harry had heard from behind Paddy. 'Who's tried?'

'Ah, there, Harry. Well, Dickson's 'ad a go isself, an' the abo 'n' Teddy Roberts there that they just took off.'

'Is Dickson paying?'

'Says he'll give a sovereign. Two bob fer anyone who 'as a go an' a sovereign fer the joker that does the job.'

Paddy was outraged. 'A sovereign, is it? That's bugger-all for a feller to get himself busted up like Teddy Roberts.'

'Well, I tell you what, Pad – it don't look like anyone else is game to try it.'

Harry broke in. 'What sort of odds d'you think people might offer, Henry?'

'Odds? On that little bastard stayin' like 'e is? Christ, Harry, I'd give yer five to one right now.'

'I'll take it. Paddy, where's the money?'

'Ah, now, wait on, Harry, wait on! That's a bad little brumby there. You wouldn't want –'

'What I want is whatever we've got – get it out at fives. Or better. I'll go and see Dickson.'

A man alongside leaned in. 'Oy, you goin' up on that thing?' Harry nodded. 'Did ya say ya wanted fives on yaself?' Harry nodded again. 'I'll have yer for a quid then. Ya bloody mad, mind, but I'll 'ave yer.'

Harry lifted an eyebrow at Paddy while the man dug into his pockets.

Dickson didn't mind who tried and when Harry told him he didn't want two bob or a sovereign but a bet, Dickson put up two guineas at once. By the time Harry had his coat off, Paddy was in the centre of a gambling-mad mob and Henry alongside him was tipping the money into a hat and scribbling down the bets on the back of a scrap of old poster.

The brumby stood, shifting uneasily, puffing little clouds of dust as he stamped a forefoot. The noise went up a little as Harry walked out and studied the horse for a moment. He was talking to it, low so that no one could hear, but Paddy had seen him do it before and watched his lips moving as his hand went out to the trailing headrope, taking it loose and gentle. Paddy had always got pleasure from seeing Harry mount a horse. There seemed to be none of that foot to the stirrup and a pause and a heaving lift. It was a quick and smooth flow from the ground to the horse's back, just like this time, the brumby lifting its head up and to the side in surprise, and a snap of laughter from the crowd.

Henry checked his watch then and said afterwards, 'Well, I reckoned he might stay ten or fifteen seconds like Teddy. Damn me, he was there just on two minutes an' 'e 'ad that broken-nose bastard walkin' round like a lady's 'ack!'

The brumby tried. Until that day he'd never had anyone on his back, and on that day he'd quickly got used to the tentative weight bearing down on him and the savaging pulls at his nose and the sting of whips across his eyes and muzzle. He knew he could get rid of those things if he fought, and he'd done it. But not now. Not with this weight, which didn't hit him and didn't kick him. Just stayed there. He tried going down and rolling, but the weight came off while he kicked and squealed in the dust and then came straight back again when he got back to his feet. And suddenly he realized he wasn't *going* to get rid of it and he was tired and the air was cold as it was sucked hard into his chest and the weight wasn't hurting him.

Harry knew it. Up on the horse's back, he could feel the sudden submission and he kneed the sweaty barrel and urged the horse forward into a canter round the dusty yard, hearing for the first time the shouts of applause and the whistles. And a voice rising high and shrill, 'Jesus, he's broke 'im. Good on ya, Breaker!'

Paddy, scarlet with joy, gave Henry five guineas for his help and sewed seventy more into his belly-band, keeping fifteen out for supplies and drinks. Not that they had to buy much that night. Everyone wanted to shout a grog for Harry Morant. Breaker Morant, that's what they were calling him.

When they came into the other pub a month or two later, the name was fixed. He was The Breaker. By then Harry had been asked several times to take on tough horses and had done so each time, always for fair pay, always with the odds against him shortening and shortening until they no longer existed. He was The Breaker, and that was that and one of the country newspapers had written a piece about him and now everyone knew him, knew who he was and what he could do.

He was different by then in many ways, aside from the plain physical changes. He still sounded 'like a Pommy bastard', still spoke quietly, still offered courtesy where it was never expected. But there were new expressions on his tongue now and new ways of looking at things. Paddy said to him one Sunday morning in a

droving camp, breakfast over and a slack day ahead of them,
'Harry, ye're a funny feller. Ye're forever washin' yerself an'
shavin' whenever ye get half a chance, an' yet ye'll eat terrible
tucker when it's given to ye, an' ye'll go filthy dirty when ye're
workin' an' ye've a tongue on ye as rough as a blacksmith's file, yet
yer a gentleman with it. Ye're a puzzle to me.'

'I'm a bit of a puzzle to myself, Paddy.' Harry stared at nothing
and there was a silence before he went on. 'The Navy teaches you
not to be too fussy. I'm here because this is where I pretty well have
to be. But I've come to like it, I think. Anyway, I accept it. It's not
so very different in some ways, I suppose ... although I do miss
some things. ...' His voice tailed away and Paddy let the silence
hang, knowing he should say nothing.

So it was the same Paddy and a different Harry who walked back
into that other pub, a full year after Harry had first come there. He
showed no feeling about that other time as they loose-tied their
horses at the rail and walked up the steps and into the babble of
the bar, half-a-dozen men greeting them and the moist-mouthed
barman coming to them with a corner-lipped smile and a rum
bottle and a 'G'day Paddy, Breaker.' Harry poured for them both
and they drank, silently, companionably, thankfully. Pushing two
hundred head of cattle the last ten miles in the dry heat had left
them in need of stillness and liquid, and the first two drinks went
down before Paddy turned onto one elbow and looked around the
dull haze of the bar-room, fuller than usual during the day because
theirs was one of three mobs brought in to the holding yards for a
little fattening before meeting the rackety train to the abattoirs
further south.

Paddy's hand stopped, the glass almost at his lips, as he stared
across the room. He nudged at Harry's side, not moving his eyes.
Harry swung his head, saw Paddy's fixed stare and swung again to
look that way. His face closed for a second or two and the knuckles
on his hand tightened the fingers round the glass. Then he relaxed,
finished his drink and smiled at Paddy.

'You really ought to say hello to him, you know.'

'Aw, now Harry ...' Paddy caught the meaning in Harry's eyes,
and nodded with deep understanding, smiling with the other man.
'Ye're quite right, boyo, quite right. Wouldn't do to ignore an old
mate now, would it?' He drowned his rum, poured another and
raised his voice. 'Hey – Sims! Is it you, me boy? How are ye then,
Sims?' Letting himself sway a little, slurring his voice, he raised his
glass above his head in salute, then pounded Harry's shoulder.
'Hey, Harry – ye're not drinkin' to me friend Sims there!'

Expressionlessly, Harry lifted his glass a couple of inches, but didn't drink. Across the room, Sims and the same group of cronies laughed and began to shove their way across, crowding close.

'If it ain't the pretty porter-boy! G'day!' Sims' smile was closer to a leer and Harry looked at him dispassionately.

'Hello. How are you, Sims?'

Hearing the voice, Sims pulled a prissy face, one hand flopping onto his hip. 'How *am* I? Oh, ai'm very faine, thenk you, my lord. Ai trust you've been keepin' well, Fancy?'

'Well enough. I'd be better if you bought me a drink.'

'Me! Me buy *you* a drink! Get out, ya bloody slack-kneed, gutless Pommy dung-fly!'

Paddy watched Harry. Motionless, expressionless, as Sims ranted on. 'I c'n see you've been out in the sun too much, it's touched yer 'ead. No, mate, you're gointa buy *me* a drink. An' me friends.' He shouted to the barman in the sudden quietness, 'Oy – this pretty cove's buyin' drinks all round. Let's 'ave some service.'

The barman moved towards them, licking his wet lips, bottle tilting over Sims' glass. Harry's hand stopped the bottle.

'Just a moment, please, there seems to be some mistake. Sims, I'd sooner give a drink to a stinking dingo than to you.'

Now the silence was total for a long moment, breaking into splinters of sound, odd shards of edgy laughter. The barman had the truncheon in his hand, waiting. It took Sims several seconds to mouth the words he wanted, his voice thick and a deep flush on his face.

'Outside you! I'm gointa kill ya!'

It was the same scene again, Paddy thought, as they shoved and heaved outside, the same street, the same sun, the same crowd ... larger now than last time, but otherwise the same. Even the same kids and dogs. Certainly the same Sims. But a different Harry now, tossing his cord coat to Paddy and the wide-brimmed hat, pulling off the grey flannel shirt and shoving back the sleeves of the long undervest. He was leaner than he had been by a little and his face and forearms were deeply burned by the outdoor months, burned and hard. Sims might have been wearing the same foul vest now as then, and Paddy could see the anger in him, spiked and vicious. Folding Harry's coat as he moved closer, Paddy noticed a small bundle of papers slipping from a pocket and pulled them free, shoving them into his own pocket without looking at them.

In the ring the two men faced one another. Again, Harry stepped forward, arms cocked, feet set, adopting the classic pose. One of

Sims' mates muttered, 'Jees, he's away again,' and Sims moved forward.

This time he used the knee, stepping in close enough, fast enough to jerk it suddenly up, both hands out for a headlock, waiting for Harry's head to drop into them as he doubled. It didn't happen. Harry moved aside, no more than a foot, enough to avoid the knee and kick sideways savagely at Sims' other ankle. The boot stopped the ankle-bone going, but Sims yelped with the pain and toppled, arms flailing. As he began to go over, Harry's forearm slashed sideways and down, rigid as a club, striking across Sims' kidneys, choking the first yell in a deep grunting groan. Harry moved back to his original position while the other man knelt holding his back with one hand, rubbing his ankle with the other. Harry waited till Sims glared up, shaping a curse, then he walked in very deliberately and clubbed a fist to the side of the kneeling man's head, rocking him across to meet the other fist, rocking him back, and again and again, smashing his face into blood and a mash of bone where the nose used to be. He stepped back again, watching as Sims shook his head, blood splashing into the dust and disappearing, spittle and a broken tooth hanging from a pulped mouth. Then he joined his hands into a single fist and swung them together, underhanded to the side of Sims' jaw. The man on his knees went silently down on his side, his jaw loose, and Harry walked away.

Paddy rushed to him, both of them ignoring the pats on Harry's back, ignoring the little group carrying Sims away, and the Irishman shook Harry's hat under his nose, clinking the coins in it.

'Oh, me son, we've made a little goldmine here! There was fools giving me twenty to one about you, d'ye know that!'

Harry took his shirt and coat, shrugging into them. 'Stop gibbering, will you, Paddy.'

'Gibbering is it? Look, boyo, will ye look at the money in here! There's easy livin' for a month in this old hat of yours!'

Harry turned away.

'Harry! Hey, Harry, where're ye off to?'

He followed, dragging at Harry's sleeve, turning him, face suddenly anxious.

'Harry, are ye all right?'

'No. No, I'm not all right.' Now, for the first time, his eyes were fierce and his face showed emotion. 'Paddy, would you say I beat him badly – Sims?'

'Beat him? Ye knocked the murderin' tripes out of him, ye know that!'

'I enjoyed it.' It was a flat statement.

'Well, of course y'enjoyed it. Why wouldn't ye? Any decent man enjoys a fight, specially if he wins it!'

'Not the fight. Feeling him go down. Feeling the bones go. The blood on him.' He looked down at his hands and wiped them on the side of his trousers. 'I enjoyed *that*, Paddy. I *liked* it.'

He turned again and walked quickly away, Paddy watching him, the hatful of coins bundled in his hand, his eyes puckered with worry.

It was another camp, one of scores they'd set up, lived in, broken and left. Ten feet from their fire, the Bogan River ran low and greening towards the settlement at Nyngan and behind them the track was dry-rutted where it led north to Bourke. There were a couple of tied lines down into the water, the floats carrying them out at sharp angles as the thin current dragged at them. There was the little noise of the river and the wet crunching as the hobbled horses grazed around themselves, and the crackle of the fire and Harry whistling quietly between his teeth as he darned an old pair of trousers. Paddy couldn't see any of it, flat on his back with his hat over his face and his hands under his head, but he could hear the small noises and he knew where they came from. His voice was muffled when he spoke.

'Aaah. There's somethin' about a Sunday mornin', wouldn't ye say?'

Harry looked up, smiling gently round the whistle but said nothing.

'There's a peacefulness about it, y'know. A – a sort of lovin' feelin'.'

The whistle stopped with a short laugh. 'You sound like a preacher, Paddy. Why don't you ride in and go to church?'

The hat tumbled to one side as Paddy jerked half up, then sat up rubbing a hand through the spikes of his hair. 'Church, is it? I misremember the last time I went to Mass. Begod! It'd take me a fortnight just to confess me sins!' He poked at the branches under the billy, glancing at Harry. 'There's one sin I could confess to you, boyo.'

'Whoa, now!' Harry bit off the end of the thread and tossed the trousers aside, tucking the needle into a tin box. 'I've enough sins of my own without being worried by yours.'

'No, now – I'm serious. I've somethin' of yours. Somethin' belongs to you.' He flapped open the saddlebag by his head and pulled out a bundle of papers. 'They came from ya pocket last week, the day you took off yer coat to fight Sims.'

Harry sat quite still, looking at Paddy. Then he held out his hand, unspeaking.

'Harry, they're damn good stuff, y'know. I didn't know you was any kind of a poet.'

'Give them to me.'

Paddy handed the little bundle across. 'It's the Irish blood in ye for certain, me son. What'll ye do with them, then?'

Harry leafed through the pages, not looking up, voice low. 'They're just scribbles.' He folded them abruptly. 'You think they're good, do you? How the hell would you know?'

'Ah, now, when did ye ever know an Irishman couldn't tell good poetry from bad? I tell ye, they put the whole of the bush in a man's head, they do. And the smell of the cattle and the feel of a horse.'

Harry looked up. 'You like them! You really do?'

'I do so.'

'Then you'd better keep them.' He squeezed the pages into a bundle and threw it at Paddy. 'Or burn them if you want. Do what you like with them.'

'Truly now – ye mean it?' Paddy was carefully unfolding the pages, pressing them down with the flat of his hand on his thigh.

'Why not? They're no use to me.'

The Sunday had gone away from them then, and another, and they'd spent a week in Bourke and teamed up with a mob heading south again, and come back past Nyngan, well down with the cattle to Orange. The boss had been pushing them hard, trying to save a day, and the animals were tired and the men were tired and the dust was sharp and hurtful in the throat and the eyes. Now that the cattle had the smell of the other cattle in the yards and the water there, they began to move along faster and the boss swirled up out of the dust-murk, tugging down the scarf over his face to shout hoarsely at them and at his drovers.

'Come on you bludgers! The sooner you get the bloody beef in there, the sooner the beer's on!' He spat dust and shouted again above the hoof noise. 'Hey, Breaker! Harry!'

Harry edged his horse alongside, the snake of the stockwhip looping through his hand. The men looked like twins, coated head to foot in red, gritty dust, sitting horses of dust in a dusty world. The boss pulled up the scarf again and leaned in so that Harry could hear his muffled voice. 'Y'stayin' over for Race Week, are ya?'

'Yes, Tom. It'll take that long to get this bloody dust out of my gullet!'

'Yair. Well, we'll be in the pub in an hour with a bit of luck. Are ya ridin' anythin' in the races, then?'

'Might be. That chap Travers, the one from Mudgee – I believe he's got a horse he wants me to push along for him.'

One of the other drovers had walked his horse in close enough to catch the last exchange. 'Y'not ridin' anythin' in the Cup, Breaker?'

'No, Alec. Not unless Travers' horse is better than I think it is.'

The boss had swung towards the second man. 'Y've knocked off then, 'ave ya, Alec? No more bloody work to do, is that it? Go on – get yer arse over there with Paddy and let's get this mob locked up. I want a beer.'

He kicked his horse away and Harry and Alec grinned at one another and followed him.

There was beer, there was rum; there would be the races; and between the rum and the races . . .

Harry heard the banging on his bedroom door in the pub as a distant drum, then as thunder then, with the shouting, realized what it was and half sat up, rubbing a hand across his face. The room was almost dark and cooling and the warm, damp hump alongside him was – was Judy. With the memory of the name he came fully awake, hearing the voice as Paddy's, hearing the renewed thumping.

'Will yet get the bloody door open, Harry? I'm goin' to break it down in a minute, so I am!'

The girl was half awake now, staring around swimmy-eyed. Harry shook her, not too gently. 'Come on, Judy, wake up now.' He lifted his voice. 'Hold on, Paddy. And stop that damn din!'

The knocking stopped and the muffled voice was quieter. 'Well, shake yerself then and open up.'

The girl was sitting up, Harry's hand still on her shoulder, and she smiled sleepily up at him, sliding closer in the bed, looping a leg across him and flattening her breasts against his chest. 'Harry?'

He kissed her lightly on the cheek and pushed her away, his voice as final as his movements. He struck a match and lit the kerosene lamp beside the bed. 'Out you get, Judy, and open that door.'

'Oh, hell.' Sulking, Judy swung to the floor, pulling the blanket with her and around herself, and wrenched back the bolt, jumping back as Paddy barged in, checking himself for a moment to look at her as the blanket slipped down under her breasts. He cupped a hand under the nearer one and planted a kiss on the corner of her mouth. She jerked away.

'Get off, you dirty old bastard, you're drunk!'

'I am, I am indeed, lass!' He turned, beaming at Harry. 'Drunk with the drink and drunk with the news.' He flourished the papers in his hand. 'Look here, will ye, Harry.'

The pink covers of the *Bulletin* were unmistakable. There were two copies of the Sydney magazine dated three and four weeks earlier and Harry folded them on the bed, not looking at them, looking at Paddy dancing in little jigging steps in front of him.

'It's the poetry, Harry – remember? The poems ye wrote back there?'

'What in hell's name are you gabbling about, you madman?'

'They're in there! They've published them! Here, look!'

He snatched up the magazines, ripping at the pages to find what he wanted, then thrust them back.

'D'ye see? Right there!'

Judy moved forward, careless of the blanket now. 'I suppose you've forgot there's a lady present, haven't you?'

Harry didn't look up from the pages, just reached out a hand and scooped some coins off the table, flipping them onto the bed near her. His voice was detached. 'You're a working girl, Judy, not a lady. You've done your work and there's your pay and you can go. And thank you.'

She grabbed at the coins, scowling, watching Paddy drag an envelope from his pocket and half-crouch over Harry.

'And there's more, me son! Will you look at this – a bank draft. Two guineas it is, made out to Bearer.'

Harry's head was still down, his eyes moving from the printed pages to the green cheque.

'Isn't that a great thing now? Your poems printed and money for the writing ... and d'ye see the name there, eh? "The Breaker". See, "The Brigalow Brigade, a bush-ballad by The Breaker".'

Harry looked up, smiling, not smiling, a little dazed.

'Ye said I could do what I wanted with them, remember? Ye did say that.'

Judy had dropped the blanket and stood there naked, looking at them. Now she picked up her dress, stepped into it and did up one of its four buttons, moving towards the door.

She pitched her voice coldly at them. 'Well, I'll leave you two fancy lads together, then. It don't look as if you need a woman here.'

Now Harry looked up at her, the half-smile going chill. 'Don't be nasty-minded, Judy. I don't like hitting women. Not even whores.' He threw her another coin. 'Go on now, there's a good lass.'

Close to tears she pulled the door shut behind her, listening to the excitement in their voices through it.

'Ye're not upset, are ye, Harry? That I sent the poems off like that?'

'Not a bit of it, Paddy. I'd never have had the nerve. There's a devil of a lot of people read the *Bulletin*.'

'There is, there is. And they'll be reading your poetry! Look at it there. "The Brigalow Brigade, a bush-ballad by The Breaker".'

With their laughter behind her, Judy wiped her face and walked away, counting the coins in her hand.

It was beginning to drizzle when Judy left, and after that there had been three days of light rain, the first for over a year. It had done almost nothing to relieve the land, sinking into the dust without running off into the creeks, raising the level in the little dams by only a fraction. But it damped the surface enough to stop the dust swirling as much as usual and the lack of even a breeze meant that the hundreds of feet and hooves at the race-track served more to pack down the red dirt than to lift it.

Paddy glanced sideways at Harry as they walked into the crowd, wondering for the hundredth time how the hell he managed to look elegant in the cheap clothes. They were essentially no different from those of most of the men there, but on him the clean moleskins and the stuff jacket looked properly cut, and his dark grey hat had a little tilt that was different somehow. It was maybe the set of the shoulders, Paddy thought, somewhere between the stiffness of a naval officer's and the easy sling of a rider's. It wasn't that Harry was tall or stately – just that he had a movement about him. And a stillness.

Out of the still face, Harry saw the crowds about him with great clarity. It seemed to him that, for the first time since he'd come to Australia, he was a person, something more than just another man. People called to him in the near-crush, most of them simply waving or smiling from a little distance, some of them elbowing closer for a handshake or a pat on the shoulder, all of them using the name he now accepted fully – The Breaker. The outback of the Australia he knew was filled with men who were recognized as 'characters', and he supposed himself to be one of them now. He was different, as all such characters were different. For the man they called Guts Robinson, there was the fact that he could eat for hours at a time and then ask when the next meal would be ready; Killer Morrowby once shot his own horse between the ears accidentally while trying to hit a little 'roo from the saddle; there was Col the Galah, a man with a beaked face and a way of ruffling himself in his clothes which gave him the look of the bush bird; Arsehole Thomas, The Sailor,

John the Lady ... there were scores of them. And now there was
Harry Morant, The Breaker. His face was quiet and smiling and he
made the appropriate answers, occasionally tipping his hat to one
of the women, but behind the mask there was an ugly grin, a twist
of the inside mouth and a glint of the inside eyes at the thought of
his wardroom friends of a few years ago, of his family – Harry
Morant, horse-breaker, stockman, boundary-rider, whore-sticker,
accepted, liked, looked up to. And now deferred to as a man of
letters because a Sydney weekly magazine had printed some of his
scribblings. Oh, the admiral would be delighted if he knew! And
wouldn't his mother love Paddy Magee, tough old hard-guzzling
Irishman out of some Wexford bog? Oddly enough, he thought, she
probably would... and then he blanked out all the thoughts of the
other times, the other places and grabbed Paddy's sleeve.

'Come on, for God's sake, let's get a drink.'

Travers stopped them before they got to the pub-stall, a red-
faced little man under a fringe of sweaty grey hair, the beer smell
leaking out of him in the heat.

'There you are, Morant! I was beginning to think you were off
somewhere writing poetry.'

His laugh was edged with beer looseness, but Harry saluted him
and made no attempt to meet his gaiety. 'Mr Travers, you know
my friend Magee, I think.'

Travers shook Paddy's hand almost absent-mindedly, his concentration on Harry and his need for him that day. Looping a hand
through Harry's arm he led him to the roped-off enclosure where
the horses for the races were hobbled, pointing to a leggy black and
looking quizzically round at Harry. Paddy ducked under the ropes
and ran a hand down the horse's neck, feeling the light dew of
excitement on him. The horse tossed his head and stepped minc-
ingly about, watching Harry who'd followed his friend and who
gentled the damp muzzle.

'Hallo there, Sunfire.' He turned to Travers. 'He looks fit, very
fit. I hope you've got your money on him.'

'He's a good horse, my boy, and he'll have the best rider. You'll
win me a tidy bundle between you, even with the odds the way they
are.' His eyes had gone past Harry and the horse and now he
called, 'Over here, Lenehan. Spare me a minute.'

He moved away from them to meet the man he'd called and
Harry looked at him, and at the girl with him, seeing that the man
was perhaps forty, neatly and expensively dressed, seeing that the
girl was young, maybe twenty at the most, and that the flowered
frock was full of her. Travers was leading them together, an arm on

Harry's shoulder now. 'John, I'd like to introduce Harry Morant to you. Morant – Mr Lenehan has Eagleton y'know, the big property to the west of here.'

Harry's hat was in his hand, his other hand outstretched for Lenehan's cool, dry grip. 'I'm honoured to meet you, sir.'

'And I you, Mr Morant. Or am I to call you Breaker?' The smile was deep and friendly, drawing the flash of Harry's in answer.

'Harry will do very well.'

'Splendid! And this is my niece. Julia, may I present Mr Morant? Harry, Miss Davis.'

The girl's eyes were the darkest green Harry had seen, almost black, and they locked onto his as her gloved hand went to his fingers. He bowed, breaking the look, but it was still there when he straightened, and her voice was almost as deep in sound as her eyes in colour, deep and low.

'Mr Morant, if you ride as well as you write poetry, I shall ask Uncle John to place a wager for me.'

'If I'm sure you're backing me, Miss Davis, I shall ride all the faster.'

Behind him, at Sunfire's head, Paddy tossed a pious glance to Heaven. A steward, one of the local men with a red ribbon tied to his hat and a sheaf of papers in his hand, was moving through the crowd now, calling for starters for the second race. Travers turned from his conversation with Lenehan, tapping Harry's arm.

'This is you, Morant. No instructions – you know better than I do what to do, my boy. Ride to win, that's all.'

'I always do, Mr Travers.'

Harry slipped off his coat, handing it with his hat to Paddy who'd been watching the young aboriginal adjusting Sunfire's saddle and bridle. Harry made that fluid move into the saddle, checking the lengths of the leathers, walking Sunfire through a few steps in a tight circle. As the ropes were lowered for the horses to move onto the track, Julia moved in close. Paddy handed up the light crop and stepped back, watching, as Julia slipped off her glove and gave Harry her hand again, smiling at him.

'Good luck, Mr Morant. And take this as a charm.'

She gave him the slim white glove. Smiling down at her he tossed the crop back to Paddy and flicked Sunfire lightly with the glove, moving him onto the track. His face closed in concentration and the people watching disappeared. There were the other horses, there was Sunfire beneath him, bunching with eagerness to be off. That was the world.

*　　　*　　　*

Galloping now down the soft flank of the hill above the property, Harry turned in the saddle to see Julia on the bay only ten feet from him, the horse running freely, her slim body relaxed in the saddle, her head back in a laugh. She reined in alongside him as he stopped, and they walked their horses together.

'Oh, that was wonderful, Harry! I don't believe I've ever ridden like that in my life!'

'You ride very well.' The horses still had the friskiness in them, fresh from the gallop, and for a few moments they let them canter, slowing them as they came onto the flat, the house half a mile away beyond the trees. Harry looked at her as she ran a hand down her long hair.

'What else do you do well?'

She hesitated, her eyes darting away from his and her hand fretting at her hair. 'I – I think I might do anything well. If you were to ask me.' Her look became almost suppliant. 'Why don't you ask me?'

She stopped her horse and reached for his rein, pulling his horse close and leaning across to him. Her lips opened on his and he could feel the depth of her breathing, but he made only the slightest response. She pulled away, anger reddening her face, and a touch of shame.

'I see. The great Harry Morant can't be bothered with a simple country girl.'

She kicked savagely at her horse, but Harry's hand on the bridle stopped the animal's move, jerking at its head so that the girl had to struggle to hold her seat till the horse quietened again. He kept his hand on her bridle.

'Julia – no, please. You misunderstand.'

'Oh? Really?' Voice cold.

'It isn't you, my dear. I – I'm afraid I'm rather out of sorts.' Releasing her bridle, he looped an arm around her, taking her to him and kissing her, hot and demanding, his tongue forcing between her lips, his arm feeling the sudden swell of heat in her body. She was pale when he let her go, breathing sharply, her eyes on him as he said, 'You see?'

She couldn't answer for a moment, calming herself. Her voice was a little shaky when she did speak. 'Yes, I see, Harry. Is it something I can help with?'

He shook his head and moved his horse forward, leading hers with him.

They left the screen of trees and Eagleton was there before them and a little below, a sprawling white house, glaring in the morning sunlight, pepper trees and three huge old gums shading a little of the front and one wing. Off to one side they could see Lenehan leaning on the white-painted rails of the horseyard, his foreman alongside him, watching as a stockman walked towards the stables. Harry's sweeping arm took in the whole scene. 'Look at that. This is the first time I've been in a gentleman's house since –' His voice was calm, but it tailed away with an edge of bitterness, and Julia caught up the unfinished sentence.

'Since you left England?'

'Since I ran away from England.'

'Why? Was it something bad you did to make you run away?'

He looked straight at her, his mouth twisting down at one corner. 'Bad enough. Running away is always bad.'

She looked away, down at the house, and waited before speaking again. 'And you miss it? All this sort of thing?'

'Miss it?' He sat very still for so long that she was about to break the silence. But he turned to her again, a hand out to her and she took it, feeling the tightness of his fingers on hers. 'Last night, little Julia, last night we dined off good china. There was silver on the table, wasn't there, and we drank a sound wine and we slept between clean sheets.' His hand left hers to check her interruption with a finger on her lips, then went back. She listened to the way his voice changed; no louder, but with tiny barbs in it now, little wicked points of irony and brutality. 'Last week – for the last hundred weeks and more – I was unshaven and there was dirt and cattle-stink in every crease of my body and lice in my clothes.' He was holding her eyes as they widened, and his grip on her was very hard. 'I slept under my horse's blanket and took my food from a tin dish. At night when it got cold, I warmed myself a bit at a time by a branchfire and I warmed my guts with grog. I –' He stopped abruptly, collecting himself, realizing he'd started to let too much creep into his voice. 'I wasn't born to do those things, Julia. I miss everything I was born to do. I thought I'd forgotten ... but I was wrong.'

She took him up at once. 'Then go home, Harry. Go back and belong again.'

'Belong? I think this is where I belong now, because I have to, you see. I have friends here of a sort, men who don't look the other way when I walk into a room. People like your uncle who takes me as I am.'

He'd begun to pull his hand away, but now she was gripping him. 'I would take you, Harry. As you are, as you were – anyway you chose to be. You know that.'

'I know. You'd be sorry.' He kissed her again, very gently. 'Believe me, you'd be sorry. I'm only good enough for the company I keep, the men I work with.' Now the bitterness in his voice was open and he made no attempt to hold it back. 'I live from one task to the next, from bottle to bottle. Woman to woman, Julia ... and not your sort of woman.'

'Suppose I was prepared to be *your* sort of woman?'

He stared at her, knowing she meant it. 'Then I would thank you deeply ... and tell you to go and find someone better.'

He spurred suddenly away from her, tearing his hand away and leaving her with her hand outstretched, the tears blurring her sight of him. By the time she smeared them away, he was halfway to where her uncle was standing, and she urged her horse into a gallop to follow him.

John Lenehan turned from the rail when he heard the hooves coming in behind him, Julia pulling her horse up alongside Harry's, and he waved at them, smiling, thinking how well they looked together. He'd enjoyed having Harry as a guest these past few days, the invitation made at the party Travers threw after Sunfire had romped home, five lengths out and going away. Morant was a different kettle of fish from most of his house-guests and the two men had hit it off well, Harry slipping back into a once-familiar routine and luxuriating in it, Lenehan glad of the chance to talk at a level he wasn't normally able to achieve outside his infrequent visits to Sydney. And Julia ... Julia was clearly deep in a romantic trance, he thought, seeing her now looking at Morant as though she wanted to eat him. But Morant had eyes only for the horse. Lenehan turned back to the yard, the young stockman now close to the rail, holding the horse's head. From behind him, Morant's voice was quiet, almost reverent.

'My God, Lenehan, that's a splendid looking thing!'

Lenehan waited till the other man had dismounted and joined him at the rail.

'That's Cavalier, Harry. Bred out of the best there is on both sides. And bloody useless.'

'I can't believe that.' Harry was studying the horse with care: a tall, broad-chested grey, but so deep a grey it was near-black, the sunlight seeming to sink into his hide, the gleams and shadows with a tinge of steel-blueness in them. He stood, stallion-proud, neck arching, bold eyes watching the men watching him.

'He won't take discipline. Oh, he'll let himself be ridden, but only till he's tired of it. Then he seems to explode, that's all. So – no use to hounds, nor on a track, nor across the hurdles. He'd have been better gelded for hacking, I think.'

'Oh, Christ, no!' There was something like anguish in Harry's voice, and Lenehan smiled at him.

'He *is* magnificent to look at, isn't he, though?'

'On my oath he is! And fast too, I'll lay odds.'

'You won't find a faster one. Jumps like Springheel Jack on top of it. But useless.'

Harry looked at him speculatively. 'You don't sound as though he's much use to you.' A carefully calculated pause and then, offhand, 'Will you sell?'

'Sell? Cavalier?'

The horse pricked his ears and Harry smiled gently at the tone of disbelief in Lenehan's voice.

'Why not? You said he was useless.'

Lenehan's look was long and careful, first at the horse, then at Harry, and there was a glitter in his eyes when he answered.

'No, I won't sell. But I'll bargain with you. Not as John Lenehan with Harry Morant, though. As Cavalier's owner with The Breaker.'

Harry didn't speak, just looked at Lenehan, level and unsmiling, waiting.

'Look, the big race is on Friday, the District Cup. With you up on him, I don't see how I could lose, and you're the only one I can think of who might stay on him that long.'

'So? What's your bargain?' Flat, almost unfriendly.

'If you do it – if you can ride him and win – by the living God, I'll *give* him to you!'

Now Harry smiled, that great flash, and he shook hands hard. 'You have a bargain.'

'Good!'

'Does he know his name?' He looked round at the horse and Lenehan looked with him.

'I wouldn't be surprised if he knew mine!'

Harry ducked under the rail and Lenehan went on. 'Watch him Harry. He's clever.'

'Get your chaps out of here, will you?'

Lenehan gestured the stockman and the foreman clear, both of them grinning at the thought that The Breaker had met his match. As Julia came to the rail, dismounted, Harry suddenly remembered she was there, feeling a touch of regret that the beautiful horse had made him forget for a minute the beautiful girl. She stood by her uncle, looking at Harry, and he stepped back to her.

'Will you excuse me, Julia?'

She nodded, her face open, her feelings plain.

'I shouldn't want to see you hurt, Harry.'

'You won't.'

He walked towards the horse, not hurrying, stopping four or five feet from him. They studied one another, both motionless, contained. Then slowly, Harry began to rub his hands together, holding them waist-high in front of him, the movement and the dry, rubbing sound pulling the horse's head and eyes to them. He kept up the rubbing, adding a soft chirrup from his lips, and his eyes lightened as the horse began to step in, stretching his neck, lowering his muzzle towards the man's hand. Harry took the rope halter gently, still chirruping and ran an easy hand over the soft muzzle and up between the eyes. His voice when he spoke was confidential and close to the pricked ear.

'Hey then, Cavalier, that's a fine name for a fine horse, isn't it, eh? Now, let's have an understanding, shall we? You're going to be my horse, Cavalier. We're going to win that Cup, you and I, and Lenehan can have the purse and the prize. We shall have one another ... what d'you say to that?'

He had the horse's head half sideways on his chest now, and his voice kept on quietly and hypnotically, just as his hand kept up its soothing massage.

'But the first thing is, I've got to ride you, old son, just so we've both got it clear who's in charge, right? And you're going to behave yourself for me, aren't you? Fine. Now, I'm just going to hop up on that good broad back of yours and you're going to do exactly as you're told, aren't you? Steady now.'

The one-piece swinging move took him up and there was a beat of suspense while Cavalier stood stock-still. Harry gathered the slack of the halter in his left hand, the right knuckling the horse's forehead gently. And then at a click of the tongue, the horse was walking easily round the yard, then trotting, responding to the very light pressure on the headrope and the urging of the man's knees. At the rail, the three men watched, shaking their heads in admiration. Julia stood by them, pale, tears on her cheeks, knuckles white. They watched through five minutes as Harry took Cavalier round, checking and wheeling him, once lifting him, forefeet clear, in a curvetting turn, trotting and walking him through figure-eights and finally bringing him to the gate and slipping down, one arm over the horse's neck, fondling him.

'No one understood him till I came along, that's all. We'll win the Cup for you, Lenehan. Make your bets big.'

*   *   *

By two o'clock on the Friday afternoon, Harry and Cavalier had spent two full days together, quartering the ground for miles around the homestead, walking diagonally up the long rises, moving along the creek-lines at a contained canter, releasing themselves together in a series of bursting gallops across the flat meadows back to the yard and the house. Harry groomed and fed and watered the horse himself and, as Julia said with a touch of petulance, did everything but sleep in the stall with him. Lenehan, even knowing Harry's reputation as he did, watched in continued amazement as Cavalier responded to every least demand made on him without once showing the desire to rebel. Paddy, putting on weight with the amount of food thrust on him and the comfort of the stockman's cottage, told him it was nothing new.

'Ye see what it is, Mr Lenehan ... there's some fellas have a nose for where gold's hid in the ground, and there's some can look at the lie of a bit of desert and find water in it. I knew an old man up on the Tweed River once could drop a net into the water and the fish would swim uphill for a mile to throw themselves in it, that's the God's truth!'

Lenehan, smiling, finished filling his pipe and handed the tobacco to Paddy, who smelled it with enjoyment.

'Ah, that's better than the old horse-turds I've been on this past month or so!' He lit up and puffed deeply, speaking in bursts of smoke. 'With Harry, now it's horses. What was them old creatures one time that was half a horse and half a fella?'

'Centaurs?'

'That's them! Right, well, Harry's a centaur in a way of speaking, and the horses they know it, d'ye see? He can talk to them and understand them, just like they was people. It's a rare gift.'

'Not his only one, either, eh, Magee?'

Paddy's face became cautious. 'Ye mean the women, sir? Ah, well now, he's not any kind of a ladies' man ye'll understand. It's just that they don't seem to be able to let him be, is all.'

'I was thinking of his poetry, in fact. But I believe I know what you mean with the other.'

Lenehan was seeing in the eye of his mind the look on Julia, wondering whether to speak to her or let her find her own way through her own problems.

By two o'clock on the Friday afternoon, the race-track was dead dry again, the full week of sun-heat and the beat of men and horses trampling the last of the dampness out of it. The District Cup was the major event and there were people from outlying places who

couldn't spare the time to be there for the whole week but who'd
ridden in for the Cup race alone.

In the small saddling enclosure, Paddy stood to Cavalier's head.
The big steel-grey horse stood quietly, already saddled, listening as
Paddy muttered to him. 'Ah, ye'll win goin' away, Cavalier, me fine
fella. And with old Harry up, you'd win on three legs anyway, ye
would.' He glanced round. 'Where the devil's that useless lump of a
blackfeller? Hey, Jackie!'

The young aboriginal, grinning yellowly, came out of a little
group of his friends and Paddy handed him the bridle. 'Now then,
you walk him about just a bit, Jackie. And every now and then you
make him jib a little bit, see – get him to kick his heels. I don't want
to see him standin' peaceful, otherwise we'll get no kind of odds
whatever, d'y'understand?' The lad nodded, his grin widening, and
Paddy ducked under the ropes, checking his old turnip watch as he
headed for the cluster of people surrounding the riders.

He touched a finger to his hatbrim as he shouldered through
them. 'Mr Lenehan, Miss Julia, I beg yer pardon. Harry, it's just
about that time, boyo. Ye'll need to be away to mount up.'

Harry nodded. 'Cavalier all right?'

'He couldn't be better 'less he grew wings.'

Harry nodded again, already remote from the chatter and excitement around him, losing himself in the race to come. Without
speaking he began to turn away.

Julia pulled off a glove.

'Harry – for good luck.'

He looked down, then up at her, not really seeing her.

'No, you keep it, Julia. Pity to break the pair.'

Paddy saw, as Harry didn't, the hurt in the girl's eyes. Harry
went on. 'Cavalier and I will make our own luck. Excuse me –'

This time Lenehan stopped him, holding out a firm hand. 'Good
luck anyway, Harry.'

'Thanks.'

His handshake was as curt as the word, and he was gone, Paddy
ducking away after him.

Lenehan cupped a hand under Julia's elbow and moved to the
roped enclosure, filled now with mounted riders, only Cavalier
waiting. Harry swung into the saddle, running a hand down the
horse's neck.

'Are ye right, Harry?'

Settling himself, Harry muttered, 'This leather doesn't seem to
be sitting quite right,' and leaned down to adjust the shortened
strap to the nearside stirrup. The raking bay on Cavalier's offside

shifted step then as it was moving forward, its shoulder brushing Cavalier's flank, and the steel-grey horse's sudden jib and lunge caught Harry head down and off-balance. He fell heavily, no chance to set himself or to roll with the fall, landing on his right arm and shoulder and there was a gasp from the crowd. Julia, white-faced, jerked away from Lenehan and under the rope, but by the time she reached him Harry was up and dusting himself, Paddy patting at him and cursing the other rider. Harry stepped away.

'Don't fuss, for Christ's sake! Give me a boost.'

His foot in Paddy's hands, he went back into the saddle, gentling the horse and gathering the reins and crop. Without a word or a glance back, he followed the field to the start.

Watching, Paddy saw the nine horses line edgily out across the track, Cavalier at number four. With the gun, eight broke clean, and there was a groan when, in the dust, it was seen that Cavalier had swung right-handed and was a length back. Lenehan swore softly, mutting, 'Come on Harry, come *on!*'

It was a mile run and at the quarter there was nothing to be seen but an occasional flash through the moving cloud of red dust on the turn. They were squinting as the horses went along the back and Lenehan pounded Paddy's arm.

'Can you see, Paddy? Damn dust –'

Julia a pair of opera glasses to her eyes, answered him. 'Cavalier's lying about halfway back, Uncle John. He's moving up, I think. Harry doesn't seem to be pushing him.'

'He's riding funny, sir.' Paddy's voice was anxious. 'I've never known him not make a run for the front by this time.'

In the swirl of the field, Harry sat easily, face still, body moving only as Cavalier's body moved. The crop was unused in his fingers. In the turn to the final quarter-mile, he learned forward a little more, seeing the three horses ahead of him, the leader a good eight lengths out, and he spoke to Cavalier.

'Sorry boy – a bad start and all my fault. Now, we're going to win this damned race, so let's get after them. Come *on*, Cavalier!'

He loosed the reins and felt the great swell of muscle beneath him respond, tucking himself down behind the horse's head, easing his weight in the saddle and seeing now nothing but the one horse ahead of him, the roll and heave of its rump. Then he was along-side, not looking but seeing from the side of his eye the other rider's arm swinging up and down and back, flailing the crop-driven horse, its head now alongside Harry's knee and then back and out of sight; and there was the red and white post like a barber's pole and they were past and he heard the shout of sound and closed his

knees, leaning back a little on the reins and feeling sick and dizzy
and clammy with sweat. He pulled Cavalier to a gentle trot, spitting wet dust from his mouth and turned him back to the crowd
and the stewards, stopping him and cocking a leg over the saddle to
slide down. The noise was swirling round him and the heat was
intense and he heard 'The Breaker' rising like a chant round his
bursting head. Then, there was Paddy, face split in a gaping grin,
and Julia, tear-streaked, her hair coming down, and Lenehan,
smiling, smiling. Lenehan grabbed at his hand and wrung it and
Harry felt the bile in the back of his mouth as Lenehan shouted in
his ear.

'Oh, well done, lad! Bloody well ridden!'

Harry's voice seemed metallic in his skull and echoing, as Lenehan
pumped his hand up and down.

'Thanks Lenehan ... I wonder ... I wonder if you'd mind
shaking the other hand? I think that arm's broken.'

And the shouting and the pain and the heat went away as he
sank to the ground.

The sling was of silk, dark blue silk, elegant and quite in contrast
with Harry's clothes. He was back in his old flannel shirt and
working trousers, comfortably-worn boots in the stirrups, old jacket
thrown across the saddle on Cavalier's back. The horse he'd ridden
in was on a lead rein behind him, a pack across its back and Paddy
was walking his horse alongside, his voice raised in a croaking
bellow of song.

The arm was almost healed now, but Harry had slipped the sling
on again knowing it would be a long day's ride, not wanting to jar
or tire the arm early in the day. Now, with the sun an hour over the
low hills behind them, he reached into the folds of silk and pulled
out a flask of brandy, passing it to Paddy.

'Here, you noisy brute – put a stopper in that hole in your face.
We'll both feel better for it.'

Paddy, still roaring, took the flask, stopping the song to tug the
cap free with his teeth and take a deep swig. His sigh was satisfied.
'Ah, now, it's a mornin' for singin' this is! I never was much of a
man for sittin' on me arse in a posh house, y'know!' He drank
again, deeply, gulping at the brandy, then held it out. 'Will ye have
some?'

'If you've quite finished, you tosspot!'

'Ah, there's a little left yet.' He passed the flask back. 'It didn't
take ye long to lose yer fancy tongue, did it now? Ye're right back
where ye was, rough-tonguein' yer best mate.' He sighed and shook

his head. 'Never mind – 'tis good to be away on the track again.'
They rode silently for a little while, Paddy stewing over something
in his mind before he spoke again.

'You now, Harry, that's a different story. Y'know ye could have
stayed there, don't ye? I could see the way ye fitted in, in amongst
the gentry and that. Ye could have lived like a proper gentleman
and written yer poetry and rode for the love of it instead of after a
lot of stinkin' cattle.' He paused, looking at Harry. 'Ye could've
married that Miss Julia. She was in a real sweat for ye, Harry.'

Harry passed the flask across again. 'Not my kind of life. I'm like
you, a bushman.'

'Ye never are! Oh, ye've the way of it right enough, and ye're a
good man on the track and a fine mate. But that's more for you –'
he cocked a thumb behind him, the way they'd ridden, ' – than this
is.'

'Might have been once. Not any more. All I'm after, Paddy, is to
whack up another cheque in the bush and drink it down at the
pub.' Even to himself, his voice sounded false, and he didn't meet
Paddy's look. He fumbled in a pocket and took out a small gold
locket on a thin wisp of chain, clicking the case open with his
thumb-nail. Julia's face smiled out at him and he felt a stab of
something like pain, remembering the warmth and closeness of her,
the tautness of her breasts under his hand, the way she panted and
pushed herself at him. Remembering her sudden panic when she
lay naked with him and he took her hand and put it on himself, the
way she whimpered, 'Harry no, no – I can't – I'm afraid. Harry –
I'm not your wife!' Remembering the wet face as she dragged her
nightgown over herself and ran from his room into the darkness of
the sleeping house.

He held the locket out so that Paddy could see the picture. 'Not
that Julia wasn't a great comfort to me ... you'd be surprised what
a tender little nurse she was. Especially at night when I couldn't
sleep for the pain.'

'Did she bring yer medicine then, in the night?' Paddy sounded
surprised.

'The best medicine for an ailing man.'

He heard himself saying it and felt hatred, self-hatred, rise like
sickness in his throat. Paddy clicked his tongue against his teeth.
'I've said it before – ye're a terrible rogue, Harry Morant. Toyin'
with a nice little lady like that. A terrible rogue.'

He shook his head again and drained the last of the brandy,
letting the flask drop into the dust of the track. Harry's fingers

worked at the locket, slipping the portrait free and letting it fall, tucking the gold trinket back into his pocket.

'I wouldn't pretend otherwise, Paddy. I'm not properly cut out for a gentleman, I'm afraid.'

Behind them, under the hooves of the led horse, the tiny picture and the empty flask lay side by side in the hoofmarks on the track.

November 1901

The afternoon had stretched itself out into a long, red-gold evening and now, with the first of the night's cold creeping in behind the dusk, Paddy was glad of the fire. It wasn't much of a house, but he'd fixed it up well and it let in no draughts and let out no warmth, and with Harlequin stalled and pile of dry logs by the grate, with a meal in his belly and a glass of grog in his hand and his old pipe drawing well, he felt mostly content. A bit of company would be nice – he thought that almost every evening, especially in the autumn, when the whole world seemed to be touched with a little loneliness, and the dullness of winter was pulling up close.

He'd not lit the lamp, and he sat there in the flame-flicker, thinking. . . . Harry on Cavalier, his waterproof and the horse's hide both the same gleaming black with the rain teeming down, and the cattle tired and up to the hocks in mud, but Harry always ready with a smile, always with a bottle of something warm tucked away in a pocket to share with Paddy, laughing into the rain, dog tired though they were. Ah, they'd drunk many a stirring drink that way, the two of them, wet and dirty-dry, working and loafing, card-playing and womanizing and gambling and fighting. Begod, that Breaker could swing a fist like a club, and he never again tried the gentleman's boxing game after that first time with Sims!

Not that he hadn't been knocked about other times, without fighting for it. The polo had done for him more than once, a madman's game for gentlemen only, with the bloody great sticks like hammers flashing about and the little ponies whipping round like watch-wheels, and somebody bound to get hurt. And there'd be the old Breaker – broken in a part of him and tucked away in bed in a hospital somewhere. Roaring at Paddy for a smuggled bottle of liquor and with half the local lassies visiting him, and him lying there in the bed in splints and a spare hand up their skirts or down their fronts and them lining up for more of it!

It seemed to him, staring into the flames, sipping at his grog, that there'd been trouble one way and another ever since they'd ridden away from Eagleton that time, and away from that little Miss Julia. Not that it was all bad – funny some of it. Like that time they went off on that pigsticking jaunt in Victoria somewhere. Harry went anyway, and himself just for the gallop and a friendly bit of a sneer. And there was Harry with this great long lump of bamboo and a pointy blade on the end of it enough to slice the tripes out of an ox, and half a dozen other men like it and all jinking about in that wicked scrub country with the rocks hidden by the scrub, after a bit of a black bastard of a humpty-backed pig! And himself dismounting for a sip out of the bottle in the saddlebag and seeing Harry alone ride into a clearing after a pig and check and the other man coming out sideways at him, walking his horse and the point of his spear under Harry's chin, very still, just pricking at a tiny spot of blood. He remembered watching frozen, too late to do anything and listening to the two of them, Harry with his head back, and the man saying, 'I should hold my horse pretty damn steady if I was you, Morant.'

And Harry lowering the point of his spear and Cavalier standing like a statue while Harry said, 'I don't think we've met, have we?'

Cool as ice, and the other man holding down the fire in him, but there was heat in his voice.

'We haven't, but I've been looking forward to it. I want to give you a little advice.'

And he'd shifted his point a bit and Harry's head went a bit further up and his back straightened all the way.

'I always take the advice of a man with a blade in my gullet.' His voice was tight, but very steady, Paddy remembered, and the other man had said, 'Good. Then stay right away from my wife. Right away. Or I'll be hunting you instead of the little pigs.'

And he'd given another touch of a jab and ridden away and Harry had sat and watched him go, rubbing his throat and tilting the spear back over his shoulder. Paddy had ridden out to him, his face white, and Harry had smiled ruefully at him and said, 'All very well ... but which one *is* his wife?'

Paddy kicked the sinking fire into life again and refilled his glass, thinking, Ah, God, he changed a lot them years did

Harry. Kept on with the poetry, though, all that time. And times, behaved like a real gentleman. Like the man he used to be once.

It had taken Harry a week to get used to being back in a city again. It was seven years since he'd landed in Sydney and the place seemed to have grown like a wild pumpkin in damp ground, sprawling tendrils everywhere. He and Paddy had wound up a three-month spell on the one property and had then moved down to the races at Bathurst, and the work and the winnings between them had left them flush, enough money as Paddy had said, 'So we can take a bit of a rest, boyo. Eat and drink in style for a month, eh? Why don't we go down to The Smoke?'

New clothes and a decent hotel room and a long lunch with the *Bulletin* people and temporary membership of the Turf Club on Lenehan's letter of introduction. Paddy watched as his friend slid easily away from the roughness of the track and into the smooth patterns of social life, seeing his enjoyment in it, although he worked hard at the pretence that it was all a lot of balderdash. He went to the Turf Club Ball and Paddy looked at him ready to leave the hotel, white tie and tails that he'd bought specially for the occasion, silk hat in a white-gloved hand and the lined cloak swirling round him as he went out to the horse-cab, and he began to wonder if the man would ever come back with him into the outback again. He needn't have worried.

The night after the ball, Harry said, 'My god, Paddy, I could do with a decent drink.'

'Well, now yer Lordship, ye've nothin' to do but ring the little bell there and one of yer slaves will bring ye some champagne in a golden slipper. Or will I ring it for ye, sir?'

'Paddy, I want a *drink*.'

And they went out, plainly dressed, and down to Woolloomooloo, where the pubs were close together and noisy and reeking and full of the oddments of Sydney – journalists and pimps, painters and sailors, whores and thieves.

By the time they'd been at the bar for an hour, Harry was flushed and half-drunk, his eyes fever-lit and no sign of the polished gentleman of the night before. The young man who'd edged in beside him caught his attention and he nudged Paddy and said, 'I say, Patrick, look at this young shaver – all fresh and dewy-eyed and drinking small beer.'

The youngster half-turned, his face colouring, and managed half a smile. Harry slapped him across the back. 'Hey, that stuff'll rot your insides, my lad. I'll buy you a proper drink.' Spreading a handful of silver on the bar he shouted for three rums, sliding one of them to Paddy and one to the young man. 'What's your name, sonny?'

'Grant, sir. Duncan Grant. And thank you.' The voice was quiet, well-enough taught, something of a lilt in it.

'Aha, a polite young Scot! Drink your rum, Duncan Grant, and tell us what a sprat like you comes to Sydney Town for.'

'I've ... I've just landed, sir. Today. I've come to work.'

'Hey, Paddy, here's a phenom ... phenomenal thing. This young man wants to *work!*'

Paddy stared owlishly across at Grant. 'Very commendable. Very. The young men of today don't seem to want that any more, so they don't. Just wanta drink. Drink's a curse, that's what it is. I'm very near teetotal meself.' He sank his face into his rum again, and Grant smiled a little.

Harry waved a hand for more drinks, his arm still looped across the young man's back. 'And what line of business are you in, may I ask, Duncan Grant?'

'None, really, sir. That is – I was working in my uncle's warehouse in London – he's an importer you see, but –'

'But you got tired of it and ran off to the Colonies? Adventure and far places and all that ... right?'

Grant nodded, smiling, the drink warming him. 'I suppose that's what it was. I've read about New South Wales and it seemed to me there were chances for ... other things out here.' Harry looked at him quizzically, and the youngster stumbled on. 'I don't mean to stay in Sydney. I ... I want to be a bushman.'

Harry's roar jerked Paddy's head around. 'Bushman! You! Hey, Paddy, this little pink thing wants to go bush!'

Paddy leaned in closer. 'Don't do it, young fella. 'Tis a terrible life. Stay here where the rum is. Get a job in a pub, why don't ye?'

Harry was running hard fingers up Grant's arm and punching him gently but with firmness on the chest. 'You're too soft, sonny. You wouldn't last a week in the brigalow!'

Grant pulled himself away, face clouding. 'I may be a little out of condition, sir ... the sea voyage ... but I'll harden I don't doubt.' Then his curiosity beat him. 'What's the brigalow?'

'What is it, sonny? It's all out there –' his sweeping arm made Grant step back again, '–the bush, the backblocks. You need to be a strong man to live out there, Duncan Grant from the warehouse.' His voice had gone up and two of the barmen moved along nearer to him, one of them frowning, holding an empty quart bottle by the neck. Paddy tugged at Harry's sleeve.

'Harry, give over will ye! Ye're creatin' a disturbance.'

The barman with the bottle leaned across, face close to Harry's. 'Oy, you! If you wanta drink, then pay yer money an' drink, right? If yer wanta shout yer 'ead off an' make a bloody shivoo, y'll 'ave to do it somewhere else. Or I'll *knock* ya fuckin' 'ead off with this, see?'

Harry stared at the bottle waving under his nose, then pushed it gently aside with one finger. 'My dear man, all I'm doing is telling this young new-chum about the bush, that's all. About living in the brigalow.'

'Yair, well keep yer voice down while yer doin' it.' He turned to Grant. 'You keep yer mate quiet, lad. An' what *'e'd* know about the bush I'd 'ate to think!'

Paddy was suddenly outraged, stretching an arm across and wagging a thick finger in the barman's face.

'Oh, ye're an ignorant man, so y'are! D'ye not know this is Harry Morant? The Breaker?'

'Yair, an' I'm the Pope, old feller. Just keep 'im quiet.'

Grant looked puzzled. 'Who's The Breaker?'

A quietly-dressed, elderly man standing close by chipped in at once. 'A balladist, young man. Harry Morant is The Breaker, a man who writes excellent bush verses.' He turned to Harry. '*Are* you, sir? Are you Morant?'

Harry sketched a bow. 'I am indeed. For what it's worth.'

'I consider it to be worth a good deal, sir, and I'm most pleased to make your acquaintance. I've admired your verses since they first appeared.'

'Very kind, very kind.' Harry was making an attempt to control the slur in his speech as he took the offered hand. Embarrassed, he tried to change the subject. 'I was just trying to tell my young friend here, Grant, about life in the brigalow, sir.'

The man smiled at Grant. 'Then you should ask Mr Morant to recite you his ballad about 'The Brigalow Brigade'.'

Grant's face lit up. 'Would you? I'd like fine to hear it if you would.'

'Oh, but ... really, this is hardly the place for recitation –'

Paddy, grinning, broke in. 'Ah, go on now, Harry! 'Twouldn't be the first time ye've spouted a piece in a pub!'

The quiet man had had their glasses refilled and slipped one into Harry's hand. Harry took a gulp, looking round at the three of them and shrugged. 'Very well, gentlemen, I shall recite!'

With his back to the bar, leaning comfortably on his elbows, he let his eyes lose the sight of the crowded, rackety bar, picturing for them the openness of the country out to the north and west, looking on to the words he'd written five years ago, a notebook balanced on his thigh as he walked his horse:

'There's a band of decent fellows
On a cattle-run outback –
You'll hear the timber smashing
If you follow in their track;
Their ways are rough and hearty
And they call a spade a spade;
And a pretty rapid party
Are the Brigalow Brigade!'

Paddy was beating time with the swing of the lines and Duncan Grant and the quiet man were both smiling, standing close. Several of the people nearby had caught something in what Harry was saying and had edged in a little and there began to be a circle of quietness about the man with his back to the bar and his head back and his voice, low but ringing:

'They are mostly short of 'sugar'
And their pockets, if turned out,
Would scarcely yield the needful
For a decent four-man 'shout'.
But they'll scramble through a tight place
Or a big fence unafraid,
And their hearts are in the right place
In the Brigalow Brigade.'

Now the ring around Harry had sucked in most of the people in the bar, and there was a murmur of 'The Breaker', and the barman had shifted along, the scowling one behind Harry at a bit of a loss. Harry's voice hadn't risen, but in the comparative quiet it rang clear in the room:

'The Brigalow Brigade are
Fastidious in their taste
In the matter of a maiden
And the inches of her waist;
She must be sweet and tender
And her eyes a decent shade –'

There were smiles all around the bar now as the words caught them, and they waited for the last line, roaring it with Harry –

'*Then her Ma may safely send her*
To the Brigalow Brigade.'

The chorus snapped Harry's head down and his eyes cleared and there were people buying drinks and calling to him and even the surly barman was smiling with the new rush of orders.

Harry flushed and frowned, the sudden attention unwelcome. His head felt clear now, and he muttered to Paddy, 'I'll join you later, back at the hotel,' and pushed his way through the crowd to the door.

A block away from the pub, Harry slowed to a stroll. He was near the Harbour and the sea-smell came strong to him, and the ship-smells – a sweet-sourness of tarred ropes and salt-steeped timbers and canvas and a thousand mixed cargoes. The night was clear and chill and the last of the rum fumes washed out of him as he walked, remembering other days in other seaport towns. He didn't hear the running feet, and the man who cannoned into him at the corner caught him off balance, sending him lurching to the wall, clutching at rough cloth. Pulling himself upright by the man's clothing, he could see in the flicker of a street-light that he was a sailor, Royal Navy, dishevelled capless and panting.

'Whoa there, Jack! What's all the hurry?'

The man wrenched at Harry's hand, his voice harsh with lack of breath. 'Lemme go, mate – I gotta find some help –'

Harry shifted his hand from the tight grip on the man's shirt and laid it hard on his shoulder, his voice crisp and cold. 'Stand still, man, and talk sense.'

The tone of the voice snapped the sailor upright and still, and he searched Harry's face in the near dark, listening.

'Now then, what's wrong?'

'We been jumped on, sir. A gang round there, round the corner a bit. They're knockin' the Jesus outa my shipmates. I've got to –'

'Show me where.'

The sailor swung away at once and Harry followed him back the way he'd come, seeing as they rounded the corner the struggling group at the end of the narrow street under another light. As he ran he summed up the scene: three matelots, one down in the gutter, the other two backed against a wall trying to hold off five – no six – bully-boys. They were so deeply immersed in what they were doing that Harry and the sailor hit them like a swinging club, taking two of them out of the fight at once. From the corner of his eye Harry saw the sailor leap, his bunched knees catching one of the men in the small of the back, his fist swinging sideways at another. Harry used the weight of his running body to drive his arm and fist at an unguarded throat, feeling his knuckles sink in and hearing the choked scream. Then it was a general mêlée, with the two other sailors, heartened by the reinforcements, coming back strongly.

When the police arrived the fight was even and Harry's eyebrow was bleeding where a short cudgel had smacked at him. His knuckles were raw and he was gasping for breath, feeling a dull ache below the breastbone where a knee had dug in.

Paddy walked along the damp stone corridor, the sergeant ahead of him, a bundle of long keys jangling in his hand. The two big cells were off to one side facing the half-dozen single cells across fifteen feet of ill-lit paving slabs. The bully-boys were in the first big cell, lounging back on the floor or on the plank seat along one wall, and they scowled silently as Paddy and the policeman went past them. In the other cell, Harry, a handkerchief still wiping drying blood from his forehead, stood straight, his back to the door, looking at the four sailors sitting in a row, heads down. His voice was crackling.

'You ought to be ashamed of yourselves! Four of Her Majesty's jacks not able to handle a bunch of wharfside ruffians like that!'

One of the sailors, the one Harry had run into, looked up apologetically. 'They caught us on the 'op, sir –'

'Be quiet! And stand up straight!'

The four of them scrambled to their feet, one standing a little crooked, a hand pushed into his side.

'Look at you! Not a hat between you and your uniforms are in a disgusting state.' He let a smile creep through. 'I'm very glad to have been of service to you.'

The sideways sailor grinned at him. 'Very pleased to have had you along sir.'

One of the others, the side of his face puffed and blackening, said, 'Beg pardon, sir, but are you – was you – er, in the Andrew, sir? The Navy?'

Harry was saved from answering by the sergeant, rattling his keys into the lock and swinging the door wide. 'Out you come, Morant. Your friend here has paid you out.'

Harry spun around. 'Paddy! Well done. Have you any money on you?' Without waiting for an answer he turned to the policeman. 'Sergeant, what's the damage for these men?'

'Same as yours. Five shillings a piece.'

'Good. Paddy, a quid. Quickly now!'

Paddy had been standing through this fast exchange, his mouth open. Now he shut it to swallow before shouting. 'Are ye out of yer mind! I'll not spend good silver on a mob of drunken sailors –'

'You'll pay for these men or I'll break your scruffy Irish neck!' The tone of command softened. 'Come on now, Paddy. You're still holding a few guineas of mine.'

Paddy stared at him, then at the sailors, and the sergeant broke in. 'Well, do you or don't you?'

Muttering under his breath and firing salvoes of fury from his eyes, Paddy fumbled coins out of his pockets and his belt. The sailors crowded round Harry, wringing his hand. The one who'd joined him in the attack said, 'Yer a toff, sir, a real toff.'

'That's all right. But you'd better tidy yourselves before you get back to your ship. Ready, Paddy?'

'Ay, I'm ready. Ready to ding you in the skull, ye madman!'

The four sailors had shuffled themselves into a line under the glance of the one with the bruised face. Now he flicked a look at the four of them and slid words from the corner of his lips.

'Right? Hup!'

As one, the four came rigidly to attention, Bruised Face whipping his hand to his forehead in salute. Very gravely, Harry tipped his battered and dusty hat to them, turned smartly on his heel and walked out. Paddy, skipping to keep up with him, let the irony sting through his voice. 'Lovely! Is the captain ready to go ashore now?'

Harry smiled straight ahead, but there was a wistfulness in it.

Sydney? But that was a long time ago. Paddy felt that the cold of this high country had got into his bones. He felt the dullness of the ache across the small of his back as he lifted the axe again, and the deep pull at his shoulders as it came down, clean-splitting the pine log. He stood surrounded knee-deep by split wood and he stopped to wipe the cooling sweat away from his face, looking down the valley to where the snow hadn't settled as it had begun to do up here on the slopes.

He'd knocked together the remains of an old wheelbarrow the week before when they moved into the hut, and he piled it high now with firewood and rolled it, squeaking and leaning, cursing when he saw the door wide open. He stamped in, slamming it behind him, and crossed to the fire, low and half-choked with ash, kneeling and poking it into life again and deliberately rattling the iron bar around to try and stir the sleeping man in the bunk there behind.

By the time he'd got the new-cut wood in and stacked and dragged in two or three bigger logs for keeping, the early sun had gone and the feathery clouds had massed and dropped, ready to snow again.

As once before – the time he had got pneumonia, years ago now – they'd spent a couple of weeks helping bring sheep down out of the upcountry – irritating work because the animals were scattered through several small valleys in the hills. Neither Paddy nor Harry much liked working sheep, but they'd found work increasingly hard to get during the last year or two because of Harry's drinking and his truculence.

Foremen and bosses had found him a problem, drinking not to be friendly or to keep the cold out, only for the sake of it and then spoiling for a fight with someone, anyone. This last job had ended with the boss deducting a good lump of Harry's pay because he'd gone grog-wild one night and just about taken the little tucker-cart to pieces with a cleaver in protest against the cook. Paddy had managed to keep them hanging on till the end and then dickered with the property-owner for the use of the hut up the slopes, planning to settle there for a while and try to dry Harry out a bit. The supplies had taken almost all the money they had, but they were snug enough for the winter if necessary and could make a fresh go of it when the thaw came.

The horses were in a lean-to behind the hut and Paddy raked the straw around, spreading fresh stuff on top of it and dropping some dry feed into the trough, his own horse standing dozing on three legs, Cavalier nosing at his hands as he mixed the feed. Through the wall he could hear Harry moving, stumbling about first, then the creak of the door, then the retching and heaving and, sighing, he went around to the front of the hut, looking at the man standing barefoot in the thin snow.

'Oh, Christ, Harry, if ye don't kill yerself tearing yer guts out like that ye'll do it be freezin' yerself to death!' He got an arm round the crouching figure and half-dragged him back inside, dropping him into the beaten old chair by the fire and throwing a blanket over him. 'Sit there a minute and try and get the blood movin' a bit inside ye. I'll clean ye up as soon as I've yer bed fixed.'

In the early evening Harry came fully awake for the first time that day. Paddy was hunched over a piece of harness, a saddler's palm on his hand, the curved needle catching the glint of the fire as he sewed. There was a food smell from the pot to one side of the heat and Harry's stomach contracted with emptiness and need as he pushed back the blankets, noticing that he was in clean underwear and socks. He toppled twice while he was pulling on his trousers and shirt, and he grunted each time. Paddy made no move other than to go on with his repairs and Harry, not speaking, ladled stew into a dish and tore off a piece of damper, slumping onto the stool at the rough table and shovelling food into his mouth, head low. He wiped the plate clean with the last of the damper and fossicked around in a box under the wallshelves, finding the rum and mixing two mugs of it with hot water and a little sugar. Paddy put the harness and sewing-gear away and lit the lamp, looking at Harry, yellow in the yellow light, stubbled and gaunt.

'Ye're a mess, Harry Morant, d'ye know that?'

'I know it.' The voice was harsh and blurry. 'There's no bastard knows it better.'

'Ah, ye're disgustin'!' He started to go on, but stopped himself and swung the chair round to face the other man across the table, sipping at the hot grog while he studied him. When he spoke again his voice was gentle. 'We been on the track a long time, Harry. There's no man I'd sooner have rode with, I tell you that straight. Ye're a helluva fella an' I love ye like a brother, but ye've made yerself a stinkin' mess, ye have.'

'Oh, for Christ's sake, Magee! I don't need you preaching at me!'

'Magee, is it? Right then – Morant!' Paddy shoved back the chair and stood over him, solid and chunky in the low light, his brows down dark across his face. 'Let me tell it to ye straight – ye're a drunk. Ye're a spendthrift, stupid, womanizin' drunk. And what with the one and the other and the lot of them, ye'll put yerself in the grave in jigtime. Ye will!'

Harry looked up at him, a twist of a smile making him look ugly somehow, and he nodded his head. 'Right!'

'Right? It's not right at all! It's a madness!'

Harry drained his mug and reached again for the bottle, but Paddy snatched it from him, holding it away where he couldn't reach, letting the anger seep out of his voice.

'Ah, now, boyo, don't ye see what ye're doin'? Ye're killin' yerself!'

'Exactly! You have the gift of clear sight, Paddy old friend, like all the mystic madmen of Ireland. I'm killing myself. And why not? Why ever the hell not? It's the only privilege I still have.' The clear irony changed to a growl. 'Give me that bloody bottle.'

'Aaah, take it, then, ye drunk fool!'

He watched as Harry poured neat rum this time and gulped at it. 'Look, Paddy,' he said, 'there's nothing I can do will ever put me up on a horse behind a Devonshire fox again, is there? Nothing will take me home again, will it? So it doesn't matter, does it?'

'Harry, the old people at home have a word for fellas like you, and the abos too. Ye're puttin' the death-wish on yerself. Ye're gallopin' to yer own drunk death is what ye're doin'.'

'I am. I am indeed.'

Harry took another deep drink. 'I am indeed.' His face was desolate and his voice entirely sober.

Late that night, with Harry snoring and bubbling, Paddy hunted out every bottle of drink he could find, smashed them on a rock and buried the pieces.

They came out of the hills in a softening and a damp warmth, new pale greens all round them and the loud sounds of downhill water proving the end of the winter.

Harry was thin but clear-eyed and Paddy felt good as he rode behind Cavalier, looking at the easy uprightness of Harry's back and hearing his whistling.

The morning after Paddy had got rid of the drink, Harry had had a fit of raging fury which would have ended in Paddy's death or serious injury had the younger man not been weakened by continual drinking and sickness. As it was, he'd done a fair amount of damage to the hut, throwing clothes and food out into the deepening snow and nearly setting fire to the place, and he'd left an aching bruise on Paddy's leg which had taken weeks to fade out. In the end he'd knocked himself out without Paddy having to hit him and for three weeks after that had spent his time either in bed or sulking silently in the chair. He stank and his beard grew in a straggly scrub and he ate only just enough to keep himself alive, glaring at Paddy when the food was put before him.

At the end of a month, still silently, he rose early one morning and by the time Paddy woke, the hut was filled with the smell of food, the fire was high and cheerful and Harry was washed and shaved and in clean clothes. Paddy made no comment till later that day, well into the afternoon, when he heard the sound of the axe and went out to where Harry, sweating and panting, was swinging away at a dead pine. Paddy was alongside him before he noticed, and he lowered the axe and wiped his streaming face with the back of a wet hand. Paddy, face serious, laid a hand on his shoulder and said, 'Welcome back, boyo,' and they both smiled.

'Ye'd better come inside and wipe that sweat off ye, and get a dry shirt on. Ye wouldn't want another cold now. I'll heat some soup – not as warming as grog, of course.'

He lifted an eyebrow at Harry who stared back, pokerfaced.

'Grog? You know I don't drink, you mad Irishman.'

And that had been that, so that now, with the opening of spring, they rode down into the valleys, pockets empty, tucker-bags almost empty and ready for work.

Harry had held off the drink for a long, hard six months, not refusing two or three beers at the end of a stiff day, but not once taking any of the hard stuff. They settled in on a property outside Yass, a sheep place, where Harry rode the boundary and strung some wire and Paddy, deciding on a bit of a rest, took on as rouseabout, spending much of his time close to the homestead.

It was the most sedate period of their lives in all the years, a settled and near-routine time, without the shifts and starts they'd begun to accept as normal. Harry began to jot down verses again and broke half a dozen new horses and seemed relaxed and comfortable. He began to talk of a trip down to Melbourne or even to Adelaide to see what the racing was like on the city tracks there.

They were back in the high lands that autumn, again to move sheep down out of the cold. It was black rock country, hard and unyielding, and underlying ribs of the slopes covered with a loose skin of sharp stones, almost bare of greenery. Above them the sky was nearly as black, looked almost as hard, and the wind had swung to come out of the north-east, whistling down the gullies and then suddenly carrying swirls of sleet in front of it and chopping across sight-lines in a blur of icy greyness.

Harry and Paddy had been moving well out on a flank, the others across a gully from them and up the slope of the ridge opposite. It had seemed to Harry that Cavalier was making hard going of it and, with the sleet and the wind pushing it directly into their faces, he felt the big horse lose the certainty of his footing, felt a slackness in his movements as they edged upwards almost blindly. He swung down, shaking his head against the tiny ice chips and turned his back to the wind, taking Cavalier's head to his chest, listening with a touch of fear to the stallion's heavy breathing, feeling the tremble in the shoulder muscles under his hand. He realized they weren't any more the great rounded bunches they had been, that Cavalier had lost weight, thinned down. He'd been three, perhaps four, when Lenehan had handed him over that day at Eagleton and that was close to nine years back. It wasn't necessarily much of an age for a horse, but he knew how Cavalier had worked, knew how hard he'd pushed him as a stock-horse, as a saddle-horse, as a race-horse. And now he felt afraid.

The breathing slowed and eased although the trembling was still there. Harry muttered, close to the steel-grey head, 'All right, old son. The devil with the sheep. We'll go back.' He lifted his head and shouted against the skirl of the sleety wind, hearing Paddy's answering call, thin and tossed about against the rocks, waiting till he loomed out of the murk, covered with the silver crystals of the settling sleet. Mutely Harry swung an arm downhill, back towards the homestead and Paddy nodded, tugging a scarf up over his face and hunching his shoulders. Harry swung into the saddle and they began to move down, letting the horses pick their own paths.

Twice Cavalier stumbled, once where he went through a crisping surface into a wet little bog of a hollow and once when a loose rock skittered away under a forehoof. Then they were almost on the flat, not at the bottom but a place where the slope eased before plunging down again. Cavalier stopped, head down and blowing gouts of steamy breath and as Harry shifted weight into one stirrup to dismount, the big horse went to his knees, a thick sigh shaking him. He tossed his head as though objecting to his own weakness and let himself slide over, lying down, his barrel heaving with the effort of breathing. Harry knelt by him. 'My poor old boy. It's too much for you, isn't it? And I'm a bastard!' The wetness in his eyes wasn't all sleet and he blinked, rubbing the horse's head. 'You shouldn't be working in this stinking weather, Cav. Let's get you home, eh? Come on now, old son, up you get.'

Paddy, riding ahead, realized he was alone and turned his horse into the gusts again, squinting to see. He came on the stooping man and the struggling horse almost before he knew they were there. He was out of the saddle at once, kneeling by Harry, running hard, expert hands over the horse. 'Ah, ye good old fella, has the cold got to ye then? All them hard miles, eh?' He looked round at Harry and lowered his voice, close to Harry's ear, as though they were in a sick-room. 'He's had enough, Harry. He needs rest—'

He broke off as Harry stood and walked around Cavalier, stooping to the old rifle in the saddle-boot, tugging it clear of the horse's body.

'Ah, ye'll not!'

'I have to, Paddy. He's gone. He's got a few years too many on him for the way I've worked his guts out. He's gone.' He checked the breech and looked down.

'If we could get him moving easy . . . get him to shelter—'

'So he can spend a year coughing himself to death? Not my horse, not Cavalier. He wouldn't want that.'

Paddy stood, holding out his hand for the rifle, but Harry shook his head. Paddy bent again, patting the horse lightly and coughing, pretending the wind was in his throat, and Harry waited till he'd moved away, kneeling then on the rocks and slipping the bit and bridle from Cavalier's mouth. He slackened the girths and let the saddle slip down, pulling his bags from it and tossing them behind him where Paddy took them up. He shoved his hand deep in the coat pocket where he kept some of the coarse brown sugar Cavalier loved and held it out. The horse had kept his eyes on the man all the time, half-arching his neck and turning his head, and now he dropped his muzzle to the sugar and licked a little of it, not finishing, letting his head drop back, sighing again. Harry lowered his head, dropping his hat alongside him, and rested his forehead against the horse's, still for a long span of seconds. Cavalier whickered softly.

Harry stood abruptly and, in the same movement, cocked the rifle and fired. There was hardly an echo, the wind taking the flat sound and throwing it away in the gullies round them. Paddy mounted, Harry's bags across the saddle in front of him, and waited, saw Harry stand still with the wind whipping at his hair, then eject the shell. Wordlessly he swung up behind Paddy, letting the rifle fall by the dead horse, leaving the saddle where it had slipped. His arms were tight around Paddy's waist and he dug the side of his face hard into the back of Paddy's shoulder as they walked slowly down in the storm.

Horses! There were maybe sixty in the mob ... not all of them fully wild. A few, perhaps a dozen, were runaways and it was those few who were making it so damned hard to push the brumbies into the rough yard at the bottom of the gully. They knew what the sapling rails were for, they recognized the gate, hanging wide on strap-leather hinges, and every time they were edged down towards it they propped and wheeled, trying to run back through the mob and sending them all scattering up the rough sides of the gully and back towards the half-dozen men behind them. Riding the dapple he had picked up as a replacement for Cavalier – a poor substitute, but he had to have a horse – Harry was half-blinded with dust and sweat. The wild horse whirling up almost directly ahead of him caught him by surprise and he let it by. Over on his right, Spencer, the man for whom they were working now, bellowed, 'Don't sit there on y'r arse, Morant, get ahold of him.'

By the time Harry had turned the wild horse, the rest of the mob were halfway through the gate, the stockwhips cracking about their heels and the men whistling and shouting. Harry quartered his dapple behind the other horse, trying not to gallop him, not to frighten him more than was necessary. As the bulk of the dust began to settle he could see his quarry more clearly and his eyes widened and he whistled between his teeth. Under the caked mud from a creek somewhere, under the dust, this was something special ... the coat was rough and thick with burrs, but it looked golden, and the mane and tail, grey-red with dirt, looked to be black below. And the horse, a stallion, moved beautifully, certain-footed and a splendid stride, long and with a raking dash in it. Clever, too, Harry half-smiled to himself, seeing how the horse checked and wheeled, changed gait, spun about, pacing him for a few strides, then stopping suddenly in the hope that Harry would go past him and leave him clear. By the time they'd worked down to the gate, Harry was smiling widely in appreciation and when he cracked his whip six feet behind the horse, it looked at him as though realizing the game was over and trotted sedately in to the yard where the rest of the mob were milling themselves to a standstill. Paddy wheeled alongside.

'Holy Jesus, that was hot work!'

Harry didn't shift his stare. 'D'ye see him, Paddy? Don't make it obvious now; just look around casually. I don't want Spencer noticing. There – by the rail – the stallion.'

Paddy shifted in the saddle for a clearer look. 'I see him. He stands out a bit from that mob of scrubs, don't he? There's breedin' there, boyo.'

'D'y see the colour under all that muck? I believe he's a true Palomino, Paddy!'

'What the hell's that when it's at home?'

'Wait and see!' He wheeled the dapple and walked over to where Spencer was watching the gate being lashed fast. 'Mr Spencer ... may I talk with you for a moment?'

Spencer, thickset and scowling, looked at him curtly. 'Make it smart then, Morant. I want to get home before dark.' He half turned to call to the rest of the men. 'Come on you lot – y'pay's here!' He turned back to Harry. 'What d'you want then?'

'I want you to keep my pay.'

Now Spencer gave Harry his full attention, staring at him, suspicious. then he grunted a laugh. 'Do you now? Well, I'll not fight you about that! What's the catch?'

'No catch. I'll take it out in horseflesh.'

'What, one of them?' Spencer's thick thumb jerked at the quietening mob and Harry nodded.

'Yes. Will you do it?'

Spencer shrugged. 'Why not? The price they're fetching nowadays, I'll be saving money. Go on, help yourself.'

Harry raised a hand in thanks, wheeled and stooped from the

saddle to undo the gate lashings, Paddy moving along with him. The stallion was watching, a little away from the bunched mob near the centre of the yard and when the gate was swung three or four feet, he moved at once, trotting through the gap. As he came through, Harry dropped a rope halter over his head and took a loop on to his saddle while Paddy shut and lashed the gate again. Spencer watched them, looking at the horse and for a moment it seemed as though he was going to speak. Harry got in first.

'My bargain, I think, Spencer – thanks! Paddy, come and make the acquaintance of – of Harlequin.'

Renmark looked inviting when they rode into the town, cool in the first long shadows of the afternoon, fresh from the light shower which had fallen earlier in the day. The dapple on a lead-rope walked behind Harlequin and Paddy's bay, down to the corner hotel in which Harry had got himself arrested a month earlier when he was on the spree after the death of Cavalier.

After the great brumby round-up they'd spent the bulk of the month twenty miles or so up the Murray River towards the Victorian border, putting up with the evening mosquitoes for the chance to camp near big water, the chance for Paddy to pull some fat fish out of the river. The chance for Harry to work with Harlequin. For three days he'd just let the stallion graze on a running-line near the camp, making no attempt to ride him or clean him, simply spending long periods talking to him, knuckling his forehead, getting him used to the cupped handful of brown sugar. He was maybe a hand shorter than Cavalier and not as huge-muscled, but he was, as Paddy said, 'A terrible elegant sort of a horse,' and there was a quick intelligence in his look. When it came to it there was really no need for him to be broken. He kicked up his heels a time or two when Harry first settled onto his back, and he spun a little and jinked about, but they both knew at once that this was a game of sorts, token gestures by both the horse and the man. Then Harry began to groom him, walking him into a shallow place where a miniature shingle beach led into the river. Paddy watched from higher up the bank, a line in his hands, his old pipe going like a smokestack, and he let the line hang slack as the horse emerged from its coat of dirt and burrs. Even though Harry had prepared him for it, he hadn't expected quite what he saw, the sleek, deep gold of the hide and the fine black silk of the mane and tail. When Harry led Harlequin back from the water, still shining wet, Paddy stared at the two of them and said quietly, 'Ah, now, ye're a pair of champions, so y'are!'

Now, as they tied the horses outside the corner hotel in Renmark, people stopped to admire Harlequin, several boys crowding close, one of them patting the Palomino's muzzle. Harry watched, smiling, till the voice beside him jerked him around.

'Morant, you're not plannin' to start any trouble, I 'ope.'

The sergeant towered over him, face grim. Harry, recovering, was all at once glad to be clean and sober. 'No, Sergeant, no trouble. Not this time.'

'Not *any* time in this town, son, take my word for it.'

'Fair enough. May I buy you a drink?'

The sergeant shifted the roll of paper under his arm and looked at his pocket-watch. 'Yair, I don't see why not. 'Bout that sorta time anyway. Good on ya.'

Paddy watched delighted at the way the pint pewter emptied into the sergeant. 'By the livin' God, ye've a hell of a swallow there, Sergeant! I've not seen a better.'

'Practice, Magee. I been doin' it a long time.' He hunched lower on his forearms, cocking a sideways look at Harry. 'Yer still on the hard stuff, I see. I'll remind ya again – no trouble.'

'Sergeant, this is a glass of rum. It's the one I bought two or three minutes ago and I shall drink it, *and* the one you buy *and* the one Paddy buys. Then I shall stop for the evening.' He downed the drink.

'I believe ya.' He waved a large hand and the glasses and his pot were refilled. 'I see the *Bulletin* got another of yer pieces in. That one about yer horse, Cavalier. I liked that.'

Harry smiled up at the big man. 'I wouldn't have suspected you of being a poetry-lover, Sergeant.'

The sergeant smiled back, 'The way I see it, if a man's got them kinda feelin's about a horse that belongs to him, then he's pretty near orright.' He lifted the pot. ''Ooray, Breaker.'

When he'd drunk the beer Paddy bought him he checked his watch again. 'Better be gettin' on. Gotta put this up yet.' He picked up the long roll of paper which he'd propped against the bar.

'What've yer got there, Sergeant – a picture is it?'

'Poster, Paddy. Notice come up from Adelaide – they're goin' up all over. Come an' 'ave a squint.'

They followed him out to the low veranda, watching as he dug around for a little box of thumb-tacks and carefully pinned the notice up near the door in the light of a pair of hanging kerosene lamps. Several other men gathered to watch, unable to read the notice till the sergeant's spread shoulders moved and the lettering stood out clear in the lamplight.

As the little crowd built, the words were buzzing back and into the bar, dragging more men out to swell the noise. Paddy listened, his eyes on Harry who was reading the notice with complete attention.

''Ey, they're callin' for volunteers, Mick!'

'What for?'

'Join the Yeomanry – go to South Africa.'

'Second South Australian Yeomanry . . . see?'

'What the fuck 'appened to the first?' A burst of laughter.

'Maybe they lost 'em!'

'Get out. I 'eard one lot's gorn already. That'd be the first.'

'Yair, well whatta they want volunteers *for*?'

'Fight the bloody Bores.'

'The who?'

'The Bores. Dutchies. In South africa.'

'Fight 'em for what?'

'I dunno, mate. Don't matter, does it – you're not goin' anyway!'

'I don't see you runnin' off to enlist neither Jacko!'

'Me! No way, digger!' More laughter. Harry was still reading, close to the poster, leaning forward a little to read the bottom lines. Paddy edged close to him.

'Harry? Ye're – ye're thinkin' of going, are ye?' His voice sounded frightened.

Harry straightened, smiling, and Paddy looked at him. It was the full, flashing smile of the young Harry, the Harry of fifteen years ago. He slapped a hand hard onto Paddy's shoulder.

'Going? Of course I'm going!'

They left Renmark just as the sun was lifting, Harry and Paddy and the two other men, a little group of people to see them away, the sergeant among them. They rode down south and west to Berri, where another man was already on the road, and then south to Loxton and then edging into the west again through Wanbi to Tailem Bend and Murray Bridge, men in ones and twos turning off tracks and out of gates to ride with them, joining them from places off the Adelaide Road, from Waikerie and Tinkarrie and Mannum, from Pinnaroo on the Victorian border and up from Meningie and Strathalbyn. By the time they topped Mount Pleasant and looked down on Adelaide and the sea, there were more than forty of them, Harry on the golden Harlequin at their head. And they rode into the city like that, along North Terrace to the white block of the Barracks with the guns pointing outwards from the gravel parade-ground corners.

Paddy waited outside the Barracks, Harlequin's rein looped over his wrist as he sat his own horse. He was edgy, nervous. Adelaide was a small and quiet city, but it still made him jumpy. Especially knowing what was coming. He looked across the gravel to the two sentries there, mounted and still, one on either side of the archway. The parade-ground was busy, even now, close to six in the evening, with a file of men in stable-gear moving across it picking up small pieces of litter, and a raucous corporal over on the other side, roaring the step to a fire-picquet marching to their post. And there was Harry, swinging towards him, a gleam of amusement in his eyes. Paddy looked at him, trim in khaki and polished leather, the boots and spurs gleaming, the side of the slouch hat clipped up and letting the last of the light fall on his face. He looked fine.

'Merciful God, 'tis a general at the very least!'

Harry's hands went to Harlequin, and he grinned at Paddy as he mounted.

'Not yet, you mad Irishman, but just you wait!' He slapped the other man on the shoulder. 'How are you, Paddy?'

'Oh, well enough, well enough.' They turned the horses and walked them along the Terrace. 'I've got the place I want, Harry, while you've been playin' soldiers. Thirty miles it is, about, and just a few acres. Enough room for a few vegetables and a run for the horses.'

Harry leaned forward. 'And how d'you like that, Harlequin, eh?' The horse heard his name and danced a little, pricking his ears. 'I wish I could take him with me, Pad. – the first lot took their own. He'd enjoy it; and God knows what sort of hacks they'll find us over there!'

'Ah, he'll be right enough with me, y'know that. There's good grass, an' I'll take care of him. Don't worry now.' They rode for a while in silence, wheeling through the parkland and heading back towards the Barracks. Harry had an hour's leave. When they saw the guardpost lights, Paddy said, 'It's been six weeks now. When are ye off then, d'ye know?'

'Tomorrow.' He didn't see Paddy's start, the look of pain. 'Big march through the city first. Will you stay over and see us go through?' Paddy coughed and covered the sudden shake in his voice with a laugh. 'Not me, boyo, not me! I don't like crowds. An' soldierin's somethin' I can do without.' He reached out and grabbed Harry's arm, pulling both horses to a stop. 'Are ye sure ye wouldn't want to cut and run now, Harry? We could be away and home tomorrow night, you and me. And Harlequin!'

'You know I couldn't do that, Paddy, even if I wanted to.' They moved on. 'Look, I've got a fresh hand of cards here, old friend. I haven't had a drink these past six weeks, did you know? I'm as fit as I've ever been. I think I'm cut out for a war. I *want* to go!'

'Ah, ye would, ye would. Well, ye'll do as ye want, Harry Morant. Ye've never done a damn thing else!'

They were back at the corner of the parade-ground. Harry sat quite still for a moment, reins slack, one hand absently sliding down Harlequin's neck. Then he dismounted and passed the rein to Paddy. 'Paddy, will you promise me about Harlequin? No one rides him till I get back. Promise?'

'Ye have my word on it. He'll not have a saddle to his back. Not till ye come home.'

Harry patted Harlequin again, and the horse nudged at his pocket with a damp muzzle, looking for the sugar which wasn't there this time.

Paddy's hand was square and hard in Harry's, the grip firm and long.

Then Harry spun about and Paddy watched him go, marching easily across the gravel in the shadows, turning for a second to wave in the archway under the light, between the mounted sentries and then gone.

Paddy looked at the empty space and said it again, quietly. 'Not till ye come home, Harry.'

SOUTH AFRICA

Under the loom of Table Mountain, the dock at Cape Town looked like an open-air madhouse. Harry leaned on the rail watching the gangs of Kaffirs walking the mooring ropes to bollards, watching the troops and the naval shore-parties scurrying about, listening to the roar of voices crossing one another in commands and curses, topped by the shrilling of whistles and the gun-thunder made by the wheels of a long string of carts and wagons on the wooden setts of the dock. There was a band playing in the shade of a warehouse and a guard drawn up in review order near them. It was probable, Harry thought, that only the guard could hear the band with all that din. Certainly from the rail of the transport only an occasional treble squeak could be picked out, the bandsmen seeming to be puppets, playing without sound.

Ted Hewett alongside him shook his head admiringly. 'You've gotta give the Pommies credit, you blokes. They really know how to make a fella fell welcome. You wouldn't get a shivoo like this anywhere else, now wouldya?'

'Bloody hope not!' Owen Fisher, on the other side of Hewett, spat down over the side of the ship. 'If this is how they carry on about unloadin' one lousy ship, what the bloody hell are they gointa to be like when it comes to a fight?'

'Harry? Oy, you're one of *them* – are they always like that?' Ted Hewett was grinning, one eye winking at Fisher.

Harry kept his face straight. 'I'll tell you, Ted. It's all a very clever ruse. They do it to confuse the enemy into thinking they don't know what's what, you see.'

Fisher spat again. 'Yair, well I'd say they're doin' a pretty fair job of confusin' *me* for a start.' From behind them a bugle sounded and Fisher pushed himself upright. 'There ya go, lads. That cruise is over an' the excursion's just about to get under way. Move along.'

'Harry an' me'll be along in a minute. You go on, Owen, if ya want.'

'Nice of you, Corporal Hewett!' Fisher's voice was quiet, but the snap in it pulled the other two upright. 'Now, you and Trooper Morant might just do me a favour. Move!'

Ted, his face assuming a wide-eyed stare of panic, saluted left-handed.

Harry bowed, deeply and gracefully, sweeping his slouch hat along the deck. Fisher's grim face cracked in a grin. 'I'll see you jokers later. If you can manage to tear yourselves away.'

He wheeled and moved along the deck, chivvying troopers to their disembarkation stations and Harry winked at Ted. 'Nice chap, Fisher. For a sergeant.'

Ted brushed his two chevrons casually. 'Yair; well now he's gone. *I'm* in charge here, Morant. And you heard what the sarge said – move!' He ducked under Harry's flat-handed swipe and they headed forward, into the mass of men forming ranks near the brow of the ship.

On the dock, the Second South Australian Yeomanry stood easy, the men turning to watch the activity round them, pointing, chattering. From the transport ship they'd just left, slings from derrick arms were lowering nets filled with ther kitbags, with boxes and bales of supplies, with odd bundles of miscellaneous military gear.

Further aft, a gang of mixed sailors and gunners were swinging out one of the six field-pieces which had come with them and there was a growing pile of material building on the dock, kaffirs swarming all over it under the tongue-lashing of a red-faced Ordnance sergeant. The wagons were rolling forward slowly, ready to be loaded and move the stuff away, and the band was still playing, behind them now and audible to some extent. Off to one side were several British officers and, from where he stood, Harry looked at them, recognizing some of the badges, some of the elegant uniforms. They were snapped up to attention almost at once, Regimental Sergeant-Major Maitland yelping at them, then stumping to where the C.O. and the officers were grouped. Half a minute later the officers were saluting and moving to their squadrons, and the C.O. was marching stiffly to meet a British staff colonel, their hands coming to their hat-brims as they met.

'Good morning, sir. Morrissey, Second South Australian Yeomanry.'

'Morning, Morrissey. Welcome to the war.' The colonel looked along the ranks of the Australians and consulted a slip of paper. 'Two hundred and eighteen, I believe?'

'Right, sir. All present and correct. No casualties, no sick; and anxious to get going, if I might say so.'

'Yes, of course.' There was no warmth in the words, only something close to condescension, and he hadn't looked up from the paper to see Morrissey's flush. 'Well, we've got some livestock for you round the corner somewhere, I daresay. You'll be in the camp-lines out to the north of the town with the rest of us, naturally.' He glanced at the waiting troops again. 'Bit – er – shoddy, are they, Morrison? Those their best uniforms?'

'Morrissey, sir. And those are the only uniforms they – *we've* got, apart from stable gear.' He tried to mask his anger.

'Ah? I thought it *was* stable gear. Never mind – the quarter-bloke might be able to find you something a little more suitable ... the officers, anyway.'

Out of the corner of his eye, Morrissey could see Fishburn, his adjutant, face scarlet with the repressed desire to hit out, but the colonel spoke again before anything happened, looking up as he tucked the paper into his pocket.

'Well, now, I'll send someone along to show you where to pick up your mounts and guide you to your lines. Oh – and the general would like you and your – er – officers to dine with him tonight.' His pale eye went up and down Morrissey. 'Informally, of course. Eight o'clock in the Mess.'

Morrissey's hand was still at the salute when the colonel flicked two fingers at him and walked away.

Fishburn let out a gust of breath. 'Jesus Christ all-bloody mighty! Sorry, sir, but if that bastard's what all these bastards are like I'm – I'm going to desert and fight on the other bloody side!'

'Hold up, Len, hold up! I don't believe there's another bastard in the world like *that* one! Let's get our blokes moving, shall we?'

Sergeant Owen Fisher looked at his horse with some disbelief. He gave it a gentle punch on the shoulder and shook his head when the mare swung a complacent eye round at him and then slumped again. Fisher walked to where his troop commander stood. 'Mr Cowan, sir, a word with you?'

'Hallo, Owen. What's your problem?'

'Me horse, sir. She's a nice old thing. 'Bout as big as a good-sized dog, she is, an' very quiet. I mean she's asleep, properly speakin'. I'm a bit afraid to get on 'er in case she falls down.'

Cowan bit back the smile as he looked up at Fisher's six-foot-three-high poker face. 'Perhaps you could carry her, Sergeant.' He lifted a hand to stem the outburst. 'Look, Owen, if you've kept your eyes open you'll have seen we're all in pretty much the same boat.'

Further along, Morrissey and the R.S.M. were in conference.

'Well, Mr Maitland, they're a job lot, aren't they? I don't think you'd make much out of them if you had *them* up for auction at y'yard, do you?'

'I asked one of those Remount johnnies where they come from, Colonel. D'y'know what he said? Said about half out of a hack stables in the city an' the rest was saved from a glue factory they've got set up here somewhere!' Maitland was a solid, tough man, but he looked like a wounded child, and Morrissey gave a ruefully sympathetic smile. 'Nothing we can do about it at the moment, anyway. Maybe I can talk to the general tonight. In the meantime, what's happened to the saddles and equipment?'

Maitland gestured to the long shed behind them and the file of men heading into it. 'Being issued now, sir. God knows what *they'll* be like!'

Gloomily, they looked at the scene, the Australian troops struggling with their new and unfamiliar equipment, the air solid with curses. A dozen N.C.O.s in British cavalry uniforms were desperately trying to show them how to stow everything.

Little Peter Pullen, the smallest man in Harry's troop, stood chin up to a Hussar corporal. 'What's this fuckin' saddle made *out* of, mate, cast iron?'

The trim corporal stared down, glowering. 'For a start, cocky, don't call me mate, call me Corporal, and stand to attention.'

'Get fucked!'

The Hussar gasped three times before he got the words clear. 'I'll have you! You miserable little Colonial bleeder, I'll have you on a charge so fast –'

'Aw, git out of it! Can't you jokers make yer own argument stick? Whaddya wanna start talkin' about charges for? Yer breeches is pretty, but yer a lotta gutless wonders!'

The Hussar's fists clenched, but he checked himself and spun round calling, 'Sergeant!'

Owen Fisher's quiet voice grated right beside him. 'Yair. What's the trouble, son?'

Eyes flicking over Fisher's tunic and chevrons, the Hussar said stiffly, 'I was calling for Sergeant Jackson of Ours.'

'Well, I'm Sergeant Fisher. Of Somebody else's mind, but I'm still one of Her Sainted Majesty's Holy Sergeants.' The voice was suddenly a whiplash. 'Stand to attention, Corporal.'

The Hussar stiffened and went rigid under Fisher's gaze as he walked slowly round him, examining him from head to toe.

'Very nice! Very nice indeed!' Several of the Australians were bunched around them now grinning, and Fisher spoke to them. 'Trooper Pullen, you midget misery, you, 'ave a good squint at this man. All of ya, 'ave a look. That's a soldier, that is. That's what British soldiers look like, see? Cavalryman, this one. See 'ow lovely 'is uniform fits, and not a mark on 'im anywhere. Brasses like gold, spurs like silver, face all scrubbed. Beautiful!' The Hussar twitched. 'Stand *still*, Corporal! Now then, you crude colonials, just because this man may not 'ave the brains of a sheep in a snowdrift, just because 'e may not 'ave the manners of a blackfeller with a bottle of gin, 'e *looks* like a soldier, so you treat 'im with proper respect, see? Don't make fun of 'im, nor yet the 'orses he's give us, nor yet the saddles an' stuff.'

Ted Hewett and Harry had drifted into the listening crowd, and Ted called out, 'Sounds like the Ten Commandments, Owen!'

'Well, 'ere's the Eleventh one then, Corporal Hewett. Get this mob moving and ready to ride out. I'm sure this corporal of cavalry will excuse us simple Colonial volunteers.' He gave the Hussar a final malevolent glare. 'Go on, son, run away, Dismiss!'

The flushed and furious Hussar stalked away, the whistles and catcalls dying as the R.S.M. moved among them suddenly.

'Sergeant Fisher, what's going on here?'

'Nothin', Sar-Major. Just thankin' that corporal there for giving us the benefit of 'is expert knowledge.'

Maitland looked at him steadily, but his eyes were gleaming. 'Good for you! Now, less chat and more action. The boss wants us away.'

That evening they sat around their gear, bellies full and pipes and rolled cigarettes thickening the air in the tent, dulling the light from the single lamp hung to the centre pole.

'Christ, my arse hasn't been as sore as this since m'father took a belt to it!' Hewett shifted from one hip to the other on the blanket padded under him.

'It's those bloody saddles – made out of teak, they are.' Peter Pullen, standing, felt his backside with care and lowered himself with even more care onto his bedroll. 'Goes right through t'the bone.'

Harry stretched himself luxuriously, flat on his back with his stockinged feet propped on the tentpole. 'The trouble with you people is you're not really used to riding. You're all aristocratic folk, y'see, used to putting your bums down on cushions, of course. Undoubtedly—' His voice choked off as Fisher tossed a loose blanket over his head, and when he dragged it off, Greville leaned across and said earnestly, 'Hey, Breaker – you're a Pommy – why the hell would they want to make saddles like them?'

'Damned if I know, Bernie. I'm inclined to think we'd be better off bareback than on those things. And don't call me a Pommy.'

Fisher, cross-legged on an ammunition-box, blew smoke into the pitch of the tent. 'T'ain't just the saddles, Harry, it's the whole bloody shebang as far as I can tell. I reckon that poor old mare I was up on 'ad sixty pounds useless weight on 'er.'

Jewett leapt at the opening. 'Git out, Owen, you weigh more than sixty pounds, mate!'

Harry's voice rose above the roar of laughter. 'It's my belief the staff's still fighting in the Crimea ... wouldn't be surprised if Florence Nightingale turned up any moment now.'

'With a few of 'er nurses, eh?'

'Gawd, I c'd use a woman just about now!'

The interrupting voice stopped the banter dead. 'Well, you lot sound happy enough.'

The man with his head through the tent-flap was a stranger; brick-red face with an enormous black moustache halving it and a dark-blue cap topping it, the field-gun badge glinting in the dull light. He looked around the silent group.

'Er, don't let me put a damper on things, mateys. Only came along to see how you was settling in.'

Owen Fisher said flatly, 'Thanks,' and the silence settled again. The man in the doorway coughed and stepped in, a haversack swinging from one hand. The three gold chevrons on his sleeve had a smaller version of the cap badge set over them. 'Farringdon. Troop Sergeant, G Battery, Royal Horse Artillery.'

'G'day.' Fisher had made no move. He let the word drop, watching as Farringdon glanced round at the silent men and cleared his throat again.

'Friendly lot of sods, aren't you? And me with a house-warming present.' He swung the haversack against his booted leg and bottles clinked.

Harry's eyes caught Fisher's, saw the gleam of laughter deep in them. The others were beginning to smile as their sergeant stood, stretching out a hand to the stranger. 'Ah – Owen Fisher, Second South Australian Yeomanry, all of us. Siddown, mate.' He shifted along the ammunition box to make way for Farrindon who unstrapped the haversack and passed out three bottles, dark and unlabelled.

Greville took one, holding it up to the light. 'What is it – oxblood?'

'It's a gift-'orse, Bernie.' Ted Hewett was working at a cork with his clasp knife. 'Don't look at its teeth, son.'

Harry held out a mug for Hewett to pour into and sipped at the dark red liquid. 'My God,' he choked, his eyes streaming. 'Take care, you lot, it's loaded.'

'Local brew.' Farringdon took a deep draught from the neck of the bottle he'd opened. 'Our Mess buys it by the dozen.' He looked at them all, considering them. 'Do I get the feeling you don't think much of us? Not that I was listening – just you had your voices up a bit.'

Harry coughed again and answered, 'I'm afraid we've had rather a bellyful of the British Army today, Sergeant Farringdon. Nothing against you, of course–'

'Specially since I bought some booze, eh?' Farringdon had cocked an ear at Harry's voice.

Little Peter Pullen took the bottle from his lips long enough to say, 'Y'see, it appears your Army's got some bloody funny ideas, mate, that's about the strength of it.'

'Not used to ridin' scraggy cattle, Sarge.' Greville's rumble rode over the top of Pullen's thin voice. 'With a cartload of rubbish tied on front an' bloody back.'

'An' saddles as sharp as a dingo's backbone.' That was Hewett, again changing hips.

Farringdon nodded solemnly. 'Uh, huh – bit soft are you?' He ignored the way the smiles disappeared. 'You'll harden, my sons. Believe me, you'll harden.'

Harry deliberately let the edge in his voice show through. 'There's a difference between hardening and setting solid. Seems to me that's what you chaps have done. Set solid – between the ears.'

In the silence, Farringdon pointed a long finger at Harry. 'That's my stuff you're drinking there. I don't have a lot of time for a man who'll miscall me while he's drinking out of my bottle.'

Feeling the tension, Owen Fisher broke in on them, turning himself to face Farringdon beside him. 'That's fair enough. What did you say your first handle was?'

'Arthur.' Farringdon hadn't taken his eyes from Harry and he was leaning a little forward towards him.

'Fair enough then, Arthur. We got no quarrel with you, mate. Have we, Morant?' He swung to Harry, barking the last words at him. Harry's grin flashed.

'No, of course not. Sorry old son – it's your lords and masters we're grumbling about.'

Farringdon relaxed, his face loosening and he drank again. 'My lords and masters, eh? You couldn't grumble any more'n we do, I tell you that!' He suddenly realized what had caught his ear before. 'Here, you're not Australian though. You're from Home.'

'A long way from Home, Arthur.'

The last of the tension went. The bottles circulated and the gunner moved to the ground, leaning back against the ammunition box. 'You'll get used to it soon enough. Once you get up against the old Boer you'll be surprised how everything seems to fall into line.'

'What's it like? Up there?' Fisher's question drew them all a little closer, all watching Farringdon.

'Like? Another bloody world! Not like any war I was ever in, I tell you that. I never fought a white man before, for a start, not in a battle I mean. Makes a difference.'

Ted Hewett, irrepressible, chipped in. 'Makes 'em easier to 'it in the dark, don't it?' ... but Farringdon didn't join in the laughter.

'You have your fun while you can, son. You'll be laughing the other side of your face before long. If you got a face left, that is.'

They were silent again, thinking about that, till Fisher spoke. 'But they're not soldiers, are they? I mean, they're not even

short-timers like us; no training nor nothing from what we've
'eard.'

'No, they're buggerall like us, Digger. No uniforms, no supply-
columns, no base camps. And no rules. Everyone of them's against
us – women, nippers, the lot.'

'But we're winning?'

Farringdon looked over at Greville. 'I dunno what you call
winning. We got a lot of country under our belt and a fair few
prisoners, but we can't seem to hold the bastards down. See, you
send out a column and there'll be twenty or thirty of the Dutchmen
up on a bit of a hill ... and you never see 'em.' His voice was low
and they craned in to listen, held by his intensity. 'A Boer can tuck
himself away in a crease in the countryside you couldn't hide a
rabbit in. And he'll wait there all day for you, right there in the sun,
no food, no water. Patient sod, he is. And when you turn up, he'll
put a bullet in you neat as range practice!' He slapped his knee with
a big hand, startling them out of their stillness. 'And then he's off
and away before you know what's happened, and half-a-dozen
good blokes with their heads blown out. More, sometimes.' He
drank deep again. 'Very dodgy bird, the old Boer.'

The general said, 'But I think we've got the measure of him,
gentlemen, we've got his measure,' and listened with obvious
pleasure to the murmur of agreement.

The Mess tent was beautifully disguised. The canvas walls were
hidden under dark blue drapes made, Morrissey suspected, from
Army issue blankets. There was a framed portrait of of the Queen
at the far end, behind the General's chair, and it was flanked by
cased colours. Two long side tables held a display of silver trophies,
and the dining table itself was a-glitter with silverware. There were
lamps burning brightly from a number of the support poles and two
candelabra of tall candles gave a warm glow to the forty or so
officers now slumping comfortably as the port circulated on a
miniature gun-limber and the cigars stung the air.

With the exception of the Australians, all the officers were in
Mess kit or regimentals, Morrissey's 2 i/c, Major Young, who'd
brought the rear party into camp late in the afternoon, had hissed
in Morrissey's ear when they arrived, 'I though you said it was
informal, Bill!' and Morrissey had whispered back, '*They* said it
was. Maybe this isn't full dress for them.' Alan Young had taken
another long look and muttered, 'What do they wear when they're
going flat out – golden armour?'

The General had made them welcome, greeting them in a haze of sherry, but the overall reception had been cool enough to keep the Australians, especially the junior officers, fairly tightly bunched before dinner. At the table, scattered among the other diners, they listened with some puzzlement to drawled conversations about parties in Cape Town, the possibility of organizing a pack of hounds for a drag, a cricket match played the previous Saturday between regiments, and a wide variety of minor scandals and major slanders. It wasn't till the port arrived that the talk turned to the campaign.

Major Young, thrusting and aggressive, listened to the general rumbling about having taken the Boer's measure, leaned forward and said, 'I understand from what we heard today, sir, that you've been taking some quite heavy casualties.'

The British officers looked at Young, a concentrated gaze filled with something close to pity, although the surgeon sitting well down the table, a sombre patch of unadorned dark blue, nodded his head. The general was unperturbed. 'Always casualties in battle, m'dear fellow.'

The surgeon's voice was a bitter intrusion. 'I don't get many Boers to treat, sir.'

''Course you don't! Bloody Boer takes 'em off with him, doesn't he, eh?' A languid Lancer major drawled down the length of the table. 'I don't really believe you can get a true picture of battle tactics, Doctor, from a vantage point in your – er – butcher's shop.'

In the spurt of laughter at the surgeon's expense, Young caught Morrissey's eye in some disgust. Morrissey shook his head and frowned for his second-in-command to keep quiet. He waited till the laughter had died before speaking up to the head of the table.

'It does seem from what we've been told that the Boer's fighting a rather unorthodox war, sir. How do we tackle him ... in the orthodox way?'

'The Boer's not fighting a war at all, Morrissey.' For the first time the general seemed to be angry. 'He's a rebel, fighting a rebellious action. No different from any other native rising, eh, gentlemen?' The murmur rose again, the Lancer major rapping the table with his fingers and sliding out a distorted 'Hear, hear!'

The general sipped at his port. 'A rising, Morrissey – and it'll be put down by punitive action, just as we've always put the natives down when they've got above themselves.'

Young couldn't stop himself. 'With respect, sir, mightn't we be better off fighting them with their own tactics? I mean if—'

The staring silence was so profound that his words seemed to sink away in it.

The staff colonel who'd met Morrissey when they disembarked sent his voice slashing along the table at Young. 'My dear, good chap! What an appalling suggestion! You couldn't seriously expect the British Army to throw away everything it stands for and go into the field like – like some collection of backwood farmers?'

Young flushed angrily under the insolent lash, but it was Ian Burgess who'd been simmering right at the end of the table, who bit back dryly.

'Maybe it's because most of us *are* backwoods farmers, sir!'

'Now, now, now, gentlemen!' The general was affable again. 'Morley here meant no disrespect. But what he said is quite correct, of course. We're not just an army – we're the British Army, all of us. And we have certain standards to maintain.'

The surgeon muttered, loud enough for almost everyone to hear, 'No matter how many men get killed.'

The general didn't hear and plunged on. 'We have certain tried and tested methods to use. We've always been successful because of our discipline and our methods, and we shall be successful again, naturally. Just you get your chaps into line with ours, learn to understand the way we do things and you'll do jolly well, jolly well indeed.'

Morrissey inclined his head. 'As you say, sir.'

The general rose and the rest shoved back their camp chairs and stood waiting. 'Well then, gentlemen, time we were in bed, I think. No horseplay for you younger chaps tonight, I'm afraid – early start in the morning, eh?'

The Australians clustered together behind Morrissey as the general moved from his place and the rest of the diners began to head down to the door. The general placed a friendly hand on Morrissey's arm. 'Colonel Morrissey, gentlemen, a pleasure to have had you as our guests. From tomorrow we shall be comrades-in-arms, what? Just you watch the way we do things, my boys, and I'm sure we shall be proud of you all!'

From behind Morrissey, the surgeon said, his voice sad, 'That's right, Colonel, just you watch the way we do things.'

The country was waiting for rain. There was a stillness in the hot air which was almost a throb, not a silence and yet not quite sound. Somewhere in it was the muted rustle of a fitful ground-breeze in paper-dry trees and the flutter of the little dikkop birds. All waiting for rain. Especially the Boers, Harry thought.

The little column straggled easily along half a mile of shade where a low ridge humped to its right, the flankers up there silhouetted occasionally against the afternoon sky as they moved. The flankers out to the left and the scouts ahead were invisible in the haze and across the long undulations of the land, but knowing they were there meant that A Squadron could relax to some extent and Harry was letting his horse walk with the others while he half-dozed.

What was it that Scottie sergeant had said the other day – that the Boer commandos were back there in the hills somewhere waiting for the rain? That was it – they wouldn't come out in any kind of strength till the grass was up and green so their horses had fodder wherever they went. Made sense.

He shifted in the saddle, easing himself, the insides of his breeches wet with sweat. The horse they'd given him back there at the Cape hadn't lasted the train journey north and he supposed himself lucky to get anything at all to ride, but the placid beast he was on now was as broad-backed as a plough-horse and uncomfortable to sit for long even at this pace. Dubbin and boiling rags and pounding with a bootheel had at least reduced the saddle to something like a seat, but the two-and-a-half foot picket pegs with their ironshod tips were still crossed behind him, lashed to the cantle regulation style and ripping at the thighs on mounting or dismounting. Under command of the Lancers as they had been, they'd found the regulations hard to get away from and they were getting tired of these pointless patrols. The one chance for action back there at the Modder River had been thwarted when they were held in reserve and sat about all day listening to the rumours rattling as sharp as the rifle-fire.

They moved out of the shade of the ridge, and the flare of sunlight pulled his head up to look up the column: Tregaskis at the head with Owen Fisher, then Burgess' troop, then young Cowan leading theirs. Beyond the head of the column a patch of flat country with another, higher ridge to the left a little.

When Tregaskis' hand went up, Harry glanced at the sun, estimating the time at about three. The column halted while the captain and Fisher checked a map, then moved forward again, wheeling left-handed on the start of its return leg; and Peter Pullen, riding to Harry's right, blinked his dusty eyes and said, 'We goin' back, are we?'

'Looks like it, Peter. Be nearly dark by the time we get there, too.'

Peter was nodding dozily when the man in front of him jerked backwards off his horse, and he reined in, startled, before any of them heard the crack of the Mauser. Harry heard a sharp hiss in the air by his head before anything else, but then it seemed as though the air was full of the hissing sounds and the echoes of rifle-fire from the ridge, now on their left. He yanked his horse's head, fighting to pull the sluggish beast towards the dead ground below the hump of the rise as Pullen went past him shouting, 'Come on, Harry – don't just bloody sit there!'

For thirty seconds there was total confusion, Tregaskis shouting unheard orders at the head of the column, Owen Fisher racing past at a hand-gallop roaring at them to dismount, two men down, one rocking in the saddle and screaming, the blood pouring down his chest from a torn throat. And then there was Cowan with Ted Hewett knee-to-knee with him, turning back along his own troop and waving and calling; 'My troop – come with me, my troop!'

By the time a dozen men had heard him and followed, Cowan and Ted were in the lee of the ridge, dismounted and staring upwards cautiously. Harry slid down alongside them, the others clumping against the rock. Cowan had his Webley in his hand and looked half grim, half boyish excited.

'Right, lads. There's a gully there, looks like cover all the way round and up to that little pimple; see it? Up we go, then.'

Ted Hewett, not smiling, said, 'Bayonets, sir?'

'Yes. Hurry now.'

Harry doubted they'd get close enough for that, but there was a feeling of muscle somehow in locking that fourteen inches of steel onto the muzzle of the Lee-Metford. Everyone had said it – the Boer doesn't like the blade.

From the other ridge, the two scouts could see back across the open patch from where they lay on their stomachs, pulled flat by the sound of the first shot. Below the ridge they could see the bulk of the column deployed along the base of the ridge, some of them beginning to inch upwards. Two little forms lay still in the dust and a riderless horse was running aimlessly loose.

'Christ, that was quick! Can you see 'em?'

The second scout squinted down and back. 'No, not a bloody sign. You can't spot that smokeless powder they use. Hey up – yair – see in that patch of rocks there? I just caught a snatch of a move.'

'Miserable bastards! They let us go right through –'

'You thank yer lucky stars they did, Mick, else you'd be down there with a hole in ya like them others.'

Staring, they saw the other movement.

'Who is it, Cowan?'

'Looks like it. Cowan an' Fisher, I think. Harry Morant. The little one must be Pete Pullen.'

'Gonna work up that gully an' get behind 'em by the look of it.'

'Y'reckon? Good luck to 'em.'

He turned onto his back and began to roll a smoke.

High up the gully, Cowan stopped, head cocked, shoulder pressed into the rock. Beyond him there was only sky over the ridge. He turned, mouthing silent orders and gesturing the men behind him into position. Fisher took four of them across to the other side of the narrow cleft and Harry closed up on Cowan, hearing the young lieutenant's shallow rasp of breath, seeing his back tense and his legs set to spring. When Cowan moved, they all went with him, bursting over the lip of the ridge. The Boers were a little below them, eight, ten of them spread along a hundred feet of false crest and the shots from their rear smacking into and round them sent them scattering at once, one of them pitching headlong, one staggering. Cowan suddenly spun about at Harry's side, gasping, his hand going to the reddening patch on his thigh. Below him, Fisher was bounding down the rocks, the others behind him, the long blades gleaming, their shouts echoing off the rocks. Harry heard the clash of a bullet on the rock above Cowan's head and felt the chips sting his face as he ducked, pulling the wounded man lower. A quick look from low behind cover showed the Boers streaming for their horses – there, in a hollow on the reverse slope – and above the horses, a youngster with a rifle. Cowan rolled over, grunting with pain, and peered over Harry's shoulder as he saw the Lee-Metford go up and steady. They both watched as the lad slammed backwards and disappeared. The Boers were away now, two of them on one horse, the rest hurtling down the rough slope to the plain below, the Australians sending a few shots after them. Cowan's voice was thin with pain.

'Good shooting, Harry. Well done. First blood, eh?'

'Only a colt, sir. Pity it hadn't been a stallion.'

He slung his rifle and stooped to pull Cowan across his back.

Cowan wasn't badly hurt, the bullet, at close range, having gone clean through the meat of his thigh without touching bone. He'd heal quickly enough and in the meantime, Owen Fisher was being chiaked about his temporary command of the troop and Ted Hewett was suddenly very serious as an acting troop-sergeant. They'd lost two dead and five wounded, one badly, in return for only one dead Boer. They'd stood around looking down at him, an elderly man with a solid grey beard, his long coat dusty and bloodstained over a work shirt and whipcord trousers. Bernie Greville had growled, 'Buggered if he looks like a soldier. Looks like old Mullins used to keep the shop at Five Corners 'n' preach Baptist on Sundays.'

Harry, belly full of stew, mind on the afternoon's deaths, walked to the edge of their camp where the medical cart stood, the rifle on his shoulder. There were two men in the cart, one moaning in his sleep, one still. Under a rough shelter of strung blankets lay the Boer boy Harry had shot, eyes wide on the doctor who'd been attached to them, an elderly Englishman from Cape Town. He was stooping over a man from Burgess' troop, tying off a bandage around the man's head, and he turned when he heard Harry's footsteps, lowering the man's head gently and rising. Harry stopped, looking down on the young Boer, a dark-haired boy, perhaps fifteen, face white and shining with sweat, the bandages across his chest and shoulder stained with dried blood.

The doctor watched for a second, then moved closer. 'Taking a look at your handiwork, Morant? The boy's shoulder's gone – you smashed the bone to pieces.'

Harry, unspeaking, stared down at the boy, meeting the sullen glare.

The doctor's voice was angry. 'I thought you came out here to fight men, not to cripple children.'

Harry turned on him slowly, slipping the rifle from his shoulder, and the doctor flinched. 'He was carrying this. Loaded. He shot young Cowan with it.' Harry held it out to the doctor. 'Look at it. It's British, a Metford. It must have belonged to one of our own people. I wonder how this – child – got hold of it? Or how many men he's shot with it?'

He swung suddenly to face the boy lying at his feet, the rifle muzzle dropping, his fingers snapping the bolt back and forward, loading and cocking. The doctor started forward convulsively, hand outstretched in appeal and the boy under the blankets froze, his mouth open in fear. Harry held the muzzle steady on the boy's head for a long, long second, then worked the bolt back again, ejecting the rounnd in the breech and reversed the rifle grasping the barrel, raising it and smashing the stock down on the ground, striking downwards again and again till the weapon broke. He threw down the pieces and walked away, the doctor, white and shaken, staring after him, the boy crying now in great, tearing sobs.

Farrier-Sergeant Pollock was a beefy man, suety, pink and white like pork, fingers like sausages and a head, as Pullen once remarked, 'Same size, same shape, same 'ardness as a chopping-block.' He spotted the man he wanted, sitting in the shade of a supply cart, and plodded across, the bulk of his shadow attracting the man's attention.

'G'day, Morant. I wanna talk to you about a little bit of a job I got in mind.'

'Haven't you heard, Sarge – we've got three days' rest. And that's just what I'm doing.' Harry stretched elaborately and relaxed again. Pollock hunkered down beside him, flopping a very big hand on his shoulder.

'Look, Morant, I've butchered steers bigger'n you. I wouldn't want to think you was being awkward or anything.'

Harry opened his eyes and looked into the steady gaze of the farrier, realizing he was serious. 'Righto. I can't beat you. I'd better join you.' He sat up and took a cigarette from a flat tin, offering one to Pollock and lighting them both. Pollock looked at him, head on one side.

'I wanna get one thing straight first. I know it's said, but I wanna be sure. You *are* the right Morant? The one they call The Breaker?' Harry nodded, wondering. 'Goodoh. then I got a job that's just your mark. I want you to pinch some horses.'

Harry stared at him. 'Hold on, now, you're not serious! I'm not a bloody horse-duffer, Pollock.'

'Simmer down, simmer down. The way I see it is if you pinch something from the Army – specially the British Army – it's not really stealing at all. D'y'agree with me?'

'Well, yes, I suppose so. But horses?'

'Right. See, the boss bailed me up just now and he says we're mounted like a lot of drunk clowns – as though we didn't know it – and he wants something done about it. He says we got three days to pull the horses into shape and I tells him it can't be done because they're no good from the off –'

'That's true enough.'

'Right. So he tells me to do something about it, and when I asks him what I'm supposed to do he says he don't much care. Just so long as I do *something*.'

'Well, that seems straightforward enough. So you're going to steal some, is that it?'

'No, son. You are.' The big hand went up, stopping Harry's reply.

'Now wait on. I can't do it – I'm too damn big and slow for this kind of a job. But *you* can. You've got a way with horses – everyone knows that. And all you'll have to do is snaffle 'em. I've done all the organizing.'

'That's very civil of you! What's it supposed to mean?'

'It means that if you take a bit of a stroll round the back edge of this place, you'll see there's a sort of a house over in the corner of the lines. It's Headquarters, and the Brass lives there and has their scoff there and there's a lot of nice clean tents roundabout where the base whallahs live. Know where I mean?'

'I think so.'

'And behind that house there's some horse lines. Very nicely laid out, they are, and there's dry standing for the beasts and two nice English sentries plodding up and down all night.'

'God in Heaven, you're not seriously talking about swiping the staff horses? You'll get me shot!'

'Never! Not if you use a bit of common. See now. We're supposed to hoof off out of here before dawn on Thursday. That gives you tonight and tomorrow night to have a good squiz at the place, then you go in and pinch the stock say about three o'clock Thursday and we're off and away.'

'Oh, bloody wonderful! You're mad, Pollock, you're a lunatic.'

'I'm also the farrier-*sergeant*, Corporal Morant, so watch your tongue.'

'But there wouldn't be anything like enough horses there —'

'Enough for the colonel and the officers, most likely. And you can take your pick of what's left. How about that?'

'Very generous.' Harry was hard put to it not to laugh at the impudence of the scheme. 'Look, I couldn't do it on my own. I'd have to have some fellows with me.'

'Up to you, son. Just so long as you get it done.'

From inside the supply cart against which Harry was leaning, Owen Fisher's voice echoed, mordant and muffled. 'Harry, you make a move without me an' I'll 'ave yer tripes for picket-ropes!'

Morissey had watched Pollock go and had called Fishburn, his adjutant.

'I'm not going to see the brigadier on my own Len. I need some help ... and I want someone else there if he turns me down.'

Headquarters, in the sprawling house Pollock had told Harry about, was an elegant and smoothly organized bustle. The general, immaculate in a scarlet tunic, greeted the two Australians cordially and spread a map across the table between them, anchoring it with — as Fishburn later told the Mess with delight — a velvet case filled with medals and decorations, a silver mug of brandy, a lady's shoe hall full of Havana cigars and a fox mask mounted on a small wooden plaque. As Fishburn said, 'You could see the old josser's whole life laid out there on the corners of the map.'

Jabbing his finger down like a drill, the general rapidly ran through a summary of his own dispositions of troops and his assumptions of where the enemy was and in what strength, then sat down, apparently exhausted by the explanation. There were no chairs on the other side of the desk and Morrissey looked down on the general when he spoke.

'That's very clear, sir, but we are sure about the Boer? That he *is* holed up across there?'

''Course we're sure! I've had vedettes from the South African Horse out that way for a week now and the Jocks have made two patrols in some force and received fire. Logical place for the Boer to be anyway, you see – all that high ground there.'

'Of course, sir, it's just that it seems a little too logical if you see what I mean.'

'No, dammit, I don't!'

'Well, if I was in their shoes, I should have a fairly strong position up here too—' Morrissey's finger sketched a line high on a rise of land almost at rightangles to the slopes the general had indicated. 'I don't believe I'd miss the chance to enfilade people attacking frontally across there.'

'Ah, yes, I see what you mean, Colonel. Quite. But I think you're giving the old Boer a little more credit than he deserves, don't you? He's not a soldier, you know.'

'Yes, sir.'

'Good. Well then, m'dear fellow, if you're quite clear—'

Fishburn muttered, 'Er, there was one other thing, sir—'

The general cocked a surprised eye at him. 'Not about the plan of attack, surely, Captain?'

Morrissey took over. 'No, not that, sir. But I was wondering – sir, may I be frank?'

'By all means, Morrissey! Don't hold back if there's something on your mind.'

'Well then, sir, you've got us brigaded with the lancers here, on the left of the centre-line. My fellows aren't cavalry, you see, not in the way your fellows understand it—'

'Oh, come now, that's too modest by half! Why, your Australian horsemen have reputations second to none. Whole Army knows that!'

'Horsemen, yes sir. But they've had no training as light cavalry-men, only as Yeomanry. We're Mounted Rifles, sir.'

'Ah now, you're quibbling, Colonel. The Lancers will be delighted to have you along, delighted! And – this is between ourselves of course – Henry Gore, their colonel, well, he's rather a fussy fellow. Won't ride with just anyone. And he told me personally that he'd be *most pleased* to take you along with him. There!'

The general beamed happily, missing the look of distaste on Morrissey's face at the thought of being 'taken along'.

'I'm sure we shall manage it, sir.'

The general was standing and an orderly appeared from nowhere at once with his hat, gloves and crop.

'There is just one other thing, sir.'

The general checked, the smile slipping easily from his instantly cold face. He made no response, just stood waiting, and Morrissey heard himself speaking rather too quickly.

'We have something of a problem with our horses. They're poor quality and the remounts we're getting are even worse—'

'I'm afraid we're all in the same boat, Morrissey. Not a decent nag to be had just now. I have written to Whitehall—'

He made a small, final gesture and began to pull on his gloves.

'Is there no chance—?'

'None whatever, Colonel. As I've just said, we're stretched to the limit.' The general let the smile slide back as he grasped Morrissey's arm, uging him towards the door, Fishburn trailing behind them with the orderly. 'Now then, what about a whisky-soda before Mess? I can't dine you tonight I'm afraid; my old regiment's putting on a dinner for me. No? Ah, then I shall see you at a later stage.'

The salute was a graceful wave of the crop and he was gone.

'Congratulations, sir.' Fishburn's voice was dry.

'Thanks. Now you see why I wanted you along. None of our blokes would believe it otherwise.'

There were four of them – Harry, Owen, Ted and little Peter – paler shadows in the deep shadows. Bernie Greville, like Pollock, had felt he was too big and awkward to come with them, but he was waiting back where the trees ran along the rear of the row of tents. There was no moon and the sky had darkened early, building rain-clouds moving in and hanging now in a thick pall that shut out the stars. Harry lowered himself quietly to the ground, pillowing his head on his folded forearms and letting his breathing slow. He felt a hand on his stockinged foot and then the others were close beside him as he slid his head around the back corner of the house smelling the horses thirty or so feet away. Looking round he could just see the others – Peter was on his left, Owen and Ted on his right, and Harry tapped Owen's shoulder and gestured for him to move. Owen's fingers touched Harry's shirt-sleeve, rubbed across the two chevrons there, then took Harry's hand to his own three chevrons, the gleam of his teeth a little bar of lightness. Without knowing whether the 'up you' signal could be seen, Harry made it into Owen's face and moved out, smiling.

Neither of the sentries heard them, shifting in their socks across the night-damp ground, up out of the blackness behind them at either end of the horse lines. A hand across the mouth pulling the head back, a knee in the small of the back and a twist to put the man down and the soft blapping noise of a flour sack with a pound of sand in it.

Ted and Peter came up, tugging their unconscious sentry with them, Ted swinging the man's rifle. Owen was already working on their man and he hissed up, 'Get his boots off. Take 'em an' the rifles an' the coats and any ammo. They'll think the Boer's been in.'

Harry had gone at once to the horses, hearing them jinking a little at the new noises, hearing a hoof pawing at the earth, a quiet snort of breath. Owen joined him as Harry's knife cut the running-line near a picket-peg and he slid the headropes off the cut end, murmuring to the sleepy horses as he did it, stroking their necks, chirruping gently to them. He worked along the lines, cutting the ropes, his face damp from the muzzles which came out to him, passing the headropes back to Owen then to Peter and Ted, just hearing them as they walked the horses quietly away into the night. Harry took the last three himself, adding in his mind till he reached thirty-four, finding it hard to suppress the laughter building in him.

As he joined the others with Bernie and the horses it began to rain and the soft hiss covered the little noises they made back to their tents where lamps were already flickering as the squadrons made ready to leave.

The colonel's galloper streaked back alongside the column, shouting for officers and troop-sergeants, his call floating behind him with the dust. Harry and Ted wheeled away from the troop, cantering ahead of them with the others towards the colonel. Morrissey looked unhappy, a paper in his hand and his mouth tight. He returned their salutes and looked round at them.

'Orders, gentleman. We're to move on up. H.Q. Troop, re-mounts and sick over in that gully there. The rest of us up on the left. We're to come under command of the Lancers.'

There was a groan from the group and a curse or two. Morrissey stared them down, waiting for silence.

'I said it was an order! We don't have to like it, but we obey it, understand? Right, column of squadrons, me leading. Go on.' He watched, waiting till the rearmost riders had reached their troop, then swung his horse about, Fishburn and Maitland behind him, at the head of the column. His raised arm moved them forward and they walked along the track, round the knoll on their left and on to the flat land sloping gently downwards towards the hills that cupped it. Glancing up as they rode into the open, Harry could see a cluster of men high on the forward slopes of the knoll, a scarlet coat, a blue coat and off to one side the sun-wink of a heliograph. Bernie Greville had followed his look and growled, 'Bloody staff. Well outa harm's way, as usual.'

They'd heard firing earlier in the morning as they'd moved up, but the valley ahead of them was silent now as they halted and Morrissey cantered forward to where the Lancers were deployed in line, the sun dancing along the rows of steel points high above the horses' heads.

Harry looked past the Lancers, lips puckering. 'They've been working at it, Bernie. Look there.' He pointed with his chin.

The ground ahead of them wasn't truly a valley. It was perhaps a mile-and-a-half long, running down to a ridge of grey-red rock which burst up out of the plain to a height of about four hundred feet, extending more than two miles across the gradual slope. At the left, the same ridge swung almost at right-angles, dipping a little at the join, then coming back towards them for close to half a mile. The knoll on which the staff stood looked as though it had broken away from this main mass in some volcanic upthrust. Away on their right was a belt of old and massy trees running along the twisted line of a watercourse.

Between them and the frontal face of the ridge, well towards the rocks themselves, they could see the pattern of the morning's work in the scattered figures lying still in the dusty grass, one or two moving a little from time to time. Beyond them and in the rubble at the base of the slope, the khaki dolls were more numerous, grouped closer. In one place there was a neat line of them.

Peter Pullen on the other side of Bernie, had edged his horse in a little close and spoke across the big man.

'Nasty sorta setup, Harry.'

'Usual Boer setup, Peter. Aren't you used to it yet?'

'Oh, *I'm* used to it all right, mate! Don't look as though them bastards is, though.' His scornful thumb jerked upwards towards the top of the knoll.

To the right of the Australian column and several hundred yards forward of them, the infantry were grouped, the men standing easy or sitting slumped on the ground while parties moved among them distributing ammunition and food. Behind them the medical wagons were busy and behind them again a couple of field-kitchens were sending up black smoke signals and the smell of stew carried back towards the Australians, mingling with the smell of spent cordite in the still air. On the ridge and its flanking ridge, there was no movement.

Morrissey rode to meet the Lancer colonel, a bulky, red-faced man with a large smile.

'Ah, Morrissey, we meet again!'

Morrissey reined in, eyes on the ground ahead of them. Without looking at Gore he said, 'I understand we're to go in with you.'

'You're to come under my command, yes.' Gore's voice was a little edged. He waved at the ridge. 'There's the Boer, along that lump of rock there. The general has put the K.O.Y.L.I.'s and the Jocks at them a couple of times, as you can see, without doing much good. So he's come to his senses and asked us to go along and winkle them out for him with the footsloggers to follow us up.'

Morrissey looked at the Lancer silently, then back at the lie of the land. Behind him, Fishburn and Maitland tried to avoid one another's eyes.

'I should be glad if you'd extend my left, Morrissey. We'll advance squadrons in line and your chaps can wheel in a bit just before the charge.'

Morrissey was still looking past Gore, but now he swung his eyes directly to him. 'I think not.'

For a moment the Lancer missed the Australian's meaning, missed the blunt denial in his tone. Then he scowled. 'What d'you mean – you think not?'

'I mean, No. I'll not be a party to anything so damn stupid.'

Fishburn heard Maitland suck in his breath and then start to whistle low and tunelessly between his teeth. Gore's scowl turned to open amazement. 'Do I understand you to be refusing my order, Colonel Morrissey?'

'You do. You're clearly out of your head even to suggest that sort of attack. We'll be cut to pieces—'

'You, of course, have a superior plan!'

'Yes. Ride hard round the ridge there. Dismount. Hit the Boer from the rear just the way he'd do it to us.'

'I see. You realize you'll have to face court martial charges for your behaviour?'

Morrissey stayed silent, and Gore turned in the saddle, waving for one of his officers to ride forward. The Lancer major rode up, saluting, and Gore said, 'This is Major Carteret, my adjutant. Carteret, I want you here as a witness. Now then, Morrissey, for your information, *we* are a regiment of cavalry, not of mounted infantry. *We* are used to obeying orders and fighting like gentlemen, not Boer rebels. Or backwoodsmen. I shall offer you one final chance to save yourself. Join my left please, Colonel Morrissey.'

'I will not have my men butchered needlessly.'

'Then you will have to be dealt with. After my regiment has taught the Boer a lesson.'

He wheeled furiously away, Carteret shrugging his shoulders and galloping after him. Morrissey spun his horse and rejoined the Australian column without speaking to Fishburn and Maitland.

High on the knoll, the general sat in a canvas chair finishing a chicken leg. Below him the scene lay stretched like a sandtable battle map and he watched as a column of horse began to edge out onto the clear ground. A staff major standing a little forward with a glass to his eye lowered it and turned to the general.

'Lancers moving out now, sir. The Australians don't seem to be with them.'

The general tossed the chicken bone to the ground and stepped forward, looking down, the rest of his staff clustering round him. A gunner major edged in and caught his eye.

'May I move my guns down now, sir? I could give the cavalry quite heavy support.'

'No, no, no, Major!' The general snapped the words impatiently without even looking at the gunner. 'I don't want those guns committed. Once you get out there the Boer will send out snipers and we shall lose you. Couldn't have that.'

'But, sir, a screen of infantry with us –'

'No, I won't have it. You'll stay where you are. The cavalry can handle this little affair.'

Furious, the gunner stalked back to his waiting battery. The staff major said, 'Still no sign of the Australians, sir.'

'Can't rely on Colonials.' The Guards captain drawled it out, face expressionless. 'Especially part-timers.'

'Ah well, gentlemen, the Lancers will have to manage on their own. Shouldn't have much trouble anyway.'

The Australians had moved fast but they heard the rataplan of Mauser fire while they were still halfway up the rear slopes of the flanking ridge. Somehow they all knew by then what had happened between Morrissey and Gore, knew it with a mixture of derision and disgust on the one hand and a swell of goodwill towards Morrissey on the other. They'd followed him at a full gallop when he wheeled them about and raced for the end of the ridge, riding under the knoll so that the staff major above them hadn't spotted them, then swinging right to dismount and begin the scramble upwards.

Cowan's troop had been sent by Morrissey to walk their horses up the less steep slopes at the very end of the ridge as a mobile follow-up force and now, as Harry's horse crested just behind Cowan and with Ted Hewett a little to his right, they saw their own men topping the rocks further round and saw the spurts of flame as the Australians began to drop fire onto the Boer positions from above and behind. By that time, though, the Lancers had come far forward in their ludicrous advance, urging their mounts up over the loose scree at the base of the ridge. From concealed positions on the forward slopes, the Boers had already poured a slashing fire into the advancing and slowing horsemen and there were two neat windrows of them lying in the rubble, men still, men twisting and yelling, horses bleeding and running and trampling.

With the shots from behind, the Boers began to drop in their turn, began to break and scatter to where their horses were, but the Australians were already there and now Cowan, yelling incoherently, waved his troop on and down. Harry kneed his horse at the downward slope. She was a big roan, a hunter, his part of the loot from the Headquarters raid, and she was used to rough going. He let the reins hang slackly looped over his left arm, bringing his rifle down and firing into the group of Boers as they cut into them, feeling the jar as the roan's shoulder knocked one of the running men flat, feeling her change pace to avoid the body, seeing a bearded face disappear in a blast of blood.

Then his magazine was empty and he reversed the rifle, swinging it like a mace across a running man's neck, hearing the clean crack, and then he was through them and the roan was running across still Lancer forms and swerving to avoid crawling Lancers. Harry slid the rifle back into the scabbard on the saddle, feeling the stock greasy with blood, and slowed the horse, seeing suddenly the lurching figure ahead of him go to its knees and struggle up again, crouching, weeping.

He yanked the horse to a stop, looking down at the man, seeing the colonel's insignia on the Lancer uniform, wet with blood at the side of the stomach. The face above was contorted, blood seeping from the hatless head over the right cheek and caking quickly. The

mouth was wide open making uncouth noises and tears were mixing with the blood. Harry walked his horse alongside, ignoring the
flick of bullets from Boers still hidden on the frontal ridge, looking
down with disgust. Leaning over he grabbed the mouthing, weeping man contemptuously, slinging him across the saddle in front of
himself, face down like a sack of rubbish. He pulled his horse away
at an angle, trotting back to the ridge, rock splinters and pieces of
metal whining above him as he rode, and he looked down on the
bloody and heaving back and spoke with hatred.

'Never mind, pretty man. They'll find you some more toy soldiers
to break, I expect.'

Henry Gore went into hospital and then back to England, broken
and mad. Carteret, his adjutant, had been killed outright in the
first few minutes of the Lancers' abortive attack and there was no
one to press charges against Morrisey. On the way back to camp –
they'd learned by then to call it 'laager' – the Yeomanry had
discussed the whole bad business and determined that if anything
happened to their colonel, they'd go after the Lancers themselves
and show them what was what! Morrissey got to hear about that, of
course, and he growled, 'By God, I believe the mad bastards
would, too!' He was smiling when he said it but there was dampness in his eyes.

They'd learnt a lot by then. Harry looked at his troop as they
moved easily across the country on patrol. They looked different
from the other troops with whom they came into contact, different
from the men they were when they arrived. Now that they were
operating under their own command, more or less, they'd discarded virtually everything they considered either useless or an
emcumbrance. They wore no tunics or braces, riding in breeches
and shirts, the sleeves up and bandoliers slung across their chests.
Their slouch hats were now unclipped, the wide brims comfortably
bent to shade their eyes and necks, and every man had somehow or
other contrived to get hold of a British greatcoat for wear during
the chill, sometimes the frost, of the open nights. Largely thanks to
Harry's group of thieves, they were well mounted and had a string
of remounts which they guarded with a terrible ferocity, so that
other marauders gave them a wide berth. They'd also managed to
'find' half-a-dozen light carts and a number of mules to pull them,
and so the men rode unencumbered by the mass of paraphernalia
considered essential by the British horsemen. What they did carry
was what they felt was vital to them and their operations – an extra
water canteen each, spare bandoliers, a bag of feed, hard rations

and some warm clothes. They were mobile, fast, self-contained and at home in the face of the country they fought in.

Owen Fisher has strolled across to where Harry was sitting, a pad on his knee, scribbling a hasty note to Paddy, and his long shadow had darkened the paper before Harry heard the footsteps on the rocky ground. 'Righto, Harry, you've got fifteen minutes.'

'Splendid! That's exactly what I need! Fifteen minutes to get this letter finished.'

'Yer can write yer memores later. You've now got fourteen and a half minutes to get yerself straightened up. Get a tunic on and fix yer 'at.'

Harry put down the pad and pencil and looked up. 'Are you taking me to a dance or something, Owen? Won't the others be jealous?'

'Fourteen minutes.'

Getting to his feet, Harry tucked the pad and pencil in his saddlebag and turned to Fisher again. 'I'm sure you'll want to tell me what it's about sooner or later, Owen. I mean, even a squadron sergeant-major isn't supposed to keep secrets from his men.'

Fisher lifted the corner of a lip in a mordant grin. 'You've been elevated, Sergeant Morant. Yer joinin' the staff.'

'I'm *what*?'

'Fact. The Old Gent with the medals sent a message to all mounted formations—' he let his voice drift into a ludicrous imitation '—Ai would be pleased if you would be so good as to be so kind as to supply to me one orficer below field rank and one sergeant to act as starf gallopers durin' the forthcomin' section.'

It had drizzled fitfully during the night and now, in the first true morning light, the sky was overcast. Harry glanced up at the clouds.

'No heliograph, of course. Why me?'

'Ah, well, y'see, the colonel says to me, 'Oo's the best sergeant for this kinda rort, Owen?' an' I tells 'im you are, of course. I says yer educated an' pretty an' can just manage to sit on yer 'orse if yer sober, see? Perfect man for the job.'

'Very civil of you. What the hell am I supposed to do.'

'Mr Burton out of B Squadron's the officer an' you're supposed to meet him up there where the colonel is in—' he checked his watch – 'ten minutes flat. Clean, bright and slightly oiled, Harry. Come on, I'll give you a hand.'

Three-quarters of an hour later Harry stood by his horse on the slope of a long spur of land rising out of the plain a little over two

miles from the river. There were four sergeants altogether, a Lancer
who kept a fair distance from Harry and two men from the South
African Horse, known to one another and deep in conversation.
Harry had walked a little away from them, hearing again what the
staff captain had said when they rode in.

'Right, you chaps. Just stand by here, will you? The general will
relay messages by officer-galloper. You people will act as supports
to them, carrying duplicates of the messages by an alternative
route. Do you all understand that?' He waited for their response.
'Good. Then you may stand easy. Somebody will arrange some
rations for you in a while, I daresay. Don't unbutton your tunics.
The general wouldn't like that.'

The general was about twenty yards away at a field-table set up
under a stretched tarpaulin, the centre of a busyness of officers and
orderlies, a bluff and square-faced man, his white hair and drooping cavalry moustache stark against the redness of his skin. Harry
watched him, wondering how it felt to command twenty thousand
men and be preparing for a major battle.

When the Yeomanry had moved into their assigned positions late
the previous evening they found themselves part of the largest force
they'd yet seen. Highlanders, Irish regiments, gunners, half a
dozen other infantry regiments and the Colonials were spread in
laager over a couple of miles of country behind the spur on which
the staff was now established and their fires reflected pinkly off the
low and weeping clouds. Ted Hewett had strolled around with
Harry and muttered, his voice unusually sombre, 'I tell you what,
mate, there's a big old stoush brewin' up here.'

'Been on the cards for some time, hasn't it, Ted? We've been
chivvying them back and back for weeks now. They'd have to stand
somewhere, surely.'

'Yair, well if I know the old Boer, they'll have picked their spot
all right. It'll be bullets for breakfast, Harry, you mark my words.'

Looking down now, Harry wondered how right Ted had been.
There was no sign of an enemy anywhere between himself and the
horizon. Directly across from where he stood the land rose quite
steeply in a series of rough folds, the top ridge perhaps six hundred
feet above the plain. Two miles away on the left, a small village
huddled, the white buildings grey in the lack of sunlight, the
massed trees in and near them showing the presence of water. The
river ran through a cleft in the hills beyond the village, the single
road across the veldt entering the village by the same cleft and

leaving as a track leading down to the river bank where a plank bridge crossed the water, perhaps thirty feet wide at that point. The river swung away just past the bridge and made a long loop, turning back again across the plain and forming a salient of land inside the loop which looked to be about a quarter of a mile on each side. There was the thin scar of a track cutting into the side of the loop nearer Harry and it ran into the water at what seemed to be a ford. Down there nothing moved on either side of the river.

Harry's horse suddenly jibbed and danced as the guns opened up and he saw the plumes of greeny-black smoke rise in and around the village. There was a battery of the Royal Horse Artillery just forward of the base of the spur and he could see the gunners serving their guns, the new lyddite shells coming out of the limbers as fast as they could be handled. Past the guns and under the arching flight of the shells, a mass of men was advancing in near-perfect order – Highlanders, Harry realized, as he caught the flash of bare knees under the khaki aprons over the kilts. Out to their left he could see a squadron of South African Horse cantering forward in a wheeling movement which would bring them in on the far side of the village. The other sergeant had moved to join him, the Lancer still staying a little apart.

One of the South Africans said, 'Well, there go our boys. Don't you wish you were with them, Dick?'

The other spat tobacco juice in a brown blob. 'I wish I was at home. And if I can't be at home, I'd just as soon be up here, my friend.'

Harry heard his name called and turned to where Lieutenant Burton, the officer he'd ridden in with, was sitting his horse.

'I'm going back down to the colonel, Morant. Thought you'd like to know our lot's being held in reserve.'

'The colonel will be pleased about that, sir, I'd think. Looks like a big affair building up down there.'

Burton looked down to the village, the troops now drawing close, the buildings almost obscured in the rising smoke. Behind the infantry there were already numbers of dead and wounded, but the formation moved forward steadily, seemingly untouched, the dull wink of the bayonets among the khaki.

'Mmmm ... from what I've just heard over there, it seems those blokes are to clear and take the village and the main force is to cross the river. The Boer seems to have left that clear.'

Harry swung his eyes across the bridge and the loop of water and the ford, then lifted them to the slopes above.

'No sign of anything there, is there, sir? But we've seen that sort of thing before.'

'Too true. Still, the Old Man seems to know what's what. Well, I'm away.'

'Do I come with you?'

'Not this time. I'll be back in twenty minutes.'

He wheeled and put his horse into a gallop down the track and Harry walked back to the others, noting that they were now looking down and away from the village.

Below them, the main body of the army was moving on the river. Coming out of the re-entrant below and behind the spur, a huge rectangle of men was edging forward, a khaki, multi-legged insect inching out onto the plain, more of them and more again till they covered a mile of country and spread across a half-mile front. Behind and around this main body, Harry could see the others, the Hussars and Dragoons wide on a flank, two batteries of field-guns jouncing and rattling behind their teams on the opposite flank and then, towards the rear and halting now as the infantry advanced, a troop of 4.7s – 12-pounder guns from the Naval Brigade, easily picked out by the uniforms and straw hats of the gunners.

There was a sudden stir over by the general's table and the raising of voices. An imperious arm waved and the Lancer captain serving as galloper moved into the group, running out a moment later and starting his horse into a walk, hopping one foot on the ground till he swung into the saddle.

The Lancer sergeant mounted, waiting for his officer, who was calling now as he rode close, 'Sergeant, take the near flank and ride for Colonel Hart of the Irish. Tell him a spotter has observed the enemy on the ridges there – some guns too. Ride, man!' The two of them were gone in a swirl of dust and Harry and the two South Africans looked at one another and then across at the slopes beyond the river.

The naval guns below them opened up and the slopes they were staring at began to fade behind a mass of the distinctively green-black smoke, but a freshening breeze which began to open the clouds above them also shifted the smoke so that the flashing blows of the shells could be seen. But that was all – there was still no sign, no movement, no response.

On the plain, halfway to the river, the gunners had now raced their guns and limbers past the head of the infantry column and perhaps two hundred yards wide of the marching men. Harry could see the two Lancers flogging and spurring their horses up the flanks towards the head of the column and stayed watching, fascinated, as a South African Horse lieutenant took one of the sergeants with a message for the gunner command to halt and engage at no closer range. The thought ran through his mind that at the rate the guns were being driven, they'd be across the ford before the gallopers reached them.

He saw the sudden darting wink of a signal from the column below and turned, seeing the heliograph in operation from close to the general's post, realizing that he was standing now in bright sunlight and that the need for his services was probably gone. Burton went trotting past him, waving a casual hand as he returned from their own regiment.

The shells were still beating into the ridges and there was still no answer, no slightest sign of the enemy. The two field batteries were now less than a quarter of a mile from the ford and Harry saw the commander's hand go up and the teams check and wheel, swinging the guns and limbers so that the muzzles faced across the water. Before the drivers had the chance to unhitch, or the crews go into action, Harry saw men and horses begin to fall.

The South African sergeant beside him gripped his arm with crushing fingers. 'Oh, Christ, the Boer's got them in rifle range! Look at it!'

'Where *are* they? Where's the fire coming from?'

With the question, they both saw the bobbing heads and the little straight lines of rifle barrels, saw the long line of men in trenches on this side of the river, trenches dug into a natural fold above the banks and invisible to the men on the plain, almost invisible from up here. The heliograph was blinking and staring now but there was no answering light from below and the tiny points of fire from the concealed riflemen stabbed into the guns, dropping men and horses in little clumps around the unfired weapons.

Four gunners fought to control the rearmost team as they kicked and plunged in panic, fought to wheel them and move away from the scythe of fire. Then they went down together, men and horses, and Harry thought he could hear the human and the animal screams, though he knew it was only his horrified imagination. Within two minutes there were only dead and wounded men and beasts there and the guns stood, whole and unserved, limbers full, muzzles forward, only four hundred yards from the Boers.

The infantry column moved stolidly on, although a body of men, about a half-company Harry thought, swung out towards the guns, closing on them with the obvious purpose of pulling them clear, rescuing them. Some of them got close, but all of them went down

without reaching the marooned batteries. Harry realized the South
African was still gripping his arm, and he prised the fingers loose,
seeing the man's white and shocked face, mouth open, and wondering whether he himself looked as ill.

The fire from the trench was now dropping onto the flank of the
infantry and there were men dropping, being stepped over, left to
lie, but the column was well advanced into the river's loop and
Harry could see that another couple of hundred yards would take
them to the ford on one side and the bridge on the other and would
mean they'd flanked the hidden rifles. The Hussars and Dragoons
were pulling in to close on the infantry front making for the bridge
to head them across.

And then the slaughter began, the same lines of heads, the same
spears of light from the same kind of unseen entrenchments all
around the loop.

More than half the column was now inside the loop and the
cavalry was well towards the bridge and they were enfiladed from
three sides, a wicked, a killing fire that struck inwards at them and
was joined by the deep bark of field-pieces from the slopes across
the river, shells dropping in to the centre and rear of the column,
boxing them in completely.

It was like harvesting, like running a line of reapers round a long
field of wheat, the blades cutting inwards towards a shrinking
centre, the fallen stalks lying in an increasingly wide band. From
the first line of fire, figures were racing out now to the abandoned
guns, swinging them, loading and firing them into the flanks of the
decimated infantry at close range, killing them with their own
weapons, their own shells. Alongside him the South African
sergeant was crying, great dry, choking sobs, hands on his knees,
head low; and Harry glanced at him, then back to the butchery
below him, seeing the Irish and the Scots and the Yorkshiremen
break and try to turn back through their own pressing ranks,
seeing the Dragoons and their horses piled like a wall near the
entrance to the bridge, the Hussars dropping behind them as they
tried to wheel between the marching, dying men and the sharp
points of fire.

Burton's voice in his ear was loud and strained. 'Come on,
Morant! Get down there, for God's sake! Make sure you reach
whoever's left and tell them to get out, get to Hell out of that death-
trap. Tell them to try for the guns, not the river. Understand – not
the river!'

Burton was gone and Harry mounted and kicked his horse away
after him, knowing it was too late. As he rode he could still see the

flash he'd had of the general's face, grey now and the white hair and moustache seeming grey and his big frame slumped in his camp-chair as he dry-washed his hands together. The clouds were in again and the 4.7s were still coughing and the shells were still hitting the slopes across the river. There was stillness from the village and it seemed clear the attack there had been successful, but in the flat Harry rode only among the bleeding and the screaming and the dead. The volume of fire ahead of him was slackening and he realized he was riding now through men coming towards him, retreating from the slaughterhouse, and he knew he could do nothing with his useless message. His horse whinnied with unease, standing among wounded and dead men, wounded and dead horses, and Harry held him still with some difficulty, watching the ghastly parade that came past him, unseeing. A sergeant in kilts marched by, eyes straight ahead, head up, leading twenty or so Highlanders, their rifles at the high port, bayonets slanting up over their left shoulders and Harry saw the sergeant's hands clamped tight across his stomach where the blood had gushed down the front of his apron and the green and yellow and mauve of his guts were sliding out of his grip. He saw a tall Dragoon, dismounted, staggering back with one hand holding the side of his face together and a light infantryman, a King's Own Yorkshireman, one leg gone at the knee, arm looped about another man's bleeding shoulders, a long and wavering line of blood seeping into the ground behind them. Just ahead of him a disembowelled horse lay kicking feebly, half a man wound into its pouring intestines; and Harry's horse checked, pawing and head tossing. Harry looked down, seeing the half-body, wondering where the legs and balls and stomach were, recognizing the smeared face as Burton's. He leaned over his horse's neck, vomiting and retching and remembering the cheerful rubbish he'd written to Paddy, back there in the other world of a couple of hours ago.

The night had that special blackness which the dark of the moon brought to a deep gully, and Harry's patrol wound slowly in file, the men barely able to see, guided only by the noise of the men ahead. Harry, in the lead, listened to the clicking rattle of the hooves over the loose stony surface and cursed under his breath, realizing how far the sound carried in the night stillness, calming himself with the knowledge that they'd been through here only two hours before on the way out without a sign of Boers anywhere. Not that that meant a bloody thing, of course.

The shots came from both sides, stabbing sudden jerks of flame into the darkness, and the patrol broke. Harry shouted over his shoulder, 'Spurs – ride for the open!' and kneed his horse ahead, trusting to her to find her own footing while he snatched the carbine from the saddle bucket. Behind him he could hear the wild clatter as the rest of them burst into what speed they could make, a thin scream rising above the gunfire and bouncing off the rock walls of the gully.

At least, he thought, the bastards can see no more than we can, and then he was clear, not so much seeing as feeling the closing walls falling away from him and picking up a little breeze on his right cheek as he rode. Again he shouted. 'Break clear, fellows. Don't try to fight 'em! Break clear and scatter!' He pulled the horse's head hard to the right, feeling and hearing the noise change as the track went away from them and they were on looser soil and grass, hearing the noise sink as the patrol – how many left? – cleared the gully. He wanted to call to them to head east, but daren't take the chance of pinpointing his own position or letting the Boer know which way they were heading; but he knew his men were all right, knew they'd find themselves and the camp.

He'd made perhaps half a mile, sweeping in a long curve south, then east, the ground rising underfoot, when the horse checked and faltered. He was out of the saddle at once, the carbine cocked, and the thought ran through his mind that this was a bitch of a place to be alone in the dark with a foundered horse. Thank the lord they'd had their old Lee-Metfords replaced with these magazine Lee-Enfields – no time for single-shot loading if he was caught out here. The exploring hand ran down the near foreleg and the horse winced, lifting the hoof up and inwards, the pulled muscle jerking with pain.

Harry took a deep breath, absently running his head down the horse's neck, considering. What he needed was a place with some cover ... no damn use trying to head across the flat like this, walking, and with the Boer out for game. If he could hole up for the night, strap the hurt leg, wait for dawn and the first of the army patrols, he'd be likely to have a chance. He looped the reins into the back of his belt, leaving both hands free, slid the bayonet out of its scabbard and locked it quietly onto his rifle muzzle, and felt for the uphill tilt of the ground, moving forward and up slowly as quietly as he could.

Three things stopped him. The barely perceptible loom of a mass of rock ahead of him, confirmed by his probing hand, was the first. Then the realization that the edge of the rock was very faintly outlined in a thin pinkish glow. Then the muted whinny of a horse.

His hand flashed back at once to his own horse's muzzle, closing on it to prevent an answering sound, and he edged forward in fractional moves, the cocked rifle steady ahead of him.

The glow came from a small shielded fire set to one side of a cupped hollow in a ring of rising roughness. A horse was stretched on its side near the fire, legs loosely hobbled, neck stretched, and another gentle whinny jerking its head up a little as Harry watched. The man hunched over the horse had his back turned, head down, and Harry's fingers went to the back of his belt, loosing the reins. He stepped out, clear of the rocks, moving his feet with great care so that the spurs wouldn't catch or clink. Ten feet from the crouching back, the bayonet and muzzle tilted down, he spoke, his voice level and crisp.

'Keep quite still. There's a rifle at your back.'

The man's hands, working at the horse's shoulder, stopped for an instant and Harry saw the blood on them in the firelight. Then they went on with their task. Harry moved to one side of the fire, placing himself so that he and the other man could see one another clearly.

'Get up! Unless you want to be shot.'

The man glanced up, a flash of eye-bright in the glow of the flames, then down again at his hands. His voice was as quiet as Harry's and showed no passion.

'Look, redneck, if you're going to shoot, then do it and be damned! If you're not, then sit down and wait. I've got a sick horse here.' Intrigued, hearing the reasonableness in what the man said, Harry lowered his rifle and moved closer, looking down. His finger was still on the trigger, the muzzle a yard from the man's neck. The horse's shoulder was bleeding fairly freely and the crouching Boer moved a hand to its head, holding it steady while the point of the knife in his other hand edged gently into the centre of the patch of blood. Without thinking about it, Harry uncocked his rifle and put it down, kneeling on the other side of the horse, his hands going to the twisting head, the little soothing chirrups coming from his lips. The other man looked steadily at him across the horse.

'Good for you, redneck.'

Harry ran a gentle hand across the wound and around it, feeling the sticky hair.

'Bullet?'

'Ricochet, I think. Not big, but pretty deep.'

'Can you reach it?'

The knife-point went deeper, moving in tiny touches from side to side. 'Just touching now. Damn, it's right into the muscle!'

Harry's fingers spread, a hand on either side of the knife-point, the wound opening under the gentle pressure. He forced the flesh down as evenly as he could, his hands and the Boer's hands touching, the blood sliding between them. The Boer sucked in his breath and the knife moved quickly, in and along and up, half an inch of rough metal coming with it, the horse jerking wildly and whinnying with the pain, Harry's horse in the darkness answering it. Harry patted the sweating neck, his other hand deep in his pocket, dragging out the flask. He pulled the stopper with his teeth and tipped a little of the spirit into the wound, feeling the horse start and try to leap up as the Boer mopped at the shoulder. Then they let the horse rise, his head swinging round as he tried to nuzzle at the wound, the Boer wiping blood away from it, ripping away a piece of rag and packing it into the jagged little hole. He looked up at Harry and they grinned at one another, two men with a task successfully done. In a spurt of flame as a small log shifted in the fire, Harry saw the square face under the flap-brimmed hat, the wide mouth over the fringe of beard, the light eyes. He thought, God, without the beard he could be old Paddy! He passed the flask across the horse's back and the Boer took a deep draught, shaking his head and coughing at the sting of the spirit.

'Ach, that's good brandy!' He took another drink. 'Looted?'

'Looted. From a British cavalry Mess!' They grinned again and Harry walked around to look at the wound. 'He's going to be stiff for a while. You won't be riding tonight.'

'He'll be well enough by dawn. He's a tough old horse, that one.'

Harry glanced around. His own horse had edged in and stood now, muzzling at the Boer's.

'Mine's lame. He'll need a strapping before it swells too much.'

The Boer nodded judiciously.

'Have you food?'

'Some corned beef. Some beans.'

'I have bread and biltong and coffee.' He looked very straight at Harry, lips pursed before he spoke again. 'Truce, redneck?'

Harry's smile was a white flash and he put out his hand. 'Truce, Boer.'

An hour later they sat leaning back against the rock, the fire between their stretched feet. The two horses were nearby, hobbled, Harry's with the paleness of a wet puttee strapped around its foreleg. The men had barely spoken, tending to Harry's horse, draining and repacking the other horse's wound, feeling for more wood for the fire, eating and drinking the shared rations. Now they sat, smoking quietly in the lee of the rock, hearing the night wind picking up to a whistle above them, knowing it was strong enough to carry the smoke and coffee smells away.

The Boer edged a coal into the fire with the toe of his boot. 'You have done this before, redneck; slept by a fire in the open.'

'How can you know that? Except that all soldiers do it sooner or later?'

'No, not as a soldier. As a life.' He gave Harry that level look again. 'Oh, it can be seen if a man looks for it. See – a man who is used to a roof over his head doesn't sit quiet like that in the open. Neither does he check where the breeze is and sit away from the smoke. Neither does he scrape his plate into the fire as soon as he has eaten. No. This you have done before.'

Harry nodded. 'Many times.'

'But not in England. In England I think they do not learn such things.'

'No. Australia.'

'So? That is why you think first for the horses. You from Australia have given us some trouble, you are not like the English ones. You are more like us.'

'Well, a lot of us are bushmen. Stockmen, cattlemen, farmers.'

The Boer's face lightened. 'That was me also – a farmer. Good farm. Cattle, goats, pigs, chickens, mealie corn, a little fruit.' He sighed. 'Good farm. *Was* a good farm.' The half-smile on his face had gone.

Harry let the silence hang a moment, but he had to ask the question. 'Was? Did our people—?'

'No.' The Boer shook his head, smiling again, grimly now. 'No, your people didn't get the chance, redneck. The Kaffirs raided; took what they could and put the torch to the rest. Killed my bywoner.' He saw the puzzled look and let the smile loose. 'My foreman.'

'And your family?'

The smile broadened, a touch of pride in the voice. 'Ah, Mamma took the big shotgun to them and the girls had each a pistol. But not in time to save Jannie. He was a good foreman. Now the women are with my sister safe, but the farm is—' His hands turned palm up, spread, tossing to the wind.

'Have you no sons to care for your women while you're away?'

The Boer barked a short laugh, eyes squinting in enjoyment.

'Oh, I have sons, my friend! Paul and Klaus and Pieter – big men, those kerls! They ride with Christiaan de Wet's commando. All with red hair.' He laughed again. 'You mind yourself if you meet three big men with red hair, soldier-boy!'

Harry said, seriously, 'I'll remember.'

They sat silent again for a minute or two, each of them staring into the fire, seeing different things. Harry broke the silence, voice sounding tired. 'It's a rotten war, this. Burning farms and home, killing men who speak the same language.'

'The same language?' The Boer's voice was tighter, a barb in it. 'So you speak the Taal then ... Afrikaans?' Harry stared at him, caught by the sudden near-vehemence. 'No, redneck, of course you don't! You're not a Boer, you're a Uitlander, a foreigner.' He shook his head, holding down the anger deliberately. 'See, my friend, the colour of the skin, even the sound of the tongue are not the matters that count. It's the way to live that counts ... the freeness. From Australia you should know what that means, as I know, as all of us here know. But those in London – how can they know? So long they have lived with their laws and their commands and their little minds in their big Empire—' the scorn was open '—they cannot know how a man can be free and happy without them.'

'You sound like some of the men I know in Australia. They talk about the English like that.'

'A strange people, the English. They make laws for themselves and their dirty little patch of an island and then they try to keep the same laws for other people in other places. That way they lost America. That way they will lose us. One day they will lose you Australians and the Canadians and all the others, even the black men in India. Either they will lose in blood or they will just give up. They cannot win.'

Harry listened to the words echoing – They cannot win – and fought down the sudden shiver.

'They're winning now. This war.'

'So, you believe that? Because they have taken so much land and so many towns and so many miles of the railway line? *Us* they haven't taken, and this is what matters. *Us* they cannot take, because they are stupid and try to fight us as they fought with Bonaparte and then the Russians. *We* are alive and we fight, and so the Englishmen cannot win.'

There was the ring of total certainty in his words, Biblical pro-nouncements, a prophet in a high place, and he was saying in a different way what Harry had heard so many soldiers say, what he'd said himself.

Yet somehow he had to make a defence. 'You know Kitchener's taken over? That might make all the difference.'

'Perhaps. You change your generals as a woman changes her hats. A new hat does not make a new woman.' He tapped out his pipe and changed his tone, smiling. 'But there will always be a place under the sky for a little fire and a pipe and a talk ... with a friend.'

Harry thought again as the Boer smiled, how much like Paddy he was, and he watched as the other man lifted his face to the sky, sniffing the now still air. 'Four hours till dawn, and then I will guide you to your people. Now we must sleep.' He began to pull a blanket over his shoulder.

'Both of us? No guard?'

'What need, my friend? If my people or your people come, one of us will speak for the other, no? Sleep.' He shrugged himself down into the blanket and Harry pulled his up to his chin. Under the blanket he felt for his belt, lying near his shoulder, and slipped his revolver from it, placing it within easy reach. He saw the movement across from him, the Boer placing his pistol also near at hand, and they smiled openly at one another and settled quietly.

The half-light of piccaninny dawn held them in a grey world, chill and damp and Harry shivered, pulling his British greatcoat closer round him. His horse was moving well enough and the Boer had cleaned his own horse's wound again half an hour ago so that it walked only a little stiffly. The Boer's hand was out suddenly, stretched wide, palm back towards Harry halting him, and both men leaned over their horse's muzzles. From somewhere in the dimensionless greyness came the guttural rattle of talk, the thick Afrikaans echoing flatly round them. The Boer listened, head cocked, and they heard the voices stop and the thin sharpness of hooves on rock, dying away soon into nothing. They rode on, still quiet, still cautious, and then the greyness opened out and became blackness below them, a blackness punctured by the small red and yellow holes of scores of fires on the plane. The Boer pointed.

'Your people, redneck.'

Harry's lip twisted. 'They don't exactly hide themselves, do they?'

'It would be easy to attack them from here.'

The Boer sounded almost wistful and Harry wondered whether they had the strength in these hills to mount an attack anyway. He followed the signposts of the fires, working out where the lines were, where the creek ran, and he smiled without real humour.

'You might have some trouble if you did attack. That dark patch on this side is where *we're* laagered. You wouldn't get past us.'

'Perhaps, perhaps not. Now you must go before the true dawn. This is where *we* patrol while it's dark. You can have it in the daytime, when we can see you properly through the sights.' The smile took the sting from the words.

Harry reached out the flask again, nearly empty now, and raised it. 'Thank you. And good luck.' He drank and passed it, watching as the Boer also raised it in a toast and drained it.

'Good luck to you, redneck. Watch out for my three big sons . . . and ride safely. Tot siens.'

'Ride safely, friend.'

They didn't shake hands, just wheeled away in opposite directions as the first tint of pink slid into the dawn greyness.

It was a cage, a large square of wired-off dust, guarded and patrolled and surrounding nothing but half-a-dozen coop-like huts at one side and perhaps three hundred inmates.

It had stood empty when the Yeomanry rode into the town but the Boers had been driven in the previous day, a long, uneven line of them, dirty and ragged, walking, not marching, between files of armed soldiers. Harry had been struck by the fact that they didn't look like prisoners then, nor now, inside the wire. There was a look and a feel about them which may have been compounded of sullenness and hate and revulsion, but which added up to pride, to self-containment. He thought of the Boer with whom he'd spent the night in camp, and could see men like him in there, behind the wire.

Most of them were bearded men, not all old but bearded in the Boer way, the face hair allowed to grow as soon as a boy turned sixteen, as soon as he was recognized as a man, a fighter, capable of taking on the British Army in all its solidity and strength.

Harry eased his way through the crowd of soldiers clustered at the wire near a corner, watching the prisoners, occasionally jeering at them. A stooped old man, bare-headed and grey-square-bearded was the centre of a swelling group of Boers, his voice rising over them as though he was preaching a sermon, his hands steadying a ragged newspaper against the fitful wind.

Near Harry a soldier called, 'Oi, Grandpa! What's all the garglin' abaht?' but the old man's voice droned on in Afrikaans above the catcalls from the watchers. Another soldier shoved his face against the wire, shouting, 'Ya got the results of the Grand National, old man?' and the laughter rose again.

The old Boer lowered the paper and stared at the men outside the cage, then moved across, standing close, the mob of prisoners following him. The two nearest sentries looked at one another anxiously and came closer, nervously fingering the bolts of their rifles. When the Boer spoke, his voice was thick, gutturally accented.

'Do you truly wish to know what I read, you rednecks?'

The man he addressed turned a mock-surprised face to his companions. 'Gawd, it walks an' talks just like a man, don't it?'

The laughter this time was just a little uneasy now that the old Boer was close, could be seen to be tired and pale. But strong.

'I read to my comrades how the world hates you British.' He flourished the paper, seeming to wave down the growl that rose from the troops. 'I read how in Germany the Kaiser gives us his blessing and how in America people collect money for our cause—'

Behind him many of the other prisoners were clenching their fists and one of them spat through the wire. The troops surged inwards and two strands of wire began to bend. One of the sentries cocked his rifle and waved at the other, an urgent wave which sent him running towards a nearby building. Beside Harry, Ted Hewett raised his voice.

''At's all very well, you old fool, but we're not English. Some of us is Australians.'

'Then that is worse, *because* you are not English! Why do you fight for them against us?' His voice rose in contempt. 'Jackals! You Australians are very bad people—'

He was close now, close to Harry, only a foot separating their faces across the wire and Harry looked hard at the contorted face.

'Why, old man? Because we fight as you do? Because we don't march about and wait for you to shoot us down as the British wait?'

The shouts of abuse were building from both sides now, the noise dragging more men to the outside of the cage. From somewhere to Harry's left a voice called, 'You're finished with fighting, you lot! It's near enough over. You've lost, mate. Why don't you admit it?'

The prisoners were still suddenly, still and silent, and the silence spread across the wire. The old Boer gripped a strand with both hands, the knuckles whitening, his beard pushing through.

'Finished? You think we have lost because we are in this cage, because you have taken back some towns? I will tell you when we will have lost, rednecks. When we are all dead, that is when! Only when you have killed us all, every one. And if you do not kill all of us, then you cannot win! See –' he pulled aside his long coat and ripped at his shirt, exposing the naked chest, grey-haired and the ribs showing through the skin. 'Shoot me now! Or one day I will shoot you.'

There was a roar from the men behind him and they all tore open their clothes, baring their chests, grinning with triumph as they saw the looks of the soldiers.

Sick, the bile in his throat, Harry shoved backwards out of the press and walked fast across the dusty square away from the cage.

'Harry! Harry Morant!'

The voice jerked him to a stop, eyebrows down in thought. Then he spun about, eyes going wide as the calling man ran to him. His hand was crushed in the other man's grip, and then they were pummelling one another and laughing, a pair of British privates watching them in disbelief. Harry leaned back, holding the other man at arm's length.

'By God and the bloody devil. Lenehan! *Captain* Lenehan!'

'And *Sergeant* Morant! Show a little respect, man!'

Their faces wide with grins they stepped apart a pace or two. Harry snapped to attention and whipped up a formal salute, answered with total gravity by Lenehan. And then they burst into hilarious laughter again, staggering away with their arms linked. The two British privates watched them go, one of them muttering, 'Fuckin' Australians. They're madder than the Boers!'

Harry pushed stockinged feet towards the wood-stove and stretched his arms rackingly above him, then slumped again.

'This is without doubt the most luxurious room I've been in in Africa! My Heavens, but you're living soft, Lenehan!'

'Only lately, m'friend, believe me! We got down here last week.' He busied himself with opening a fresh bottle. 'We've had quite a busy time lately, as a matter of fact. You know, they finally decided if they wanted to get the job done properly, they'd better send for the old New South Wales Lancers.'

'We heard you'd been quite badly cut about. Was it sticky?'

'Oh, sticky enough.' He flicked Harry's tunic where it hung over the back of a chair, looking at the clasp on the breast. 'You've been seeing a bit of action too. Was this for picking up that Lancer lunatic?'

Harry nodded. 'Quite some time ago. I've a new job now.'

'Oh? Safe?'

'Safe as the Bank of England. Staff galloper. None of your comman-as-muck soldier-men for me nowadays. I only mix with the Brass Hats.' His voice went low and bitter. 'And a dull bloody lot they are too.'

'Dull? Wouldn't have thought that was the word. From the little we've seen of 'em I'd have said they were very pretty.'

'I'll give you that – they're lovely to look at! Trouble is they're all corpses above the collars.'

'Not Kitchener, from what I hear. He'll soon put a short fuse under 'em.'

'I believe you could put a cartload of gunpowder under 'em and they wouldn't even hear the bang!'

'Ah, now, let's not spoil a reunion by talking about that lot. Where's that old rascal of an Irishman you used to ride with? Out here?'

'Not Paddy! No. He's at home near Adelaide.' He reached for his tunic and took a picture from his pocket. 'He sent me this a little while ago. That's Harlequin with him.'

Lenehan looked at the stiff pose, Paddy in a much-creased suit, the black and golden head of the horse near his shoulder. 'Fine looking horse that.'

'The finest. Never been ridden by anyone except me. Never will be.' He gulped at his drink, then said brusquely, 'I had to shoot Cavalier. Sorry, Lenehan.'

'Yees. Well, it comes to all of us, doesn't it?' He looked embarrassed. 'Er – did you know Julia married? She has three boys.'

Harry's smile was reminiscent, gentling his face. 'Julia. I'd almost forgotten Julia.'

'Well, she didn't forget you. Her oldest lad is called Harry. She didn't think you'd mind.'

Harry looked up, seeing Lenehan's dry smile, and dragged the cushions from behind his head, shying it across the room at the other man. It flew across the opening door, almost catching the newcomer in the face, a lean and smilingly quizzical face behind a bar of black moustache.

The man shut the door and leaned against it, looking at them. 'I know Australians are supposed to be uncouth, but it can be carried too far, old son!'

He stared inquiringly at Harry, and Lenehan moved forward.

'Burleigh, come in, come in, do! You two should meet Harry, this is Bennet Burleigh of the London *Daily Telegraph* and this is Harry Morant, an old friend from Australia. Also known as The Breaker.'

Harry shook hands, liking the other man on sight. 'I've read some of your dispatches. You seem to have a very clear understanding of the war, sir.'

'Do I? I only see it from the sidelines. You chaps are *in* it. And don't for God's sake call me 'sir' – makes me sound like your grandfather! Why do they call you The Breaker?'

Lenehan broke in. 'Wait till you see him on a wild horse ...
you'll know.'

Burleigh had found a glass and poured a large drink, sucking it
down with obvious relish. 'How on earth am I supposed to see a
wild horse out here? I've never seen a worse collection of hacks in
my life. They don't even taste good! They won't let me write about
it, of course. My editor says it might cause despondency at home!'

Harry waved a generous hand. 'You'd better come and see our
horse lines. We manage rather well.'

'I wish I knew how!'

Lenehan laid a hand on Harry's shoulder. 'Ah, well, it's a mixture of skill, cunning—'

'And outright theft!' Harry hardly looked repentant, and they
settled down laughing. Lenehan put fresh wood into the stove.

'What are you doing this far from the action, Burleigh? Not like
you.'

'Oh, every now and then I like to come back to where the
comforts are and spend a day or two watching the antics of the
Gilded Staff. I'm waiting for that crucial moment when they cross
over into the nineteenth century to join the rest of us. No sign of it
yet, I'm afraid.'

Harry watched him while he spoke, the face solemn but the eyes
dancing.

'The sign will never come, Burleigh; not unless old Kitchener
sets to and boots the lot of 'em out.'

'I saw Kitchener in London – great tall chap with the coldest
eyes I've ever seen and a voice like God.' He drank, recalling the
man. 'They say he's got a plan....'

Harry interrupted. 'Plan be buggered! They've all got plans,
most of them a century out of date! Can't they see the way to fight
these people is on their own terms? Irregular units. Fast riding. No
baggage, no spit-and-polish, no manoeuvres in review order. Hit
'em hard and move away – *that's* all the plan they need. We've got
more men by thousands. We could break 'em in no time like that!'

He leaned forward and stabbed the poker fiercely into the grate
of the stove, while Lenehan and Burleigh looked at one another
across his back. Burleigh said, 'Pity you're a sergeant, Morant. You
should be a general.' There was no malice in what he said, and
Harry smiled up at him, clanging the poker down.

'I shan't be a sergeant much longer. I'm to be commissioned.'

'Congratulations.'

'Well done, Harry! In your own regiment?'

'No. They're off home in a few weeks – enlistment's up.

Quite a few staying on one way or another. I put in for the Cape Police.'

Burleigh had been studying him quietly. 'Then it shouldn't be hard to get you detached for a bit should it?'

'Detached? What the devil for?'

'Oh, I don't know. Come riding round with me for a bit. Have a looksee at things. Give me the benefit of your fiery opinions – that sort of thing. Would you like to?'

'Can you get whisky?'

'My dear chap I can get anything, ... except information out of the staff!'

'Then I'm your man!'

Staring into the grey-blue wisps of smoke rising under the panni-kin, Harry wondered how many fires he'd lit, how many meals he'd cooked like this, out in the open. All the way up the coast and inland in New South Wales, he thought, and on up north and west into Queensland and down again across Victoria and into South Australia ... and the eye of his mind blurred them all into one picture, spinning right up to now, the last of many impressions of a hundred fires in a hundred parts of South Africa. Like this one, a neat little fire, set in a rough ring of flattish stones on which the pannikin and a billy could rest, dry grass for kindling, little gum branches for flame, some knotty thorn-tree branches for solidity and a banking of fried horse-turds to hold the heat in and raise the slightly acrid smoke that helped keep the flies away. His mind had walked carefully through all these details while his hand stirred the meat stew in the pannikin and his chin sank lower ... and it was Burleigh's voice which jerked him upright, a hand grabbing in-stinctively for the rifle near his foot, then relaxing.

'God, that smells good! What is it?'

Burleigh was stretching and twisting himself upright, the two hours' sleep under the thorn tree's shade leaving him now wide-awake and hungry.

Harry shook his head, dispelling the daydreams of the afternoon heat, noticing how much longer the shadows had grown. 'Don't be inquisitive. It might spoil your appetite.' He spooned thick meat into their dishes and Burleigh sniffed deeply.

'Well, it still smells good. As long as it's no one we know.'

They ate in silence, watching the blue fingers of shadow creep along the plain and down the tilt of land behind them where it rose into the foothills of the great range further back, listening to the calls of the first of the night birds. Burleigh leaned forward to toss a handful of tea into the billy.

'You should have shaken me earlier, Harry. I've some work to do, you know.'

'About what? The war?' He inflated his voice. '"A dispatch from the back of the front by our sleeping partner and holiday correspondent, Bennet Burleigh." I don't believe either one of us has the slightest idea what's happening to the war, Ben.'

Burleigh sat up, smirking a little. 'Ah, that's the trouble with you ordinary chaps – the brutal and licentious soldiery. No mastery of Grand Strategy, let alone tactics. *We*, the correspondents, *we* know everything about the war, even if we're nowhere near it.' He dragged a large notecase from his pack and flourished it. 'Here you have the garnered wisdom of the past year, my Military Morant, the gleanings of a supreme intelligence, saved for just such a moment! Before we go back, I shall have transmuted this into pluperfect prose about which my editor will rhapsodize, the staff with enthuse, Her Majesty will doubtless confer on me a significant Order and the public will rush shouting into the streets!'

'With nooses tied and cabbages to throw!'

The past five days had brought these two men close, Burleigh watching with admiration Harry's self-possession as they moved across the land, seeing his skills at bushcraft and adaptation, at providing food, at settling them in some degree of comfort each afternoon. He liked his quietness. Harry had enjoyed the conversation, the irreverence of the correspondent's comments on senior soldiers and statesmen, his scorn for the timidity of his editor, his clear liking for the soldiers, the men who were working the rough end of the war. Each of them had the same dry humour and the liking was mutual and deepening. Harry waited now till Burleigh had eaten and had poured the black tea, adding lime from a flask and rum from a bottle, then he took the pad of papers by his side and said, 'I've saved you a job, Ben. Here—' and tossed the pad across, moving a couple of branches so that the fire spurted high. They were many miles from any likely Boer activity, only twenty miles from camp and on the British side of the sprawl of troops across the countryside. Burleigh leaned in towards the firelight at the heading on the first page: 'Kitchener's New Proposal for the Conduct of the War', looked up, startled, then down again and became absorbed, while Harry considered their position. Even where they were in a short fold in the plain and with a screen of trees to one side of them, even this far from the last reported Boer parties, he knew they needed to take some care and he checked his rifle and both revolvers, planning to bank the fire low as soon as the light had gone. About an hour, he thought.

Burleigh rested the pad on his knee, eyes blank, then suddenly focusing brightly on Harry.

'Did you write this? Good God!' He studied Harry's look of mock modesty. 'Damn my eyes! It's good, it's bloody good!'

'Then you'd better put your name to the bottom of it. Wouldn't do for me to be known as the author.'

'Oh, but look here, Harry, I can't do that! This is splendid stuff, quite masterly, really. Right in my style too, you bugger!'

'So much the better — no one will know, will they? Take it in payment for getting me away from Base for this past week. I've enjoyed it. And you *did* bring the whisky . . . which you might now be good enough to pass!'

He woke in the silent darkness, the taste of the whisky still in his mouth, and knowing something was wrong. Habit kept him still, eyes only slitted open, ears wide for sounds . . . Burleigh snoring quietly to his right and a hiss of breeze in the dry grasses. Nothing else — except he knew there was something. His hand slid very gently up under the blanket to the revolver by his shoulder and he winced as a boot crushed down on his wrist. The voice above him was deep and matter-of-fact.

'Stand up rednecks! Up, quickly!'

A boot kicked into the fire and in the little flare Harry could see there were four of them, one standing over Burleigh, another by the fire with a rifle levelled across the scene, the last bringing their horses to stand, all headroped together with the Boer ponies. Harry looked at the man who'd roused him, judging him to be the leader, seeing the solid features, the hard eyes, red with the fireglow, the tight mouth.

'My friend is no soldier. Let him go. He's only a civilian writer.'

The Boer looked briefly at Burleigh. 'A writer for the newspapers of London?' He accepted Burleigh's nod. 'As bad as a soldier then. I have seen the lies that his sort has written about us.' He saw Burleigh's dispatch-case and, in a swift move hooked it to him with his boot-heel and kicked it into the fire. Burleigh's involuntary move forward bought two rifle muzzles close to his chest and the Boer leader laughed without humour.

'If you don't like the treatment, scribbler, you should have stayed safe in England.'

Harry had taken half a step forward, mouth open to object, but the leader's butt moved through a short, vicious arc into his ribs, doubling him over with the pain. Burleigh saw the mad flare of light in Harry's eyes. The Boer leader stood over the crouched man.

'You keep your English mouth shut, hear? We will eat and sleep a little before I decide what to do with you. And don't worry about being rescued, rednecks; your nearest friends are seven miles away and my brother's patrol will have them by now. Turn around.'

The two men were manhandled together, rifle-muzzles forcing them to move, and their hands were tied behind them. A rawhide rope was lashed two or three times round their chests as they stood back-to-back, and then the leader's hands on their shoulders crammed them down to the ground, sitting awkwardly, knees high, away from the fire. Two of the Boers were systematically going through their saddlebags, pulling out the little food they had left, taking the clothes, tossing other things aside. The prisoners watched as the Boers began to prepare food. Burleigh, his head craning back and half-turned, whispered, 'What d'you suppose they'll do, Harry?' He tried to keep his voice calm, but Harry heard the slight tremble in it and thought, No point in not telling him the truth.

'Knife us, I should think, Ben. Makes no noise ... and saves bullets.'

Burleigh's back tensed against his, then relaxed. 'That bloody Boer was right, wasn't he? I should have stayed at home!'

Harry's grin was dry. He moved his head with care, looking around the patch of near-dark ground beyond his stretched legs. His bedroll was about six feet from him and he could see what he was looking for, just clear of the blanket. When the Boer boot had held his wrist down, no one had picked up the revolver he'd been reaching for and now he strained his foot towards it, realizing at once that it was too far away. He twisted his head, holding his voice to a bare murmur.

'Ben, listen! My gun's over there on the ground. I can't reach it. We have to get closer somehow. When I give you the word, start a scrap. Start arguing with me and be prepared for me to pull you about a bit, d'you hear?'

'Yes, all right. But your hands are tied—'

'Shut up and stop worrying! Now, go!'

Over by the fire, the four Boers heard the sudden outburst, Burleigh shouting, 'You stupid bastard! If it hadn't been for you we wouldn't —' He was jerking at his bonds, seeming to want to turn and hit at Harry, who pulled back, also shouting.

'Keep your dirty mouth shut, you bloody moaning civilian. I'd sooner have old Dutchie here than you!'

Their struggles had toppled them sideways, heads away from the fire and three feet nearer the blankets when the leader stood over them again, sneering.

'No wonder you can't fight us, English! You are too busy fighting each other. Now be quiet!' He turned away, then turned back and kicked Harry savagely just below the ribs. 'And don't call me Dutchie!'

Harry was gasping from the pain of the kick and he took a moment to gather himself before muttering again, 'No good, Ben, I've got to get about two feet further this way.' He felt the slight shrug in Burleigh's shoulders as the journalist whispered back, 'Oh, well, here we go again.'

This time they began struggling silently, writing and kicking at one another, and all four Boers moved quickly to look down at them. The leader was holding his reversed rifle, the butt menacingly over their heads, his voice angry.

'Mad English, stop it! You stop it now or I'll bang you on the head!'

The wriggling men lay still as the Boers went growling back to the fire. Burleigh spat dust from the side of his mouth and whispered, 'Well?'

'Got it! I kicked it about four or five feet to the left there. Now it's just a matter of waiting.'

The first grey light saw the Boers stirring, one of them mending the fire and the smell of coffee reaching the prisoners, their mouths watering as they listened to their captors drinking and chewing on the last of Harry's rations. Then the leader and one of the others had jerked them upright, laughing as their stiff limbs wobbled under them. The sun was beginning to edge up, sliding colours into the greyness as the leader poked them in the ribs with his rifle-muzzle.

'All right, my little English, strip! Take off your clothes. Everything off, and quickly.'

The man with him slackened their chest ropes and cut through the ties around their wrists and they stood chafing the skin, dragging the circulation back again. Harry could see the four Boers were all ragged enough ... the leader and the man with him watching them closely, the third man stamping down the fire and the last of them tightening the girths on the horses and swinging the bags onto their backs. The leader prodded at them again. 'Come

on, no wasting time. We can use those clothes to fool more stupid
soldiers. Get them off.'

They began to strip, Harry hopping first on one foot, then on the
other as he tugged at his socks, each hop taking him six inches
nearer the clump of scrub where he could just see the dew-pearls on
the pistol. Urged by the rifle-muzzle Burleigh was standing in his
drawers, stooping now for his socks. Harry had socks and trousers
off and unbuttoned his shirt, watching as the other man near the
leader answered a companion's call to help him with the horses.
Harry's hands went to the bottom of his shirt and he tugged it up
over his head, feeling the morning's coolness on his skin. He was
perhaps two feet from the Boer leader when he pulled the shirt free,
arms taking it upright above him, and then instantly sweeping it
down across the rifle-muzzle as he threw himself sideways and
backwards towards the hidden gun. He rolled, feeling the pebbles
and the sharp grass-edges cutting into his thighs and buttocks, but
the gun was in his hand, cocked and the barrel up in a shining line
as the Boer, raging, swept the flannel shirt away from his hands
and his rifle. The two fired almost together and Harry felt the sting
of the bullet as it struck a small rock near his shoulder ... and saw
the Boer's throat go away on one side in a spurt of red. His second
snap shot caught the man at the fire in the thigh and there was
Burleigh beside him, the Boer leader's dropped rifle steady in his
hands, and the other two Boers letting the horses go, grabbing for a
second for guns, then raising their hands while they looked down,
shocked, at the bubbling throat of their leader. Harry stood up and
looked at the man by his feet. 'He'll be dead in five minutes. Forget
him. Ben, get dressed while I hold these beauties. Then we'll take
them along, I think.'

The little room at the end of the railway platform was stifling, the
one window giving only onto a shed a few feet away from it, the air
motionless and thick. Behind the desk, behind the massed piles of
papers, the colonel was red and sweating, his tunic patched across
the chest and shoulders and under the arms with black stains and
his balding head and thick face running with sweat. He glared at
the captain who followed his knock at the door with a rushed
entrance, envying his slimness and youth, wondering why the
young shit wasn't fighting instead of working here at the railhead
like an old man. The captain seemed agitated.

'Sir – excuse me, sir, there's a war correspondent to see you. And
a sergeant. Australian.'

The colonel wondered what the hell the young fool was grinning at. 'I've got no time to talk to correspondents and colonial sergeants, Maxwell. Chuck 'em out!'

'Yes, sir. But they asked me to tell you – sir, they say they've got a present for you. To be given personally, sir.'

The colonel threw his pen into the desk-top like a dart, running wet hands down his wet face.

'What the bloody Hades are you talking about, man? Oh, for God's sake let's have them in, then.'

The captain swung the door and Harry and Burleigh walked in, Harry saluting smartly, Burleigh nodding, a finger to his hat-brim. Before the colonel could speak, the two men moved a little apart and led in three Boers, watching the colonel's eyes widen, hearing the smothered laughter from the outer office, seeing the captain's great crack of a smile. The Boers were stark naked except for their hats and boots, and the rough bandage around the thigh on one of them. Their bodies were red-scorched with the sun through which they'd walked and their faces mixed fury with desperation. The colonel closed his mouth, slapped the desk with both hands, sending papers flying everywhere and exploded in a huge guffaw, choking and gasping till he could speak.

'By the living God, Sergeant . . . what's your name, man?'

'Morant, sir. Second South Australian Yeomanry, detached.'

'Detached for what . . . collecting naked Boers?' He roared with laughter again.

'No, sir, pending commissioned transfer into the Cape Police. This is Mr Bennet Burleigh of the London *Daily Telegraph*.

'Well, Sergeant Morant Detached, if I could do it I'd make you a major in the field, I would! A bloody general! I'd hang a medal on you, by Jesus and the Apostles!' He turned, scarlet, to Burleigh. 'You too, sir, if you weren't a stinki – sorry – if you weren't a civilian.'

Burleigh was quite unperturbed. 'That's perfectly all right, Colonel. I've got my best story in years, thanks to Morant here.'

'Quite, quite. Very proper attitude! Maxwell, get these – these – children of nature out of here and find 'em some clothes.' He looked at the red-raw backsides of the prisoners as they were led out by the grinning captain and roared again with laughter.

'God, that's done me a power of good! Now then, Morant, where d'you belong, eh? I'll get a signal to your C.O. You too, Burleigh?'

'Thank you sir. My commanding officer's Colonel Morrissey, but he's in the field. I'm due for leave, sir.'

Burleigh said, 'I'll travel with Morant, if I may, Colonel. I want a bath and a telegraph.'

Answering the colonel's shout, the smiling captain returned.

'Those laddies are locked in that empty stores hut, sir. They're all standing. ...'

Harry and Burleigh kept straight faces, but the colonel went into another jerk of laughter, fighting his way out of it at last.

'Leave, eh, Morant? By the Lord Harry you deserve it. You'll both lunch with me first, though – bugger the protocol, Maxwell! I want to hear all about it. Then we'll get you on a train for Base. Maxwell – a compartment, mind, not just a couple of seats. Back to Australia for you, my lad!'

Harry smiled quietly down at the Colonel. 'Not Australia, sir. I'm going home.'

ENGLAND

It rained lightly as the train pulled away from Exeter, a thin mist of rain that swallowed the cathedral in a gulp and took the city with it before thinning further to let the sun begin to show through. The greens were all dark and fresh and the cart-roads to the farms and the ploughed or fallow fields were red, the soft bronze-red of West Country clay. Harry, alone in the compartment, tugged at the leather strap that held the window closed and leaned out, sucking his lungs full of the smells, grinning at the lushness of it all, the neatness of the line curving away ahead into a toy greystone tunnel.

There were oaks and beeches growing thickly up there where the road and the rail ran across the Torridge, high with the last of the spring rains and the salmon weirs splashing with the leaping fish. The last time he'd made this journey he'd been a lad, with a pocketful of warnings from people to whom he owed money and a confrontation with his father looming. By God! he thought, I was scared that day! A Post Captain in a rage was no welcome for a one-ship lieutenant. ...

He settled back, considering that he was still a lieutenant, and the captain was now a retired admiral, but what a whole whirling world of difference there was between them. He'd chosen to change into uniform that morning, wanting to make it plain that he was coming back in Service, as he'd been when he left, and he straightened the blue tunic now, glancing down at the campaign medals and the clasps, at the fine cut of the pale khaki whipcords and the chestnut of the boots. He was damned if he sneaked home in mufti, not after the last year, certainly. The carriage porter slid back the compartment door, grinning in, a massive watch in his hand. 'Rackon us'll be pullin' in to Bideford 'bowt seven minutes now, sir. I s'll get thee bags down, s'll I?' The broad burr brought a smile to Harry's face and he stood, stretching, as the man pulled down his cases and slid the tin trunk to one side, dropping a half-sovereign into his hand and gravely returning the one-finger salute. In the little oval mirror above his seat he stared at himself, realizing he was nervous, smoothing back his hair, feeling the light damp of sweat on his hands and forehead. The khaki slouched hat with the big silver badge, chinstrap just under the bottom lip, made him look less anxious, and he scowled, then laughed. Out there, in the pale sunlight now, the land rose towards Appledore and Westward Ho and below his feet he could feel the first juddering as the brakes began to lock the wheels. Bideford. Home.

Head out of the window, holding his hat against the wind, the brim curling away from his face, Harry could see only steam, sweeping back with the smoke from the stack and blotting out the station platform in a cloud of grey and white. There were noises and voices up there, the squeal of the braking wheels and a bell ringing and a voice calling 'Bideford – Bideford Station!' and then the red gravel end of the platform cut through the smoke and the stone side of a building and a large-lettered sign and the steam and the smoke were in his eyes and he could feel them stinging with the moisture, the dampness on his cheeks and he ran the back of his hand across his face and swung the door wide and stepped out, standing stock-still, crying without shame.

The three of them there. Father, shoulders stooped a little now, whiskers white, a solid figure in Donegal tweeds, his hard hat square on his head. Father staring at him, gripping the old black cane like a sword. Mother was tiny still, a bird of a woman, her small gloved hands strangling the life out of her purse, her face as wet with tears as his own. And Helen, topping mother by a head, a slim and stately young woman where he'd left a little girl. And they stood there, ten feet apart while the world moved, and then there was no distance between them at all and mother's arms were about his neck and he could feel the crêpe-paper fineness of her face against his and her lips covering his and hear the little murmuring wordless noises and Helen, an arm around each of them and weeping and laughing and saying in a crackly sort of voice, 'Oh, Harry, welcome home, welcome home!'

And then they loosened, the arms and the lips, and there was father and Harry realized that he'd pulled off his hat when he left the train and he put it back on and pulled himself upright and stared at the old man levelly and saluted him, holding the hand there at the brim of his hat for a long, long moment. And father very stiffly, face unmoved, raised his own hand and took off his hat to his son and then threw the hat to the ground and ran the three steps between them and they met chest to chest there on the platform while the people around them stared and Damn the people to Hell and the white whiskers rasped against Harry's cheek and he felt his father tremble and shake but the grip of the arms was strong on him. Harry leaned back.

'Father . . .? May I come home, sir?'

The light eyes were brimming, but the voice was a growl. 'Don't be bloody silly, boy! You *are* home! Helen, pick up my hat!'

The house had never been big, not when it was built somewhere in the mid-1700s, not when it had been added to nearly a century later by Harry's grandfather, the plain, neatly columned front with a low wing on either side. The poplars along the drive were taller and the laurels had grown and thickened and the ancient and twisted oak among whose branches the boy Harry had climbed was gone, the hole of its passing filled now with roses in a formal bed. More than anything yet, Harry realized how the loss of that old oak marked the loss of the years.

Leitch the coachman had managed to edge alongside Harry as he left the carriage, managed to mutter, 'Raight glad to see you 'ome agen, Muster 'Arry,' and the roll of the voice out of the corner of the almost still lips suddenly reminded Harry of the man . . . no, the lad, who'd worked about the stables once, staring up at the young master with wide round eyes. And then there was Parker, old Parker, his back as stiffly upright as ever, his pink face purpling with the effort not to grin, allowing himself only a smile with his bow and a quiet, 'The staff wishes me to welcome you back, sir. It's very good to see you. *Very* good, sir, old times come again.' Harry shook hands but could only nod, standing there at the foot of the eight wide, shallow steps, looking up at the house, at the servants waiting there, his throat swollen with an insane desire to shout and to cry and to laugh.

Helen had wanted to come upstairs too, but his mother had said firmly, 'No, dear, you just go and freshen yourself and make sure

luncheon is ready. I'll take Harry to his room,' and they'd walked
up the curve of the staircase, her hand trembling a little on his arm,
the thin sunlight striking as it always did late in the morning along
the upper hall with the two side-tables and the pictures of grandfather Morant and grandfather Chetwynd and the very bad painting of father's first command, a sloop, *Virginia*. The first door on the
left was father's room and the second was mother's and the door
opposite those two had always been known as the sewing-room,
though mother was much more likely to be writing letters, drinking
endless cups of tea or chattering.

Then there was Helen's room on the right and beyond mother's
bedroom, Miss Tunstall's, the Nanny, the door wide now so that
Harry could see it was obviously a room used by Helen ... a white-
and-gold piano, an easel and some racked canvases. Then the end
door on the right, the corner room that looked out over the wing at
that end, its window offering easy access to that lower roof and to
the roof of the greenhouse behind it and the forbidden night-world,
poaching-world beyond that.

'It's still your room Harry, my dear. It always has been.' His
mother's gentle hands on his face pulled him down as she kissed
him. 'We'll wait luncheon for you ... but not too long. We've a long
time to make up for. But you're home now, my son.' She kissed him
again and was gone, hurrying down the hall, through the sunbars.

Now he lay on his back in the bed that had always had a little lump
on the left side of the mattress no matter how often it was turned,
and he knew where everything was. Everything as he had left it.

He'd let his mother turn down the stairs and then pushed open
the door, eyes closed for a second and feeling the sun on the lids. he
didn't open them till he was inside.

A big, square room on the corner of the old house, the bed with
the same dark blue counterpane with the light blue pattern on it
over in the far corner. The desk, once his grandfather's, in the
opposite corner in the angle between the windows. The enormous
old wardrobe filling all the wall up to the doorway. The cabinet
of shelves and the campaign chest which had been his mother's
brother's. The white and gold striped wallpaper a little more faded.
Everything clean, everything neat ... fresh flowers in two bowls,
roses in a big one on the chest and a little jar of periwinkles on the
round table by the bed. Books tidily on the shelves and papers
straight on the desk; and the smell of the lavender his mother always
wore everywhere in the room. He stood there, knowing she had been
here not just today, not just to make sure it was right, but many times.

The windows were beginning to assume shapes, less-than-black rectangles against the more-than-black of the room and Harry shook himself lower in the bed, pressing and curving his body not just into the sheets and under the blankets but into the house itself, into the country, into the life. He remembered quite clearly the last time he was in this room, the room in which he'd grown up. He'd taken the coach from Dartmouth up to Exeter and then another rattling and bumping its way across to Barnstaple. Hiring a horse there he used all but a few shillings of the little money he had left, but it meant he could time his ride down to Bideford, skirting the town and coming onto his father's land from the seaward side. The spinney at the top of Seven Crosses Hill had given him a clear view of the house and gardens spread a mile below and he'd spent six chilly, hungry hours there, the smoke from the kitchen chimneys blowing up towards him, carrying, so he imagined, the smells of lunch with it. It was well after two that afternoon that he'd seen the light carriage wheel round to the steps and the boxes and cases being lashed on behind. That was better than he'd thought – it meant his parents were off, probably for the weekend, and there'd be no real need for hurry. Not that he'd wanted to prolong things.

Parker had seen him ride down the hill and through the little pear orchard and was waiting on the steps when he dismounted, his uniform crumpled and damp from the night's travel and the long morning in the trees.

'Oh, Mister Harry, the Captain's left sir, and Lady Dorothy – to the Amorys, sir, for the shooting.'

'It's all right Parker. I'm not on leave,' he had said. 'Just overnight. Get someone to rub this beast down and feed him, will you?'

He'd run up the steps, not wanting to talk, not wanting to face the puzzled look, and had heard Parker calling for a groom. Harry had his tunic off by the time Parker came tapping at the door carrying the leather valise with the H.H.M. stamped on it.

'Your bag, sir. I'll have a bath drawn directly; and you'll be wanting some dinner?'

'See what you can find me now for a start – anything. Some cold meat and some bread and cheese. Up here on a tray. And some cider, please.'

By the time the butler had brought the tray the room was a shambles. Harry had sold the rest of his clothes two days before, sneaking into the dingy pawnbroker's at Dartmouth and out again with three guineas jingling thinly in his pocket. Almost everything he'd left at home was too small for him now, but he'd piled some socks and drawers and shirts on the bed, leaving the rest strewn around.

Parker put the tray down on the chest, looking around with a worried frown. 'Is there something wrong, Mister Harry? Something I can do?'

Parker had been a footman when Harry began to walk, as much a part of the family as any relative. Harry had tried a smile, knowing that it wasn't working, knowing too that if Parker sent a groom riding to the Amorys on a fresh horse, his father would very likely be back here by nightfall.

'No, nothing wrong, Parker – not really. Look, I've changed my mind. I shan't stay over, so don't get cook started on one of her Fattening Young Harry feasts. I'll eat here while I sort myself out and then be off. I'd like Rajah saddled, please.'

'But sir—'

'No buts, man! Just do as I say!' He saw the wounded look and cursed his abruptness. 'Look, Parker, I *am* in a touch of bother but I shall only need a day or two to sort it out, believe me. Just get along and see to Rajah for me, eh?'

He bustled the man out and locked the door, sick at the lying, and tore at the sliced beef on the tray while he went on cramming things into his valise. A rapid search through all his pockets and the various drawers in the room yielded a little over eight pounds and he sat on the disordered bed finishing the cider and looking round, wondering about a note. Below the window he'd heard voices and looked out seeing Rajah, his own hunter, being held there, Parker and the groom talking together. Damn, he'd have to ride away in uniform, otherwise they'd suspect even more. He'd crammed on his hat, snatched at the valise and then, not able to go otherwise, crossed to the desk and scrawled on a piece of paper, 'Dearest Mother and Father, I'm truly sorry. Goodbye. All my deepest love, Harry.'

Then he'd slammed the door and run downstairs and ridden away. . . .

Now he was back.

He slid out of bed, feeling the morning chill and shrugging into the dressing-gown of his father's which had been on his bed last night. With the curtains pulled back the first of day looked clear, a dew-fost on the lawns just beginning to sparkle, and he leaned against the side of the window looking out, forcing himself to believe, remembering the words he'd once said to Paddy in a smelly hut high on a winter hill across the world. . . . Nothing will take me home again, will it? So it doesn't matter, does it? But it did, it mattered, and he felt the quick start of tears again, smiling to think how old Paddy would love to see that!

There was enough light for him to see his unshaven face in the mirror. His mother had left all the old invitations, stuck in the frame ...'request the pleasure of the company of ...' '... Hunt ball ...', a pink and deckle-edged one '... the birthday of their daughter Felicia ...' and the scrawl across the corner of it – '*Please* come! F.'

He pulled the bell-cord and bundled the invitations together into a drawer till the tap at the door came. It was a new face, smiling and saying, 'Ayliffe, sir. Footman these three years. 'Morning, sir.'

'Oh, yes. Good morning, Ayliffe. See if you can find me some hot coffee, will you? Nothing to eat. I'll come down to breakfast later.'

'Very good sir. Draw your bath?'

'After the coffee, please.'

'Yessir.' The smile was back, wider. 'Big day today, sir.'

Not that Harry saw much of the events in the house during that day. The thought of suddenly being thrown back into the wild waters of the county's social swim made him nervous, his mind refusing to let him forget how long he'd been gone and under what terms he'd left. The one dominant thought was the hurt to his mother if people should choose not to accept invitations, or come in order to bite on some tasty old meat of scandal. But by the time he'd bathed and breakfasted alone, it was clear from the neat double-stack of acceptances on the table in the hall that the place would be packed that evening. The whole ground floor was a whirling scuttle of servants and Harry got out as fast as he could, a startled lad in the stables saddling a steady-looking mare for him and the gravel of the drive spurting as he cantered away.

By the time he got back the poplars were sliding long pencils of shadow across the lawns. The great double-doors were standing wide to the warm air and the hall was a banked mass of flowers, the eight man-high brass candlesticks that his father had brought back years ago from Hong Kong spaced about, candles as thick as Harry's wrist waiting to be lit. Parker was there looking as though he had just come fresh from a special fitting at a superb tailor's, and a constant stream of maids and footmen moved to and from him for the quiet and unruffled answers to their questions. He waved two of them away as he saw Harry and came forward, taking his hat and gloves and passing them behind him to a youngster who seemed to move with him like the Dog Star with the moon.

'Mister Harry, Lady Dorothy asked me to let you know she thought you were very sensible to get away into the fresh air and out of the – er – turmoil, sir. She and Miss Helen are dressing.'

'Been a bit of a madhouse, has it, Parker?'

'Busy, sir, busy enough. But we've managed very well.' Just a tiny touch of pride there, Harry thought, Parker the Centre of the Universe. Probably right, too.

'The admiral suggested you might like to take a sandwich and a glass of sherry with him, sir. In his dressing-room.' The raised eyebrow was question and answer all in one. Will he do it . . . and if not what will I tell the old gentleman? I'll think of something.

Harry clapped him affectionately on the arm. 'I'll be there in five minutes. Just a quick wash first, right?'

Harry dawdled over his wash. He hadn't been alone with his father since he got home and he felt rather like a schoolboy on holidays after a poor term report. He straightened his shoulders, crossed the upper hall and tapped at his father's door, not waiting for an answer before going in. There was a quiet fire in the grate and Harry remembered how his father had always felt the chill, the legacy of years spent away from England under blood-thinning suns. The admiral was propped comfortably in an armchair to one side of the fire, feet up on a stool, a tattered old gown round him and a tray of chicken sandwiches on a low table alongside, with a decanter and glasses.

'Father, may I come in?'

'In or out, boy, but shut that damn door! Draught's like a sword.' He poured some of the very pale sherry and waved at the other armchair. 'Sit down, Harry, and have something.'

It was awkward for them both as they sat sipping and chewing at the sandwiches, staring into the fire, each wanting to start, neither knowing how. It was Harry who broke the silence, leaning forward to refill the glasses, eyes down as he spoke.

'It's very good to be home, Father.'

The admiral coughed, and again. 'Good to have you here, boy. Dammit, I don't suppose I should be calling you 'boy' should I? Not any more. You've grown well, Harry.'

'In a number of ways, Father. I've – I've not always done things you'd approve of.'

The old man smiled for the first time, the heavy face softening at once. 'You never did, you bloody young rogue! Always went your own way.' With the smile they both relaxed.

'I was pretty much of a fool, Father. You do know how sorry I am for . . . all that business, don't you? I – must have hurt you badly.'

'You did, boy. Hurt your mother worse. I'm stronger stuff, of course. You should have told me about it, not run off like—' He stopped, not wanting to say words that would sting, then went on, his voice quiet. 'Harry, it's all past and done. No point in dragging

it all up again – it's over. We've missed you here, all of us, and your
mother looks twenty years younger now you're home again. And
you've done good things, boy. I'm proud of you.'

He blinked, staring back again into the fire, and Harry was
astonished at the fierce stab of affection he felt for the old man
opposite, saying gentle things. The silence this time was longer, but
there was a comfortable softness in it and when the admiral said,
'Well then – what was it all like? Australia and the war and all
that?' Harry began to talk, the fire lowering, the room darkening,
their heads closer together, the old man often breaking into a
barking laugh. At one stage he said, 'By the God, that feller Magee
sounds like a sensible chap! I think I should like him,' and Harry
suddenly realized that his father and Paddy would probably get on
like lifelong friends. And for a moment, he missed Paddy deeply.

Then the tapping at the door and Parker saying, 'Excuse me, Sir
George – Lady Dorothy asked me to let you know it is getting a
little late,' and Harry stood and his father stood by him, a little
shorter with his stoop. Parker's eyes were alight as he saw the old
man's arm across Harry's shoulders, pushing him affectionately
out of the door. 'Go on with you, you smooth-tongued young devil!
Get your fancy duds on! There are people coming to stare at you.
And watch the old women, boy! They'll be wanting to grab you off
for their daughters!'

The long morning room was to the right of the hall and, to the left,
the dining room and then the library. The tall panelled doors
between all these rooms had been leafed back so that the whole
wide front of the house splayed light and music and noise out into
the gardens and along the arc of the drive. Sheltered behind a bank
of shrubs, an eight-piece orchestra was lilting its way through a
polka and the two long buffet tables were surrounded by a constant
shift of people, the three men and two maids behind the food slicing
and serving with barely a pause. The punchbowls were on the oak
table by the library wall with Parker standing nearby, a careful eye
cocked on the man attending to the bar. There were several tubs of
ice, the gilt caps of the wine bottles glinting out of the blue-
whiteness, and a silver tray for the cluster of whisky and brandy
bottles.

Parker had listened, sometimes with amusement, sometimes
with anger, to the splinters of conversation piercing the overall
fabric of the noise. A bonelessly elegant young man had slid past
him, balancing three glasses of champagne and drawling to the girl
giggling with him. 'I'm told he actually worked as some kind of

farm labourer. I mean, as *a workman!*' The girl had glanced at Harry, tall by his mother's side, and said, her eyes running up and down him, 'Well, it doesn't seem to have hurt him, Arthur.' Another girl was asking her escort, 'What *is* that funny uniform Harry's wearing?' The young man in infantry scarlet with the green facings and the three Devonshire castles of the 11th of Foot, said, 'His sister tells me it's the Cape Police, of all things. Not properly military at all, of course.' 'Pears he's been commissioned into them.'

One of the older women swam out of the stream and anchored herself by Harry, a thin hand on his arm. 'Shall you be home for long, Lieutenant Morant?'

'Six months, Lady Wemyss. I have that much leave.'

'How very nice for your dear mother.' Her fan tapped his shoulder. 'You must call on me soon. I've a niece I want you to look over.'

Harry caught her look and they laughed together. 'I knew a man in New South Wales, Lady Wemyss, who used to talk to me about horses in just that way.'

'Ah, well, you might find the similarity doesn't end there, young man. I'm afraid my niece isn't exactly a great beauty.'

'But you'd like me to – er, look her over?'

'Oh, indeed yes! Teeth and stance and so on. You might even run a hand over her fetlocks!' She gave a great guffaw of laughter and Harry's mother turned inquiringly, meeting Harry's smile as Lady Wemyss moved away.

'Is old Elizabeth being coarse again, Harry dear?'

'Not really, mother. Just inviting me to make a bid for a niece of hers. With a touch-trial first.'

'Harry! How awful!'

'Yes, I gathered she was.'

His mother giggled and he kissed her, edging into the crush. Over by the bar-table, Parker heard a beefy Grenadier say, rather too loudly, to one of the admiral's young cousins, 'Don't see what the fuss is about really. Out of some strange Colonial Yeomanry into the African police and everyone treats him like bloody Wellington! Quite extraordinary!'

The cousin, a quiet man in the blue and gold of a commander's full-dress rig, looked with care at the Guardsman. 'Ah, well, he *has* seen some action, y'see. Bit different from Palace duties, I imagine.' Parker thought, Good for the Navy, and leaned back a little to the tight group of chattering girls behind him.

'Helen told me he's written a lot of poetry ... some of it quite ...
well, you know—'

'Really! Oh, I'd love to persuade him to read me some of it!'

A third voice said, drily, 'From what I've heard of Harry Morant,
you wouldn't have any trouble persuading him to do anything ...
not with your bosom cut that low, dear!'

'Good –then I shall have to do something about it, shan't I?'

Parker watched her pass him, a plump girl, pouting her chest so
that her very full breasts almost leapt out of the blue silk, thrusting
them ahead of her to where Harry was moving towards the door at
the end of the library, the door to his father's study. He smiled with
quiet enjoyment as Harry passed through the door, leaving the girl
tight-lipped and scowling.

Harry pushed the door almost shut behind him, muting the
sound of the violins and the conversations out there. The study was
immediately below his bedroom, another big square corner room,
rich now with the cigar-smoke overlaying the old leather smells
from the two walls of shelves and the headiness of port and brandy
fumes. His father was leaning against the mantelpiece, his frock-
coat unbuttoned, listening with the rest of the seven or eight elderly
men there to one of his near neighbours. General Sawyer's face was
almost exactly the same scarlet as his tunic and his eyes were
sending pale-blue flashes of fire around the group.

'I'm not saying the Boer *can't* fight, dammit! What I'm saying is
that he *don't* fight! He shoots a bit and hides a bit and bloody well
runs away!'

The lean old man across the group was in the regimentals of the
Duke of Cornwall's Light Infantry, his throat and chest glittering
with the cheerful ribbons and shining metal of a dozen past cam-
paigns. He opened his tight lips just enough to rasp out, 'Well, if
that ain't fighting, John, you'd better have another look at the
casualty lists. Half the Army's been shot to pieces – and that's *since*
Botha surrendered!'

'Gentlemen,' the admiral broke in, 'all I can say is things must
be in damn bad shape for the Army to have to call in a Naval
Brigade to help them out! Bluejacket gunners, by the God! fighting
on land!'

The tubby man at the other end of the mantelpiece leaned
forward, bald head gleaming. 'Ah, that was just to let your sailor-
boys see a bit of real action, Morant –'

'Real action my arse!' General Sawyer was spraying tiny drops of
port as he sputtered. 'There ain't any real action any more! It's all
this – this commando stuff the Boer's started. No discipline, no

uniforms, elect their own officers, all over the place like a pack of mangy dogs!'

The admiral chipped in forestalling any of the others. 'Well, Kitchener'll soon put a stop to it all. D'you see today's report in the *Telegraph*? That chap Burleigh says K's ordered a line of block-houses right across the fighting front.'

'What the blazes is the good of blockhouses? Only hampers the troops – you can't form line in a bloody blockhouse!'

'Well, I don't know, John. Burleigh says they're going to clear the whole damn countryside and toss all the civilians into camps of some kind so the old Boer can't sneak about and get supplies and so on.'

'Supplies, is it? He'll have no trouble about that, not with the bloody Kaiser shipping him guns through the Portuguese at Delagoa Bay. Mark my words, gentlemen, the Kaiser's going to have to answer for the way he's supporting those damn rebels!'

The tubby man leaned forward again. 'I just hope Kitchener gives our cavalry a chance to get at 'em. From what I hear from my old regiment, there hasn't been a single decent cavalry action yet. Just not using 'em!'

Harry had been listening quietly, his face twisted cynically at the edge of the group, when the quiet voice came from the far side, away from the light of the two desk-lamps and the fire.

'What a load of manure!'

General Sawyer started and glared. 'What's that? Speak up, young feller!'

The voice said, a little louder, 'Sorry, sir. I said I'm not so sure.'

Harry grinned and shifted to see who had spoken, but his father had pulled the other man forward by the arm and Harry saw a tall and slender man, hair the colour of tow, face thin and sunburnt. His Hussar blues clung to him and the furred pellise across his left shoulder partly concealed the light silk sling holding his wrist. The admiral said, 'I don't believe you know young Hunt, John. General Sawyer, gentlemen – Captain Geoffrey Hunt. On leave, like Harry.' He turned to the general. 'Hunt's been out there, you know ... the Cape.'

The general hadn't taken his eyes from the young Hussar, only nodding at the introduction, Hunt's last words still clear in his mind. Now he shoved his red face forward.

'What do you mean – you're not sure?'

Harry was struck by the quality of repose in Hunt, standing, elegant and relaxed in the circle of older and more senior officers. It wasn't insolence, he thought, but it wasn't a long way from it. Hunt looked back at General Sawyer.

'I was considering the remark about the cavalry not being used, sir.' He half turned and made the slightest of bows to the tubby man. 'I can assure you, all of you, from personal experience that we are indeed being used. And used very badly.'

The tubby man's voice rose above the murmur, shrill with indignation. 'Damn your impertinence! What d'you mean – used badly?'

Harry edged a little closer, seeing that Hunt's face was entirely calm and that he faced the obvious hostility around him almost with enjoyment, looking down on the bald head of the tubby man and answering him directly.

'Sir, with respect, we've been used in regimental and brigade advances just as though the Boer didn't have expert marksmen with the best Mauser magazine rifles. *And* Maxim guns in concealed positions. We've been ridden at the centre of strongpoints where we couldn't see the enemy at all – never did see him. We've been used as though nobody's learned a thing since Balaclava.'

The silence was thick with anger and embarrassment. Hunt alone seemed unmoved and it was Harry who spoke, deliberately.

'How would *you* suggest using the cavalry?'

'Send 'em home.' The immediate response brought a growl from the others, with Sawyer stepping close to Hunt, snarling at him.

'Send 'em home? I find it difficult to believe that an officer—'

Harry pitched his voice just high enough to top the other man's. 'And replace them with what, Hunt?'

'Mounted infantry, of course. *We're* no damn use against the Boer. You can't charge uphill into rocks and get a point into an invisible man who's shooting at you.' He swung to look round them. 'As a piece of first-hand information, gentlemen, let me advise you that the Boer can find his mark in good light at a comfortable thousand yards. He aims generally for the thigh or the leg, so that his round passes through the man and gets the horse too. Disgusting, isn't it?' The mockery in his voice was open now. 'No, the answer's mounted infantry. Horses to get 'em in there, dismount 'em and tackle the Boer with well-trained riflemen – magazine rifles would be nice – and machine-guns.'

The tubby man was almost dancing with rage. 'I'm – I *was* – a Dragoon, sir. I'm glad I wasn't a Hussar, if you're an example of the Light nowadays. You should be—'

Again Harry interrupted. 'I beg your pardon, sir, but I have to say that Captain Hunt is voicing the opinion of almost everyone who's actually fought against the Boer, especially the younger officers. The situation's a little different when you're actually there, of course.' He'd said it as coldly as he could and just had time to catch Hunt's wink before the admiral moved forward, determined to relieve the tension.

'Er – Harry, why don't you and young Hunt go and – er – enjoy the dancing?'

Taking the cue, Harry nodded around the group. 'Of course, Father. Gentlemen, I'm sure you'll excuse us. You must have many memories to recapture.'

His father walked him to the study door, Hunt following them. The admiral's whisper was loud enough for only Harry to hear. 'You young snot-nose! Now I shall have to settle 'em down. But you were right, boy! Stand up to 'em.'

Harry gripped his father's shoulder hard for a second, knowing suddenly how much alike they were, and slipped out of the study, heading straight for the bar. He gestured at an opened bottle and the man poured champagne into two glasses, a blue-and-gold arm reaching past Harry for the second one. Hunt said, 'I say, you must be Morant, the long-lost-son-of-the-house fellow.'

Harry kept his face straight. 'You're not really a British cavalry officer, are you?'

Hunt drank down the champagne and passed the glass back to be refilled, using his empty hand to make a sweeping gesture at himself. 'I must be. All this glory could never grace a footslogger!'

Harry shook his head in apparent disbelief. 'I'd never have believed the day would come when I'd hear a cavalry-man talking sense! You astound me – and I'm bloody glad to meet you!'

They gripped hands hard, neither of them noticing the girl who'd moved close to them, her hair as light as Hunt's, her eyes as blue and the old-gold gown hugging her to the hips before flaring out in a golden swirl. She spoke across Hunt to Harry.

'Then I hope you'll be just as bloody glad to meet the rest of the family.'

Both men wheeled, startled, and Hunt's voice was sharp. 'Margaret! Behave yourself!' He turned to Harry. 'My apologies – my sister doesn't stand much on ceremony.'

The girl blew him a little kiss. 'Don't be mealy-mouthed, Geoffrey. Introduce the nice gentleman properly, please.'

Harry didn't wait for the introduction. He made a leg, the deep bow almost a caricature. 'Morant, Miss Hunt. Harry Morant. And I'm delighted to meet the rest of the family, I promise you. I don't believe I've ever heard a lady say 'bloody' before.'

'Then you've led a rather sheltered life, Harry Morant – which I find difficult to believe. Besides, I'm not much of a lady.'

Hunt sounded outraged. 'Now look here, Margaret! Morant—'

He realized they were ignoring him completely, Harry staring down at the girl, only an inch or two shorter than himself, deliberately letting his look dwell on her breasts. She stood, hands by her sides, aware of his inspection and accepting it calmly, chin up to study his face. Hunt whistled tunelessly between his teeth, turned to the bar and held up three fingers to the man there. He turned back, a glass of champagne in his hand, to find them gone, moving easily together in the waltz the violins were sighing over. He stared after them for a moment then downed the champagne, then the second, then picked up the third. Parker watched him, smiling, and the smile widened as he looked past the young Hussar to Harry and Margaret Hunt.

Harry couldn't describe it, even to himself. The sense of well-being, of satisfaction, of something like completion, was so much around him that he could only accept it, wrapping himself in the almost tangible blanket of enjoyment. Sometimes it seemed to him that he was dead and in the Heaven he'd been told about as a little boy, a place where the sun always shone, the birds always sang and no one was ever unhappy.

Within a week of getting home he'd snatched up the thousand loose threads of his old life, plaiting them into strong ropes, binding himself once more to the things and the people he'd never expected to see again, and he found the long years behind him were sliding away fast, sliding backwards into a piece of his mind that belonged to someone else, like a book he'd read or a play he'd seen. The real present was being home again. And Geoffrey. And Margaret, most of all Margaret.

When they swung away from her brother in that first waltz, they moved into a separate world. Harry looked down into her face, looking up into his, and began a smile. Margaret quite deliberately turned him into an angle of the crowded room, a corner where the lights reached less well, and moved herself against him, laying the full length of herself onto his body, still moving in the rhythm of the dance, so that he could feel the swell of her breasts and the roll of her thighs. He tightened his grip on her, staring down at the eyes that hadn't shifted from his own.

'Do you know what you're doing?'

Then she smiled, widely and with a happy triumph.

'Oh, yes, Harry Morant, I know exactly what I'm doing. Don't you?'

And she'd pressed herself to him again, then twirled him back into the crush.

It had gone on for weeks, the days spinning away in a reel of pleasure, Harry and Margaret constantly together, Geoffrey almost always with them, the county ladies buzzing and winking over their teacups, the Hunts and the Morants delighted, the engagement ring a sharp fire of diamonds and the women lost in a wild fantasy of fashions for the proposed wedding.

And it went sour.

July brought early rain and cold winds and the two men rode back to the house with their cloaks dripping. The train had hissed wetly away into the mist with their families, hellbent for a frenzy of London shopping, and the house seemed strangely quiet. In Harry's room the fire cracked and glowed and they kicked off their boots and let the warmth wrap them. Geoffrey slumped into one of the two big chairs with a relaxed sigh, propping his stockinged feet on the fender. Harry had walked in the window and stood staring out at the trees tossing in the wind which was throwing handfuls of rain at the windows. He didn't turn when Parker came in with a tray of coffee, the paper and a small bundle of letters. He glanced at Harry's stiff back and coughed gently.

'Er, coffee, Mr Harry?'

'Thanks, Parker. Just leave it, will you?' His back was still to the room. 'Oh – and put some brandy out, will you please?'

'Yes, sir.' Harry could hear the clink of the decanter and glasses. 'The morning post is here, sir. One for Captain Hunt, sent on for you, sir.'

Harry looked around and nodded as Parker passed the letter to Geoffrey, then swung back to stare emptily out of the wet window again. Hunt waited till Parker had closed the door behind him before speaking, the unopened letter balanced in his fingers.

'Harry. Something wrong?'

'No. Just this damned rain, I think.'

Geoffrey poured coffee, clattering the cups.

'Well, then, sit down for God's sake. Have some coffee.'

Harry swung round and slumped in the other chair, reaching for the decanter and pouring two stiff shots of brandy. He ignored the little pile of mail till Hunt asked, 'Aren't you going to open your letters?' then riffled through them and dropped them on the floor by his chair.

'Oh, just the usual ration of bills and invitations.'

He drank his brandy and poured another at once, not touching his coffee, and the silence stretched. Hunt leaned forward to poke down a log. 'I suppose by the time Margaret gets back she'll have bought half the fashion houses in Town.'

Harry grunted.

'She's used to spending pretty freely, Harry. Won't be cheap keeping her.'

'I suppose not. We'll manage.'

'Er – perhaps I shouldn't ask, but as the prospective best man – how long an engagement d'you two have in mind?'

'Engagement? Oh, Hell, I don't know! Haven't really pinned things down to a date yet.'

'Oh, I see.' Hunt shifted uncomfotably. 'You don't mean – er – you're not . . .?'

'No, of course not, Geoffrey, don't be bloody daft! We're engaged and we're going to be married. I'm just not sure when, that's all.' He gulped down brandy and refilled once more.

Hunt started to speak, thought better of it and followed Harry's example, watching the other man cross back to the window and stare out again at the driving rain.

He called across the room. 'I suppose it's as hot as Hell in Pretoria.'

Harry spun about, almost smiling. 'That's funny. I was just thinking the same thing. I think I've got what the troops call itchy feet.'

He slumped into his armchair again, unfolding the newspaper across his knees while Hunt stared at him, one eyebrow raised, a grin twisting one side of his mouth. 'Itchy feet, is it, Harry? I think I've got what *I* call guilty conscience.'

'What the devil have you got to be guilty about?'

'Oh, all this. All part of what's been fretting me for some time. Sitting on my bum doing nothing. Enjoying myself – or pretending to. My arm's in fine shape now . . . I ought to be back at work.'

'Back in action, d'you mean?'

'I suppose I do.'

'That's a damn silly thought! You've still got weeks of leave. Me too.

'Christ! You sound thoroughly miserable about it! I believe you feel just the same way I do.'

'Don't be ridiculous!' Harry rattled the newspaper up in front of his face, holding it there for a minute or two before dropping it again. 'You're right of course. Geoff. I don't think I can take another week of this . . . dinners and parties and soirées and all the rest of it!'

'Exactly! We're not meant to lie about, Harry. We're meant to be doing something. We should be back in harness.'

'Listen to this – *The Times*. "Now that the first of the enclosed areas has been completed the strength of the Commander-in-Chief's plan is evident. The Boer forces under De La Rey have been forced to move back from the clear and protected country and have been thrown upon very meagre resources. Nonetheless, they continue to fight a hard and savage guerilla action.'" He crumpled the newspaper and tossed it across the floor. 'I keep thinking of our chaps out there and wondering what the bastard hell I'm doing here!'

'I know.' Hunt's voice was quiet. 'I know just what you mean.'

Harry made no answer and Hunt, tightening his lips as he looked across at his friend's grim face, ripped the flap of the letter Parker had given him, noticing that it came from the Cape. His yell jerked Harry's head up.

'Oy, Harry, listen to this – it's from MacEvoy, one of our people at Kitchener's H.Q.! He says, "and there's a great deal of conversation about a new formation to be raised called the Bush Veldt Carbineers. They say it's already recruiting both officers and men and that it's to be a highly irregular affair working well away from Base. You can imagine the effect it's having on some of the old diehards." Harry? Did you hear that?'

Harry was leaning forward. 'Highly irregular, did he say?'

'That he did! "Highly irregular" and ... where is it ... "well away from Base."'

Harry's hands slapped onto his knees and he jerked to his feet, a look of amazement on his face. 'My God, someone's woken up at last!' Hunt's groan pulled him around.

'All very well ... but we're not there, dammit! If only—'

'If only be *damned*! We can soon *be* there, can't we?'

'How? You mean – cancel our leave? Can we?'

Harry stalked forward grinning and his hand took Hunt's shoulder hard. 'Of course we can! Shall we?'

They stared at one another, eyes brightening, the grins spreading. Then Harry was at the door shouting. 'Parker! Parker – find me a shipping list, quickly! And get my trunk out! Oh – and Parker – get someone to bring Captain Hunt's horse round at once.' He slammed the door in Parker's bewildered face and laughed at the gaping Hunt. 'You'd best get home and pack, my son!'

Hunt was tugging on his damp boots, laughing. 'We're really going to do it? God, how marvellous!'

Harry pulled him up and began jigging him around the room in

a wild polka, the two of them chanting 'Highly irregular' till the
entire house seemed to shake and they fell gasping against the door
and Harry opened it and began shoving Hunt out, urging him to
hurry.

Hunt gasped, 'Harry, what about Margaret?'

Harry stood stock still, face suddenly sober. 'Margaret? Margaret
will understand, Geoff.'

Below them in the stables, the horses were shifting quietly in their
stalls, and there was the hissing crunch of teeth in a feedbox. Up
here, in the loft, the cracks and chinks in the roof let in slim shafts of
pale sunlight across which dust and wispy ends of hay floated.
Margaret's fist pounded at his shoulder.

'No, I *don't* understand! I don't understand it at all, Harry!'

'Darling ...'

'Keep away!' She wrenched herself around, her back half turned
to him. 'How can grown men be such fools! Such – such children!'
Turning back to him she shook her head in puzzlement. 'Harry,
you're supposed to love me. We're engaged to be married ...'

'I *do* love you and you know it!' He held her fast, his fingers
gripping her shoulders. 'And we *will* be married –'

Struggling against his grip, she panted at him. 'And in the
meantime you must run off back to your damn war! It's not sense –
not fair!'

He managed to reach her cheek with a kiss. 'Margaret, please ...
surely you understand it's the chance of a lifetime?'

With a sudden violent move she pulled free, staring at him.
'Chance of a lifetime! Oh, you – you schoolboy, you!'

Angered by the scorn in her voice he leaned away from her,
letting his voice chill. 'You seem to forget I'm still a serving soldier.
And there *is* a war going on.'

'And you're on leave from it—'

'A leave which I feel it necessary to cancel. As does your brother.'

'Then you're both fools!'

'We're both quite old enough to make logical decisions.'

'Logical! And I can go to Hell, I suppose?'

'And you can—' Abruptly he leaned towards her again, softening. 'You can surely wait for me? With her silence his anger
returned. 'Look, I'm not a tame hack that you can hobble to ride
just when you feel like it!'

As she swung her head a shaft of light struck fire from her eyes.
'Oh, tell the truth, Harry. You're escaping! You're running away –

again! You're quite happy to bed me but you're scared to wed me, that's the truth of it, isn't it?'

She stopped on a gasp, suddenly frightened of what she's said, frightened of his reaction. But his voice was sad and not much above a whisper. 'That's not so, Margaret. You know it isn't so.'

And she was in his arms and the tears were shaking her as his hand stroked her hair.

'Harry ... Harry, why do you have to go?'

SOUTH AFRICA

After the sunlight, the Bush Veldt Carbineers headquarters was almost dark, a sergeant looming suddenly from behind a table on their right and a dim figure at the end of the room. Harry's hand was halfway to the salute when the figure leapt up and almost ran towards them.

'Hallo, Harry! Welcome to the Bad Boys' Club!'

Lenehan looked older, thinner, greyer, but the smile was as wide and as welcoming and the handshake hard. Harry stared, open-mouthed, finally managing. 'Well, I'm damned! Are you the boss?'

'Indeed I am – you're all mine. I've been waiting for you.' He half turned. 'You must be Hunt?'

'Yes, sir, Geoffrey Hunt. Am I classed as a Bad Boy now?'

'Oh, the old fuddy-duddies seem to think we're all either bad or mad in this show. Come in, come in, find a chair.'

Harry slumped, tunic unbuttoned and looked at Lenehan. 'Major now, I see. I though you'd taken your discharge and gone home long since.'

'Thought about it. Then they offered me this and I couldn't resist it.'

Geoffrey leaned forward. 'Caught us the same way, sir. Are we the last?'

'Just about.' Lenehan waved at the sergeant. 'Potter, go and ask the other officers to step in, will you? And the sar-major, please.' He turned back as the sergeant went. 'Still a few odds and sods to come, but you're the last of the officers. Actually, the whole blasted show's made up of odds and sods, I think you'll know one or two of them, Harry. Some of 'em are a bit rough ... but you'll find out for yourselves soon enough.' The mutter of voices and clink of spurs could be heard outside and Lenehan forestalled the knock by calling, 'Come straight in, you chaps.'

Harry was to learn these men intimately in the weeks that followed, but he never forgot his first sight of them, the impression at this first meeting that someone had gone out of his way to collect a job lot of junior officers for a nasty task ... George Witton, slight and slim and foxy-faced, with a fuzz of gingery hair and artillery badges; Tom Fletcher, all angles and brown-leather skin, managing to look like a gypsy, even in his N.S.W. Lancer's uniform; the great blacksmith's bulk of Peter Handcock swelling through his Bushman's tunic, through ropes of hands jutting from the sleeves which still carried the outlines of a farrier-sergeant's chevrons and insignia; Alec Picton, plump and gentle-looking, like a schoolmaster, round-eyed as though astonished to find himself at war; Ivor Summers, a slender reed of a lad, thin fair hair flopping across a red-burnt face above an elegantly-cut Lancer tunic. They clumped into the little, airless room, raising the temperature perceptibly, and draped themselves across the desk and against the walls and cupboards. Geoffrey caught Harry's eye in a look that said, unmistakably, Jesus! What *have* we got into?

The touch on Harry's elbow was light but firm and he turned, feeling a sudden gush of emotion in the throat as Owen Fisher smiled at him – an apparently unchanged Owen, one side of the thin mouth crooked up in a grin, one black eyebrow up above it.

'Owen – by God, Owen! What the hell are you doing here?'

Fisher saluted, but Harry grabbed his hand down and wrung it, unable to stop smiling. Fisher gestured slightly with his head to take in the others, watching with interest and some amusement.

'As you see, Harry – sorry, sir. Came along for the fun. Good to see you again.'

Harry, with Geoffrey on one side of him and Owen on the other, felt that things couldn't be bad.

Lenehan's briefing was concise and pungent, his finger sweeping across the sketch map pinned to the wall as he showed them their area of operations. Kitchener's plan was well advanced, great sections of countryside cleared of all Boers, crops and farms, even small villages burnt, and the inhabitants moved back into huge camp areas. The commandos had been forced out of this growing belt of devastation, pushed away from the settlements and farms which had sheltered and fed them, which had been their depots and command-posts. And while the massive juggernaut of the armies pounded forward slowly and irresistibly, the Boer troops were moving back and around and away, into the rough country, the higher country, where they were difficult to reach. And, despite reduced numbers and almost non-existent supplies, they were still darting down in fast raids, wreaking havoc on the lines of communication, cutting into the flanks of the main forces, living off British food, firing British ammunition.

The Bush Veldt Carbineers were to fight them at their own game. In quick stabs, Lenehan's finger marked their battleground on the map ... a waste of dust and rock and scrap vegetation, a tangle of single-beast tracks, a sweep of hills arcing round at both ends to a half-dry river. One far boundary was a spur railway-line, and the main track south cut into it at an angle forming another bound. It looked like tough and hardworking campaigning, and the group of men sucked in their breath and whistled gently as the scope of their area became clear. Lenehan looked sombrely at them.

'Yes, I know, it's bloody enormous, isn't it?'

Tom Fletcher, slumped in a corner like an old brown saddlebag, broke the considering silence. 'How many of us will there be, Major?'

'When we're full up, a hundred odd, including us.'

Fletcher's voice was dry. 'Ah, then they'll give us a week or two to win the war for 'em, I s'pose.'

Lenehan overrode the ripple of laughter. 'It's not as bad as it sounds. The last intelligence puts the Boer round here mainly,' his hand flickered across the sweep of rocky hills, 'about four hundred they reckon, but in small groups, scattered. We've got to stop 'em getting together. If we don't – well, we shall be in the shit!'

'What about my guns, sir? When do we get them?' It was George Witton, ginger head bobbing up across the room, and Lenehan hung onto a pause before answering.

'I'm sorry, George – we don't, I'm afraid.' He forestalled Witton's objection. 'I know you and your fellows came as gunners, but that's not the sort of fight we're likely to get into. Of course, you're free to go back to your regiment as soon as you wish—'

'Good God, no!'

There was a roar of laughter at Witton's indignant squeak and he sank back out of sight, his face scarlet. Harry called across the room, 'What about the men, sir?'

'Mixed bag – just like us. They're going to need a bit of shaping up.' He listened to the murmur that rose. 'I think we all are,

gentlemen.' The others stilled at the more formal address, and
Lenehan let his voice become a little crisper, pulling them back into
the feeling of command. 'I intend to work in troop patrols when we
get going, but I'm allowing two weeks for us to shake down and get
to know one another. Hunt, you're next senior rank, so you're now
second-in-command for your sins. We'll manage without an adjutant. The rest of you will be allocated as soon as I can sort it out.
Questions?'

Peter Handcock's voice was a heavy rumble. 'Horses, sir. What
are they like?'

'I don't know, Peter. We haven't got more than a dozen yet. Tell
you what – I'll leave The Breaker to find some for us, eh, Harry?
Think you can do that?'

Harry kept his face straight. 'Shouldn't be surprised, sir.'

Owen's lopsided smile was back and Geoffrey noticed the slanted
look of appraisal that came up from Fletcher, although he said
nothing. It was Handcock, shouldering through the rest who said,
'Hey, are you *that* Morant? Well, it's a pleasure to serve with you!'
and who wrapped Harry's hand in one of his own enormous ones,
shaking it till Harry had to ask him to stop. Under the cover of the
general murmur of chatter, Geoffrey whispered to Harry, 'Didn't
realize you were famous, old boy. I shall have to mind my manners.'
Harry hissed back at him, 'You'd better mind your flapping tongue,
Captain Hunt, sir, or I'll clip it for you. As soon as my hand
heals ...' and he looked down ruefully at his fingers, reddening
again as the blood came back into them.

Lenehan had been right. The men did need shaping up and the ten
days that followed that first meeting were a continual grind. Fisher,
squadron sergeant-major, never seemed to raise his voice, but its
flat rasp was there all day, barbed and prodding, as he put the
troops through basic drills time and time again, shaking them back
into routines they thought happily forgotten, pushing them to the
point of exhaustion, stripping what little fat there was away from
them and drawing fast responses and unhesitating movements.
They split the duties, each of the officers taking a spell at the
drilling, as much for their own needs as for the men, but each of
them also spending time on their special skills. So Peter Handcock
took over the horses as they came in, setting up a little smithy and
ending his days black and reeking, his huge body browning to an
oak colour and his hair bleaching paler and paler. George Witton,
deprived of his guns, scrounged a couple of discarded limbers and a
collection of broken and rusted parts and, with a couple of his

gunners, more or less invented a Maxim and a Hotchkiss. Alec Picton made their maps, riding hundreds of miles with a couple of men who'd run chains for Government surveys, borrowing instruments, stealing paper and spending long evenings turning out probably the only detailed maps of that part of the world. The wispy Ivor Summers asked for and got permission from Lenehan to use the six Lancers he'd brought with him as a reconnaissance troop, disappearing with them for three and four days at a time and coming back with his men exhausted and himself seemingly dustproof, heatproof and immune from thirst and hunger, to give Lenehan information about Boer detachments in the sort of detail which meant he must have been within touching distance of them. Harry, with Tom Fletcher, rode out every morning and came back every evening with horses. Neither man would say where they came from, although Fletcher usually muttered, 'Ah, we found 'em strayin' out in the bush,' and grin ... but Handcock and his assistants spent a fair part of their time running out new brands.

Geoffrey Hunt got to know the track from the B.V.C. area to Field H.Q. intimately. Once the morning routine was over, he'd jam a saddlebag with that day's pile of requests, indents and reports and ride out, spending his days chasing equipment, ammunition, weapons, rations, and vainly trying to speed the movement of their action orders. After ten days he threw himself down on his camp-bed one night, his normally good-natured face screwed up in disgust. Harry, propped on an elbow in the other bed and reading a month-old newspaper grinned across at him.

'You look like a sulky kid who's been kept in after school.'

'Oh, shut up, for Christ's sake!'

Harry's eyebrows shot up and he pretended to cower. 'Oh, please, Captain Hunt, sir, please don't hit me! I'm sorry if I offended your Hussarship!'

For a long moment it looked as though Geoffrey was going to hit him, then the scowl gave way to a rueful laugh. 'Sorry, Harry. It's just that I really didn't come back to act as a dogsbody messengerboy, you know. God, I think I'd sooner be at one of old Mrs Darby's dinner parties. At least there'd be some decent food!'

'Ah – hah!' Harry swung himself upright. 'Now we have the truth of it! Gallant Hussar misses action! Under pressure, Captain Hunt admits he'd rather be feeling knees under dinner-table than carrying out necessary wartime tasks!' The pillow caught him full across the face before he could duck.

Later, lying half-asleep in the dark, Harry spoke quietly. 'Geoff, you're not sorry, are you? About coming back?'

'No. Wouldn't be anywhere else for quids. You?'

'No. Except for Margaret.'

The name hung in the still dark and Harry felt the quiver in his body as he thought of her, thought of her willingness and warmth, and rolled savagely onto his side, trying to force himself into sleep.

By the end of the second week, the Volunteers looked a much more workmanlike body of men. Differences in uniform had been simply overcome – everyone, officers and men alike, wore plain khaki tunics and breeches, and rank badges were the simplest cloth ones. No one wore shiny brass or pipeclay and the only distinguishing feature about them as a unit was the strip of green cloth each man wore as a puggaree around his bush hat. Rifles and pistols were standard issue and most of the men carried either bayonets or long knives as well, while George Witton's two little guns travelled lashed to either side of a home-made limber which could, if necessary, be handled over rough ground by two or three men. Watching them ride out just after dawn one morning on a field exercise, Lenehan noticed how quiet they were, how well they sat the fair horses they rode, how few orders were given beyond simple hand movements, and he was satisfied. He turned to Hunt. 'Geoffrey, I'm coming with you today. We will, by God, beard the general in his unsavoury lair and bloody well force him to give us some work to do. Come on!'

Riding easily at the head of Geoffrey's troop, Harry saw Lenehan and Hunt move out along the track to Field H.Q. and silently wished them luck. He knew the men were sick to death of drills and exercises, just as he knew they needed some action as a unit to pull them really tight. He wondered how his own men would work together, wondered about the trouble-makers, wondered whether he'd done the right thing.

Earlier that week he'd sat half-slumped in the saddle watching Owen Fisher put the troop through their paces. The two files of fifteen men had halted their horses and were sitting to attention, but from where he sat, Harry could see that three of the troopers in the rear file were muttering to one another, their horses jibbing a little out of line. The end man had already been before Harry twice during days of duty as orderly officer – Booth, a dark-faced and surly man from London with a record as a trouble-maker. When Harry had once asked him why he'd re-enlisted, Booth smiled unpleasantly and answered, 'Chance to make some money, sir.' The tone had made it plain he had loot in mind. Now, as Harry started to edge his horse forward, Fisher's voice snapped out.

'Booth! When I want two of us talking at once I'll let you know!'

Harry, closer than Fisher, heard the low-voiced snarl in reply. 'Bloody nice of you, mate!'

Fisher wheeled his horse as Harry rode up, and saluted. 'Troop present and correct, sir.'

'Thank you, Sar-Major.' He dropped his voice as he answered the salute.

'I wouldn't say Booth's all that correct, Owne, would you?'

'Bloody nuisance, that man, Harry. Needs a bit of action to work it out of his system.'

'Well, we all need that.'

'True enough. Just the same, I'd be happier with Booth somewhere else, I think. Trouble-maker, he is.'

'Good soldier, though? In a scrap, I mean?'

Fisher considered. 'Yair. I reckon he could look after himself.'

'Well, we might be able to make use of him then, mightn't we?'

Harry reined his horse back a little and swung to face the troop, pitching his voice up a little. 'All right, you blokes, sit easy. Well, it looks as though we might get off this damned square before long and start tackling the Boer again.' He sensed the stir and gave it a moment to settle. 'You can take it that this is probably close to the end of training. You can start thinking about some real work.'

There were a few grins among the listening men. 'I'm going to assume that we'll be on the track tomorrow, so we'll stand down now and take it slack for the rest of the day.' The grins widened and there was a mutter of appreciation. 'All right, properly at ease now. Fall them out, Sar-Major.'

As soon as Owen had dismissed the men, Harry muttered to him, 'Tell Booth I want to see him now; behind the supply shed.'

Fisher's face was immobile, but his eyes were smiling as he nodded.

Harry heard the man coming and set himself. As Booth rounded the corner of the shed on the edge of their area, Harry's hands shot out, locking hard into the front of Booth's tunic, forcing his chin up and back, and Harry pivoted, slamming him flatbacked against the shed wall so that the breath burst out of him in a great grasp. He held the man there, almost on tiptoe, face purpling and hand plucking uselessly at Harry's wrists, while he spoke to him, quietly and conversationally.

'Trooper Thomas Booth, slum-boy and trouble-maker, right? Right?' He slammed him against the shed again till Booth nodded tightly. 'Well, Trooper Thomas Booth, you're making a nuisance of yourself, you and your nasty friends. You're not behaving yourself, lad, not the way I want you to behave, and I'm going to have to teach you a lesson, eh?' He threw Booth contemptuously from him and watched as the man controlled his breathing and straightened his tunic, his stare at Harry malevolent.

Still panting a little, Booth spat out, 'That's contrary to the Articles, that is, *Mister Morant*! You struck me – you could be locked up for that!'

'Indeed I could – if you could prove it, Booth. But there aren't any witnesses, you see – just you and me. Now then, you're a strong lad and you've got all sorts of ideas of your own. Here's your chance to try them out. Come on, let's see just how good you are.'

For a moment Booth tensed, fists clenching, setting himself for a spring. Then he relaxed. 'Oh no, oh no, you don't! You'll not get Tommy Booth on striking a superior officer! Not on your life, cully!'

Harry smiled coldly. 'Good! Bears out what I thought – you've got a brain in your head. Now let's see if you can start using it. You've got a year's service, Booth. You ride well and apart from your disgusting bad manners, you make quite a respectable soldier. But you've got to learn who's the boss, Booth. Understand?' Booth stared back at him, trying to hold his gaze, then nodded. Harry bore straight in.

'The answer is "Yes, sir"'

'Yes. Sir.'

'Ah, now we're getting along famously. We shall be friends yet, you and I. And just to show you how friendly I can be, I'm going to make you up to corporal.' He watched the wash of amazement on the man's face and smiled grimly. 'I'm going to give you some responsibility. Make you give a few orders. You'll like that, won't you, Corporal Booth?'

The other man was silent, mouth open, eyes blinking. 'Lost your tongue, man? Never mind. I don't want to be thanked. Just you take care, though, and behave yourself. You've got something to lose now, you see.' His voice suddenly snapped. 'Straighten yourself up!'

Booth pulled himself together, composing his face but unable to hide the suspicion in his eyes. Harry held down a grin. 'Good. Now, just to show there's no ill-feeling, let's shake hands on it, shall we?'

He stretched his hand and Booth instinctively met it. Harry slid his grip along, moving into the hollow where Booth's thumb ended and across the little joints at the back of the hand, locking his own fingers in and down, hard and steadily, seeing Booth's eyes go wide, then fill with tears of pain, his face twisting. Harry was expressionless and he kept his voice low and friendly.

'I'm sure you'll remember who's in charge here, won't you, Corporal?'

Dropping his hand, he turned on his heel and was gone.

Now, glancing back, he could see Booth with Dawes and Rattray, his two cronies, riding together. There'd been no further overt trouble from any of them but Harry sensed the hatred in Booth whenever they were near and again he wondered whether he wouldn't have done better to get rid of him. Shrugging the thought away, he wheeled of the track, gesturing the troop to follow him.

Dinner had been over an hour ago and the little Mess hut was thick with tobacco-smoke, hanging in blue swirls in the still heat of the night. Harry was resting on his shoulderblades in the wreck of an easy chair someone had salvaged, idly watching Peter Handcock hunched over a letter, the pen almost invisible in his massive fingers. Witton and Summers were bickering quietly across a chess-board and the others were trying to find something new to read in the pile of ancient newspapers and journals. All heads raised and swung as they heard the horses canter in. When Lenehan and Hunt came through the door, everyone was up and surrounding them at once, Witton gesturing to the orderly for two whisky-sodas. The latecomers were dusty and obviously tired and Lenehan shoved his officers aside impatiently, slumping into Harry's chair and taking the drink from the orderly.

'For God's sake, chaps, let's get our breath! Thanks George – cheers everyone!' He gulped the drink down. 'All around, please, orderly.'

Harry caught Geoffrey's eye and felt a surge of relief at the beaming smile and the wink that went with it. He leaned in towards Lenehan.

'Well, sir, what's the word?'

Lenehan let the others fall silent while he sipped at his second drink. Then, 'We're off!'

There was an immediate hubbub, Handcock capering round with little Alec Picton till the room shook. The orderly darted out to spread the word and ran back in a moment later with two fresh bottles. Lenehan rose and crossed to a table, hitching himself onto it and yelling at them to calm down. In the comparative quiet he said, 'Look, this isn't a bloody picnic outing we're going on, you know—'

Summers' boyish voice crossed his. 'Well, we – we have rather been waiting, sir.'

'Well, the waiting's over. We've been cleared by H.Q. and Geoffrey has the orders here . . .' he stretched out his hand for the bundle of papers and rustled through them to find what he wanted . . . 'orders to "engage in actions against the enemy by means of vigorous and offensive patrolling".'

It was half a minute before Geoffrey, balancing on a rickety chair, could lift his voice above the noise. 'We did try to find out what that meant exactly, but there wasn't a manjack there prepared to commit himself!'

Witton called out, 'Good enough. Leaves us a pretty free hand, don't it?'

'Sir! Sir, did you see K himself?' Ivor Summers sounded more than ever like an excited schoolboy.

Geoffrey answered, 'Kitchener? Oh, we *saw* him all right – at a very considerable distance. He's got a flock of aides and secretaries ten deep to keep common soldiers like us away from him!'

'But he did sign the orders?'

Lenehan took up Harry's question. 'He did. Or to be strictly accurate, somebody signed them for him. And as George suggests, we've got a pretty free hand, the way I see it. So, we start tomorrow. Two patrols.' There was an immediate silence as he looked round. 'One's mine with George as 2 i/c and Geoffrey will take the other out with Harry.' He frowned down the swell of complaints from the others. 'You'll all get your turns, never fear. We shall all be out inside a week.' Not letting anyone interrupt, he went straight on, 'There's one other thing. No prisoners.' The silence was intense and he spoke quietly into it. 'That's what we were told at H.Q. – no prisoners will be taken.'

Again it was Summers who spoke. 'They can't be serious! That's unheard of!'

Tom Fletcher, businesslike as always, asked, 'Did they put that in the orders, sir?'

'Not in the written orders, no. But we were told, Geoffrey and I, that Kitchener wants it made plain. Anyone under arms or sheltering an armed man is to be shot at once.'

'To Hell with that!' Harry's voice was tight with rage. 'Sorry sir, but—'

'That's all right, Harry, I quite agree. If they shoot, then we shoot them. Otherwise, we take prisoners – on my authority. We might be irregular but that doesn't make us bloody barbarians.' There was a slackening of tension. 'Now then, what about a stirrup-cup?'

*   *   *

In the first light of the next morning, Geoffrey, leading his patrol, turned to Harry and said, 'There's something to be said for it you know – this no prisoners thing.'

'You're never serious! You mean just shoot 'em?'

'Yes. Why not?'

Hunt's voice was quite flat and Harry stared at him in surprise.

'Is this the Gentle Geoffrey, Meek and Mild? Ravening round the countryside like a murdering Mongol?'

Hunt stared back at him levelly. 'I'm serious, Harry. Remember how often we've talked about fighting them on their own terms? I think that's just about what I meant. They don't hesitate to shoot our wounded. By God, you've seen it happen! Why should we hold back?'

'You couldn't do it, Geoff. None of us could.'

'Depend on the circumstances, wouldn't it?' He half smiled. 'Perhaps that's the difference between us professionals and you toy soldiers.'

'Hmmm. I'll remember that the next time I see you handing over your bullybeef to some hairy old Boer brigand.'

The soft thump of hooves came from wide on the flank and they reined in, waiting for the scout to reach them. He swung alongside in a cloud of dust, the grey beginning to turn gold in the light of the new sun. 'Farm just across that little rise, sir. Small place – don't look much.'

Geoffrey checked his map and nodded. 'Right, thank you. Back you go.' As the scout cantered away, Hunt turned. 'Harry, take your half and circle round to the south there, will you? I'll give you a couple of minutes to position then I'll come in on this track. We should be there just about nicely together.'

Harry saluted solemnly and, just as solemnly, asked, 'Do we take prisoners, sir?'

Hunt smiled widely. 'Only the young and pretty ones.'

Harry, wheeling his half-troop away, was smiling too ... but the thought was there that old Geoffrey was a harder customer than he looked. Harry wondered whether he himself was as hard as he thought.

Harry led his half-troop through a thin screen of scrubby trees to one side of the farmhouse as Geoffrey's half swung through the gate on the track. An old Boer came out onto the stoep, watching silently as the troops moved in. Owen Fisher, riding with Geoffrey that day, fanned his hand outwards and four men took post wide beyond the fence corners. The rest of them dismounted and led their horses into a patch of shade, then spread out quickly. Geoffrey, Harry and Fisher sat their horses, waiting till the quick inspection was over, then swung down. Fisher beckoned two troopers to follow them as they moved towards the stoep. The old man there snatched off his hat, jerking his head in a kind of bow.

'Good day, mynheeren. Will you come inside.?'

He gestured at the open door, bobbing his head. Geoffrey and Harry, hands on pistol-butts, stopped outside the door and Fisher led the two troopers inside, rifles ready. Geoffrey and Harry followed them in.

It was cool and dim in there, a wide square kitchen with a low fire muttering in the stove, the huge chimney sucking the heat away. An old woman stood grimly to one side, a younger woman by her and two children half-hidden behind them. It was silent except for the heavy ticking of an old clock on the overmantel. The troopers slid to either side of the door, covering the room. Geoffrey sketched a perfunctory salute to the women and the old man stepped towards him.

'There is nothing here for soldiers, mynheer.'

Ignoring him, Geoffrey nodded to Fisher who pushed through the door across the room and began a rough search. The old man started after him, then swung back. 'Why do you search my house like this? For what do you search?'

Geoffrey's smile was cold. 'You don't know, of course.'

'I am a farmer.' He spread his hands and hunched his shoulders. 'How should I know the ways of soldiers?'

'Well, Mynheer Boer, the ways of soldiers are these – to search for guns, for ammunition, for hidden fighters, for supplies. But you know of none of those things, of course.'

'I have said I am a farmer only. I know nothing of these other things.'

'Then I may just shoot you for *not* knowing.' The old man stepped back hastily and the woman gasped. Harry looked in astonishment at his friend. He had spoken flatly and without a trace of emotion and Harry felt he meant what he had said. He pursed his lips in a noiseless whistle. This was the 'professional soldier' with a vengeance.

Owen Fisher came back into the room, slipping his pistol into its holster and shaking his head minutely. Geoffrey strolled about the dim room, lifting and dropping the lid of a storage bin, flicking open a cupboard door, the children's eyes, enormous, following him as he went. He stopped at the overmantel, tapping his pistol muzzle against the bobbled fringe, staring at the family photograph there, the people in the room posed in a formal group with three young men. He lifted the picture down and looked at it, speaking with his back to the room.

'There are no young men on your farm. Have you no sons?'

The old man barely hid his smile. 'Oh, ja, I have three fine sons, mynheer. See, there in the picture.'

Geoffrey turned, also smiling faintly and handed the picture to Harry who put it back on the mantel. Geoffrey walked close to the old man.

'Where are they, these three fine sons?'

'Oh, Petrus, the oldest – the father of these little ones here – Petrus is in Pietersburg. He sells two oxen and buys a horse. In the place of those your soldiers have taken from us.'

'And the others?'

'Josef and Nicolas are working for a friend of mine on the other side of the valley. Just for a few weeks.'

Hunt nodded in apparent understanding. 'Of course.' He strolled to a corner where a gun-rack stood empty. 'No sons here. No horses. And no guns?' And he turned again to the old man.

'These also the soldiers have taken.'

'Which soldiers, old man – ours or yours?'

The old man made no answer and Hunt flicked an eyebrow at Harry and Owen as he moved to the doorway. 'I shall want water for my men.'

'Of course, mynheer, of course. There is a barrel of fresh water just outside here.'

He darted forward, obviously glad to get them out of his house and Geoffrey followed him. Harry, seeing Owen Fisher move back into the room, paused to watch. Fisher walked to the younger woman and gently shifted her to one side so that he could see the children ... a girl of perhaps five and a boy a year or two older. Digging into a tunic pocket, Fisher brought out a slab of thick toffee and held it out to them, seeing the eyes grow big and round, staring first at the toffee then up at their mother. The mother's hands went around the children's shoulders, pulling them close and Fisher straightened, shrugging. He put the toffee on the table by the children and made for the door. Harry saw the little girl's hand sneaking out, but the mother's hand was there first and she snatched up the sticky sweetmeat, tossing it into the stove. She spat after Fisher and Harry, face wrinkling in disgust, turned away outside.

The old man was at a big water-butt by the end of the stoep, its lid partly aside, baling water out into a couple of tin jugs. Two of the troopers were filling canteens from the jugs as Harry mounted, and he unlooped his canteen and passed it down, walking his horse alongside Geoffrey's as they waited. He leaned closer.

'Geoff, I believe you *would* have shot that old bloke.'

Hunt didn't turn his head and his voice was calm. 'Yes. If he'd given me the slightest reason, I think I would.'

Wondering about it, Harry watched the watering, and a sudden sharp look on the Boer's face caught his attention. It was almost a smile, just for a second, almost a smile of . . . what? Triumph? He watched closely, accepting his own dripping canteen back without shifting his gaze. He uncapped the canteen and lifted it to his mouth, seeing the sudden dart of the old man's eyes, then he kneed his horse gently forward and leaned down, holding out the canteen.

'Here, drink some, old man.'

The Boer looked up, not moving, and spoke politely. 'Thank you mynheer. I am not thirsty.'

'Not for thirst. For a toast – to your three fine sons.'

Geoffrey had stepped his horse closer and the men had stopped to watch, sensing something happening. The Boer still made no move and Harry straightened, calling.

'Sergeant-Major Fisher!' Owen shouldered through the men. 'Give this old man a drink.' He handed the canteen to Fisher and drew his pistol, cocking it deliberately. Fisher held the canteen to the old Boer's face.

'Here y'are, Grandad, take a swig of this.'

The Boer jerked his head away, staring up at Harry. 'Mynheer, I do not wish to drink, believe me!'

Harry said, 'Old man, I believe you. Drink!' And he lowered the pistol's muzzle till it was centred on the Boer's forehead. The man snatched at the canteen and made some pretence at drinking, his eyes locked on the pistol. Then he threw it aside and tried to run, a dozen hands on him at once. Harry looked down at him.

'Give him a drink. A good stiff one.'

Harry grinned a little at Geoffrey's inquiring glance above the struggling men but said nothing, watching as they held the Boer still and forced the neck of the canteen between his lips, pinching his nostrils closed so that he had to open his mouth. He swallowed, and again, then gagged and retched and, as the men let him go, dropped to his knees vomiting.

Harry holstered his pistol. 'Tip that water-barrel over, some of you men.'

A couple of the troopers got their shoulders to the butt and rocked it till it swung off its blocks onto its side, the staves and hoops cracking apart and the water dashing out to disappear almost at once in the dust. A deep growl came from the watching men as they saw the mass of filth in the wrecked barrel ... a well-decomposed bird of some kind, and what was obviously the contents of the farm's sanitary bucket. On the stoep, the man's family had watched the scene and now the old woman ran forward to her husband, clutching at him protectively. Geoffrey's face was white with revulsion. Harry said, 'I imagine the well will be clean, Geoff,' and was answered only by a nod. Then Geoffrey looked round.

'Right. Corporal, take four men empty every canteen and refill them at the well. Sergeant-Major, we'll have that ox butchered right away please. Send someone into the house for some cloth to wrap the beef in. And I want the poultry collected.'

As Fisher saluted and the men began to move, Harry caught Geoffrey's sleeve. Geoffrey turned to him, unsmiling.

'Don't worry Harry, I'm not going to shoot them, though God knows I should! But I *am* going to teach them a lesson.' He called, 'Corporal Booth, I want all the rest of the livestock, no matter what – get everything over by that well. When the canteens are full, kill the stock.'

Booth grinned. 'Yes sir. Kill the stock it is, sir.'

'Oh, and Booth – the dogs too.'

'Kill 'em? The dogs, sir?'

'Everything. And cut the guts open. Then throw the bodies into the well.'

He jerked his horse around and rode to the gate, his back turned to the farm.

Booth muttered to Dawes and Rattray. 'Fancy shooting the dogs, eh? I'll lay you that was Bloody Breaker Morant's lousy idea.'

Now that they were close the sound had lost its ghostliness. From the back there, back in the flat dark out of which they'd ridden, the sound had come catlike, a thin and inhuman skirl in the blackness, snapped into unequal lengths by the skittishness of the night wind. They hadn't seen the light till they moved through the trees, and right to that moment there wasn't a man among them could have said from which spike of the compass the sound was coming. The dim and yellow light tied it down for them and Harry urged his horse forward a little faster, glad that he knew where he was heading.

Moving cautiously down the loose scree slope into the shallow valley, Harry knew he and his men were very tired, just as he knew that they were never careless any more. There were fewer of them now, the flame-stabs in past nights had thinned them a little, but they were sinew-taut. They rode without talking, falling easily into the night-patrol formation, wide of one another, no two men in file, no man completely out of sight, no points or flanks to be picked off by a silent knife or a thin rope.

Plump little Alec Picton had gone that way, relieving one of his men out on a flank and stumbled over half an hour later, stripped to the drawers, his head grotesquely sideways on his pudgy neck and the rawhide buried in the cut flesh. Patterson, a quiet trooper from Auckland had gone unquietly, bubbling a pink froth into the night, his voice full of aerated lung-blood as he gasped how a Boer had been riding alongside him. Whatever their past experience had been, they'd all learned something these past hard weeks, they'd all seen things that held them quiet. In the sudden and unexpected fight at Van Maal's Post, when the place erupted nearly fifty Boers, Ivor Summers had been dismounted, had lost his carbine, had emptied his pistol and with his back against a corner-post in the angle of a fence, had fought five men with a rake, whipping his lender body about like a demented swordsman, his shoulder bleeding from a bullet graze. And when Harry had cantered up and burst into the Boers, blowing one man's head apart, Ivor had cursed him for getting brains and blood all over a good tunic. Peter Handcock had gone silently berserk in that fight, picking up a Boer and using him like a flail, walking in among the thick of them and swinging the broken corpse as though he was beating a carpet, his face deathly still and a frown of concentration pulling his brows down. When it was over he remembered none of it and cried when they told him. Tom Fletcher, leathery and sardonic, had taken to riding with a stockwhip looped over his shoulder, and Harry had seen him ride into the direct fire of a group of Boers, the metal tips of the lash cutting wickedly till the Boers broke and ran, yelping and demoralized. And Harry had seen Geoffrey in action, unruffled, deliberate and unhesitating, as often as not with an unlit cheroot jutting from the corner of his lips and a cold mercilessness keeping him firing at the enemy as long as there was a movement to fire at.

As the half-troop crossed the narrow floor of the almost flat valley, the light ahead of them brightened and the building stood out a fraction darker against the dark sky. The singing had stopped a couple of minutes earlier but now started again, the solid cadence of the hymn ringing out, nothing ghostly about it now. 'A Sure Stronghold is My God', they sang ... forty or so of them, Harry thought, as he peered through the window of the simple wooden church; praising their God and not a fit man among the lot of them.

Harry's sergeant, Parker, had moved the men around fast and silently in an arc twenty feet wide of the church and was waiting for Harry at the door. Grinning without humour, Harry waited till the 'Amen' was fading, then slammed the door back and stepped inside, the shuffle of feet and a wild squeak from the harmonium the only sounds for the moment. It was a narrow-shouldered building, unadorned and shabby, the uncomfortable rough-hewn pews leading down to a small platform – a lectern, a plain table with a massive old Bible on it, and the harmonium. Behind the lectern, the Predikant stared at them for a long breath, then ignored them, coughing out the harsh gutturals of the Taal as he began his sermon. The congregation at once turned to him. The soldiers might just as well not have existed. Harry gestured, and Parker and a couple of troopers moved down the sides of the church, one of the men snatching his hat off with an embarrassed look at Harry, standing still in the doorway, pistol in his hand, his eyes on the dyed hessian curtain behind the Predikant.

On the other side of the curtain, the children had frozen at the first alien sounds. The hessian covered the door leading to the small room at the end of the church, a storeroom of sorts, with a couple of broken pews in it and some empty boxes. There were five children. Two boys, perhaps twelve, were in the pit in the ground, the wooden flap held up by an older girl. Another girl stood near the door and the fifth boy, not more than ten, was motionless just outside the door, hand clamped hard over the muzzle of the donkey there, harnessed into the shafts of a flat cart. He was the only one who could see outside, the only one who could see the mounted soldier walking his horse along the fence, head turning, carbine ready. The second soldier swung dimly into sight and the boy heard him call, not knowing he was hearing Corporal Booth.

'Well, you goin'ta be all bloody night, Mick?'

The first rider turned back. 'Nothing here, Corp. They're all in there.'

'Aagh, we oughta put a match to the place. Get rid of a double lot of trouble in one go – bleedin' Boers and Biblebashers all in one. Come on!'

The boy waited till they went, then hissed into the storeroom. At once the other children began to move, the boys in the pit passing up the rifles and the bandoliers, the girls passing them out, the other boy sliding them soundlessly into the bed of the cart and pulling old sacks over them. Beyond the door and the curtain they could hear the rumble of the Predikant's voice.

The voice didn't falter as Harry walked down the narrow aisle, but the passionate hands became knuckled fists. Skirting the lectern, Harry stepped up onto the platform behind the preacher and flicked the hessian aside, seeing the door there, nailed up, trying it and finding it fast. He waved to Parker, signing him to get outside and check the other side.

The children heard the rattling of the door and hurriedly passed out the last two rifles, dropping the lid on the pit and edging a box over it. Four of them slipped noiselessly away along the fence side of the church, and the fifth one, the boy, hand again over the donkey's muzzle, began to lead the animal away, the cart's wheels nearly silent in their axle-beds of grease.

As Harry reached the door of the church again, the sermon ended and the harmonium gasped and sucked in air and belched a sour chord. The first notes of the hymn came with the shots and the singing stopped abruptly. Glaring back at the Predikant, Harry saw him gesturing fiercely and the music rose round him again as he ran outside.

Two shots, then another, and some shouting and the pounding of hooves and the mad bray of a donkey. Harry stood still by his horse, waiting, and they brought the wagon to him, Booth leading the donkey, two other men carrying Parker. In the yellow flare from the window Harry could see Parker's chest dark with the gush of blood and knew he'd lost a good sergeant. Booth gestured with a thumb.

'In the wagon, Mr Morant. It's only a bloody kid. He shot the sarge.'

Harry stepped close and looked down. 'Oh, Christ!'

The boy was slim and weighed very little as Harry cradled him, the torn throat still pumping blood which he could feel seeping through to his skin. He walked back to the church, the gap-mouthed head lolling against his shoulder and walked again down the aisle. The singing didn't falter and the Predikant's eyes were fixed on a point above Harry as he sang. Down the aisle and to the front and turned and hold the little body out to the people. The singing went on, seeming to rise louder, and though there were tears on the faces, the mouths kept opening and closing and the singing went on as Harry dropped the boy's body on the table and ran from that terrible church.

As they rode away, Parker's body in the cart on the Boer rifles, the singing was still there, swelling into the night.

It was the morning after the next before he had a chance to write to Parker's wife, sitting on an ammunition box outside the tent he shared with Geoffrey. Beyond them the men of their troop were relaxing, knowing there was something planned for that night. Geoffrey, back propped against a saddle, watched Harry seal the letter and put it to one side with a small canvas bag of Parker's personal belongings. He tossed away the end of the cheroot.

'That's a job I hate more every time.'

'Writing to the next-of-kin? Yes, I know how you feel … never really know what to say to them.'

'Who was that – Parker?'

'Mmm. Only been married six months, I believe.'

'Dear Widow Parker, I regret to inform you your husband was shot by a Boer boy aged eleven who was killed in our counter-attack. God!' He turned his head away and they sat unspeaking till they heard the sounds of horses coming into the bivouac and stood up, stretching and slapping dust. Hunt said, 'That'll be Peter with Owen Fisher and the rest of the men for tonight. We might as well let them all know about it now, I suppose.'

Looking across the sprawling ring of men, Owen Fisher thought again what a well-matched pair Hunt and Morant were for this kind of work. Between them they showed everything that was needed – Harry's dash and fire, Hunt's cold calculation and the undoubted boldness of them both. The night was likely to be a hard one and he was glad enough to have these two men to lead them. They were crouched together now on the far side of the ring, comparing their maps, Harry looking chunkier than he was against the slim height of Hunt, elegant as always, as plainly dressed as the rest of them but in khaki cut specially for him, the breeches neatly patched in many places but worn in preference to Army issue. Now Hunt stepped forward.

'Right, pay attention. We're going after the Dutchman in some style tonight. The word is that there's a clutch of them concentrating at De Koven's. We don't know how many but we'll assume a fair crowd. And there's another lot meetin at Klinger's, across the ridge from De Koven's. I think you all know the ground there well enough, but Mr Morant has maps for you to look at later. You'll notice that the major has sent Mr Handcock along with an extra half-troop and the sergeant-major and we're going to go for both places at once.' He let the murmur rise while he lit a cheroot, then quieted them and went on, scratching a diagram in the dust with a stick. 'Now then, the farms are about a mile and a half apart, but there's the ridge and a dry gully between them. I shall take my troop and Mr Fisher's people to De Koven's and the rest of you will hit Klinger's with Mr Morant. Questions?'

One of the men called, 'What about Mr Witton's lot, sir? They coming with the pompom?'

'No; we though about it but I think they'd be more trouble than enough on that ridge. And if we get close enough in they'd be a danger to us anyway.'

'Hot meal before we go, sir?'

'Yes; and eat up well, lads. It'll probably be a long night.' He caught Owen's eye. 'Yes, Mr Fisher?'

'I brought up some – er – medical supplies sir. The major's compliments.'

Geoffrey grinned. 'If that means what I think it means, there'll be a rum issue when we stand-to. No rum in the canteens, please, you N.C.O's.'

The lounging men stood as Geoffrey and Harry moved away to where Peter was checking the horses.

The last red sunlight was smeared across the edge of the sky when the rum went round to the men standing by their horses' heads along the track. Corporal Booth, sucking the thick liquor through his teeth, scowled at the two men in his file. 'Stupid bastards! Why can't they leave well enough alone? Another night chasing the fucking Dutchy!'

Rattray pushed his nose down into the tin mug, inhaling the rum fumes. 'If we left 'em alone they'd be down on us before we knew what was what.'

'Get out of it. Them Boers are buggered, mate! We been runnin' 'em ragged. They couldn't damage a girls' school!'

Dawes, his ferret-face twitching, broke in. 'I could – by God I could!'

Booth sneered at him. 'Oh, you're always crutch-hungry, you are, Sid! Anyway, that something else we won't get tonight.'

Rattray finally gulped down his rum and licked his lips. 'Ah, there's always a flopsie around the Boers, Tom, y'know that. They do the cookin', among other things.'

Dawes snapped out a thin laugh. 'Gawd, y'not fussy, are ya? Them old crows, they're all made of leather.'

The corporal spat into the dust by his boot. 'Aside from which, Mr Captain Bloody Hunt and Mr Lieutenant Bloody Morant wouldn't like it!' he spat again. 'I tell you, this coulda been a very handsome few months, this could, if it hadn't been for them toffee-noses.' He screwed up his face and affected a drawl. 'No lootin', chaps, an' hands off the gentlewomen! Christ!'

The word came down the line to mount, and they swung up into their saddles. Rattray settled himself and leaned closer to Booth. 'Well, one thing, Tom – you'll not catch me chasin' after a bullet tonight. Me for a nice thick rock.'

'Yeah, well leave room for me mate. And Sid.'

At the head of the column, Harry and Geoffrey were comparing their watches.

'All clear then, Harry? One hour to get into position. No noise, no action, till you hear my three signal shots.'

'Right you are. Just don't keep us hanging around all night. Ready, Peter?'

Handcock nodded and Hunt raised his hand. Quietly the file of horsemen moved out of the bivouac area, separating almost at once into their two columns.

The moon was still low and only in its first half, but it was a clear night and there was starshine and the shadows were black enough for the ground ahead of them to be visible in relief: a slope, dropping about thirty feet in the hundred down to the fence. Beyond that Klinger's farm humped black and solid. No lights, no movement, but the slim breeze lifting towards them from down there carried the smell of woodsmoke to where Harry lay with Peter Handcock. Harry held his watch close to his face, then leaned sideways to whisper in Handcock's ear.

'Ten minutes yet, Peter, but you'd best get along to your blokes now and start working down. I'm going to move down now with my people. I want to get in the lee of that barn before the party starts. Give it another couple of minutes and then bring your lot down to the fence-line.'

He felt, rather than saw, Peter's nod as he elbowed himself back to where his half-troop was waiting, and he checked them quickly before beginning to work transversely down the slope, heading for the clump of trees which would screen their passage to the barn.

They were still twenty yards from the trees when the single shot came.

Across the ridge and the gully, Geoffrey Hunt had positioned his men quickly for the close move on De Koven's farm. It was a more awkward attack approach than Harry's, since the farm buildings were placed in a rough square with a yard in the centre, and the gully took a sharp swing alongside the main building, running away behind it and giving an excellent cover for anyone needing to get out fast. Owen Fisher had held his watch up to show Geoffrey there was a little more than ten minutes left and Geoffrey nodded, deliberately relaxing.

Ten yards back and to the left, Booth, Rattray and Dawes had found their rock, a solid shoulder jutting out of the slope, and they were stretched behind it, Booth and Rattray still and silent, Dawes fidgeting and jumpy.

'How long d'you reckon, Tom?'

Booth pulled away. Dawes' mouth was close to his face and his breath was rancid. 'I don't know. Too bloody soon I expect. Shut up and keep still.'

Dawes wriggled away a foot or two, edging his head around the base of the rock and trying to see ahead. His fingers played nervously with the safety of his cocked rifle and, as he half knelt for a view, the rifle slipped from his sweaty hand and toppled a yard down the rock slope. The safety was off and the shot sounded as loud as the last trump.

Geoffrey whipped round, squinting into the dark, aware of the noise in the farmhouse ahead and below, aware of a dart of light as a door opened and shut, of shouting. He heard Owen call, 'What bloody fool did that?' and he shouted himself, 'All right Sergeant-Major, let 'em rip!' He aimed his pistol into the sky and fired three rapid shots as his men began to slip and rattle past him, the stabs of their fire cutting through the darkness.

Harry had frozen at the sound of the first shot, trying to determine where it had come from, hearing nothing for a long breath, then the three shots together.

'Christ, they're early!' He stood up, calling, 'Move in, Peter – move in now. Open fire!'

The fight at Klinger's was half over almost as soon as it began. Within seconds of Harry's call, the two men sent down into the farmyard had put a match to the pile of hay alongside the barn and the dry stuff went up like a giant torch lighting the whole area. The dozen or so men tumbling out of the house were easy targets. Three of the went down at once, another staggered and was grabbed by two of his friends. Only one got away into the night and the rest bolted back inside. A moment later they began returning fire from the farmhouse windows, but it was clear they wouldn't be able to hold out long. Harry hadn't fired a shot by the time he found Peter again, settled on the far side of the barn away from the hay fire. Peter grinned.

'No trouble, Harry. Have 'em out of there in five minutes.'

'Yes, it looks good enough. Peter, I think there's something wrong over on Geofrey's side – that early shot. I think —'

Peter's great hand suddenly closed on his arm and his head cocked. In a lull in the firing Harry caught the sound, the unmistakable heavy stammer echoing off the rocks.

'Oh, God, they've got a Maxim there! They'll cut the guts out of Geoff's lads!'

Peters face was tight.

'I'll take whoever's clear, Harry —'

'Take 'em all, Peter, all except these blokes here!' He gestured at the half-dozen men nearby. 'Go on, *move*! I'll be there as fast as I can.'

He didn't wait to see them go, hearing the shouts and the scatter of hooves as he moved among the men left, still firing into the farm. He grabbed Mulholland, a stocky and competent corporal.

'Listen, Mulholland, Captain Hunt's in trouble and I'm leaving you in charge here. You're a sergeant now.'

'Goodoh, sir. She'll be right.'

'Get it cleared up fast and get your men over to De Koven's. If you've got prisoners and they won't move, break their bloody legs and leave 'em.'

'We'll sort 'em out, sir. Be there in no time.'

Harry ran for his horse, hearing Mulholland ordering three of his men to speed up the rate of fire and cover his advance to the farm.

The firing at De Koven's had stopped by the time Harry's horse, blowing hard, had reached the top of the ridge. There was a tongue of flame licking out of a window at the end of the house and he could see figures moving together in the yard. He plunged down the slope, jerking the horse back onto its haunches as he came on a group of men standing and lying by a clump of rocks.

He grabbed a trooper's shoulder as he hit the ground. 'Where's Mr Hunt?'

'Don't know, sir. Down there was the last time I seen him.' He getured down towards the farm, now beginning to burn fiercely.

'Where are the N.C.O.'s?'

Booth moved in before the man could answer. 'I think I'm the only one left, sir. Since the sar-major got hit.'

'Where's Captain Hunt, Booth?'

'Must be with the others, sir. They had a Maxim.'

Harry began to run down towards the burning farm. Just inside the gate a man was kneeling by three still figures and he looked up, recognizing Harry, and beckoning him urgently. In the flame-light as he knelt, Harry could see Owen Fisher, face wrenched with pain. Owen plucked at him with a weak hand and Harry took it, feeling the chill wetness of it.

'Owen, quiet now, man. We'll get you back in a bit.'

Fisher's mouth gasped for words. 'Hu—Hunt —'

Harry bent lower. 'Where? Where is he, Owen?'

The mouth shut, clenching against the pain and Harry looked down, feeling sick as he saw the bloody and tangled mess of Fisher's belly. The sweaty fingers tightened in his and the gasping voice came.

'We – we went against the farm, Harry – the Maxim. Hit us with the Maxim.' Anger lent him strength and his voice became louder. 'They wouldn't back us up, the bastards —'

Harry could hear the shuffle of boots as men gathered round and the sharp sound of hooves drawing close. 'Who, Owen? Who wouldn't?'

Fisher tried to lift himself and Harry slid an arm behind his shoulders, propping him. He stared round, his head wobbling, his eyes fierce in their need to see clearly, and he jerked his chin at Booth.

'Him. And his mates ... wouldn't support us. Mr Hunt was hit —'

He fainted then and Harry laid him back gently, wiping his hands on his breeches as he stood. He remembered the sound of horses and called over his shoulder.

'Sergeant Mulholland are you there?'

'Sir!'

'Bring Corporal Booth here, please.'

Harry looked round the yard. They'd taken a number of casualties and there was a growing line of still or moaning figures by the fence. Several of the troopers were scouting nearer the buildings. Mulholland coughed quietly alongside Harry and he took a deep breath and swung to face Booth, standing at attention. Mulholland was holding two rifles and Booth's empty fingers were clenching and unclenching. He spoke as soon as Harry looked at him.

'Sir, we was advancing and that Maxim opened up and a lot of the men was hit. I didn't know Mr Hunt was hit, sir. I saw Fisher go down and I – I pulled the others back, sir. To – to regroup and attack again.'

Harry looked past him, speaking to the others. 'Is that what happened?'

There was a moment's uneasy silence in which Dawes and Rattray glanced at one another and shifted a little away from Booth. One of the troopers spoke out of the ruck.

'Not properly, sir. Mr Fisher was yelling for us to come again –
we heard him. He shouted he was hit and for us to rush the flank –
get Mr Hunt.'

Booth burst in. 'I had to make a decision, sir. It would have been
murder to go into that bloody Maxim —'

It wasn't till Peter Handcock loomed up by him that Harry
realized he hadn't seen him there till then. The big man's head was
down and when he looked up, Harry saw his face was wet with
tears and wrinkled like a baby's.

'Harry, we found Geoffrey. Over there behind the farm. They
must have dragged him in and then left him when they shot
through.'

They walked together round to the back of the building and
Peter pointed, standing there weeping as Harry went the extra
couple of yards alone. Geoffrey was lying a few feet away from the
back door and Harry felt the bile coming into his throat and pain
grip his stomach. He bent over, gagging, then straightened, sucking
in air and fighting for control. His voice was quite steady when he
called.

'Bring Booth here.'

He groped in his pockets, finding his message-pad and a stub of
pencil and waited till Booth was standing there, his lips trembling.
Harry jerked a finger downwards.

'Kneel down.' Booth hesitated and Harry's rage overcame him,
so that he shouted into the man's white face. *'Kneel down, you shit!'*
and his hand on Booth's shoulder forced the man to his knees
alongside Hunt's body. Harry thrust the pad and pencil at him.

'Now write this, Booth.' There was no sound from the watching
men as Harry dictated, speaking coldly and steadily, his eyes fixed
on Hunt in torment.

'Captain Hunt's body was struck by a bullet at close range. It
passed through his right shoulder. This was a simple wound and
did not cause his death. When found the body was stripped naked.
The sinews at the back of both his knees and ankles had been
severed. The forehead was bruised and the right cheekbone
crushed. Captain Hunt had been castrated.'

He choked and spun away, vomiting onto the ground. Peter
Handcock, wet eyed, gestured to the men and two of them came
forward, kneeling by the kneeling Booth to roll Hunt's body in a
blanket and carry it away. Peter watched as Harry walked to his
horse, mounting as though he was exhausted and walking it away
up the slope. He turned to Mulholland.

'I gather you're a sergeant now, Les.' The other man nodded

silently. 'Right – send someone you can rely on to stay with Mr Morant and get a galloper away for a couple of carts for the wounded. Then let's get this mess cleared up.'

It was almost dawn when they were finished and the flames from the burning buildings were beginning to pale as the sky lightened. The men stood by their horses, not talking, faces drawn and tired in the dawn chill. There were eight graves in a row beside the track and another a little further away under a scrubby tree. Harry stood bare-headed and slump-shouldered looking down at it, at the rifle jammed muzzle-down into the pile of rocks. Peter Handcock stepped forward, touching his arm gently and Harry straightened painfully, then shook himself and took a deep breath. He walked to his horse and pulled himself up into the saddle, waiting till the men had mounted before speaking. Then he looked along them, face set.

'Don't bring me any more prisoners.'

He turned his horse's head along the track.

'Y'ave 'ardly touched a thing, Mr Morant, sir.' Craddock's crinkled nut of a face showed his concern as he shuffled the tin plates about on the folding table. 'That was a nice bitta corned beef 'ash, that was.'

Harry neither answered nor moved, sitting slouched in a canvas chair, glass in one hand, bottle in the other, and Craddock thought he looked like an old man. He clattered the plates together and let a note of reproof creep into his words.

'Y'got to eat somethink, sir. Y'can't go without eatin'. Y'll get sick.'

He waited for some response from Harry but there was none. Craddock sighed, twisting his lips in thought. 'Will I make some fresh tea, sir, eh? Nice strong cuppa —'

The bottle slammed down on the table, shaking it and slopping gravy off the edge of the plate, and Harry stared at the little man with dull anger. 'Oh, for the love of God, stop jabbering! You sound like an old woman.' He saw the wounded look and shut his eyes, calming himself before speaking again. 'All right, all right, I'm sorry, Craddock. Just clear that stuff out of here.'

He got up and stalked to the side of the little hut, looking down on his bed, littered with loose gear and clothing. The open trunk alongside it was half-packed with Geoffrey's things and Harry turned away from it, sick of the business of making Geoffrey finally gone.

'Craddock, go and ask Mr Handcock to come in.'

'Yessir. Er, fresh tea, Mr Morant?'

The murderous look sent him scuttering from the hut and Harry poured himself another drink, carrying the glass as he walked idly about, picking up papers and clothes and putting them down again in other places. Handcock's voice took him by surprise and the thought shot through his mind not for the first time that for all his bulk, the man moved like a cat.

'Did you want me, Harry?' The rumbling voice was tentative, and Handcock stood only halfway through the door. In the days since they'd got back from De Koven's, Harry had been almost unapproachable, although they all knew Lenehan had spent an hour with him late that afternoon.

Harry waved the glass. 'Yes. Come in.' He watched Handcock walk to the table and stand awkwardly, shifting his massive weight from foot to foot. 'Don't stand there like a bloody tree, man! You give me the jumps.'

Not speaking, Handcock sat, chewing at his lower lip and Harry felt a swell of self-hatred, knowing how easily the man was hurt. 'I'm sorry, Peter. I'm – I'm a bit off tonight.'

'That's all right.' He glanced at the mess. 'D'you want some help?'

'No, thanks. I'm nearly finished. There's some other stuff at H.Q., but they'll look after that, I suppose.' He swept the loose items off the bed into the trunk and kicked the lid down. 'Not much to show, is there?' Abruptly, he moved back to the table and slumped down in the other chair. 'I'm to take over Geoffrey's troop.'

'Yes, we expected that. I'm glad.'

'Are you? You may not be. You're to be my second-in-command.'

'I'm still glad.'

Harry looked up, meeting the big man's level stare, then looked away, unwilling to accept or share emotion. He poured whisky into a second glass and pushed it across the table.

'I'd like you to move in here, Peter. Sorry – I mean, would you like to move in here?'

'Well, look, I don't want to push in, Harry.'

'No question of that – it makes sense. We're going to be working pretty closely together, Peter.'

'Yes, well, of course. I'll be happy to.' He gulped down his drink and stood, towering and seeming to fill the room. 'I'll go and get my gear shifted. Won't be long.'

He paused, seeing Harry wanted to speak, seeing the difficulty he

was having. 'Peter, thanks. I don't think being on my own would
do me much good just now.'

Handcock's grin was understanding. 'That's all right. But don't
push yourself to hard.'

'Me? Don't worry about that.' His face went stony. 'It's the
bloody Boer who's going to get pushed hard.'

Handcock remembered those words as he watched Harry make
them live, driving the troop unmercifully in his chase. The easy-
going humour he'd always shown, the readiness for a prank, the
thought for his men and their mounts, were all gone; he was
drinking heavily again and eating only when somebody put food in
front of him and he looked gaunt and grey, twitching with a
nervous energy that kept him from sleep and comfort. He seemed in
any kind of ease only when they were on the track, only when they
found Boers, and then he became an icy demon.

He left the troop with Peter for two days while he caught the
train to the hospital in the town seventy miles south, where Owen
Fisher was being kept. When he came back he sat slumped on his
bed, elbows on his knees, hands slack and head hanging, and his
voice was dull.

'Owen and I came out here together, you know Peter . . . he was a
good friend. Now he's lying in that bed there, half a man, while
they try to keep him alive. His guts are in pieces and they keep
pumping stuff into him to deaden the pain, but it doesn't. His hair's
nearly all fallen out and you can see his skull showing through his
face and he's mad and he stinks.' Harry looked up and Peter was
shocked at the naked torture on his face. 'And he was crying, Peter
– Owen Fisher crying.'

He never spoke of Geoffrey, except late one afternoon when they
had searched a house on the edge of a little dorp and found an old
Snider rifle tucked behind a cupboard. The woman of the house
said she hadn't known it was there. Perhaps her dead husband had
left it, but Harry had turned her out with her two half-grown boys
yoked to a cartful of their belongings and a little girl crying in her
arms, and had then broken a lamp against a wooden wall and
watched the burning oil spread. Standing outside as her home
burnt and the troops walked their horses back and across the little
vegetable garden, the woman, dry-eyed, had stared up at Harry
and cried out, 'You are a pagan, a heathen! You make war on
women and children! You destroy food!' She spat and made horns
with her fingers at her forehead. 'You are a son of the Devil!'

Harry spoke down to her coldly. 'Not my choice, Madam. It's an arrangement made between some of your people and my friend, Captain Hunt.'

He saluted and turned away, and Handcock felt chill as he watched him.

Gradually, though, he seemed to pull himself back, and the news that Owen Fisher was progressing left him almost cheerful. A rider had come into their camp late the previous night carrying the news about Owen among his messages and now, in the clear softness of a Sunday morning, Harry decided they'd rest for the day, and the men lay sprawled comfortably around in the shade of some trees by a small creek, spelling the three lookouts every couple of hours.

Harry was dozing when he heard a flurry of voices and sat up, knuckling the sleep from his eyes. Mulholland was leading a small group of men across, a Boer in the middle of them and Harry stirred Peter into wakefulness as they approached. Mulholland hunkered down by them.

'Got a Dutchman, sir. Dawes spotted him and bailed him up.'

Dawes was standing with a self-satisfied grin. Since Booth had gone, his posting away quickly arranged by Lenehan, Dawes had been at pains to keep himself well out of the way, not even having much to do with the very subdued Rattray. Now, though, he'd brought in a prisoner and hoped that might help him. Harry ignored him completely, studying the Boer, a filthy, slew-eyed young man in an overlong greatcoat which fell loosely to his ankles. Standing up, Harry pulled the crushed cabbage-tree hat off the man's head, looking at the loose lips and the trickle of slobber on the stubbled chin. Beside him, he heard Peter's snort of disgust.

'Oh, God, he's a lunatic!'

Harry turned to Dawes, whose grin was fading.

'Where did you find this? And why drag it back here?'

Dawes stuttered. 'He – he was carrying a rifle sir, and ammunition. I thought —'

'All right, don't go on about it.' Harry pulled up a box, sitting and studying the Boer, who grinned stupidly at him.

'What's your name?'

The man's voice was thin and jerky. 'Oh, I am Hennie Visser, mynheer. I am a soldier like you.'

Harry's face twitched with disgust. 'Hardly. Whose commando are you with, Visser?'

'My uncle Piet's commando, mynheer. I am a scout and a very good shot —'

'God help your Uncle Piet, then!'

The man giggled and Harry looked away.

'Mulholland! Take this softhead away. Give him something to eat ... we'll take him back to the cage with us.'

Peter sighed with quiet relief, thinking how, a week or two ago, Harry would have had the man shot for carrying a weapon and Harry, as though knowing what was in his mind, said, 'Wouldn't be worth the waste of a bullet, Peter. Christ, the Boer must be getting pretty hard up!'

It had been decided that they'd ride back to Base in the cool of the evening and they ate well at lunch, planning on a couple of hours' sleep while the sun was high. Harry and Peter leaned back against a tree, smoking, relaxed, across the little glade from the men. The prisoner, Visser, sat at the edge of the troops' circle, a tin plate of food under his chin, his lip slobbering. Mulholland walked across.

'All fed except the scouts, sir. I'll relieve them in ten minutes or so. What time for stand-to?'

'Oh, four, I think. That'll get us back into camp around nine in comfort.'

'One or two of the horses are looking a bit knocked up, sir.'

Peter broke in. 'I'll come and have a look at them in a minute, Les.'

Harry yawned and stretched. 'We won't push them, anyway. I'd like to – to —'

His voice slowed and stopped and the other two followed his stare. Across the glade, Visser had finished eating and was standing, hat off and greatcoat rolled into a bundle to be used as a pillow. Under the coat he was wearing a khaki tunic and breeches, unlaced and hanging loose above bare legs and an old pair of ammunition boots. Harry's move to him was deadly fast and Peter scrambled after him, seeing him spin Visser around. Peter's breath caught in his throat as he realized what had snatched at Harry. The tunic and breeches were military, finely-cut khaki, filthy and sweat-stained, but unmistakable. The patches on the breeches were neat under the grime and the sleeves and collar of the cavalry tunic showed darker markings where badges and brevets had been cut away. Visser, not knowing what was happening, shrank away from the menace in Harry's stare, sinking down onto his bundled coat, but Harry's whisper froze him.

'Stand up, Visser!' Harry reacheddown with both hands, seizing the Boer's upper arms and jerking him to his feet, his face wincing in pain. The hands tore open the front of the tunic and Peter could see past Harry's arm, the faded but clear label inside: 'Gieves, London. G. G. R. Hunt.'

Harry threw the man down onto his back, treading him down and holding the tunic open with his foot so that everyone could see the label. His voice was hoarse.

'For pity's sake, get Geoffrey's clothes off that thing!'

Peter tugged at his soulder, feeling the muscles tense and locked.

'Harry, calm down – he could have —'

Harry ignored him, watching as two of the men tugged the uniform away from Visser's squirming body, leaving him in a torn pair of foul drawers.

'Put him over there!' Harry pointed to a slimp tree about ten feet away.

No one moved and he drew and cocked his pistol, his voice low and shaking.

'I said, put him over there.'

Visser, blank face distorted and wet, was dragged kicking to the tree, where he stood half-crouched.

Harry walked to one of the saddles nearby and dragged the rifle from its scabbard. He moved back and tossed it into Visser's chest, the halfwit cradling it instinctively against him.

'You, Visser! Shoot!'

The man blinked and wept and held the rifle out to return it.

'Shoot, God damn you to hell!'

Clumsily Visser fumbled with the bolt and Harry stepped a pace closer and fired into his face, blasting the head into a splash of red and white which fanned backwards against the tree, the body arcing back incredibly under the blow and falling clumsily. Harry stepped closer again and methodically emptied the other five chambers into the chest and the belly, and no one moved in those few seconds.

He looked round at them.

'Bury it.'

No one moved still, as he walked away, reloading his pistol. By his own saddle he turned and called back to them.

'Mr Handcock, I want that carrion covered up. And we'll ride as soon as it's done.'

Half a mile away, the two Boers tucked into a cleft in the rocks across the creek, stared at one another. The younger one, his bearded face black with rage, slid his rifle forward and jerked up the backsight, but his companion pressed the barrel down, shaking his head. For a moment they struggled silently then the younger man yielded and rested his head on his arm, cursing fiercely. The older man patted his shoulder and jerked his head back to where their horses were tethered, and they wormed their way back, the picture of what had happened clear in their minds.

Lenehan folded the bundle of maps into the scuffed leather case and buckled it down.

'Right then, Harry, that's it. I'll be gone about six days I should think – maybe a day or two longer. You can't rush those idiots at H.Q. Any problems?'

'No John. It's all in hand. Give Owen my regards, won't you?'

'I'll do that, never fear. And Harry, watch yourself. That story about the man Visser. Well, you know what I mean.'

'Yes I know.' Lenehan looked at him, seeing the flint hardness there, and choked back any further comments.

They were at a junction of two tracks, the first time in weeks that the entire B.V.C. had been together. The eighty-odd men were standing easy by their horses, the officers grouped by George Witton's limber nearby. Lenehan was to go to Field H.Q. with half-a-dozen troopers as escort and Harry would command in his absence. Lenehan handed him the case.

'Well, the maps are all marked and up to date.' The rattle of wheels and hooves pulled their heads around to the cart that was being trotted down the line of troops, a corporal leading the two skinny horses in the shafts. 'Hallo, what's all this?'

The corporal saluted.

'Stopped this old cove just behind the ridge, sir. Says he's a Bible-basher.'

'All right, thanks. You can leave him here.'

The corporal trotted away and the rest of the officers drew closer as Lenehan and Harry stepped forward, looking up at the man on the box of the cart.

'Who are you?'

The man, his long black coat and black wide-brimmed hat dusty, looked down at Lenehan, a hand stroking through the grey beard. 'I am Jacob Hesse, sir. A pastor and missionary of the Lutheran Church, travelling in the name of God.'

'You're not a Boer, sir. Are you from Holland?'

'No, I am from Berlin. I wish to pass through.'

His English was heavily accented but quite clear and he spoke with determination; almost, Harry thought, arrogance.

Lenehan nooded. 'I see. Excuse me for a moment. Er – won't you get down and have a cup of coffee?'

'Thank you, no. Please to let me pass.'

'Shortly.'

He moved aside, the others closing on him.

'What d'you think?'

Ivor Summers spoke quietly.

'He looks a little like my old history tutor, sir. Shouldn't he have some papers on him?'

'He'd better have. Harry?'

'Why don't you leave him to me? It's my pidgin now and there's no reason for you to hang about.'

Lenehan looked at him consideringly. 'Yes, all right. But be careful, Harry.' He stepped back and said, 'Your command, Mr Morant,' returning the salutes and mounting. 'Right, Sergeant, let's have our detachment, please.' Looking down, he smiled. 'Enjoy yourselves; and take no chances, Harry.'

Harry watched the little group of horsemen trot away, then turned back to where the old man sat grimly on the cart.

'My name is Morant, Lieutenant Morant. I'm in command here now. Will you come down, please?'

The old man shook his head. 'I do not wish to come down, Herr Leutnant. I wish only to go about God's work.'

'And I don't wish to have you lifted down Herr . . . Hesse? I wish only to go about *my* work.'

Hesse tried to stare Harry out, but his gaze dropped and his head with it. Tight-mouthed he clambered down, one of the troopers helping him. After a hesitation he took off his hat and gave a jerky little bow. Harry punctiliously saluted.

'You have some papers of identity, sir?'

'Ja.' He fumbled inside his long coat, handing over an oilskin packet. 'They will tell you only what I have already said.'

Harry skimmed rapidly through the papers: a German passport, a travel visa signed by someone at General Headquarters, an impressive piece of parchment with the Prussian crest on it. He handed them back and waved to Mulholland.

'Sergeant, you might take a look in that cart, please.'

Hesse watched the sergeant and two troopers rummaging through his gear, his face flushed with annoyance.

'I have only supplies, there, Herr Leutnant – personal things, Bibles —'

'No guns? No ammunition?'

'I am a man of God, mein Herr. I do not deal with guns. They are of the Devil. It is such men as you who deal with them.'

Witton broke in. 'All very well, pastor, but your people in Germany are doing a bit of devil-dealing too, you know.'

The old man looked around them. 'I do not speak of war or politics. There are now people in this land who have not homes and have not families and who need the help of the good God. This I go to give them.'

Mulholland spoke from the cart. 'Nothing there, sir, only what he said.'

Hesse pulled on his hat and drew himself up. 'So I may go forward now?'

Harry cocked an eye at the others. Peter rumbled at the missionary, 'It's thick with Boers out there, you know. Not safe.'

'They are Christians, young man, children of my Church.'

'They're also touchy on the trigger,' broke in Harry. 'Once you pass here, people don't wait to ask questions. If they don't recognize you at once, they shoot. They even shoot Christians.'

One of the troopers snorted, and Hesse flushed again.

'I tell you Herr Leutnant, I am not concerned with shooting.'

'I can't give you an escort.'

'Thank you, I have my Escort. You will permit me ...?'

The man had a simple dignity now, and Harry shrugged and stepped aside, watching him clambering up again and accepting the reins from a trooper.

He made a last attempt. 'You do understand, pastor ... it's at your own risk. I won't have a patrol along that track for several days.'

'I will pray for God's forgiveness for you all.'

They watched the cart go, bumping away along the narrow track with a cloud of dust rising to hide it.

'I have a feeling I shouldn't have let him go.'

George Witton ran his hand through his gingery fuzz and spat dust away from his lips. 'Couldn't really stop him, could we? Sanctimonious old sod!'

'Let's hope his God's riding with him.' Fletcher sounded solemn for a change, and Harry looked at him, grinning wryly.

'Well, He's unlikely to be riding with us, Tom.' He raised his voice. 'Mount 'em up, Sergeant Mulholland – work to do!'

An hour later, a single shot out of the sun took Tom Fletcher just ahead of his right ear. Harry looked down at the shallow grave and said, 'I wish that padre was here. He might like to thank his God for His children's work.'

The scout was calling as he galloped in.

'Road block, sir, 'Bout quarter of a mile up the track. Round that way.'

Captain Gregory's hand shot up and the column halted. He signalled the scout to go on his tracks and waited while his lieutenant and the troop-sergeant joined him. Behind him the mounted infantrymen sat alert, carbines cocked.

Gregory sniffed at the dry air; trying, as he always did, to get the feel of the place. Nothing.

'Right – usual drill. I'll go up the middle this time. Eyes open for signals, please.'

Nodding, and without fuss, the two others wheeled away, pulling the column off into three sections, the sergeant leading out wide to the left to cut across the curve and behind a slope, the lieutenant taking his men up the hill on the right. Gregory gave them a few moments to get well under way and waved his own men forward along the track.

Up on the hill, edging just his head above the crest-line, the lieutenant looked down on the block. A cart, tipped on one side and slewed across the track, its contents spilled and scattered. Traces cut, and no horses. The sergeant's party just working into sight below and to the right.

The sergeant saw the toppled cart almost as quickly. From his angle he could also see the humped black body in its lee and the grotesque black birds trenching obscenely into it. He halted his men and looked up, waving to the lieutenant and waiting.

Captain Gregory led his party slowly round the curve, looking up to the hilltop for the all clear, then out to the left for the second reassurance. He moved forward and the three groups converged on the cart, the vultures rising with an ugly clatter ahead of them. By the time Gregory had dismounted the sergeant was kneeling by the body, face disgusted, hands busy. Gregory forced himself to look down, a handkerchief at his nose.

'Anything, Sergeant Matthews?'

'Bible in the pocket, sir ... foreign. And papers.' He passed up the book and an oilskin packet. 'Been shot, sir. One in the back, high up – here.' He half rolled the body so that Gregory could see the hole in the black coat, just below the shoulder. Lower than that, almost central, much of the man's back was gone in a gaping shambles. 'That lot's from the other shot, in the chest, sir. Close range by the look of it.'

Gregory nodded, looking round to see that the lieutenant had men spread well on lookout and searching the nearby ground. He opened the packet of papers, then stared up, startled.

'Good Lord, it's a padre! German.' He wheeled on the watching men. 'All right – get this cart off the track, some of you. Matthews, see if there's anything in his boxes and things. And get a blanket round him. Quickly.'

The lieutenant strolled across, face grave, tossing something in one hand.

'I say, Greg, there was this. Lying just over there.'

Gregory looked at the bent and smelly can, shreds of bully beef inside it with a few ants crawling stickily about. He looked at the label.

'Our issue. Oh, damnation!'

'There's a fair amount of that stuff leaks away to the Boer, you know. Doesn't necessarily mean . . .'

'I know. I know. Still and all . . . where'd you find it, exactly?'

They walked to where two or three men were still peering in amongst the scrub and small rocks. One of them bent suddenly, picked up something small and passed it silently to Gregory. It was the twisted strip of dark green puggaree cloth, sweat-stained and ravelled from old knots.

The lieutenant looked at it, sombre.

'Hardly likely any of our chaps would shoot a padre, surely?'

'After these past few months, I believe some of 'em would shoot the Archibishop of Canterbury.' He turned away, calling again to the sergeant.

'Matthews, I shall want you to take that body back to Head-quarters. You'd better put a couple of the horses to that cart and take half-a-dozen men. Let the colonel know what's happened, please, as soon as you get in. I'll give you a note to him and another for the provost-marshal.'

Harry was in his tent scribbling a report when Handcock stuck his head through the flap.

'Column riding in, Harry.'

Outside, squinting into the afternoon sun, they studied the approaching horsemen. Handcock grunted.

'Bloody Pommies! Two days late! Suppose they kept stopping for tea and sandwiches on the way.'

'Stop picking, Peter. They may have run into trouble.' He shaded his eyes against the glare. 'Seem to be more than we expected.'

The column moved into the camp area, a long double-file of mounted infantry, a young captain at their head with a grim-faced major alongside him. As they led under a couple of tall old trees, Harry could see the major was wearing a provost brassard. Behind him was a section of men in the white crossbelts of the field police.

Wondering, he slipped on his hat and stepped forward saluting and smiling as the two officers dismounted, the police following them.

'Hallo, there ... we've been waiting to hand over to you! I'm Morant.'

The others returned his salute and the captain made to take Harry's outstretched hand, but in his fractional hesitation the major spoke.

'Lieutenant Morant, I'm Malleson, assistant provost-marshal.'

'Good afternoon, sir. Trouble?'

'Very possibly. Is all your command here?'

'Yes, sir. We've been waiting for —'

The major broke in, tugging a paper from his belt-pouch.

'I should like to see all the officers, please. Immediately.'

Puzzled at the man's formality, Harry gestured the others forward. 'Of course, sir. Gentlemen —'

Malleson looked at them as they stepped forward. 'Lieutenant Morant, would you report your officers to me formally, please?'

Harry looked a query at the young captain who licked his lips and looked past him. Shrugging, he drew himself to attention. 'Sir – Lieutenants Handcock, Witton, Summers and Morant reporting as requested.'

The four saluted as one, Malleson carefully answering. 'Thank you. Gentlemen, I must notify you that I am now placing you all under open arrest.' His hand moved a little from his side and his policemen moved closer. 'Will you hand over your side-arms, please?'

For a second the silence was complete, Malleson staring into their shocked faces. Then Harry exploded. 'What the bloody hell are you talking about? I'm sorry sir, but what in God's name is going on?'

'Your side-arms, please, gentlemen. I'd be most reluctant to place you under close arrest, but I'm prepared to if you make it necessary.'

Harry stared at him and around, noticing how the policemen were now in an arc, three wide on either side of the major. He looked at the others, shaking his head. Ivor Summers stepped half a pace forward.

'Look here, sir, what are the charges?'

Malleson was suddenly embarrassed. 'You will be advised of the charges at Field Headquarters —'

Now George Witton stepped in, ginger eyebrows lowering. 'But that's quite contrary to Queen's Rules and Regulations —'

'Please! I'm acting under direct orders from the Field Commander. Now, side-arms, if you will.'

The M.I. captain spoke from behind Malleson's shoulder. 'Look Morant, I'd advise you to go along. It's just something —'

Malleson's voice was abrupt. 'If you don't mind, Gregory.' Then, to the four men facing him, more softly, he said, 'I don't like this any more than you do, but I'm afraid I don't have any latitude in the matter. Orders.' He held up the paper.

'Harry tried again. 'Major, my C.O. is at Field Headquarters and I feel sure —'

'Major Lenehan is being detained under inquiry.'

There was another silence, the British troops motionless on their horses, the men of the B.V.C. clustering close. Harry saw Mulholland, face worried, and Dawes, an unpleasant grin twitching his mouth. He shrugged and pulled out his pistol, slipping the lanyard over his head and handing it across, butt foremost. The other three followed his lead.

Harry tried to keep his voice light. 'I've no idea what this is about, but I suppose this is the quickest way to get it sorted out.'

Malleson was obviously relieved. He passed the pistols back to one of his men and sagged a little. 'Thank you, gentlemen. I'm sure I have your word you'll cause no trouble and attempt no escape.' He waited for their nods. 'Now, if you'll get your necessary things together, we'll move as soon as we've had a meal.'

'What about my men?'

Gregory came to him, a sheet of buff paper in his hand. 'Er – I've been given temporary command of your chaps, Morant. I'll bring them into Field H.Q. in a few days. I've one patrol to make first.'

'I see. Well, look after them, won't you?'

'They'll be all right.'

Peter, watching Harry, saw the effort at control, saw the little patches of white around his lips, prayed he would hold himself in ... then sighed in relief as Harry smiled, pitching his voice so everyone could hear, making it cheerful.

'Well, the last time I was arrested it was for being drunk and disorderly in South Australia! This time I'm as sober as a judge and as dry as a bone! Would I be permitted to offer you gentlemen a drink?'

The sentry to one side of the metal-strapped door slapped his rifle-butt under the lamplight as Lenehan and the orderly officer approached. The orderly officer, his crimson sash the only warm splash of colour, produced a pass and the sentry banged a flat hand on the door behind him. There was the metal jangle of keys and the grating sound of a bar sliding before the door swung and a corporal of Field Police checked the pass, then saluted them through.

They were halted again on the far side of the room where a sergeant took the pass and they signed the Duty Book, then moved on behind the corporal through the rest room, empty at that moment and to the other door. The corporal's knock brought a face to the barred grille with a nod and a hand sliding a long steel key through the bars.

The corporal unlocked the door, slamming and locking it again behind them. 'This way, sir.'

Lenehan didn't move, looking down the corridor to where another armed man sat with his back against the far door. He suddenly shouted, his voice ringing and bouncing off the stone and metal.

'B.V.C.! Are you there, my chaps?'

The echoes were alone for a second, then there was a sudden clash and shout, Harry Morant's voice above it all.

'John! John Lenehan, welcome to Liberty Hall!'

Lenehan rounded on the orderly officer.

'Open these bloody doors, man! Come on, smartly now!'

Watched with care by the guards at either end of the corridor, the cell doors were unlocked and the men allowed into one big cell at the far end on the right, pounding at Lenehan's back, wringing his hands, questions falling over one another in a jumble until he managed to shout them into a grinning silence. He looked at the orderly officer. 'I say, there's really no need for you to hang about, is there?'

''Course not, sir. I shall have to lock you in, I'm afraid.'

Lenehan nodded and the door clanged as the young officer left, turning the key on them. There was a little awkward silence as Lenehan stared round at the four of them.

'Well, are you all right?'

Ivor Summers smiled lazily. 'It makes a nice change from chasing Brother Boer, sir. We don't even have to sleep on the ground.

'But we *would* like to know what's happening.' George Witton needed a haircut and he brushed the ginger fringe out of his eyes, Handcock nodding alongside him. Harry hadn't spoken and Lenehan cocked an eye at him, meeting that wide flash of a grin. Harry gripped his arm.

'What about you? Are you in the clear?'

'Yes, I am now. I feel badly about not being with you fellows . . .

but then I can probably be more use out of here. They tell me I shall be called as a witness anyway.'

Peter Handcock's rumble sounded even deeper in that closed room.

'Witness to what, sir? What are we supposed to have done?'

'You mean they haven't —' The rattle of the key in the lock interrupted him and they all turned as the orderly officer led another man in, neat, compact seeming almost dainty in his spotless uniform.

Lenehan let out a gust of relief. 'Well, thank Heavens for that!' He shook the newcomer's hand firmly and faced the others. 'Gentlemen, this is Ian Thomas of the New South Wales Lancers. Major Thomas, may I introduce —'

He was stopped again as Thomas stepped forward, his hand upraised.

'All right John, let's leave the amenities for a moment.' The voice bore no relationship to the man's size and apparent delicacy. It was strong and vibrant and he used it as an actor does, pitching it with care for the most effect. 'We'll all get to know one another soon enough, gentlemen. I'm a lawyer. I'm a very good lawyer and I'm going to defend you.' He watched the reactions on their faces for a second, then whipped round suddenly on the orderly officer. 'Look here, Captain I-Don't-Know-Your-Name ... go and see the commandant and tell him I want some chairs and tables in here. And some lamps ... writing materials. By God! these gentlemen aren't criminals. You're supposed to be guarding them, not burying them!'

The orderly officer's mouth opened and closed but no sound came from it.

Thomas snapped at him, 'Go on, man, gallop about a bit!'

Aware of the prisoners' surprised grins, the captain flushed and made for the door.

Half-an-hour later the big cell looked more like a Mess anteroom, with half-a-dozen chairs around a trestle-table, a green cloth covering the boards. Ther were two layback chairs on either side of a small side-table, and some other oddments of furniture, hastily collected, were piled in the corridors waiting for this first meeting to end. Lenehan and Thomas had both brought cigarettes and tobacco and the prisoners were luxuriating in a thick haze of blue smoke as they leaned around the table, looking to Thomas at its head. He finished scrawling a note in the scratch-pad in front of him and slammed the flap of his dispatch case closed on it, leaning back and looking quickly around them.

'Right! So much for the pettifogging details. Let's have your questions first, shall we?'

'When do we get out of this place?'

'What the hell are we doing in here anyway?'

Harry and George had spoken together and Thomas checked them. 'I don't know how long you'll be held here. I do know why. You're being held under field arrest on charges arising from a Court of Inquiry into a number of deaths of Boer civilians. I've already told you that.'

'But it's a lot of balls!' Peter's voice was indignant.

'Very probably. Nonetheless, the Court has ordered you further held pending continuation of inquiries.'

Harry let an edge of irritation creep into his voice. 'Come on now, Major, you can swallow all the formal flapdoodle. What's the situation in plain language?'

The others murmured agreement and Thomas grinned at them without real mirth.

'Simple language, eh? Well then – someone's stewing something up.'

George snorted. 'And what's that supposed to mean?'

'It means that rigmarole at the Court of Inquiry where they gibbered at John Lenehan there, all of that was a lot of claptrap. Didn't mean a damn thing as far as I'm concerned. There's something else hatching, and they're hanging onto you people while they sort themselves out.'

Lenehan leaned forward, face anxious. 'Can they do that?'

'Properly speaking, no. But there's a war on you know, the bloody-minded men in the Judge Advocate-General's office *are* doing it! I'm having the devil's own job —'

He bit the words off short as the guard corporal knocked and entered, a flat package in his hand, a long envelope on top of it.

'Letter for you, sir, and a package for Major Lenehan.'

Lenehan ripped open the envelope, smiling as he handed letters across the table. He'd not told them about his arrangement to collect their mail in case something went wrong, but now there was something for each of them and they chattered and laughed over their letters like schoolboys at the end of term. Harry looked at his two envelopes ... one from Margaret and one from Paddy. Smiling quietly he tucked them away to read later and leaned close to Lenehan.

'What have you really heard, John?'

Lenehan hesitated, then spoke quietly. 'I wasn't going to mention it, but the word is out that there's going to be a court martial.'

'But that's absurd!' Lenehan frowned a caution to Harry to keep his voice down, and he controlled himself with an effort. 'It's absurd,' he repeated. 'I mean there was only an inquiry because everyone knows old Kitchener's a stickler for military form!'

'Harry, it's only what they're saying in the H.Q. Mess. That there's to be a court martial and . . .'

His voice died away as he realized the others had stopped their chatter and had heard him. Ivor Summers was pale. He was the only professional soldier among them, a British officer at that, and the sound of a court martial had a peculiarly horrifying ring about it to him. 'But good God, we only did what we were told!'

Handcock's voice was loud with rage. 'You know that, sir – the orders were clear enough!'

'Lenehan tried to answer but George Witton cut in. 'Not as though we were the only ones, even if there *was* any truth in it at all. And every damn civilian over the age of six was out to get *us!*'

Harry's head had swung to the others and he now spoke to them all. 'The point is, can they make any charges stick against us, anyway? Surely they'll never do it?'

'They're going to have a bloody good try.'

Thomas had been silent since he had opened his letter, but the others hadn't noticed in their elation at receiving mail, then in their fury. Now his voice was flat and dry and it silenced them at once. Thomas was staring down at the papers, his hands flat on either side of them, and when he looked up his face was grave.

'Gentlemen, I have now received information from the office of the Judge Advocate-General. I am advised that you are severally and together to be arraigned before a Field General Court Martial on a date to be set.'

George, as usual unable to contain himself, burst out. 'What the fuck's a Field General Court Martial?'

Thomas looked at each of them in turn before answering, keeping his voice deliberate and uninflected. 'It's a court comprised of three officers. It has the power to impose a sentence of death.' He went on looking at them in complete silence, reading the shock and puzzlement in their stares.

'Why?' It was Harry, asking for them all. 'What for?'

Thomas pretended to consult the pages in front of him before he answered. He found it difficult to hold down his own sense of outrage. 'The material brought forward at the Court of Inquiry will be taken into account and there will be three separate charges to which you must answer. These concern the deaths of certain Boer civilians on two occasions.' He paused again, again looking round at them. 'The principal charge concerns one, Jacob Hesse, a German national —'

Peter interrupted. 'Hesse? Harry, that's that crazy old missionary —'

Thomas overrode the interruption. '— was found shot to death in suspicious circumstances within the area of operations of the Bush Veldt Carbineers under temporary command of Lieutenant H. H. Morant. You are being charged with his murder.'

It was rather like being locked inside a stone, Harry thought, like being a fly in ambergris. The floor beneath his feet was stone in slabs and the walls were stone blocks. The ceiling was of heavy wooden planks, but they were grey-painted and had the look and closeness of stone around him, like the door, strapped wood and metal bars. The single window was high and narrow and close-barred and he had to stand on the end of the hard bunk to look out of it, seeing nothing but the flat waste of beaten earth on that side of the prison, and a few lights from the town in the hollow beyond. Each of the cells had an oil-lamp on a hook by the door and the yellowness fell at a sharp angle through the bars, striping one corner with poor light.

Harry propped himself there to look through the letters again, trying to feel from Margaret's words something of home, something of her warm flesh and the comfort of her body and her love. This letter had taken seven weeks to reach him here, in a stone box, and the last of her scent had gone from it somewhere on the way. She hadn't known then about Geoffrey's death and he could only feel an emptiness when he re-read her messages to the man under the tree, out of the world, inside the past.

And yet Paddy's carefully-formed writing, the letters large and rounded and a little aslant across the pages, Paddy's letter brought him all the smells of the bush somehow. Even there, even barred and blocked, the simple letter seemed to carry with it something of freedom.

Harlequin is doing well and I sometime find it hard to keep my promise which you placed on me not to saddle him up and go for a good old run. Im sure he would like that Harry old friend and you migt care to give it some of your thinking. Last Thurs. old Mac Taylor from out by Downs River was thro this way and stayd here with me for three days. We had a fine time talking on the old days and he sents you his Very Best Respects. I showd him all the newspaper pices I been keeping in

a box about your Exploits and those of the Gallant Boys which left from here. He was glad to hear you are now an officer which I said was No Surprise to me and he agreed. Where are you now Harry and what are you doing? I have it reckoned out that you will be halfway to being up with your Enlistment and look to see you Home again with your Lovely Lady. Harlequin and me will be pleased for that day to come. Write soon and remember Your Old Friend, P. Magee (Paddy).
P.S. Are you writeing any Poems still?

He found the light was poorer than he thought as he folded the letter, unwilling to admit to himself that his eyes were wet. When the guard walked along the boot-banging corridor a few minutes later turning off all the lamps except those at the ends, Harry lay on his bunk fully dressed, and stared at the far wall, seeing the barred lines of the window creep out of the first blackness and listening to Thomas' voice in his head telling him he would be charged with murder.

By now the big cell had come to be called the Common Room and the three weeks which had gone by had given it a lived-in look, almost one of comfort. The four men were allowed to move freely between their own cells and the big one until ten at night, and they took their meals together there, Thomas having arranged for the Commandant's Mess to provide for them. Hasleton, the Commandant, had become a friend – an elderly colonel, pining for the active days when he'd commanded his own infantry regiment and considerably out of sympathy with what he called 'Arse-faced Authority locking up good young fighting officers.'

At Christmas, he'd gone out of his way to bring them something of the traditional cheer, providing them with a pudding and a fine turkey, cold ham, glazed sweets, several bottles of wine and some excellent brandy. Thomas had brought a stunted tree in a box, its lack of relationship to a fir tree considerably disguised by the small decorations he'd managed to fasten to it and the gaily-wrapped packages below it, cigars and books. John Lenehan had arrived with a bundle of letters for them and parcels from Ivor's family, and on Christmas morning, the guard sergeant, his face scarlet with shyness, had carted in a box of gifts from the several Officers' Messes in and near the town. The four prisoners felt, for the first time, that they weren't alone, that there was a great swell of friendly feeling around them – and not simply because of the time of the year.

But it was a short interlude and by Boxing Day the prison feeling was back with them, stronger for the previous day's gaiety. On Christmas night, Harry, Peter and George had lain silently in their cells listening to Ivor sobbing quietly.

They'd settled into a routine of sorts. Lenehan would call on them every day with newspapers and letters and gossip, often staying for a meal. Thomas, too, made at least one visit each day, even when there was no real need for it, and they'd come to appreciate the toughness of this dapper little man and his no-nonsense methods. The food was good and they were able to supplement it occasionally when one or other of them was able to arrange for some funds. What they all missed most was the company of other people, the chance to talk outside their own confined circle, the chance to walk somewhere other than on the baked earth beyond the prison wall for a half-hour a day and under guard. Chess and bridge, reading and writing letters, reminiscing – everything grew stale quickly and they found in the third week that they were spending less time together. They were all scared of abrading one another, of becoming quarrelsome. But they met for dinner each evening, scrupulously cleaning up and dressing as well as they could, making of the unelaborate meals a ritual of normality, trying to lose sight of the bars and the drab stonework as they sat around the table in the Common Room, a couple of plain candlesticks from the Commandant's quarters softening the circumstances a little. And they tried to keep the conversation general, away from the war and their immediate problems, each of them able to contribute an aspect of talk, of life, which was new to the others. Inevitably, though, it seldom lasted a whole evening. Always they'd drift back to the fighting.

Thomas had brought them a box of cigars this evening and now, with the dinner things cleared away, they sat puffing into a lapse in the talk.

Handcock, bulking over the table on his elbows, admired the length of his ash and spoke casually to Thomas. 'What's this rumour about Kitchener halting operations, Ian?'

'Not a rumour.' The others cocked their ears. 'Not a halt either, really.'

George had never tanned easily and the past three weeks' confinement had left his fair skin almost white. He grinned crookedly out of that pale face. 'Well, that makes almost as much sense as the average High Command statement.'

Thomas smiled back, nodding his head in rueful agreement. 'No, it's just that he's got everyone sitting more or less still, that's all.

The blockhouse line's finished, the country's cleared, the camps are full and the place has got a garrison of sorts every twenty feet or so it seems.'

'And the old Boer's doing nothing, is that it?'

Thomas snorted at Harry's question. 'Hardly. He's just moved back into your stamping-ground and he runs out every now and chews us up and runs back again.'

'Splendid!' Harry let the sarcasm knife out. 'They keep us stabled here and our men sitting on their backsides waiting for their enlistments to run out and the bigwigs chaffer over the politics of it all. And the Dutchman goes on doing what he was doing last year!'

There were silent nods from the others, even Ivor Summers. They'd noticed how much quieter he'd become, his lazy humour seeming to have gone completely these days.

The mood lifted when Lenehan walked in a moment later, a bundle of journals under his arm. 'Here, you blokes, papers are in.' He sat down, accepting the cup of coffee Thomas poured him and riffling among the newspapers to find the one he was looking for. 'There's some rather odd news from Burleigh in the *Telegraph*.' He folded the paper flat and pulled a candle closer to read. '"... and it is believed that the Kaiser has made the strongest personal representations to His Majesty to follow the German Government's recommendations to Downing Street in the matter of the death of the missionary, Hesse. Informed sources in Berlin report that the essence of these communications is of reparations rather than of justice. ..."' He stopped and looked up at them.

Peter rumbled, 'Pity we hadn't stopped that bloodly Bible-bird that day, Harry.'

Harry was savage in reply. 'Pity we hadn't *shot* the bastard! And put him underground and forgotten about him! We'd have saved all this bother.'

Thomas frowned across at him. 'Hardly a sensible attitude, Harry – and it won't help if anyone outside here hears you.'

'Oh, for God's sake!' Harry shoved his chair back, toppling it, and went to his own cell, slamming the door hollowly behind him.

He could hear them still as he stood perched on the end of his bunk, looking through the window-bars without seeing anything. He could hear the thick silence which followed his walk-out and then the gradual growl of conversation for a while, even a laugh or two. But the 'Goodnights' came quickly and the rattle of footsteps and the locking of the end door, and then near silence as the others drifted back to their cells. It was only when he realized that there was slightly more light in his cell that Harry looked round, seeing the loom of Peter standing in the doorway.

'Harry? All right?'

He stepped off the bunk, sitting on it and leaning his back against the cool stone wall, his knees pulled up.

'Hardly, Peter. I'm in prison . . . hadn't you noticed?' The bitterness rang in that hard room and he rose again to stare out into the night, speaking back across his shoulder. 'Sorry. I'm afraid I get a bit edgy when I'm cooped up for too long.'

Peter settled on the other end of the bunk and lit a pipe, his silence companionable, undemanding. Harry's voice softened as he half turned from the bars.

'It's a bit like the country the other side of Adelaide, over the hills.'

'Mmm, a lot of South Africa's like home, hadn't you noticed? Makes me quite homesick sometimes.' Peter chewed his words round the stem of the pipe. 'You wouldn't be homesick for Australia though, would you, Harry?'

'Oh, it's not the places I miss so much. It's things I miss and the way I like to do them. People, too.'

'Know what you mean. All this must be unpleasant for your fiancée. . . .'

'Margaret?' He looked down at the big man in the dim light. 'You know Geoffrey Hunt was her brother?'

'That must have been a hard blow on its own. How's she taking all this?' The pipe-stem took in the cell, the prison, their lives.

'Taking it? As you'd expect, of course. But it's finished. I've written to her and told her it's finished. I wouldn't want to bring her more trouble.'

'That's a bit down, itsn't it, Harry? The court can't do anything to us. They've nothing at all to go on.'

'Oh? Go and have another look at that piece of Burleigh's.' He turned to the window again, chin on his folded arms on the ledge, face close to the bars and the night breeze. 'Wonder how Harlequin is? Be a grand night for a gallop.'

Thomas was back immediately after breakfast the next morning to tell them the Court would begin to sit the next day and to take them again through the procedures and the material he'd collected. In the previous weeks he'd talked to each of them separately several times, covering page after page of paper with his dashing script, checking and cross-checking everything. It wasn't until he'd collated everything they'd told him that he met with all of them together

and with Lenehan present. He looked pleased on that day, slapping
the neatly ribboned pages together on the table.

'Well, you're all square as far as I'm concerned. Not that I didn't
expect it, but it's reassuring to know one's clients are cutting from
the whole cloth. I just wanted you all to know I'm completely
confident of your stories and I don't doubt the Court will be too.
Splendid!'

On this day he spent most of the daylight hours with them,
picking at lunch, answering every question patiently, turning up
references for them, trying to impress them with the impartial
justice of the law, working to build their confidence, to lift them out
of the worry and depression of the weeks gone by. It was particularly hard with Summers and Thomas followed him into his cell,
closing the door behind them.

'Mind if I spend a minute with you, Ivor?'

'Take your time, Ian. I'm not going anywhere.'

There was no humour there, only a resigned listlessness.

'Well, actually you are, my lad. You're going in front of that
Court and then home. Before too long, I shouldn't wonder.'

'Perhaps.'

'Oh, come now, Ivor, you mustn't mope like this! Good God, if
you answer the Court that way they'll – they'll smack your bottom
and send you to bed!'

A thin smile rewarded him and he pressed on. 'I realize it looks
unpleasant for you, but you wouldn't be the first officer to have
made a damn good career after being cleared by a court.'

'You're sure we're going to be cleared?'

'Aren't you? Don't you believe they've no case against you?'

'I know I've – we've – done nothing wrong.'

'Well, then!'

Ivor's face came alive for a moment.

'You're a good chap, Ian. I'm sure they won't let any of us down
in any way. It's just that I don't believe there's anything left for me
in the Army after all this. There'll always be – you know – hints,
stories.'

'Be damned to them! Fight back!'

'I think my fighting days are over. Whatever happens.'

Thomas was appalled when he realized Ivor Summers was
crying.

Breakfast was a strange meal next morning, the four of them
alternately chattering as though they were going on a trip, then
lapsing into deep silences. In a way, Harry supposed, they were

taking a trip. The Court was to sit in the building beside the prison, a meeting-hall of some kind, and this would be the first time they'd been outside the walls for more than the daily half-hour's exercise, the first time they would have seen people other than Lenehan, Thomas and the prison staff.

Hasleton came to see them as they were finishing breakfast, pouring himself tea and injecting a mood of belligerent cheer, eyes beaming in the scrubbed pink face, fingers plucking at the tobacco stains on his white moustache.

'Well now, laddies, off you go, eh? Up against Arse-faced Authority! Almost wish I was with you, begod! I'd tell those blinders a thing or two, spending their time chivvying good fighting officers about instead of letting them get on with their work! Not good enough! I tell you what, now, I know the fella who's sitting over this Court – 'bout as much use as a eunuch's cock!' He suddenly realized that that was hardly a comforting statement and made haste to recover. 'Mark you, he's fair! Got to be truthful – he's a wank and an arsehole, but not an unfair man!'

His confusion, far from depressing them, brought them to laughter and they were still laughing when Lenehan arrived. He listened to them for a second, hearing the thin, faint edge of hysteria.

Then Hasleton caught the eye of the sergeant at the door and abruptly pulled himself upright, tugging down the flaps of his tunic and putting on his cap. He walked to the door and turned to face them, coughing loudly till he had their attention.

'Gentlemen, I must inform you that I am about to parade you for handing over to your escort. Perhaps you'd be good enough to collect your requirement and stand by your cell doors?' He was flushed with embarrassment as they filed past him.

The guards led them out of the corridor and through the rest room into the hall. The outer doors were closed and the day guard was drawn up along one wall, armed and at attention. Facing them, the Commandant and the orderly officer stood together with a young captain in Rifle green who stepped crisply forward as the prisoners halted.

'Good morning, gentlemen. I'm Crookes of the Sixtieth, Escort Commander. I should very much like to be able to stand down my men – if I may have your word . . .?' He let the question hang and Harry glanced around at the others, seeing their immediate agreement.

'That's kind of you. Of course you have our word.'

'Splendid. Then we'll stroll across as soon as I've signed you

out.' He returned to the guard sergeant and scribbled his name
where the man's finger was poised on the great ledger, then turned
back to the Commandant, his salute seeming to make the air
crackle.

'Thank you, sir. The Prisoners' Escort is ready.'

Hasleton winked approvingly as he casually flopped a salute in
return. 'Well done, young Crookes. Off you go.'

The doors swung and Crookes led them out, a Rifles sergeant
bringing the men there to a crashing attention. Crookes waved an
airy hand at him and said, 'All right, Sergeant, Dismiss,' and led
them along the wall at a saunter, rather like a prefect taking a
group of junior boys along to see the headmaster, Lenehan thought
as he followed behind.

Crookes smiled easily around him. 'We'll be doing this every day
till the Court rises, you fellows. Do please let me know if there's
anything I can do to – er – ease things along, won't you? Can't
discuss proceedings, of course, or smuggle hacksaws or anything of
that kind. Anything else though, within reason.' Waving aside their
thanks, he looked at Ivor inquiringly. 'I know you, don't I? You're
Summers, you were at school with my ass of a little brother –
Simon.'

Ivor's face flushed with pleasure. 'Good lord, yes! I'd no idea –
how is he? We were really quite good friends, you know.'

'So I gathered from his letter. Knew I was in these parts and
asked me to look you up and tell you not to fret and so on. He'll be
bucked up no end when he knows I've seen you.'

'Is he out here? On service?'

'Yeees ... doing rather depressingly well for a tiddler. Gunner,
you know.'

Watching Ivor's animation, Harry blessed the chance that had
brought Crookes to them. As they walked between the guards
outside the Court, they all, strangely, felt an ease that had been
noticeably absent for some time.

Malleson, the assistant provost-marshal who'd arrested them,
was standing just inside the doorway and accepted Crookes' salute
as he came forward.

''Morning. You've been tolerably well looked after, I hope?'

'For prisoners, yes, sir.' George was unable to keep the sharpness
from his tongue and Malleson gave him a dry smile.

'Witton, isn't it? Yes, well, I'm afraid we have to accept the fact
that you *are* prisoners, gentlemen, until the Court decides otherwise, of course. The provost-marshal has appointed me to be here
throughout proceedings. You understand that your – er – quarters

and Colonel Hasleton come under his jurisdiction, and the rules require the presence of an officer from his staff.' They nodded in understanding as both Lenehan and Thomas joined them, listening silently as Malleson continued.

'I can see by the fact that you arrived under this officer's escort only that you've paroled yourselves to him. I'm directed by the convening officer to let you all know that no one desires these proceedings to be any more onerous than is absolutely necessary. Proper military forms will be observed, natually, but otherwise I think we'd all prefer that things moved along as comfortably as possible.'

Harry, biting back the temptations to say they'd be more comfortable with the positions reversed, restrained himself to nothing more than an uninflected, 'Thanks.'

Malleson accepted it with a quick nod. 'You are, nominally, in the charge of the provost-marshal – which means in my charge as things stand. Captain Crookes is your escort and I don't propose to interfere in any way with the arrangements he makes with you for your movements between these two buildings, as long as there is no trouble of any kind.' He let the last words hang for long enough to let it be plain they were a warning, then smiled suddenly and disarmingly, and relaxed the stiffness of his stance. 'It's always a bloody business, this. I'm afraid I have to be a bit pompous about it at the start, but I'm sure you'll understand the need. I'd really prefer you to think of yourselves as being in my care, rather than in my charge. Good luck to you.'

He was gone quickly, a solid and erect man marching through the door across the hall. Crookes muttered, 'Good chap, that. Mustn't be put off by all the provost-marshal stuff. Malleson's quite human for a bobby.'

Thomas paused by them long enough to say, 'Feeling better now? Good. Lots of people on our side, you know.' Then he followed Malleson.

A moment later Crookes led them off into a side room, the one window firmly closed and locked and the only furniture a bare table and a number of hard chairs. Crookes perched himself on a corner of the table and passed cigarettes around.

'Be a little while, I should think.' He nodded to the second door in the room. 'Court's in there. They'll be ploughing through all the paperwork for a bit before they send for us.' He sent a long streamer of smoke up to the ceiling and smiled round at them. 'One thing about a Field Court like this – none of that follol with swords and gloves and so on. Much more comfortable this way.'

It was plain that he was trying to keep the feeling light, not to let them think about the day, but they were silent, George and Ivor sitting side by side, gazing vacantly ahead, Peter patrolling in his strangely silent way and Harry drawn irresistibly to the window.

Beyond them, inside the court-room, there was a shuffling of feet and a low rattle of talk. The knock at the door was startling when it came and they were all on their feet at once, staring at the sergeant there, holding the door wide and saying to Crookes, 'President would like the accused paraded now, sir, please.'

Crookes stood, tall and suddenly sombre, stubbing his cigarette into an empty tin on the table.

'Right, sergeant, thank you.' He turned to the four. 'Well, then, gentlemen, time we went in.'

Through the open door they could hear a sharp voice calling. 'The Court is open,' and an increase in the noise as a number of people moved in from the hall. Crookes gave them an encouraging little smile.

'Straight line, please. I'm going to march you in.'

A moment later, Harry leading with Crookes on his right, they stepped smartly into the Court, marching a dozen steps, halting on the quiet command and turning right, standing at attention facing the long table. From somewhere off to one side, just out of Harry's range of vision, three men moved to stand behind the table, its length covered in green baize, a number of heavy books and several pads of paper and some pencils scattered along its length. The three turned, facing the four accused men – a Buffs major, elderly and solid: a Gunner captain, thin-faced, fair-headed; another captain, thickset and freckled under his tan, his tunic bearing the double-headed eagle of the King's Dragoon Guards.

They spaced themselves out behind three of the four chairs there, and another man moved in to stand by the empty chair to the major's right. His tunic was plain, the General Staff badges and lack of medal ribbons giving no indication to his status, only the major's crowns showing his rank. The Buffs major glanced at the others, sat and gestured to them to sit and Crookes' gentle touch on his elbow turned Harry and the other three to a row of chairs behind them. In a few seconds of turning and sitting, Harry could see that there were several rows of chairs in the body of the court-room and he caught a glimpse of the dozen or so faces there, none of them known to him. Thomas was at a small table to the right, a younger officer bent over the papers there with him. To the left, a similar table was empty, but a moment later two men walked quickly to it, their arms full of files and books and sat down.

Crookes leaned close and whispered, 'Prosecuting officer; name of Llewellyn.'

The Buffs major's voice was brisk and clear as he glanced around the room, his fingers pulling a sheet of paper from the open file in front of him.

'I should like silence, please. I shall now read the order for the convening of this Court.' He cleared his throat in the hush that followed, then read, quickly and almost without inflection:

'"On Active Service, this nineteenth day of January, 1902. Whereas it appears to me, the undersigned, an officer in command of His Majesty's Forces in South Africa, on active service, that the persons named in the annexed schedule, being subject to Military Law, have committed the offences in the said schedule mentioned; and whereas I am of opinion that it is not practicable that such offences should be tried by an ordinary General Court Martial; I hereby convene a Field General Court Martial to try the said persons, and to consist of the officers hereunder named. President, Major James Courtney Bainbridge, the Royal West Kent Regiment; members, Captain Leonard Edward Briggs-Cope, the 205th Field Battery, the Royal Artillery, and Captain the Honourable Michael Stuart Patrick Holding, the King's Dragoon Guards." This Convening Order is signed "Kitchener, General Officer Commanding and Convening Officer".' He placed the paper neatly at the bottom of the file and looked directly at the four men. Crookes leaned forward a little to glance at Thomas who stood, gesturing to the four to stand also.

The major, now known to them as Bainbridge, and the president of the Court, checked a new sheet of paper before him. 'Lieutenant Harry Harbord Morant, Bush Veldt Carbineers, you now have the opportunity to challenge all or any member of this Court now convened. Do you wish to make any such challenge?'

Thomas had briefed them on this point and it was clear in their minds. One after the other they answered 'No' to the president's question, Ivor Summers stuttering and flushing scarlet.

Then they sat while the room grew warmer round them, watching and listening as the president introduced the lean, grey-haired major by his side as the appointed Judge Advocate, and as he, in turn, swore in the president and the two members of the Court.

To Harry the whole thing had the feel of unreality about it, the swimming feeling of half-waking from sleep after a heavy night of drinking. The people around them appeared less than tangible somehow, mouthing echoing words and making unusual motions. The court orderly, the sergeant who'd called them from the side room, was standing rigidly in the at-ease position off to one side and Harry watched him fascinated, seeing the fly crawling across his face and seeing too the man's fight not to move to brush it away, the corner of his lips twitching as he puffed at the insect without dislodging it. Harry wanted to dash across and brush the fly off and the desire grew and grew in him till he had to grip the edges of his chair to keep himself still. When the low talk and the shuffling of papers at the long table stopped, he dragged a long breath of relief into his lungs at the thought that now something was going to happen.

'The accused will stand.'

They rose, unconsciously stiffening themselves to meet the president's level stare along the four of them.

'Number 918, Lieutenant Harry Harbord Morant, the Bush Veldt Carbineers, you are charged on three counts. Charge Number One is of the unlawful destruction of civil property during the months of October and November 1901 within the area of military operations designated as Area 6 in Field Operational Order 132; Charge Number Two is of being instrumental in causing the unlawful deaths of certain civilian persons, namely one Christiaan De Beer, aged eleven, and one Hendrik Visser, aged Twenty-six, within the same designated Area; Charge Number Three is of the unlawful murder by shooting of a German civil person, namely Jacob Hesse, aged sixty-one, within the same designated Area. How do you plead to the first charge?'

'Not guilty.'

'How do you plead to the second charge?'

'Not guilty.'

'How do you plead to the third charge?'

'Not guilty.'

Bainridge entered each plea meticulously on the paper in front of him and looked up again. 'Do you wish to apply for an adjournment on the ground that any of the rules relating to procedure before trial have not been complied with, and that you have been prejudiced thereby, or on the ground that you have not had sufficient opportunity for preparing your defence?'

In one wild second Harry recalled the arguments they'd had with Thomas about the way they'd been arrested without knowing on what grounds, how they'd been held for six days without information and without being allowed to talk with one another or receive visitors, and he remembered Thomas saying, 'Drag all that up and we'll alienate the Court at once. They'll know about it, because I'll make it my business to *make* them know about it. Keep mum and they'll think the better of you for it.' Now he breathed deeply again and shook his head.

'No, thank you, sir.'

The routine dragged on, each of the others being charged in precisely the same way and being asked exactly the same questions, each of them answering as Harry had done. A light mutter of talk had risen behind them during this and when the president had signed to the four of them to sit down again, he frowned over their heads and raised his voice.

'This is a military Court. The persons entitled to speak here are those directly concerned with the charges and proceedings, and no one else. At all. If conversation continues among the visitors – who are here by courtesy, I would remind you – I shall have the Court cleared.'

He waited to be sure there was absolute silence, his mouth grim under his moustache, then spoke directly to the four. 'I'm sure you defending officer has been at pains to explain the procedure of this Court, but I will go through it quickly so that the members and I may be sure you know what is happening. The prosecuting officer, Major Llewellyn, will first of all conduct his examination, the examination-in-chief. The defending officer may cross-examine each witness and the proscuting officer may then re-examine if he wishes. Evidence for the defence will then be brought and the same procedure will apply. Witnesses will be brought into the Court as required. At the end of all evidence, the two counselling officers will sum up their cases, after which I may or may not present my own summation. I shall keep a record of the proceedings and I shall consult with the Judge Advocate here,' he nodded to his right, 'should the Court require information on specific points of law. The Judge Advocate will take no other part in these proceedings.' He paused and studied them with care. 'I consider this to be a court of military law – and of justice. No reasonable legal or military request will be denied to the accused, but I expect proper behaviour within the Court at all times. Is all of this clearly understood?' He accepted their nods with no change of expression and Harry remembered Hasleton's opinion of the man – 'A wank and an arsehole, but not unfair.' Bainbridge spoke again. 'Major Thomas – Major Llewellyn – you have established, I understand, that none of the accused has been tried before now with any of the offences listed in the schedule?' Thomas and Llewellyn glanced at one another for a second, then said, 'Yes sir' simultaneously.

'Good, Then I think we may proceed, gentlemen. Major Llewellyn —'

For more than an hour-and-a-half, Llewellyn spoke fluently and in a surprisingly gentle voice, the Welsh cadences becoming more marked when he made emotional points in his background story. Harry found himself leaning back, relaxing, listening with fascination to that singing voice telling a story which, after the first few minutes, seemed to be just that – a well-told tale, an entertainment. Llewellyn took the Court through the raising of the B.V.C., dwelling lyrically on the type of war they had fought and in what fierce terrain and under what physical hardships. He painted an engrossing picture of their operations against the larger backdrop of the conduct of the campaign as a whole, and stressed the success of their actions in meeting the Boer on his own terms. Once the president interrupted as Llewellyn paused for a sip of water.

'Major Llewellyn, I wasn't aware that we needed this detailed statement about circumstantial affairs. Do you propose to continue for long before calling evidence to the charges?'

Llewellyn dropped his chin on his chest and considered before replying.

'Mr President, I am perhaps going to considerable lengths to establish the – er – circumstantial affairs, because I feel it is essential for the Court to understand clearly some of the things which caused these charges to be brought against the four accused officers. I have no wish to prolong proceedings, sir, but I am sure this explanation in advance will enable the Court to see points made later in a much clearer light.'

Bainbridge grunted and waved to him to continue, and Llewellyn did, at the same pace and in the same almost eulogizing way. Harry, puzzled, glanced at the others to see that they were in the same case. George Witton caught his look and raised his gingery eyebrows high, shrugging his shoulders a little. Beyond him, Harry was surprised to see Ian Thomas slumped in his chair, his face twisted in a fierce scowl.

At lunch in the side room, Thomas cleared the point for them. 'Clever little bastard, that Llewellyn. He's silk, you know – King's Counsel. What he's done is steal a good deal of our thunder, d'ye see that? He's put you people in a bloody good light – you and the B.V.C. – and I can't get at him for that. I can't even capitalize on it much. Now he'll start calling witnesses and begin to pull you to pieces and he'll try to give the Court the impression that he's doing it unwilling – that he's conforming to the letter of the law and being forced, in all honesty, to argue your guilt *even though* you're a band of gallant heroes!'

The court-room seemed strangely familiar when they were taken back into it after their lunch, as though it was a place in which they'd spent much of their lives. Within seconds of the president's nod, Llewellyn called his first witness and the sergeant, acting as court orderly, called through the main door of the room, 'Captain Viljoen, please.' Viljoen, a flat-backed little man in the khaki of the South African Horse, took the oath and stood steadily, impassively answering Llewellyn's opening questions in monosyllables as the prosecuting officer took him briefly through his background as a Transvaal-born soldier against the Boers.

'And are you presently in command of an irregular unit of horse in the Northern Transvaal?'

'I am.'

'This unit is known as Viljoen's Horse, and is established on lines very similar to those of the Bush Veldt Carbineers?'

'The name is right. As to the rest I don't know.'

'I see. Well, perhaps you will tell us briefly of your establishment, Captain Viljoen.'

'Yes. I have one hundred and ten all ranks. We work as four troops and engage in offensive patrol activity in our area —'

'That's the one designated as Area Seven in the Field Operational Orders?'

'Yes. Area Seven. We are under order to engage the enemy as we do.'

'These are written orders?'

'Yes.'

'Do they include any order which states that you shall not take prisoners?'

'No.'

'*Do* you take prisoners?'

'Often.' There was a flicker of a smile on the still face.

'Have you ever, within your command, shot, or ordered the shooting of prisoners, civil or military.'

'No.'

'Thank you.' Llewellyn's wave to Thomas was both graceful and condescending.

Thomas stood directly in front of Viljoen and looked at him hard. 'You are locally-born, Captain Viljoen, yet you fight on the British side. May I ask why?'

Llewellyn was on his feet at once, but the president gestured him to sit down again before he could protest. Viljoen's lips tightened a little. 'It is a matter of belief, of conscience.'

'I see. You do not believe the Boer cause – the cause of your own people – is the right one to follow?'

'No.'

'And you have engaged in military activity for British arms since the outbreak of hostilities?'

'Not since the outbreak, no.'

'No. Since the formation of the first of the irregular units, such as your own and the Bush Veldt Carbineers, is that right?'

'Yes.'

'A late decision.' Thomas' tone was dry and Harry caught the glances among the members of the Court. 'How many prisoners has your unit brought in, Captain?'

'How many? I don't know ... a number. It has been several months —'

'More than a hundred?'

'Possibly.'

Thomas held his hand behind him and his junior passed a paper to him. Without looking at it he pressed on. 'If I suggested one hundred and nineteen, would that sound right to you?'

'It could well be.' Viljoen's eyes were on the paper and Thomas now looked down at it.

'One hundred and one women and children. Eighteen men, all over the age of sixty-five with the exception of one man who was crippled in both legs.' He stared at Viljoen whose face was now reddening. 'These are the official returns, Captain. Do you agree with them?'

'I – I must. They are official.'

Thomas passed the paper to the president.

'In how many actions has your command engaged?'

'I could not say, not without the records.'

Again, Thomas' hand went back and received a clipped bunch of papers. He passed them to Viljoen.

'These *are* the records, Captain. Please correct me if I'm wrong. In the past five months, your command has engaged in a total of sixty-one patrols of which thirty-eight have resulted in actions of a minor or major kind. Is that correct?'

Viljoen waved the sheaf of papers. 'If that is what the record says, yes.'

'It is. And in that time, during those actions, no prisoners under arms were taken by your command?'

'The Boer fights hard. He fights to kill and we do the same.'

'Thank you, Captain Viljoen. I take that to mean that you agree that during that time, in thirty-eight actions, *no prisoner under arms were taken by your command.*'

He sat down at once, and Llewellyn rose to re-examine. 'Captain

Viljoen, have any charges of any kind relating to the treatment of prisoners, civil or military, ever been brought against you or any person under your command?'

'No, sir. None.' With obvious relief, Viljoen spoke loudly, assertively, and Llewellyn, smiling a little, sat down. Viljoen, excused, was a little less flat-backed when he left the Court.

During the rest of that afternoon, Llewellyn called officers from four other irregular commands, establishing with each of them the pattern of their operations as being similar to those of the B.V.C. In none of these cases was Thomas able to move as he had against Viljoen. All of the men were British and all had fought against the Boer from the outset. The records of their actions showed that many prisoners had been taken, and the best Thomas could do was compare their figures with those prepared by Lenehan to show that, on balance, they were much the same.

When the Court adjourned that evening, all that Harry could feel was that the work they'd done in the field had been made to look shabby, and he was beginning to hate the softly singing voice of Llewellyn.

It took Llewellyn five days to work his way through his witnesses, five days with a weekend interrupting them, and the four men sat through the hours in the court-room bewildered at the parade of people brought in to testify to their crimes. During the weekend, Ivor Summers said in a suddenly petulant voice, 'Well, I don't care! After what those people have said this week, I just don't care a stuff any more about any of it! If the world wants to think I'm that kind of blackguard, the world can go to hell!'

Harry looked across their common room at Thomas. 'That chap Llewellyn *has* been dredging, hasn't he?'

'A good lawyer does, Harry – part of his trade. I've done a bit myself.'

'All very well, but fancy dragging in those women! Of course we routed them out ... we had to. God damn it, Kitchener did the same thing on a bloody sight grander scale than we ever did – turned people out, burned their houses, burned their crops, took their stock. Isn't that what we were there for?'

George broke in. 'Ah, yes, but you see, Harry, it's not the Brass that's in there on trial. It's us.' His voice had grown waspish in the past few days. 'Unless Ian proposes to call Kitchener in evidence. Ian?'

'Hardly. But I think you're losing sight of the fact that Llewellyn hasn't been able to establish a single valid point. So far, anyway.

We've been able to counter all along, and always with the business of precedent, of accepted fact through the Army. He hasn't hurt us yet, you know.'

George reddened with anger. 'Hurt *us*? You make it sound as though you're being tried too! He has hurt *us*, you know. Not you – *us!*' And he half ran back to his own cell, leaving a dull silence behind him. Thomas pursed his lips and looked at the others.

'I'm sorry. I hope you understand what I mean?'

Harry nodded and Ivor sat as though he'd heard nothing. Peter stood and stretched his great frame till the bones cracked.

'Don't worry, Ian. We know you're doing everything you can. It's just that it sounds so – you know, dirtifying. All that stuff . . . it makes us sound like a lot of shits.'

On the morning of the fifth sitting day, Llewellyn rose at the outset and said, 'Mr President, I shall conclude my evidence today. I have three final witnesses. May we have Colonel Burnham Harrison called, please?'

Harrison was tall and stooped, an ageing man who looked like a mild-mannered schoolmaster and who attested that he was on the headquarters secretariat and that his responsibility was the drafting of orders and the supervision of their dispatch.

'And you held this same position at the time of the formation of the unit designated the Bush Veldt Carbineers, and drew up their operational orders?'

'Yes, that is so. I handed the orders myself to Major Lenehan, the Officer Commanding that formation.'

'Mr President, I have here copies of those orders from Colonel Harrison's files, their veracity agreed to by my learned friend.' He passed the papers to Bainbridge. 'These orders, Colonel, have only one thing to say about the treatment of captured persons. Would you be so good as to read the relevant section from my copy?'

Harrison took the orders, and pulled a pair of thin spectacles onto his nose and peered down, his fingers searching.

'Ah, yes. Number Seven, which states – and I remember this quite clearly – "Persons captured under arms against British forces in the field shall be treated as laid down in the Manual of Military Law. Persons found to be sheltering or otherwise aiding such persons under arms shall be arrested and placed within the jurisdiction of the nearest Provost Marshal or Garrison Commandant."' He stared up over the glasses and Llewellyn took over at once.

'Did Major Lenehan question any part of these orders when you handed them to him?'

'Quite the contrary. He seemed delighted to receive them. He had been badgering us for some days and was anxious to get into the field. Captain Hunt —'

'Did he read the orders in your presence?'

'No, he handed them to Captain Hunt and went immediately to talk with the quartermaster, I believe.'

'Thank you, Colonel. No further questions.'

Thomas made his point at once. 'Colonel Harrison, you tried to say something about Captain Hunt when my learned friend interrupted you. Would you tell us now what it was you wished to say?'

The president's voice was sudden and curt. 'One moment, Major Thomas, please. I'm not sure you can follow that line of questioning. . . . It's – er – second-hand or something, isn't it?' He directed the last part of the the query at the Judge Advocate beside him and they heard his voice for the first time, precise and with a slight hissing of sibilants.

'Colonel Harrison has mentioned Captain Hunt's name as being present at the time the orders were handed to Major Lenehan and has said further that the orders were passed to the captain. It would seem then that the captain's presence and action were introduced into the evidence drawn by the prosecuting officer and that the defending officer may follow that line as long as it has direct application.' He leaned back and became immobile again, seeming almost to disappear. The president coughed and signalled to Thomas to go on.

'Well, Colonel. About Captain Hunt?'

'Yes, well, I simply wanted to say that Hunt did read through the orders in my presence, and he too seemed delighted with them.'

'He asked no questions about them?'

'Not to my recollection, no.'

'And you vouchsafed no additional information?'

'None whatever. It was all there.' Harrison sounded offended, as though the comprehensiveness of his work had been questioned, and Thomas let a silence build before his next question.

'Now then, Colonel, I ask you to consider carefully before answering my next question. Did you yourself tell Captain Hunt, or did you hear anyone else in a position of responsibility tell him that no prisoners were to be taken?'

'Certainly not! That's a most reprehensible suggestion!'

'Is it within your knowledge that it was Headquarters policy to advise that prisoners taken under arms should not be brought in?'

'No, it is not!'

'Thank you, Colonel. Mr President, may it be noted please that I may wish to recall this witness at a later stage?'

Trooper Dawes came into the court-room uneasily, his peaked face pale and twitching. He'd found clean khakis from somewhere and they were a size too large for him, adding to his general air of awkwardness. It was clear he was frightened and Llewellyn took some care to calm him by making the first few questions simple and innocuous. Dawes relaxed visibly and Llewellyn moved in.

'Were you pesent, Dawes, at the church at Duival's Kloof on the night on which the boy Chritiaan De Beer was killed?'

'I dunno what the kid's – the boy's name was, sir, but I was at the church all right.'

'There was a service in progress?'

'Yes sir. Hymns and prayers, all in Dutch.'

'In Afrikaans, yes. Can you tell us how the boy was killed?'

'Didn't see it meself, sir, not the shooting proper. I was round the front. Mr Morant and Sergeant Parker and a coupla the men went inside the church and then after a bit, the sergeant came out and went up the side and round the back. Then there was this firing and yellin' and the next thing, they was carryin' Parker back all bleedin' and the boy layin' in his own cart. He was dead, sir, first time I seen 'im.'

'And what happened then?'

'Well, Mr Morant grabs the corp and he drags it inside the church and some of us followed 'im to see what was gointa 'appen. He walks in there while they was singin' a hymn and he throws the corp on the altar sort of ting.'

Harry started up, his face white, but Crookes' firm hand pulled him back into his seat, and the rifleman's face, serious now, warned him to be still and silent.

Llewellyn moved back to his chair, an eyebrow cocked at Thomas. The president's face was grim as Thomas stood in front of Dawes.

'Trooper Dawes, I just want to clear up one or two minor points, if you'll help me?'

'Yes, sir, a course.' Dawes' smile was cockily friendly.

'Thank you. I think you said you didn't see the actual shooting?'

''At's right, sir. It 'appened round the back.'

'How many shots?'

'About three, I think.'

'All from your own troops?'

'No, sir, there was a Mauser first. Couldn't mistake it.'

'This was, presumably, the shot which killed Sergeant Parker?'

'Musta been, I s'pose, sir, yes.'

'So it seems logical to assume that someone – possibly the boy himself – fired first, killing the sergeant, and that he himself was killed by the return fire?'

The Judge Advocate and the president had been leaning together as Thomas spoke and now the president interrupted. 'Don't answer that question, Dawes. Mr Thomas, I'm advised that the question is entirely out of order since any answer by Trooper Dawes would have to be pure conjecture. You may continue.'

Harry could see Llewellyn's half-smile as Thomas went on. 'You've said, Dawes, that Lieutenant Morant *threw* the boy's body onto an altar.'

''At's right, sir.'

'Mr President, the paper numbered A6 in your file is a disposition by Lieutenant George Cann, Royal Engineers, together with several perspective drawings and plans made by him at the church in question. You will see there is no altar within the church, simply a table upon a platform.' The president nodded, passing the papers along the table as Thomas turned back to Dawes.

'Properly speaking then, the body was placed up this *table*?'

'Well, yessir. I only thought —'

'Placed, Dawes? Or thrown?'

'Well, sir, depends what you mean. Dropped, I s'pose.'

'Yes, of course. The boy's body was *not* "thrown on the altar", but dropped on the table?'

'Yessir.' Dawes was quieter, his eyes watchful.

'The – er – cart in which the body was brought from the back of the church. Was there anything in it other than the body?'

'Yessir. 'Bout twenty rifles, some of 'em our issue, an' a lot of bandoliers.'

'Thank you, Dawes. You've been most helpful.'

Llewellyn wasn't going to leave it at that. 'Just before you're excused, Trooper Dawes, let's be quite clear. You were on patrol under Lieutenant Morant's command, some of you entered a church while a service was in progress and as a result of this an eleven-year-old boy was shot to death?'

'Right, sir.'

'I have no more questions, sir, but I may wish to recall Trooper Dawes later.'

It was eleven o'clock when Llewellyn called Booth, and the hot room seemed to Harry to become stifling suddenly. Booth looked well, spotlessly clean, his hair and moustache neatly-trimmed, the chevrons on his sleeve pipeclayed, his medal ribbons gay on his chest. Llewellyn took him quickly through the preliminaries, then through the actions at the church, apparently seeking to do no more than confirm the impression he'd striven for with Dawes' evidence. Thomas looked puzzled, but approached Booth with confidence.

'Corporal, you joined the B.V.C. as a trooper, isn't that so?'

'Yes, sir. Transferred at my own request sir – chance to see a bit more action.'

Harry, watching the members, saw Holding, the Dragoon, give a pleased little smile. Thomas went straight on.

'You were in Lieutenant Morant's troop?'

'Yes, sir, I was. Best troop in the unit.'

'Please restrict yourself to answering my questions, Corporal. You were promoted corporal within that troop ... by whom?'

'Mr Morant, sir. It was his half-troop then, of course. Captain Hunt was in com —'

Bainbridge cut across the flow. 'The defending officer has asked you to restrict yourself to answering the questions asked, Booth. I'm telling you to do so.'

'Sir!'

Thomas looked happier. 'Lieutenant Morant promoted you to the rank of corporal?'

'Yes, sir.'

'On the night of the combined action of De Koven's Farm and Klinger's Farm, the night on which Captain Hunt was killed, did Lieutenant Morant carry out any unusual punishment upon you?'

'No, sir.'

'Did he require you – indeed, order you – to kneel down by Captain Hunt's body and write a description of it at his dictation?'

'Yes, sir.'

'And you didn't consider that unusual?'

'Well, sir – Mr Hunt and him was friends. He was upset.'

Even Holding looked sceptical at the falsity of the tone.

'So that you made no effort to report Lieutenant Morant's actions or to seek redress for them?'

'No, sir. No reason to.'

'No reason to.' He paused. 'Am I to take it then that you agreed with Lieutenant Morant's actions, that you respected him as your immediate commander.'

'Yes, sir. Always. He got me my stripes, after all.'

Thomas waived a resigned hand and sat down, still puzzled.

Llewellyn's re-examination wiped away the puzzlement and re-placed it with anger. Llewellyn rocked on his heels in front of Booth, smiling at him.

'At the end of the action referred to by Major Thomas, Booth, the action in which Captain Hunt was killed, and *following* Lieu-tenant Morant's subjecting you to an indignity under stress of emotion —'

Thomas was on his feet at once and the Judge Advocate, with a nod from Bainbridge, raised a finger to him, addressing Llewellyn.

'That is not permissible, Major Llewellyn, as I'm sure you know. The Court has a right to an apology and should caution you about procedure.'

Llewellyn was unruffled. 'Of course, sir. My apologies, Mr President, and I accept your caution. Now, Corporal Booth, what were the final events that night at De Koven's, please?'

'Well, we got the wounded tied up and into a couple of carts, we rounded up all the livestock and we buried the dead. Nine al-together, sir.'

'Including Captain Hunt?'

'Yes, sir. Buried 'em all on a bit of a hill there.'

'And Lieutenant Morant was present throughout this?'

'Well, not properly speakin', sir. He sort of went off by himself after – after we found Mr Hunt. Then he come back when the buryin' was done.'

'And did what? Said a prayer, perhaps?'

'No, sir. Not a prayer. He spoke to us though – the men.'

'Can you tell us what he said?'

'Yes, sir. He said, "Don't bring me any more prisoners".'

There was a buzz, quietened at once by Bainbridge's scowl.

'Those were his exact words? "Don't being me any more prisoners"?'

'Yes, sir.'

Harry could hear himself saying it, looking down on Geoffrey's grave, the farmhouse burning below them.

Dawes, recalled by Llewellyn, was voluble about the incident with Visser.

'Well, sir, he was like a wild animal, Mr Morant was —'

Thomas was on his feet immediately, hand in the air in protest and the Judge Advocate nodded, hissing something to Bainbridge. The president spoke directly to Dawes. 'Trooper Dawes, you are not permitted to make remarks like that about the accused. You'll confine yourself to describing the events without giving us personal comments about people. Go on.'

'Yes, sir — sorry, sir. Anyway, this loony, Visser, 'e was just standin' there when Mr Morant run over an' grabbed at 'im an' tore 'is jacket open. An' then he sorta glared at 'im an' 'e tole us to get the clothes off 'im — Visser's clothes, that is.'

Llewellyn was quiet, gentle. 'And did you remove Visser's clothes?'

'Not me, no, sir. Some of the others — Sergeant Mulholland was one — they pulled 'em off and the poor geezer was stood there in 'is drores an' 'e was cryin'.'

Llewellyn let it sink in, nodding several times before speaking. 'Was Visser armed?'

'Not then 'e wasn't, no, sir. But Mr Morant 'e slung a rifle at 'im an' then 'e just up an' shot 'im. Right in the phiz — the face, sir. An' then 'e went on shootin' 'im till 'is gun was empty.'

Llewellyn made him go through it again, stressing points with him till everyone in the court had the gruesome picture clearly in mind. Then he waved him to Thomas.

'Trooper Dawes, these clothes Visser was wearing — did you recognize them?'

'No, sir. Khaki, they was, an' old ... coulda been any sorta clothes.'

'British Army uniform?'

'Coulda been, I suppose sir. I wouldn't be sure.'

'Did you see any identifying mark on them or in them — a label perhaps?'

'No, sir. Some of the lads reckoned they see Mr 'Unt's name in 'em, but I never.'

'And what happened to the clothes afterwards?'

Dawes smiled.

'Oh, Sergeant Mulholland took 'em an' burned 'em, sir.'

Llewellyn sat back satisfied and declined to re-examine.

They sat silent through lunch, Crookes attempting to raise a smile with his inconsequential chatter and failing miserably. Ian Thomas didn't join them at all and they filed back into the courtroom after the recess, still silently. For the first time Harry felt a deep sense of depression.

Llewellyn had advised the Court of the closure of his parade of witnesses immediately before the lunch break and now Thomas walked easily to a central spot, seeming to anchor his small feet firmly, not speaking till he was set.

'Mr President, I do not propose to speak at length about the background to the charges brought against the accused. My learned friend has already done that admirably.' Llewellyn's smile was broad. 'Neither do I propose to speak of the military virtues of these men, for their uniforms and decorations attest to these. At the outset I want to state simply that they have entered pleas of Not Guilty to all the charges brought against them. *They* do not believe themselves to be guilty of crimes or offences. *I* do not believe it – and it is my conviction that the Court will not believe it by the end of these proceedings. Now, with the Court's approval, and that of my learned friend, I wish to change the stated order of call of my witnesses.'

Bainbridge glanced at the Judge Advocate who muttered to him. Thomas and Llewellyn were waved forward and for a moment or two there was a low consultation, then Llewellyn, clearly angry, stamped back to his chair. Thomas, face impassive, turned to the court orderly, listening as he raised his voice through the doorway.

'Call Corporal Thomas Booth.'

Harry spun around, staring, then back to look at the others, all of them showing their astonishment. Booth marched back in, concern on his face. Bainbridge checked Thomas and spoke across him to Booth.

'Corporal Booth, the defending officer has asked for your recall and for you to appear and to testify as a witness for the defence. I am advised that this cannot be so unless you agree to do so. In the interest of truth and of justice, I can see no reason for you *not* to agree, but, of course, the decision rests with you.'

The implication was plain and Booth's discomfort was just as plain, his eyes flickering between Bainbridge and Llewellyn, who pointedly looked away. Bainbridge snapped, 'Well, Corporal?'

Booth swallowed. 'Sir, I – I don't think I should.'

'Major Thomas?'

'Mr President, members of the Court, I have no desire to press the point. I would, however, request that Corporal Booth remain within the body of the Court subject to the president's discretion as to his recall.'

Again the whispered consultation along the table, the Judge Advocate's hissing sibilants the only distinguishable sounds, then Bainbridge nodded. 'Very well, Corporal, you may be excused, but you will remain within this room.' He waited till Booth had found a seat in an otherwise empty row. 'Now, Major Thomas.'

'Thank you, sir. My first witness is Sergeant Gordon Connelly.'

The court orderly startled everybody by marching briskly forward to the witness chair instead of calling the name, and Thomas left it to the last moment before explaining.

'This is Sergeant Connolly, sir. The court orderly.'

The Judge Advocate leaned almost entirely across the table. 'Now, now, Major thomas. The sergeant has been present throughout the testimony given. It would be entirely improper —'

'With respect, sir. Sergeant Connelly approached me in some distress during the luncheon recess with information which I feel it is vital for the Court to hear, otherwise I would not have taken this most unusual step.'

'I am in some doubt, Major, whether his testimony would be admissible, even so.'

'With your permission, sir, I have here copies of the sergeant's sworn statement to me, before witnesses. If I may pass them to you, and one to my learned friend, to assist you deliberations?' Without waiting for an answer, he stepped forward, placing papers on the table, then turned and carried one sheet to Llewellyn. For a full minute no one moved or spoke. Then the Judge Advocate looked up and said something quietly to Bainbridge, who nodded his head. The two captains behind the table made the same indication and Bainbridge spoke.

'Major Llewellyn, we would value your opinion in this.'

Llewellyn, his face dark with anger, stalked a little forward from his table. 'Mr President, I see no need for Sergeant Connelly to testify. I should like to assure the Court and my learned friend that, had I known of this earlier, I should not have called Corporal Booth as a witness. With the Court's permission, I would suggest that the defending officer read the sergeant's sworn statement and that it be accepted into the record of proceedings.' He nodded curtly to Thomas and sat down.

Bainbridge looked approving. 'The Court agrees. You may be excused, Sergeant. Major Thomas, please read the statement.'

That vibrant voice of Thomas' rang in the otherwise fully silent room. '"This statement was made voluntarily by Number 25986, Sergeant Gordon Connelly, the Wiltshire Regiment, in the presence of Major Ian Thomas, New South Wales Lancers, Captain Jeremy Andrews, the Scots Guards and Regimental Sergeant-Major Angus Charles Fergusson, the Scots Guards, at Pietersburg on Tuesday, 24th January, 1902. I, Gordon Connelly, solemnly swear and testify that on this day while on duty as court orderly at Pietersburg, I was in the presence of Corporal Thomas Booth, a witness for the prosecution at the Field General Court Martial there being held. During the lunch recess on this day, Corporal Thomas Booth did say, in my presence and hearing, the following words: 'That'll do for them, I reckon. I tell you, I'd walk from

Spelonken to Pretoria to see Morant in front of a firing-squad.'
Corporal Booth then spat and walked away."'

Thomas looked up and there was a shuffle in the Court as
everyone, it seemed, turned to where Booth sat, deathly pale.

Bainbridge spoke directly to him. 'Corporal Booth, this will
become a matter for a separate Court of Inquiry. Is the assistant
provost-marshal present?' Malleson stood up at the back of the
room. 'You will place Corporal Booth under open arrest pending
that Court. Sergeant Connelly, you are relieved of duty as court
orderly, and I shall write a note of commendation on your conduct
to your commanding officer. Thank you. I think, gentlemen, the
Court should adjourn now until nine tomorrow morning.'

In the common room that evening, even Ivor seemed happy, and
Thomas was gleeful.

'It's just what we needed. Pure luck, of course, but just what we
needed. It's got everyone with you now, lads, all the sympathy in
the world!'

Hasleton, beaming, slapped Thomas' shoulder. 'I told you – I
told you what he was like, didn't I? Said he was a prick – but fair!'

Dinner that evening was the gayest for some time and when
Lenehan arrived he was greeted with shouts of joy and they talked
above one another in a swell of sound trying to explain what had
happened. Peter noticed Lenehan's apparently listless reaction,
and rumbled across the table at him.

'Come on now, John, It's good news!'

'Yes. I'm glad. But I'm afraid I've some bad news, too.' He
swung sideways to face Harry.

'It's Owen Fisher. He died this afternoon.'

Sleep wasn't easy that night. Owen's face kept swimming out of the
darkness ... lean and brown and with the lopsided grin ... and
then the naked weeping face he'd seen weeks before in the hospital.
The messages since then had said he'd been improving but Lenehan
had told them that Owen would never have been whole, or wholly
sane, again, that his lucid times were less and less frequent and that
he had no feeling for life. He'd just screamed one last time and died.
When Harry did fall asleep, he dreamed of screaming faces.

The scream was a high yell, nearby, and overlaid with the sharp
crackle of rifle fire. Harry scraped the gum of sleep from the corners
of his eyes as he leaned against the wall, peering from the barred
window, seeing nothing but the usual barren night-time scene
there, then leaped for the door. In the corridor the night-guards

were running to where someone was hammering for the main door to be unlocked and Harry shook the bars shouting, 'What the devil's going on?' The others joined his shouts and the echoes rang and jolted back along the stones. Then there was more light and voices and keys in the locks and the four of them were in the corridor, Peter gigantically naked, the others in their drawers and the duty sergeant was standing aside to let the orderly officer through, mouth grim and eyes startled.

'Right – let's have quietness, please.'

In the moment's silence, the gunfire beyond the walls could be heard louder and closer and there was a bugle ringing somewhere and, faintly, the jumbled thump of hooves.

'We're under attack. The Boers are coming in past us; probably on the other side of the valley, too. The commandant would like you all to get dressed quickly, please.'

'How many of them?'

Harry's voice was crisp and it halted the others, already turning back to their cells.

'No idea. A hell of a lot, by the sound of it. Hurry, please. I'll be back immediately.'

In the cell, on the outside of the building, the fighting noises were certainly louder and from the edge of the window Harry saw a dark clump of horsemen stretched at a full gallop across the flat and heading down towards where the lights were coming up fast in the town. There was continuous firing in the dip and out of his sight, but the night sky was glowing a little down there with the start of a fire. Harry jerked on his trousers, shirt and boots and ran back into the corridor, finding the others already there and the orderly officer just coming back through the door from the guard's rest room. He was breathing fast.

'Gentlemen, it looks as though —' There was the singing scream of metal on stone as a bullet tore through a cell window and threw itself against the wall of the corridor, bouncing away with a diminishing yelp. They all ducked and the orderly officer took up where he'd stopped, his mouth tilting in a tight grin. '— as though we're under attack ourselves. Colonel Hasleton has asked me if you'll accept weapons under parole and assist in the defence of this place.'

Peter growled, 'Give me something to shoot with, for Christ's sake, and let's get on with it.'

Within seconds, rifles and bandoliers had been passed through to them and they stood for a second, smiling at one another at the feel of it, then automatically turned to Harry. He looked at the orderly officer and nodded.

'Right – you'll have work to do. I'll take over here if you like. Can we get onto the roof?'

'You might – from the back, anyway. Sergeant, get that end door open.'

They ran down the corridor to the far end, the sergeant struggling with the stiff lock, then they were outside, the night cool and loud around them. Harry looked up and nodded again.

'We can manage. Off you go.' Without waiting to see the other two race away, he tossed his rifle to Peter and stood back a couple of feet. Peter and George, their own rifles on the ground, held Harry's like a bar between them. He took a short step, jumped onto the horizontal rifle with one foot and the other two hoisted. His hands went up to the stone coping set well above the doorway and he could feel the shove against his feet as the others hoisted the rifle, pushing him up till he grasped the roof parapet and jerked a leg over, dragging himself across and immediately turning and hanging head down to take the rifles as they were passed. Peter lifted George effortlessly and Harry grabbed his wrists, pulling him up and over. Ivor came up like a feather and Harry called down at Peter's upturned face.

'See if you can find us a Maxim, and a couple of boxes for you to stand on. You're too bloody big for us to drag you up.'

The grin from below seemed to light the night.

'Yair, I'm big and beautiful all right, Harry. Back in a minute.'

Harry rolled back to look around him.

The parapet was no more than two feet high and the pitch of the iron roof ran down into it all the way round, the skylights which lit their corridor by day set into it on either side of the ridge. Between the bottom edge of the iron and the inside of the parapet there was perhaps two feet of flat space which acted as a gutter, the down-piping holes puncturing it at intervals. His urgent wave took the other two after him as he scuttled along that space, moving above their cells to the front corner of the building. The noise was louder now and, risking a quick look over the edge, Harry could see that there was fire coming from the small clump of trees on the far side of the road and from the house, partly wrecked, a little further along. A sudden spurt of flame showed him that there were some Boers in the gully alongside the road. Below them, in the room above the entrance, there was the muffled sound of the return fire and away across the flat where they'd taken their daily exercise, the sound was building into what seemed like a heavy fight. Harry sat in the gutter considering for a moment.

'They're across the road there and in that old house. George, you stay in this corner; and Ivor, you slide along about halfway and you should be able to lob into them easily. They'll spot you as soon as you start firing, so watch yourselves. I'm going back to see if Peter's done any good.'

He could hear the two rifles open up behind him as he slithered back.

Below, outside the back door, Peter was staring up, two men with him and the bulk of a Maxim between them.

'Harry? I've got the bugger. If we get the wheels and the shield off we might be able to get it up there.'

'Fine. Go ahead and try.'

He watched as the axle-pins were banged out, the trail un-coupled and the steel protector plate pulled off. One of the men lashed a rope round the muzzle and breech and threw the end up to Harry. A moment later Peter was alongside him, pushed up on the shoulders of the men he'd brought along and he took the rope and called down, 'Right – let's give it a burl.' Lifted from below and with Peter's huge muscles heaving steadily from above, the bulky body of the gun came up fast and they wrestled it across the parapet.

'I'll take this, Harry; you bring the belts.'

Peter stood, the Maxim cradled in his arms, his shoulder muscles forcing his shirt tight and his face gleaming with sweat; and Harry, struggling with a box of ammunition belts behind him, shook his head in admiration at the great man's strength and surefootedness in that narrow gutter-way.

Bullets began to hiss and sing past them, ripping into and bounc-ing from the iron roof with tearing clangs, but they were at the front corner within a couple of minutes, George wriggling aside to let Peter lower the Maxim onto the parapet, then taking the box from Harry and quickly feeding a belt end into the breech. Peter, grin-ning like a mischievous schoolboy, pulled back the cocking handle and squinted along the barrel, depressing it towards the gully and the trees and snapping a short test burst.

Harry banged him hard on the shoulder.

'Good man, Peter. Go to it. George, you stay and load. I'm going up with Ivor.'

Boer bullets were smacking into the stonework just below them and still ripping above their heads into the iron roof, but the heavy stammer of the Maxim took effect very quickly. From the other end of the roof where he and Ivor kept up an accurate fire, speeding up the rate whenever the Maxim stopped for reloading, Harry could see there were now several small fires burning in the town. But he could tell also that the fighting was moving back towards them, that the Boer attack had been held and was being beaten back. A moment or two later, a large group of horsemen came up out of the dip, scattering as they rode fast across the flat towards the road, scattering wider and many of them falling as Peter's fire went in among them. One horse checked and staggered, then veered wildly towards the prison before going down, the rider leaping free and running, head down and arms pumping. Harry squinted, locking his sights on to the speeding figure and squeezed the trigger gently, feeling the butt come back into his shoulder, seeing the little manikin fall, the legs kicking and jerking. He lowered the rifle and muttered, 'Go on, scream, you bastard. That's for Owen.'

There was a ladder propped against the roof for them to come down by and half-a-dozen men went up it then to recover the Maxim and the ammunition belts. Outside the back door, Hasleton, tunic unbuttoned over his nightshirt, stood smiling, the orderly officer and several soldiers and field police with him. They were all dishevelled and sweaty.

George jumped off the ladder and flicked a friendly finger at the Commandant. 'I tell you what, Colonel – I didn't think I liked this place well enough to fight for it!'

Ivor, his face happier than it had been for weeks, chipped in. 'Like it or not, it's the only place we've got, George!'

Hasleton cleared his throat. 'Gentlemen, most gallant, most gallant. I'm deeply indebted to you. We all are.' He insisted on shaking their hands.

Peter, smoke-blackened, growled, 'That's all right, sir – made quite a change,' and Harry added, 'It's what we're supposed to be doing after all, sir.'

Hasleton looked suddenly embarassed as he stepped back a pace. 'Yes, of course . . . that's quite so. Er – I wonder, gentlemen —' His eyes went to the weapons in their hands and they realized what he meant, realized that the men behind Hasleton were all armed and close. He went on stumbling, 'Little though I like it, lads – er – I'm afraid I must ask you —' he let it die away, his hand sketching a gesture towards their rifles. Harry, his face stony, held his rifle across his body, muzzle down. His fingers went to the bolt, working it fast, sending a stream of shining cartridges in an arc. Then he simply opened his hands and let the weapon drop and turned, walking into the dark corridor, into his cell and slamming the door behind him.

* * *

The sitting of the Court the following morning showed things in a new light, perhaps because everyone in the room had been awake for a good part of the night, many of them actively engaged in the fight with the Boers, now known to have been a strong force under Beyers, beaten back with quite heavy losses but leaving considerable damage behind them and a number of British wounded and dead.

Thomas addressed the Court as soon as it was in session.

'Mr President, gentlemen, I want to depart, if I may, from the business of presentation of evidence in defence of the accused in order to speak briefly about their conduct last night. Everyone here knows of the events which took place; some will not know that these men, accused and imprisoned on charges which the prosecution has not been able to substantiate, willingly gave their parole and accepted weapons in the defence of the very prison in which they are being held. In the defence, Mr President, of this town and its inhabitants and its military installations. If it is desired, I can call the prison commandant, Colonel Hasleton, and the men under his command, to testify to the gallantry of the accused and to the importance of their contribution to the defeat of the enemy last night. I do not think that will be necessary – it is already common knowledge. Sir, I quote to the Court the words of England's greatest soldier, Arthur Wellesley, the Duke of Wellington. The Iron Duke himself said, and recorded for posterity,"The performance of a duty of honour and trust after knowledge of a military offence ought to convey a pardon."' He paused, looking at them, Bainbridge and the Judge Advocate watching him expressionlessly, Holding, the Dragoon, nodding seriously, Briggs–Cope, the youngest member of the Court, looking down as he doodled on a pad. '*Ought to convery a pardon*, sir. Wellington's own words and his own feelings. Since it is undoubted that these men performed a duty of honour and trust after knowledge of a military offence *which has not been proven*, I ask whether this Court is not prepared, is not, in fact, willing, to follow the Duke's dictum. I ask that the accused be granted an immediate pardon.'

He sat down in a weighted silence and no one moved until Bainbridge seemed to shake himself into speech.

'The Court is sensible of the conduct of the accused last night. I am going to adjourn to seek the advice of the Judge Advocate and his staff. The accused and all Court officers will remain close to this room for recall, please.'

*   *   *

They waited for two hours in the side room. Crookes assuring them that the longer the delay, the more likely the Court would be to accept Thomas' request. Thomas himself spent only a few minutes with them, but seemed quite light-hearted and when they filed back into the court-room, the four men themselves felt a wash of hope. It didn't last. Bainbridge leaned forward on the table and directed his words to Thomas.

'The Court has gone thoroughly into this matter and wishes to commend the accused on their actions during last night. There is, however, no question of a pardon and the proceedings will continue.' Harry heard Ivor's low cry above the mutter from the people in the court-room behind him and Thomas strode forward scowling.

That evening at dinner in their common room, George said, 'Remember what Ian told us right at the start ... something's stewing up, he said. He was bloody right. They're stewing *us* up!' Hasleton looked in long enough to thank them again and to denounce the Court in blistering terms, but none of them felt like talking and they went early to their cells.

Harry thought about that day, about the way the Court had seemed to change its attitude. Throughout Llewellyn's period, virtually no questions had come from the long table, but today, Bainbridge and occasionally Holding had intervened a number of times to question witnesses themselves. The atmosphere had been one almost of hostility. Lenehan had been called early and had been eloquent in praise of his officers' work. Bainbridge had broken in to Thomas' line.

'Major Lenehan, no one is disputing their soldierly qualities or their bravery in action. I remind you, however, that the charges against these men are because of actions which were *not* soldierly. We've been told by Colonel Harrison of Headquarters that the orders he drafted for you were explicit and contained no reference to the treatment of prisoners other than those in the Field Orders. We have also been told – at second-hand – that Captain Hunt stated that *he* had been instructed that no prisoners were to be taken. I would like to know whether you were told anything of that kind?'

'No, sir. I had no direct conversation with Colonel Harrison about our orders. But Captain Hunt came to me as soon as he had spoken with the colonel and advised me of the "no prisoners" information.'

'In other words, Hunt was the only one to hear this supposed statement?'

'Yes, sir. But I had no reason to doubt —'

'And Captain Hunt is now, unfortunately, dead?'

'Yes, sir, he is.'

George Witton had, not unexpectedly, lost his temper. Holding had asked leave of the president and questioned George.

'Were you present during the incident in the church at Duival's Kloof?'

'I was not.'

'Were you present when the man Visser was shot?'

'No.'

'Were you present during the interrogation of the missionary – er – Hesse?'

'I was there when he was brought in and when he left – but there was no interrogation.'

'Really? You realize that all three charges laid apply to you, although you say you were not present on two particular occasions?'

'I do – and I'm damned if I see why! None of us should be here —'

Bainbridge's voice was icy. 'Lieutenant Witton, I warn you that you must behave yourself. Unless you conduct yourself in a proper military manner and show this Court the respect due to it, the consequences will be serious.'

George gaped at him. 'Serious! What the hell do you think they are now?'

Thomas leapt up and quietened George, making apologies to the Court and managing to prevent things becoming worse. They were bad enough.

When Bainbridge spoke to Ivor, it was with an ill-concealed contempt.

'You are a British officer, Lieutenant Summers, a regular Army officer, and might be expected to have a clearer understanding of the forms of war. Yet, if the testimony we have is correct, you made no attempt to intervene in the interrogation of Jacob Hesse or the subsequent events. Why is that?'

Ivor was white-faced and clammy with sweat. 'Sir, with respect, there was *no* interrogation of Hesse, as Lieutenant Witton has already pointed out. And I don't know what the – the – subsequent events were.'

'You say that on oath?'

'I do, sir.'

Bainbridge made no reply, but wrote something on his pad with great deliberation.

Peter Handcock seemed taller than the president, even sitting down, and his broad, square face was set grimly when Bainbridge questioned him.

'In the matter of the shooting of the man Hendrik Visser – you were present?'

'Yes, sir.'

'What part did you take?'

'None, sir. No active part, that is.'

'What part was taken by any person present, other than Lieutenant Morant?'

'None, sir.'

'What part was taken by Lieutenant Morant?'

'He shot Visser, sir. And quite rightly.'

'I will not accept that comment, Lieutenant Handcock. You said, 'He shot Visser' . . . after what kind of trial?'

'Trial, sir? I don't follow?'

'Was the court at the trial of Visser constituted like this?' Bainbridge waved his hand about. 'Were the appropriate paragraphs of the King's Regulations observed?'

Peter glanced around him and let his look dwell on the officers behind the table.

'Was it like this? No, sir, not half so handsome. We were out fighting Boers, not sitting comfortably behind barbed-wire entanglements. We got 'em and we shot 'em under rule 303.'

There was a titter from the spectators, silenced by Bainbridge's glare, which he then turned on Peter.

'Rule 303, what does that mean?'

'A 303 cartridge, sir. Very effective.'

Harry grinned, but there was no answering smile from Thomas.

The succeeding two days brought a string of B.V.C. troopers to the Court, men who testified almost without deviation to the real events at the church, at De Koven's and with Hesse, reducing Dawes' story to its true dimensions and even further discrediting Booth. Despite persistent questioning from the Court and from Llewellyn, one man after another told the same thing and Mulholland proved an excellent witness, reporting in great detail on the finding of Hunt's body and the effect on Harry, and on the later events with Visser in Hunt's uniform. But while Thomas was able to extract all this with ease and was able to build a solid base of matching testimony, Llewellyn was just as able to reduce much of it by pointing out that the stress of emotion had little to do with commission of the acts.

When Thomas put Harry up, there was a stir. Everyone realized that this was likely to be the crux of the whole affair, that Morant was the key figure. Thomas, after discussing it with Harry the night before, had determined to use Llewellyn's own tactics and try to cut the ground from under the feet of the opposition by direction his questions as *they* would likely to do and establish Harry's situation clearly.

'Of those accused here, Lietenant Morant, is it true to say that you are the only officer who was present during the circumstances leading to the major charges – at the church, De Koven's Farm and the deaths of Visser and Hesse?'

'Perfectly true, yes.'

'Is it equally true that there were three men who could very largely substantiate the untruth of the charges against you – Captain Geoffrey Hunt, Squadron Sergeant-Major Owen Fisher and Sergeant Stanley Parker?'

'That is so.'

'And that all these valuable witnesses are dead?'

'Yes. They're dead.' Harry felt a wave of desolation as he said it.

'So that your testimony, which affects not only yourself but the other accused, stands, in some respects, materially unsupported?'

'It does.'

'And you are on oath and realize that this Court is searching only for the truth in these matters?'

'Yes.'

'Then I ask you, Lieutenant Morant, whether you are guilty of the destruction of civil property by burning or other methods?'

'Yes, I am, if guilty's the word. In the ordinary way of these things, when we discovered a place with arms in it or with Boer troops in it or with evidence to show the enemy had been given aid, we cleared the people and livestock from it and burnt it.'

'Was this practice isolated to your area of operations?'

'Not by half! It's quite standard – look at the clearing of the ground ahead of the blockhouse line!'

'Thank you. Now I ask you whether you are guilty of the death of the boy Christiaan De Beers at the church at Duival's Kloof?'

'I am not, and neither was anyone under my command, except that they returned the boy's killing fire.'

'And you are guilty of the death of Hendrik Visser?'

'Of *his* death, yes, as an act of war.'

'An act of war, you say?'

'Yes, of retributive war. He was armed and wearing the clothing of a British officer who had been mutilated and killed by Boers.'

'And are you guilty of the death of Jacob Hesse?'

'No, in no way. We tried to stop him going forward, in fact.'

Thomas turned to Bainbridge. 'Mr President, I would like to waive further examination of Lieutenant Morant and request, on his behalf, that he may make a statement to the Court.'

Bainbridge frowned, but nodded, and Thomas gave Harry an encouraging wink. Harry straightened and looked at each of them in turn. Briggs-Cope looked away; Bainbridge stared over his head; the Judge Advocate stared back, lips pursed, and Holding smiled faintly.

'Mr President and gentlemen, I only want to say this, that you can't blame the young 'uns – these others here. They just carried out their orders as I did – and they had to do that.' His voice went up a little. 'We all carried out orders – they obeyed mine and thought they were obeying those of headquarters. Captain Hunt told all of us we'd been directed not to bring in prisoners, and he and I discussed that – discussed the wrongness of such an order. None of us obeyed that one order, and that's likely to be the only crime of which we're guilty in military law. I did not carry out that order until my best friend was brutally murdered, and then I resolved to do exactly as I had been told. But if anyone is to blame, then it is only me.'

No one behind the long table spoke. Bainbridge nodded towards Llewellyn who walked forward almost reluctantly.

'Lieutenant Morant, the vigour and earnestness of your statement convinces me that no words of mine will alter what you say. I shall ask only three questions of you, and then only to corroborate earlier statements made in this Court. Did you shoot to death Hendrik Visser?'

'I did. For good reason.'

'Please, answer the questions and no more. Did you shoot to death Hendrik Visser?'

'Yes.' Harry's chin was up and his face grim.

'While in temporary command of the Bush Veldt Carbineers, were you actively patrolling in the area designated as Area Six, the area in which Jacob Hesse was shot?'

'Yes.'

'Close to the body, two items were found – an empty British bully beef tin and this —' he drew from his pocket the length of ravelled green cloth which Gregory's lieutenant had found, and which had been lying on his table since the first day. He held it before Harry. 'Is this puggaree band similar in every way to those worn by members of the Bush Veldt Carbineers?'

Harry stared at it.

'It's a piece of green cloth.'

'Exactly similar to those worn by you and your men?'

'Yes.'

'Thank you. That is all I wish to know.'

Thomas rose to re-examine and handed Harry a small paper package.

'Lieutenant Morant, would you please unwrap this package and show the Court the contents?'

Harry pulled out a strip of dark green cloth.

'Now would you read the slip of paper enclosed with it, please?'

Harry smiled gently as he read. 'Received from Major I. F. Thomas the sum of twopence for one yard of dark green cotton. Signed, L. Braun from Braun's Stores, Pietersburg.'

'Thank you. Nothing further, Mr President.'

'Very well. The Court will adjourn until nine o'clock tomorrow morning for summing-up by defence and prosecution. We shall hope, gentlemen, to keep tomorrow's proceedings as brief as is reasonable so that the Court may also sum up. Adjourned.'

'Reluctantly, Mr President, I'm forced to submit that the evidence heard from Colonel Harrison is worthless and irrelevant. A certain conversation said to have taken place between the colonel and the late Captain Hunt, and reported by Hunt immediately to Major Lenehan and later to other officers under his command, was denied by Colonel Harrison. I suggest there has been ample testimony to show that Colonel Harrison was, to be charitable, forgetful of what had actually happened. Attempts have been made throughout these proceedings to link the four accused in responsibilities for a series of so-called 'crimes', and yet there has been no valid evidence to show that crimes were committed, only acts of war – although there *has* been evidence to show that not all the accused were present at these places when the alleged crimes were committed. Attempts have been made to suggest there was no justification for the shooting of Hendrik Visser, although there has been more than enough testimony to the facts of his being an armed enemy when captured in the dress of a *murdered* British officer. No attempt has been made by the Court to consider fairly the conduct of the accused during the Boer attack on this settlement, nor to consider the extreme stress and provocation placed upon one of them, Lieutenant Morant, by the brutal and savage murder of his friend and troop commander.'

Thomas had been speaking for little more than a quarter of an hour, his vibrant voice controlled, never raised but reaching every ear in the room. 'Further, gentlemen, the charges brought against each of the officers accused implies their complicity in alleged crimes, implies that each of them was, if not directly guilty, guilty as an accessory before or after certain alleged facts ... not one of which has been proven here! Lieutenant Morant, acting in temporary command of the Bush Veldt Carbineers at the time of the arrest of the four accused, has gallantly stated that he alone is to blame for any fault; but it is my assertion that none of these men is to blame for anything, unless carrying out their duties in the face of hazard and hardship is a matter for blame. And following their arrest – an arrest made in the field, within sight of the Boer rifles, in front of their own men, an arrest made *without explanation*, Mr President – following that, these brave men were subjected to close confinement and without the benefit of advice or friendship or even information for a period of several days! This hardly seems the way of British military justice. Gentlemen, I submit that the facts are quite clear. The boy Christiaan De Beers was shot during a military engagement in which he himself bore and used arms against our troops, killing one of them. The man Hendrik Visser was shot as an enemy combatant, bearing arms and clearly implicated in the murder of a British officer. The man Jacob Hesse was shot by unknown persons after he had disregarded the warnings given him by the accused about proceeding further into enemy-held territory. None of the accused did other than obey what he took to be his legal orders. If the Court holds that these men were mistaken in their views about what they were entitled to do, then certainly the accused are open to censure. But not to a charge of murder.'

Thomas sat down to a shuffle of feet and a buzz of muted comment and Llewellyn, responding to Bainbridge's nod, moved slowly forward.

'Mr President, members of the Court, let me say at once that the matter of the military conduct of the accused, in general, is not and has not been in dispute. Had there been any doubt of their gallantry, their actions during the attack here recently would have dispelled that and, in fairness to them and to my learned friend, I must add my voice to those which have said that Wellington's dictum might well have been taken into stronger account as a result of that night's work.'

There was a gasp from the spectators and a quick handclap before Bainbridge slammed his hand down on the table, and again. His face was angry.

'That is quite enough! There *will* be silence in this Court!' He waited until there was no sound, then pointed at Llewellyn who went on undisturbed, the Welsh in his voice more marked now.

'Having said that, sir, I trust it will be clear that I do not in any way feel that the accused have been brought here wrongly charged, nor do I believe they are other than guilty as charged. Emotional attempts to plead stress and hardship and the loss of close friends do not weight against the Manual of Military Law. Such things are the lot of every soldier on active duty in the field. There is not one grain of evidence to show that the yound lad, De Beers, eleven years old, sir, fired the shot that killed Sergeant Parker, or indeed, fired any shot then or at any other time. Yet he was killed. There is not a shred of evidence to show that there was a connexion between the death of Captain Hunt and the wearing of his clothes by Visser. He could have come by the clothes through purchase, barter, even theft, yet the accused chose to believe he was concerned in Hunt's death and Visser was killed. Summarily. Without trial.' He walked slowly to his table and took a drink of water, then walked just as slowly back to the same spot before continuing.

'There is, however, more than a shred of evidence to connect the accused with the dastardly killing of Jacob Hesse, a man of the church engaged on a godly mission. There is a length of cloth. Only one formation of troops in this entire area of operations wears such a distinctive insignia ... and those troops were under the temporary command of one of the accused while the other three accused were on service with him! In answer to my learned friend, let it be said that, gallantry aside, a boy and two men, one a missionary, were shot to death in the area in which a military formation was operating. Troops from that formation were present on each occasion. The accused are the officers in command of those troops. I think those facts speak for themselves.'

Harry could see Ian Thomas straightening his files and books and papers and he leaned to Peter and whispered, 'That's it, then, old son. One way or the other.' Peter rumbled back, 'You make it sound like there's a choice! I hope you're right!'

Bainbridge had consulted with the other members and now leaned forward again. 'The Judge Advocate will sum up for the Court.'

That sibilant voice from the prim lips was brief.

'There is little to add from the Court. We have noted the conflict of evidence as between defence and prosecution witnesses, and the Court has already instructed that action be taken in the matter of the testimony of Corporal Thomas Booth and that his evidence not be taken into account in these proceedings. The Court has also noted the remarks made by both defending and prosecuting officers as to the words attributed to the Duke of Wellington, and wishes to point out with clarity that these words are no more than that. *Obiter dicta* cannot replace the law, no matter how high the standing of the speaker. Finally, the Court has clearly in mind that the charges which have been brought against the accused are based soundly upon absolute requirements within the Manual of Military Law ... and they will be considered in that light and in that light only, whether they be true charges or not.'

He leaned back, becoming at once the same greyish figure he had been throughout, muttering a few words to Bainbridge and then rising and leaving, a shade of a man.

Bainbridge shuffled his papers.

'The Judge Advocate has left the court in the presence of the accused and separately from the members of the Court, as required. The members of the Court will now retire to consider their verdict and the accused will be returned to the jurisdiction of the provost-marshal. This Court is now closed.'

When they were signed back into the prison building by the guard sergeant, there were half-hidden smiles around them. Crookes, who usually left them there with a cheerful 'Cheerio, see you in the morning' hung about while they filed through the door, through the rest room and into the cell corridor beyond. For the four of them there was a sense of end-of-term, of annual holiday, of a task completed ... not a happiness, simply a feeling of something over and done with.

It was Ivor who found the surprise.

Harry, peeling off his tunic, heard Ivor's high voice calling from the common room.

'I say, come here, you people, in the common room!' And then a ring of laughter.

They crowded in, their faces cracking into smiles as they saw the table, a strip of white running alone the centre of the green baize over the boards, a bowl of flowers in the centre between Hasleton's candlesticks, two flat plates of savouries and a large silver tray with glasses and three bottles of sherry on it.

Hasleton's voice behind them was a benign boom. 'Well, go on, go on! In you go, laddies. It's over and I thought we'd better have a bit of a celebration!' He pushed past them, the cork coming out of a sherry bottle quickly, the pale liquor splashing as he spoke. 'I just thought we'd have a bit of a drink to the confusion of Arse-faced Authority, eh?' Crookes was there and John Lenehan and Ian

Thomas, balancing on his small feet, a quiet smile on his face and there was suddenly a party and the slap and clatter of crossed conversations and the sweet heaviness of tobacco smoke and laughter, while the afternoon sky became the evening sky and the sherry disappeared and they relaxed for the first time in weeks.

But that wasn't all. Hasleton kept chuckling and grinning and hinting at 'better things yet, laddies' until, a little after seven, his own batman and orderly appeared to clear the table and began setting it and they kept coming and going till Hasleton could contain himself no longer and, face flushed with the wine, shouted, 'Right, then, gentlemen. Shall we dine?'' and bustled about pushing them into chairs around the candlelit table, thumping himself down at the head and beaming across the smoking roast that his orderly put before him, his hands flashing the carving knife and fork like fencing foils.

It was an astonishing evening. Burleigh arrived while Hasleton was carving and there were roars of applause and shout for another chair and another setting and applause for the bottle of brandy he'd brought. When the grinning orderly carried in a huge dish of strawberries nested in ice, there was more applause, swelling into a shout of joy when the batman staggered after him, a tub of ice cradled in his arms and the necks of six bottles of champagne jutting from it. Hasleton stared.

'Oi, Carter, what's this, what's this? S'posed to be four bottles of bubbly, ain't there?'

Carter, the batman, lowered the tub with a grunt and dug an evelope from his pocket. 'The other two come about an hour ago, sir. Message with 'em.'

Hasleton tore the envelope open and pulled a candlestick closer, peering at the note, then suddenly slamming his hand on the table so that the plates and glasses jumped and rattled, roaring with glee.

'Listen to *this*, you terrible people, you! *This* is the news of the minute!' He flourished the paper, then read, '"For the Gentlemen of the Bush Veldt Carbineers, with our apologies for their inconvenience and our sincere Good Wishes for their Successful Futures".' He smiled widely round at them, his eyes almost disappearing behind his flushed cheeks. 'And it's signed "Michael Holding and Leonard Briggs-Cope" ... not so bloody arse-faced after all, eh?' There was an instant of stunned silence, and then they burst into cheers and laughter, Peter grabbing wispy Ivor, lifting him clear of the floor and waltzing round the table with him, yelling, 'There you are, son – the bloody Court sent us champagne! *Now* you can cheer up!'

Later, glutted with food and wine and laughter, they sat quietly in a haze of cigar smoke, sipping at Burleigh's brandy. Crookes looked around at them, the candles burning low now and their faces smoother in the mellow light.

'Well, it's all over bar the shouting, you fellows. What are you going to do when they've apologized and let you out?'

'I know bloody well what I shall do.' Peter, huge in the candle shadow, his voice deeper than ever, spoke up at once. 'When I get home I'm going to start finding out about motors. Everyone thinks they're just a bit of a fad, see, but I reckon they're the coming thing. There'll be motors all over the place before ten years've gone. Horses are going out. Don't see much point in going back to blacksmithing, myself, so it'll be motors for me. The quicker the better.'

George, his hair standing on end and his face redder than his eyebrows, slapped Peter's shoulder. 'Right, Peter! I'm going back to farming – I reckon if I can handle soldiers I can handle sheep again – an' when you get your first motor running, you can damned well come and visit me! If the thing works, I'll buy one, by God! Sooner run sheep in a motor than a saddle!'

There was a laugh and Lenehan, in the little pause that followed it, said, 'Ivor? You'll go on soldiering, of course.'

Summers looked the way he used to look, languid and almost fragile, his eyes lit with laughter, 'I should think I'll have to, John. Don't know anything else. I remember Daddy telling me once that I was the thirty-first Summers of one kind or another to live in the Army. Never really thought about *not* being in the Army, so I shall go on. Wind up as an antique colonel in Brighton, I expect – gout and a liver and half a pension.'

'Not so much of the antique colonel, you young sprout!' Hasleton's smile was benevolent. 'Harry, you're keepin' pretty mum down there. What about you?'

Harry had been half listening to the others, his head down over a pencil and a sheet of paper. Now he looked up and focused properly on them. 'Me, I shall hoof back to Australia with John, here, collect my old friend Magee and my horse and take 'em back to England and hunt a few foxes. Might write a book. Wait for another war. I think chaps like me only really function properly when there's a war going on.' None of them asked him if marriage figured anywhere in his plans, but Lenehan leaned over, looking down at the paper under Harry's hand.

'Started the book already, Harry?'

'This? No, this is just a scribble. I thought it might seem appropriate to the occasion.'

Urged by the others, he rose, a little unsteadily, the paper in one hand, a dripping candle in the other.

'Right then – pay attention. I dedicate this rhyme to all my friends present, and anyone with the wit to take its meaning.

> *In prison cell I sadly sit —*
> *A damned crestfallen chappy!*
> *And own to you I feel a bit —*
> *A little bit – unhappy!'*

There were cries of mock-commiseration, and he shouted over them,

> *'It really ain't the place nor time*
> *To reel of rhyming diction —*
> *But yet we'll write a final rhyme*
> *While waiting cru-ci-fixion!'*

George called, 'Bring on your hammer and nails!' and Peter gagged him with a spread hand that almost covered his face. Harry read on,

> *'No matter what end they decide —*
> *Quicklime or boiling oil, sir,*
> *We'll do our best when crucified*
> *To finish off in style, sir!'*

'Hear, hear!' from Hasleton at the head of the table.

> *'But we bequeath a parting tip*
> *As sound advice for such men*
> *Who come across in transport ship*
> *To polish off the Dutchmen!*
> *If you encounter any Boers*
> *You really must not loot 'em —*
> *And if you wish to leave these shores*
> *For pity's sake, don't shoot 'em!'*

The great gush of laughter swelled and boomed along the corridor and through the walls to the night-guard, grinning at their posts.

It couldn't be heard in Bainbridge's quarters where he sat at his desk, Holding and Briggs-Cope opposite him. They'd dined together, carefully keeping the conversation away from the trial, and now were sitting sombrely, their papers spread before them. Bainbridge looked up.

'Well, then, Briggs-Cope, junior member first. General feelings, please.'

The young gunner hesitated. 'Er – they're not really general feelings at all, sir. I think I'm pretty clear in my mind about it.'

'You *think* you are? You'll need to be more definite than that, you know.'

'Yes, I know. Well, the main thing is – there doesn't really seem to be anything that can be called *proof* does there? Aside from Visser – and even then I'm inclined to feel we must give Morant the benefit of the doubt, all things considered.'

'Do you?' Bainbridge's voice was flat and cold, and he stared at Briggs-Cope till the younger man looked down. 'Holding, what about you?'

'I'm forced to agree about the lack of actual proof, you know. The first charge is nonsense, surely ... we've all done that sort of thing, and K has made it part of the policy. The boy's death was clearly accidental – and his own stupid fault anyway, by the sound of it – and Visser was shot quite deservedly, in my opinion. It's the Hesse business I'm not sure about.'

Bainbridge leaned back, balancing a pencil below his chin.

'It looks to me as though neither one of you is very sure about anything. I'm going to help you clear your minds. The Hesse business, as you call it, Holding, is one of crucial importance. For more than just the obvious reasons.'

He leaned right forward to them and began to talk, quietly and forcefully.

Half a mile away in prison, Crookes leaned elegantly against the wall alongside the very mellow Hasleton, watching as the others fought and struggled in a game of touch-rugger with a rolled-up tunic as the ball.

'Certainly lettin' off steam, sir, wouldn't you say?'

Hasleton belched comfortably. 'They need to, young Crookes. Poor bastards, locked up in this place all this time and then subjected to all that palaver by those cock-faces out there! Let 'em rip. I don't care if they wreck the bloody prison!'

The tunic-ball came flying out of the tangle of bodies towards them and Crookes caught it neatly, his lean face suddenly smiling very youthfully. 'Oh, good, sir. Then if you'll excuse me —' He howled like and banshee and dived full tilt into the laughing scum.

February had opened in a swirl of heat and a letting-down of
emotions. The party to mark the end of the hearing had left them
all with sore heads, and the routine of the days in the court-room
was no longer there, so that they quickly became bored, a boredom
coloured with the sick shades of apprehension, despite Lenehan's
assurances.

'Oh, come now, the talk in the Mess is that the delay's because
Bainbridge hasn't been well. They say he's got a bit of a cold and
has been kept to his bed. Everyone says that they're bound to wipe
all the charges out.'

Ian Thomas was less sanguine, but far from gloomy. 'The way I
see it, they'll want to make something stick after all the fuss they've
kicked up, so they'll plump for something easy. Probably squash
the charges in general and stick Harry with a severe reprimand and
that'll be that.'

Privately he wasn't so sure. That Bainbridge had been isolated in
his quarters was common knowledge, but Ian also knew that the
Judge Advocate had been a frequent visitor and that Briggs-Cope
and Holding had been there every day. None of them appeared in
the Mess.

And then the word came, Thomas and Hasleton arriving on a
sultry Tuesday afternoon, with the formal pronouncement that the
Court would reconvene the following morning at nine to deliver its
findings.

Ivor burst out, 'Does that mean we can get out of here tomorrow
– you know, if it's all squashed?' He looked pathetically young and
eager.

'Well, what happens is that you're paraded in front of the Court
and they read of their findings and then you're brought back here
until the whole thing's confirmed.'

'Oh, Christ – paperwork!' George's waspishness had come back.
'How long's that likely to take?'

'Well, the rules say that the convenor of the Court has to confirm
the findings – that's Kitchener – but they also say any officer
superior in rank to the president can do it if there's a reason.'

'Is there?' Harry was apparently relaxed, but Thomas could see
the tension? Oh, well, yes – distance and time, you see. It's close
enough to two hundred miles along the roads, and it has to be done
in person, by signature. Telegraph's no good.'

'So somebody local will do it?'

'Yes, the brigadier, I expect. Or a visiting officer if there's one
passing through of enough rank ... takes the onus off the local
chap, y'see.'

Thomas didn't realize till he was on the way out of the building that his last remark sounded a little ominious.

Crookes was back in the morning, and they went through the familiar routine almost with relief, knowing that something was happening to break the long day's monotony. The courtroom, when they were marched in, seemed quite crowded and Harry noticed Bainbridge looked pale and unwell. The chair next to his was empty ... and then he realized that the two captains flanking Bainbridge had the look of sickness too and he felt his stomach lurch unaccountably. The first formalities quickly over, the four sat, while the men behind the long table leaned their heads together, Bainbridge pointing to a bundle of forms in front of him, then nodding and looking up. When he spoke, his voice was slightly hoarse.

'The accused will stand.' He watched them levelly as they rose, instinctively straightening themselves, a short, firm line staring at him.

'Lieutenant Ivor Compton Summers, Twelfth Lancers, detached Bush Veldt Carbineers.' They all heard Ivor's breath suck in between his teeth. 'The Court finds the charges against you as follows: Charge Number One, Not Guilty; Charge Number Two, Not Guilty; Charge Number Three, Guilty —' he stopped abruptly as Ivor's gasping moan ran through the still room, then bore on. 'Guilty, but with mitigating circumstances.' He made no pause, no change in inflection as he said, 'Lieutenant Gerald George Witton, Colonial Horse Artillery, detached Bush Veldt Carbineers, the Court find the charges against you as follows: Charge Number One, Not Guilty; Charge Number Two, Not Guilty; Charge Number Three, Guilty, but with mitigating circumstances.' Harry could feel Peter's bulk tense alongside his shoulder. 'Lieutenant Peter Handcock, Bushmen's Regiment, detached Bush Veldt Carbineers, the Court finds the charges against you as follows: Charge Number One, Not Guilty; Charge Number Two, Not Guilty; Charge Number Three, Guilty as charged.'

There was a low grunt, deep in Peter's chest and Harry could only think and think again, My God, they've stuck Peter – they've done for him! He heard the relentless voice rasping his own name and the findings against him, and it sounded like an echo of the previous statement, while his mind spun with vertigo in the knowledge that big, friendly Peter had been smashed. And then he realized it was no echo, that Bainbridge had finished speaking and that the last words had been directed at him – 'Guilty as charged'.

And then Bainbridge was speaking again, saying, 'The Court's findings in these procedures were unanimous,' and he was scratching his signature across the bottom of a form and sliding it to Holding and then to Briggs–Cope for their signatures, while he spoke passionlessly. 'The Court directs that prisioners to be returned to their place of confinement within the jurisdiction of the provost-marshal pending confirmation of these findings and handing down of sentences.'

Malleson was there suddenly with Crookes, both grim, Crookes' eyes as sad as a spaniel's all at once, and there was an armed guard outside, and Thomas, stock-still at the door, his face covered with a film of sweat and Harry suddenly realized that Bainbridge hadn't referred to the four of them as 'the accused'. He'd called them 'the prisioners'.

Hasleton was waiting for them as they were marched into the entrance hall and signed for, Crookes silently shaking hands with each of them in turn. The old colonel's head was shaking and his lips trembled under his moustache as Malleson whispered to him off to one side, then he pulled himself upright, nodding, and walked across to them.

'Gentlemen, under instructions from the provost-marshal, I must inform you that you may no longer be allowed the privilege of the large cell in this establishment as a common meeting room. You will be confined to your own cells except for statutory periods of exercise which you will take individually. This will apply during the remainder of your stay here.' He swallowed, then muttered, loud enough for only the four of them to hear, 'Oh, the crawling shits! I'm so sorry, laddies.' He spun on his heel, signalling to the duty sergeant, and they were marched to their cells.

There was no exercise. It was just after ten by the entrance hall clock when they went in. Harry sat on his bunk, watching the slow sweep of the shadows of the window-bars across the floor, wondering in a mildly puzzled way how people could be so stupid as to find Peter guilty of anything ... any of them, but Peter, huge and gentle, Peter most of all. He had no idea of the circling of time and when the keys rattled along the corridor and he looked at his watch, he was surprised to find it was close to noon. He heard the steps and saw the heads go past, down to Ivor's cell at the end and then back, a glint of sun on Ivor's very fair, thin hair, and the slamming of the door and then a silence. The whole prison seemed to be still, waiting, and the noise of the return seemed overwhelming. Harry was hard against his cell door, his face pressed to the chill bars and he could see the tears coursing down Ivor's face.

Peter, in the next cell, shouted angrily, 'What've they done to you, Ivor? What's happening?'

Summers stopped abruptly, face contorted. 'They've cashiered me! They're sending me to Hell!' then stumbled forward again, the guards not looking at him, returning a moment later with George, pale, slit-lipped.

Peter called again to Ivor, but there was only the sound of soft weeping, and he went back to his door, cramming himself against the bars like Harry, both of them waiting, not speaking. George stopped outside his own cell door when they came back and called in a bitter cry, 'Mitigating circumstances, fellows – all they're going to do is send me to prison for life. That's all!'

Harry felt sick, felt his guts churn and his throat construct, the sweat breaking out on his face as he struggled not to vomit. By the time he'd gained control, Peter had gone along the corridor and through the loud door and into the silence beyond it. Ivor was still crying and George shouted at him, 'Oh, for Christ's sake, Ivor, I'll change places with you!'

Then there was Peter again, his eyes wrinkled in puzzled concentration, his lips pursed. He passed Harry unspeaking and went straight into his cell, not answering Harry's cry.

Malleson was beyond the door and he led Harry to a side room, knocked and took him through. The sallow-faced colonel at the table looked up and nodded. 'My name is Corcoran and I'm the provost-marshall. I have to advise you that the findings of the Field General Court Martial before which you were arraigned have been confirmed, the confirmation being made by Brigadier Arthur Bernard Doyle, garrison commander. Under the regulations governing this action, it was deemed that there was no reason to delay confirmation owing to the distance between Court and the present whereabouts of the convenor. Do you understand?'

Harry nodded, and Corcoran glanced down at the form he held. 'You have been advised that you have been found guilty as charged of Charge Number Three in the proceedings against you. The verdict of the Court, unanimously reached is that you, Harry Harbord Morant, being found guilty of the murder of Jacob Hesse, shall be put to death by firing party, the sentence to be carried out at Pietersburg on the next day after this confirmation. March out.'

When Thomas turned, Lenehan was shocked by his appearance. All the dapper trimness was gone. His tunic was unbuttoned and it and the shirt beneath it were dark with sweat; his skin was pale and somehow shrunken, so that he looked thinner and unshaven and his hair was tangled at the top and back of his head where he'd been running his hand through it. He stared at Lenehan, gave him an absent nod and turned back to lean again over the corporal at the Morse key and the signaller alongside him with a pencil poised over a pad of message forms. Lenehan pushed through the counter-flap to their bench at the back and stood beside Thomas, looking down.

Thomas spoke without turning his head. 'Nothing, John – absolutely bugger all! We've sent three signals in the past two hours and all we're getting back is acknowledgements. Here look.'

He thrust some crumpled papers at Lenehan who flattened them to read the pencilled messages. The first was timed at 1.05, addressed to the Commander-in-Chief, H.Q., Pretoria, and it said, 'Urgently request consideration deferment sentence Morant Handcock pending appeal highest authority. Thomas, Defending Officer, Pietersburg.' The second was timed at 1.55 and was the same message, preceded by, 'Repeat stress urgency earlier message.' The third, timed twenty minutes ago, at 2.40 read, 'Request urgent permission to make direct appeal His Majesty in case of Morant Handcock and your most urgent notification no promulgation execution order pending same.' The answer in each case had come within ten minutes of the receipt of the signals at Headquarters – the laconic 'Acknowledged.'

Lenehan dropped the papers and said, 'What else? Shouldn't I ride to Pretoria, or get the train?'

'Two hundred miles? And try getting the gilded bloody staff to rouse K from his virtuous couch?'

'No, I suppose not.' His voice was tired. 'Ian, it has to be some sort of ghastly mistake. We must be able to do *something*!'

'I'm doing it, damn it!' He straightened, his hand massaging the small of his back. 'I'm sorry, John – I feel a bit like Judas, and I expect he got a bit short-tempered when he heard them carpentering the cross.' He moved through the counter to the door, pulling Lenehan with him away from the two signallers. 'I don't believe there's been any kind of mistake, my friend. I believe poor Harry and Peter – and the other two, come to that – have been put up like sacrificial bloody lambs on somebody's political altar. I –'

The stutter of the Morse key and the corporal's cry came together and they ran back to the bench, leaning across the men's backs as the sharp rattling was translated into hasty writing on the pad. Thomas reached down and grabbed the page as the man finished writing.

'Not before time! Here – it's from Kelly, Adjutant-General's office –"Reference your request deferment of sentence pending appeal His Majesty. Must advise cable facilities ex-Pretoria extremely limited. Further advise unlikelihood appeal successful."' The key was rattling again as Thomas read on savagely. '"C. in C. absent these Headquarters tour of inspection outstations probably returning Friday. Kelly." Friday! Oh, how fucking convenient!'

The corporal glanced up.

'Sir, there's another one ... it's personal to you from General Kelly.'

Thomas snatched the form from the other man.

'"Personal. No copy retained Headquarters. Deeply regret situation and aware your feelings. Shared here by many but orders give no choice. C. in C's absence most unfortunate and no telegraph link his position. Orders originated beyond this Headquarters and appear impossible appeal. Have done all possible. Kelly."' Thomas pushed the form into his pocket in a damp and crumpled ball. 'That's it, then, John. Those daft words of Harry's the other night were right, weren't they? Remember? ... "while waiting crucifixion"?' He looked round at the two solemn-faced signallers. 'Thank you both. I'm sure you'll realize the need to keep close mouths about the last message ... no copies, no chat?'

'Not to worry, sir.' The corporal's nod was joined by the signaller's.

'We'll keep mum, and we're very sorry about it, sir.'

'Thank you again.'

Lenehan noticed that, despite the heat, Ian Thomas was shivering.

Burleigh's normally good-natured face was a black scowl as he loomed over the uncomfortable brigadier in the garrison commandant's office.

'You do realize, I'm sure, what the effects of this sort of thing could be?'

'My dear Burleigh, I realize only too well. Just as you must realize the sort of position in which you're placing me. I'm under orders, man. I may be in local command, but that's the top and the bottom of it. I can't fight Headquarters!'

'Can't or won't? Were you under orders to confirm that damnable sentence?'

The brigadier shifted awkwardly, looking away, and Burleigh stared at him, surprise wiping away the anger suddenly.

'By the Living God, I believe you were!' He felt for a chair and sat silent for nearly a minute while the other man watched him,

licking his lips nervously. When Burleigh spoke again his tones
were level and polite.

'I am making formal advances now, sir. On behalf of my newspaper, I request your permission to use telegraph facilities to
dispatch a story to my editor in London, via Pretoria.'

The brigadier stared back at him, tightening his lips.

'I'm sorry, Mr Burleigh. I repeat, the facilities are not available
at this time for other than military traffic.'

'Then I request a first priority on those facilities. Will you give
me some indication when they *will* be available?'

'I can't do that. Headquarters will make that decision.'

'After tomorrow morning, no doubt.' He stood, his downward
look contemptuous. 'I shall let you have a written request within a
quarter of an hour. I hope you'll be prepared to let me have your
answer in writing – fully – as quickly as possible. He walked to the
door and turned. 'I'd hate to have to sleep with a military conscience tonight.'

The brigadier sat still, listening to the echoes of the door's slam.

At four o'clock, the orderly officer and two guards unlocked
Harry's cell and took him out for exercise.

He'd spent most of the time since pecking at his lunch staring out
of the window at nothing, trying to get his mind to adjust to not
being there any more, not being anywhere. He looked at the young
orderly officer vacantly for a second or two, shaking his head, then
blinked and came back to the present.

'Exercise? No, thanks. I'd rather not.'

'I'm sorry, Morant, the provost-marshall has said it's a regulation. He says you're to have half-an-hour outside.'

'Does he? And suppose I refuse?'

The orderly officer looked momentarily confused, then recovered
himself, his shoulders tightening.

'I'm sure you wouldn't want to do that. It would be – awkward.
For me.'

Harry looked at him, realizing the truth of that, and smiled
quietly.

'Yes, of course. I'm sorry, old son. Lead on.'

They strolled in a wide circle around the flat pan of baked earth
in the late afternoon sun, and he found he was glad he was outside
for a while, glad to feel the heat and the first lift of a cool breeze to
gentle it, glad to be stretching his legs. The guards walked behind
and the orderly officer paced alongside, making no attempt to talk,

but offering a cigarette and showing he'd be prepared to chat if Harry wanted to.

Peter was being brought in as Harry was signed into the book. He looked just as tall, but less solid somehow, as though the flesh and muscles were hanging on the great bones rather than being packed hard there.

'Hallo, Harry. Been walking?'

'Yes. You?'

'Yes, out that side. They don't seem to want us to mix now, do they?'

'Doesn't look like it. George and Ivor's turn next, I suppose.'

The duty sergeant glanced across at the orderly officer, but no one said anything as they were led back into the corridor and to their cells. Then Harry noticed the two end doors were standing wide open and saw the orderly officer's quick look, and he stopped outside his own cell.

'Have they gone walking already?'

'Er – yes, they have as a matter of fact.' He shifted his glance.

'Where? Not where I was –'

Peter, in his own cell doorway, listening, rumbled, 'And not on my side.'

'Look, will you go back in, please, you fellows? We can't stand about out here.'

Harry gripped the door, the bones of his hands jutting through the white skin.

'Have they gone? Have they been taken away?'

A pause. Then, 'Yes. Yes, I'm very much afraid they have. While you two were out.'

Peter's voice was thick with fury. 'You miserable, crawling, Pommy bastards! Wouldn't even show enough stinking guts to let us say goodbye to our mates! Christ, I hate the whole shit-mouthed mess of you!' He shook the heavy door till the hinges grated and the guards stepped close, rifles ready.

'Peter!' Harry barked it out like a command and the big man stopped at once, standing with his arms hanging and his face crumpled.

'That won't do any good, old lad. Although I agree – it was a cur's trick.' He rounded on the orderly officer. 'I suppose you knew?'

'Yes. I'm ashamed to say I did, but I'd no choice. The provost-marshal decided there was to be no fuss.'

Harry could see the pain in the young man's eyes. He was an infantryman and was simply serving a twenty-four hour duty as one of a string of young officers to take a turn.

'Where've they gone, do you know?

'Train to Pretoria. On to the Cape then, I imagine. It – they gave Summers some civil clothing to wear. It didn't fit too well.' He turned his head.

'Yes, well, it's done, isn't it? Thank you for telling us. Not your fault.'

He turned his back and walked into the cell, standing with his back turned and his head in the oblique shaft of afternoon sunlight.

Lenehan watched Harry's hands, firm and steady as they tidied the last of his meagre belongings into neat little piles.

'Did – did Ian come, Harry?'

'Yes, about an hour ago. He was pretty cut up, I'm afraid.'

'He feels guilty ... like Judas, he said.'

'He shouldn't be. He did a marvellous job. No one could have done more than he did. He was just up against too much, that's all – we all were. Dear old Hasleton's Arse-faces.' He grinned without any humour at all. 'You heard about Ivor and George?'

'I saw them. At the train.'

'How were they?'

'As you'd expect, Harry. They both asked me to say their good-byes to you. Poor Ivor asked us all to pray for him ... it's affected him very badly. They'll be in Pretoria tomorrow morning.'

'Yes, well, we won't see much of tomorrow morning, will we?' He opened his writing-pad. 'Look, will you take these letters for me, John? And I want you to make sure whatever cash is due to me goes into this one for Paddy.' Lenehan nodded, mute. 'I've asked him to let Harlequin go. ...' He turned, his head down, and fussed need-lessly with his folded clothes. 'The others are to my people ... and ... and Margaret.' He held one envelope in his fingers. 'I'd written one to you too, old man. Didn't think I'd see you again, somehow.' He dropped the envelope on the bed. 'You won't need it now. I just wanted to ask you to see Paddy and the fellows at the *Bulletin* for me. And to thank you for your friendship.'

Lenehan found he couldn't answer, only nod, his eyes blurring, as Harry tore a couple of pages from his writing-case and crumpled them onto the floor near the door. He handed the case to Lenehan and piled some other things onto it ... his leather box, his wallet and his old gunmetal cigarette case. There was a knock at the cell door and a guard looked in.

'Padre's here, sir.'

Harry faced Lenehan.

'Time to go, John. Give my love to Julia.' Lenehan's fingers were crushing his own. 'And, John, thank you for Cavalier.'

Lenehan's foot brushed against the little ball of crumpled paper Harry had tossed down and, as the padre came in, he managed to bend quickly and pick it up without Harry noticing. He walked quickly away down the corridor for the last time.

The padre stood uncertainly for a moment, looking at Harry's back.

'May I talk with you, lad? It's Harry, isn't it?'

Harry turned slowly and sat on the end of the bunk, leaning back against the wall under the window.

'It is, Padre, but you won't do much business with me, I'm afraid.'

'You're very close to the Infinite, Harry.'

'As close as I've ever been. But then, we always are, aren't we?'

The Padre's face was thin and intelligent, and he almost smiled, nodding in recognition of the remark.

'Would you like to pray?'

'For what, Padre? Another crack of the whip?'

'You could pray for God's mercy.'

'No, thanks. I'm quite sure if there *is* a God, he knows what he's doing. And if there isn't – what's the point of praying, anyway?'

'Is there nothing I can offer you?'

'A hacksaw mightn't be a bad idea.' The padre was startled at the sudden flashing smile. 'No – nothing, I'm afraid. But thank you for coming, Padre. Go and have a word with Peter.'

'I shall. And I shall pray for you.'

'I can't stop you. You might try one for the Court while you're about it. I shouldn't think they'll be sleeping much tonight.'

The Padre shook his head sadly and rapped on the door. Harry, looking away, heard him go to Peter's door . . . and realized his own door hadn't been closed. The orderly officer was standing there, a bottle of brandy in his hand. He held it out.

'The Commandant sent this down.' He gave the bottle to Harry and stood there still. 'Look, Morant – we all think – I mean –'

'I know. Thank you. And tell old Hasleton he's a damned decent fellow, will you?'

The door closed and Harry thoughtfully pulled the cork, sniffing appreciatively at the fine cognac. He tipped the neck over his tin mug, emptying half the bottle into it so that the brandy came right to the rim, then took the bottle to the door, calling for the guard sergeant. The man came down, staring at Harry through the bars.

'Sergeant, be a good chap will you. Take this to Mr Handcock
for me . . . after the padre's gone, eh?'

'Yes, sir, glad to.' He reached through the bars for the bottle.
'Sir?'

'Something wrong?'

'Yessir. The men – they think – we *all* think – well, it's bloody
bad business, sir, that's what!'

'Yes, I suppose it is. But I'm afraid everyone thinks so except the
Powers That Be. Thank you . . . and the men.'

The sergeant stamped away, passing the padre as he came from
Peter's cell. A moment later, Peter's bass roar echoed up the
corridor.

'Good on you, Harry. Drink hearty!'

'You too, Peter. Chin up!'

Outside the prison, the sentry saluted Lenehan as the door closed
behind him and he walked slowly to one side, standing in the light
of a lamp, the bullet-marks on the walls above his head still raw.
He shifted the little pile of Harry's things and carefully unfolded
the crumpled sheets of paper he'd snatched from the cell floor,
tilting them to the light and bending his head to read, not realizing
he was reading aloud, the sentry's head turning as Lenehan read.

> *When I am tired, and old, and worn,*
> *And harassed by regret;*
> *When blame, reproach and worldlings' scorn*
> *On every side are met;*
>
> *When I have lived long years in vain*
> *And found life's garland's rue,*
> *May be that I'll come back again*
> *At last – at last – to you!*
>
> *When all the joys and all the zest*
> *Of youthful years have fled,*
> *May be that I shall leave the rest*
> *And turn to you instead;*
>
> *For you, dear heart, would never spurn*
> *(With condemnation due!)*
> *If, at the close of all, I turn*
> *Homeward – at last – to you!*

When the other faces turn away
And lighter loves have passed,
When life is weary, old and grey
I may come back – at last!

When cares, remorse, regrets are rife—
Too late to live anew—
In the sad twilight of my life
I will come back – to you!

The writing was neat, unaltered, as though Harry had thought it all in his mind exactly before putting it down. But there was a scrawled line diagonally across the bottom of the page, the writing fierce and angry: 'But I won't, Margaret, I won't!'

The sentry heard the anguished, 'Oh, Christ!' from Lenehan and saw him bend his head, and called out, 'Are you all right, sir?'

Lenehan put the pages in his tunic pocket and lifted his head. 'Oh yes, I'm just fine, thank you.'

When the sentry told his mates about it later, he said, 'I dunno about fine – he sounded as though he'd just been gut-shot!'

There had been muted noises in the night on the flat ground beyond the prison and, with the first of the true light, Harry could see from his perch on the end of the bunk, the two thick posts which had been set into the ground there, a couple of hundred feet away. There was something gleaming near the top of each of them.

He hadn't slept, yet he didn't feel tired. In some way he felt more alert, more aware than he'd ever felt, holding on to, breathing deeply of all the time left to him. Unless something very unexpected should happen. They brought breakfast just after six, a guard carrying the tray in without looking at him, and he'd been surprised to find he was ravenously hungry, clearing the food quickly and calling to ask for more tea. The same guard had brought him hot water in a jug and he'd washed and shaved carefully, changing into the clean breeches and shirt he'd kept out the night before, giving his boots a final buff with the discarded shirt and folding his sleeves back neatly above his elbows. He felt clean and light and vigorous, the thought in his mind that it was such a waste to destroy a firm body with years of action in it yet.

There was little noise in the prison and he made no attempt to call out to Peter, hearing the muted sounds of his movements in the next cell above the thick silence which seemed to envelop the place.

He'd kept his watch and he looked at it when the door at the end of the corridor opened and the steps came towards him ... seven-thirty.

The orderly officer was pale, the black smudges under his eyes darker for the pallor, and he swung the door and stood back, not speaking. Harry stepped out, taking one backward look at the cell, at the scuff marks where his boot-toes had dug into the wall the many times he'd stood up there to look out; at his initials, cut into the stone of the window ledge with a nail during an interminable day. By the time he'd turned back, Peter was there beside him, the guards all around them. Peter was pale, too, but smiling, and he boomed, 'Morning, Harry. Fine day for it.' Harry grinned back at him, feeling a great affection for this big, calm man, and said, 'Good company, too, Peter.' Then they were moving down towards the door at the far end, the door through which they'd gone the night of the Boer attack, and Peter looked up and back as they went through, remembering the scramble up there and the muscle-cracking lift of the stripped-down Maxim. Hasleton was there and the sallow-faced provost-marshal, Corcoran, and Malleson, solid and erect and miserable. He was carrying the big ledger from the entrance hall, and the orderly officer signed them out. Finally. Malleson handed the ledger to a guard and Hasleton walked to them.

'Harry – Peter. My dear laddies. I'm ashamed of my uniform for the first time.' he coughed loudly, wringing their hands. 'God bless you both, boys.' Then the guards were about them again, and they were moving around the corner and becoming a part of the cere-mony there.

One of the guards stumbled on a loose stone and Peter smiled sideways at him, rumbling, 'Pick up the step there, son,' but that was all that was said while they marched crisply towards those two posts, the gleam now clearly visible as a steel hook set in the front of each post about a foot from the top. Behind them, Hasleton and Corcoran had moved around along the side wall of the prison, below the windows of the cells, and some distance away to their left there was a file of men halting and turning right into line facing the posts. Harry and Peter looked at them, recognizing the Balmorals and the flash of tartan under the khaki aprons.

They hadn't known Malleson was marching with them until they were halted by the posts and turned to see him there, a field policeman with him stepping forward and moving behind them. Two of the guards urged them gently back and they felt hands taking their wrists.

Harry cocked an eyebrow at the white-faced orderly officer.

'Mayn't we have a smoke?'

The young man looked at Malleson who nodded and came forward, his case open to them, and they felt the thongs slacken. He lit their cigarettes for them, deliberately standing in front of them to try to obscure their view of the Highlanders, but they could hear the snap of the commands there, each of them preceded by the readying words, 'Firing party ...'

Peter took only two or three drags, deep ones, and dropped the cigarette. Harry puffed once more at his and they smiled their thanks to Malleson, whose face remained unchangingly sad. Peter's hand was dry and big around Harry's as steady as his look. 'Goodbye, Harry. It's been a good time. I'm glad we were friends.'

Harry looked up at him.

'Goodbye, Peter. If there's anything after this, I hope we can share it.'

Then the thongs were round their wrists and the posts were hard and cool against their backs. The field police sergeant moved in front of them and passed a broad leather strap around each chest, someone behind taking the slack of the loop and raising it, not tight but firm, holding them upright, and Harry realized what the hooks were for. Malleson and the orderly officer stepped aside and they were looking across the brown barrenness before them to the firing party.

A sergeant was moving along the line, handing something to each man, and they could see then the single action as each of the men in the line pushed a round into the breech of his rifle. One of them is a blank, Harry thought, and every man there will live the rest of his life not knowing whether he's killed one of us or not. The Highland officer passed down the line inspecting each man briefly, then marched to one side, standing stiffly, his sword a slash of clean silver light. The sergeant positioned himself to the officer's right and a pace behind him.

Harry suddenly realized the padre was there, stepping forward to speak to them. Peter turned his head away and Harry said, 'Goodbye, Padre' and looked past him. The man sighed and blessed them both quietly and walked away to the prison wall where Hasleton stood, Malleson, Corcoran and the orderly officer joining them there, a drab little group against the white wall. At the far end, the front corner of the prison, there was a knot of men ... they could see Lenehan there, and Thomas and Crookes, and Mulholland and half a dozen of the B.V.C. troopers and some others. The road ran past them, a little below their level, but they could see the tops of the trees and the chimney of the wrecked house from which they'd driven the Boers. And they could hear in the still morning air the tattoo of galloping hooves there, too, and everyone's head swung as the rider came in sight, an officer on a lathered horse, a blue-and-white dispatch brassard on his arm and a flat leather case strapped across his back. Harry heard Peter's hiss of indrawn breath and quirked his lips in a mirthless smile, looking straight ahead of him as the rider galloped up to the prison and past it and away, down into the town. The police sergeant was there again, two wide black cloths dangling from his hand, but they both shook their heads and he stowed them into a pocket, taking from another pocket two white discs of thick paper and a couple of long pins. Breathing heavily he stepped close, avoiding their eyes, and pinned a disc to each man's chest, a little to the left of the breastbone, then stepped back and quickly away.

There was a silence and Harry was looking up into the sky, deep and warmly blue. The voice sounded a thousand miles away when it called the firing party to the aim, and he looked down again, surprised to see them so close, the muzzles staring at him. He pitched his voice down to them.

'Shoot straight, you bastards. Don't make a mess of us!'

They saw the flame, but not the smoke which followed it.

March 1902

It had rained just a little during the night, but now, in the late morning, the sky was clearing fast and there was sunlight. Paddy walked sluggishly down the footworn track from the house to the rail fence, feeling that the brightness was wrong, that there should be black clouds and rain and thunder, something stormy and fearsome. The last newspapers to arrive were spread on the table back there in the house, with the untouched food and the cold mug of tea, and Lenehan's letter and Harry's letter were crushed in his hand as he walked, because he didn't realize his fists were clenched and his shoulders hunched.

Across there in the green shadow, there was a flicker of movement and he whistled gently, waiting for the golden shape to come through the shadows. Harlequin danced and sidled out, one big eye fixed on Paddy as he went through his pretence of not wanting to come close, till he realized the man wasn't playing, was just standing there, staring down at the letters in his hand.

Paddy lifted his head, letting Harlequin nose against his cheek, and he dredged a handful of coarse brown sugar from his pocket, walking with it in his hand to the gate, putting the letters away and slipping the bar to let the gate swing wide. The golden horse stepped delicately through, his turning head and his eyes showing that he was puzzled at this variation. He came close, outside the rails, and put his silky muzzle down into Paddy's cupped hand, while the man gentled him.

'Well, there, Harlequin, lad, that's the end of yer sugar ration. I made Harry a promise an' I'm going to keep it, so I am. Ye shan't be rode by anyone other than Breaker Morant ... that was me word, remember?' The horse tossed his head as though agreeing and Paddy looped a hand into his thick black mane and walked him away from the yard, well out to where the land rolled down to the creek on one side and swelled up in a bald, grassy hill on the other. He swung the horse around, facing him up the hill, and patted his neck.

'Go on now, fella. Ye're as free as he is now. Away ye go!'

Harlequin stood there, looking at Paddy a forefoot pawing gently at the ground. He whinnied a question and swung his head, looking around him.

'Go, Harlequin, go!'

Paddy slapped the firm rump and the horse started away, trotting, stopping, looking back. Then he began to run, a long and easy gallop, across the face of the hill till he stood on the skyline, the sun on the deep golden sheen of his hide. He called once, a high neigh, then he turned and was gone below the crest and there was only the sky.

Paddy walked back to the house alone.

Now that you've finished ...

There are one or two things you may be interested in knowing.

Harry Morant and Peter Handcock *were* executed by a firing party from the Cameron Highlanders, at Pietersburg on the morning of 27th February, 1902. They're buried near where they were shot.

The real George Witton went to prison on the Isle of Wight, serving nearly three years of his life sentence, then being released in haste and secrecy after petitions and a great deal of political pressure had been brought to bear.

There *was* a Major Thomas – not Ian, though – and he was disgusted at the whole miserable affair, and wrote of his conviction that the executions were carried out for international policy reasons.

And there was, of course, a Kitchener. During his visit to Australia in 1910 he was asked to unveil a memorial to Boer War dead at Bathurst, in New South Wales. It's recorded that he refused to unveil the memorial to those volunteers unless the name of Lieutenant Peter Handcock was removed from the roll and, to the shame of the men who ordered it done, it was removed. It was replaced afterwards and I've seen it there, centrally placed on a separate strip of bronze.

I've been to all sorts of sources for material for this book. The poems quoted *were* written by Morant and I found them, together with a wealth of other stuff, in the only factual record of any worth about these events, *Breaker Morant–A Horseman Who Made History*, written by F.M. Cutlack, out of print and kindly loaned to me by the publishers, Ure Smith.

Finally, if there seem to be errors in fact of military law and its methods, they're either because I am at fault, or because the way in which it was interpreted in the case of Morant and Handcock seems to have been grievously wrong.

Since their execution, no Australian soldier has been tried on a capital charge by a British Army Court.

Wentworth Falls,
Blue Mountains,
N.S.W.
1972.